THE
ADVENTURES OF

INDIANA JONES AND THE RAIDERS OF THE LOST ARK™

Campbell Black

Adapted from the screenplay by Lawrence Kasdan
Based on a story by George Lucas and Philip Kaufman

INDIANA JONES AND THE TEMPLE OF DOOM™

James Kahn

Adapted from the screenplay by Willard Huyck & Gloria Katz
Based on a story by George Lucas

INDIANA JONES AND THE LAST CRUSADE™

Rob MacGregor

Adapted from the screenplay by Jeffrey Boam
Based on a story by George Lucas and Menno Meyjes

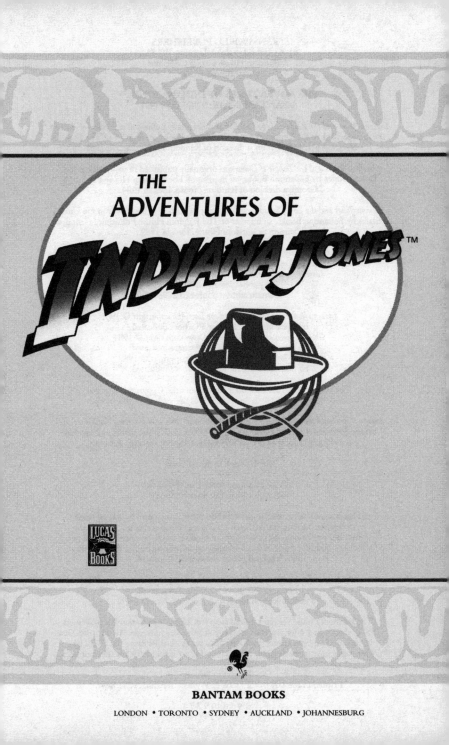

THE ADVENTURES OF

INDIANA JONES™

LUCAS BOOKS

BANTAM BOOKS

LONDON • TORONTO • SYDNEY • AUCKLAND • JOHANNESBURG

TRANSWORLD PUBLISHERS
61–63 Uxbridge Road, London W5 5SA
A Random House Group Company
www.rbooks.co.uk

**THE ADVENTURES OF INDIANA JONES™
A BANTAM BOOK: 9780553819991**

Indiana Jones and the Raiders of the Lost Ark was originally published as *Raiders of the Lost Ark* in paperback in the United States by Ballantine Books, an imprint of The Random House Publishing Group, a division of Random House, Inc., in 1981.

Indiana Jones and the Temple of Doom was originally published in paperback in the United States by Ballantine Books, an imprint of The Random House Publishing Group, a division of Random House, Inc., in 1984.

Indiana Jones and the Last Crusade was originally published in hardcover in the United States by Ballantine Books, an imprint of The Random House Publishing Group, a division of Random House, Inc., in 1989.

This edition originally published in Del Rey trade paperback in the United States by Del Rey, an imprint of The Random House Publishing Group, a division of Random House, Inc., New York.
First publication in Great Britain
Bantam edition published 2008

Indiana Jones and the Raiders of the Lost Ark copyright © 1981
by Lucasfilm Ltd. & ® or ™ where indicated.
Indiana Jones and the Temple of Doom copyright © 1984
by Lucasfilm Ltd. & ® or ™ where indicated.
Indiana Jones and the Last Crusade copyright © 1989
by Lucasfilm Ltd. & ® or ™ where indicated.

The authors have asserted their right under the Copyright, Designs and Patents Act 1988 to be identified as the authors of this work.

Indiana Jones and the Raiders of the Lost Ark, *Indiana Jones and the Temple of Doom*, and *Indiana Jones and the Last Crusade* are works of fiction. Names, places and incidents are either products of the author's imagination or are used fictiously.

Book design by Katie Shaw

A CIP catalogue record for this book
is available from the British Library.

Addresses for Random House Group Ltd companies outside the UK can be found at: www.randomhouse.co.uk
The Random House Group Ltd Reg. No. 954009

The Random House Group Limited supports The Forest Stewardship Council (FSC), the leading international forest certification organisation. All our titles that are printed on Greenpeace approved FSC certified paper carry the FSC logo. Our paper procurement policy can be found at www.rbooks.co.uk/environment

Typeset in Janson
Printed in the UK by CPI Cox & Wyman, Reading, RG1 8EX.

2 4 6 8 10 9 7 5 3

INDIANA JONES
AND THE
RAIDERS OF THE
LOST ARK™

ONE

South America, 1936

THE JUNGLE was darkly verdant, secretive, menacing. What little sunlight broke the high barriers of branches and twisted vines was pale, milky in color. The air, sticky and solid, created a wall of humidity. Birds screamed in panic, as if they had been unexpectedly trapped in some huge net. Glittering insects scurried underfoot, animals chattered and squealed in the foliage. In its primitive quality the place might have been a lost terrain, a point unmapped, untraveled—the end of the world.

Eight men made their way slowly along a narrow trail, pausing now and then to hack at an overhanging vine or slice at a dangling branch. At the head of this group there was a tall man in a leather jacket and a brimmed felt hat. Behind him were two Peruvians, who regarded the jungle cautiously, and five nervous Quechua Indians, struggling with the pair of donkeys that carried the packs and provisions.

The man who led the group was called Indiana Jones. He was muscular in the way one might associate with an athlete not quite beyond his prime. He had several days' growth of dirty blond beard and streaks of dark sweat on a face that might once have been handsome in a facile, photogenic fashion. Now, though, there were tiny lines around the eyes, the corners of the mouth, changing the almost bland good looks into an expression of character, depth. It was as if the contours of his experience had begun, slowly, to define his appearance.

Indy Jones didn't move with the same caution as the two Peruvians—his confidence made it seem as if he, rather than they, were the native there. But his outward swagger did not impair his sense of alertness. He knew enough to look occasionally, almost imperceptibly, from side to side, to expect the jungle to reveal a threat, a danger, at any moment. The sudden parting of a branch or the cracking of rotted wood—these were the signals, the points on his compass of danger. At times he would pause, take off his hat, wipe sweat from his forehead and wonder what bothered him more—the humidity or the nervousness of the Quechuas. Every so often they would talk excitedly with one another in quick bursts of their strange language, a language that reminded Indy of the sounds of jungle birds, creatures of the impenetrable foliage, the recurring mists.

He looked around at the two Peruvians, Barranca and Satipo, and he realized how little he really trusted them and yet how much he was obliged to depend on them to get what he wanted out of this jungle.

What a crew, he thought. Two furtive Peruvians, five terrified Indians, and two recalcitrant donkeys. And I am their leader, who might have done better with a troop of Boy Scouts.

Indy turned to Barranca and, though he was sure he knew the answer, asked, "What are the Indians talking about?"

Barranca seemed irritated. "What do they always talk about, Señor Jones? The curse. Always the curse."

Indy shrugged and stared back at the Indians. Indy understood their superstitions, their beliefs, and in a way he even sympathized with them. The curse—the ancient curse of the Temple of the Chachapoyan Warriors. The Quechuas had been raised with it; it was intrinsic to their system of beliefs.

He said, "Tell them to be quiet, Barranca. Tell them no harm will come to them." The salve of words. He felt like a quack doctor administering a dose of an untested serum. How the devil could he know that no harm would come to them?

Barranca watched Indy a moment, then he spoke harshly to the Indians, and for a time they were silent—a silence that was one of repressed fear. Again, Indy felt sympathy for them: vague words of comfort couldn't dispose of centuries of superstition. He put his hat back on and moved slowly along the trail, assailed by the odors of the jungle, the scents of things growing and other things rotting, ancient carcasses crawling with maggots, decaying wood, dying vegetation. You could think of better places to be than here, he thought, you could think of sweeter places.

And then he was wondering about Forrestal, imagining him coming along this same path years ago, imagining the fever in Forrestal's blood when he came close to the Temple. But Forrestal, good as he had been as an archaeologist, hadn't come back from his trip to this place—and whatever secrets that lay contained in the Temple were locked there still. Poor Forrestal. To die in this godforsaken place was a hell of an epitaph. It wasn't one Indy relished for himself.

He moved along the trail again, followed by the group. The jungle lay in a canyon at this point, and the trail traversed the canyon wall like an old scar. There were thin mists rising from the ground now, vapors he knew would become thicker, more dense, as the day progressed. The mists would be trapped in this canyon almost as if they were webs spun by the trees themselves.

A huge macaw, gaudy as a fresh rainbow, screamed out of the underbrush and winged into the trees, momentarily startling him. And then the Indians were jabbering again, gesticulating wildly with their hands, prodding one another. Barranca turned and silenced them with a fierce command—but Indy knew it was going to be more and more difficult to keep them under any kind of control. He could feel their anxieties as certainly as he could the humidity pressing against his flesh.

Besides, the Indians mattered less to him than his growing mistrust of the two Peruvians. Especially Barranca. It was a gut instinct, the kind he always relied on, an intuition he'd felt for most of the journey. But it was stronger now. They'd cut his throat for a few salted peanuts, he knew.

It isn't much farther, he told himself.

And when he realized how close he was to the Temple, when he understood how near he was to the Idol of the Chachapoyans, he experienced the old adrenaline rushing through him: the fulfillment of a dream, an old oath he'd taken for himself, a pledge he'd made when he'd been a novice in archaeology. It was like going back fifteen years into his past, back to the familiar sense of wonder, the obsessive urge to understand the dark places of history, that had first excited him about archaeology. A dream, he thought. A dream taking shape, changing from something nebulous to something tangible. And now he could feel the nearness of the Temple, feel it in the hollows of his bones.

He paused and listened to the Indians chatter again. They too know. *They know how close we are now.* And it scares them. He moved forward. Through the trees there was a break in the canyon wall. The trail was almost invisible: it had been choked by creepers, stifled by bulbous weeds that crawled over roots—roots that had the appearance of growths produced by some floating spores randomly drifting in space, planting themselves here by mere whim. Indy hacked, swinging his arm so that his broad-bladed knife cracked through the obstructions as if they were nothing more than fibrous papers. Damn jungle. You couldn't let nature, even at its most perverse, its most unruly, defeat you. When he paused he was soaked in sweat and his muscles ached. But he felt good as he looked at the slashed creepers, the severed roots. And then he was aware of the mist thickening, not a cold mist, not a chill, but something created out of the sweat of the jungle itself. He caught his breath and moved through the passage.

He caught it again when he reached the end of the trail.

It was there.

There, in the distance, shrouded by thick trees, *the Temple*.

For a second he was seized by the strange linkages of history, a sense of permanence, a continuum that made it possible for someone called Indiana Jones to be alive in the year 1936 and see a construction that had been erected two thousand years before. Awed. Overwhelmed. A humbling feeling. But none of these descriptions was really accurate. There wasn't a word for this excitement.

For a time he couldn't say anything.

He just stared at the edifice and wondered at the energy that had gone into building such a structure in the heart of a merciless jungle. And then he was shaken back into an awareness of the present by the shouts of the Indians, and he swung round to see three of them running back along the trail, leaving the donkeys. Barranca had his pistol out and was leveling it to fire at the fleeing Indians, but Indy gripped the man's wrist, twisted it slightly, swung the Peruvian around to face him.

"No," he said.

Barranca stared at Indy accusingly. "They are cowards, Señor Jones."

"We don't need them," Indy said. "And we don't need to kill them."

The Peruvian brought the pistol to his side, glanced at his companion Satipo and looked back at Indy again. "Without the Indians, Señor, who will carry the supplies? It was not part of our arrangement that Satipo and I do menial labor, no?"

Indy watched the Peruvian, the dark coldness at the heart of the man's eyes. He couldn't ever imagine this one smiling. He couldn't imagine daylight finding its way into Barranca's soul. Indy remembered seeing such dead eyes before: on a shark. "We'll dump the supplies. As soon as we get what we came here for, we can make it back to the plane by dusk. We don't need supplies now."

Barranca was fidgeting with his pistol.

A trigger-happy fellow, Indy thought. Three dead Indians wouldn't make a bit of difference to him.

"Put the gun away," Indy told him. "Pistols don't agree with me, Barranca, unless I'm the one with my finger on the trigger."

Barranca shrugged and glanced at Satipo; some kind of silent communication passed between them. They'll choose their moment, Indy knew. They'll make their move at the right time.

"Just tuck it in your belt, okay?" Indy asked. He looked briefly at the two remaining Indians, herded into place by Satipo. They had trancelike expressions of fear on their faces; they might have been zombies.

Indy turned toward the Temple, gazing at it, savoring the moment. The mists were becoming denser around the place, a conspiracy of nature, as if the jungle intended to keep its secrets forever.

Satipo bent and pulled something out of the bark of a tree. He raised his hand to Indy. In the center of the palm lay a tiny dart.

"Hovitos," Satipo said. "The poison is still fresh—three days, Señor Jones. They must be following us."

"If they knew we were here, they'd have killed us already," Indy said calmly.

He took the dart. Crude but effective. He thought of the Hovitos, their legendary fierceness, their historic attachment to the Temple. They were superstitious enough to stay away from the Temple itself, but definitely jealous enough to kill anybody else who went there.

"Let's go," he said. "Let's get it over with."

They had to hack and slash again, cut and slice through the elaborately tangled vines, rip at the creepers that rose from underfoot like shackles lying in wait. Sweating, Indy paused; he let his knife dangle at his side. From the corner of his eye he was conscious of one of the Indians hauling back a thick branch.

It was the scream that made him swing abruptly round, his knife raised in the air now. It was the wild scream of the Indian that made him rush toward the branch just as the Quechua, still yelling, dashed off into the jungle. The other remaining Indian followed, crashing mindlessly, panicked, against the barbed branches and sharp creepers. And then they were both gone. Indy, knife poised, hauled back the branch that had so scared the Indians. He was ready to lunge at whatever had terrified them, ready to thrust his blade forward. He drew the branch aside.

It sat behind the swirling mist.

Carved out of stone, timeless, its face the figment of some bleak nightmare, it was a sculpture of a Chachapoyan demon. He watched it for a second, aware of the malevolence in its unchanging face, and he realized it had been placed here to guard the Temple, to scare off anybody who might pass this way. A work of art, he thought, and he wondered briefly about its creators, their system of beliefs, about the kind of religious awe that might inspire something so dreadful as this statue. He forced himself to put out his hand and touch the demon lightly on the shoulder.

Then he was conscious of something else, something that was more disturbing than the stone face. More eerie.

The silence.

The weird silence.

Nothing. No birds. No insects. No breeze to shake sounds out of the trees. A zero, as if everything in this place were dead. As if everything had been stilled, silenced by an ungodly, destructive hand. He touched his forehead. Cold, cold sweat. Spooks, he thought. The place is filled with spooks. This was the kind of silence you might have imagined before creation.

He moved away from the stone figure, followed by the two Peruvians, who seemed remarkably subdued.

"What is it, in the name of God?" Barranca asked.

Indy shrugged. "Ah, some old trinket. What else? Every Chachapoyan household had to have one, didn't you know?"

Barranca looked grim. "Sometimes you seem to take this very lightly, Señor Jones."

"Is there another way?"

The mist crawled, rolled, clawed, seeming to press the three men back. Indy peered through the vapors, staring at the Temple entrance, the elaborately primitive friezes that had yielded to vegetation with the passage of time, the clutter of shrubs, leaves, vines; but what held him more was the dark entrance itself, round and open, like the mouth of a corpse. He thought of Forrestal passing into that dark mouth, crossing the entranceway to his death. Poor guy.

Barranca stared at the entranceway. "How can we trust you, Señor Jones? No one has ever come out alive. Why should we put our faith in you?"

Indy smiled at the Peruvian. "Barranca, Barranca—you've got to learn that even a miserable gringo sometimes tells the truth, huh?" And he pulled a piece of folded parchment out of his shirt pocket. He stared at the faces of the Peruvians. Their expressions were transparent, such looks of greed. Indy wondered whose throats had been cut so that these two villains had managed to obtain the other half. "This, Barranca, should take care of your faith," and he spread the parchment on the ground.

Satipo took a similar piece of parchment from his pocket and laid it alongside the one Indy had produced. The two parts dovetailed neatly. For a time, nobody spoke; the threshold of caution had been reached, Indy knew—and he waited, tensely, for something to happen.

"Well, amigos," he said. "We're partners. We have what you might call mutual needs. Between us we have a complete map of the floor plan of the Temple. We've got what nobody else ever had. Now, assuming that pillar there marks the corner—"

Before he could finish his sentence he saw, as if in a slowed reel of film, Barranca reach for his pistol. He saw the thin brown hand curl itself over the butt of the silver gun—and then he moved. Indiana Jones moved faster than the Peruvian could have followed; his motions a blur, a parody of vision, he moved back from Barranca and, reaching under the back of his leather jacket, produced a coiled bullwhip, his hand tight on the handle. His movements became liquid, one fluid and graceful display of muscle and poise and balance, arm and bullwhip seeming to be one thing, extensions of each other. He swung the whip, lashing the air, watching it twist itself tightly around Barranca's wrist. Then he jerked downward, tighter still, and the gun discharged itself into the ground. For a moment the Peruvian didn't move. He stared at Indy in amazement, a mixture of confusion and pain and hatred, loathing the fact that he'd been outsmarted, humiliated. And then, as the whip around his wrist slackened, Barranca turned and ran, racing after the Indians into the jungle.

Indy turned to Satipo. The man raised his hands in the air.

"Señor, please," he said, "I knew nothing, nothing of his plan. He was crazy. A crazy man. Please, Señor. Believe me."

Indy watched him a moment, then nodded and picked up the pieces of the map.

"You can drop your hands, Satipo."

The Peruvian looked relieved and lowered his arms stiffly.

"We've got the floor plan," Indy said. "So what are we waiting for?"

And he turned toward the Temple entrance.

The smell was the scent of centuries, the trapped odors of years of silence and darkness, of the damp flowing in from the jungle, the festering of plants. Water dripped from the ceiling, slithered through the mosses that had grown there. The passageway whispered with the scampering of rodent claws. And the air—the air was unexpectedly cold, untouched by sunlight, forever shaded. Indy walked ahead of Satipo, listening to the echoes of their footsteps. Alien sounds, he thought. A disturbance of the dead—and for a moment he was touched by the feeling of being in the wrong place at the wrong time, like a plunderer, a looter, someone intent on damaging things that have lain too long in peace.

He knew the feeling well, a sense of wrongdoing. It wasn't the sort of emotion he enjoyed entertaining because it was like having a boring guest at an otherwise decent dinner party. He watched his shadow move in the light of the torch Satipo carried.

The passageway twisted and turned as it bored deeper into the interior of the Temple. Every now and then Indy would stop and look at the map, by the light of the torch, trying to remember the details of the layout. He wanted to drink, his throat was dry, his tongue parched—but he didn't want to stop. He could hear a clock tick inside his skull, and every tick was telling him, *You don't have time, you don't have time . . .*

The two men passed ledges carved out of the walls. Here and there Indy would stop and examine the artifacts that were located on the ledges. He would sift through them, discarding some expertly, placing others in his pockets. Small coins, tiny medallions, pieces of pottery small enough to carry on his person. He knew what was valuable and what wasn't. But they were nothing in comparison to what he'd really come for—the idol.

He moved more quickly now, the Peruvian rushing behind him, panting as he hurried to keep up. And then Indy stopped suddenly, joltingly.

"Why have we stopped?" Satipo asked, his voice sounding as if his lungs were on fire.

Indy said nothing, remained frozen, barely breathing. Satipo, confused, took one step toward Indy, went to touch him on the arm, but he too stopped and let his hand freeze in midair.

A huge black tarantula crawled up Indy's back, maddeningly slowly. Indy could feel its legs as they inched toward the bare skin of his neck. He waited, waited for what seemed like forever, until he felt the horrible creature settle on his shoulder. He could feel Satipo's panic, could sense the man's desire to scream and jump. He knew he had to move quickly, yet casually so Satipo would not run. Indy, in one smooth motion, flicked his hand over his shoulder and knocked the creature away into the shadows. Relieved, he began to move forward but then he heard Satipo's gasp, and turned to see two more spiders drop onto the Peruvian's arm. Instinctively, Indy's whip lashed out from the shadows, throwing the creatures onto the ground. Quickly, Indy stepped on the scuttling spiders, stomping them beneath his boot.

Satipo paled, seemed about to faint. Indy grabbed him, held him by the arm until he was steady. And then the archaeologist pointed down the hallway at a small chamber ahead, a chamber which was lit by a single shaft of sunlight from a hole in the ceiling. The tarantulas were forgotten; Indy knew other dangers lay ahead.

"Enough, Señor," Satipo breathed. "Let us go back."

But Indy said nothing. He continued to gaze toward the chamber, his mind already working, figuring, his imagination helping him to think his way inside the minds of the people who had built this place so long ago. They would want to protect the treasure of the Temple, he thought. They would want to erect barricades, traps, to make sure no stranger ever reached the heart of the Temple.

He moved closer to the entrance now, moving with the instinctive caution of the hunter who smells danger on the downwind, who feels peril before he can see signs of it. He bent down, felt around on the floor, found a thick stalk of a weed, hauled it out—then reached forward and tossed the stalk into the chamber.

For a split second nothing happened. And then there was a faint whirring noise, a creaking sound, and the walls of the chamber seemed to break open as giant metal spikes, like the jaws of some impossible shark, slammed together in the center of the chamber. Indiana Jones smiled, appreciating the labors of the Temple designers, the cunning of this horrible trap. The Peruvian swore under his breath, crossed himself. Indy was about to say something when he noticed an object impaled on the great spikes. It took only a moment for him to realize the nature of the thing that had been sliced through by the sharp metal.

"Forrestal."

Half skeleton. Half flesh. The face grotesquely preserved by the temperature of the chamber, the pained surprise still apparent, as if it had been left unchanged as a warning to anybody else who might want to enter the room. Forrestal, impaled through chest and groin, blackened blood visible on his jungle khakis, death stains. Jesus, Indy thought. Nobody deserved to go like this. Nobody. He experienced a second of sadness.

You just blundered into it, pal. You were out of your league. You should have stayed in the classroom. Indy shut his eyes briefly, then stepped inside the chamber and dragged the remains of the man from the tips of the spikes, laying the corpse on the floor.

"You knew this person?" Satipo asked.

"Yeah, I knew him."

The Peruvian made the sign of the cross again. "I think, Señor, we should perhaps go no further."

"You wouldn't let a little thing like this discourage you, would you, Satipo?" Then Indy didn't speak for a time. He watched the metal spikes begin to retract slowly, sliding back toward the walls from which they'd emerged. He marveled at the simple mechanics of the arrangement—simple and deadly.

Indy smiled at the Peruvian, momentarily touching him on the shoulder. The man was sweating profusely, trembling. Indy stepped inside the chamber, wary of the spikes, seeing their ugly tips set into the walls. After a time the Peruvian, grunting, whispering to himself, followed. They passed through the chamber and emerged into a straight hallway some fifty feet long. At the end of the passageway there was a door, bright with sunlight streaming from above.

"We're close," Indy said, "so close."

He studied the map again before folding it, the details memorized. But he didn't move immediately. His eyes scanned the place for more traps, more pitfalls.

"It looks safe," Satipo said.

"That's what scares me, friend."

"It's safe," the Peruvian said again. "Let's go."

Satipo, suddenly eager, stepped forward.

And then he stopped as his right foot slipped through the surface of the floor. He flew forward, screaming. Indy moved quickly, grabbed the Peruvian by his belt and hauled him up to safety. Satipo fell to the ground exhausted.

Indy looked down at the floor through which the Peruvian had stepped. Cobwebs, an elaborate expanse of ancient cobwebs, over which lay a film of dust, creating the illusion of a floor. He bent down, picked up a stone and dropped it through the surface of webs. Nothing, no sound, no echo came back.

"A long way down," Indy muttered.

Satipo, breathless, said nothing.

Indy stared across the surface of webs toward the sunlit door. How to cross the space, the pit, when the floor doesn't exist?

Staipo said, "I think now we go back, Señor. No?"

"No," Indy said. "I think we go forward."

"How? With wings? Is that what you think?"

"You don't need wings in order to fly, friend."

He took out his whip and stared up at the ceiling. There were various beams set into the roof. They might be rotted through, he thought. On the other hand, they might be strong enough to hold his weight. It was worth a try, anyhow. If it didn't work, he'd have to kiss the idol good-bye. He swung the whip upward, seeing it coil around a beam, then he tugged on the whip and tested it for strength.

Satipo shook his head. "No. You're crazy."

"Can you think of a better way, friend?"

"The whip will not hold us. The beam will snap."

"Save me from pessimists," Indy said. "Save me from disbelievers. Just trust me. Just do what I do, okay?"

Indy curled both hands around the whip, pulled on it again to test it, then swung himself slowly through the air, conscious all the time of the illusory floor underneath him, of the darkness of the pit that lay deep below the layers of cobwebs and dust, aware of the possibility that the beam might snap, the whip work itself loose, and then . . . but he didn't have time to consider these bleak things. He swung, clutching the whip, feeling air rush against him. He swung until he was sure he was beyond the margins of the pit and then he lowered himself, coming down on solid ground. He pushed the whip back across to the Peruvian, who muttered something in Spanish under his breath, something Indy was sure had religious significance. He wondered idly if there might exist, somewhere in the vaults of the Vatican, a patron saint for those who had occasion to travel by whip.

He watched the Peruvian land beside him.

"Told you, didn't I? Beats traveling by bus."

Satipo said nothing. Even in the dim light, Indy could see his face was pale. Indy now wedged the handle of the bullwhip against the wall. "For the return trip," he said. "I never go anywhere one way, Satipo."

The Peruvian shrugged as they moved through the sunlit doorway into a large domed room, the ceiling of which had skylights that sent bands of sunlight down on the black-and-white tiled floor. And then Indy noticed something on the other side of the chamber, something that took his breath away, filled him with awe, with a pleasure he could barely define.

The idol.

Set on some kind of altar, looking both fierce and lovely, its gold shape glittering in the flames of the torch, shining in the sunlight that slipped through the roof—*the idol.*

The Idol of the Chachapoyan Warriors.

What he felt then was the excitement of an overpowering lust, the desire to race across the room and touch its beauty—a beauty surrounded by obstacles and traps. And what kind of booby trap was saved for last? What kind of trap surrounded the idol itself?

"I'm going in," he said.

The Peruvian now also saw the idol and said nothing. He stared at the figurine with an expression of avarice that suggested he was suddenly so possessed by greed that nothing else mattered except getting his hands on it. Indy watched him a moment, thinking, *He's seen it. He's seen its beauty. He can't be trusted.* Satipo was about to step beyond the threshold when Indy stopped him.

"Remember Forrestal?" Indy said.

"I remember."

He stared across the intricate pattern of black-and-white tiles, wondering about the precision of the arrangement, about the design. Beside the doorway there were two ancient torches in rusted metal holders. He reached up, removed one, trying to imagine the face of the last person who might have held this very torch; the span of time—it never failed to amaze him that the least important of objects endured through centuries. He lit it, glanced at Satipo, then bent down and pressed the unlit end against one of the white tiles. He tapped it. Solid. No echo, no resonance. Very solid. He next tapped one of the black tiles.

It happened before he could move his hand away. A noise, the sound of something slamming through the air, something whistling with the speed of its movement, and a small dart drove itself into the shaft of his torch. He pulled his hand away. Satipo exhaled quietly, then pointed inside the room.

"It came from there," he said. "You see that hole? The dart came from there."

"I also see hundreds of other holes," Indy said. The place, the whole place, was honeycombed with shadowy recesses, each of which would contain a dart, each of which would release its missile whenever there was pressure on a black tile.

"Stay here, Satipo."

Slowly, the Peruvian turned his face. "If you insist."

Indy, holding the lit torch, moved cautiously into the chamber, avoiding the black tiles, stepping over them to reach the safe white ones. He was conscious of his shadow thrown against the walls of the room by the light of the torch, conscious of the wicked holes, seen now in half-light, that held the darts. Mainly, though, it was the idol that demanded his attention, the sheer beauty of it that became more apparent the closer he got to it, the hypnotic glitter, the enigmatic expression on the face. Strange, he thought: six inches high, two thousand years old, a lump of gold whose face could hardly be called lovely—strange that men would lose their minds for this, kill for this. And yet it mesmerized him and he had to look away. Concentrate on the tiles, he told himself. Only the tiles. Nothing else. Don't lose the fine edge of your instinct here.

Underfoot, sprawled on a white tile and riddled with darts, lay a small dead bird. He stared at it, sickened for a moment, seized by the realization that whoever had built this Temple, whoever had planned the traps, would have been too cunning to booby trap only the black tiles: like a wild card in a deck, at least one white tile would have been poisoned.

At least one.

What if there were others?

He hesitated, sweating now, feeling the sunlight from above, feeling the heat of the torch flame on his face. Carefully, he stepped around the dead bird and looked at the white tiles that lay between himself and the idol as if each were a possible enemy. Sometimes, he thought, caution alone doesn't carry the day. Sometimes you don't get the prize by being hesitant, by failing to take the final risk. Caution has to be married with chance—but then, you need to know in some way the odds are on your side. The sight of the idol drew him again. It magnetized him. And he was aware of Satipo behind him, watching from the doorway, no doubt planning his own treachery.

Do it, he said to himself. What the hell. Do it and caution be damned.

He moved with the grace of a dancer. He moved with the strange elegance of a man weaving between razor blades. Every tile now was a possible land mine, a depth charge.

He edged forward and stepped over the black squares, waiting for the pressure of his weight to trigger the mechanism that would make the air scream with darts. And then he was closer to the altarpiece, closer to the idol. The prize. The triumph. And the last trap of all.

He paused again. His heart ran wildly, his pulses thudded, the blood burned in his veins. Sweat fell from his forehead and slicked across his eyelids, blinding him. He wiped at it with the back of his hand. A few more feet, he thought. A few more feet.

And a few more tiles.

He moved again, raising his legs and then gently lowering them. If he ever needed balance, it was now. The idol seemed to wink at him, to entice him.

Another step.

Another step.

He put his right leg forward, touching the last white tile before the altar.

He'd made it. He'd done it. He pulled a liquor flask from his pocket, uncapped it, drank hard from it. This one you deserve, he thought. Then he stuck the flask away and stared at the idol. The last trap, he wondered. What could the last trap be? The final hazard of all.

He thought for a long time, tried to imagine himself into the minds of the people who'd created this place, who'd constructed these defenses. Okay, somebody comes to take the idol away, which means it has to be lifted, it has to be removed from the slab of polished stone, it has to be *physically* taken.

Then what?

Some kind of mechanism under the idol detects the absence of the thing's weight, and that triggers—what? More darts? No, it would be something even more destructive than that. Something more deadly. He thought again; his mind sped, his nerves pulsated. He bent down and stared around the base of the altar. There were chips of stone, dirt, grit, the accumulation of centuries. Maybe, he thought. Just maybe. He took a small drawstring bag from his pocket, opened it, emptied out the coins it contained, then began to fill the bag with dirt and stones. He weighed it in the palm of his hand for a while. Maybe, he thought again. If you could do it quickly enough. You could do it with the kind of speed that might defeat the mechanism. If that was indeed the kind of trap involved here.

If if if. Too many hypotheticals.

Under other circumstances he knew he would walk away, avoid the consequences of so many intangibles. But not now, not here. He stood upright, weighed the bag again, wondered if it was the same weight as the idol, hoped that it was. Then he moved quickly, picking up the idol and setting the bag down in its place, setting it down on the polished stone.

Nothing. For a long moment, nothing.

He stared at the bag, then at the idol in his hand, and then he was aware of a strange, distant noise, a rumbling like that of a great machine set in motion, a sound of things waking from a long sleep, roaring and tearing and creaking through the spaces of the Temple. The polished stone pedestal suddenly dropped—five inches, six. And then the noise was greater, deafening, and everything began to shake, tremble, as if the very foundations of the place were coming apart, splitting, opening, bricks and wood splintering and cracking.

He turned and moved quickly back across the tiles, moving as fast as he could toward the doorway. And still the noise, like desperate thunder, grew and rolled and echoed through the old hallways and passages and chambers. He moved toward Satipo, who was standing in the doorway with a look of absolute terror on his face.

Now everything was shaking, everything moving, bricks collapsing, walls toppling, everything. When he reached the doorway he turned to see a rock fall across the tiled floor, setting off the darts, which flew pointlessly in their thousands through the disintegrating chamber.

Satipo, breathing hard, had moved toward the whip and was swinging himself across the pit. When he reached the other side he regarded Indy a moment.

I knew it was coming, Indy thought.

I felt it, I knew it, and now that it's about to happen, what can I do? He watched Satipo haul the whip from the beam and gather it in his hand.

"A bargain, Señor. An exchange. The idol for the whip. You throw me the idol, I throw you the whip."

Indy listened to the destruction behind him and watched Satipo.

"What choices do you have, Señor Jones?" Satipo asked.

"Suppose I drop the idol into the pit, my friend? All you've got for your troubles is a bullwhip, right?"

"And what exactly have *you* got for *your* troubles, Señor?"

Indy shrugged. The noise behind him was growing; he could feel the Temple tremble, the floor begin to sway. The idol, he thought—he couldn't just let the thing fall into the abyss like that.

"Okay, Satipo. The idol for the whip." And he tossed the idol toward the Peruvian. He watched as Satipo seized the relic, stuffed it in his pocket and then dropped the whip on the floor.

Satipo smiled. "I am genuinely sorry, Señor Jones. Adios. And good luck."

"You're no more sorry than me," Indy shouted as he watched the Peruvian disappear down the passageway. The whole structure, like some vengeful deity of the jungle, shook even more.

He heard the sound of more stones falling, pillars toppling. *The curse of the idol*, he thought. It was a matinee movie, it was the kind of thing kids watched wild-eyed on Saturday afternoons in dark cinemas. There was only one thing to do—one thing, no alternative. You have to jump, he realized. You have to take your chances and jump across the pit and hope that gravity is on your side. All hell is breaking loose behind you and there's a godawful abyss just in front of you. So you jump, you wing it into darkness and keep your fingers crossed.

Jump!

He took a deep breath, swung himself out into the air above the pit, swung himself hard as he could, listened to the *swish* of the air around him as he moved. He would have prayed if he were the praying kind, prayed he didn't get swallowed up by the dark nothingness below.

He was dropping now. The impetus was gone from his leap. He was falling. He hoped he was falling on the other side of the pit.

But he wasn't.

He could feel the darkness, dank smelling and damp, rush upward from below, and he threw his hands out, looking for something to grip, some edge, anything to hold on to. He felt his fingertips dig into the edge of the pit, the crumbling edge, and he tried to drag himself upward while the edge yielded and gave way and loose stones dropped into the chasm. He swung his legs, clawed with his hands, struggled like a beached fish to get up, get out, reach whatever might pass now for safety. Straining, groaning, thrashing with his legs against the inside wall of the pit, he struggled to raise himself. He couldn't let the treacherous Peruvian get away with the idol. He swung his legs again, kicked, looked for some kind of leverage that would help him climb up from the pit, something, anything, it didn't matter what. And still the Temple was falling apart like a pathetic straw hut in a hurricane. He grunted, dug his fingers into the ledge above, strained until he thought his muscles might pop, his blood vessels burst, hauled himself up even as he heard the sound of his fingernails breaking with the weight of his body.

Harder, he thought.

Try harder.

He pushed, sweat blinded him, his nerves began to tremble. Something's going to snap, he thought. Something's going to give and then you'll find out exactly what lies at the bottom of this pit. He paused, tried to regroup his strength, rearrange his waning energies, then he hauled himself up again through laborious and wearisome inches.

At last he was able to swing his leg over the top, to slither over the edge to the relative safety of the floor—a floor that was shaking, threatening to split apart at any moment.

He raised himself shakily to a standing position and looked down the hallway in the direction Satipo had taken. He had gone toward the room where Forrestal's remains had been found. The room of spikes. The torture chamber. And suddenly Indy knew what would happen to the Peruvian, suddenly he knew the man's fate even before he heard the terrible clang of the spikes, even before he heard the Peruvian's awful scream echo along the passageway. He listened, reached down for his whip, then ran toward the chamber. Satipo hung to one side, impaled like a grotesquely large butterfly in some madman's collection.

"Adios, Satipo," Indy said, then slipped the idol from the dead man's pocket, edged his way past the spikes and raced into the passageway beyond.

Ahead, he saw the exit, the opening of light, the stand of thick trees beyond. And still the rolling sound increased, filling his ears, vibrating through his body. He turned, astounded to see a vast boulder roll down the passageway toward him, gathering speed as it coursed forward. *The last booby trap*, he thought. They wanted to make sure that even if you got inside the Temple, even if you avoided everything the place could throw at you, then you weren't going to get out alive. He raced. He sprinted insanely toward the exit as the great stone crushed along the passageway behind him. He threw himself forward toward the opening of light and hit the thick grass outside just before the boulder slammed against the exit, sealing the Temple shut forever.

Exhausted, out of breath, he lay on his back.

Too close, he thought. Too close for any form of comfort. He wanted to sleep. He wanted nothing more than the chance to close his eyes, transport himself into the darkness that brings relief, dreamless and deep relief. You could have died a hundred deaths in there, he realized. You could have died more deaths than any man might expect in a lifetime. And then he smiled, sat up, turned the idol around and around in his hands.

But worth it, he thought. Worth the whole thing.

He stared at the golden piece.

He was still staring at it when he saw a shadow fall across him.

The shadow startled him into a sitting position. Squinting, he looked up. There were two Hovitos warriors looking down at him, their faces painted in the ferocious colors of battle, their long bamboo blowguns held erect as spears. But it wasn't the presence of the Indians that worried Indy now; it was the sight of the white man who stood between them in a safari outfit and pith helmet. For a long time Indy said nothing, letting the full sense of recognition dawn on him. The man in the pith helmet smiled, and the smile was frost, lethal.

"Belloq," Indy said.

Of all the people in the world, Belloq.

Indy looked away from the Frenchman's face for a moment, glanced down at the idol in his hand, then stared beyond Belloq to the edge of the trees, where there were about thirty more Hovitos warriors standing in a line. And next to the Indians stood Barranca. Barranca, staring past Indy with a stupid, greedy smile on his face. A smile that turned slowly to a look of bewilderment and then, more rapidly, to a cold, vacant expression, which Indy recognized as signaling death.

The Indians on either side of the traitorous Peruvian released his arms, and Barranca toppled forward. His back was riddled with darts.

"My dear Dr. Jones," Belloq said. "You have a knack of choosing quite the wrong friends."

Indy said nothing. He watched Belloq reach down and pick the idol from his hand. Belloq savored the relic for a time, turning it this way and that, his expression one of deep appreciation.

Belloq nodded his head slightly, a curt gesture that suggested an incongruous politeness, a sense of civility.

"You may have thought I'd given up. But again we see there is nothing you can possess which I cannot take away."

Indy looked in the direction of the warriors. "And the Hovitos expect you to hand the idol over to them?"

"Quite," Belloq said.

Indy laughed. "Naïve of them."

"As you say," Belloq remarked. "If only you spoke their language, you could advise them otherwise, of course."

"Of course," Indy said.

He watched as Belloq turned toward the grouped warriors and lifted the idol in the air; and then, in a remarkable display of unified movement that might have been choreographed, rehearsed, the warriors laid themselves face down on the ground. A moment of sudden stillness, of primitive religious awe. In other circumstances, Indy thought, I might be impressed enough to hang around and watch.

In other circumstances, but not now.

He raised himself slowly to his knees, looked at the back of Belloq, glanced quickly once more at the prostrate warriors—and then he was off, moving fast, running toward the trees, waiting for that moment when the Indians would raise themselves up and the air would be dense with darts from the blowguns.

He plunged into the trees when he heard Belloq shout from behind, screaming in a language that was presumably that of the Hovitos, and then he was sprinting through the foliage, back to the river and the amphibian plane. Run. Run even when you don't have a goddamn scrap of energy left. Find something in reserve.

Just run.

And then he heard the darts.

He heard them shaft the air, whizzing, zinging, creating a melody of death. He ran in a zigzag, moving in a serpentine fashion through the foliage. From behind he could hear the breaking of branches, the crushing of plants, as the Hovitos pursued him. He felt strangely detached all at once from his own body; he'd moved beyond a sense of his physical self, beyond the absurd demands of muscle and sinew, pushing himself through the terrain in a way that was automatic, a matter of basic reflex. He heard the occasional dart strike bark, the scared flapping of jungle birds rising out of branches, the squeal of animals that scampered from the path of the Hovitos. Run, he kept thinking. Run until you can't run anymore, then you run a little further. Don't think. Don't stop.

Belloq, he thought. *My time will come.*

If I get out of this one.

Running—he didn't know for how long. Day was beginning to fade.

He paused, looked upward at the thin light through the dense trees, then dashed in the direction of the river. What he wanted to hear more than anything now was the vital sound of rushing water, what he wanted to see was the waiting plane.

He twisted again and moved through a clearing, where he was suddenly exposed by the absence of trees. For a moment, the clearing was menacing, the sudden silence of dusk unsettling.

Then he heard the cries of the Hovitos, and the clearing seemed to him like the center of a bizarre target. He turned around, saw the movement of a couple of figures, felt the air rush as two spears spun past him—and after that he was running again, racing for the river. He thought as he ran, *They don't teach you survival techniques in Archaeology 101, they don't supply survival manuals along with the methodology of excavation.*

And they certainly don't warn you about the cunning of a Frenchman named Belloq.

He paused again and listened to the Indians behind him. Then there was another sound, one that delighted him, that exalted him: the motion of fast-flowing water, the swaying of rushes. *The river!* How far could it be now? He listened again to be certain and then moved in the direction of the sound, his energies recharged, batteries revitalized. Quicker now, harder and faster. Crashing through the foliage that slashes against you, ignore the cuts and abrasions. Quicker and harder and faster. The sound was becoming clearer. The water rushing.

He emerged from the trees.

There.

Down the slope, beyond the greenery, the hostile vegetation, the river.

The river and the amphibian plane floating up and down on the swell. He couldn't have imagined anything more welcoming. He moved along the slope and then realized there wasn't an easy way down through the foliage to the plane. There wasn't time to find one, either. You had to go up the slope to the point where, as it formed a cliff over the river, you would have to jump. Jump, he thought. What the hell. What's one more jump?

He climbed, conscious of the shape of a man who sat on one wing of the plane far below. Indy reached a point almost directly over the plane, stared down for a moment, and then he shut his eyes and stepped out over the edge of the cliff.

He hit the tepid water close to the wing of the plane, went under as the current pulled him away, surfaced blindly and struck out toward the craft. The man on the wing stood upright as Indy grabbed a strut and hauled himself out of the water.

"Get the thing going, Jock!" Indy shouted. "Get it going!"

Jock rushed along the wing and clambered inside the cockpit as Indy scurried, breathless, into the passenger compartment and slumped across the seat. He closed his eyes and listened to the shudder of engines when the craft skimmed the surface of the water.

"I didn't expect you to drop in quite so suddenly," Jock said.

"Spare me the puns, huh?"

"A spot of trouble, laddie?"

Indy wanted to laugh. "Remind me to tell you sometime." He lay back and closed his eyes, hoping sleep would come. But then he realized that the plane wasn't moving. He sat upright and leaned forward toward the pilot.

"Stalled," Jock said.

"Stalled! Why?"

Jock grinned. "I only fly the bloody thing. People have this funny impression that all Scotsmen are bloody mechanics, Indy."

Through the window, Indy could see the Hovitos begin to wade into the shallows of the river. Thirty feet, twenty now. They were like grotesque ghosts of the riverbed risen to avenge some historic transgression. They raised their arms; a storm of spears flew toward the fuselage of the plane.

"Jock . . ."

"I'm bloody well trying, Indy. I'm trying."

Calmly, Indy said, "I think you should try harder."

The spears struck the plane, clattering against the wings, hitting the fuselage with the sound of enormous hailstones.

"I've got it," Jock said.

The engines spluttered into laborious life just as two of the Hovitos had swum as far as the wing and were clambering up.

"It's moving," Jock said. "It's moving."

The craft skimmed forward again and then began to rise, with a cumbersome quality, above the river. Indy watched the two warriors lose their balance and drop, like weird creatures of the jungle, into the water.

The plane was rising across the tops of trees, the underdraft shaking the branches, driving panicked birds into the last of sunlight. Indy laughed and closed his eyes.

"Thought you might not make it," Jock said. "To tell you the bloody truth."

"Never a doubt in mind," Indy said, and smiled.

"Relax, now, man. Get some sleep. Forget the bloody jungle."

For a moment, Indy drifted. Relief. The relaxation of muscle. A good feeling. He could lose himself in this sensation for a long time.

Then something moved across his thigh. Something slow, heavy.

He opened his eyes and saw a boa constrictor coiling itself in a threatening way around his upper leg. He jumped upright quickly.

"Jock!"

The pilot looked round, smiled. "He won't hurt you, Indy. That's Reggie. He wouldn't harm a soul."

"Get it away from me, Jock."

The pilot reached back, stroked the snake, then drew it into the cockpit beside him. Indy watched the snake slide away from him. An old revulsion, an inexplicable terror. For some people it was spiders, for some rats, for others enclosed spaces. For him it was the repulsive sight and touch of a snake. He rubbed at the sweat newly formed on his forehead, shivering as the water soaking his clothes turned abruptly chill.

"Just keep it beside you," he said. "I can't stand snakes."

"I'll let you in on a wee secret," Jock said. "The average snake is nicer than the average person."

"I'll take your word for it," Indy said. "Just keep it away from me."

You think you're safe, then—a boa constrictor decides to bask on your body. All in a day's work, he thought.

For a while he looked out of the window and watched darkness fall with an inscrutable certainty over the vast jungle. You can keep your secrets, Indy thought. You can keep all your secrets.

Before he fell asleep, lulled by the noise of the engines, he hoped it would not be a long time before his path crossed once again with that of the Frenchman.

TWO
Berlín

IN AN OFFICE on the Wilhelmstrasse, an officer in the black uniform of the SS—an incongruously petite man named Eidel—was seated behind his desk, staring at the bundles of manila folders stacked neatly in front of him. It was clear to Eidel's visitor, who was named Dietrich, that the small man used the stacks of folders in a compensatory way: they made him feel big, important. It was the same everywhere these days, Dietrich thought. You assess a man and his worth by the amount of paperwork he is able to amass, by the number of rubber stamps he is authorized to use. Dietrich, who liked to consider himself a man of action, sighed inwardly and looked toward the window, against which a pale brown blind had been drawn. He waited for Eidel to speak, but the SS officer had been silent some time, as if even his silences were intended to convey something of what he saw as his own importance.

Dietrich looked at the portrait of the Führer hanging on the wall. When it came down to it, it didn't matter what you might think of someone like Eidel—soft, shackled to his desk, pompous, locked away in miserable offices—because Eidel had a direct line of access to Hitler. So you listened, and you smiled, and you pretended you were of lesser rank. Eidel, after all, was a member of the inner circle, the elite corps of Hitler's own private guard.

Eidel smoothed his uniform, which looked as if it had been freshly laundered. He said, "I trust I have made the importance of this matter clear to you, Colonel?"

Dietrich nodded. He felt impatient. He hated offices.

Eidel rose, stretched on his tiptoes in the manner of a man reaching for a subway strap he knows to be out of range, then walked to the window. "The Führer has his mind set on obtaining this particular object. And when his mind is set, of course . . ." Eidel paused, turned, stared at Dietrich. He made a gesture with his hands, indicating that whatever passed through the Führer's mind was incomprehensible to lesser men.

"I understand," Dietrich said, drumming his fingertips on his attaché case.

"The religious significance is important," Eidel said. "It isn't that the Führer has any special interest in Jewish relics per se, naturally." And here he paused, laughing oddly, as if the thought were wildly amusing. "He has more interest in the *symbolic* meaning of the item, if you understand."

It crossed Dietrich's mind that Eidel was lying, obscuring something here: it was hard to imagine the Führer's being interested in *anything* for its symbolic value. He stared at the flimsy cable Eidel had allowed him to read a few minutes ago. Then he gazed once more at the picture of Hitler, which was unsmiling, grim.

Eidel, in the manner of a small-town university professor, said, "We come to the matter of expert knowledge now."

"Indeed," Dietrich said.

"We come to the matter, specifically, of archaeological knowledge."

Dietrich said nothing. He saw where this was leading. He saw what was needed of him.

He said, "I'm afraid it's beyond my grasp."

Eidel smiled thinly. "But you have connections, I understand. You have connections with the highest authorities in this field, am I right?"

"A matter of debate."

"There is no time for any such debate," Eidel said. "I am not here to argue the matter of what constitutes high authority, Colonel. I am here, as you are, to obey a certain important order."

"You don't need to remind *me* of that," Dietrich said.

"I know," Eidel said, leaning against his desk now. "And you understand I am talking about a certain authority of your acquaintance whose expertise in this particular sphere of interest will be invaluable to us. Correct?"

"The Frenchman," Dietrich said.

"Of course."

Dietrich was silent for a time. He felt slightly uneasy. It was as if the face of Hitler were scolding him now for his hesitance. "The Frenchman is hard to find. Like any mercenary, he regards the world as his place of employment."

"When did you last hear of him?"

Dietrich shrugged. "In South America, I believe."

Eidel studied the backs of his hands, thin and pale and yet indelicate, like the hands of someone who has failed in his ambition to be a concert pianist. He said, "You can find him. You understand what I'm saying? You understand where this order comes from?"

"I can find him," Dietrich said. "But I warn you now—"

"Don't warn *me*, Colonel."

Dietrich felt his throat become dry. This little trumped-up imbecile of a desk clerk. He would have enjoyed throttling him, stuffing those manila folders down his gullet until he choked. "Very well, I *advise* you—the Frenchman's price is high."

"No object," Eidel said.

"And his trustworthiness is less than admirable."

"That is something you will be expected to deal with. The point, Colonel Dietrich, is that you will find him and you will bring him to the Führer. But it must be done quickly. It must be done, if you understand, *yesterday*."

Dietrich stared at the shade on the window. It sometimes filled him with dread that the Führer had surrounded himself with lackeys and fools like Eidel. It implied a certain cloudiness of judgment where humans were concerned.

Eidel smiled, as if he was amused by Dietrich's unease. Then he said, "Speed is important, of course. Other parties are interested, obviously. These parties do not represent the best interests of the Reich. Do I make myself clear?"

"Clear," Dietrich said. Dietrich thought about the Frenchman for a moment; he knew, even if he hadn't told Eidel, that Belloq was in the south of France right then. The prospect of doing business with Belloq was what appalled him. There was a smooth quality to the man that masked an underlying ruthlessness, a selfishness, a disregard for philosophies, beliefs, politics. If it served Belloq's interests, it was therefore valid. If not, he didn't care.

"The other parties will be taken care of if they should surface," Eidel was saying. "They should be of no concern to you."

"Then that is how I'll treat them," Dietrich said.

Eidel picked up the cable and glanced at it. "What we have talked about is not to go beyond these four walls, Colonel. I don't have to say that, do I?"

"You don't have to say it," Dietrich repeated, irritated.

Eidel went back to his seat and stared at the other man across the mountain of folders. He was silent for a moment. And then he feigned surprise at finding Dietrich seated opposite him. "Are you still here, Colonel?"

Dietrich clutched his attaché case and rose. It was hard not to feel hatred toward these black-uniformed clowns. They acted as if they owned the world.

"I was about to leave," Dietrich said.

"*Heil Hitler*," Eidel said, raising his hand, his arm rigid.

At the door Dietrich answered in the same words.

THREE
Connecticut

INDIANA JONES sat in his office at Marshall College.

He had just finished his first lecture of the year for Archaeology 101, and it had gone well. It always went well. He loved teaching and he knew he was able to convey his passion for the subject matter to his students. But now he was restless and his restlessness disturbed him. Because he knew exactly what it was he wanted to do.

Indy put his feet up on the desk, deliberately knocked a couple of books over, then rose and paced around the office—seeing it not as the intimate place it usually was, his retreat, his hideaway, but as the cell of some remote stranger.

Jones, he told himself.

Indiana Jones, wise up.

The objects around him seemed to shed their meaning for a time. The huge wall map of South America became a surreal blur, an artist's dadaist conception. The clay replica of the idol looked suddenly silly, ugly. He picked it up and he thought: For something like *this* you laid your life on the line? You must have an essential screw loose. A bolt out of place.

He held the replica of the idol, gazing at it absently.

This mad love of antiquity struck him all at once as unholy, unnatural. An insane infatuation with the sense of history—more than the *sense*, the need to reach out and touch it, hold it, understand it through its relics and artifacts, finding yourself haunted by the faces of long-dead artisans and craftsmen and artists, spooked by the notion of hands creating these objects, fingers that had long since turned to skeleton, to dust. But never forgotten, never quite forgotten, not so long as you existed with your irrational passion.

For a moment the old feelings came back to him, assailed him, the first excitement he'd ever felt as a student. When? Fifteen years ago? sixteen? twenty? It didn't matter: time meant something different to him than it did to most people. Time was a thing you discovered through the secrets it had buried—in temples, in ruins, under rocks and dust and sand. Time expanded, became elastic, creating that amazing sense of everything that had ever lived being linked to everything that existed in the now; and death was fundamentally meaningless because of what you left behind.

Meaningless.

He thought of Champollion laboring over the Rosetta stone, the astonishment at finally deciphering ancient hieroglyphics. He thought of Schliemann finding the site of Troy. Flinders Petrie excavating the pre-dynastic cemetery at Nagada. Woolley discovering the royal cemetery at Ur in Iraq. Carter and Lord Carnarvon stumbling over the tomb of Tutankhamon.

That was where it had all begun. In that consciousness of discovery, which was like the eye of an intellectual hurricane. And you were swept along, carried away, transported backward in the kind of time machine the writers of fantasy couldn't comprehend: your personal time machine, your private line to the vital past.

He balanced the replica of the idol in the center of his hand and stared at it as if it were a personal enemy. No, he thought: you're your own worst enemy, Jones. You got carried away because you had access to half of a map among Forrestal's papers—and because you desperately wanted to trust two thugs who had the other half.

Moron, he thought.

And Belloq. Belloq was probably the smart one. Belloq had a razor-blade eye for the quick chance. Belloq always had had that quality—like the snakes you have a phobia about. Coming out unseen from under a rock, the slithering predator, always grasping for the thing he hasn't hunted for himself.

All that formed in the center of his mind now was an image of Belloq—that slender, handsome face, the dark of the eye, the smile that concealed the cunning.

He remembered other encounters with the Frenchman. He remembered graduate school, when Belloq had chiseled his way to the Archaeological Society Prize by presenting a paper on stratigraphy—the basis of which Indy recognized as being his own work. And in some way Belloq had plagiarized it, in some way he had found access to it. Indy couldn't prove anything because it would have been a case of sour grapes, a rash of envy.

1934. Remember the summer of that year, he thought.

1934. Black summer. He had spent months planning a dig in the Rub al Khali Desert of Saudi Arabia. Months of labor and preparation and scrounging for funds, putting the pieces together, arguing that his instincts about the dig were correct, that there were the remains of a nomadic culture to be found in that arid place, a culture pre-dating Christ. And then what?

He closed his eyes.

Even now the memory filled him with bitterness.

Belloq had been there before him.

Belloq had excavated the place.

It was true the Frenchman had found little of historic significance in the excavations, but that wasn't the point.

The point was that Belloq had stolen from him again. And again he wasn't sure how he could prove the theft.

And now the idol.

Indy looked up, startled out of his reverie, as the door of his office opened slowly.

Marcus Brody appeared, an expression of caution on his face, a caution that was in part concern. Indy considered Marcus, curator of the National Museum, his closest friend.

"Indiana," he said and his voice was soft.

He held the replica of the idol out, as if he were offering it to the other man, then he dropped it abruptly in the trash can on the floor.

"I had the real thing in my hand, Marcus. The real thing." Indy sat back, eyes shut, fingers vigorously massaging his eyelids.

"You told me, Indiana. You already told me," Brody said. "As soon as you came back. Remember?"

"I can get it back, Marcus. I can get it back. I figured it out. Belloq has to sell it, right? So where's he going to sell it? Huh?"

Brody looked tolerantly at him. "Where, Indiana?"

"Marrakesh. Marrakesh, that's where." Indy got up, indicating various figures that were on the desk. These were the items he'd taken from the Temple, the bits and pieces he'd swept up quickly. "Look. They've got to be worth something, Marcus. They've got to be worth enough money to get me to Marrakesh, right?"

Brody barely glanced at the items. Instead, he put out his hand and laid it on Indy's shoulder, a touch of friendship and concern. "The museum will buy them, as usual. No questions asked. But we'll talk about the idol later. Right now I want you to meet some people. They've come a long way to see you, Indiana."

"What people?"

Brody said, "They've come from Washington, Indiana. Just to see you."

"Who are they?" Indy asked wanly.

"Army Intelligence."

"Army *what?* Am I in some kind of trouble?"

"No. Quite the opposite, it would seem. They appear to need your help."

"The only help I'm interested in is getting the cash together for Marrakesh, Marcus. These things have to be worth *something*."

"Later, Indiana. Later. First I want you to see these people."

Indy paused by the wall map of South America. "Yeah," he said. "I'll see them. I'll see them, if it means so much to you."

"They're waiting in the lecture hall."

They moved into the corridor.

A pretty young girl appeared in front of Indy. She was carrying a bundle of books and was pretending to look studious, efficient. Indy brightened when he saw her.

"Professor Jones," she was saying.

"Uh—"

"I was hoping we could have a conference," she said shyly, glancing at Marcus Brody.

"Yeah, sure, sure, Susan, I know I said we'd talk."

Marcus Brody said, "Not now. Not now, Indiana." And he turned to the girl. "Professor Jones has an *important* conference to attend, my dear. Why don't you call him later?"

"Yeah," Indy mumbled. "I'll be back at noon."

The girl smiled in a disappointed way, then drifted off along the corridor. Indy watched her go, admiring her legs, the roundness of the calves, the slender ankles. He felt Brody tug at his sleeve.

"Pretty. Up to your usual standards, Indiana. But later. Okay?"

"Later," Indy said, looking reluctantly away from the girl.

Brody pushed open the door of the lecture hall. Seated near the podium were two uniformed Army officers. They turned their faces in unison as the door opened.

"If this is the draft board, I've already served," Indy said.

Marcus Brody ushered Indy to a chair on the podium. "Indiana, I'd like to introduce you to Colonel Musgrove and Major Eaton. These are the people who've come from Washington to see you."

Eaton said, "Good to meet you. We've heard a lot about you, Professor Jones. Doctor of Archaeology, expert on the occult, obtainer of rare antiquities."

"That's one way to put it," Indy said.

"The 'obtainer of rare antiquities' sounds intriguing," the major said.

Indy glanced at Brody, who said, "I'm sure everything Professor Jones does for our museum here confirms strictly to the guidelines of the International Treaty for the Protection of Antiquities."

"Oh, I'm sure," Major Eaton said.

Musgrove said, "You're a man of many talents, Professor."

Indy made a dismissive gesture, waving a hand. What did these guys want?

Major Eaton said, "I understand you studied under Professor Ravenwood at the University of Chicago?"

"Yes."

"Have you any idea of his present whereabouts?"

Ravenwood. The name threw memories back with a kind of violence Indy didn't like. "Rumors, nothing more. I heard he was in Asia, I guess. I don't know."

"We understood you were pretty close to him," Musgrove said.

"Yeah." Indy rubbed his chin. "We were friends . . . We haven't spoken in years, though. I'm afraid we had what you might call a falling out." *A falling out*, he thought. There was a polite way to put it. A falling out—it was more like a total collapse. And then he was thinking of Marion, an unwanted memory, something he had yet to excavate from the deeper strata of his mind. Marion Ravenwood, the girl with the wonderful eyes.

Now the officers were whispering together, deciding something. Then Eaton turned and looked solemn and said, "What we're going to tell you has to remain confidential."

"Sure," Indy said. Ravenwood—where did the old man fit in all this fragile conundrum? And when was somebody going to get to the point?

Musgrove said, "Yesterday, one of our European stations intercepted a German communiqué sent from Cairo to Berlin. The news in it was obviously exciting to the German agents in Egypt." Musgrove looked at Eaton, waiting for him to continue the narrative, as if each was capable of delivering only a certain amount of information at any one time.

Eaton said, "I'm not sure if I'm telling you something you already know, Professor Jones, when I mention the fact that the Nazis have had teams of archaeologists running around the world for the last two years—"

"It hasn't escaped my attention."

"Sure. They appear to be on a frantic search for any kind of religious artifact they can get. Hitler, according to our intelligence reports, is obsessed with the occult. We understand he even has a personal soothsayer, if that's the word. And right now it seems that some kind of archaeological dig—highly secretive—is going on in the desert outside Cairo."

Indy nodded. This was sending him to sleep. He knew of Hitler's seemingly endless concern with divining the future, making gold out of lead, hunting the elixir, whatever. You name it, he thought, and if it's weird enough, then the crazy little man with the mustache is sure to be interested in it.

Indy watched Musgrove take a sheet from his briefcase. He held it a moment, then he said, "This communiqué contains some information concerning the activity in the desert, but we don't know what to make of it. We thought it might mean something to you." And he passed the sheet to Indy. The message said:

TANIS DEVELOPMENT PROCEEDING.

ACQUIRE HEADPIECE, STAFF OF RA,

ABNER RAVENWOOD, US.

He read the words again, his mind suddenly clear, suddenly sharp. He stood up, looked at Brody and said, incredulously, "The Nazis have discovered Tanis."

Brody's face was grim and pale.

Eaton said, "Sorry. You've just lost me. What does Tanis mean to you?"

Indy walked from the podium to the window, his mind racing now. He pushed the window open and breathed in the crisp morning air, feeling it pleasingly cold in his lungs. *Tanis. The Staff of Ra. Ravenwood.* It flooded back to him now, the old legends, the fables, the stories. He was struck by a barrage of knowledge, information he'd stored in his brain for years—so much that he wanted to get it out quickly, speed through it. Take it slow, he thought. Tell it to them slowly so they'll understand. He turned to the officers and said, "A lot of this is going to be hard for you to understand. Maybe. I don't know. It's going to depend on your personal beliefs, I can tell you that much from the outset. Okay?" He paused, looking at their blank faces. "The city of Tanis is one of the possible resting places of the lost Ark."

Musgrove interrupted: "Ark? As in Noah?"

Indy shook his head. "Not Noah. I'm talking about the Ark of the Covenant. I'm talking about the chest the Israelites used to carry around the Ten Commandments."

Eaton said, "Back up. You mean *the* Ten Commandments?"

"I mean the *actual stone tablets,* the original ones Moses brought down from Mount Horeb. The ones he's said to have smashed when he saw the decadence of the Jews. While he was up in the mountain communing with God and being shown the law, the rest of his people are having orgies and building idols. So he's pretty angry and he breaks the tablets, right?"

The faces of the military men were impassive. Indy wished he could imbue them with the kind of enthusiasm he was beginning to feel himself.

"Then the Israelites put the broken pieces in the Ark and they carried it with them everywhere they went. When they settled in Canaan, the Ark was placed in the Temple of Solomon. It stayed there for years . . . then it was gone."

"Where?" Musgrove asked.

"Nobody knows who took it or when."

Brody, speaking more patiently than Indy, said, "An Egyptian pharaoh invaded Jerusalem around 926 B.C. Shishak by name. He *may* have taken it back to the city of Tanis—"

Indy cut in: "Where he may have hidden it in a secret chamber they called the Well of the Souls."

There was a silence in the hall.

Then Indy said, "Anyway, that's the myth. But bad things always seemed to happen to outsiders who meddled with the Ark. Soon after Shishak returned to Egypt, the city of Tanis was consumed by the desert in a sandstorm that lasted a year."

"The obligatory curse," Eaton said.

Indy was annoyed by the man's skepticism. "If you like," he said, trying to be patient. "But during the Battle of Jericho, Hebrew priests carried the Ark around the city for seven days before the walls collapsed. And when the Philistines supposedly captured the Ark, they brought the whole shooting works down on themselves—including plagues of boils and plagues of mice."

Eaton said, "This is all very interesting, I guess. But why would an American be mentioned in a Nazi cable, if we can get back to the point?"

"He's *the* expert on Tanis," Indy said. "Tanis was his obsession. He even collected some of its relics. But he never found the city."

"Why would the Nazis be interested in him?" Musgrove asked.

Indy paused for a moment. "It seems to me that the Nazis are looking for the headpiece to the Staff of Ra. And they think Abner has it."

"The Staff of Ra," Eaton said. "It's all somewhat farfetched."

Musgrove, who seemed more interested, leaned forward in his seat. "What is the Staff of Ra, Professor Jones?"

"I'll draw you a picture," Indy said. He strode to the blackboard and began to sketch quickly. As he drew the chalk across the board, he said, "The Staff of Ra is supposedly the clue to the location of the Ark. A pretty clever clue into the bargain. It was basically a long stick, maybe six feet high, nobody's really sure. Anyhow, it was capped by an elaborate headpiece in the shape of the sun, with a crystal at its center. You still with me? You had to take the staff to a special map room in the city of Tanis—it had the whole city laid out in miniature. When you placed the staff in a certain spot in this room at a certain time of day, the sun would shine through the crystal in the headpiece and send down a beam of light to the map, giving you the location of the Well of the Souls—"

"Where the Ark was concealed," Musgrove said.

"Right. Which is probably why the Nazis want the headpiece. Which explains Ravenwood's name in the cable."

Eaton got up and began moving around restlessly. "What does this Ark look like anyhow?"

"I'll show you," Indy said. He went quickly to the back of the hall, found a book, flipped the pages until he came to a large color print. He showed it to the two military officers. They stared in silence at the illustration, which depicted a biblical battle scene. The army of the Israelites was vanquishing its foe; at the forefront of the Israelite ranks were two men carrying the Ark of the Covenant, an oblong gold chest with two golden cherubim crowning it. The Israelites carried the chest by poles placed through special rings in the corners. A thing of quite extraordinary beauty—but more impressive than its appearance was the piercing and brilliant jet of white light and flame that issued from the wings of the angels, a jet that drove into the ranks of the retreating army, creating apparent terror and devastation.

Impressed, Musgrove said, "What's that supposed to be coming out of the wings?"

Indy shrugged. "Who knows? Lightning. Fire. The power of God. Whatever you call it, it was supposedly capable of leveling mountains and wasting entire regions. According to Moses, an army that carried the Ark before it was invincible." Indy looked at Eaton's face and decided, This guy has no imagination. Nothing will ever set this character on fire. Eaton shrugged and continued to stare at the illustration. Disbelief, Indy thought. Military skepticism.

Musgrove said, "What are your own feelings about this . . . so-called power of the Ark, Professor?"

"As I said, it depends on your beliefs. It depends on whether you accept the myth as having some basis in truth."

"You're sidestepping," Musgrove said and smiled.

"I keep an open mind," Indy answered.

Eaton turned away from the picture. "A nut like Hitler,

though . . . He might really believe in this power, right? He might buy the whole thing."

"Probably," Indy said. He watched Eaton a moment, suddenly feeling a familiar sense of anticipation, a rise in his temperature. *The lost city of Tanis. The Well of the Souls. The Ark.* There was an elusive melody here, and it enticed him like the seductive call of a siren.

"He might imagine that with the Ark his military machine would be invincible," Eaton said, more to himself than to anybody else. "I can see, if he swallows the whole fairy tale, the psychological advantage he'd feel at the very least."

Indy said, "There's one other thing. According to legend, the Ark will be recovered at the time of the coming of the true Messiah."

"The true Messiah," Musgrove said.

"Which is what Hitler probably imagines himself to be," Eaton remarked.

There was a silence in the hall now. Indy looked once more at the illustration, the savagery of the light that flashed from the wings of the angels and scorched the retreating enemies. A power beyond all power. Beyond definition. He shut his eyes for a second. What if it *was* true? What if such a power *did* exist? Okay, you try to be rational, you try to work it like Eaton, putting it down to some old fable, something circulated by a bunch of zealous Israelites. A scare tactic against their enemies, a kind of psychological warfare even. Just the same, there was something here you couldn't ignore, couldn't shove aside.

He opened his eyes and heard Musgrove sigh and say, "You've been very helpful. I hope we can call on you again if we need to."

"Anytime, gentlemen. Anytime you like," Indy said.

There was a round of handshakes, then Brody escorted the officers to the door. Alone in the empty hall, Indy closed the book. He thought for a moment, trying at the same time to suppress the sense of excitement he felt. *The Nazis have found Tanis*—and these words went around and around in his brain.

The girl, Susan, said, "I really hope I didn't embarrass you when you were with Brody. I mean, I was so . . . obvious."

"You weren't obvious," Indy said.

They were sitting together in the cluttered living room of Indy's small frame house. The room was filled with souvenirs of trips, of digs, restored clay vessels and tiny statues and fragments of pottery and maps and globes—as cluttered, he sometimes thought, as my life.

The girl drew her knees up, hugging them, laying her face down against them. Like a cat, he thought. A tiny contented cat.

"I love this room," she said. "I love the whole house . . . but this room especially."

Indy got up from the sofa and, hands in his pockets, walked around the room. The girl, for some reason, was more of an intrusion than she should have been. Sometimes when she spoke he tuned her out. He heard only the noise of her voice and not the meaning of her words. He poured himself a drink, sipped it, swallowed; it burned in his chest—a good burning, like a small sun glowing down there.

Susan said, "You seem so distant tonight, Indy."

"Distant?"

"You've got something on your mind. I don't know." She shrugged.

He walked to the radio, turned it on, barely listening to the drone of someone making a pitch for Maxwell House. The girl changed the station and then there was dance-band music. Distant, he thought. Farther than you could dream. Miles away. Oceans and continents and centuries. He was suddenly thinking about Ravenwood, about the last conversation they'd had, the old man's terrible storm, his wrath. When he listened to the echoes of those voices, he felt sad, disappointed in himself; he'd taken some fragile trust and shattered it.

Marion's infatuated with you, and you took advantage of that.

You're twenty-eight, presumably a grown man, and you've taken advantage of a young girl's brainless infatuation and twisted it to suit your own purpose just because she thinks she's in love with you.

Susan said, "If you want me to leave, Indy, I will. If you want to be alone, I'll understand."

"It's okay. Really. Stay."

There was a knock on the door; the porch creaked.

Indy moved out of the living room along the hallway and saw Marcus Brody outside. He was smiling a secretive smile, as if he had news he wanted to linger over, savor for as long as he could.

"Marcus," Indy said. "I wasn't expecting you."

"I think you were," Brody said, pushing the screen door.

"We'll go in the study," Indy said.

"What's wrong with the living room?"

"Company."

"Ah. What else?"

They entered the study.

"You did it, didn't you?" Indy said.

Brody smiled. "They want you to get the Ark before the Nazis."

It was a moment before Indy could say anything. He felt a sense of exaltation, an awareness of triumph. *The Ark.* He said, "I think I've been waiting all my life to hear something like that."

Brody looked at the shot glass in Indy's hand for a moment. "They talked with their people in Washington. Then they consulted me. They want you, Indiana. They want *you.*"

Indy sat down behind his desk, gazed into his glass, then looked around the room. A strange emotion filled him suddenly; this was more than books and articles and maps, more than speculation, scholarly argument, discussion, debate—a sense of reality had replaced all the words and pictures.

Brody said, "Of course, given the military mind, they don't exactly buy all that business about the power of the Ark and so forth. They don't want to embrace any such mythologies. After all, they're soldiers, and soldiers like to think they're hard-line realists. They want the Ark—and I'll quote, if I can—because of its 'historic and cultural significance' and because 'such a priceless object should not become the property of a fascist regime.' Or words to that effect."

"Their reasons don't matter," Indy said.

"In addition, they'll pay handsomely—"

"I don't care about the money, either, Marcus." Indy raised a hand, indicated the room in a sweep. "The Ark represents the elusive thing I feel about archaeology—you know, history concealing its secrets. Things lying out there waiting to be discovered. I don't give *that* for their reasons or their money." And he snapped his fingers.

Brody nodded his head in understanding. "The museum, of course, will get the Ark."

"Of course."

"If it exists . . ." Brody paused a moment, then added, "We shouldn't build our hopes up too high."

Indy stood up. "I have to find Abner first. That would be the logical step. If Abner has the headpiece, then I have to get it before the opposition does. That makes sense, right? Without the headpiece, *voilà*, no Ark. So where do I find Abner?" He stopped, realizing how quickly he'd been talking. "I think I know where to start looking—"

Brody said, "It's been a long time, Indiana. Things change."

Indy stared at the other man for a second. The comment was enigmatic to him: *Things change.* And then he realized Marcus Brody was talking about Marion.

"He might have mellowed toward you," Brody said. "On the other hand, he might still carry a grudge. In that case, it's reasonable to assume he wouldn't want to give you the headpiece. If in fact he has it."

"We'll hope for the best, my friend."

"Always the optimist, right?"

"Not always," Indy said. "Optimism can be deadly."

Brody was silent now, moving around the room, flicking the pages of books. Then he looked at Indy in a somber way. "I want you to be careful, Indiana."

"I'm always careful."

"You can be pretty reckless. I know that as well as you. But the Ark isn't like anything you've gone after before. It's bigger. More dangerous." Brody slammed a book shut, as if to emphasize a point. "I'm not skeptical, like those military people—I think the Ark has secrets. I think it has dangerous secrets."

For a second Indy was about to say something flippant, something about the melodramatic tone in the other man's voice. But he saw from the expression on Brody's face that the man was serious.

"I don't want to lose you, Indiana, no matter how great the prize is. You understand?"

The two men shook hands.

Indy noticed that Brody's skin was damp with sweat.

Alone, Indy sat up late into the night, unable to sleep, unable to let his mind rest. He wandered from one room of the small house to another, clenching and unclenching his hands. After all these years, he thought, all this passage of time—would Ravenwood help him? Would Ravenwood, given that he had the headpiece, come to his assistance? And behind these questions there lingered still another one. Would Marion still be with her father?

He continued to go from room to room until finally he settled in his study and put his feet up on the desk, looking at the various objects stuffed in the room. Then he closed his eyes for a moment, tried to think clearly, and rose. From a bookshelf he removed a copy of Ravenwood's old journal, a gift from the old man when the two were still friends. Indy skimmed the pages, noticing one disappointment listed after another, one excavation that hadn't lived up to its promises, another that had revealed only the most slender, the most tantalizing, of clues to the whereabouts of the Ark. The outlines of an obsession in these pages; the heartbreaking search for a lost object of history. But the Ark could flow in your blood and fill the air you breathed. And he understood the old man's single-mindedness, his devotion, the kind of lust that had led him from one country to another, to one hope after another. The pages yielded up that much—but there was no mention of the headpiece anywhere. Nothing.

The last item in the journal mentioned the country of Nepal, the prospect of another dig. Nepal, Indy thought: the Himalayas, the roughest terrain on earth. And a long way from whatever the Germans were doing in Egypt. Maybe Ravenwood had stumbled onto something else back then, a fresh clue to the Ark. Maybe all the old stuff about Tanis was incorrect. Just maybe.

Nepal. It was a place in which to start.

It was a beginning.

He fingered the journal a moment longer, then he set it down, wishing he knew how Abner Ravenwood would react to him.

And how Marion would respond.

FOUR

Berchtesgaden, Germany

DIETRICH WAS UNEASY in the company of René Belloq. It wasn't so much the lack of trust he felt in the Frenchman, the feeling he had that Belloq treated almost everything with equal cynicism; it was, rather, the strange charisma of Belloq that worried Dietrich, the idea that somehow you *wanted* to like him, that he was drawing you in despite yourself.

They were seated together in an anteroom at Berchtesgaden, the Führer's mountain retreat, a place Dietrich had never visited before and which filled him with some awe. But he noticed that Belloq, lounging casually, his long legs outstretched, gave no sign of any similar feeling. Quite the opposite—Belloq might have been sitting sprawled in a cheap French café, in fact in the kind of place where Dietrich had found him in Marseilles. No respect, Dietrich thought. No sense of the importance of things. He was irritated by the archaeologist's attitude.

He listened to a clock tick, the delicate sounds of chimes. Belloq sighed, shifted his legs around and looked at his wristwatch.

"What are we waiting for, Dietrich?" he asked.

Dietrich couldn't help talking in a low voice. "The Führer will see us when he's ready, Belloq. You must think he has nothing better to do than spend his time speaking to you about some museum piece."

"A museum piece." Belloq spoke with obvious contempt, staring across the room at the German. How little they know, he thought. How little they understand of history. They put their faith in all the wrong things: they build their monumental arches and parade their strutting armies—failing to realize you cannot deliberately create the awe of history. It is something that already exists, something you cannot aspire to fabricate with the trappings of grandeur. The Ark: the very thought of the possibility of discovering the Ark made him impatient. Why did he have to speak with this miserable little German house painter, anyhow? Why was he obliged to sit through a meeting with the man when the dig had already begun in Egypt? What, after all, could he learn from Hitler? Nothing, he thought. Absolutely nothing. Some pompous lecture, perhaps. A diatribe of some kind. Something about the greatness of the Reich. About how, if the Ark existed, it belonged in Germany.

What did any of them know? he wondered.

The Ark didn't belong anywhere. If it had secrets, if it contained the kind of power it was said to, then he wanted to be the first to discover it—it wasn't something to be lightly entrusted to the maniac who sat, even now, in some other room of this mountain lodge and kept him waiting.

He sighed impatiently, shifting in his chair.

And then he got up, walked to the window and looked out across the mountains, not really seeing them, noticing them only in an absent way. He was thinking of the moment of opening the box, looking inside and seeing the relics of the stone tablets Moses had brought down from Mount Horeb. It was easy to imagine his hand raising the lid, the sound of his own voice—then the moment of revelation.

The moment of a lifetime: there was no prize greater than the Ark of the Covenant.

When he turned from the window, Dietrich was watching him. The German noticed the odd look in Belloq's eyes, the faint smile on the mouth that seemed to be directed inward, as if he were enjoying an immensely private joke, some deep and amusing thought. He realized then how far his own lack of trust went—but this was the Führer's affair, it was the Führer who had asked for the best, the Führer who had asked for René Belloq.

Dietrich heard the clock chime the quarter hour. From a corridor somewhere inside the building, he heard the sound of footsteps. Belloq turned expectantly toward the door. But the footsteps faded and Belloq cursed quietly in French.

"How much longer are we supposed to wait?" the Frenchman asked.

Dietrich shrugged.

"Don't tell me," Belloq said. "The Führer lives his life by a clock to which we ordinary men have no access, correct? Perhaps he has visions of his own private time, no? Perhaps he thinks he has some profound knowledge of the nature of time?" Belloq made a gesture of despair with one hand, then he smiled.

Dietrich moved uncomfortably, beset by the notion that the room was wired, that Hitler was listening to this insane talk. He said, "Does nothing awe you, Belloq?"

"I might answer you, Dietrich, except I doubt you would understand what I was talking about."

They were silent now. Belloq returned to the window. Every moment stuck here is a moment less to spend in Egypt, he thought. And he realized that time was important, that news of the dig would spread, that it couldn't be kept secret forever. He only hoped that German security was good.

He looked at the German again and said, "You haven't fully explained to me, as a matter of interest, how the headpiece is to be obtained. I need to know."

"It is being taken care of," Dietrich said. "People have been sent—"

"What kind of people, Dietrich? Is there an archaeologist among them?"

"Why, no—"

"Thugs, Dietrich? Some of your bullies?"

"Professionals."

"Ah, but not professional archaeologists. How are they to know if they discover the headpiece? How are they supposed to know it isn't a forgery?"

Dietrich smiled. "The secret lies in knowing *where* to look, Belloq. It doesn't entirely depend on knowing *what* you're looking for."

"A man like Ravenwood is not easily coerced," Belloq said.

"Did I mention coercion?"

"You didn't have to," Belloq said. "I appreciate the need for it, which is enough. In certain areas, I think you'll find that I am not a squeamish man. In fact, if I say so myself, quite the opposite."

Dietrich nodded. Again there were footsteps outside the door. He waited. The door was opened. A uniformed aide, dressed in that black tunic Dietrich so disliked, stepped inside. He said nothing, merely indicated with a backward nod of his head that they were to follow him.

Belloq moved toward the door. The inner shrine, he thought. The sanctum of the little house painter who has dreams of being the spirit of history but who fails to realize the truth. The only history in which Belloq was interested, the only history that made any sense, lay buried in the deserts of Egypt. With luck, Belloq thought. With any luck.

He saw Dietrich move ahead. A nervous man, his face as pale as that of someone stepping, with as much dignity as he can muster, to his own execution.

The thought amused Belloq.

FIVE
Nepal

THE DC-3 CRUISED over the white slopes of the mountains, skimming now and then through walls of mist, banks of dense cloud. The peaks of the range were mostly invisible, hidden in the frosty clouds, clouds that seemed motionless and solid, as if no wintry wind could ever disperse them.

A devious route, Indy thought, staring out his window, and a long one: across the United States to San Francisco, then Pan Am's China Clipper, arriving after many stops in Hong Kong; another rickety plane to Shanghai, and finally this aging machine to Katmandu.

Indy shivered as he imagined the frigid bleakness of the Himalayas. The impossible crags, the unmapped gulleys and valleys, the thick snow that covered everything. An inconceivable environment, and yet life flourished here, people survived, labored, loved. He shut the book he'd been reading—the journal of Abner Ravenwood—and he looked along the aisle of the plane. He put his hand in the back pocket of his jacket and felt the wad of money there, what Marcus Brody had called "an advance from the U.S. military." He had more than five thousand dollars, which he'd begun to think of as persuasion money if Abner Ravenwood hadn't changed in his attitude toward him. A touch of bribery, of *la mordida*. Presumably the old man would be in need of money, since he hadn't held any official teaching post, so far as Indy knew, in years. He would have gone through that great scourge of any academic discipline—the pain of finding funds. The begging bowl you were obliged to rattle all the time. Five grand, Indy realized, was more money than he'd ever carried at any one time. A small fortune, in fact. And it made him feel decidedly uncomfortable. He'd never had more than a cavalier attitude toward money, spending it as quickly as he made it.

For a time he shut his eyes, wondering if he would find Marion with her father still. No, it wasn't likely, he decided. She would have grown up, drifted away, maybe even married back in the States. On the other hand, what if she was still with her father? What then? And he found himself suddenly unwilling to look Ravenwood in the eye.

All those years, though. Surely things would have changed.

Maybe not, maybe not with somebody as singleminded as Abner. A grudge was a grudge—and if a colleague had an affair with your daughter, your child, then the grudge would be long and hard. Indy sighed. A weakness, he thought. Why couldn't you have been strong back then? Why did you have to get so carried away? So involved with a kid? But then, she hadn't seemed like a kid, more a child-woman, something in her eyes and her look suggesting more than a girl going through adolescence.

Drop it, forget it, he thought.

You have other things on your mind now. And Nepal is just one step on the way to Egypt.

One long step.

Indy felt the plane begin to drop almost imperceptibly at first, then noticeably, as it ploughed downward toward its landing spot. He could see emerging from the snowy wastes the thin lights of a town. He shut his eyes and waited for that moment when the wheels struck ground and the plane screamed along the runway as it braked. Then the plane was taxiing toward a terminal building— no more than a large hangar that had apparently been converted into an arrivals-and-departures point. He got up from his seat, collected his papers and books, took his bag from beneath the seat and began to move down the aisle.

Indiana Jones didn't notice the raincoated man just behind him. A passenger who had embarked in Shanghai and who, throughout the last part of the journey, had been watching him down the aisle.

The wind that ripped across the airfield was biting, piercing through Indy. He bent his head and hurried toward the hangar, holding his old felt hat in place with one hand, the canvas bag in the other. And then he was in the building, where it wasn't much warmer, the only heat seeming to be that of the massed bodies crammed inside the place. He quickly passed through the formalities of customs, but then he was thronged by beggars, children with lame legs, blind kids, a couple of palsied men, a few withered humans whose sex he couldn't determine. They clutched at him, imploring him, but since he knew the nature of beggars from other parts of the world, he also knew it was best to avoid dispensing gifts. He brushed past them, amazed by the activity inside the place. It was as much a bazaar as an airport building, stuffed with stalls, animals, the wild activity of the marketplace. Men burned sweetbreads over braziers, others gambled excitedly over a form of dice, still others seemed involved in an auction of donkeys—the creatures were tethered miserably together in a line, skin and bone, dull eyes and ragged fur. Still the beggars pursued him. He moved more quickly now, past the stalls that belonged to money-changers, to vendors selling items of unrecognizable fruits and vegetables, past the merchants of rugs and scarves and clothing made from the hide of the yak, past the primitive food-stands and the cold-drink places, assailed all the time by smells, by the scent of burning grease, the whiff of perfume, the aromas of weird spices. He heard someone call his name through the crowd and Indy paused, swinging his canvas bag lightly to warn the beggars off. He stared in the direction of the voice. He saw the face of Lin-Su, still familiar even after so many years. He reached the small Chinese man and they shook hands vigorously. Lin-Su, his wrinkled face broken into a smile that was almost entirely toothless, took Indy by the elbow and escorted him through a doorway and out onto the street—where the wind, a savage, demented thing, came howling out of the mountains and scoured the street as if it were bent on an old vengeance. They moved into a doorway, the small Chinese still holding Indy by the arm.

"I am glad to see you again," Lin-Su said in an English that was both quaint and measured, and rusty from lack of use. "It has been many years."

"Too many," Indy said. "Twelve? Thirteen?"

"As you say, twelve . . ." Lin-Su paused and looked along the street. "I received your cable, of course." His voice faded as his attention was drawn to a movement in the street, a shadow crossing a doorway. "You will pardon this question, my old friend: Is somebody following you?"

Indy looked puzzled. "Nobody I'm aware of."

"No matter. The eyes create trickery."

Indy glanced down the street. He didn't see anything other than the shuttered fronts of small shops and a pale light the color of a kerosene flame falling from the open doorway of a coffeehouse.

The small Chinese hesitated for a moment, then said, "I have made inquiries for you, as you asked me to."

"And?"

"It is hard in a country like this to obtain information quickly. This you understand. The lack of lines of communication. And the weather, of course. The accursed snow makes it difficult. The telephone system is primitive, where it exists, that is." Lin-Su laughed. "However, I can tell you that the last time Abner Ravenwood was heard from, he was in the region around Patan. This much I can vouch for. Everything else I have learned is rumor and hardly worth discussion."

"Patan, huh? How long ago?"

"That is hard to say. Reliably, three years ago." Lin-Su shrugged. "I am very apologetic I can do no better, my friend."

"You've done very well," Indy said. "Is there a chance he might still be there?"

"I can tell you that nobody had any knowledge of him leaving this country. Beyond that . . ." Lin-Su shivered and turned up the collar of his heavy coat.

"It helps," Indy said.

"I wish it could be more, naturally. I have not forgotten the assistance you gave me when I was last in your great country."

"All I did was intervene with the Immigration Service, Lin-Su."

"So. But you informed them that I was employed at your museum when in fact I was not."

"A white lie," Indy said.

"And what is friendship but the sum of favors?"

"As you say," Indy remarked. He wasn't always comfortable with Oriental platitudes, those kinds of comments that might have been lifted from the writings of a third-rate Confucius. But he understood that Lin-Su's Chinese act was performed almost professionally, as if he were speaking the way Occidentals expected him to.

"How do I get to Patan?"

Lin-Su raised one finger in the air. "There I can help you. In fact, I have already taken the liberty. Come this way."

Indy followed the little man some way down the street. Parked against a building there was a black car of an unfamiliar kind. Lin-Su indicated it with pride.

"At your disposal I place my automobile."

"Are you sure?"

"Indeed. Inside you will find the necessary map."

"I'm overwhelmed."

"A small matter," Lin-Su said.

Indy walked round the car. He glanced through the window and looked at the broken leather upholstery and the appearance of springs.

"What make is it?" he asked.

"A mongrel breed, I fear," Lin-Su said. "It has been put together by a mechanic in China and shipped to me at some expense. It is part Ford, part Citroën. I think there may be elements of a Morris, too."

"How the hell do you get it repaired?"

"That I can answer. I have my fingers crossed it never breaks down." The Chinese laughed and handed a set of keys to Indy. "And so far it has been reliable. Which is good, because the roads are extremely bad."

"Tell me about the roads to Patan."

"Bad. However, with any luck you will avoid the snows. Follow the route I have marked in the map. You should be safe."

"I can't thank you enough," Indy said.

"You will not stay the night?"

"I'm afraid not."

Lin-Su smiled. "You have . . . what is that word? Ah, yes. A deadline?"

"Right. I have a deadline."

"Americans," he said. "They always have deadlines. And they always have ulcers."

"No ulcers yet," Indy said, and opened the car door. It creaked badly on its hinges.

"The clutch is stiff," Lin-Su said. "The steering is poor. But it will take you to your destination and bring you back again."

Indy threw his bag onto the passenger seat. "What more could a man ask from a car, huh?"

"Good luck, In-di-an-a." It was like a Chinese name, the way Lin-Su pronounced it.

They shook hands, then Indy pulled the car door shut. He turned the key in the ignition, listened to the engine whine, and then the car was going. He waved to the small Chinese, who was already moving down the street, beaming as if he were proud to have loaned his car to an American. Indy glanced at the map and hoped it was accurate because he sure couldn't expect highway signs in a place like this.

He drove for hours along the rutted roads Lin-Su had marked on the map, aware as darkness fell of the mountains looming like great spooks all around him. He was glad he couldn't see the various passes that swept down beneath him. Here and there where snow blocked the road he had to edge the car through slowly, sometimes getting out and scraping as much snow from his path as he could. A desolate place. Bleak beyond belief. Indy wondered about living here in what must seem an endless winter. The roof of the world, they said. And he could believe it, except it was a mighty lonesome roof. Lin-Su apparently could stand it, but then it was probably a good place for the Chinaman to have his business, the importing and exporting of lines of merchandise that were sometimes of a dubious nature. Nepal—it was where all the world's contraband came through, whether stolen objects of art, antiquities or narcotics. It was where the authorities turned eyes that were officially blind and forever had their palms held out to be slyly greased.

Through the margins of sleep Indy drove, yawning, wishing he had some coffee to keep him going. Mile after dreary mile he listened to the springs of the mongrel car creak and squeal, to the squelch of tires on the snow. And then unexpectedly, before he could check his destination on the map, he found himself on the outskirts of a town, a town that had no designation, no sign, no name. He pulled the car to the side of the road and opened the map. He switched on the interior light and realized he must have reached Patan because there wasn't any other sizable community marked on Lin-Su's map. He drove slowly through the straggling outskirts of the place, dismal huts, constructions of windowless clay shacks. And then he reached what looked like the main thoroughfare, a narrow street—little more than an alley—of tiny stores, passageways that led off at sinister angles into shadows. He stopped the car and looked around him. A strange street—too silent in some way.

Indy was suddenly conscious of another car cruising behind him. It passed, swerved as if to avoid him, picked up speed as it moved. When it disappeared he realized it was the only other car he'd seen all the way. What a godforsaken hole, he thought, trying to imagine Abner Ravenwood living here. How could anybody stand this?

Somebody moved along the street, coming toward him. A man, a large man in a fur jacket, who swayed from side to side like a drunk. Indy got out of the car and waited until the man in the fur jacket had come close to him before speaking. The man's breath smelled of booze, a smell so strong that Indy had to turn his face to the side.

The man, like somebody expecting to be attacked, stepped suspiciously away. Indy held his arms out, hands upturned, a gesture of harmlessness. But the man didn't come any closer. He watched Indy warily. A man of mixed heritage, the shape of the eyes suggesting the Orient, the broad cheekbones perhaps indicating some Slavic mix. Try a language, Indy thought. Try English for a start.

"I'm looking for Ravenwood," he said. This is absurd, he said to himself: the dead of night in some deserted place and you're looking for somebody in a language that probably makes no sense. "A man called Ravenwood."

The man stared, not understanding. He opened his mouth.

"Do. You. Know. Somebody. Called. Ravenwood?" Slowly. Like speaking with an idiot.

"Raven-wood?" the man said.

"You got it, chum," Indy said.

"Raven-wood." The man appeared to suck the word as though it were a lozenge of an exotic flavor.

"Yeah. Right. Now we stand here all night and mumble, I guess," Indy said, cold again, tiredness coursing through him.

"Ravenwood." The man smiled in recognition and turned, pointing along the street. Indy looked and noticed a light in the distance. The man cupped one hand and raised it to his mouth, the gesture of a drinker. "*Ravenwood*," he said over and over, still pointing. He began to nod his head vigorously. Indy understood he was to go in the direction of the light.

"Much obliged," he said.

"Ravenwood," the man said again.

"Yeah, right, right," and Indy moved back to the car.

He got in and drove along the street, stopped at the light the man had indicated, and only then realized it emerged from a tavern, outside of which, incongruously, hung a sign in English: THE RAVEN. The Raven, Indy thought. The guy had made a mistake. Confused and drunk, that was all. Still, if it was the only joint open in this hick burg, he could stop and see if anybody knew anything. He got out of the car, aware of the noise coming from inside the tavern now, the rabbling kind of noise created by any congregation of drinkers who've spent their last several hours devoted to the task of wasting themselves. It was a noise he enjoyed, one he was accustomed to, and he would have liked nothing better than to join the revelers inside. Uh-uh, he said to himself. You haven't come all this way to get loaded like a lost tourist checking the local lowlife. You've come with a purpose. A well-defined purpose.

He moved toward the door. You've been in some weird places in your time, he told himself. But this takes the blue ribbon for sure. What he saw in front of him as he stepped inside was an odd collection of boozers, a wild assortment of nationalities. It was as if somebody had picked up a scoop, dipped it into a jar filled with mixed ethnic types and spilled it here in the mad, lonely darkness of the wilderness. This one *really* takes the cake, Indy laughed to himself. Sherpa mountain guides, Nepalese natives, Mongols, Chinese, Indians, bearded mountain climbers who looked like they'd fall off a stepladder in their present condition, various furtive kinds of no obvious national origin. This is Nepal, all right, he thought, and these are the drifters of the international narcotics trade, smugglers, bandits. Indy shut the door behind him, then noticed a huge stuffed raven, wings spread viciously, mounted behind the long bar. A sinister memento, he thought. And something troubled him, the odd similarity between the name of Abner and the name of this bar. Coincidence? He moved further into the room, which smelled of sweat and alcohol and tobacco smoke. He detected the sweet, aromatic scent of hashish in the air.

Something was going on at the bar, where most of the clientele was gathered. Some kind of drinking contest. Lined up on the bar was a collection of shot glasses. A large man, shouting in an Australian accent, was stumbling against the bar even as he raised his hand and blindly fumbled for his next drink.

Indy moved nearer. A drinking contest. And he wondered who the Australian's opponent might be. He pushed his way through, trying to get a look.

When he saw, when he recognized the opponent in the contest, he felt a moment of dizziness, a giddiness that was tight in his chest, a stab, a quick ache. And for a second the passage of time altered, changed like a landscape painted long ago and left untouched. An illusion. A mirage. And he shook his head as if this movement might bring him back to reality.

Marion.

Marion, he thought.

The dark hair that fell around her shoulders in loose, soft waves; the same large intelligent brown eyes that surveyed the world with a mild skepticism, an incredulity at what passed for human behavior—eyes that always appeared to look inside you, as if they might perceive your innermost motivation; the mouth—perhaps only the mouth was a little different, a little harder, and the body a little fuller. But it was Marion, the Marion of his memory.

And here she was involved in an insane drinking contest with a bear of an Australian. He watched, hardly daring to move, as the throng around the bar made bets on the contest. Even to the most innocent spectator, it must have seemed wildly unlikely that the Australian could be outdrunk by a woman barely more than a couple of inches over five feet tall. But she was throwing back drinks, matching the man glass for glass.

Something inside him, something that lay hard in the center of him, became suddenly soft. He wanted to drag her away from the lunacy of the place. No, he told himself. She's not a child anymore, she's not Abner's daughter now—she's a woman, a beautiful woman. And she knows what she's doing. She can take care of herself—here, even in the middle of this motley crew of burnt-out cases and bandits and boozers. She tossed down another drink. The crowd roared. More money was thrown down on the bar. Another roar. The Australian staggered back, reached for a drink, missed and toppled backward like an axed tree. Indy was impressed. He watched as she tossed her black hair back, picked up the money from the bar and shouted at the drinkers in Nepalese; and although he didn't know the language, it was obvious from her tone of voice she was telling them that their sport was over for the evening. But there was one glass left on the counter and they weren't going to move until she'd drunk it.

She stared around them, then she said, "Bums." And she drank the glass down. The crowd roared again, then Marion waved her arms in the air and the mob began to disperse, grumblingly, moving toward the door. The barman, a tall Nepalese character, was making sure they left, ushering them out into the night. He had an ax handle in one hand. In a joint like this, Indy thought, you might need more than an ax handle to ensure closing time.

Then the bar was empty, the last stragglers having gone out.

Marion went behind the bar, raised her face and looked at Indy.

"Hey, didn't you hear me? You deaf or something? Time's up. You understand? *Bairra chuh kayho?*"

She began to move toward him. And then, the light of recognition on her face, she paused.

"Hiya, Marion," he said.

She didn't move.

She simply stared at him.

He was trying to see her now as she was, not remember her as she had been, and the effort was suddenly difficult. He felt tight again, this time in his throat, as if something had congealed there.

"Hello, Marion," he said again. He sat down on a barstool.

For a second he imagined he saw some old emotion in her eyes, something locked there in her look—but then what she did next astonished him. She made a hard fist of her hand, swung her arm at great speed and struck him with a solid right to the side of his jaw. Dizzy, he fell from the stool and lay sprawled across the floor, looking up at her.

"Nice to see you, too," he said and, rubbing his jaw, grinned.

She said, "Get up and get out."

"Wait, Marion."

She stood over him. "I can do it a second time just as easy," she said, making a fist again.

"I bet," he said. He rose to his knees. The jaw was damn sore. Where had she learned to hit that way? Where had she learned to drink so well, come to think of it? *Surprise, surprise*, he thought. *The girl becomes a woman and the woman turns out to be a terror.*

"I don't have anything to say to you."

He rose now and rubbed dirt from his clothes. "Okay, okay," he said. "Maybe you don't want to talk to me. I can understand that—"

"That's insightful of you."

That bitterness, Indy thought. Did he deserve that bitterness? Yeah, maybe, he realized.

"I came to see your father," he said.

"You're two years too late."

Indy was aware of the Nepalese bartender nursing his ax handle. A menacing character altogether.

"It's okay, Mohan. I can handle this." She gestured contemptuously at Indy. "Go on home."

Mohan laid the ax handle on the bar. At her nod, he shrugged and left.

"What do you mean 'two years too late'?" Indy asked slowly. "What's happened to Abner?"

For the first time something in Marion softened. She exhaled slowly, breathing out an old sadness. "What do you think I mean? An avalanche got him. What else could get him? It's only fitting—he spent his whole damn life digging. As far as I know he's probably still up the side of that mountain, preserved in the snow."

She turned away from him and poured herself a drink. Indy sat down on the barstool again. *Abner dead.* It was inconceivable. He felt as if he'd been struck again.

"He became convinced his beloved Ark was parked halfway up some mountain." Marion sipped her drink. He could see some of her hardness, some of that exterior shell, begin to crack. But she was fighting it, fighting the display of weakness.

She said, "He dragged me, a kid, halfway round the world on his crazy digs. Then he pops off. He didn't leave me a penny. Guess how I lived, Jones? I worked here. And I wasn't exactly the bartender, you understand?"

Indy stared at her. He wondered what he was feeling now, what kind of strange sensations were moving inside him. They were unfamiliar to him, alien. She suddenly looked terribly fragile. And terribly beautiful.

"The guy that owned the place went crazy. *Everybody* goes crazy here sooner or later. So when they dragged him away, guess what? He leaves me this place. All mine for the rest of my natural. Can you imagine a worse curse?"

It was too much for Indy to absorb at once, too much to take in. He wanted to say something that might comfort her. But he knew there weren't any words.

"I'm sorry," he said.

"Big deal."

"I'm really sorry."

"I thought I was in love with you," she said. "And look what you did with that sacred piece of knowledge."

"I didn't mean to hurt you."

"I was a child!"

"Look, I did what I did. I'm not happy about it, I can't explain it. And I don't expect you to be happy about it, either."

"It was wrong, Indiana Jones. And you knew it was wrong."

Indy was silent, wondering how you could ever apologize for past events. "If I could go back ten years, if I could undo the whole damn thing, believe me, Marion, I would."

"I knew you'd come through that door sometime. Don't ask me why. I just knew it," she said.

He put his hands on the bar. "Why didn't you go back to the States, anyhow?" he asked.

"Money. Pure and simple. I want to go back in some kind of style," she said.

"Maybe I can help. Maybe I can start to do you some good."

"Is *that* why you came back?"

He shook his head. "I need one of the pieces that I think your father had."

Marion's right hand came up swiftly, but this time Indy was ready and caught her wrist.

"Sonofabitch," she said. "I wish you'd leave that crazy old man in peace. God knows you caused him enough heartache when he was alive."

"I'll pay," he said.

"How much?"

"Enough to get you back to the States in style, anyhow."

"Yeah? Trouble is, I sold all his stuff. Junk. All of it. He wasted his whole life on junk."

"Everything? You sold everything?"

"You look disappointed. How does *that* feel, Mr. Jones?"

Indy smiled at her. Her second of triumph pleased him in some way. And then he wondered if she was telling the truth about selling Abner's stuff, if it was all really so valueless.

"I like it when you look dejected," she said. "I'll buy you a drink. Name it."

"Seltzer," he said, and sighed.

"Seltzer, huh? Changed days, Indiana Jones. I prefer scotch myself. I like bourbon and vodka and gin, too. I'm not much for brandy. I'm off that."

"You're a tough broad now, aren't you?"

She smiled at him again. "This ain't exactly Schenectady, friend."

He rubbed his jaw once more. Suddenly he was tired of the fencing. "How many times can I say I'm sorry? Would it ever be enough?"

She pushed a glass of soda toward him and he drank from it with a grimace. Then she leaned against the bar, propped on her elbows. "You can pay cash money, can you?"

"Yeah."

"Tell me about this thing you're looking for. Who knows? Maybe I can locate the guy I sold the stuff to."

"A bronze piece in the shape of the sun. It has a hole in it, slightly off center. There's a red crystal in it. It comes from the top of a staff. Does it sound familiar?"

"Maybe. How much?"

"Three thousand dollars."

"Not enough."

"Okay. I can go as high as five. You get more when you return to the States."

"It sounds important."

"It could be."

"I have your word?"

He nodded.

Marion said, "I had your word once before, Indy. Last time we met you gave me your word you'd be back. Remember that?"

"I *am* back."

"The same bastard," she said.

She was silent for a time, moving around the side of the bar until she was standing close to him. "Give me the five grand now and come back tomorrow."

"Why tomorrow?"

"Because I said so. Because it's time I started to call some shots where you're concerned."

He took out the money, gave it to her. "Okay," he said. "I trust you."

"You're an idiot."

"Yeah," he sighed. "I've heard that."

He got down from the stool. He wondered where he was going to spend the night. In a snowbank, he supposed. If Marion had her way. He turned to leave.

"Do one thing for me," she said.

He turned to look at her.

"Kiss me."

"Kiss you?"

"Yeah. Go on. Refresh my memory."

"What if I refuse?"

"Then don't come back tomorrow."

He laughed. He leaned toward her, surprised by his own eagerness, then by the sudden wildness of the kiss, by the way she pulled at his hair, the way her tongue forced itself between his lips and moved slickly against the roof of his mouth. The kiss of the child was long gone; this was different, the kiss of a woman who has learned the nature of lovemaking.

She drew herself away, smiled, reached for her drink.

"Now get the hell out of my place," Marion said.

She watched him go, watched the door close behind him. She didn't move for a time; then she undid the scarf she wore around her neck. A chain hung suspended between her breasts. She pulled on the chain, at the end of which there was a sun-shaped bronze medallion with a crystal set into it.

She rubbed it thoughtfully between thumb and forefinger.

Indy trembled in the freezing night air as he went toward the car. He sat inside for a time. What was he supposed to do now? Drive around this hole until morning? He wasn't likely to find any three-star hotel in Patan, nor did he relish the idea of spending the night asleep in the car. By morning he'd be frozen solid as a Popsicle. Maybe, he thought, I'll give her some time and then she'll soften and I can go back; maybe she can show me some of that hospitality for which innkeepers are supposed to be famous. He cupped his hands and blew into them for heat, then he started the engine of the car. Even the rim of the steering wheel was chilly to touch.

Indy drove off slowly.

He didn't see the shadow in the doorway across the street, the shadow of the raincoated man who had boarded the DC-3 in Shanghai, a man by the name of Toht who had been sent to Patan at the express request of the Third Reich Special Antiquities Collection. Toht moved across the street, accompanied by his hired help—a German thug with an eyepatch, a Nepalese in a fur jacket and a Mongolian who carried a submachine gun as if anything that might move in his line of vision would automatically be a target.

They paused outside the door of The Raven, watching Indiana Jones's car depart in a flare of red taillights.

Marion stood reflectively in front of the coal fire, a poker in her hand. She stabbed at the dying flames and suddenly, despite herself, despite what she considered a weakness, she was crying. That damn Jones, she thought. Ten years down the road, down a hard bloody road, he comes dancing back into my life with more of his promises. And the ten years collapsed, time flicked away like the pages of a book, and she was remembering how it had been back then—fifteen years old and fancying herself in love with the handsome young archaeologist, the young man her father had warned her about. She remembered his saying, "You'll only get hurt, even if you'll get over it in time." Well, the hurt had been true and real—but the rest of it wasn't. Maybe it was true what they sometimes said, that old wives' tale—maybe you never really forgot the first man, the first love. Certainly she had never forgotten the delicious quality, the trembling, the feeling that she might die from the sheer anticipation of the kiss, the embrace. Nothing had touched that wicked heightening of the senses, that feeling of floating through the world as if she were insubstantial, flimsy, as if she might be transparent when held up to light.

She decided she was being stupid, crying, all because Mr. Big Shot Archaeologist comes strutting through the door. The hell with him, she said to herself. He's only good for the money now.

Confused, she went to the bar. She slipped the chain from her neck, laid the medallion on the bar. She picked up the money Indy had left and, reaching behind the bar, put it inside a small wooden box. She was still staring at the medallion, which lay in the shadow of the huge taxidermic raven, when she heard a noise at the door. She whipped quickly around to see four men come in, and at once she understood that there was trouble and that the trouble had come in the wake of good old Indiana Jones. What the hell has he landed me in? she wondered.

"We're closed. I'm sorry," she said.

The one in the raincoat, who had a face like an open razor, smiled. "We didn't come for a drink," he said. His voice was heavily accented, German.

"Oh." And she watched the razor's companions, the Nepalese and the Mongolian (dear God, he has a machine gun), poke around the place. She thought of the medallion lying on the surface of the bar. The guy with the eye patch passed very close to it.

"What do you want?" she asked.

"Precisely the same thing your friend Indiana Jones is looking for," the German said. "I'm sure he must have mentioned it."

"No, I'm sorry."

"Ah," the man said. "Has he acquired it, then?"

"I don't think I understand you," she said.

The man sat down, drawing his raincoat up. "Forgive me for not introducing myself. Toht. Arnold Toht. Jones asked about a certain medallion, did he not?"

"He might have done . . ." She was thinking about the gun that lay on the ledge behind the stuffed raven, wondering how quickly she could reach it.

"Don't play silly games with me, please," Toht said.

"All right. He's coming back tomorrow. Why don't you come back then too, and we'll hold an auction, if you're *that* interested."

Toht shook his head. "I'm afraid not. I have to have the object tonight, Fräulein." He rose and looked in the fire, bending, lifting the poker from the embers.

Marion pretended to yawn. "I don't have it. Come back tomorrow. I'm tired."

"I am sorry you're tired. However . . ." He motioned with his head. The Mongolian caught Marion from behind, pinning her arms at her back, while Toht pulled the red-hot poker from the fire and moved toward her.

"I think I see your point," she said. "Look, I can be reasonable—"

"I'm sure, I'm sure." Toht sighed as if he were a man weary of violence, but that sound was misleading. He advanced toward her, still holding the poker close to her face. She could feel its heat against her skin. She twisted her face to the side and struggled against the grip of the Mongolian, but he was too strong.

"Wait, I'll show you where it is!"

Toht said, "You had your opportunity for that, my dear."

A sadist of the old school, she thought. The medallion doesn't matter a bit to him, only the sight of that poker searing my face. She struggled again, but it was useless. Okay, she decided, you've lost everything else, you might as well lose your looks, too. She tried to bite the big man's arm, but he simply slapped the side of her face, stinging her with an open palm that smelled of wax.

She stared at the poker.

Too close. Five inches. Four. Three.

The sickening smell of hot metal.

And then—

Then it all happened too quickly for her to follow for a moment, an abrupt series of events that occurred in a blur, like an ink drawing that has been caught in the rain. She heard a crack, a violent crack, and what she saw was the European's hand go up in the air suddenly, the poker flying across the room to the window, where it wrapped itself in the curtains and started to smolder. She felt the Mongolian release her and then she realized that Indiana Jones had come back, that he was standing in the doorway with that old bullwhip of his in one hand and a pistol in the other. Indiana Jones, just like the damn cavalry coming at the last possible moment. *What the hell kept you?* she wanted to scream. But now she wanted to move, she had to move, the room was filled with all manner of violence, the air was charged like the atmosphere of an electrical storm. She swung over the bar and reached for a bottle just as Toht fired a gun at her, but the bullets were wild and she rolled over on the floor behind the counter in a rage of shattered glass. Gunfire, deafening, loud, piercing her ears.

The Mongolian, cumbersome, leveled his submachine gun. He's aiming for Indy, she realized, directly at Indy. Something to hit him with, she thought. She reached instinctively for her barman's ax handle and struck the Mongolian across the skull as hard as she could, and he went down. But then there was somebody else in the bar, somebody who'd come crashing through the door like it was made of cardboard, and she raised her face to see somebody she recognized, a Sherpa, one of the locals, a giant of a man who could be bought by anybody for a couple of glasses of booze. He came through, a whirlwind, tackling Indy from behind, crushing him to the floor.

And then Toht was shouting, "Shoot! Shoot both of them!"

The man with the eye patch sprang to life at Toht's command. He had a pistol in his hand and it was clear he was about to follow Toht to the letter. Just as she panicked, a strange thing happened: in an unlikely conspiracy of survival, Indy and the Sherpa reached for the fallen gun simultaneously, their hands clasping it. Then they turned it against their assailant and the weapon fired, striking Eye Patch, a direct hit in the throat with a force that threw him across the room. He staggered backward until he lay propped against the bar with an expression on his face that suggested a pirate keelhauled during a drunken binge.

Then the struggle was on again, the unnatural joining of forces, the weird truce, brought to an end. The pistol had fallen away from the hands of Indy, and the Sherpa, and they were rolling over and over together as each tried to grab the elusive gun. But now Toht had a clear shot at Indiana. She picked up the submachine gun that had dropped from the Mongolian's shoulder and tried to understand how it worked—how else could it work, she thought, except by pulling the trigger! She opened fire, but the weapon kicked and jumped wildly. Her shots sizzled past Toht. Then her attention was drawn to the flames spreading from the curtains toward the rest of the bar. Nobody's going to win this one, she thought. This fire is the only thing likely to come out ahead.

From the corner of her eye she watched Toht crouch at the end of the bar as the flames were bursting all around him, searing the bar. He's seen it, she thought. He's seen the medallion. She watched his hand snake toward it, saw the expression of delight on his face, and then suddenly he was screaming as the fire-blackened medallion scorched his palm, burned its shape and design, its ancient words, deep into his flesh. He couldn't hold it. The pain was too much. He staggered toward the door, clutching his burned hand. And then Marion looked back toward Indy, who was struggling with the Sherpa. The Nepalese was circling them, trying to get a clear shot at Indy. She tapped the submachine gun, but the weapon was useless, spent. The pistol, then. The pistol behind the stuffed raven. Through flame and heat she reached for it, turned, listened to the bottles of booze explode around her like Molotov cocktails, took aim at the Nepalese. One true shot, she thought. One good and true shot.

He wouldn't keep still, the bastard.

Now smoke was blinding her, choking her.

Indy kicked the Sherpa, rolling away from him, and then the Nepalese had a clear target—Indy's skull. Now! Do it now!

She squeezed the trigger.

The Nepalese rose in the air, blown upward and back by the force of the shot. And Indy looked at her gratefully through the smoke and flame, smiling.

He grabbed his bullwhip and his hat and yelled, "Let's get the hell out of here!"

"Not without that piece you wanted."

"It's here?"

Marion kicked a burning chair aside. From overhead, in a spectacular burst of flame, a wooden beam collapsed, throwing up sparks and cinders.

"Forget it!" Indy shouted. "I want you out of here. Now!"

But Marion darted toward the place where Toht had dropped the medallion. Coughing, trying not to breathe, her eyes smarting and watering from the black smoke, she reached down and picked up the medallion in the loose scarf that hung round her neck. And then she looked for the wooden money-box.

"Unbelievable!" Ashes. Five grand up in smoke.

Indiana Jones grabbed her by the wrist, dragging her through the fire toward the door. "Let's go! Let's go!" he screamed.

They made it out into the chill night air just as the place began to crumble, as smoke and fire poured upward into the darkness in a wild display of destruction. Cinders, glowing embers, burning timbers—they danced through the fiery roof toward the moon.

From the other side of the street Indy and Marion stood and watched it.

She noticed he still had his hand around her wrist. That touch. It had been so long, so much time had dwindled away, and even as she remembered the contact, the friction of his skin upon hers, she fought the memory away. She took her arm from his hand and moved slightly away.

She stared at the bonfire again, and said nothing for a time. Timbers crackled with the sound of pigs being scorched over spits. "I figure you owe me," she said, finally, "I figure you owe me plenty."

"For starters?"

"For starters, this," and she held the medallion toward him. "I'm your partner, mister. Because this little gismo is still my property."

"Partner?" he said.

"Damn right."

They watched the fire a little longer, neither of them noticing Arnold Toht slinking away through the alleys that ran from the main street—slinking like a rat heading through a maze.

In the car Marion said, "What next?"

Indy was silent for a moment before he answered, "Egypt."

"Egypt?" Marion looked at him as the car moved through the dark. "You take me to the most exotic places."

The silhouettes of mountains appeared; a pale moon broke the night sky. Indy watched clouds disperse. He wondered why he felt a sudden apprehension, a feeling that passed when he heard Marion laugh.

"What's the joke?"

"You," she said. "You and that bullwhip."

"Don't mock it, kid. It saved your life."

"I couldn't believe it when I saw you. I'd forgotten about that ratty old whip. I remember how you used to practice with it every day. Those old bottles on the wall and you standing there with the whip." And she laughed again.

A memory, Indy thought. He recalled the odd fascination he'd had with the bullwhip ever since he'd seen a whip act in a traveling circus as a seven-year-old kid. Wide-eyed in wonder, watching the whip artist defy all logic. And then the hours of practice, a devotion that nobody, himself included, could truly explain.

"Do you ever go anywhere without it?" she asked.

"I never take it to class when I have to teach," he said.

"I bet you sleep with it, huh?"

"Now, that all depends," he said.

She was silent, staring out into the Himalayan night. Then she said, "Depends on what?"

"Work it out for yourself," Jones said.

"I think I get the picture."

He glanced at her once, then returned his eyes to the pocked road ahead.

SIX

The Tanis Digs, Egypt

A HOT SUN scorched the sand, burning on the wasteland that stretched from one horizon to the other. In such a place as this, Belloq thought, you might imagine the whole world a scalded waste, a planet without vegetation, without buildings, without people. *Without people.* Something in this thought pleased him. He had always found treachery the most common currency among human beings—consequently, he had trafficked in that currency himself. And if it wasn't treachery people understood best, then its alternative was violence. He shaded his eyes against the sun and moved forward, watching the dig that was taking place. An elaborate dig—but then, that was how the Germans liked things. Elaborate, with needless circumstance and pomp. He stuck his hands in his pockets, watching the trucks and the bulldozers, the Arab excavators, the German supervisors. And the silly Dietrich, who seemed to fancy himself overlord of all, barking orders, rushing around as if pursued by a whirlwind.

He paused, watching but not watching now, an absent look in his eyes. He was remembering the meeting with the Führer, recalling how embarrassingly fulsome the little man had been. *You are the world's expert in this matter, I understand, and I want the best.* Fulsome and ignorant. False compliments yielding to some deranged Teutonic rhetoric, the thousand-year Reich, the grandiose historic scheme that could only have been dreamed up by a lunatic. Belloq had simply stopped listening, staring at the Führer in wonderment, amazed that the destiny of any country should fall into such clumsy hands. *I want the Ark, of course. The Ark belongs in the Reich. Something of such antiquity belongs in Germany.*

Belloq closed his eyes against the harsh sun. He tuned out the noises of the excavations, the shouts of the Germans, the occasional sounds of the Arabs. The Ark, he thought. It doesn't belong to any one man, any one place, any single time. But its secrets are mine, if there are secrets to be had. He opened his eyes again and stared at the dig, the huge craters hacked out of sand, and he felt a certain vibration, a positive intuition, that the great prize was somewhere nearby. He could feel it, sense its power, he could hear the whisper of the thing that would soon become a roar. He took his hands from his pockets and stared at the medallion that lay in the center of his palm. And what he understood as he stared at it was a curious obsession—and a fear that he might yield to it in the end. You lust after a thing long enough, as he had lusted after the Ark, and you start to feel the edge of some madness that is almost . . . almost what?

Divine.

Maybe it was the madness of the saints and the zealots.

A sense of a vision so awesome that all reality simply faded.

An awareness of a power so inexpressible, so cosmic, that the thin fabric of what you assumed to be the real world parted, disintegrated, and you were left with an understanding that, like God's, surpassed all things.

Perhaps. He smiled to himself.

He moved around the edge of the excavations, skirting past the trucks and the bulldozers. He clutched the medallion tight in his hand. And then he thought about how those thugs dispatched by Dietrich to Nepal had botched the whole business. He experienced disgust.

Those morons, though, had brought back something which served his purposes.

It was the whimpering Toht who had shown Belloq his palm, asking for sympathy, Belloq supposed. Not realizing he had, seared into his flesh, a perfect copy of the very thing he had failed to retrieve.

It had been amusing to see Toht sitting restlessly for hours, days, while he, Belloq, painstakingly fashioned a perfect copy. He'd worked meticulously, trying to recreate the original. But it wasn't the real thing, the *historic* thing. It was accurate enough for his calculations concerning the map room and the Well of the Souls, but he had wanted the original badly.

Belloq put the medallion back inside his pocket and walked over to where Dietrich was standing. For a long time he said nothing, pleased by the feeling that his presence gave the German some discomfort. Eventually Dietrich said, "It's going well, don't you think?"

Belloq nodded, shielding his eyes again. He was thinking of something else now, something that disturbed him. It was the piece of information that had been brought back, by one of Dietrich's lackeys, from Nepal. *Indiana Jones.*

Of course, he should have known that Jones would appear on the scene sooner or later. Jones was troublesome, even if the rivalry between them always ended in his defeat. He didn't have, Belloq thought, the cunning. The instinct. The killing edge.

But now he had been seen in Cairo with the girl who was Ravenwood's daughter.

Dietrich turned to him and said, "Have you come to a decision about that other matter we discussed?"

"I think so," Belloq said.

"I assume it is the decision I imagined you would reach?"

"Assumptions are often arrogant, my friend."

Dietrich looked at the other man silently.

Belloq smiled. "In this case, though, you are probably correct."

"You wish me to attend to it?"

Belloq nodded. "I trust I can leave the details to you."

"Naturally," Dietrich said.

SEVEN
Cairo

THE DARK was warm and still, the air like a vacuum. It was dry, hard to breathe, as if all moisture had evaporated in the heat of the day. Indy sat with Marion in a coffeehouse, rarely taking his eyes from the door. For hours now, they had been moving through back streets and alleys, staying away from the central thoroughfares—and yet he'd had the feeling all the time that he was being watched. Marion looked exhausted, drained, her long hair damp from sweat. And it was clear to Indy that she was becoming more and more impatient with him: now she was staring at him over the rim of her coffee cup in an accusing fashion. He watched the door, scrutinized the patrons that came and went, and sometimes turned his face upward to catch the thin passage of air that blew from the creaking overhead fan.

"You might have the decency to tell me how long we're going to creep around like this," Marion said.

"Is that what we're doing?"

"It would be obvious to a blind man that we're hiding from something, Jones. And I'm beginning to wonder why I left Nepal. I had a thriving business, don't forget. A business you torched."

He looked at her and smiled and thought how vibrant she appeared when she was on the edge of anger. He reached across the small table and touched the back of her hand. "We're hiding from the kind of jokers we encountered in Nepal."

"Okay. I buy that. But for how long?"

"Until I get the feeling that it's safe to go."

"Safe to go where? What do you have in mind?"

"I'm not exactly without friends."

She sighed and finished her coffee, then leaned back in her chair and shut her eyes. "Wake me when you've made up your mind, okay?"

Indy stood up and pulled her to her feet. "It's time," he said. "We can leave now."

"Brother," she said. "Just as I was trying to get some beauty sleep."

They went out into the alleyway, which was almost deserted.

Indy paused, looking this way and that. Then he took her by the hand and began to walk.

"You want to give me some idea of where we're headed exactly?"

"The house of Sallah."

"And who is Sallah?"

"The best digger in Egypt."

He only hoped Sallah still lived in the same place. And beyond that there was another hope, a deeper one, that Sallah was employed in the Tanis dig.

He paused at a corner, a junction where two narrow alleys branched away from one another. "This way," he said, still pulling at Marion's arm.

She sighed, then yawned. She followed.

Something moved in the shadows behind them, something that might have been human. It moved without noise, gliding quickly over the concrete; it knew only to follow the two people who walked ahead of it.

———

Indy was welcomed into Sallah's house as if only a matter of weeks had passed since they last met. But it had been years. Even so, Sallah had changed very little. The same intelligent eyes in the brown face, the same energetic cheerfulness, the hospitable warmth. They embraced as Sallah's wife, a large woman called Fayah, ushered them inside the house.

The warmth of the greeting touched Indy. The comfortable quality of the house made him feel at ease immediately, too. When they sat down at the table in the dining room, eating food that Fayah had produced with all the haste of a culinary miracle, he looked over at the other table in the corner, where Sallah's children sat.

"Some things change after all," he said. He placed a small cube of lamb into his mouth and nodded his head in the direction of the kids.

"Ah," Sallah said. His wife smiled in a proud way. "The last time there were not so many."

"I can remember only three," Indy said.

"Now there are nine," Sallah said.

"Nine," and Indy shook his head in wonderment.

Marion got up from the table and went over to where the children sat. She talked to each of them, touched them, played briefly with them, and then she came back. Indy imagined he saw some kind of look, something indeterminate yet obviously connected with a love of children, pass between Marion and Fayah. For his part he'd never had time for kids in his life; they constituted the kind of clutter he didn't need.

"We have made a decision to stop at nine," Sallah said.

"I'd call that wise," Indy said.

Sallah reached for a date, chewed on it silently for a moment and then said, "It really is good to see you again, Indiana. I've thought about you often. I even intended to write, but I'm a bad correspondent. And I assumed you were even worse."

"You assumed right." Indy reached for a date himself. It was plump and delicious.

Sallah was smiling. "I won't ask you immediately, but I imagine you haven't come all the way to Cairo just to see me. Am I correct?"

"Correct."

Sallah looked suddenly knowing, suddenly sly. "In fact, I would even place a bet on your reason for being here."

Indy stared at his old friend, smiled, said nothing.

Sallah said, "Of course, I am not a gambling man."

"Of course," Indy said.

"We don't talk business at the table," Fayah remarked, looking imposing.

"Later," Indy said. He glanced at Marion, who appeared half-asleep now.

"Later, when everything is quiet," Sallah said.

There was a silence in the room for a second, and then suddenly the place was filled with noise, as if something had erupted at the table where the kids sat.

Fayah turned and tried to silence the pandemonium. But the kids weren't listening to her voice, because they were busy with something else. She rose, saying, "We have guests. You forget your manners."

But they still didn't hear her. It was only when she approached their table that they became silent, revealing in their midst a small monkey sitting upright in the center of the table, chewing on a piece of bread.

Fayah said, "Who brought this animal in here? Who did it?"

The children didn't answer. They were busy laughing at the antics of the creature, which strutted around with the bread in its paws. It bounced over, performed a perfect handstand and then leaped from the table and skipped across the floor to Marion. It jumped up into her lap and kissed her quickly on the cheek. She laughed.

"A kissing monkey, huh?" she said. "I like you too."

Fayah said, "How did it get here?"

For a time none of the children spoke. And then the one that

Indy recognized as being the oldest said, "We don't know. It just appeared."

Fayah regarded her brood with disbelief. Marion said, "If you don't want to have the animal around—"

Fayah interrupted. "If you like it, Marion, then it's welcome in our home. As you are."

Marion held the monkey a moment longer before she set it down. It regarded her in a baleful way and immediately bounced back into her lap.

"It must love you," Indy said. He found animals only slightly more bothersome than children, and not quite so cute.

She put her arms around the small creature and hugged it. As he watched this behavior, Indy wondered, Who could hug a monkey that way? He turned his face toward Sallah, who was rising from the table now.

"We can go out into the courtyard," Sallah said.

Indy followed him through the door. There was trapped heat in the walled courtyard; at once he began to feel lethargic, but he knew he had to fight the tiredness a little longer.

Sallah indicated a raffia chair and Indy sat down.

"You want to talk about Tanis," Sallah said.

"You got it."

"I assumed so," Sallah said.

"Then you're working there?"

Sallah was quiet, looking up into the night sky for a time.

"Indy," he said. "This afternoon I personally broke through into the Map Room at Tanis."

This news, though he had somehow expected it, nevertheless shook him. For a time his mind was empty, thoughtless, as if all perceptions, all memories, had fled into some dark void. *The Map Room at Tanis.* And he thought of Abner Ravenwood after a while, of a lifetime spent searching for the Ark, of dying in madness because the Ark had possessed him. Then he considered himself and the strange jealous reaction he had begun to experience, almost as if *he* should have been the first to break through into the Map Room, as if it were *his* right, like a legacy Ravenwood had passed down to him in some obscure way. Irrational thinking, he told himself.

He looked at Sallah and said, "They're moving fast."

"The Nazis are well organized, Indy."

"Yeah. At least they're good at something, even if it's only following orders."

"Besides, they have the Frenchman in charge."

"The Frenchman?"

"Belloq."

Indy was silent, sitting upright in his chair. *Belloq*. Wasn't there anywhere in the world the bastard wouldn't turn up? He felt angry at first, and after that something else, a feeling he began to enjoy slowly, a sense of competition, the quiet thrill of seeing the opportunity to get even. He smiled for the first time. *Belloq, I'll get you this time*, he thought. And there was a hard determination in the prospect.

He took the medallion from his pocket and passed it to Sallah.

"They might have discovered the Map Room," he said. "But they won't get very far without *this*, will they?"

"I take it this is the headpiece of the Staff of Ra?"

"That's right. The markings on it are unfamiliar to me. What do you make of it?"

Sallah shook his head. "Personally, nothing. But I know someone who would. I can take you to meet him tomorrow."

"I'd appreciate that," Indy said. He took the medallion back from Sallah and put it in his pocket. Safe, he thought. Without this, Belloq might just as well be blind. A fine sense of triumph there, he told himself. *René, this one is all mine*. If I can arrange some way to get around the Nazis.

He asked, "How many Germans are involved in the dig?"

"A hundred or so," Sallah said. "They are also very well equipped."

"I thought so." Indy closed his eyes and sat back. He could feel sleep press in on him. I'll think of something, he said to himself. Soon.

"It worries me, Indy," Sallah said.

"What does?"

"The Ark. If it is there at Tanis . . ." Sallah lapsed into silence, an expression of suppressed anguish on his face. "It is not something man was meant to disturb. Death has always surrounded it. Always. It is not of this world, if you understand what I mean."

"I understand," Indy said.

"And the Frenchman . . . he's clearly obsessed with the thing. I look in his eyes and I see something I cannot describe. The Germans don't like him. He doesn't care. He doesn't even seem to notice anything. The Ark, that's all he ever thinks about. And the way he watches everything—he misses nothing. When he entered the Map Room . . . how can I describe his face? He was transported into a place where I would have no desire to go myself."

Out of nowhere, shaken out of the hot dark, there was an abrupt wind that blew grit and sand—a wind that died as sharply as it had risen.

"You must sleep now," Sallah said. "My house is yours, of course."

"And I'm grateful."

Both men went indoors; the house was quiet.

Indy walked past the room where Marion was sleeping; he paused outside the closed door, listening to the faint sound of her breathing. A child's breathing, he thought—and he had a flash of Marion years ago, when their affair, if that was the word, had taken place. But the desire he felt right then was a different thing altogether: it was a desire for the woman now.

He was pleased with the feeling.

He passed along the corridor, followed by Sallah.

The child is buried, he thought; only the woman lives now.

Sallah asked, "You resist temptation, Indy?"

"Didn't you know about my puritan streak?"

Sallah shrugged, smiled in a mysterious way, as Indy closed the door of the guest room and went toward the bed. He heard Sallah move along the corridor, then the house was silent. He closed his eyes, expecting sleep to come in quickly—but it didn't. It remained an elusive shadow just beyond the range of his mind.

He turned around restlessly. Why couldn't he just let go and sleep? *You resist temptation, Indy?* He pressed his knuckles against his eyelids: he turned around some more, but what he kept seeing inside his head was a picture of Marion sleeping quietly in her room. He got out of bed and opened the door. Go back to bed, Indy, he said to himself. You don't know what you're doing.

He stepped out into the corridor and walked slowly—a burglar on tiptoe, he thought—toward Marion's room. Outside her door he paused. Turn around. Go back to your insomnia. He twisted the handle, entered the room and saw her lying on top of the bed covers. Moonlight flooded the room like a silver reflection thrown by the wings of a vast night moth. She didn't move. She lay with her face to one side, arms across her stomach; the light made soft shadows around her mouth. Go back, he thought. Get back now.

Beautiful. She looked so beautiful, vulnerable, there. A sleeping woman and the touch of the moon—a dizzying combination. He found himself going toward the bed, then sitting on the edge of the mattress. He stared at her face, raised his hand, placed the tips of his fingers lightly against one cheek. Almost at once she opened her eyes.

She said nothing for a time. Her eyes seemed black in the room. He put a finger over her lips.

"You want to know why I'm sitting here, right?" he asked.

"I can hardly begin to guess," she said. "You've come to explain the intricacies of Mr. Roosevelt's New Deal? Or maybe you expect me to swoon in the moonlight."

"I don't expect anything."

She laughed. "Everybody expects something. It's a little lesson I picked up along the way."

He lifted her hand, felt it tremble a little.

She didn't say anything as he lowered his face and kissed her on the mouth. The kiss he received in return was quick and hard and without emotion. He drew his face away and looked at her for a time. She sat up, drawing a bedsheet over herself. The nightdress was transparent and her breasts were visible—firm breasts, not those of a child now.

"I'd like you to leave," she said.

"Why?"

"I don't have to give reasons."

Indy sighed. "Do you really hate me that much?"

She stared at the window. "Nice moon," she said.

"I asked you a question."

"You can't just trample your way back into my life, Indy. You can't just kick over all the props I've made for myself and expect me to pick up the pieces of the past. Don't you see that?"

"Yeah," he said.

"That's my lecture. Now I need some sleep. So go."

He got up slowly.

When he reached the door he heard her say, "I want you too. Don't you think I do? Give it some time, okay? Let's see what happens."

"Sure," and then he stepped out into the corridor, unable to silence the echo of disappointment that seemed to roll inside his head. He stood in the moonlight that came in slivers through the window at the end of the hallway, and he wondered—as his desire began to fade—whether he'd made an ass of himself. It wouldn't be for the first time, he thought.

She couldn't sleep after he'd gone. She sat by the window and stared at the skyline of the city, the domes, minarets, flat roofs. Why did he have to try this soon, anyhow? The damned man had never learned patience, had he? He was as reckless in matters of the heart as he was in everything else. He didn't understand that people needed time; it might not be the great healer, but it was a lot better than iodine. She couldn't just haul herself out of the past and land, like some alien creature from a far galaxy, in the rude awakening of Indiana Jones's present. It had to be mapped more gently.

If there was anything to be taken; if there was anything to be mapped.

The figure moved quickly through the cloakroom where Indy and Marion had left their suitcases and belongings. It moved with unnatural stealth, opening cases, sifting through clothes, picking up pieces of paper, examining them with laborious slowness. It did not find what it had been trained to discover. It understood it had to look for a particular shape—a drawing, an object, it didn't matter as long as it had the shape. When it found nothing, it understood its owner would be disappointed. And that would mean a lack of food. That might even mean punishment. It made a picture of the shape once more in its brain: the shape of the sun, small marks around it, a hole in the center. It began to rummage again.

Again, it found nothing.

The monkey skipped lightly into the corridor, removed some items of food scraps from the table where it had played before with the pretty woman, then swung out through an open window and into the dark.

EIGHT

Cairo

THE AFTERNOON was sunny, the sky almost a pure white. Whiteness reflected from everything, from walls, clothing, glass, as if the light had become a frost that lay across all surfaces.

"Did we need the monkey?" Indy asked. They were going quickly through the crowded street, passing the bazaars, the merchants.

"It followed me, I didn't exactly *bring* it," Marion said.

"It must be attached to you."

"It's not so much *me* it's attached to, Indy. It thinks you're its father, see? It's got some of your looks, anyhow."

"My looks, your brains."

Marion was silent for a while before asking, "Why haven't you found yourself a nice girl to settle down with and raise nine kids?"

"Who says I haven't?"

She glanced at him. It pleased him to think he saw a brief flash of panic on her face, of envy. "You couldn't take the responsibility. My dad really had you figured, Indy. He said you were a bum."

"He was being generous."

"The most gifted bum he ever trained, but a bum anyhow. He loved you, you know that? It took a hell of a lot for you to alienate him."

Indy sighed. "I don't want to rehash it, Marion."

"I don't want that, either," she said. "But sometimes I like to remind you."

"An emotional hypodermic, is that it?"

"A jag, right. You need it to keep you in your place."

Indy began to walk more quickly. There were times when, despite his own defenses, she managed to slide just under his skin. It was like the unexpected desire he'd felt last night. I don't need it, he thought. I don't need it in my life. Love means some kind of order, and you don't want order when you've become accustomed to thriving on chaos.

"You haven't told me where we're going yet," Marion said.

"We meet Sallah, then we go see Sallah's expert, Imam."

"What I like is how you drag me everywhere," Marion said. "It reminds me of my father sometimes. He dragged me around the globe like I was a rag."

They reached a fork in the street. All at once the monkey pulled itself free of Marion's hand and ran through the crowd in quick, loping movements.

"Hey!" Marion shouted. "Get back here!"

Indy said, relieved, "Let it go."

"I was just getting used to it."

Indy gave her a dirty look, caught her by the hand and made her keep up with him.

The monkey scuttled along, slipping through the crowds that jammed the street. It avoided the outstretched hands of people who wanted to touch it, then it turned a corner and stepped into a doorway. There it leaped into the arms of the man who had trained it. He had trained it very well. He held it against his body, popped a confection in its mouth and then moved out of the doorway. The monkey was better than a bloodhound, and a hundred times smarter.

The man looked along the narrow street, raising his face toward the rooftops. He waved.

From a nearby rooftop somebody waved back.

Then he patted the animal. It had done its job very well, following the two who were to be killed, tracking them as diligently as a predator but with infinitely more charm than that.

Good, the man thought. Very good.

Indy and Marion turned into a small square, a place cramped by the stalls of vendors, the crowds of shoppers. Indy stopped suddenly. That old instinct was working on him now, working over his nerve ends, making him tingle. *Something is about to happen*, he thought.

He looked through the crowds. Exactly what?

"Why have we stopped?" Marion asked.

Indy said nothing.

This crowd. How could he tell anything from this bunch of people? He reached inside his jacket and gripped the handle of the bullwhip. He stared into the crowd again. There was a group that moved toward him, moved with more purpose than any of the ordinary shoppers.

A few Arabs. A couple of guys who were European.

With his sharp eyesight, Indy saw the flash of something metallic and he thought, *A dagger*. He saw it glint in the hand of an Arab who was approaching them quickly. Indy hauled the whip out, lashed, listened as it split air with the sound of some menacing melody; it curled around the hand of the Arab and the dagger went slicing harmlessly into nowhere. But then there were more people advancing toward them and he had to think fast.

"Get out of here," he said to Marion, and gave her a quick shove. "Run!"

But Marion wasn't running. Instead, she seized a broom from a nearby stall and swung it into the throat of another Arab, who slumped to the ground.

"Go," Indy said again. "Go!"

"The hell I will," she said.

There were too many of them, Indy thought. Too many to fight, even with her help. He watched the blade of an ax swing, and he struck with the whip again, this time around the Arab's neck. He pulled tight and the man moaned before he dropped. And then one of the Europeans was on him, trying to drag the whip from his hand. Indy swung his leg high, smashing his foot into the man's body. The man clutched his chest and fell backward into a fruit stall, toppling amid spilled and squashed vegetables that looked like a mad still life. Indy noticed a gate in a wall and reached for Marion, pushing her through it, then drawing the bolt so she couldn't get out despite her cries and protestations. He looked around the square, striking with his whip, knocking away the props of stalls. Chaos, utter chaos, and he loved it. A blade swung at him and he ducked just in time, hearing the steel whistle above his head. Then he flicked his whip and wrapped it around the Arab's ankles, bringing him down in a pile of scattered vases and broken jars, while the merchant screamed angrily.

He surveyed the wreckage. He wondered if there were any more takers. The urge for action he felt was exalting.

Nobody moved except the merchants who had seen their stalls wrecked by some lunatic with a bullwhip. He began to back away, moving toward the door in the wall, reaching for the bolt as he did so. He could hear Marion banging on the wood. But before he could slide the bolt, a burnoosed figure lunged toward him with a machete. Indy raised his arm to fend off the blow, catching the man by the wrist and struggling with him.

Marion stopped banging and backed away from the door, looking for some other access to the square. Damn Indy, she thought, for thinking he's got some God-given right to protect me! Damn him for an attitude that belongs to the Middle Ages! She turned down the narrow alleyway in which she found herself and then stopped dead: an Arab was walking toward her, walking in quick, menacing steps. She slipped down the nearest alley, heard the man coming up from behind.

A dead end.

A wall.

She hoisted herself onto the top of the wall, listening to the Arab grunt as he chased her. She scrambled over, got to the other side, hid herself in an alcove between buildings. The Arab unsuspectingly went past her and, after a moment, Marion peered out. He was coming back again, this time in the company of one of the Europeans. She stepped back inside the alcove, breathing hard even as she tried despairingly to still her lungs, to stop the rattle of her heart. What do you do in a situation like this? she thought. You hide, don't you? You plain hide. She had stepped back further into the alcove, seeking the shadows, the dark places, when she encountered a rattan basket. Okay, she thought, so you feel like one of the Forty Thieves, but there was an old saying about any port in a storm, right? She climbed inside the basket, pulled the lid in place and remained there in a crouching position. Be still. Don't move. She could hear, through the slits in the rattan, the sound of the two men skulking around. They spoke to one another in an English so broken, she thought, as to be in need of a major splint.

Look here.

In this place I already looked.

She remained very still.

What she didn't see, what she couldn't see, was the monkey sitting on a wall that overlooked the alcove; she could hear it chattering suddenly, wildly, and it was a few moments before she understood what the noise was. That monkey, she thought. It followed me. The affectionate betrayal. Please, monkey, go away, leave me alone. But she felt herself being raised up now, the basket lifted. She peered through the narrow slats of the basket and saw that the Arab and the European were her bearers, that she was being carted, like refuse, on their shoulders. She struggled. She hammered with her fists against the lid, which was tight now.

In the bazaar Indy had pushed the man with the machete aside; but the place was in turmoil now, angry Arab merchants milling around, gesticulating wildly at the crazy man with the whip. Indy backed away against the door, fumbled for the bolt, saw the machete come toward him again. This time he lunged with his foot, knocking the man backward into the rest of the crowd. Then he worked the door open and was out in the alley, looking this way and that for some sign of her. Nothing. Only two guys at the other end of the alley carrying a basket.

Where the hell did she go?

And then, as if from nowhere, he heard her voice call his name, and the echo was strangely chilling.

The basket.

He saw the lid move as the two carriers turned the corner. Briefly, a strange chattering sound drew his attention from the basket, and he looked upward to see the monkey perched on the wall. It might have been deriding him. He was filled with an overwhelming urge to draw his pistol and murder the thing with one well-placed shot. Instead, he ran quickly in the direction of the two men. He took the same turn they had made, seeing how fast they were running ahead of him with the basket wobbling between them.

How could those guys move so quickly while they carried Marion's weight? he wondered. They were always one turn ahead of him, always one step in front. He followed them along busy thoroughfares filled with shoppers and merchants, where he had to push his way through frantically. He couldn't lose sight of that basket, he couldn't let it slip away like this. He pushed and shoved, he thrust people aside, he ignored their complaints and outcries. Keep moving. Don't lose sight of her.

And then he was conscious of a weird noise, a chanting sound that had somber undertones, a certain melancholy to it. He couldn't place it, but somehow it stopped him; he was disoriented.

When he started to move again, he realized he had lost her. He couldn't see the basket now.

He started to run again, pushing through the crowd. And the strange sound of the lament, if that was what it was, became louder, more piercing.

At the corner of an alley he stopped.

There were two Arabs in front of him carrying a rattan basket.

Immediately, he drew his whip and brought one of them down, hauled the whip away, then let it flash again. It cracked against the other Arab's leg, encircling it, entwining it like a slender reptile. The basket toppled over and he stepped toward it.

No Marion.

Confused, he looked at what had spilled out of the thing.

Guns, rifles, ammo.

The wrong basket!

He backed out of the alley and continued up the main street of bazaars, and the odd wailing sound became louder still.

He entered a large square, overwhelmed by the sudden sight of misery all around him: a square of beggars, the limbless, the blind, the half-born who held out stumps of arms in front of themselves in some mindless groping for help. There was the smell of sweat and urine and excrement here, a pungency that filled the air with the tangibility of a solid object.

He crossed the square, avoiding the beggars.

And then he had to stop.

Now he knew the nature of the moaning sound.

At the far side of the square there was a funeral procession moving. Large and long, obviously the funeral march of some prominent citizen. Riderless horses hauled the coffin, priests chanted from the Koran, keening women walked up front with their heads wrapped in scarves, servants moved behind, and at the rear, cumbersome and clumsy, came the sacrificial buffalo.

He stared at the procession for a time. How the hell could he go through that line?

He looked at the coffin, ornate, opulent, held aloft; and then he noticed, through a brief break in the line, the basket being carried by the two men toward a canvas-covered truck parked in the farthest corner of the square. It was impossible to be sure over the noise of the mourners, but he thought he heard Marion screaming from inside.

He was about to move forward and shove his way through the procession when it happened.

From the truck a machine gun opened fire, raking the square, scattering the line of mourners and the mob of beggars. The priests kept up their chant until the blasts burst through the coffin itself, sending splinters of wood flying, causing the mummified corpse to slide through the broken lid to the ground. The mourners wailed with renewed interest. Indy zigzagged toward a well on the far side of the square, squeezing off a couple of shots in the direction of the truck. He slid behind the well, popping up in time to see the rattan basket being thrown into the back of the truck. Just then, almost out of his line of vision, barely noticeable, a black sedan pulled away. The truck, too, began to move.

It swung out of the square.

Before it could go beyond his sight, Indy took careful aim, an aim more precise than any other in his lifetime, and squeezed the trigger. The driver of the truck slumped forward against the wheel. The truck swerved, hit a wall, rolled over.

As he was about to move toward it, he stopped in horror.

He realized then he could never feel anything so intense in his life again, never so much pain, so much anguish, such a terrible, heavy sense of numbness.

He realized all this as he watched the truck explode, flames bursting from it, fragments flying, the whole thing wrecked; and what he also realized was that the basket had been thrown into the back of an ammunitions truck.

That Marion was dead.

Killed by a bullet from his own gun.

How could it be?

He shut his eyes, hearing nothing now, conscious only of the white sun beating against his closed lids.

He walked for what seemed like a long time, unknowing, uncaring, his mind drifting back time and again to that point where he had leveled the gun and shot the driver. Why? Why hadn't he considered the possibility that the truck might be carrying something dangerous?

You ruined her life when she was a girl.

Now you've ended it when she was a woman.

He walked the narrow streets, the alleys thronged with people, and he blamed himself over and over for the death of Marion.

It was more pain than he could think about, more than he could bear. And he knew of only one remedy. He knew of only one reliable form of self-medication. So he found himself walking toward the bar where, earlier, he had arranged to meet Sallah. That seemed locked in some dim past now, another world, a different life.

Even a different man.

He saw the bar, a rundown place. He stepped inside and was assailed by thick tobacco smoke, the smell of spilled booze. He sat on a stool by the bar. He ordered a fifth of bourbon and drank one monotonous glass after another, wondering—as he grew more inebriated—what it was that made some people tick while others were as animated as broken clocks; what was that clockwork so necessary to successful relationships that some people had and others didn't. He let the question go around in his mind until it shed its sense, floating through alcoholic perceptions like a ghost ship.

He reached for another drink. Something touched his arm and he twisted his head slowly to see the monkey on the bar. That stupid primate to which Marion had become so witlessly attached. Then he remembered that this idiot creature had splashed a kiss on Marion's cheek. Okay, Marion liked you, I can tolerate you.

"Want a drink, you baboon?"

The monkey put its head to one side, watching him.

Indy was aware of the barman watching him as if he were a fugitive from a nearby asylum. And then he was aware of something else, too: three men, Europeans—Germans, he assumed, from their accents—had crowded around him.

"Someone wishes your company," one of them said.

"I'm drinking with my friend here," Indy said.

The monkey moved slightly.

"Your company is not requested, Mr. Jones. It is *demanded*."

He was hauled from the stool and rushed into a back room. Chattering, squealing, the monkey followed. The room was dim and his eyes smarted from smoke.

Someone was sitting at a table in the far corner.

Indy realized that this confrontation had been inevitable.

René Belloq was drinking a glass of wine and swinging a chain on which hung a watch.

"A monkey," Belloq said. "You still have admirable taste in friends, I see."

"You're a barrel of laughs, Belloq."

The Frenchman grimaced. "Your sense of repartee dismays me. It did so even when we were students, Indiana. It lacks panache."

"I ought to kill you right now—"

"Ah, I understand your urge. But I should remind you that I did not bring Miss Ravenwood into this somewhat sordid affair. And what is eating you, my old friend, is the knowledge that *you* are responsible for that. No?"

Indy sat down, slumping into the chair opposite Belloq.

Belloq leaned forward. "It also irks you that I can see through you, Jones. But the plain fact is, we are somewhat alike."

Through blood-shot eyes Indy stared at Belloq. "No need to get nasty."

"Consider this," Belloq said. "Archaeology has always been our religion, our faith. We have both strayed somewhat from the so-called true path, admittedly. We are both given to the occasional . . . dubious . . . transaction. Our methods are not so different as you pretend. I am, if you like, a shadowy reflection of yourself. What would it take to make you the same as me, Professor? Mmm? A slight cutting edge? A sharpening of the killer instinct, yes?"

Indy said nothing. Belloq's words came to him like noises muffled by a fog. He was talking nonsense, pure nonsense, which sounded grand and true because it was delivered in a French accent that might be described as quaint, charming. What Indy heard was the hissing of some hidden snake.

"You doubt me, Jones? Consider: What brings you here? The lust for the Ark, am I correct? The old dream of antiquity. The historic relic, the quest—why, it might be a virus in your blood. You dream of things past." Belloq was smiling, swinging a watch on a chain. He said, "Look at this watch. Cheap. Nothing. Take it out into the desert and bury it for a thousand years and it becomes priceless. Men will kill for it. Men like you and me, Jones. The Ark, I admit, is different. It is a little removed from the profit motive, of course. We understand this, you and I. But the greed is still in the heart, my friend. The vice we have in common."

The Frenchman stopped smiling. There was a glassy look in his eyes, a distance, a privacy. He might have been conducting a conversation with himself. "You understand what the Ark is? It is like a transmitter. Like a radio through which one might communicate with God. And I am very close to it. Very close to it, indeed. I have waited years to be this close. And what I am talking about is beyond profit, beyond the lust of simple acquisition. I am talking about communicating with that which is contained in the Ark."

"You buy it, Belloq? You buy the mysticism? The power?"

Belloq looked disgusted. He sat back. He placed the tips of his fingers together. "Don't you?"

Indy shrugged.

"Ah, you are not sure, are you? Even you, you are not sure." Belloq lowered his voice. "I am more than sure, Jones. I am *positive*. I don't doubt it for a moment now. My researches have always led me in this direction. I *know*."

"You're out of your mind," Indy said.

"A pity it ends this way," Belloq said. "You have at times stimulated me, a rare thing in a world so weary as this one."

"That thought makes me happy, Belloq."

"I'm glad. Truly. But everything comes to an end."

"Not a very private place for murder."

"It hardly matters. These Arabs will not interfere in a white man's business. They do not care if we kill each other off."

Belloq rose, smiling. He nodded his head in a curt way.

Indy, stalling for time, for anything, said, "I hope you learn something from your little parley with God, Belloq."

"Naturally."

Indy braced himself. There wasn't time to turn swiftly and try for his pistol, and even less time to reach his bullwhip. His assassins sat directly behind him.

Belloq was looking at his watch. "Who knows, Jones? Perhaps there will be the kind of hereafter where souls like you and me meet again. It amuses me to think that I will outwit you there as well."

There was a sound from outside now. It was an incongruous sound, the collective chattering of excited young children, a happy sound Indy associated with a Christmas morning. It wasn't what he expected to hear in the death chamber.

Belloq looked toward the door in surprise. Sallah's children, all nine of them, were trooping into the room and calling Indy's name. Indy stared as they surrounded him, as the smaller ones clambered on his knees while the others made a circle in the manner of frail human shields. Some of them began to climb on his shoulders. One had managed to drape himself over Indy's neck in a piggyback-ride style, and still another was hugging his ankles.

Belloq was frowning. "You imagine you can back out of here, do you? You imagine this insignificant human bracelet will protect you?"

"I don't imagine anything," Indy said.

"How utterly typical," Belloq answered.

They were pulling him toward the door now, he was being tugged and yanked even as they were shielding him. Sallah! It must have been Sallah's plan to risk his children and send them into this bar and contrive to get him safely out somehow. How could Sallah have taken such a risk?

Belloq was sitting once again, arms folded. The look on his face was that of a reluctant parent at a school play. He shook his head from side to side. "I will regale the next meeting of the International Archaeological Society with the tale of your disregard for the laws governing child labor, Jones."

"You're not even a member."

Belloq smiled, but only briefly. He continued to stare at the children and then, as if he were deciding something, turned toward his accomplices. He raised his hand, a gesture that indicated they should put their weapons away.

"I have a soft spot for dogs and children, Jones. You may express your gratitude in some simple form, which would suit you. But small children will not become your saviors when we next meet."

Indy was moving back rapidly. And then he slipped out, with the kids clutching him like a precious toy. Sallah's truck was parked outside—a sight that filled Indy with delight, the first event of the day that even remotely lifted his spirits.

Belloq finished his glass of wine. He heard the truck pull away. As the sound died in the distance he thought, with an insight that surprised him vaguely, that he was not yet ready to kill Indy. That the time was not exactly ripe. It hadn't been the presence of the children at all—they hardly mattered. It was rather the fact that he wanted, somewhere in a place he did not quite fathom, a remote corner of understanding, to spare Jones, to let the man live a little longer.

There are some things, after all, worse than death, he thought.

And it amused him to ponder the agony, the anguish, that Jones would be going through: there was the girl, for one thing—which would have been punishment enough, torture enough. But there was also the fact, just as punishing, perhaps even more so, that Jones would live to see the Ark slip through his fingers.

Belloq threw back his head and laughed; and his German accomplices, their appetite for killing unsatisfied, stared at him in bewilderment.

In the truck Indy said, "Your kids have a sense of timing that would outdo the U.S. Marines, Sallah."

"I understood the situation. I had to act quickly," Sallah said.

Indy stared at the road ahead: darkness, thin lights, people parting from the path of the truck. The kids were in the back, singing and laughing. Innocent sounds, Indy thought, remembering what he wanted to forget.

"Marion . . ."

"I know," Sallah said. "The news reached me earlier. I'm sad. More than sad. What can I say to console you? How can I help your grief?"

"Nothing helps the grief, Sallah."

Sallah nodded. "I understand, of course."

"But you can help me in other ways. You can help me beat those bastards."

"You have my help, Indiana," Sallah said. "Any time at all."

Sallah was silent for a moment, driving the last stretch to his house.

"I have much news for you," he said after a while. "Some isn't good news. But it concerns the Ark."

"Hit me with it," Indy said.

"Soon. When we reach my house. And later, if you wish, we can visit the house of Imam, who will explain the markings to you."

Indy lapsed into a weary silence. He had a hangover already beginning, a violent throb in the center of his skull. And, if his senses had been sharper, his intuition less blunted by booze, he might have noticed the motorcycle that had followed the truck from the bar. But even if he had, he would not have known the rider, a man who specialized in training monkeys.

When the children had been sent indoors, Indy and Sallah went out into the walled courtyard. Sallah walked around the yard for a time before he paused by the wall and said, "Belloq has the medallion."

"What?" Immediately Indy felt inside his pocket and his fingers touched the headpiece. "You're wrong."

"He has a copy, a headpiece like yours, a crystal at the center. And there are the same markings on the piece as on the one you have."

"I can't understand it," Indy said, appalled. "I always believed there were no pictures anywhere. No duplicates. I don't get it."

Sallah said, "There's something else, Indiana."

"I'm listening."

"This morning Belloq went inside the map room. When he came out he gave us instructions about where we were to dig. A new spot, away from the general dig."

"The Well of the Souls," Indy said, in a resigned way.

"I imagine so, if he made the calculations in the Map Room."

Indy began beating the palms of his hands together. He turned once again to Sallah, taking the medallion from his pocket. "Are you sure it looked like this?"

"I saw it."

"Look again, Sallah."

The Egyptian shrugged and took the headpiece and stared at it for a time, turning it over in his hand. He said, "There may be a difference."

"Don't keep it from me."

"I think that Belloq's medallion had markings on one side only."

"Are you sure?"

"I'm reasonably sure."

"Now," Indy said, "all I need to know is what the markings mean."

"Then we should go to the house of Imam. We should go now."

Indy said nothing. Followed by Sallah, he left the courtyard and stepped out into the alley. He felt an urgency now. The Ark, yeah—but it was more than just the Ark now. It was for Marion. If her death was to make any sense, he had to get to the Well of the Souls before Belloq.

If death could ever make sense, he thought.

They climbed into Sallah's truck, and as they did, Indy noticed the monkey in the back. He stared at it. Wasn't it ever going to be possible to lose the thing? Pretty soon it would get around to learning human speech and calling him Dad. A echo in there caused him pain: Marion's little joke about the creature having his looks.

The monkey chattered and rubbed its forepaws.

After the truck had gone a little way, the motorcycle emerged from the darkness and followed.

The house of Imam was located on the outskirts of Cairo, built on a slight rise; it was an unusual construction, reminding Indy a little of an observatory. Indeed, as he and Sallah, followed by the monkey, walked toward the entranceway, he noticed an opening in the roof of the house from which there emerged a large telescope.

Sallah said, "Imam has many interests, Indiana. Priest. Scholar. Astronomer. If anyone can explain the markings, he can."

Ahead, the front door was opened. A young boy stood there, nodding his head as they entered.

"Good evening, Abu," Sallah said. "This is Indiana Jones." A brief, courteous introduction. "Indiana, this is Abu, Imam's apprentice."

Indy nodded, smiled, impatient to meet the scholar—who appeared at that moment at the end of the hallway. An old man in threadbare robes, his hands gnarled and covered with the brown spots of age; his eyes, though, were lit with curiosity and life. He bowed his head in a silent greeting. They followed him into his study, a large room strewn with manuscripts, pillows, maps, an-

cient documents. You could feel it here, Indy thought: a lifetime of
dedication to the pursuit of knowledge. Every moment of every
day a learning experience. Nothing wasted. Indy passed the medallion to Imam, who took it silently and carried it to a table at the
back of the room where a small lamp was lit. He sat down, twisting
the thing between his fingers, squinting at it. Indy and Sallah sat
down on some cushions, the monkey between them. Sallah
stroked the creature's neck.

Silence.

The old man took a sip of wine, then wrote something quickly
on a small piece of paper. Indy twisted around, watching impatiently. It seemed Imam was examining the headpiece as if time
were of no interest to him.

"Patience," Sallah said.

Hurry, Indy thought.

The man parked his motorcycle some way from the house. He
slipped alongside the house to its rear, looking in windows until he
found the kitchen. He pressed himself close to the wall, watching
the boy, Abu, rinse some dates at the sink. He waited. Abu put the
dates in a bowl, then placed the bowl on the table. Still the man
didn't move, more shadow now than substance. The boy picked up
a decanter of wine, several glasses, placed them on a tray, then left
the kitchen. Only then did the man move out of the shadows. He
took a bottle from his cloak, opened it, and, after looking around
the kitchen, stealthily poured some liquid from the bottle over the
bowl of dates. He paused for a second. He heard the sound of the
boy returning, and quickly, as silently as he entered, he slipped
away again.

Imam still hadn't spoken. Indy occasionally looked at Sallah, whose
expression was that of a man accustomed to periods of enormous pa-

tience, periods of waiting. The door opened. Abu came in with a decanter of wine and glasses and set the tray down on the table. The wine was tempting, but Indy didn't move for it. He found the silence unsettling. The boy went out and when he next came back he was carrying food—plates of cheese, fruit, a bowl of dates. Sallah absently picked at a piece of cheese and chewed on it thoughtfully. The dates looked good, but Indy wasn't hungry. The monkey moved away, settling beneath the table. Silence still. Indy leaned forward and picked up one of the dates. He tilted his head back, tossed the date in the air and tried to catch it in his mouth as it fell—but it struck the edge of his chin and bounced away across the floor. Abu gave him a strange look—as if this Western custom was too insane to fathom—then picked up the date and dropped it in an ashtray.

Hell, Indy thought. My coordination must be shot.

"Look. Come over here and look," Imam suddenly said.

His strange hoarse voice broke the silence with the solemn authority of a prayer. It was the kind of voice to which one responded without thinking twice.

Over his shoulder, Indy and Sallah watched Imam point to the raised markings. "This is a warning . . . not to disturb the Ark of the Covenant."

"Just what I need," Indy said.

He bent forward, almost touching the frail shoulders of Imam.

"The other markings concern the height of the Staff of Ra to which this headpiece must be attached. Otherwise, the headpiece by itself is of no use." Indy noticed the old man's lips were faintly blackened, that he rubbed them time and again with his tongue.

"Then Belloq got the height of the Staff from his copy of the medallion," Indy said.

Sallah nodded.

"What do the markings say?" Indy asked.

"This was the old way. This means six kadam high."

"About seventy-two inches," Sallah said.

Indy heard the monkey moving around the food table, picking

at assorted bits and pieces. He went over and picked up a date, grabbing it before the monkey reached it.

"I am not finished," Imam said. "On the other side of the head-piece there is more. I'll read it to you. 'And give back one kadam to honor the Hebrew God whose Ark this is.' "

Indy's hand stopped halfway to his mouth. "You're sure Belloq's medallion has markings on one side only?" he asked Sallah.

"Positive."

Indy started to laugh. "Then Belloq's staff is twelve inches too long! They're digging in the wrong spot!"

Sallah laughed too. The men hugged one another as Imam watched them, unsmiling.

The old man said, "I do not understand who Belloq is. I can only tell you that the warning about the Ark is a serious one. I can also tell you that it is written . . . those who would open the Ark and re-lease its force will die if they look upon it. If they bring themselves face to face with it. I would heed these warnings, my friends."

It should have been a solemn moment, but Indy was suddenly too elated at the realization of the Frenchman's error to absorb the old man's words. A triumph! he thought. Wonderful. He wished he could see the look on Belloq's face when he couldn't find the Well of the Souls. He tossed a date in the air, opening his mouth.

This time, he thought.

But Sallah's hand picked the date out of the air before it could enter Indy's mouth.

"Hey!"

Sallah gestured toward the floor under the table.

The monkey lay there in a posture of death. It lay surrounded by date pits. Faintly one paw flickered, trembled, then the animal's eyes closed slowly. After that it didn't move again.

Indy turned his face toward Sallah.

The Egyptian shrugged and said, "Bad dates."

The Tanis Digs, Egypt

THE DESERT MORNING was burning, the stretches of sand shimmering. A landscape, Indy thought, in which a man would have every right to claim he saw mirages. He stared at the sky as the truck rattled along the road. He was uncomfortable in the burnoose he'd borrowed from Sallah, and he wasn't entirely convinced that he could pass himself off as an Arab anyhow—but anything was worth a shot. He turned around from time to time to look at the other truck that followed. Sallah's friend Omar drove the second truck; in the back of it were six Arab diggers. There were another three in Sallah's truck. Let's hope, he thought, that they're as trustworthy as Sallah says.

"I am nervous," Sallah said. "I do not mind confessing it."

"Don't worry too much."

"You're taking a huge risk," Sallah said.

"That's the name of this game," Indy remarked. He looked up at the sky again. The early sunlight beat the sands with the force of a raging hammer.

Sallah sighed. "I hope we cut the staff to the correct size."

"We measured it pretty well," Indy said. He thought of the five-foot stick that lay right then in the back of the truck. It had taken them several hours last night to cut the thing, to whittle the end so that the headpiece would fit. A strange feeling, Indy thought, placing the medallion on the stick. He had felt a sharp affinity with the past then, imaging other hands placing the same medallion in exactly that way so long ago.

The two trucks came to a halt now. Indy got out and walked back to the truck driven by Omar; the Arab stepped down, raising his arm in greeting. And then he pointed to a spot in the distance, a place where the terrain was less flat, where sand dunes undulated.

"We will wait there," Omar said.

Indy rubbed his dry lips with the back of his hand.

"And good luck," the Arab said.

Omar got back into his truck and drove away, trailing a storm of dust and sand behind the vehicle. Indy watched it go. He went back to where Sallah was parked, climbed in; the truck moved slowly for a mile or so, then it stopped again. Sallah and Indy got out, crossed a strip of sand, then lay down and looked across a depression in the land beneath them.

The Tanis excavations.

It was elaborate, extensive; it was obvious, from the amount of equipment below, the numbers of workers, that the Führer wanted the Ark badly. There were trucks, bulldozers, tents. There were hundreds of Arab diggers and, it seemed, just as many German supervisors, incongruous in their uniforms somehow, as if they deliberately sought discomfort out here in the desert. The land had been dug, holes excavated, then abandoned, foundations and passageways unearthed and then deserted. And beyond the main digs was something that appeared to be a crude airstrip.

"I've never seen a dig this size," Indy said.

Sallah was pointing toward the center of the activity, indicating a large mound of sand, a hole at its core; a rope had been slung around it, suspended between posts.

"The Map Room," he said.

"What time does the sun hit it?"

"Just after eight."

"We don't have much time." He looked at the wristwatch he'd borrowed from Sallah. "Where are the Germans digging for the Well of the Souls?"

Sallah pointed again. Some way beyond the main activity, out in the dunes, were several trucks and a bulldozer. Indy watched for a while. Then he stood up. "You've got the rope?"

"Of course."

"Then let's go."

One of the Arab diggers took the wheel of the truck and drove it slowly toward the digs. Between the tents Indy and Sallah got out. They moved stealthily toward the Map Room, Indy carrying the five-foot staff and wondering how long he could contrive to be inconspicuous with so long a piece of wood in his hand. They passed several uniformed Germans, who hardly paid any attention to them: they were grouped together, smoking and talking in the morning sunlight. When they had gone a little further, Sallah indicated that they should stop: they had reached the Map Room. Indy looked around for a moment and then walked, as casually as he could, toward the edge of the hole—the ceiling of the ancient Map Room. He peered down inside, held his breath, and then looked at Sallah, who produced a length of rope from under his robes and tied one end of it around an oil drum located nearby. Indy lowered the staff inside the hole, smiled at Sallah and took one end of the rope. Sallah watched grimly, face covered in perspiration. Indy began to lower himself inside the Map Room.

The Map Room at Tanis, he thought. At some other time he might have been awed by the mere thought of actually being in this place; at some other time he might have paused to look around, might have wanted to linger—but not now. He reached the floor and tugged on the rope, which was immediately pulled up. Damned hard, he thought, not to get excited by this place—an elaborate frescoed room lit by the sunlight streaming in from overhead. He moved across the floor to where the miniature model of the city of Tanis was laid out: a remarkable map cut out of stone, immaculate in detail, so well constructed you could almost imagine miniature people existing in those buildings or walking those streets. He couldn't help but be astonished by the craftsmanship of the map, the patience that must have gone into the construction.

Alongside the map was a line created by embedded mosaic tiles. There were evenly spaced slots in this line, each accompanied by a symbol for a time of the year. The slots had been made to accommodate the base of the staff. He took the headpiece from his robes, reached for the staff and looked at the reflected sunlight that had already begun to move slowly across the miniature city at his feet.

It was seven-fifty. He didn't have much time.

Sallah had gathered the rope, bunched it in his hands and begun to move back toward the oil drum. He barely heard the jeep that came up alongside him, and the loud voice of the German startled him.

"Hey! You!"

Sallah tried to smile dumbly.

The German said, "You, right. What are you doing there?"

"Nothing, nothing." He inclined his head in a gesture of innocence.

"Bring that rope over here," the German said. "This damn jeep is stuck."

Sallah hesitated, then he untied the rope and carried it toward the jeep. Already another vehicle, a truck, had appeared; it stopped some feet in front of the jeep.

"Tie the rope from the jeep to the truck," the German said.

Sallah, sweating, did so. The rope, he thought: the precious rope is being tugged away. He listened to the engines of the two vehicles, watching the wheels squirm in the sand. The rope was pulled taut. What was he going to do to get Indy out of the Map Room without a rope?

He followed the jeep a little way across the sand, failing to notice he was standing beside a kettle of hot food cooking over an open flame. There were several German soldiers seated around a table and one of them was calling to him to bring some food. Helplessly, he watched the German.

"Are you deaf?"

He bowed subserviently and lifted the heavy kettle, carrying it toward the table. What he was thinking about was Indy trapped in the Map Room; what he was wondering about was how, without a rope, he could get the American out.

He began to serve, trying to ignore the insults of the soldiers. He served hurriedly. He spilled food across the table and was cuffed around the side of the head for his efforts.

"Clumsy! Look at my shirt. Look what you've spilled on my shirt."

Sallah lowered his face. Mock shame.

"Get some water. Hurry."

He rushed away to find water.

Indy took the headpiece and fitted it carefully to the top of the staff. He placed the base of the staff in one of the mosaic slots and listened to the sound of the wood clicking against the ancient tile. The sunlight caught the top of the headpiece, the yellow beam moving within a fraction of the tiny hole in the crystal. He waited. From overhead he could hear the sounds of voices shouting. He blocked them out. Later, if he had to, he'd worry about the Germans. But not now.

The sunlight pierced the crystal, throwing a bright line across the miniature city. The line of light was altered and broken by the prism of the crystal—and there, in those miniature buildings and streets, it fell across one spot in particular. Red light, glowing against a small building, which, as if by some ancient chemistry, some old artistry, began to glow. In amazement he watched this effect, noticing now some markings of red paint among the other buildings, markings that were fresh and clean. *Belloq's calculations*.

Or *mis*calculations: the building illuminated by the headpiece was eighteen inches closer than the last red mark left by the Frenchman.

Terrific. Perfect. He couldn't have hoped for anything better. Indy went down on his knees beside the miniature city and took a tape measure from his robes. He strung the tape between Belloq's last mark and the building glowing in sunlight. He made his calculations quickly, scribbling on a small notepad. Sweat burned on his face, dripped across the backs of his hands.

Sallah didn't go for water. He scampered between tents, hoping none of the Germans would stop him again. Panicked, he began to look for a rope. He didn't find one. No rope, nothing in sight. He scurried here and there, slipping and sliding in the sand, praying that none of the Germans would notice his peculiar behavior or call on him to perform some menial task. He had to do something fast to get Indy out. But what?

He paused. Between a couple of tents lay several hampers, their lids open.

No rope, he thought; so in such circumstances you improvise.

When he'd made sure he wasn't being watched, he moved toward the hampers.

Indy snapped the wooden staff in two and stuck the headpiece back into his robes. He placed the pieces of wood in a far corner of the

Map Room, then he went to a spot directly under the hole and stared upward at the bright sky. The brilliant blue blinded him momentarily.

"Sallah," he called out, caught between a shout and a whisper.

Nothing.

"Sallah."

Nothing.

He glanced around the room for an alternative way out, but there wasn't one as far as he could see. Where was Sallah?

"Sallah!"

Silence.

He watched the opening; he blinked against the harsh light, waited.

There was a sudden movement above. Then something began to fall from the hole and for a second he thought it was the rope, but it wasn't: instead, what he saw descending was a bunch of clothing tied together, clumsily knotted to create a makeshift rope—shirts, tunics, pants, robes and—of all things—a swastika flag.

He caught hold of the line, tugged on it, and then began to climb. He surfaced, dropping flat on his stomach as Sallah started to haul the line of clothing out. Indy smiled and the Egyptian stuffed the makeshift rope inside the oil drum. Then Indy rose and followed Sallah quickly between some tents.

They didn't see the German who was walking up and down with an expression of dark impatience on his face.

"You! I'm still waiting for that water!"

Sallah spread his hands apologetically.

The German turned to Indy. "You're another lazy bastard. Why aren't you digging?"

Sallah moved toward the German while Indy, bowing in wonderful subservience, hurried off in the other direction.

He moved quickly now, his robes flapping as he rushed between tents. And from behind, as if some suspicion had just been aroused, some crime suspected, he could hear the German calling after him. *Wait. Come back here.* Indy thought, The last thing I intend to do is come back, dummkopf. He hurried along the tents, caught between his unwillingness to look suspicious and his urge to start digging for the Well of the Souls, when two German officers appeared ahead of him. Damn, he thought, pausing, watching them stop to talk, light cigarettes. His way was blocked.

He slipped along the sides of the tents, hugging such shadow as he could find, and then he moved through an opening, a doorway, and stepped inside one of the tents. He could wait here at least for a few minutes until the way was clear. Those two Krauts could hardly stand out there smoking and talking all day.

He wiped sweat from his forehead, rubbed the damp palms of his hands against his robes. For the first time since he'd entered the place, he considered the Map Room: he thought of that weird sense of timelessness he'd felt, an experience of being somehow suspended, afloat—as if he himself had become a trapped object in the jar of history, preserved, perfect, intact. The Map Room at Tanis. In a way it was like discovering that a fairy tale had some basis in reality—the legend at the heart of which there is truth. The thought touched him in a fashion he found a little humbling: you live in the year 1936, with its airplanes and its radios and its great machines of war—and then you stumble across something so simply intricate, so primitively elaborate, as a miniature map with one specific building designed to glow when struck by light in a certain way. Call it alchemy, artistry or even magic—however you cut it, the passage of centuries hadn't improved anything very much. The movement of time had merely slashed at the roots of some profound sense of the cosmic, the magical.

And now he was within reach of the Well of the Souls.

The Ark.

He wiped his forehead again with the edge of his robes. He peered through the slit in the tent. They were still there, smoking, talking. When the hell would they find a reason to move on?

He was pondering a way out, trying to think up a means of making an exit, when he heard a noise from the other corner of the tent. A strange grunting, a stifled noise. He turned around and peered across the tent, which he had convinced himself was empty.

For a moment, a moment of disbelief, wild incredulity, he felt all his pulses stammer and stop.

She was sitting in a chair, tied to it by crisscrossing ropes, a handkerchief bound tightly around her mouth. She was sitting there, her eyes imploring him, flashing messages at him, and she was trying to speak to him through the folds of the handkerchief pressed against her lips. He crossed the floor quickly, untied the gag and let it fall from her mouth. He kissed her and the kiss was anxious, long, deep. When he pulled his face away, he laid the palm of his hand flat against her cheek.

When she spoke her voice faltered. "They had two baskets . . . two baskets to confuse you. When you thought I was in the truck I was in a car . . ."

"I thought you were dead," he said. What was that sensation he felt now—unfathomable relief? the lifting of guilt? Or was it pure pleasure, gratitude, that she was still alive?

"I'm still kicking," she said.

"Have they hurt you?"

She seemed to struggle with some inner anxiety. "No—they haven't hurt me. They just asked about you, they wanted to find out what you knew."

Indy rubbed his jaw and wondered why he detected an odd hesitation in Marion. But he was still too excited to pause and consider it.

"Indy, please get me away from here. He's evil—"

"Who?"

"The Frenchman."

He was about to untie the rope when he stopped.

"What's wrong?" she asked.

"Look, you'll never understand how I feel right now. I'll never be able to find words for that. But I want you to trust me. I'm going to do something I don't like doing."

"Untie me, Indy. Please untie me."

"That's the point. If I let you loose, then they're going to turn over every particle of sand around here to find you and I can't afford that right now. And since I know where the Ark is, it's important I get to it before they do, then I can come back for you—"

"Indy, no!"

"You only need to sit tight for a little longer—"

"You bastard. Turn me loose!"

He slipped the gag back over her mouth and tightened it. Then, kissing her once more on the forehead, ignoring her protests, her grunts, he stood upright. "Sit tight," he said. "I'll be back."

I'll be back, he thought. There was a very old echo there, an echo that went back ten years. And he could see doubt in her eyes. He kissed her again, then moved toward the opening in the tent.

She thumped her chair on the floor.

He went outside; the German officers had gone.

Overhead, the sun was stronger now. It beat down insanely.

Alive, he thought: she's alive. And the thought was something that soared inside his head. He began to rush, moving away from the tents, from the excavations, out into the burning dunes, out into that place where he had a rendezvous with Omar and his diggers.

He took the surveyor's instrument from the back of Omar's truck and erected it on the dunes. He aligned it with the Map Room in the distance, and consulting the calculations he had made, he got a fix on a position some miles out in the desert, out in untouched sand considerably closer than the spot where Belloq was mistakenly digging for the Well of the Souls. *There*, he thought. The exact place!

"Got it!" he said, and he folded the instrument and stuck it back in the truck. The place was well hidden from Belloq's dig, concealed by the rise of the dunes. They could dig unobserved.

As he was climbing into the truck, Indy noticed a figure appear over the dunes. It was Sallah, robes flapping, hurrying toward the truck.

"I thought you were never coming," Indy said.

"I almost didn't," Sallah said, climbing in back.

"Let's go," Indy told the driver.

When they had gone out into the dunes they parked the truck. It was a barren spot in which to be looking for something so exciting as the Ark. Overhead the sun was incandescent, the color of an exploding yellow rose; and that was what it suggested in its intensity, a thing about to burst loose from the sky.

They went to the spot which Indy had calculated. For a short time he stood and stared at it—dry sand. You could never dream of anything growing here. You could never imagine this ground yielding up anything. Certainly not the Ark.

Indy went to the truck and took out a shovel. The diggers were already moving toward the spot. They had leathery faces, burned faces. Indy wondered if they managed to live beyond forty in a place like this.

Sallah, carrying a spade, walked alongside him. "I believe they might come here only if Belloq realizes he's working in the wrong place. Otherwise, there would be no good reason."

"Who ever heard of a Nazi needing a good reason?"

Sallah smiled. He turned and gazed across the dunes; miles of nothing stretched away. He was silent for a moment. Then he said, "Even a Nazi would need a good reason to wander in this place."

Indy struck the ground with the point of his spade. "He'd still need a requisition and have it signed in triplicate in Berlin." He looked at the diggers. "Let's go," he said. "Let's get on with this."

They began their dig, heaping sand, laboring hard, furiously, pausing only to drink water that had already turned warm in the camel-skin bags. They dug until the light had gone from the sky; but the same heat remained, tethered to the sand.

Belloq sat in his tent, drumming his fingertips on the table that held maps, drawings of the Ark, sheets of paper covered with the hieroglyphics of his calculations. There was a dark mood of frustration inside him; he was edgy, nervous—and the presence of Dietrich, as well as Dietrich's lackey Gobler, didn't help his frame of mind much. Belloq rose, went to a washbasin, splashed water across his face.

"A wasted day," Dietrich said. "A wasted day . . ."

Belloq toweled his face, then poured himself a small shot of cognac. He stared at the German, then at the underling Gobler, who seemed to exist only as a shadow of Dietrich.

Dietrich, undeterred, went on: "My men have been digging all day—and for what? Tell me, for what?"

Belloq sipped his drink, then said, "Based on the information in my possession, my calculations were correct. But archaeology is not the most exact of sciences, Dietrich. I don't think you entirely understand this fact. Perhaps the Ark will be found in an adjoining chamber. Perhaps some vital piece of evidence still eludes us." He shrugged and finished his drink. Usually he loathed the way the Germans nit-picked, the way they always seemed to hover around him as if they expected him to be a seer, a prophet. Now, however, he understood their change in mood.

"The Führer demands constant reports of progress," Dietrich said. "He is not a patient man."

"You may cast your mind back to my conversation with your Führer, Dietrich. You may well recall I made no promises. I simply said that things looked favorable, nothing more."

There was a silence. Gobler moved in front of the kerosene lamp, throwing a huge shadow that Belloq found curiously menacing. Gobler said, "The girl could help us. After all, she was in possession of the original piece for years."

"Indeed," Dietrich said.

"I doubt if she knows anything," Belloq said.

"It is worth a try," Gobler said.

He wondered why he found their treatment of the girl so unsettling to him. They had used her barbarically—they had threatened her with a variety of tortures, but it seemed apparent to him that she had nothing to tell. Was this some soft spot, some awful weakness, he had toward her? The thought appalled him. He stared at Dietrich for a moment. How very badly they live in fear of their sorry little Führer, he thought. He must strut through their dreams at night—if they dreamed at all, a prospect he couldn't quite believe. They were men stripped of imagination.

"If you don't want to be concerned with the girl, Belloq, I have someone who can undertake the task of discovering what she knows."

It was no time to parade a weakness, a concern for the woman. Dietrich went to the opening of the tent and called out. After a moment the man named Arnold Toht appeared, extending his arm in a Nazi salute. In the center of his palm was the scar, burned-out tissue, in the perfect shape of the headpiece.

"The woman," Dietrich said. "I believe you know her, Toht."

Toht said, "There are old scores to settle."

"And old scars," Belloq said.

Toht self-consciously lowered his hand.

When it was dark and a pale desert moon had come up over the horizon, a moon of muted blue, Indy and his Arabs stopped digging. They had lit torches, watching the moon begin slowly to darken as clouds passed in front of it; after that there was lightning in the sky, strange lightning that came in brief forks and flashes, an electric storm summoned, it seemed, out of nowhere.

The men had dug a hole that revealed a heavy stone door flush with the bottom of the pit. For a long time nobody said anything. Tools were produced from the truck and the diggers forced the stone door open, grunting as they labored with the weight of the thing.

The stone door was pulled back. Beneath the door was an underground chamber. *The Well of the Souls.* It was about thirty feet deep, a large chamber whose walls were covered with hieroglyphics and carvings. The roof of the place was supported by huge statues, guardians of the vault. It was an awesome construction, and it created, in the light of the torches, a sense of bottomlessness, an abyss in which history itself was trapped. The men moved their torches as they peered down.

The far end of the chamber came into view, barely lit. There was a stone altar that held a stone chest; a floor covered with some form of strange dark carpeting.

"The chest must contain the Ark," Indy said. "I don't understand what that gray stuff is all over the floor."

But then, in another flash of lightning, he saw; he shook, dropping his torch down into the Well, hearing the hiss of hundreds of snakes.

As the torch burned, the snakes moved away from the heart of the flame. More than hundreds, thousands of snakes, Egyptian asps, shivering and undulating and coiling across the floor as they answered the flame with their savage hissing. The floor seemed to move in the flicker of the torch—but it wasn't the floor, it was the snakes, striking backward from the flame. Only the altar was untouched by snakes. Only the stone altar seemed immune to the asps.

"Why did it have to be snakes?" Indy asked. "Anything but snakes, anything else. I could have taken almost anything else."

"Asps," Sallah said. "Very poisonous."

"Thanks for that piece of news, Sallah."

"They stay clear of the flame, you notice."

Pull yourself together, Indy thought. You're so close to the Ark you can *feel* it, so you face your phobia head on and do something about it. A thousand snakes—so what? So what? The living floor was the embodiment of an old nightmare. Snakes pursued him in the darkest of his dreams, rooting around his innermost fears. He turned to the diggers and said, "Okay. Okay. A few snakes. Big deal. I want lots of torches. And oil. I want a landing strip down there."

After a time, lit torches were dropped into the Well. Several canisters of oil were dropped into the spaces where the snakes had slithered away from the flames. The diggers then began to lower a large wooden crate, rope handles attached to each corner, into the hole. Indy watched, wondering if a phobia were something you could swallow, digest, something you could ignore as though it were the intense pain of a passing indigestion. Despite his resolve to go down there, he shuddered—and the asps, coiling and uncoiling, filled the darkness with their sibilant sound, a sound more menacing than any he'd ever heard. A rope was lowered now: he stood upright, swallowed hard, then swung out on the rope and down into the Well. A moment later Sallah followed him. Beyond the edges of the flames the snakes wriggled, slid, snakes piled on snakes, mountains of the reptiles, snake eggs hatching, shells breaking to reveal tiny asps, snakes devouring other snakes.

For a time he hung suspended, the rope swaying back and forth, Sallah hanging just above him.

"I guess this is it," he said.

Marion watched as Belloq entered the tent. He came across the floor slowly and studied her for a while, but he made no move to untie her gag. What was it about this man? What was it that caused a sensation, something almost like panic, inside her? She could hear the sound of her heart beat. She stared at him, wishing she could just close her eyes and turn her face away. When she had first met him after being captured, he had said very little to her—he had simply scrutinized her in the way he was doing now. The eyes were cold and yet they seemed capable, although she wasn't sure how she knew this, of yielding to occasional warmth. They were also knowing, as if he had gone far into some profound secret, as if he had tested reality and found it lacking. The face was handsome in the way she might have associated with pictures in romantic magazines of Europeans wearing white suits and sipping exotic drinks on the terraces of villas. But these weren't the qualities that touched her.

Something else.

Something she didn't want to think about.

Now she closed her eyes. Marion couldn't bear to be so closely stared at, she couldn't bear to think of herself as an object of scrutiny—perhaps like some archaeological fragment, a sliver of clay broken loose from the jigsaw of an ancient piece of pottery. Inanimate, a thing to be classified.

When she heard him move she opened her eyes.

He still didn't speak. And her uneasiness grew. He moved across the floor until he was standing directly over her, then he put his hand forward very slowly and slipped the gag from her lips, sliding it softly and teasingly from her mouth. She had a sudden picture, one she didn't want to entertain, of his hand caressing the fold of her hip. No, she thought. It isn't like that at all. But the image remained in her head. And Belloq's hand, with the certainty of the successful lover, gently drew the gag from her mouth to her chin and then he was untying the knot—everything performed slowly, with the kind of casual elegance of a seducer who senses, in some predatory way, the yielding of his prey.

She twisted her head to the side. She wanted to cut these thoughts off, but she seemed incapable of doing it. I don't want to be attracted to this man, she thought. I don't want him to touch me. But then, as he moved his fingers beneath her chin and began to stroke her throat, she realized she was incapable of fighting. I won't let him see it in my eyes, she told herself. I won't let him see this in my face. Despite herself, she began to imagine his hands drifting across the surface of her body, hands that were strangely gentle, considerate in their touches, intimate and exciting in their promises. And suddenly she knew that this man would make a lover of extraordinary unselfishness, that he would bring out of her the kind of pleasures she hadn't ever experienced before.

He knows it, she thought. He knows it, too.

He brought his face close. She could smell the sweetness of his breath. No no no, she thought. But she didn't speak. She knew she was leaning forward slightly, anticipating the kiss, her mind dancing, her desire intense. It didn't come. There wasn't a kiss. He had bent down and was beginning to untie her ropes, moving in the same way as before, letting the ropes fall to the ground as if they were the most erotic of garments.

Still he hadn't spoken.

He was looking at her. There was a light in his eye, the faint touch of warmth she'd imagined before—but she couldn't tell if it was real or if it was something he used, a prop in his repertoire of behavior.

Then he said, "You're very beautiful."

She shook her head. "Please . . ." But she didn't know if she was begging to be left alone or if she was asking him to kiss her, and she realized she'd never experienced such a confusion of emotion in her entire life. Indy, why the hell hadn't he rescued her? Why had he left her like this?

Repelled, attracted—why wasn't there some hard and fast borderline between the two? Signposts she could read? It didn't matter: there was a melting of distinctions in her thoughts. She saw the contradiction and she understood, with a sense of horror, that she wanted this man to make love to her, to teach her what she felt was his deep understanding of physical love; and beyond this, there was the feeling that he could be cruel, an insight that suddenly didn't matter to her either.

He brought his face closer again. She looked at his lips. The eyes were filled with understanding, a comprehension she hadn't seen in a man's face before. Already, even before he kissed her, he knew her, he could look into her. She felt more naked than she'd ever felt. Even this vulnerability excited her now. He came nearer. He kissed her.

She wanted to draw away again.

The kiss—she closed her eyes and gave herself to the kiss—and it wasn't like any other kiss in her life. It moved into a place beyond the narrow limits of lips and tongues. It created spaces of bright light in her head, colors, webs of gold and silver and yellow and blue, as if she were watching some impossible sunset. Slow, patient, unselfish. Nobody had ever touched her before. Not like that. Not even Indy.

When he drew his face away, she realized she was holding him tightly. She was digging her nails into his body. And the realization came as a shock to her, a shock that brought a sudden sense of shame. What was she doing? What had possessed her?

She stepped back from him.

"Please," she said. "No more."

He smiled and spoke for the first time: "They intend to harm you."

It was as if the kiss had never existed. It was as if she had been manipulated. The abrupt letdown she experienced was the wild drop in a roller-coaster ride.

"I managed to persuade them to give me some time alone with you, my dear. You're a very attractive woman, after all. And I don't want to see them hurt you. They're barbarians."

He came closer to her again. No, she thought. Not again.

"You must tell me something to placate them. Some information."

"I don't know anything . . . how many times do I have to tell them?" She was dizzy now, she needed to sit down. Why didn't he kiss her again?

"What about Jones?"

"I don't know anything."

"Your loyalty is admirable. But you must tell me what Jones knows."

Indy came swimming back into her vision.

"He's brought me nothing but trouble . . ."

"I agree," Belloq said. He reached for her, held her face between his hands, studied her eyes. "I think I want to believe you know nothing. But I cannot control the Germans. I cannot hold them back."

"Don't let them hurt me."

Belloq shrugged. "Then tell me *anything*!"

The tent door flapped open. Marion looked at the figure of Arnold Toht standing there. Behind him were the Germans she had come to know as Dietrich and Gobler. The fear she felt was like some sun burning in her head.

Belloq said, "I'm sorry."

She didn't move. She simply stared at Toht, remembering how badly he'd wanted to hurt her with the poker.

"Fräulein," Toht said. "We have come a long way from Nepal, no?"

Stepping backward, she shook her head in fear.

Toht advanced toward her. She glanced at Belloq, as if to make some last appeal to him, but he was going from the tent now, stepping out into the night.

Outside, Belloq paused. It was odd to be attracted by the woman, strange to want to make love to her even if the act had begun out of the desire to extract information from her. But after that, after the first kiss . . . He stuck his hands in his pockets and hesitated outside the tent. He wanted to go back inside and make those worms stop what they were about to do, but his attention was suddenly drawn to the horizon.

Lightning—lightning concentrated strangely in one place, as if it had gathered there deliberately, directed by some meteorological consciousness. A congregation of lightning, spikes and forks and flashes spitting in one spot. He bit on his lower lip, deep in thought, and then he went back inside the tent.

Indy moved toward the altar. He tried to ignore the sound of the snakes, a mad noise—made more insane by the eerie shadows thrown by the torches. He had splashed oil from the canisters across the floor and lit it, creating a path among the snakes; and now these flames, thrusting upward, eclipsed the lightning from overhead. Sallah was behind him. Together they struggled with the stone cover of the chest until it was loose; inside, more beautiful than he'd ever imagined it to be, was the Ark.

For a time he couldn't move. He stared at the untarnished gold angels that faced one another over the lid, the gold that coated the acacia wood. The gold carrying-rings affixed to the four corners shone brilliantly in the light of his torch. He looked at Sallah, who was watching the Ark in reverential silence. More than anything else now Indy had the urge to reach out and touch the Ark—but even as he thought it, Sallah put his hand forward.

"Don't touch it," Indy exclaimed. "Never touch it."

Sallah drew his hand away. They turned toward the wooden crate and removed the four poles that were attached to the corners. They inserted the poles into the rings of the Ark and raised it, grunting at the weight of the thing, then levering it from the stone chest into the crate. The fires were beginning to die now and the snakes, their hissing beginning to sound more and more like a solitary upraised voice, were slipping toward the altar.

"Hurry," Indy said. "Hurry."

They attached the ropes to the crate. Indy tugged on one of the ropes, and the crate was pulled up out of the chamber. Sallah took the next rope and quickly made his ascent. Indy reached for his exit rope, pulling on it to be certain of its support—and it *fell*, itself snakelike, from the opening at the top into the chamber.

"What the hell—"

From above, the Frenchman's voice was unmistakable: "Why, Dr. Jones, whatever are you doing in such a nasty place?"

There was laughter.

"You're making a habit of this, Belloq," Indy said.

The snakes hissed closer. He could hear their bodies slide across the floor.

"A bad habit, I agree," Belloq said, peering down. "Unhappily, I have no further use for you, my old friend. And I find it suitably ironic that you're about to become a permanent addition to this archaeological find."

"I'm dying of laughter," Indy shouted up.

He continued to squint upward, wondering if there were any exit from this . . . and he was still wondering when he saw Marion being pushed from the edge of the hole, falling, dropping. He moved quickly and broke her fall with his body, sliding to the ground as she struck him. The snakes edged closer. She clung frantically to Indy, who could hear Belloq arguing from above.

"She was mine!"

"She is of no use to us now, Belloq. Only the mission for the Führer matters."

"I had plans for her!"

"The only plans are those that concern Berlin," Dietrich said back to Belloq.

There was a silence from above. And then Belloq was looking down into the chamber at Marion.

His voice was low. "It was not to be," he said to her. Then he nodded at Indy. "Indiana Jones, *adieu!*"

Suddenly the stone door to the chamber was slammed shut by a group of German soldiers. Air was sucked out of the Well, torches went out, and the snakes were moving into the areas of darkness.

Marion clutched Indy tightly. He disentangled himself, picking up two torches that were still lit, passing one to her.

"Just wave the torch at anything that moves," he said.

"*Everything* is moving," she said. "The whole place is slithering."

"Don't remind me."

He began to fumble around in the dark, found one of the oil canisters, splashed the oil toward the wall and lit it. He stared at one of the statues above, feeling the snakes encroach ever closer to him.

"What are you doing?" Marion asked.

He poured what remained of the oil in a circle around them and set it ablaze.

"Stay here."

"Why? Where are you going?"

"I'll be back. Keep your eyes open and get ready to run."

"Run where?"

He didn't answer. He moved backward through the flames to the center of the room. Snakes flicked around his heels, and he swung his torch desperately to keep them away. He stared up at the statue, which reached close to the ceiling. From under his robes he took his bullwhip and lashed it through the half-light, watching it curl around the base of the statue. He tugged on it to test its strength, then he began to climb one-handed, the torch in his other hand.

He hauled himself up and twisted once to look down at Marion, who stood behind the dwindling wall of flame. She looked lost and forlorn and helpless. He made it to the top of the statue when a snake appeared around the face of the statue—hissing directly into Indy's eyes. Indy shoved his torch into its head, smelled the burning of reptile flesh, watched the snake slip from the smooth stone and fall away.

He jammed himself in place, his feet stuck between wall and statue. *Let it work*, he thought. Snakes were climbing up around the statue, and his torch—failing badly—wouldn't keep them away forever. He flailed with it, striking this way and that, hearing snakes drop and fall into the chamber. Then the torch slipped from his grasp and flickered out as it dropped. Just when you need a light, you don't have one, he thought.

And something crawled over his hand.

He yelled in surprise.

As he did so, the statue gave way, came loose from its foundation and swayed, shivered, tilting at a terrifying angle to the roof of the chamber. Here we go, Indy thought, holding onto this statue as if it were a wild mule. But it was more like a log being clutched in a stormy sea—and it fell, it fell while he struggled to hold on, gathering speed, toppling past the startled Marion, who stood in the dying fires, whizzing past her in the manner of a tree felled by a lumberjack, breaking through the floor of the Well and crashing into darkness beyond. Then the voyage astride the statue stopped abruptly when the broken figure hit bottom, and he slid off, stunned, rubbing the side of his head. He fumbled around in the dark for a moment, aware of faint light filtering through the ragged hole from the Well. Marion was calling to him.

"Indy! Where are you?"

He reached through the hole as she peered into it.

"Never ride by statue," he said. "Take my advice."

"I'll make a point of it."

He caught her hand and helped her in. She held the torch over her head. It was a poor light now—but enough for them to see they were inside a maze of interconnected chambers running at angles beneath the Well, catacombs that tunneled the earth.

"So where are we now?"

"Your guess would be as good as mine. Maybe they built the Well above these catacombs for some reason. I don't know. It's hard to say. But it's better than snakes."

A swarm of distressed bats flew out of the dark, winging around them, beating the air like lunatics. They ducked and passed into another chamber. Marion flapped her hands over her head and screamed.

"Don't do that," he said. "It scares me."

"How do you think it makes *me* feel?"

They went from chamber to chamber.

"There has to be some way out," he said. "The bats are a good sign. They have to find the sky outside for feeding purposes."

Another chamber, and here the stench was sickening. Marion raised her torch.

There were moldering mummies in their half-wrapped bandages, rotting flesh hanging from yellowed bindings, mounds of skulls, bones, some of them with half-preserved flesh clinging to their surfaces. A wall in front of them was covered with glistening beetles.

"I can't believe this smell," Marion said.

"You're complaining?"

"I think I'm going to be sick."

"Great," Indy told her. "That'd cap this experience nicely."

Marion sighed. "This is the worst place I've ever been."

"No, *back there* was the worst place you've ever been."

"But you know what, Indy?" she said. "If I had to be here with anybody . . ."

"Got you," he cut her off. "Got you."

"That's right. You do."

Marion kissed him gently on the lips. The softness of her touch surprised him. He drew his face back, wanted to kiss her again— but she was pointing excitedly at something, and when he turned his face he saw, some distance away, the merciful sight of the desert sun, a dawn sun, white and wonderful and promising.

"Thank God," she said.

"Thank who you like. But we've still got work to do."

The Tanis Digs, Egypt

THEY MOVED among the abandoned excavations, closer to the airstrip that had been hacked out of the desert by the Germans. There were two fuel trucks on the strip, a tent supply depot, and someone—clearly a mechanic to judge from his coveralls—standing at the edge of the runway with his hands on his hips, his face turned toward the sky. And then someone else was moving across the strip toward the mechanic, a figure Marion recognized as Dietrich's aide, Gobler.

Abruptly, there was a roaring noise in the sky, and from their position behind the abandoned dig, Marion and Indy saw a Flying Wing make an approach to land.

Gobler was shouting at the mechanic: "Get it gassed up at once! It has to be ready to fly out immediately with an important cargo!"

The Flying Wing came down, bouncing along the strip.

"They're going to put the Ark on that plane," Indy said.

"So what do we do then? Wave good-bye?"

"No. When the Ark gets loaded, we'll already be on the plane."

She looked at him quizzically. "Another of your schemes?"

"We've come this far—let's keep going." They moved, scurrying to a place just behind the supply tent. The mechanic was already putting blocks in front of the tires of the Flying Wing. The German attached the fuel hose to the plane. The propellers were spinning, the engine still roaring in a deafening way.

They moved even closer to the strip now, neither of them seeing another German mechanic, a fair-haired young man with tattooed arms, come up behind them. He crept toward them with the wrench upraised, his target the base of Indy's skull. It was Marion who saw his shadow first, saw it fall in a blur in front of her; she shouted. Indy turned as the wrench started to drop. He sprang to his feet, grabbed the swinging arm and wrestled the man to the ground while Marion skipped away behind some crates, watching, wondering what she could do to help.

Indy and the man rolled out across the strip. The first mechanic moved away from the plane, stood over the two wrestling figures and waited for the chance to launch a kick at Indy—but then Indy was up, agile, turning on the first man and knocking him down with a two-fisted shot. But the man with the tattooed arms was still eager to fight, and they struggled together again, rolling toward the rear of the plane, where the reverse propellers were spinning in a crazy way.

You could be mincemeat any second now, Indy thought.

He could feel the vicious blades carve the air around him as daggers through butter.

He tried to push the young guy back from the props, but the kid was strong. Grunting, Indy caught the kid by the throat and pressed hard, but the German swung away and came back again with a renewed vitality. Marion, watching from the crates, saw the pilot climb out of his cockpit and take a Luger from his tunic, leveling it, looking for a clear shot at Indy. She rushed across the strip, heaved one of the tire blocks from under the wheels and struck the pilot on the side of the skull with it, and he went down, dropping back into the cockpit, settling on the throttle so that the engine revved even harder.

The plane began to roll, rotating as if frustrated around its only set of tires that were still blocked. Marion reached for the edge of the cockpit to keep from slipping into the props, then she bent inside and tried to push the unconscious pilot away from the throttle.

Nothing. He was too heavy. The plane was threatening to go out of control and tilt, probably squashing Indy, or cutting him to thin ribbons into the bargain. *The things I do for you, Indy,* she thought. And she stepped into the cockpit, striking the plexiglass shield, causing it to slide shut above her. Still the plane was swinging, the wing moving dangerously over the place where Indy was fighting with the German. Panicked, she saw him knock the man down, and then he was up once more only for Indy to punch him backward . . .

Into the propeller.

Marion shut her eyes. But not before she saw the blades carve through the young German, sending up a spray of blood. And still the plane was rolling. She opened her eyes, tried to get out of the cockpit, realized she was stuck. She hammered on the lid, but nothing happened. *First a basket, now a cockpit,* she thought. *Where does it end?*

Indy raced toward the plane, watching it tilt, shocked to see Marion hammering against the inside of the cockpit. Now the wing, breaking, tilting, sliced into the fuel truck, breaking it open with the final authority of a surgeon's knife, spilling fuel across the strip like blood from an anesthetized patient. Indy began to run, skidding over the gasoline. He struggled for balance, slipped, got up and began to run again. He leaped up onto the wing and clambered toward the cockpit.

"Get out! This whole thing's going to blow!" he shouted at her.

He reached for the clasp that would open the cockpit from the outside.

He forced it, struggled with it, assailed by the strong smell of fuel flowing from the truck.

Trapped, Marion watched him imploringly.

———

The wooden crate, surrounded by three armed German soldiers, stood outside the entrance to Dietrich's tent. Inside, in a flurry of activity, papers were being packed, maps folded, radio sets dismantled. Belloq, standing inside the tent, watched the preparation for departure in an absent-minded fashion. His mind was concerned entirely with what lay inside the crate, the very thing he could hardly wait to examine. It was hard to restrain his impatience, to keep himself in check. He was remembering now the ritual preparations that had to be observed when opening the Ark. It was strange how, through the years, he had been making himself ready for this time—and strange, too, to realize how familiar he had become with the incantations. The Nazis wouldn't like it, of course—but they could do what they wanted with the Ark after he'd finished with it. They could pack it off and store it in some godawful museum for all he cared.

Hebraic incantations: they wouldn't like that at all. And the thought caused him some amusement. But the amusement didn't last long because the contents of the crate once more drew his attention. If everything he had ever learned about the Ark was true, if all the old stories concerning its power were correct, he would be the first man to make direct communication with that which had its source in a place—an infinite place—beyond human understanding.

He stepped out of the tent.

In the distance, flaring like a column of fire that might have been directed from heaven, there was a vast explosion.

He realized it was coming from the airstrip.

He began to run, driven with anxiety, toward the strip.

Dietrich came up behind him, followed by Gobler, who'd been at the strip only several minutes ago.

The fuel trucks had exploded and the airplane was a fiery wreck.

"Sabotage," Dietrich said. "But who?"

"Jones," Belloq said.

"Jones?" Dietrich looked bewildered.

"The man has more lives than the proverbial cat," Belloq said. "But a time must come when he has used them all up, no?"

They watched the flames in silence.

"We must get the Ark away from here at once," Belloq said. "We must put it on a truck and go to Cairo. We can fly from there."

Belloq stared a moment longer at the carnage, wondering at Indiana Jones's sense of purpose, his lavish gift of survival. One had to admire the man's tenacious hold on life. And one had to beware of the cunning, the fortitude, that lay behind it. It was always possible, Belloq thought, to underestimate the opposition. And perhaps all along he had underestimated Indiana Jones.

"We must have plenty of protection, Dietrich."

"Of course. I'll arrange it."

Belloq turned. The flight from Cairo was a lie, of course—he had already radioed instructions ahead to the island, without Dietrich's knowledge. It was a bridge he would cross when he reached it.

The only thing of any consequence now was that he should open the Ark before it was sent to Berlin.

There was wild confusion among the tents now. German soldiers had run to the airstrip and, in disarray, were returning. Another group of armed men, their faces darkened from the smoke of the ruin, had begun to load a canvas-covered truck with the Ark: Dietrich supervised them, shouting orders, his voice raised to a nervous pitch. He would be relieved and happy when this wretched crate was finally safe in Berlin, but meantime he didn't trust Belloq—he'd noticed some fierce light of purpose, a devious prupose, in the Frenchman's eyes. And behind this purpose something that looked manic, distant, as if the archaeologist had gone deeper into communing with himself. It was a look of madness, he thought, somewhat alarmed to realize he'd seen a similar look on the Führer's face when he'd been in Bavaria with Belloq. Maybe they were alike, this Frenchman and Adolf Hitler. Maybe their strength, as well as their madness, was what separated them from ordinary men. Dietrich could only guess. He stared at the crate going inside the truck now and he wondered about Jones—but Jones had to be dead, he had to be entombed in that dreadful chamber, surely. Even so, the Frenchman seemed convinced that the American had been behind the sabotage. Maybe this animosity, this rivalry, that existed between those two was yet another aspect of Belloq's lunacy.

Maybe.

There was no time to ruminate on the Frenchman's state of mind now. There was the Ark and the road to Cairo and the dread prospect of further sabotage along the way. Sweating, hating this dreary desert, this heat, he shouted once more at the men loading the truck—feeling somewhat sorry for them. Like himself, they were a long way from the Fatherland.

Marion and Indy had found their way behind some barrels, watching the Arabs run back and forth in confusion, watching the Germans load the truck. Their faces were blackened from the convulsions of the explosion and Marion, visibly pale even beneath the soot, had an appearance of extreme fatigue.

"You took your damn time," she complained.

"I got you out, didn't I?"

"At the last possible moment," she said. "How come you always leave things till then?"

He glanced at her, rubbed his fingertips in her face, stared at the soot imbedded in the whorls of his fingerprints, then he turned back to peer at the truck. "They're taking the Ark somewhere— which is what I'm more interested in right now."

A bunch of Arabs were running past now. Among them, to his pleasure and surprise, Indy saw Sallah. He stuck out his foot, tripping the Egyptian, who tumbled over and got up again with a look of delight on his face.

"Indy! Marion! I thought I'd lost you."

"Likewise," Indy said. "What happened?"

"They barely pay the Arabs any attention, my friend. They assume we are fools, ignorant fools—besides, they can hardly tell one of us from the other. I slipped away and they weren't paying close attention in any case."

He slid behind the barrels, breathing hard.

"I assume you caused the explosion?"

"You got it."

"You don't know they are now planning to take the Ark in the truck to Cairo?"

"Cairo?"

"Presumably Berlin afterward."

"I doubt Berlin," Indy said. "I can't imagine Belloq allowing the Ark to reach Germany before he's dabbled with it."

An open staff car drew up alongside the truck. Belloq and Dietrich got inside with a driver and an armed guard. There was the sound of feet scuffling across the sand; ten or so armed soldiers climbed up into the rear of the truck with the Ark.

"It's hopeless," Marion said.

Indy didn't answer. Watch, he told himself. Watch and concentrate. *Think.* Now there was a second staff car, top open, with a machine-gun mounted in the back; a gunner sat restlessly behind it. In the front of this car Gobler was positioned behind the wheel. Alongside Gobler was Arnold Toht.

Marion drew her breath in sharply when she saw Toht. "He's a monster."

"They are all monsters," Sallah said.

"Monsters or not," she answered, "it looks more and more hopeless by the moment."

Machine gun, armed soldiers, Indy thought. Maybe something was possible. Maybe he didn't have to accept hopelessness as the only answer. He watched this convoy begin to pull out, swaying over the sands.

"I'm going to follow them," he said.

"How?" Marion asked. "You can run that fast?"

"I have a better idea." Indy got up. "You two get back to Cairo as fast as you can and arrange some kind of transportation to England—anything, a ship, a plane, I don't care."

"Why England?" Marion said.

"There are no language barriers and no Nazis," Indy said. He looked at Sallah. "Where can we meet in Cairo?"

Sallah looked thoughtful for a moment. "There is Omar's garage, where he keeps his truck. Do you know the Square of Snakes?"

"Gruesome," Indy said. "But I couldn't forget *that* address, could I?"

"In the Old City," Sallah said.

"I'll be there."

Marion stood up. "How do I know you'll get there in one piece?"

"Trust me."

He kissed her as she caught his arm. She said, "I wonder if a time will come when you'll stop leaving me?"

He skipped away, weaving between the barrels.

"We can use my truck," Sallah said to Marion after he'd gone. "Slow but safe."

Marion stared into space. What was it about Indy that so affected her, anyhow? He wasn't exactly a tender lover, if he could be called a lover of any kind. And he leaped in and out of her life in the manner of a jumping-bean. So what the devil was it? Some mysteries you just can't get to the bottom of, she thought. Some you don't even want to.

Indy had seen the stallions tethered to poles in a place between the abandoned airstrip and the excavations: two of them, a white Arabian and a black one, shaded from the sun by a strip of green canvas. Now, having left Marion and Sallah, he ran toward the stallions, hoping they'd still be there. They were. My lucky day, he thought.

He approached them cautiously. He hadn't ridden for years and he wondered if it was true that horseback riding, like bicycle riding, was something you never forgot once you'd learned it. He hoped so. The black stallion, snorting, pounding the sand with its hooves, reared up as he came near; the white horse, on the other hand, regarded him in a docile way. He heaved himself up on its white back, tugged at its mane, and felt it buck mildly, then move in the direction of his tugging. Go, he thought, and he rode the animal out of the canvas shelter, digging its sides with his heels. He galloped the animal, forcing it across the dunes, down gulleys, over ridges. It moved beautifully, responding to his gestures without complaint. He had to cut the convoy off somewhere along the mountainous roads between here and Cairo. After that—what the hell?

There was much to be said for spontaneity.

And the thrill of the chase.

The convoy struggled along a narrow mountain road that rose higher and higher, moving through hairpin turns that overlooked passes whose depths caused vertigo. Indy, astride the stallion, watched it go; it labored, grinding upward, some distance below him. And the guys in the trucks, uniformed zombies that they might be, still had rifles, and you had to respect, with great caution, any armed man. Especially when they were component parts of a small army and you—with more reckless courage than reason—were alone on an Arabian horse.

He urged the steed down a slope now, a slope of scrub and shale and soft soil, and its hooves created tiny avalanches. Then he hit the strip of road behind the rear staff car, once again hoping he wouldn't be seen. Fat chance, he thought.

He made the animal weave just as the gunner in the rear car

opened fire, spraying the soft surface of the road with bullets that made the horse dance. The bullets echoed against the sides of the mountain. He drove the horse harder now, almost breaking the animal, and then he was passing the staff car, seeing the surprised faces of the Germans inside. The gunner swung his machine gun and it spluttered, kicked, running out of ammunition as he blasted futilely away at the man on the horse. Toht, seated beside the driver, pulled a pistol, but Indy was already obscured from the staff car by the truck, riding alongside the cab now. The German fired the pistol anyway. His shots ripped through the canvas of the truck.

Take your chance now, Indy thought. He jumped from the animal, spun through the air, caught the side of the cab and swung the door open as the armed guard riding with the driver tried to raise his rifle. Indy grappled with him for the weapon, twisting it this way and that while the guard grunted with the effort of a combat in which he didn't have the privilege of using his gun. Indy twisted hard; he heard the sudden sickening sound of wrists breaking, the cry of the man's pain, and then Indy forced the guard to drop from the cab out onto the road.

Now the driver.

Indy struggled with him, a stout man with gold teeth, as the steering wheel spun and the truck lunged toward the precipice. Indy reached for the wheel, pulling the truck back, and the driver struck him hard on the face.

Indy was stunned a moment. The driver tried to brake. Indy kicked his foot away. And then they were struggling together again as the wheel went into a purposeless spin and the truck swerved. In the staff car behind, Gobler had to swing his wheel to avoid the truck—a spin so sharp and so abrupt that the gunner in the rear was flipped from the side of the auto and over the edge of the cliff. He fell like a kite weighted with lead, arms outstretched and wind rushing through his hair, and the sound of his scream echoed in the canyon below.

In the lead staff car, Belloq turned to see what was going on. Jones, he thought: it had to be Jones, still trying to get the Ark. The prize will never be yours, friend, he thought. He stared at Dietrich, then he looked back once more, but sunlight obscured the view into the cab of the truck behind.

"I think there is a problem," Belloq said casually.

The car reached a summit, made a hairpin turn, struck the frail guardrail at the edge and bent it. The driver managed to get the car straight again, while the armed guard, seated in the rear of the car, leveled his submachine gun and trained it on the window of the cab.

Belloq restrained him: "If you shoot, you may kill the driver. If you kill the driver, your Führer's little Egyptian prize will very likely plummet over the side. What would I tell them in Berlin?"

Looking worried, Dietrich managed to nod in a grim way. "Is this more of your American friend's antics, Belloq?"

"What he hopes to achieve against such odds escapes me," Belloq said. "But it also scares me."

"If anything happens to the Ark . . ." Dietrich didn't finish his sentence, but he might have drawn an index finger, like a blade, across his larynx.

"Nothing will happen to the Ark," Belloq said.

Indy had his hands around the driver's neck now and the truck once again went out of control, spinning toward the broken guardrail, striking it flat, stirring up a cloud of dense dust before Indy caught the wheel and brought the truck back from the edge. In the staff car at the rear, the dust blinded Gobler and Toht— Toht, who was still holding his pistol in a useless manner.

Gobler, his throat thick from the dust, coughed. He tried to blink the dust out of his eyes. But he blinked too late. The last thing he saw was the broken guardrail, the last thing he heard the abrupt, fearful scream of Toht. The staff car, inexorably drawn to the edge of the pass as an iron filing to a magnet, went through the guardrail and dipped into space, seeming to hang for a second in some travesty of gravity before dropping, dropping and dropping, exploding in a wild burst of flame as it bounced down the side of the pass.

Damn, Indy thought. Whenever he tackled the driver, the truck almost carried them to certain death. And the guy was strong, the stoutness concealing a layer of muscle, hard muscle. From the corner of his eye, Indy was conscious of something else. He glanced at the side mirror—soldiers were clambering around the side of the truck, hanging on through fear and determination, making their way toward the cab. In one savage burst of strength, Indy shoved the driver away, slid the door open behind the wheel and kicked him out of the cab. The man bounced away in dust and screams, arms thrashing the air.

Sorry, Indy thought.

He seized the wheel and pressed the gas, gaining on the front staff car. Then there was a sudden darkness, a short tunnel cut into the side of the mountain. He swung the truck from side to side, scraping the walls of the tunnel, hearing the cries of the soldiers as they were smashed against walls, as they lost their grip on the side of the truck. Indy wondered how many other soldiers were still in the rear of his truck. Impossible to count. Out of the tunnel now, back in the hard daylight, he drove against the staff car, bumped it and watched the face of the armed guard as he looked upward, pointed—*he was pointing at the top of the truck.*

He's blown it, Indy thought. If there are more soldiers on the top of this truck, that guy has just blown the scheme. Better safe than sorry, he told himself, suddenly slamming on the brakes, locking the wheels, making the truck skid to a halt. He saw two soldiers thrown from the roof of the truck, shattered against the side of the mountain.

They were coming down from the high mountain road now. Indy put his foot on the gas, pressuring the staff car, bumping it; a good feeling, he thought, to know they won't take a chance on killing you because of your precious cargo. He enjoyed the sudden sensation of freedom, banging again and again at the rear bumper of the car, watching Belloq and his German friends being shaken, rattled. But he knew he'd have to get ahead of them sooner or later. Before Cairo, he'd have to be in front of them.

He thrust the truck forward again, hammering the staff car. The road was leveling out as it dropped from the mountain heights: in the far distance, dim as yet in outline, he could see the haze of the city. The dangerous part, the worst part now: if they ran no risk of watching him plunge the truck and its cargo down a steep pass, then they'd almost certainly try to kill him now, or at least run him off the road.

As if prompted by the thought, a form of treacherous telepathy, the armed guard opened fire. The bullets of the submachine gun shattered the glass, ripped through the canvas fabric, drove deep into the body of the truck. Indy heard them *zing* past him, but he ducked anyway, an instinctive thing. Now, for sure, he needed to get out in front. The road twisted still, going into a sharp bend just ahead. Hold on, he told himself. *Hold tight and make it here.* He gave the truck as much gas as he could and swung the vehicle around the staff car, hearing another whine of bullets, and then he was hitting the car and seeing it go off the road, where it slid down a short embankment.

One step completed. But he knew they'd get back on the road and come after him again. He glanced in his side mirror: yeah, sure enough. They were slithering back up from the incline, reversing across the road, straightening, coming after him. He shoved the gas pedal to the floor. Give me all you've got, he thought. And then he was on the outskirts of the city, the staff car immediately behind him. City streets: a different ball game.

Narrow thoroughfares. He drove quickly through them and sent animals and people flying, turning over stalls, baskets, the fruits of merchants and vendors, scattering beggars in his way. Pedestrians scurried into doorways when the truck wheeled through; then he was threading ever more narrow streets and alleys, looking for the square where Omar had his garage, replaying the geography of Cairo in his mind. A blind beggar suddenly capable of sight—a holy miracle—jumped out of the way, dropping his begging bowl and raising his dark glasses to peer at the truck.

He pushed the truck harder. The staff car still came on.

He swung the wheel. Another narrow alley. Donkeys jumped out of the path of the truck, a man fell from a stepladder, a baby in its mother's arms began to howl. Sorry, Indy thought. I'd stay and apologize in person, but I don't find it convenient right now.

Still he couldn't lose the staff car.

Then he was in the square. He saw the sign of Omar's garage, the door hanging wide open, and he drove the truck quickly through. The door was shut tight immediately as he brought the truck to a whining halt. Then several Arab boys with broomsticks and brushes began to erase the tracks of the vehicle while Indy, wondering if he'd made it, sat slumped behind the wheel in the darkness of the garage.

The staff car slowed, crossed the square and continued on its way, Belloq and Dietrich scrutinizing the streets with expressions of anguish and loss.

In the back of the truck, safe in the crate, the Ark began to hum almost inaudibly. It was as if within it, locked away and secure, a piece of machinery had spontaneously begun to operate. Nobody heard the sound.

It was dark when Sallah and Marion arrived at the garage. Indy had fallen asleep briefly in a cot Omar had provided, waking alone and hungry in the silent darkness. He rubbed his eyes when an overhead lamp was turned on. Marion had somewhere washed and brushed her hair and looked, well, Indy thought, *stunning*. She stood over him when he opened his eyes.

"You look pretty beat up," she said.

"A few surface cuts," he answered, sitting up, groaning, realizing that his body ached.

But then Sallah entered the room and Indy suddenly pushed aside his tiredness and his pain.

"We have a ship," Sallah said.

"Reliable?"

"The men are pirates, if I may use the phrase loosely. But you can trust them. Their captain, Katanga, is an honorable man—regardless of his more doubtful enterprises."

"They'll take us *and* the cargo?"

Sallah nodded. "For a price."

"What else?" Indy, stiff, got up. "Let's get this truck down to the harbor."

He gazed at Marion a moment, then he said, "I have a feeling that our day isn't quite finished yet."

In the ornate building that housed the German Embassy in Cairo, Dietrich and Belloq sat together in a room more commonly used by the Ambassador, a career diplomat who had survived the purges of Hitler and who, all too gladly, had vacated the room for their purposes. They had been sitting in silence for some time now, Belloq gazing at the portrait of Hitler, Dietrich restlessly smoking Egyptian cigarettes.

From time to time the telephone rang. Dietrich would answer it, replace it, then shake his head in Belloq's direction.

"If we have lost the Ark . . ." Dietrich lit another cigarette.

Belloq rose, walked around the room, waved a hand dismissively. "I will not countenance that prospect, Dietrich. What has happened to your wonderful Egyptian spy network? Why can't they find what your men so carelessly lost?"

"They will. I have every faith."

"Faith. I wish I had some of it myself."

Dietrich closed his eyes. He was weary of the sharp edge of Belloq's mood; and fearful, even more, of returning empty-handed to Berlin.

"I cannot believe such incompetence," Belloq said. "How could one man, acting alone—*alone*, remember—destroy most of a convoy *and* disappear into the bargain? Stupidity. I can hardly believe it."

"I've listened to this already," Dietrich said, annoyed.

Belloq walked to the window and stared out across the darkness. Somewhere, wrapped in this impenetrable Cairo night, was Jones; and Jones had the Ark. *Damn him.* The Ark could not be let go now; even the prospect caused him a chill, a sensation of something sinking inside him.

The telephone rang again. Dietrich picked it up, listened, and then his manner changed. When he hung up he looked at the Frenchman with a vague expression of vindication on his face. "I told you my network would turn something up."

"Did they?"

"According to a watchman at the docks, an Egyptian named Sallah, the friend of Jones, chartered a merchant steamer by the name of the *Bantu Wind*."

"It may be a ruse," Belloq said.

"It may be. But it's worth looking into."

"We don't have anything else anyhow," Belloq said.

"Then shall we go?"

They left the Embassy hurriedly, reaching the docks only to discover that the tramp steamer had sailed an hour ago. Its destination was unknown.

The Mediterranean

IN THE CAPTAIN'S CABIN of the *Bantu Wind*, Indy stripped to the waist, and Marion dressed his assorted cuts and wounds with bandages and a bottle of iodine. He stared at her as she worked, noticing the dress she'd changed into. It was white, high-necked, somewhat prim. He found it appealing in its way.

"Where did you get that, anyhow?" he asked.

"There's a whole wardrobe in the closet," she said. "I get the feeling I'm not the first woman to travel with these pirates."

"I like it," he said.

"I feel like a—*ahem*—a virgin."

"I guess you look like one."

She regarded him a moment, pressing iodine to a cut. Then she said, "Virginity is one of those elusive things, honey. When it's gone, it's gone. Your account is well and truly spent."

She stopped working on him, sat down, poured herself a small glass of rum from a bottle. She sipped it, watching him as she did so, seeming to tease him over the rim of the glass.

"Did I ever apologize for burning down your tavern?" he said.

"I can't say you did. Did I ever thank you for getting me out of that burning plane?"

He shook his head. "We're even. Maybe we should consider the past closed, huh?"

She was silent for a long time.

"Where does it hurt?" she asked tenderly.

"Everywhere."

Marion softly kissed his left shoulder. "Here?"

Indy jumped a little in response. "Yes, there."

Marion leaned closer to him. "Where *doesn't* it hurt?" And she kissed his elbow. "Here?"

He nodded. She kissed the top of his head. Then he pointed to his neck and she kissed him there. Then the tip of his nose, his eyes. Then he touched his own lips and she kissed him, her mouth gently devouring his.

She was different; she had changed. This was no longer the wild touch he'd encountered in Nepal.

Something had touched her, softened her.

He wondered what it had been.

He wondered at the change.

The crated Ark lay in the hold of the ship. Its presence agitated the ship's rats: they scurried back and forward pointlessly, trembling, whiskers shivering. Still silent as a whisper, the same faint humming sound emerged from the crate. Only the rats, their hearing hypersensitive, picked up on the sound; and it obviously scared them.

On the bridge, as the first light of dawn streaked the ocean, Captain Katanga smoked a pipe and watched the surface of the water as if he were trying to discern something that would have been invisible to landlocked men. He let the sun and the salt spray play against his face, streaks of salt leaving white crystalline traces on his black skin. There was something out there, something emerging from the dark, but he wasn't sure what. He narrowed his eyes, stared, saw nothing. He listened to the faintly comforting rattle of the ship's weary engines and thought of a failing heart trying to pump blood through an old body. He considered Indy and the woman a moment. He liked them both, and besides, they were friends of Sallah's.

But something about the cargo, something about the crate, made him uneasy. He wasn't sure what; he only knew he'd be glad to get rid of it when the time came. It was the same unease he experienced now as his eyes scanned the ocean. A vague pulse. A thing you just couldn't put your finger on. But there was something out there just the same, something moving. He knew it even if he couldn't see it.

He smelled, as certainly as the salt flecks in the air, the distinctive odor of danger.

He continued to watch, his body poised in the manner of a man about to jump from a high diving board. A man who cannot swim.

When Indy woke, he watched Marion for a time. She was still asleep, still looking virginal in the white dress. She had her face tilted to one side, and her mouth was slightly open. He rubbed at his bandages where his skin had begun to itch. Sallah had had the foresight to fetch his clothes, so he changed into his shirt now, made sure the bullwhip was secure at his back, then put on the leather jacket and played with the rim of the battered felt hat.

A lucky hat, he thought sometimes. Without it, he would have felt naked.

Marion turned over, her eyes opening.

"What a pleasant sight," she said.

"I don't feel pleasant," he answered.

She stared at his bandages and asked, "Why do you always get yourself into such scrapes?"

She sat up, stroking her hair, looking round the cabin. "I'm glad to see you changed clothes. You weren't convincing as an Arab, I'm afraid."

"I did my best."

She yawned and stretched and rose from the cot. He thought there was something delightful in the movement, a quality that touched him—touched him obliquely, in an off-center way. She reached for his hand, kissed the back of it, then moved around the cabin.

"How long are we going to be at sea?" she asked.

"Is that a literal or a metaphorical question?"

"Take it any way you like, Jones."

He smiled at her.

And then he understood that something had happened: while he'd been so involved in the act of introspection, the ship's engines had stopped and the vessel was no longer moving.

He rose and rushed to the door, clambering onto the deck and then the bridge, where Katanga was staring across the ocean. The captain's pipe was unlit, his face solemn.

"You appear to have some important friends, Mr. Jones," the man said.

Indy stared. At first he couldn't make anything out. But then, following the sweep of the captain's hand, he saw that the *Bantu Wind*, like a spinster courted by an unwanted entourage of voracious suitors, was surrounded by about a dozen German Wolf submarines.

"Holy shit," he said.

"My sentiments exactly," Katanga said. "You and the girl must disappear quickly. We have a place in the hold for you. But quickly! Get the girl!"

It was too late: both men noticed five rafts, with armed boarding parties, circle the steamer. Already the first Nazis were climbing the rope ladders that had been dropped. He turned, ran. Marion was uppermost in his mind now. He had to get her first.

Too late—the air was filled with the sound of boots, German accents, commands. Ahead of him he saw Marion being dragged from the cabin by a couple of soldiers. The rest of the soldiers, boarding quickly, rounded the crew on deck, guns trained on them. Indy melted into the shadows, slipping through a doorway into the labyrinth of the ship.

Before he vanished, his brain working desperately for a way out, he heard Marion curse her assailants; and despite the situation, he smiled at her spirit. A good woman, he thought, and impossible to subdue entirely. He liked her for that.

He liked her a lot.

Dietrich came on board, followed by Belloq. The captain had already given his crew a signal not to resist the invaders. The men clearly wanted to fight, but the odds were against them. So they lined up sullenly under the German guns as Belloq and Dietrich strode past, shouting orders, sending soldiers scampering all over the ship for the Ark.

Marion watched as Belloq approached her. She felt something of the same vibrations as before, but this time she was determined to fight them, determined not to yield to whatever sensations the man might arouse in her.

"My dear," Belloq said. "You must regale me with the tale—no doubt epic—of how you managed to escape from the Well. It can wait until later, though."

Marion said nothing. Was there no end in sight to this whole sequence of affairs? Indy apparently had a marvelous talent for dragging wholesale destruction behind him. She watched Belloq, who touched her lightly under the chin. She pulled her face away. He smiled.

"Later," he said, passing on to where Katanga stood.

He was about to say something when a sound seized his attention and he turned, noticing a group of soldiers raise the crated

Ark from the hold. He fought the impatience he felt. The world, with all its mundane details, always intruded on his ambition. But that was going to be over soon. Slowly, reluctantly, he took his eyes from the crate as Dietrich gave the order for it to be placed aboard one of the submarines.

He looked at Katanga. "Where is Jones?"

"Dead."

"Dead?" Belloq said.

"What good was he to us? We killed him. We threw him overboard. The girl has more value in the kind of marketplace in which I dabble. A man like Jones is useless to me. If his cargo was what you wanted, I only ask that you take it and leave us with the girl. It will reduce our loss on this trip."

"You make me impatient," Belloq said. "You expect me to believe Jones is dead?"

"Believe what you wish. I only ask that we proceed in peace."

Dietrich had approached now. "You are in no position to ask anything, Captain. We will decide what we wish to decide, and then we must consider the question of whether we will blow this ancient ship out of the water."

"The girl goes with me," Belloq said.

Dietrich shook his head.

Belloq continued: "Consider her part of my compensation. I'm sure the Führer would approve. Given that we have obtained the Ark, Dietrich."

Dietrich appeared hesitant.

"If she fails to please me, of course, you may throw her to the sharks, for all I care."

"Very well," Dietrich said. He noticed a brief expression of doubt on Belloq's face, then signaled for Marion to be taken aboard the submarine.

Indy watched from his hiding place in an air ventilator, his body hunched and uncomfortable. Boots scraped the deck unpleasantly close to his face—but he hadn't been discovered. Katanga's lie seemed feeble to him, a desperate gesture if a kind one. But it had worked. He peered along the deck, thinking. He had to go with the submarine, he had to go with Marion, with the Ark. How? Exactly how?

Belloq was watching the captain closely. "How do I know you are telling the truth about Jones?"

Katanga shrugged. "I don't lie." He stared at the Frenchman; this one he didn't like at all. He felt sorry for Indy for having an enemy like Belloq.

"Have your people found him on board?" the seaman asked.

Belloq considered this; Dietrich shook his head.

The German said, "Let us leave. We have the Ark. Alive or dead, Jones is of no importance now."

Belloq's face and his body went tense a moment; then he appeared to relax, following Dietrich from the deck of the tramp steamer.

Indy could hear the rafts leaving the sides of the *Bantu Wind*. Then he moved quickly, emerging from his place of concealment and running along the deck.

Aboard the submarine Belloq entered the communications room. He placed earphones on his head, picked up the microphone and uttered a call signal. After a time he heard a voice broken by static. The accent was German.

"Captain Mohler. This is Belloq."

The voice was very faint, distant. "Everything has been prepared in accordance with your last communication, Belloq."

"Excellent." Belloq took the headphones off. Then he left the radio room, walking toward the small forward cabin, where the woman was being held. He stepped inside the room. She sat on a bunk, her expression glum. She didn't look up as he approached her. He reached out, touched her lightly under the chin, raised her face.

"You have nice eyes," he said. "You shouldn't hide them."

She twisted her face to the side.

He smiled. "I imagined we might continue our unfinished business."

She got up from the bunk, went across the room. "We don't *have* any unfinished business."

"I think we do." He reached out and tried to hold her hand; she jerked her arm free of him. "You resist? You didn't resist before, my dear. Why the change of heart?"

"Things are a little different," she answered.

He regarded her in silence for a time. Then he said, "You feel something for Jones? Is that it?"

She looked away, staring vacantly across the room.

"Poor Jones," Belloq said. "I fear he's destined never to win anything."

"What is that supposed to mean?"

Belloq went toward the door. There, on his way out, he turned around. "You don't even know, my dear, if he's alive or dead. Do you?"

Then he closed the door and moved into the narrow passageway. Several seamen walked past him. They were followed by Dietrich, whose face was angry, stern. It amused Belloq to see this look: in his anger, Dietrich looked preposterous, like an enraged schoolmaster powerless to punish a recalcitrant pupil.

"Perhaps you would be good enough to explain yourself, Belloq."

"What is there to explain?"

Dietrich seemed to be struggling with an urge to strike the Frenchman. "You have given specific orders to the captain of this vessel to proceed to a certain supply base—an island located off the

African coast. It was my understanding that we would return to Cairo and then fly the Ark to Berlin on the first available flight. Why have you taken the liberty of changing the plan, Belloq? Are you suddenly under the impression that you are an admiral in the German navy? Is that it? Have your delusions of grandeur gone that far?"

"Delusions of grandeur," Belloq said, still amused by Dietrich. "I hardly think so, Dietrich. My point is that we open the Ark before taking it to Berlin. Would you be comfortable, my friend, if your Führer found the Ark to be empty? Don't you want to be sure that the Ark contains sacred relics *before* we return to Germany? I am trying to imagine the awful disappointment on Adolf's face if he finds nothing inside the Ark."

Dietrich stared at the Frenchman; his anger had passed, replaced by a look of doubt, incredulity. "I don't trust you, Belloq. I have never trusted you."

"Thank you."

Dietrich paused before going on: "I find it curious that you want to open the Ark on some obscure island instead of taking the more convenient route—namely Cairo. Why can't you look inside your blessed box in Egypt, Belloq?"

"It wouldn't be fitting," Belloq said.

"Can you explain that?"

"I could—but you would not understand, I fear."

Dietrich looked angry; he felt his authority once more had been undermined—but the Frenchman had the Führer as an ally. What could he do, faced with that fact?

He turned quickly and walked away. Belloq watched him go. For a long time the Frenchman didn't move. He felt a great sense of anticipation all at once, thinking of the island. The Ark could have been opened almost anywhere—in that sense Dietrich was correct. But it was appropriate, Belloq thought, that it should be opened on the island. It should be opened in a place whose atmosphere was heavy with the distant past, a place of some historic importance. Yes, Belloq thought. The setting had to match the moment. There had to be a correspondence between the Ark and its environment. Nothing else would do.

He went to the small supply cabin where the crate lay.

He looked at it for a while, his mind empty. What secrets? What can you tell me? He reached out and touched the crate. Did he simply imagine he felt a vibration from the box? Did he simply imagine he heard a faint sound? He closed his eyes, his hand still resting on the wooden surface. A moment of intense awe: he could see some great void, a sublime darkness, a boundary he would step across into a place beyond language and time. He opened his eyes; the tips of his fingers tingled.

Soon, he said to himself.

Soon.

The sea was cold, swirling around him in small whirlpools created by the submarine's motions. Indy hung to the rail, his muscles aching, the wet whip contracting in water and clinging, too tightly, to his body. You could drown, he thought, and he tried to remember whether drowning was said to be a good way to go. It might arguably be better than hanging to the rail of the submarine that could plunge abruptly into the depths. At any moment, too. He wondered if heroes could apply for retirement benefits. He hauled himself up, swinging his body onto the deck. Then it struck him.

His hat. His hat had gone.

Don't be superstitious now. You don't have time to mourn the passing of a lucky hat.

The sub began to submerge. Perceptibly, it was sinking like a huge metallic fish. He rushed across the deck, water at his waist now. He reached the conning tower, then began to climb the ladder. At the top of the turret he looked down: the sub was still sinking. Water was rushing, wildly swirling foam, toward him. The turret was being consumed by the rising water, and then the radio mast was sinking too. He moved, treading water, to the periscope. He hung on to it as the vessel continued to sink. If it went under entirely, then he was lost. The periscope started to go down, too. Down and down, while he gripped it. Please, he thought, please don't go down any further. But this is what comes of trying to stow yourself away on a German submarine. You can't expect the old red-carpet treatment, can you?

Freezing, shivering, he hung on to the periscope; and then, as if some merciful divinity of the ocean had heard his unspoken prayers, the vessel stopped its dive. It left only three feet of the periscope out of water. But three feet was something to be thankful for. Three feet was all he needed to survive. *Don't sink any deeper,* he thought. Then he realized he was talking aloud, not thinking. It might have been, in other circumstances, funny— trying to hold a rational conversation with several tons of good German metal. *I'm out of my mind. That's what it is. And all this is just hallucination. A nautical madness.*

Indy took the bullwhip and lashed himself to the periscope, hoping that if he fell asleep he wouldn't wake to find himself on the black ocean bottom, or worse—food for the fishes.

The cold seeped through him. He tried to stop his teeth from knocking together. And the bullwhip, heavy with water, was cutting into his skin. He tried to remain alert, prepared for whatever contingency might arise—but weariness was a weight in him now, and sleep seemed the most promising prospect of all.

He shut his eyes. He tried to think of something, anything, that would keep him from dropping off—but it was hard. He wondered where the submarine was headed. He sang little songs in his head. He tried to remember all the telephone numbers he'd ever known. He wondered about a girl named Rita he'd almost married once: where was she now? A lucky escape there, he thought.

But he was weary and the thoughts circled aimlessly.

And he drifted off into sleep, despite the cold, despite his discomfort. He drifted away, the sleep dreamless and dead.

When he woke it was daylight and he wasn't sure how long he'd slept, whether he'd slept a whole day away. He could no longer feel his body: total numbness. And his skin was puckered from the water, fingertips soft and wrinkled. He adjusted the bullwhip and looked around. There was a land mass ahead, an island, a semi-tropical place—halcyon, he thought. He stared at the rich foliage. Green, wonderful and deep and restful. The submarine approached the island, skimming into what looked like a cave. Inside, the Germans had built a complete underground supply base and submarine pen. *And there were more uniformed Nazis on this dock than you could have found in one of Hitler's Nuremberg extravaganzas.*

How could he fail to be seen?

He quickly drew himself clear of his whip, and he slipped into the water. He submerged, realizing he'd left his whip attached to the scope. The whip and the hat: it was a day for sad farewells to treasured possessions, for sure.

He swam toward the island, trying to remain underwater as much as he could. He saw the sub rise as it went toward the dock. Then he was stumbling onto the beach, glad to feel earth under him again, even if it was the earth of some Nazi paradise. He made his way over the sand to a high point where he had a good view of the dock. The crate was lifted from the sub, supervised by Belloq, who appeared to live in anxious expectation of somebody's dropping his precious relic. He hovered around the crate like a surgeon over a dying patient.

And then there was Marion, surrounded by a bunch of uniformed fools who were pushing her forward.

He sat down in the sand, hidden by rushes that grew on the edge of the dunes.

Inspiration, he thought. That's what I need now.

In a good-sized dose.

TWELVE

A Mediterranean Island

IT WAS LATE AFTERNOON when Belloq met Mohler. He was not entirely happy with the idea of Dietrich's being involved in the conversation. The damned man was certain to ask questions, and his impatience had already begun to make Belloq nervous, as though it were contagious.

Captain Mohler said, "Everything has been prepared in accordance with your instructions, Belloq."

"Nothing has been overlooked?"

"Nothing."

"Then the Ark must be taken to that place now."

Mohler glanced a moment at Dietrich. Then he turned and began to supervise a group of soldiers while they placed the crate in a jeep.

Dietrich, who had been silent, was annoyed. "What does he mean? What preparations are you talking about?"

"It need not concern you, Dietrich."

"Everything connected with this accursed Ark concerns me."

"I am going to open the Ark," Belloq said. "However, there are certain . . . certain preconditions connected with the act."

"Preconditions? Such as?"

"I don't think you should worry, my friend. I don't want to be the one responsible for overloading your already much-worked brain."

"You can spare me the sarcasm, Belloq. Sometimes it seems to me that you forget who is in charge here."

Belloq stared at the crate for a time. "You must understand—it is not simply the act of opening a box, Dietrich. There is a certain amount of ritual involved. We are not exactly dealing with a box of hand grenades, you understand. This is not any ordinary undertaking."

"What ritual?"

"You will see in good time, Dietrich. However, it need not alarm you."

"If anything happens to the Ark, Belloq, *anything*, I will personally pull the hanging rope on your scaffold. Do you understand me?"

Belloq nodded. "Your concern for the Ark is touching. But you needn't worry. It will be safe and delivered to Berlin finally, and your Führer can add another relic to his lovely collection. Yes?"

"You better be as good as your word."

"I will be. I will be."

Belloq looked at the crated Ark before staring into the jungle beyond the dock area. It lay in there, the place where the Ark would be opened.

"The girl," Dietrich said. "I also hate loose ends. What do we do with the girl?"

"I take it I can leave that to your discretion," Belloq said. "She is of no consequence to me."

Nothing is, he thought: nothing is of any consequence now, except for the Ark. Why had he bothered to entertain any kind of sentiment for the girl? Why had he even remotely troubled himself with the idea of protecting her? Human feelings were worthless compared to the Ark. All human experience faded into nothing. If she lived or died, what did it matter?

He experienced the same delicious sense of anticipation as before: it was hard, damnably hard, to take his eyes from the crate. It lay in the back of a jeep, magnetizing him. I will know your secrets, he thought.

I will know all your secrets.

Indy skirted the trees at the edge of the dock area. He watched Marion, flanked by her Nazi escorts, get inside a jeep. The jeep was then driven off into the jungle. Belloq and the German climbed into another jeep and, moving steadily behind the vehicle that held the Ark, went off in the same direction as Marion. Where the hell are they going? Indy wondered. He began to move silently through the trees.

The German appeared in front of him, a materialization looming over him. He reached for his holster, but before he could get his pistol out, Indy picked up the branch of a tree, a slab of rotted wood, and struck him hard across the throat. The German, a young man, put his fingers to his larynx as if surprised, and blood began to spill from his mouth. His eyes rolled backward in his head, then he slipped to his knees. Indy hit him a second time across the skull, and he toppled over. What do you do with an unconscious Nazi? he wondered.

He stared at the man for a time before the notion came to him. Why not?

Why not indeed?

The jeep that carried Belloq and Dietrich moved slowly through a canyon.

Dietrich said, "I am unhappy with this ritual."

You will be even more unhappy soon, Belloq thought. The trappings of what you so trivially call a ritual will cause a knot in your wooden brain, my friend.

"Is it essential?"

"Yes," Belloq said.

Dietrich just stared at the crate in the jeep ahead.

"It may console you to consider the prospect that by tomorrow the Ark will be in your Führer's hands."

Dietrich sighed.

The Frenchman was insane, he was convinced of this. Somewhere along the way the Ark had warped whatever judgment he might have had. You could see it in his eyes, hear it in the clipped way of talking he seemed to have developed in recent days, and you could sense it in the oddly nervous gestures he continued to make.

Dietrich wouldn't be happy until he was back, mission complete, in Berlin.

The jeep came out into a clearing now, a clearing filled with tents and camouflaged shelters, barracks, vehicles, radio masts; a swarm of activity, soldiers rushing everywhere. Dietrich surveyed the depot proudly, but Belloq was oblivious to it all. The Frenchman was staring beyond the clearing to a stone outcropping on the other side—a pinnacle some thirty feet high with a flat slab at the top. Into the sides of the slope some ancient tribe, some lost species, had carved primitive steps. The appearance was like an altar—and it was this fact that had brought Belloq here. An altar, a natural arrangement of rock that might have been designed by God for the very purpose of opening the Ark.

He couldn't speak for a time. He stared at the rock until Captain Mohler came and tapped him on the shoulder.

"Do you wish to prepare now?" the German asked.

Belloq nodded. He followed the German to a tent. He was thinking of the lost tribe that had cut those steps, that had left its own relics scattered here and there, in the form of broken statues suggesting forgotten divinities, across the island. The religious connotations of the place were exactly right: the Ark had found a place that matched its own splendor. It was correct: nowhere else could have been better.

"The white silk tent," Belloq said. He touched the soft material.

"As you ordered," Mohler said.

"Fine, fine." And Belloq stepped inside. A chest sat in the middle of the floor. He opened the lid and looked inside. The ceremonial robe was elaborately embroidered. In wonder, he leaned forward to touch it. Then he looked at the German.

"You've followed my orders thoroughly. I am pleased."

The German had something in his hand: an ivory rod about five feet in length. He passed it to Belloq, who fingered the inlaid carvings of the piece.

"Perfect," Belloq said. "The Ark has to be opened, in accordance with sacred rites, with an ivory rod. And the one who opens the Ark must wear these robes. You did very well."

The German smiled. "You will not forget our little arrangement."

"I promise," Belloq said. "When I return to Berlin I will personally speak to the Führer about you in the highest possible terms."

"Thank you."

"Thank *you*," Belloq said.

The German regarded the robes a moment. "They suggest a certain Jewishness, don't they?"

"They should, my friend. They are Jewish."

"You will make yourself very popular around here with those things on."

"I am not interested in a popularity contest, Mohler."

Mohler watched as Belloq slipped the robes over his head, watched as the ornate brocade fell all around him. It was a total transformation: the man had even begun to look holy. Well, Mohler thought, it takes all sorts. Besides, even if he were mad, Belloq still had access to Hitler—and that was all that mattered.

"Is it dark outside?" Belloq asked. He felt peculiar, distanced from himself, as if his identity had begun to disintegrate and he'd become a stranger in a body that was only vaguely familiar.

"Soon," the German said.

"We must start at sunset. It's important."

"They have carried the Ark to the slab, as you wanted, Belloq."

"Good." He touched the robes, the upraised stitches in the material. Belloq—even his name seemed strange to him. It was as if something spiritual, immaterial, had begun to consume him. He was floating outside of himself, it seemed—a perception that had the intensity, as well as the vagueness, of a narcotic response.

He picked up the ivory rod and stepped outside of the tent.

Almost everywhere, the German soldiers stopped in their activities and turned to look at him. He faintly understood the vibrations of repulsion, the animosity directed to his robes. But once again this notion reached him across some great distance. Dietrich was walking at his side, saying something. And Belloq had to concentrate hard to understand.

"A *Jewish* ritual? Are you crazy, man?"

Belloq said nothing. He moved toward the foot of the ancient steps; the sun, an outrage of color as it waned, hung low in the distance, touching everything with a bewildering array of oranges and reds and yellows.

He moved to the first step, glancing briefly at the German soldiers around him. Klieg lights had been set up, illuminating the stairs, the Ark. Belloq was certain, as he looked at it, that he heard it humming. And he was almost sure that it began to emit a glow of some kind. But then something happened, something distracted him, pulled him back to earth; a movement, a shadow, he couldn't be sure. He swung around to see one of the soldiers behave in a strange fashion, moving in a hunched way. He wore his helmet at an awkward angle, as if he sought to conceal his face. But it wasn't just this that so distracted Belloq, it was a weird sense of familiarity.

What? How? He stared—realizing that the soldier was struggling under the weight of a grenade launcher, which he hadn't noticed at first in the dying light. But that strange sense, that itch—what did it mean? A darkness crossed his mind. A darkness that was lit only when the soldier removed his helmet and leveled the grenade launcher up the steps at the Ark—the Ark, which had been de-crated and looked vulnerable up on the slab.

"Hold it," Indy shouted. "One move from anybody and I blow that box back to Moses."

"Jones, your persistence surprises me. You are going to give mercenaries a bad name," Belloq said.

Dietrich interrupted. "Dr. Jones, surely you don't think you can escape from this island."

"That depends on how reasonable we're all willing to be. All I want is the girl. We'll keep possession of the Ark only until we've got safe transport to England. Then it's all yours."

"If we refuse?" Dietrich wanted to know.

"Then the Ark and some of us are going up in a big bang. And I don't think Hitler would like that a bit."

Indy began to move toward Marion, who was struggling with her bonds.

"You look fine in a German outfit, Jones," Belloq said.

"You look pretty good in your robes too."

But somebody else was moving now, approaching Indy from behind. And even as the girl began to scream in warning, Belloq recognized Mohler. The captain threw himself at Indy, knocking the weapon from his hand and bringing him to the ground. Jones—a gallant heart, Belloq thought, a reckless courage—lashed out at the soldier with his fist, then drove his knee upward in Mohler's groin. The captain groaned and rolled away, but Indy was already surrounded by soldiers, and although he fought them, although he fell kicking amid a bunch of helmets and jackboots, he was overpowered by numbers. Belloq shook his head and smiled in a pale way. He looked at Indy, who was being pinned by soldiers.

"A good try, Jones. A good effort."

And then Dietrich was coming through the ranks. "Foolish, very foolish," he said. "I cannot believe your recklessness."

"I'm trying to give it up," Indy said. He struggled with the soldiers who held him: useless.

"I have the cure for it," Dietrich said. He took his pistol from its holster, smiling.

Indy stared at the gun, then glanced at Marion, who had her eyes shut tight and was sobbing in a broken way.

Dietrich raised the pistol, aimed.

"Wait!"

Belloq's voice was thunderous, awesome, and his face looked malign in the intense light of the klieg lamps. The gun in Dietrich's hand was lowered.

Belloq said, "This man has been an irritation to me for years, Colonel Dietrich. Sometimes, I admit, he has amused me. And although I would also like to witness his end, I would like him to suffer one last defeat. Let him live until I have opened the Ark. Let him live that long. Whatever treasures may lie in the Ark will be denied him. The contents will be hidden from his view. I enjoy the idea. This is a prize he has dreamed of for years—and now he will never get any closer to it. When I have opened the Ark, you can dispose of him. For now, I suggest you tie him up beside the girl." And Belloq laughed, a hollow laugh that echoed in the darkness.

Indy was dragged to the statue and bound against it, his shoulder to Marion's.

"I'm afraid, Indy," she said.

"There's never been a better time for it."

The Ark began to hum, and Indy turned to watch Belloq climb the steps to the altar. It galled him to think of Belloq's hands on the Ark, Belloq opening it. *The prize.* And he would see none of it. You live a lifetime with the constant ambition of reaching a goal, and then, when it's there, when it's in front of you, *wham*—all you have left is the bitter taste of defeat. How could he watch the insane Frenchman, dressed like some medieval rabbi, go up the steps to the Ark?

How could he *not* watch?

"I think we're going to die, Indy," Marion said. "Unless you've figured something out."

Indy, barely hearing her, said nothing: there was something else now, something that was beginning to intrude on his mind—the sound of humming, low and constant, that seemed to be emerging from the Ark. How could that be? He stared at Belloq as the robed figure climbed to the slab.

"So how do we get out of this?" Marion asked again.

"God knows."

"Is that a play on words?" she said.

"Maybe."

"It's a hell of a time to be making bad jokes, Jones." She turned to him; there were circles of fatigue under her eyes. "Still. I love you for it."

"Do you?"

"Love you? Sure."

"I think it's reciprocal," Indy said, a little surprised at himself.

"It's also somewhat doomed," Marion said.

"We'll see."

Belloq, remembering the words of an old Hebraic chant, words he'd remembered from the parchment that had had the picture of the headpiece, started to sing in a low, monotonous way. He chanted as he climbed the steps, hearing the sound of the Ark accompany his voice, the sound of humming. It was growing in intensity, rumbling, filling the darkness. The Ark's power, the Ark's intense power. It moved in Belloq's blood, bewildering, demanding to be understood. The power. The knowledge. He paused near the top of the steps, chanting still but unable to hear his own voice now. The humming, the humming—it was growing, slicing through the night, filling all the silences. Then he climbed more, reached the top, stared at the Ark. Despite the dust of centuries, despite neglect, it was the most beautiful thing Belloq had ever seen. And it glowed, it glowed, feebly at first and then more brightly, as he looked at it. He was filled with wonder, watching the angels, the shining gold, the inner glow. The noise, too, rumbled through him, shook and surprised him. He felt himself begin to vibrate, as if the tremor might cause him to disintegrate and go spinning out into space. But there wasn't space, there wasn't time: his entire being was defined by the Ark, delineated by this relic of man's communication with God.

Speak to me.

Tell me what you know, tell me what the secrets of existence are.

His own voice seemed to be issuing from every part of his body now, through mouth, pores, blood cells. And he was rising, floating, distinct from the rigid world of logic all around him, defying the laws of the universe. *Speak to me. Tell me.* He raised the ivory rod, placing it under the lid, then labored to pry the lid open. The humming was louder now, all-consuming. He didn't hear the klieg lights explode below, the showers of broken glass that fell like worthless diamonds into the darkness. The humming—the voice of God, he thought. *Speak to me. Speak to me.* And then, as he worked with the rod, he felt suddenly blank, as if he hadn't existed until this moment, as if all memories had been erased, blank and strangely calm, at peace, undergoing a sense of oneness with the night around him, linked by all kinds of connections to the universe. Bound to the cosmos, to all matter that floated and expanded and shrank in the farthest estuaries of space, to exploding stars, spinning planets, and even to the unknowable dark of infinity. He ceased to exist. Whoever Belloq had been, he was no longer. He was nothing now: he existed only as the sound that came from the Ark. The sound of God.

"He's going to open it," Indy said.

"The noise," Marion said. "I wish I could put my hands to my ears. What is that noise?"

"The Ark."

"The Ark?"

Indy was thinking about something, an eclipsed memory, something that shifted loosely in his mind. What? What was it? Something he'd heard recently. *What?* The Ark. Something to do with the Ark. *What what what?*

The Ark, the Ark—try to remember!

Up on the slab, at the top of the crude steps, Belloq was trying to open the lid. Lamps were exploding in violent showers of sharded glass. Even the moon, visible now in the night sky, seemed like an orb about to erupt and shatter. The night, the whole night, was like a great bomb attached to the end of a short fuse—a lit fuse, Indy thought. What is it? What am I trying to remember?

The lid was opening.

Belloq, sweating, perspiring in the heavy robes, applied the ivory rod while he kept up the chant that was inaudible now under the noise of the Ark. The moment. The moment of truth. Revelation. The mysterious networks of the divine. He groaned and raised the lid. It sprung open all at once and the light that emanated from within blinded him. But he didn't step away, didn't step back, didn't move. The light hypnotized him as surely as the sound mesmerized him. He was devoid of the capacity to move. Muscles froze. His body ceased to work. *The lid.*

It was the last thing he saw.

Because then the night was filled with fire rockets that screamed out of the Ark, pillars of flame that stunned the darkness, outreaches of fire searing the heavens. A white circle of light made a flashing ring around the island, a light that made the ocean glow and whipped up currents of spray, forcing a broken tide to rise upward in the dark. *The light, it was the light of the first day of the universe, the light of newness, of things freshly born, it was the light that God made: the light of creation.* And it pierced Belloq with the hard brightness of an inconceivable diamond, a light beyond the sorrowful limitations of any precious stone. It carved at his heart, shattered him. And it was more than a light—it was a weapon, a force, that drove through Belloq and lit him with the power of a billion candles: he was white, orange, blue, savaged by this electricity that stormed from the Ark.

And he smiled.

He smiled because, for a moment, he *was* the power. The power absorbed him. There was no distinction between the man and the force. Then the moment passed. Then his eyes disintegrated in the sockets, leaving black sightless holes, and his skin began to peel from the bone, curling back as if seized by a sudden leprosy, rotting, burning, scorched, blackened. And still he smiled. He smiled even as he began to change from something human to something touched by God, touched by God's rage, something that turned, silently, to a layer of dust.

When the lights began to shaft the dark, when the entire sky was filling with the force of the Ark, Indy had involuntarily shut his eyes—blinded by the power. And then all at once he remembered, he remembered what had eluded him before, the night he'd spent in the house of Imam: *Those who would open the Ark and release its force will die if they look upon it* . . . And through the noise, the blinding white pillars that had made the stars fade, he'd called to Marion: *Don't look!*

Keep your eyes closed!

She had twisted her face away from the first flare, the eruption of fire, and then, even if what he said puzzled her, she shut her eyes tight. She was afraid, afraid and overawed. And still she wanted to look. Still she was drawn to the great celestial flare, to the insane destruction of the night.

Don't look—he kept saying that even as she felt herself weaken.

He kept repeating it. Screaming it.

The night, like a dynamo, hummed, groaned, roared; the lights that seared the night seemed to howl.

Don't look don't look don't look!

The upraised tower of flame devastated. It hung in the sky like the shadow of a deity, a burning, shifting shadow composed not of darkness but of light, pure light. It hung there, both beautiful and monstrous, and it blinded those who looked upon it. It ripped eyes from the faces of the soldiers. It turned them from men into uniformed skeletons, covering the ground with bones, the black marks of scorches, covering everything with human debris. It burned the island, flattened trees, overturned boats, smashed the dock itself. It changed everything. Fire and light. It destroyed as though it were an anger that might never be appeased.

It broke the statue to which Indy and Marion were tied: the statue crumbled until it ceased to exist. And then the lid of the Ark slammed shut on the slab and the night became dark again and the ocean was silent. Indy waited for a long time before he looked.

The Ark was shining up there.

Shining with an intensity that suggested a contented silence; and a warning, a warning filled with menace.

Indy stared at Marion.

She was looking around speechlessly, staring at what the Ark had created. Wreckage, ruin, death. She opened her mouth, but she didn't speak.

There was nothing to say.

Nothing.

The earth around them hadn't been scorched. It was untouched.

She raised her face to the Ark.

She reached very slowly for Indy's hand and held it tight.

Washington, D.C.

S UN STREAMED through the windows of Colonel Musgrove's office. Outside, across a thick lawn, was a stand of cherry trees, and the morning sky was clear, a pale blue. Musgrove was seated behind his desk. Eaton had a chair to the side of the desk. There was another man, a man who stood leaning against the wall and who hadn't uttered a word; he had the sinister anonymity of a bureaucrat. He might have been rubberstamped himself, Indy thought, *Powerful Civil Servant* in thick black letters on his brow.

"We appreciate your service," Musgrove said. "And the cash reimbursement—we assume it was satisfactory?"

Indy nodded and glanced first at Marion, then at Marcus Brody.

Brody said, "I don't understand yet why the museum can't have the Ark."

"It's someplace very safe," Eaton said evasively.

"That's a powerful force," Indy told him. "It has to be understood. Analyzed. It isn't some game, you know."

Musgrove nodded. "We have our top men working on it right now."

"Name them," Indy said.

"For security reasons I can't."

"The Ark was slated for the museum. You agreed to that. Now you give us some crap about top men. Brody there—he's one of the best men in this whole field. Why doesn't he get a chance to work with your *top men*?"

"Indy," Brody said. "Leave it. Drop it."

"I won't," Indy said. "This whole affair cost me my favorite hat, for openers."

"I assure you, Jones, that the Ark is well protected. And its power—if we can accept your description of it—will be analyzed in due course."

"Due course," Indy said. "You remind me of letters I get from my lawyers."

"Look," Brody said, sounding strained, "all we want is the Ark for the museum. We want some reassurances, too, that no lasting damage will be done to it while in your possession—"

"You have them," Eaton said. "As for the Ark going to your museum, I'm afraid we will have to rethink our position."

A silence. A clock ticking. The faceless bureaucrat fiddled with his cuff links.

Indy said quietly, finally, "You don't know what you're sitting on, do you?"

He rose and helped Marion out of her chair.

"We'll be in touch, of course," Eaton said. "It was good of you to come. Your services are appreciated."

Outside in the warm sunlight, Marion took Indy's arm. Brody shuffled along beside them. Marion said, "Well, they aren't going to tell you anything, so maybe you should forget all about the Ark and get on with your life, Jones."

Indy glanced at Brody. He knew he had been tricked out of something that should have been his.

Brody said, "I guess they have their own good reasons for holding on to the Ark. It's a bitter disappointment, though."

Marion stopped, raised her leg and scratched her heel a moment. She said to Indy, "Put your mind on something else for a change."

"Like what?"

"Like this," she said, and kissed him.

"It's not the Ark," he said and smiled. "But it'll have to do."

The wooden crate was stenciled on the side: TOP SECRET, ARMY INTEL, 9906753, DO NOT OPEN. It sat on a dolly, which the warehouseman pushed in front of him. He hardly paid any attention to the crate. His was a world filled with such crates, all of them meaninglessly stenciled. Numbers, numbers, secret codes. He had become more than immune to these hieroglyphics. He looked forward only to his weekly check. He was old, stooped, and very few things in life engrossed him. Certainly none of these crates did. There were hundreds of them filling the warehouse and he had no curiosity about any of them. Nobody did, it seemed. As far as he could tell nobody ever bothered to open any of them anyhow. They were stacked and left to pile up, rising from floor to ceiling. Crates and crates, hundreds and hundreds of the things. Gathering dust, getting cobwebbed. The man pushed his dolly and sighed. What difference did another crate make now? He found a space for it, slipped it in place, then he paused and stuck a finger in his ear, shaking the finger vigorously. Damn, he thought. He'd have to get his hearing checked.

He was convinced he'd heard a low humming noise.

INDIANA JONES

AND THE

TEMPLE OF DOOM™

ONE

Out of the Frying Pan . . .

Shanghai, 1935

THE NIGHTCLUB had that wild and smoky air. Ladies and gentlemen and not so gentle men, of every nationality, and some no nation would claim, sat, formally attired, at tables that were scattered around the dance floor. Cigarette girls with long legs, bouncers with long faces, exotic food, tuxedoed waiters, laughter soft and loud, champagne and broken promises and opium lacing some of the tobacco—that was the flavor to the smoke. A decadent place, in a time of deep decay. But still, *très gai*. Like the last party before the apocalypse. In a few years the world would be at war.

Along the side wall, Deco curves and Oriental arches weaved around to form private booths, or step-up balconies. The bar was off to the back. Up front, beside the kitchen doors, stood the bandstand, slightly raised, and beside it, directly before the dance floor, was the stage.

Flanking the stage were two giant, carved wooden statues: Chinese warlords slouching on their thrones, sporting golden broadswords, smiling coolly, as if presiding over these festivities.

Beside the stage-left statue, an enormous gong hung by two

thick cords, from the ceiling almost to the floor. In bas-relief on its face, an angry dragon hovered above a great mountain. Beside the gong stood a muscular attendant in harem pants, the striker resting across his bare chest.

Facing front, center stage, its mouth open wide, was the head of a huge dragon. Its great eyes bulged frantically in different directions, its *papier-mâché* antennae quivered in uneasy resonance with the clatter of the room, its paper-lantern scales rippled back to the curtains.

And now smoke began to issue from its maw.

Ceremoniously, the attendant struck the gong.

Fire-red light suffused the steam filling the dragon's mouth. The smoky light poured down the steps, off the stage, onto the dance floor, as the band began playing.

And then, slowly, through the jaws of the beast, out of its fiery snarl, emerged the woman.

She was twenty, maybe twenty-five. Green-blue eyes, dark blond hair. She wore a high-necked, fitted gold-and-red sequinned gown, with matching gloves, spike heels, butterfly earrings. She paused at the dragon's lip, reached overhead to tug coyly on one of its upper teeth, then stepped forward with a sultry purr. Her name was Willie Scott. She was a knockout.

A dozen girls danced down the stairs that winged the dragon's head. They fluttered fans before their exquisitely painted faces; they wore thigh-length golden kimonos, showing more than a glimpse of silk stocking, as Willie started to sing:

> *"Yi wang si-i wa ye kan dao*
> *Xin li bian yao la jing bao jin tian zhi*
> *Dao*
> *Anything goes."*

The crowd was mostly inattentive, but Willie mostly didn't care. She went through her moves like a pro, up the steps and down, growling her song, while her mind wandered in the smoke that swirled over the stage, floating thickest around the set-creature's head, like the dreams of the dragon. In her mind, this was no sleazy Shanghai night-spot: it was a Grand Stage. And these two-bit hoofers behind her were a tight chorus line, and it was back in the States, and she was the glamorous star, rich and adored and dazzling and independent and . . .

The smoke cleared a little. Willie remembered where she really was.

Too bad for this mob, she thought. *They're too low down to appreciate a class act when it taps right up to their table.*

The bandleader cued her, and she went into her last chorus, pulling out a red scarf, taunting the audience from behind it.

"Anything goes!"

The band wrapped it up; the crowd applauded. Willie bowed. The three men at the front table clapped politely, managing to turn their lips up without smiling: the gangster Lao Che, and his two sons.

Vile scoundrels, dressed in the faintest veneer of *beau monde*.

Willie winked at them.

Or, more specifically, at Lao Che, who was currently her mealticket.

He nodded back at her—but then something else caught his eye, and a shadow held his face. As Willie ran back upstairs and offstage, she followed Lao Che's gaze, to see what it was that engendered his disfavor.

It was a man, entering the club, walking down the staircase at the back of the room. He wore a white dinner jacket with a red carnation in the lapel, black pants, vest, bow tie, shoes. Willie couldn't see much more than that, except that the man seemed to carry himself pretty well. He gave her a bad feeling, though. She wondered if he was some kind of cop.

She saw him reach the bottom of the stairs, where he was greeted by a waiter, just as she made her exit off stage. Her last thought on the matter was: *Well, he's pretty, but he looks like trouble.*

Indiana Jones stepped off the elevator and walked down the stairway into the Club Obi Wan just as the floor show was ending. He watched the twelve red-and-gold-clad dancers scurry out of sight to loud applause, smiled to himself: *Hey, don't run off now, ladies, I just got here.*

Nonchalantly, he finished descending the stairs, but his eyes scanned the room like a chary cat.

It was as he remembered it, only more so: the dissolute horde, the hollow revelry; these were the people of a dying tribe. He wondered if even their artifacts would last, if his own counterpart, in a thousand years, could dig up their boxes and jewelry and picture the life in this room. *Picture the lowlife, that is,* he thought, his eyes coming to rest on Lao Che's table.

When he reached the bottom of the stairs, a waiter came up to him. The man was young, though his hairline was thinning; slight of build, though there was something dangerous about him; half-Chinese, half-Dutch. His name was Wu Han.

He bowed slightly to Indiana, with a vacant smile of greeting, and spoke so that only Jones heard: "Be careful."

Indy nodded back absently, then walked toward Lao Che's group. They reseated themselves as he approached. The applause ended.

"Dr. Jones," said Lao Che.

"Lao Che," said Indiana Jones.

Lao was pushing fifty. Several layers of high living puffed out his cheeks and belly, but it was all hard under the surface. Like lizard meat. He wore a black silk brocade dinner jacket, black shirt, white tie. His eyes were heavily lidded, reptilian. On his left little finger he wore the gilt signet ring of the royal family of the Chang Dynasty—Indy noted this with professional admiration.

To Lao Che's left was his son, Kao Kan, a younger version of the old man: stocky, impassive, ruthless. On Lao's right sat his other son, Chen. Chen was tall, thin almost to the point of ghost-liness. The white scarf hanging loosely around his neck made Indy think of the tattered swathing that sometimes clung to long-shriveled corpses.

Lao smiled at Indy. "Nee chin lie how ma?"

Chen and Kao Kan laughed malignantly.

Indy smiled in return. "Wah jung how, nee nah? Wah hwey hung jung chee jah loonee kao soo wah shu shu." He turned the joke around on Lao Che.

The three seated men became silent. Lao stared at Indy with venom. "You never told me you spoke my language, Dr. Jones."

"I don't like to show off," Indy deadpanned.

Two bodyguards appeared, frisked him quickly, and faded out of sight again. He didn't like that, but he'd expected it. He sat down across from Lao.

A waiter arrived at the table with a large dish of caviar and a bucket of chilled champagne, which he set beside Lao.

The smile returned to the crime-lord's face. "For this special occasion I have ordered champagne and caviar." He stared at Indy with a strange intensity as he went on. "So it is true, Dr. Jones: you found Nurhachi."

Indy leaned forward slightly. "You *know* I did. Last night one of your boys tried to take Nurhachi without paying for him."

Kao Kan brought his left hand up and rested it on the table. It was newly bandaged. It was newly missing an index finger.

Lao Che seethed, nodding. "You have insulted my son."

Indy sat back. "No, you have insulted me. But I spared his life."

Lao gazed at Indy like a cobra at a mongoose. "Dr. Jones, I want Nurhachi." He placed a wad of bills on the lazy Susan that occu-pied the center of the table, and spun it around until the money rested in front of Indy.

Indy put his hand down on the pile, felt the thickness of the wad, converted his estimate to dollars, came up short. Way short. He revolved the turntable back to Lao, and shook his head. "This doesn't even begin to cover my expenses, Lao. I thought I was dealing with an honest crook."

Kao Kan and Chen swore angrily in Chinese. Chen half-stood.

Suddenly an elegant, gloved hand rested on Lao's shoulder. Indy let his eyes glide up the smooth arm to the face of the woman standing behind Lao; she stared directly back at Indy. "Aren't you going to introduce us?" she said softly.

Lao Che waved Chen back down to his seat. "Dr. Jones, this is Willie Scott," said Lao. "Willie, this is Indiana Jones, the famous archaeologist."

Willie walked around toward Indy as he rose to greet her. In the moment of the handshake, they appraised each other.

He liked her face. It had a natural beauty weathered by natural disasters, like a raw gem after a flood, crystal-rough and waiting for a setting. She wore a diaphanous butterfly barrette that seemed to grow out of the substance of her hair; Indy took this to indicate a certain extravagance to her personality, if not actual flightiness. She wore gloves; Indy saw this as a statement on her part: "I do a lot of handling, but I don't touch." She wore expensive perfume, and a sequinned dress cut high in front and low—real low—in back; Indy took this to mean she came on cool, and left you with a nice memory. She was with Lao Che. To Indy, this signaled alarm.

Willie saw at once this was the guy she'd noticed coming in at the end of her act. Her initial impression of him was even stronger now: good-looking, but so out of place the air was practically shattering around the table. She couldn't figure his place, though. Archaeologist? That didn't wash. He had an interesting scar across his chin; she wondered how he'd got it. She was a connoisseur of interesting scars. And he sure had nice eyes, although she couldn't quite figure out the color. Sort of green-hazel-gray-sky-with-gold-flecks. Clear and hard and finally unreadable. Too bad, really. Any way you sliced it, he looked like seven miles of bad road.

She let her stare drift from his interesting scar to his unhazel eyes. "I thought archaeologists were funny little men always looking for their mommies," she teased.

"Mummies," he corrected.

They sat down.

Lao interrupted their brief conversation. "Dr. Jones found Nurhachi for me and is about to deliver him . . . now."

Indy was about to reply when he first felt, and then saw, the small round mouth of Kao Kan's gun pointing at him, waiting to speak. Indy didn't want to hear what the pistol had to say, though, so he grabbed a two-pronged carving fork from a nearby trolley as Willie was talking.

"Say, who's Nurhachi?" she asked innocently, still unaware of the imminent explosion.

In the next moment, she became aware. Indiana pulled her close, and held the fork to her side.

Willie held her breath a moment. To herself she said, *I knew it I knew it I knew it*. To Lao she said softly but urgently, "Lao, he's got a fork on me."

Indy spoke in monotone to Kao Kan. "Put the gun away, sonny." He increased the pressure with his weapon.

Willie felt the prongs dent her skin. She strove to keep the fear out of her voice. "Lao, he's got a fork in me." She didn't think he'd actually use it, but you could never tell with men and their toys.

Lao Che gave his son a look; the boy put the gun down.

Indy pressed. "Now I suggest you give me what you owe me, or . . . anything goes." Then, to Willie: "Don't you agree?"

"Yes," she whispered icily.

"Tell *him*," Indy suggested.

"Pay the man," she told Lao.

Without saying a word, Lao took a small pouch from his pocket, put it on the turntable, sent it around to Indy and Willie. Indy motioned to her with his head; she picked up the sack and emptied a handful of gold coins out onto the table.

Indy was stone-faced. "The diamond, Lao. The deal was for the diamond."

Lao smiled, shrugged defeat, took a squat silver box from his vest pocket, put it on the turntable.

In the moment that Indiana's eyes were focused on the box, Kao Kan tipped a tiny bottle of white powder into the champagne glass beside him. And as the turntable passed him on its way to Indy, Kao Kan set the glass down on it, next to the coins and the silver box.

When the cache arrived before them, Willie opened the box. Inside was a hefty yet delicate diamond. "Oh, Lao," she breathed.

Diamonds were her delight and howling demon. They were hard, but brilliantly lovely. They were clear; they held every color. They were the magical reflection of her very self. And yet they were eminently practical: a diamond like this could make her rich, and blessedly independent from jerks like the yo-yos at this table.

Indy stabbed the fork into the table and picked up the jewel, pushing Willie away on her chair, back to her original position. She stared at him frostily. "You're a real snake." She'd finally placed the color of his eyes.

He ignored her to examine the gemstone. Perfectly cut, each facet representing a different plane of the ancient universe: unflawed, unmarred, unyellow. The university had been hunting a long time for this little bauble.

"Now," hissed Lao Che. "Bring me Nurhachi."

Indy waved to Wu Han, the waiter who'd originally met him at the entrance of the club. Wu Han came forward, a linen napkin draped over his left arm, a tray balanced on his right. In the center of the tray stood a small jade casket.

Willie's sense of intrigue was beginning to overcome her anger. Money, coins, jewels, threats . . . and now this exquisite miniature. "Who on earth *is* this Nurhachi?" she demanded.

Indy removed the small casket from Wu Han's tray, set it on the turntable, rotated it toward Lao Che. "Here," he smiled. "Here he is."

Willie watched it pass her on its way to Lao Che. "Must be kind of a small guy," she muttered.

Lao pulled the canister before him. His sons leaned close. Lao spoke quietly, reverentially, almost to himself. "Inside this sacred coffin are the remains of Nurhachi, the first Emperor of the Manchu Dynasty."

Indy picked up the champagne glass beside him and lifted it magnanimously in toast. "Welcome home, old boy." He drank.

Ashes? Willie thought. *That's the big deal? Ashes?* As far as she was concerned, there was no percentage in dwelling over things past. Present and future were the only tenses that mattered. The rest was supremely boring at best. She began to make up her face.

Lao grinned sharply at Indy. "And now, you will give me back the diamond."

The room felt like it was getting a bit warm to Indy. He pulled his collar away from his throat. "Are you developing a rare sense of humor, or am I going deaf?"

Lao held up a small blue vial.

That caught Willie's eye. *More treasures?* she wondered. "What's that?"

"Antidote," snapped Lao.

"Antidote to what?" Indy asked suspiciously. He suddenly had a premonition.

"To the poison you just drank," Lao sneered.

Willie got that worried feeling in her gut, that hell-in-a-handbasket feeling. "Poison!" she rasped. "Lao, what are you doing? I *work* in this place." But not for long, that feeling told her.

Indy put a finger into his champagne and rubbed the glass: a gritty residue coated the bottom.

"The poison works fast, Dr. Jones," Lao cackled.

Indy put the diamond on the table; held out his hand. "C'mon, Lao."

Chen picked up the diamond, stared into its glittering depth, smirked with satisfaction, put it back down, rotated the turntable toward his father. On its way past Willie, *she* picked it off the tray to study it. She'd never held a diamond this large before. This perfect. It almost hummed in her hand.

Lao had lost interest in the stone, though; he was still fixated on the casket before him. "At last, I have the ashes of my honored ancestor."

Indy was getting more than impatient. Yellow spots were starting to dance in his vision. "The antidote, Lao." Lao ignored him.

This wasn't going right. Jones felt shaky, felt his options slipping away. In a flash, he grabbed the fork off the table and held it once more to Willie's ribs. "Lao," he rumbled.

"Lao," she echoed.

Lao Che, Kao Kan, and Chen only laughed. "You keep the girl," said Lao. "I find another one."

Willie stared at Lao as if she were just now understanding something she'd really known all along. "You miserable little hood," she said.

Wu Han suddenly stepped forward. "Please," he smiled at Lao. They all turned to see, under the tray on his arm, concealed from the restaurant at large, a gun. Pointing directly at Lao Che.

"Good service here," said Indy.

"That's no waiter," Willie suddenly realized. The fork was still in her side. Everyone was edgy; she didn't know which way to jump.

"Wu Han's an old friend," murmured Indiana. "The game's not up yet, Lao. The antidote."

As Indy reached out his hand, there was a loud POP at the next table. They all turned to look; a sodden American had just opened a bottle of champagne, and the foam was spraying over his two giggling lady companions. Waiters there opened more bottles; more loud reports, more spray, more laughter.

Indy returned his attention to his own table. He was feeling increasingly queasy, while next to him, he noticed, Wu Han was looking positively pale. "Wu Han, what is it—" he began—but before he could finish, Wu Han collapsed to the table.

It was only then that Indy saw the smoking gun in Chen's hand withdrawing under a napkin.

"Indy!" gasped Wu Han.

As Wu Han fell forward, Indiana stood, grabbed him, and lowered the wounded comrade into his own chair. "Don't worry, Wu Han," he whispered. "I'm going to get you out of here."

"Not this time, Indy," the dying man choked. "I followed you on many adventures, but now, into the great unknown mystery I go first."

And so he died.

Indy laid his friend's head down on the table. He felt flushed, sweaty.

Lao could hardly contain his glee. "Don't be so sad, Dr. Jones. You will soon join him."

Indy's legs suddenly became quite rubbery, and he staggered backwards.

Kao Kan chuckled. "Too much to drink, Dr. Jones?"

Indy stumbled back farther, colliding with the drunk at the next table. Even the deathly gaunt Chen smiled to see their startled faces peering dizzily at each other. In a rage, Jones pushed the drunk away, bumping into another waiter who was serving the adjoining table from a trolley—serving liqueur-soaked flaming pigeons on a skewer. Indy thought: *If nothing else, I'm gonna wipe that smile off Chen's filthy face.* In a single motion, he grabbed the flaming pigeon skewer, whirled around, hurled it at Chen.

The skewer buried itself to the fiery-pigeon-hilt in Chen's chest.

There was this long, suspended moment: the crowd's din hushed, suddenly vaguely aware of its own impending convulsion; the people surrounding Lao's table froze, like a held breath, poised on the vision of this wraithlike Chinese man in a dinner jacket, impaled on a silver spear, flaming birds casting his startled face in a queer and morbid light.

Then everything happened at once.

Willie screamed reflexively. The woman at the next table, seeing the matched skewer of Pigeon Flambé on the trolley beside her and, perhaps wondering who was next in line to get spiked, likewise shrieked. The rest of the restaurant exploded in chaos. Shouts, breaking glass, running, confusion . . . like the inside of Pandora's Box before the lid was removed.

Indy dove across the table to grab the small blue tube of antidote, but it skittered over the glassy surface, off onto the floor. Indy found himself face to face with Lao. He grabbed the vile gangster by the lapels and snarled hoarsely at him: "Hoe why geh faan yaan." *Very-bad-against-law-person.*

"Ndioh gwok haat yee," spat Lao. *Foreign beggar.*

Kao Kan grasped Indy around the neck, but Jones cold-cocked him with a left hook. One of Lao's henchmen pulled Indy up from behind and, in so doing, kicked the vital blue liquid across the floor. Kao Kan's gun fell under the table.

A number of issues were racing through Willie's mind at this point: Lao was a scum she was glad to be rid of; she could forget about keeping her job at this place; she'd been right about this Jones character from the beginning; and if she kept a cool head, she might just get away with the diamond.

She stuck her hand into the fray on the table, picked up the diamond. She hardly had time to feel it, though, before Indy and the henchman he was wrestling crashed by her, knocking the jewel out of her hand, onto the dance floor.

"You fool," she gasped—talking simultaneously to Indy and herself—and dove after her fleeting fortune.

The band began to play, as if they thought the party was just getting rolling.

Indy rolled onto the next table with Lao's guard. The strongarm punched him in the jaw, stunning him; Indy swung back blindly, striking the cigarette girl, who'd fallen on top of them. The henchman threw Indy off the table, into a dinner trolley that started wheeling, from his momentum, toward the bandstand.

He careened through the bedlam like a flying apparition. The wind against his face revived him some, cooled the toxic perspiration on his forehead. The people he passed were starting to look a little distorted to him, though. He saw the vial on the floor—or did he imagine it?—but sailed right on by.

His flight was halted abruptly by crashing into the bandstand. He got up in time to see Lao's guard about to nab him, so he grabbed the big double bass in time to bash the guard into oblivion.

He stood there a moment, getting his bearings, when his eyes fell upon the vial, lying out there in the midst of the melee. He jumped for it.

In that moment, it was kicked away. In the next moment, Indy came up on his hands and knees facing Willie on *her* hands and knees.

"The antidote," said Indy.

"The diamond," Willie responded.

Indy noticed the stone near his hand, but it was immediately kicked between a dozen pairs of legs.

"Nuts," muttered Willie, crawling off after it. Indy plowed on in the opposite direction.

Lao finally made it past the shouting throng to the front door, and shouted. Almost instantly a cadre of his hoodlums ran in, awaiting instruction.

The band played on (minus the bass). Right on cue, the twelve dancing girls shuffled gaily out of the dragon's mouth and down onto the dance floor. Some party.

Indy chose the same cue to push himself up off the floor, and into the chorus line. He was feeling quite faint now. The sight of Lao's men pouring through the entrance carrying hatchets gave him a new surge of adrenaline, however; he was able to stumble back over to the bandstand.

Three hatchet men hurled their weapons at him, but he ducked behind one of the statues. Quickly, he grabbed a cymbal and sailed it back at a fourth hatchet-bearer, hitting the assassin in the head, knocking him cold. Knocking him very cold, in fact; the thug slumped into a huge ice bucket, scattering ice cubes all over the floor.

All over the diamond. Willie moaned with frustration, scrabbling through hundreds of ice nuggets, searching desperately for the now camouflaged diamond. What she found was the blue vial.

From the stage, Indy saw her pick it up. "Stay there!" he yelled at her. Please.

Their eyes met. It was a moment of decision for Willie. Who was this guy? He'd come into her life ten minutes ago, come on to her, held a fork on her, given her a touch of her first major-league precious stone, cost her her man (no loss) and her job (no sweat), and now she held his life in her hand. And he did have those eyes.

She stuck the vial down the front of her dress for safekeeping.

But no way was she going to stop looking for that diamond. She trudged off once more through the piles of ice.

Kao Kan woke up. He found his gun on the floor, turned slowly, saw Indy. Still a bit unsteady, he raised the gun, to fire across the room.

Indy saw him in time, though. He backed up to the side of the stage, pulled the release rope hanging there. And then, madly, with dream-slowness and a sense of disjointed dream-logic, balloons began floating down from the ceiling. Hundreds of colored balloons. Kao Kan lost sight of his target behind the curtain of this stately barrage.

They obscured everything in their steady, deliberate drift. Indy moved laterally, toward the place Willie had recently occupied. No Willie there, though. Only two more thugs.

One karate-chopped him, but he put the goon down with a jab to the solar plexus. He threw the other one into an angry waiter, and slumped against the balcony wall.

The poison was eating him up. He felt ashen pale, trembly. His stomach was cramping and he wanted to pass out. No, no. He had to find Willie. He had to get the vial.

He threw a glass of cold water on his face. It helped a little.

This was beginning to turn into a real situation, now. He saw four more gang members run in.

Kao Kan, meanwhile, was in a fury. He wanted his brother's murderer dead, but his arm was still shaking too much to get off a clear shot. Fortunately, he noticed that one of his gang cohorts was carrying a machine gun. Maniacally he raced over to the stairs, took the weapon from the man, and walked into the confusion, shouting, "Where is he? I'll kill him."

People who saw the gun started to scatter. The balloons were thinning out, now, too; in a few moments, Kao Kan and Indy saw each other. As Kao began to shoot, Indy dove over the ledge of the balcony, near the huge hanging gong.

Bullets tore into the balcony. Indy huddled behind the great bronze shield. People were screaming, hitting the floor, heading for cover.

When the first burst was over, Indy leaped over to the statue of the lounging warrior, pulled the golden broadsword from its hand, and with two quick slashes cut the cords that suspended the giant gong from the ceiling; it dropped to the floor with a resounding *chung*.

He jumped down behind it as bullets entered its bronze face. Then, sheltering himself on its back side, he slowly wheeled it across the floor, toward where Willie was still scurrying furiously.

Machine-gun bullets kept clanging against the surface of Indy's enormous shield. As it rolled, it gained momentum; he had to run to stay hidden. It made a monster noise, this lumbering gong, deflecting the gunfire.

Willie heard the awesome sound and looked up to see the mammoth disk bearing down on her. *So this is it*, she thought. *Crushed by a renegade gong during a cabaret riot.*

Indy grabbed her arm at the last second, though, pulling her behind the shield with him. Bullets ricocheted as Lao's men jockeyed for better firing positions among the overturned tables.

Willie hollered. Indy looked ahead. Directly before them stood an entire panel of floor-to-ceiling stained-glass windows. She shouted, "I don't want—"

But there was no time to debate. The rolling gong crashed through the towering panes; a moment later, Indy grabbed Willie around the waist and dove with her through the opening.

It was free-fall for ten feet, followed by a tumble down a sloping tiled roof; and then over the edge.

Their entwined bodies plummeted two more stories, ripping through a second-floor awning, smashing through a bamboo balcony, finally thudding to rest into the backseat of a convertible Duesenberg parked directly in front of the building.

Willie sat up in a hurry, completely amazed to be alive, to find herself staring into the equally astonished face of a twelve-year-old Chinese boy wearing a New York Yankees baseball cap, staring back at her from the front seat.

"Wow! Holy smoke! Crash landing!" said Short Round.

"Step on it, Short Round!" said Indy, rising more slowly.

"Okey doke, Indy," said the kid. "Hold on to your potatoes!"

With a great grin, Short Round swiveled around, turned his baseball cap bill-backwards, and stepped on the gas.

Tires squealing, they tore off into the Shanghai night.

TWO
A Boy's Life

SHORT ROUND was just having an average day.

He'd gotten up early that morning—around noon—and gone to work. Work was on the premises of the Liu Street opium den.

Short Round didn't really have all that much to do there in the afternoons. Only a few customers at such a daylight hour, plus a few more sleeping it off from the night before. Short Round brought them tea; or walked them out to rickshaws; or guarded their clothing in the next room, for pennies—except that occasionally he helped himself to more than pennies from the goods he was guarding: occasionally he helped himself to articles of interest.

Among other things, Short Round was a thief.

Not a thief in the strictest sense, of course. He liked to think of himself more along the lines of Robin Hood, the hero in the movie he'd seen seven or eight times at the Tai-Phung Theater. It was simply that one of the poor people he gave to was himself.

At least, such was his thought that morning, during the Liu Street den's long afternoon lull. The sweet smoke hung in thin layers above two stupefied patrons who slumped on the bare wooden cots, one an old Chinese man, one a young Belgian. Short Round was sitting on their belongings in the adjoining room, wondering about breakfast, when it occurred to him there might be something to eat in the Belgian man's bag. He was just rifling through it when the bag's owner walked in. The man did not seem pleased.

Nor did he seem dopey. In fact, he seemed rather irate. Short Round knew enough about these encounters to know that explanations were not usually fruitful, so he left by the window . . . with the Belgian's passport stuck (quite by accident) to his fingers.

The Belgian chased after him.

Short Round loved a good chase. Made him feel wanted. He ran down the rear alley, the indignant client on his tail. Over a fence, up two more winding back streets; the man stayed with him. Up a fire escape along the side of an ancient wood building—all the way up, to the roof. The Belgian was right behind.

Short Round took off across the roofs. Sloping, tiled, gabled— this was the most fun yet; he slid, scooted, swung around chimneys like a monkey in the trees. Rooftops were Short Round's specialty.

His pursuer lost distance, but not sight. Short Round came to the edge of the last roof: sheer drop, four stories. The Belgian closed the gap. Short Round scurried up the slope, over the peak, down the other side. Same drop-off.

Except a few feet below, coming out the top window of the building, was a clothesline, stringing across the alley to the window of the building on the other side.

Just like Robin Hood! Wow! Holy smoke! Short Round hopped down to the clothesline, dangled there a second, then brachiated along a string of flapping silk pajamas to the window across the way while his pursuer swore in Flemish from the roof ledge behind him.

Short Round dove in the window, turned, gave the fuming man a million-dollar smile in payment for his passport, and called out to him: "Very funny! Very funny big joke!"

The man was not amused. People had no sense of humor anymore. Short Round apologized for the disturbance to the incredulous family he'd just barged in on. Then with propriety that seemed incongruous, considering his flying entrance, he bowed, and left by the front door.

Out on the street, shadows were growing long. Fish vendors were packing up, their wares beginning to smell; night people hadn't yet begun to stir. This was Short Round's favorite time. It was the hour of the doves.

Every day around now, hundreds of doves would accumulate in the courtyard of the monastery near the Gung Ho Bar. They made the most wondrous aggregate cooing, like the murmurings of a thousand satisfied Persian cats. It was a sound Short Round associated with being rocked by his mother, though he couldn't remember why. He hadn't had any family for many years.

Except Dr. Jones, of course. Dr. Jones was his family now.

Short Round suspected Indy was actually a reincarnation of the lower god Chao-pao, He-Who-Discovers-Treasures. But Short Round himself claimed Chao-pao as an ancestor, so he and Indy were closely related in any case.

He walked out of the Place of Doves, over to the Gung Ho Bar. This was where he and Indy had first met. He entered the bar. In the back booth, sipping a cup of ginseng tea, Indy was now seated, waiting. Short Round ran up to him with a big grin, took the seat opposite.

"Indy, I get passport for Wu Han!" he whispered excitedly. He handed over the Belgian's passport.

Indy looked it over, raised his eyebrows. "Shorty, where'd you get this? I thought I told you not to steal anymore."

"No steal," the boy protested. "Man give me. He not need anymore."

Short Round looked so ingenuous, so hurt, Indy almost believed him. In any case, he pocketed the documents for Wu Han.

Short Round beamed. That was one of the reasons he loved

Indy. He and Indy, they were birds of a feather: they both had a knack for transferring the ownership of lost items, finding new homes for valuables that had resided in one place too long.

Indy was going to find a new home for Short Round, for example. He was going to take Short Round to America.

Indy squinted at him now. "Okay, kid, you sure I can count on you for the plane tickets?" He gave the boy money to purchase their tickets.

"Easy like pie, Indy. I just get my Uncle Wong's car; then I talk to ticket man; then I wait for you at club."

"Right out front." Indy nodded. "An hour before dawn. You got a watch?"

"Sure okay."

"Well, you make sure to tell your uncle thanks for the use of his car again."

"Oh, he don't mind. We leave for America soon?"

"Yeah, pretty soon. Delhi, first. Now get going; I've got to meet a man about a box."

Short Round left the bar; Indy stayed. Short Round ran six blocks to the house of a German diplomat he knew superficially— knew not at all, actually, except he'd shined the man's shoes at one of the classier brothels the week before, and there had overheard the honorable consul tell the madame that he was leaving town for a fortnight to visit relatives in Alsace.

When Short Round got to the house, he walked around back. He crawled into the garage through the small cat-door that was cut in the bottom panel of the side entrance. Inside the garage, he spent about ten minutes playing with the young cat, dragging a little woolen mouse on a string back and forth in front of it, until it pounced. When the excited kitten finally retreated, with its prize, to a hidden corner under the stairs, Short Round opened the garage doors wide. Then he hot-wired the car.

It was a cream-colored 1934 Duesenberg Auburn convertible, an easy ride to wire. Easy or not, he'd already taken this one for a spin with Indy several times this week. Now he hunkered down under the dash, crossing leads until the connection sparked and the engine roared into life. It made Short Round feel like the boy in the fairy tale who lived in the belly of a dragon: he closed his eyes, listened to the pistons rumbling, smelled the smoke of the electrical short-circuit, felt the dark enclosure wrap over him in the shape of a fire-hardened dragon-stomach. . . .

Scaring himself, he squirmed up to the seat, put the car in reverse, backed out of the garage, let the car idle, closed the garage doors again, turned down the circular drive, and headed for the open road.

He could barely see above the steering wheel or reach the pedals, but barely was all he needed. The city streets became residential, then quickly rural, in the fading afternoon light. This was Short Round's second favorite time of day: when the sun burned orange as a red coal, just before the earth gobbled it up again for the night.

By early evening he was standing in a small British airport office, negotiating for three tickets with a small British airport official named Weber.

"I hardly think I could make room for someone of *your* stature," the officious Briton began.

Short Round gave him most of Indiana's money. "Not for me. For Dr. Jones, the famous professor. This very important government case. I his assistant."

Weber still looked skeptical, but took the money. "Well, I'll see what I can do."

"You do good, Dr. Jones put you in his book. Maybe you get a medal." He winked.

Weber seemed taken aback by this strange little manipulator. "I'll do what I can, but I'm not certain I can get three seats on the same plane with such short notice."

Short Round winked again, and slipped Weber the last of Indy's wad of bills as a bribe. He also let Weber see the dagger half-hidden in his belt. Weber felt distinctly disconcerted accepting a payoff from a twelve-year-old gangster; nonetheless, he took the money.

"Yes, I'm sure the accommodations can be arranged." He

smiled. He wondered when the London Office was going to transfer him back to civilization.

Short Round bowed to Weber most graciously, then shook the man's hand, then saluted smartly, his fingertips to the visor of his baseball cap. Then he ran back to the Duesenberg and drove back to town.

He left the car parked in the warehouse of a friend who owed him a favor. Night was just opening its eyes. Short Round thought of the daytime as a sleeping rascal who awoke, each night, with a great hunger. Short Round's third favorite time was all night.

He ambled down to the docks. A boy had to be careful here—boys were much in demand, for forced sea duty, or other disreputable occupations—but it was a good place for a wily boy to get a free supper. And, like the night, Short Round was getting hungry.

He scavenged a small, flat plank from the garbage behind one of the bars, and took it down to where the oily water lapped right up against the quais. He squatted there in the shadows, his feet submerged, waiting. After five minutes passed quietly—during which time he prayed to Naga, the Dragon-King, who inhabited and guarded this sea—he suddenly slapped the board against the surface of the water, hard, several times.

In a second, a juicy moonfish rose, belly-up, to the shallow, stunned by Short Round's concussions. He grabbed the fish by the tail, yanked it out of the water, smacked it against the piling. Then, crouching in the sand a few feet away, he slit it open with his dagger, and feasted on the tender yellow meat. He wondered if they had moonfish in America.

Thinking of America made him think of movies. It was hours before he had to meet Indy yet, so he decided to wander down to the Tai-Phung Theater, to see if anything new was playing. The Tai-Phung showed mostly American films, mostly for the international crowd that populated the banking or diplomatic sections of the city. The Tai-Phung is where Short Round learned most of his English.

He couldn't read the marquee when he got there—he couldn't read at all, hardly, except for the little bits Indy was teaching him—

but the letters looked different from the markings that had been there last time he'd looked, so he decided to go check it out.

He crawled in the high bathroom window at the back of the building by standing on two garbage cans outside. Once in, he lowered himself down to the toilet tank, then to the floor. He offered to shine the shoes of the man sitting, a bit shocked, on the pot, but the man politely refused. Short Round scooted under the door of the stall, and out into the theater.

He sat in an aisle seat, near the exit, for quick departure if that should be necessary. He slumped down so the ushers who knew him by face wouldn't spot him right away. He popped a lump of bubble gum in his mouth. He settled back to watch the movie.

It was a nifty show. This private eye named Nick kept making very funny big jokes to his wife, Nora, very pretty lady. They had a silly dog, too, named Asta. Nick was drinking another martini at a big party where the bad guys were lurking, when a fancy couple sat down right in front of Short Round, blocking his view.

He was about to move to another seat when he noticed the woman put her purse down in the space between the two chairs. This looked too easy to pass up. Short Round waited ten minutes—until they got absorbed in the film—then reached forward and slid the pocketbook back to his lap.

It was a silver lamé evening bag with a mother-of-pearl clasp. Short Round clicked it open, quickly rummaged through it. Wow! What great luck! There was a jeweled makeup compact with a small watch set into its back. Just what he needed to check the time for his meeting with Indy—when the little hand was on the four, and the big hand on the twelve. (Indy was teaching him numbers, too. Numbers were easier.)

This was a very good omen: it portended well for the rest of the night. Short Round gave a brief prayer of thanks to Chao-pao, his patron deity, He-Who-Discovers-Treasures. Then he stood, began panting loudly, and fell in the aisle, draping his arm over the woman's chair.

"My word!" she gasped.

"Lady, big man just steal your purse!" Short Round panted, dropping the purse at her feet. "I catch him and take back for you. He hit me, but I get away. Here your purse." He nudged it toward her with his knee, then he collapsed.

"You poor child!" she said, quickly looking in the wallet at the bottom of the handbag. All the money was still there.

"Shhh!" said her companion, trying to ignore the distraction, feeling it was always the wisest course to disregard the overtures of these street urchins.

The woman arched an eyebrow at her escort. Short Round whimpered in apparent pain. The woman gave Short Round two dollars. "There you are, you sweet thing," she spoke as if she were confiding. "That's for being so brave and honest."

"Thanks, lady," said Short Round. He stuffed the bills in his pants, jumped up, ran out the door. The lady, briefly startled, went back to her movie.

Outside, the night was flexing. Paper lanterns, incense, jugglers, hookers, hawkers. Short Round, feeling a lot like Nick Charles, approached a streetwalker who had one slit up the side of her dress, another up the side of her smile.

"Hey, sugar, got a cigarette?" He winked at her.

She was about to retort, had a second thought, reached into her bag, pulled out a stick of gum, and flipped it to him.

"Oh, boy!" he exclaimed, pocketing the prize. "Thanks, lady!" He ran off, ready for anything. What a night!

For a dollar he bought a top that played music and flashed lights as it spun. Three boys went after him for it, though. He had to hit one of them over the head with the toy as he was climbing over a fence to get away. End of chase; end of toy.

He was left holding the broken top handle. This he threw as far as he could, back down the alley he'd been chased, and that was pretty far. Someday he'd be as good a pitcher as the great Lefty Grove: Short Round, too, was a southpaw.

His other dollar he gave to an old woman who sat, begging, on a doorstep. It upset him to see old beggars, especially grandmothers. Family was more important than anything, of course. His own grandmother was gone, but what if *she* were begging on a stoop somewhere. It was important to remember this.

The old woman bowed to Short Round; he thanked her for allowing him to honor her.

It began to rain, a fine rain. Short Round hurried back to the warehouse in which he'd parked the Duesenberg. Several men sat in a circle near the far wall. One of them was casting the I Ching.

Short Round watched him for an hour. The man threw the yarrow stalks for each person there, but when Short Round asked for his own path to be read, the man refused.

Short Round took a nap behind some bales of tea for a while, put to sleep by the cheery mumblings of a band of sailors throwing dice in a nearby alcove. Dice, I Ching: same thing. When he awoke, he saw a young couple kissing beside another stack of bales against the wall. He watched them for a few minutes. They seemed very happy. He wondered if they had any children.

From the doorway, Short Round heard the static of an old radio. He walked over. The small box sat on the ground plugged into the wall; beside it a drunk American sailor crouched, tuning it to an almost inaudible station that replayed smuggled American recordings. Breaking up over the air waves now was another adventure of The Shadow, who knew what evil lurked in the hearts of men, and who could cloud men's minds. Shorty loved this program; he listened whenever he could. The sailor kicked him away, though. This was apparently a private show.

Anyway, it seemed like it was getting late. He looked at the watch he'd found: time to go. He started up the car and eased it out into traffic. The rain had stopped.

He got to the club right when he was supposed to. No Indy, though. The doorman tried to make him move the car away from the front door, but he gave the doorman the jeweled compact-timepiece, so the doorman said he could stay there for a bit, if he didn't cause any trouble.

Then Indy dropped in. With the lady.

"Wow! Holy smoke! Crash landing!" said Short Round.

"Step on it, Short Round!" said Indy.

Tires squealing, they tore off into the Shanghai night.

Willie couldn't believe it. "For crying out loud, a *kid's* driving the car?!"

"Relax, I've been giving him lessons," Indy said nonchalantly.

"Oh, that makes me feel a *lot* safer," she nodded.

As Short Round swerved around the next corner, Willie was thrown against Indiana. Without losing a beat, he put his hand down the front of her dress.

Willie became indignant. "Listen, we just met, for crissake." Some men . . .

"Don't get your hopes up. Where's the antidote?" It was hard feeling around in there; his fingertips were numb with poison. Too bad.

He rubbed the glass vial with his palm, rolled it into his fingers, pulled it from her bra, screwed off the lid, tipped it to his lips, and swallowed. "Ech."

"You don't look very good."

"Poison never agrees with me." He wiped his mouth on his sleeve. "Short Round, pull a right and head for the Wang Poo bridge."

"Check! Gotcha!" the kid shouted back. When he drove fast, he tried to look just like James Cagney.

Indy peered out the back window and noticed a large black sedan in pursuit. "Looks like we got company."

Willie was suddenly depressed. If Lao caught her now, he'd *really* be hacked off. The club was a shambles, she'd lost the diamond, the kid was going to crash the car any minute, she had two broken nails . . . that was it. The last straw. She could cope with all the rest, but how was a girl supposed to get a job singing when she looked like—

She looked at herself in the reflection of the side window. Even worse than she thought. Tears began to well up in her eyes; tears of anger. "Look at what you've done to me," she seethed. "My lipstick is smeared, I broke two nails, there's a run in my stocking."

Gunfire shattered the rear window, spraying them with glass. Indy and Willie crouched low; Short Round was already too low in his seat to be visible from behind.

"Somehow I think you've got bigger problems," muttered Indiana, reaching for his shoulder bag. He pulled out a pistol, began firing back through the broken window. "There, Shorty!" he barked. "Through the tunnel!"

They screeched through the darkened tunnel. The pursuit car stayed right with them, its headlights burning like spectral eyes.

"What're we going to do?" cried Willie. "Where're we going?" The magnitude of the calamity was just setting in.

"The airport," Indy snapped. "No, look out, Short Round! Left, *left*!" He reached over the front seat, put a hand on the wheel, helped Short Round navigate. Then, more softly: "You're doin' all right, kid."

Willie sank lower.

The Duesenberg emerged on a crowded square: ten thousand merchants, beggars, hookers, sailors, thieves, buyers, and coolies with rickshaws wandered gaily amidst the jumble of bright paper lanterns, calligraphed banners, storefronts, and produce stands. They all scattered when the Duesenberg came roaring by.

Some of them scattered back over the street in the Duesenberg's wake—enough to totally clog the thoroughfare by the time the black sedan came barreling in. It crashed headlong into a vegetable stand, then swerved and skidded against the curb, finally coming to a halt in a swarm of peddlers.

Indy peered out the back window. "Looks like chop suey back there." Willie was afraid to look.

They put some distance on the stalled pursuer. Out onto the highway now; some fast, open countryside.

"Shorty, you called the airport?"

"Sure, Indy. Mr. Weber get seats for you, me, and Wu Han."

"Wu Han's not coming, Shorty."

Short Round considered this. Wu Han wouldn't have run; he was too loyal. Therefore he was either dead, captured, or holding off the bad guys—all very honorable occupations for Wu Han to have chosen. In any case, it was up to Short Round alone now to protect their beloved comrade and spirit-brother. "Don't worry, Indy," he assured. "Short Round number-one bodyguard now."

Willie braved a glance out the back. Far in the distance, tiny headlights rounded a curve and followed them. "I'll take the extra seat," she said dryly. Her options seemed distinctly limited. "Where are we going, anyway?"

"Siam," said Indy, reloading his gun.

"Siam?" she complained. "I'm not dressed for Siam." She wanted to complain more, actually, but no gods, demigods, or justices in the whole pagan universe seemed to want to listen or care just now, much less the deranged yahoo beside her. She looked over at him suspiciously. Outside, on the road, a sign flew by: NANG TAO AIRPORT. The headlights behind them seemed to be gaining.

Well, maybe it would work out. She'd never been to Siam. . . .

Short Round wheeled the car up a gravel drive toward the airfield. Just past a small cargo area. Out on the runway, a trimotor was revving its engines. The Duesenberg squealed to a stop on the apron; the three of them jumped out. Short Round carried Indy's shoulder bag.

At the boarding gate, the young English airline official ran up to meet them. "Dr. Jones, I'm Weber, I spoke with your . . . assistant." He eyed Short Round curiously for a moment, then continued. "I managed to find three seats; unfortunately they're in a cargo plane full of poultry."

"Is he kidding?" Willie protested.

"Madam," Weber began officiously, "it was the best I could do on such short—" He stopped suddenly, and smiled. "My heavens, aren't you Willie Scott, the famous vocalist?"

Willie was completely taken aback, then instantly charmed:

here, smack-dab in the middle of the worst day in a while, was a fan. "Well, yes, I am, actually." She blushed.

"Miss Scott," Weber fawned, "I've so enjoyed your perform-ances. In fact, if you don't mind my saying it—"

Willie was just beginning to think it maybe hadn't been quite such a bad day after all when Jones shot off his mouth again.

"You can sign autographs, doll. Shorty and I have to go."

Indy and Shorty took off for the plane. Willie hesitated for a second, but quickly found her allegiance when she saw the black sedan squeal into the airport. In her sweetest voice, with a look of majesty worn well, she said to Weber, "It's always swell meeting a fan, Mr. Weber, but I really must run now." And then, coarsely, to Indy: "Goddammit, wait for me!"

She hightailed it toward the plane. Weber waved. Willie jumped on.

The black sedan screeched to a halt at the fence of the loading area. Lao Che hopped out, followed by several henchmen with guns. The commotion—and the guns—aroused the notice of two airport policemen, who slowly wandered toward the car. Lao Che looked across the tarmac at the taxiing plane in time to see Indy give him a neat salute and slam the cargo bay shut.

Lao Che's men looked to him for orders, for rage. He only smiled, though. As the plane swung around to gain speed up the runway, he could plainly see its legend inscribed along the fuselage of the blind side: LAO CHE AIR FREIGHT.

Rolling past, the pilot saw Lao standing on the field, and saluted his boss. Laughing deeply, Lao Che returned the salute.

The plane lifted off with a roar, silhouetted crisply against the first orange light of dawn.

They flew west.

Willie huddled in her damp, sequinned dress, looking for warmth while dozens of crated and nervous chickens kept attacking her. "Quit pecking at me, you dumb clucks, or you're gonna be sitting on plates with mashed potatoes." This was really too much.

The worst part was it brought her back to her beginnings—on a chicken farm in Missouri. Dirty, no-account, nowhere chickens.

Her mother used to tell her that was where she belonged, that no amount of dreaming, or aching to be somewhere else, was ever going to get her off the farm. It would take a miracle to do that, her mother told her, and there were no such things as miracles.

It was no miracle that Willie won the county beauty queen contest when she was eighteen, though: she was just simply the most beautiful girl in the county.

With her prize money she went to New York, to be an actress and a dancer. No miracles there, though; everyone in New York wanted that, it seemed. So Willie drifted west.

She fell in with bad company in Chicago, had to leave in sort of a hurry. Which got her off on the wrong foot in Hollywood—which is a bad foot to start off on if you're a dancer.

So it was either back to Missouri or keep drifting west. And one thing Willie knew for certain was that of all the places in the world where miracles didn't exist, they didn't exist in Missouri.

She hitched a ride with a snazzy dresser who promised her the Orient was wide open. Well, that much was true, she'd found out: like a big hole.

She never saw a miracle in Shanghai, either, but things had finally begun working out. She'd developed a nice little local reputation; she had a following. She had a suitor or two. She had prospects.

But that was all ancient history. Now, instead of prospects, she had retrospects. Now she had chicken feathers in her mouth. And it tasted just like Missouri.

The door opened at the rear of the plane; out stepped Indiana Jones. He had changed.

Now he wore a beat-up leather jacket over a khaki shirt, work-pants and work-boots, a gray snap-brim hat, a leather bag across his shoulder, an old army holster at his waist. He walked forward carrying the rolled-up tuxedo in one hand, and a coiled bullwhip in the other.

He sat down between Willie and Shorty, dumping the formal wear on the floor, hanging the whip up on a coat peg.

"So, what're you supposed to be, a lion tamer?" sneered Willie with some amusement. Men were such boys.

"Since I was nice enough to let you tag along, why don't you give your mouth a rest. Okay, doll?" He patted her leg condescendingly. She was definitely starting to get on his nerves.

She removed his hand from her thigh. This guy obviously had only one thing on his mind—and this wasn't the time, it wasn't the place, it wasn't the guy. She picked up his dinner jacket from the floor. "I'm freezing. What do you mean, tag along? From the minute you walked into the nightclub, you haven't been able to keep your eyes off me." She started toward the rear of the plane, wrapping the coat around her shoulders.

"Oh, yeah?" said Indy.

He smiled, lay back against a wall of chicken crates, tipped his hat down over his eyes, and went to sleep.

The cockpit door opened a crack. The copilot stared intently into the cargo hold.

He saw Willie sleeping on a pillow of sequins near the rear, curled up now in Indy's dark formal pants, white dress shirt, and tuxedo jacket; Indy was asleep portside, his hat over his face, chicken feathers dotting his coat, and Shorty was sleeping peacefully beside him in sneakers, baseball cap, quilted pants, and a frayed, cotton coolie jacket, his head resting on Indy's shoulder.

The copilot looked over at the pilot, who was receiving radio instructions from his employer. The pilot looked back at the copilot and nodded.

The copilot picked up a large wrench, hefting it as he scrutinized Jones. After a moment, his second thoughts got the better of him; he put down the wrench and drew a knife from his belt.

As the copilot started out the door, Indiana rolled over. The copilot pulled back.

The pilot swore in Chinese, handed his assistant a .45 automatic. The copilot studied the gun, asked if the woman and the kid had to go too. The pilot nodded. The copilot felt this would engender some bad karma, and said so. The pilot vehemently disagreed. They had words. References were made to each other's ancestors.

Ultimately the pilot took his gun back, ordered the copilot to take over the controls, and went to do the job himself.

Indiana still slept soundly. As the pilot took a step toward him, an egg rolled out of a high overhead crate and fell—fell two inches to a wad of rag, then rolled end over end along an inclined plank, dropped to a finely balanced nest, teeter-tottered down to a narrow ledge, hovered an instant, and finally plunged. Without waking, without moving a muscle more than necessary, Indy held out his hand and caught the egg before it hit the ground.

Indiana Jones was not without flaw, but he had a sense for falling eggs.

It was a feat that stopped the pilot in his tracks. Amazed and afraid of this dangerous sorcerer, he backed up two steps, smiling sheepishly at the copilot. They discussed the matter calmly; they made suggestions. They had their orders. But they decided it was a matter best left to the gods.

The pilot pushed the lever on the instrument panel that emptied the fuel tanks. The copilot fitted them both up with parachutes. Then, quietly, they walked to the rear of the plane.

Willie awoke in time to blearily see the copilot enter the aft bay, closing the curtains behind him. She rolled over to go back to sleep, when she noticed the pilot emerge from the cockpit, walk back, and disappear through the same curtains.

It seemed rather odd to her. It wasn't that big an airplane; she didn't think any more crew could fit up there. Hmm. No more crew. "I wonder who's flying the plane, then."

She got up, walked forward, stuck her head inside the cockpit door. Nobody flying the plane.

She slammed the door shut with a yelp. "There's nobody flying the plane!"

Short Round, ever vigilant, woke up as soon as she shouted. Indy, still groggy from the aftereffects of the poison, kept sleeping.

Willie rushed to the back of the plane. She parted the curtains. There stood the two and only crew on the brink of the open cargo door, parachutes strapped to their backs.

"Oh, my God! Don't go! Help, Indiana! Wake up, the pilot's bailing out!"

Shorty ran over to her. Wow! No joke! The pilot was abandoning ship.

Groggily, Indy opened his eyes. "We there already?"

In a flash Willie was shaking him, waking him, beseeching him. "Nobody driving . . . jumping . . . parachutes. . . . Do something!" This cowboy had to be good for something; surely this was a flight jacket he was wearing. Surely he knew how to fly this old bus.

Indiana got up and ran back to the open curtains. Nobody there. Just two chutes billowing open in the clear sky beyond.

He ran up to the cockpit, Willie at his heels. In an instant he appraised the situation and slipped into the pilot's seat, at the controls, with absolute confidence.

Willie was teary-eyed with gratitude. Laughing, nodding, seeing there was a reason, after all, for this dubious doctor to exist. With a sigh of relief to her own question, she asked: "You know how to fly?"

Indy surveyed the control panel, turned a couple of knobs, flipped a switch, took the wheel. "No." Then, ingenuously: "Do you?"

Willie turned white; she felt her stomach rising.

Indy flashed a big bad smile, though. "Just kidding, sweetheart.

I got everything under control. Altimeter: check. Stabilizer: roger. Air speed: okay. Fuel—"

There was a long pause. Willie hadn't exactly gotten over his little joke about not knowing how to fly yet, so she was in no mood for humor now. But then this silence on Indy's part did not, in any case, sound like a humorous silence.

"Fuel?" said Willie. "Fuel? What about the fuel?"

Indiana stood up slowly. Willie followed his gaze out the window: the last engine sputtered to a stop. All the props were motionless. The plane began to nose downward.

"We've got a problem," said Indiana.

He walked past Willie, into the hold. "Shorty!"

Short Round ran up breathless. "I already check, Indy. No more parachutes." Maybe they could grow wings, like when the Monkey-God Wo-Mai gave wings to the silkworms so they could become moths, to escape their earthly prison.

Indy began to rummage through all the storage lockers.

In the cockpit, Willie was jerked rudely out of her catatonia by the almighty ludicrous vision of a snowy mountain looming immediately ahead of the windshield. "Indiana!" she bellowed, less as a call for help than as a last moment of human contact before annihilation.

The gods were generous, though. The plane barely missed the peak, knocking a noseful of snow from the highest pinnacle, clearing the crest by inches.

Willie's heart nearly stopped. She ran from the cockpit, to see Indy pulling a huge wad of yellow canvas from one of the storage bins. Printed across its side were the words EMERGENCY LIFE RAFT. "Are you nuts?" she screamed at him in fury.

He ignored her. "Give me a hand, Shorty," he told the boy.

The two of them dragged the folded canvas over to the open cargo door, as Willie kept shouting, "Are you crazy, a life raft! We're not *sinking*, we're crashing!"

"Get over here, damn it!" he ordered. "Short Round, come on, grab onto me tight."

Short Round encircled Indy's waist from behind. This crash would be better than anything in *Wings*, which Shorty had seen four times.

Willie hesitated a moment before deciding that no matter what else, she didn't want to die alone.

"Wait for me!" the little girl in her called. She grabbed her gold dress—no point in not having something to wear, just in case—ran over and threw her arms around Indiana's neck, so that she and Shorty were both hugging him from behind.

Indy clutched the bunched-up life raft in front of him as he perused the mountainside rushing close, now, beneath their sinking aircraft. Fifteen feet above the ground. Ten, and diving. Seven.

Indy jumped with all his strength, pulling the inflation cord.

Short Round closed his eyes, ready to fly.

THREE
The Sacred Stone

THEY SPILLED from the hatch. As the plane skimmed over the slopes out of control, the raft popped open into its full, bloated form, acting suddenly as a spoiler—a great bulbous kite, soaring against the rushing air, dangling these three terrified souls over eternity.

Short Round made a secret promise to Madame Wind, Feng-p'o, the Celestial Being responsible for keeping them aloft with her bags of swirling breezes.

A hundred yards away, the cargo plane kissed the earth, exploding into a tremendous conflagration of rock, steel, roast chicken. A moment later, the life raft skidded into a snowbank, bounced, flew, hit again, and took off at speed down the pristine slopes.

Indiana held on to the front while Willie and Shorty each had handfuls of ripcords. They rocketed down the mountainside like a bobsled for a few minutes, finally crossing the timberline. It was snowy forest, now. Willie looked up for less than a second before deciding she didn't want to look again.

Shorty was scared and excited all at once. This was just like the foiled escape in *Ice Creatures From Venus*. But Indy would pull them through. Short Round didn't have to look to know that. Indy was the ultimate clutch hitter—probably better, even, than Lou Gehrig.

They bounced over a snow-hidden log and took to the air again, directly toward a large tree. Indy tugged fiercely at the perimeter rope, rolled on his side, somehow managed to swerve the raft so it caromed off the snow-drifted edge of the tree. They slid straight down the next bank.

The downhill run continued. They slowed considerably, splashing through first a small stream, then some leafy ground cover. When they entered a clearing at half-speed, finally near the end of the ordeal, Indy chanced to smile at the others with relief.

"Indy, you the greatest," admired Short Round. Better even than Robin Hood.

Indy beamed at Willie. "Sometimes I amaze even myself."

"I'll bet," she replied weakly.

"Indy!" Short Round yelled.

Indy turned just as they crashed through a tangle of bushes, becoming airborne once again—over the edge of a sheer cliff. None of them looked down.

They dropped in a gentle parabolic curve for probably not as long as it felt, coming finally to rest, with a splash, on a wide bed of water. White water.

The raft plunged immediately into the raging torrent, battering rocks, spinning over roaring waves, twisting between narrow gaps of craggy stone. They held on tightly, choking and sputtering, as the rapids tore them down falls, into boulders, over thundering cascades.

Every ounce of energy was devoted to holding on. No thought to steering, to repositioning, to prayers or recriminations. Just keeping those fingers closed on those ropes.

And then there was one heart-stopping bounce—and the raft seemed to slow. It drifted out of the main stream, over toward a backwater, a sort of small bay on the river. The three bedraggled passengers lay totally still in the bottom of the raft.

Short Round, battered and exhausted, lifted his young head a few inches, to ascertain the safety of his charge. "Indy?"

Indiana coughed once. "Okay, Shorty. I'm okay."

Willie moaned. She was drenched to the bone—they all were—her hair soaked and stringy, her clothes dripping. She felt like a total mess.

"You all right?" Indiana asked her.

"No," she winced. "I'm not cut out for this kind of life." *It was nice of you to ask, though*, she thought. "Where are we, anyway?"

The raft floated to a gentle stop at the shore—more precisely, at a pair of dark legs standing on the shoreline.

Indy squinted up into the sun to see who was attached to the legs. "India," he whispered.

"Holy cow," Willie exclaimed. "India? How do you know we're in—" She rolled over to find herself staring up at the strange, withered face of an old, bony-thin man. She gasped.

The man wore a tattered robe. Around his neck hung strings of fantastic beads. His skin was dark umber, aged as time. He looked like a witch doctor.

An eerie wind rose up howling all around them. Suddenly the old man placed his palms together—Willie jumped—and moved his wedded hands up to touch his forehead.

Willie and Short Round watched, mystified, as Indiana, in like manner, returned the shaman's silent greeting.

They walked now, the shaman and four turbaned peasants, followed by Indy, carrying his bullwhip; Short Round, carrying Indy's bag; and Willie, carrying her evening gown and heels. It was a gutted, rocky path they took, through barren, rolling hills. Scrub covered the landscape in patches; an occasional fruitless tree. The air smelled dusty.

Short Round walked comfortably, taking three paces to each of Indy's two. It wasn't easy following in the footsteps of such a one, but Short Round was up to the task, for he loved Indy. Indy had befriended him when he hadn't a friend, trusted him when he'd earned no trust. And Indy was going to take him to America.

They were on their way now. Short Round could hardly believe it. America: where everyone had shoes and hats, rode in cars, knew how to dance, shot straight, made jokes, played hard, held true, looked great, talked smart, ate well, took chances that paid off. That's where Short Round was going.

He'd guard Indy tenaciously until they got there. Then, once Indy didn't need a bodyguard anymore, Short Round figured he'd just be Indy's son; that way he could continue to take care of Indy without having to drive to work every day. The only problem with this plan was that if Indy became Shorty's father, a mother would be needed. A wife. Like yin needed yang. Like Nick Charles had Nora; Fred Astaire had Ginger Rogers. Robin and Marian. Gable and Harlow. Hsienpo and Ying-t'ai.

It was in the context of these envied and archetypal pairings that Short Round cast his eye on Willie in a new light.

She might be just right for Indy. She was pretty enough; she'd gone the distance, so far. She might do okay for a mom. She and Indy could adopt him, and they could all live on the Twentieth Century Limited, riding the rails back and forth to New York City. It could be a good life. Short Round would have to consider her carefully for the job. He would give it some thought.

Willie, meanwhile, was feeling enormous relief to be alive, even if it *was* in a big desolate nowhere. Several times during the past night she might as easily have been *dead* in a big desolate nowhere, and alive was definitely better. She felt the warm stone on her bare feet, she felt the glorious sun on her face, she felt absolutely in intimate touch with her very life. She felt hungry.

She wondered if Indy had any food in his bag or jacket. Walking faster, to catch up with him, she saw he was talking to the shaman.

Actually, the shaman was talking to Indy. "Mama okey enakan bala; gena hitiyey." Indiana wasn't exactly fluent in this dialect, but he understood it all right: "*I was waiting for you*," the shaman was saying. "*I saw it in a dream. I saw the aeroplane fall out of the sky by the river. I saw this in my dream.*" The old man kept repeating it over and over.

Willie reached them, listened a moment. "What'd he say?" she asked.

"They've been expecting me," said Indy. He looked puzzled.

"What do you mean—how?"

"The old man saw it in a dream."

"Dream," she scoffed. "Nightmare is more like it."

Indy squinted. "He said they were waiting at the river; they were waiting for the plane to fall down."

It was a bewildering statement. Willie shook her head. "Where was I? Was I in the dream?"

Indiana smiled at her. *Actresses*, he thought. He didn't know any more than she did, though, so there didn't seem much use in speculation. He just kept walking.

Willie, to ease her growing discomfort, just kept talking. "That's all? So how'd the dream end? How do we get out of here? When do we eat? I'm famished. What about me?"

The rocky ground turned to parched clay. Soon a hot wind swirled dust eddies all around them as the clay became thin soil, cracked and blighted. And finally, at the foot of these ravaged hills, they came to the village.

Mayapore village: like the soil, cracked and blighted.

They walked down a dessicated road through the town. A sense of devastation was palpable. Pitiful villagers stood in groups of three or four, watching the strangers being brought in. Watching without hope.

Women pulled buckets from dry wells, coming up with sand.

Miserable dogs skulked between huts of crumbling clay, daub, and wattle. Patient vultures lurked in a few scraggly trees. It was worse than a drought. It was a deathwatch.

Indiana noticed several villagers staring at Short Round, or pointing. A few haggard women seemed to be crying, though they shed no tears, for their bodies would not easily give up such precious water. Indy drew Shorty closer to him; these signs made him uneasy for the boy. Suddenly he realized why.

There were no children in the village.

Short Round saw it, too. He grew frightened by the odd attention, and worried for Indy's safety. He was Indy's bodyguard now, after all. He pulled closer, to keep an eye on his old friend, as the wretched population looked on.

They were shown into a small stone hut with three pallets on the floor. It had no windows, so was fractionally cooler than the arid exterior.

"Sleep now," the shaman told them, "for your journey has made you tired. Later we will eat, and talk. But for now, sleep." He left them without another word.

Indy translated for his companions.

"But I'm so hungry," whimpered Willie.

"Try counting lamb chops," suggested Indiana, lying down on the earth.

It must have worked, for soon they were all asleep.

Black clouds thick with ash clotted across the blood-red sunset.

Indiana, Willie, and Short Round sat tensely on broken stools in a hut with a thatched roof but no walls, only stone arches, encouraging whatever evening breeze there was to enter. Half a dozen elders were silhouetted on the dirt floor around them, some women, some men. Central to these was the village Chieftain, an ancient white-haired man who carried the anguish of all his people on his face.

The Chieftain gave commands. Three more women scuttled in, set wooden bowls before the visitors. No bowls were placed before the elders.

Willie looked expectant. "I sure hope this means dinner."

"Estuday. Estuday," Indy said to the women. *Thank you.*

As he spoke, the women were, in fact, ladling food into the dishes of the guests. It was a grayish gruel mixed with yellow rice and a bit of moldy fruit rind. Willie stared at it in despair. "I can't eat this."

"That's more food than these people have to eat in a week," Indy advised her. "They're starving."

"I can see that," she replied tersely. "What I fail to see is how my depriving them of this meal is going to help that plight—especially when it makes me gag just to look at it." As it was, the entire situation made her completely lose her appetite. How could she possibly take this meager portion from these wasting souls? It had never been this bad on the farm in Missouri; even so, these weathered faces brought back unwanted memories. Willie wished she were somewhere else.

"Eat it," Indy ordered.

"I'm not hungry," Willie insisted.

The village elders looked on.

Indy smiled thinly. "You're insulting them and embarrassing me. Eat it."

She could have cared less about embarrassing Jones, but she had no desire to add affront to the poverty of the village. She ate. They all did.

The Chieftain smiled with satisfaction. "Rest here before you go on," he said in English.

"We'd appreciate that," nodded Indiana. So the Chief spoke English. The British must have been nearby at one time.

"We not rest," Short Round piped up. "Indy is taking me to America. We go now. We go America." He just wanted to make sure that was the ground rule here, and understood as such, before anyone came up with any other thoughts on the matter.

"We go *to* America," Willie corrected his grammar. She hadn't actually let herself think of it before now, but it all of a sudden sounded like a pretty damn good idea. Manhattan, maybe.

"America. America," nodded the Chieftain, comprehending the notion only vaguely.

"Relax, kid," Indy said to Shorty, dropping his hat on the boy's head. Then to the chief: "Can you provide us with a guide to Delhi? I'm a professor and I have to get back to my university."

"Yes. Sajnu will guide you."

"Thank you."

The shaman spoke now. "On the way to Delhi you will stop at Pankot." It was spoken as if it were already fact, as if he were merely reporting something that had already happened.

Indiana noted the change in tenor. "Pankot isn't on the way to Delhi," he said carefully.

"There, you will go to Pankot Palace," the shaman went on as if Indy hadn't said a word.

Indy tried a new tack. "I thought the Palace had been deserted since 1857."

"No," the shaman corrected. "There is a new Maharajah now, and again the Palace has the dark light. It is as a hundred years ago. It is this place that kills my village."

Indy was having trouble picking up the thread. "I don't understand. What's happened here?"

The shaman spoke slowly, as if explaining to a small child. "The evil starts in Pankot. Then like monsoon it moves darkness over all country."

"The evil. What evil?" said Indy. He could hear the shaman speaking on two levels, but the levels kept shifting; Indy had the feeling he was trying to see through broken glasses.

Short Round didn't like the direction of this conversation one bit. "Bad news. You listen to Short Round, you live longer." He especially didn't like the interest Indy was showing in the subject. Evil was something you didn't play around with. Evil didn't care if you could shoot straight, or run fast.

The shaman continued. "They came from Palace and took Sivalinga from our village."

"Took what?" broke in Willie. She, too, was getting interested: there was a drama unfolding here, like a dark stage play. She had the sense she was being auditioned for a part.

"A stone," Indy explained. "A sacred stone from the shrine that protects the village."

"It is why Krishna brought you here," the shaman nodded.

Indy wanted to set him straight on that account, though. "No. We weren't brought here. Our plane crashed."

Short Round agreed with this assessment. He said "Boom!" and fluttered his fingers down into the palm of his other hand, to make the explanation more graphic for these simple people.

Indy clarified further. "We were sabotaged by—"

"No," stated the shaman, like a patient teacher to a dim pupil. "We pray to Krishna to help us find the stone. It was Krishna who made you fall from sky. So you *will* go to Pankot Palace and find Sivalinga and bring back to us."

Indiana started to object. But then he looked at the sad, pleading Chieftain, the starving peasants, the tortured elders, all watching him helplessly. And he looked, too, once more, into the deep unwavering eyes of the old shaman.

Darkness fell. They all rose; the Chieftain led the way to the edge of the village, accompanied by peasants, elders, and guests. Torches flared throughout the assemblage, like furied spirits. Dogs howled mournfully; the stars seemed far away.

They approached a house-sized boulder, with a small dome-shaped altar cut into it. Shorty walked close beside Indiana, confused and apprehensive.

"Indy, they made our plane crash?" he whispered. "To get you here?"

"It's just superstition, Shorty," he reassured the boy. "Just a ghost story. Don't worry about it."

Short Round wasn't reassured. He knew ghost stories—tales of mountain demons, and ancestral wandering spirits, stories his brothers had told him before the night they disappeared, stories he'd heard on the street after his family was all gone, after they themselves had been stolen away by thunder-goblins. Stories from shadowy alleyways, and the backs of bars. Stories that came to life at night, when the ghosts came out.

Shorty spoke a silent petition to the God of the Door of Ghosts, the deity who kept vagrant spirits from entering our world . . . or allowed them to pass.

When the group reached the carved niche, the shaman made a gesture of devotion. Short Round began climbing up the rockface to look into this primitive shrine—just to be sure there were no ghosts inside that might be a threat to Indy—but Indiana pulled him back down to earth, giving him a cautionary look.

"They took the Sivalinga from here?" Indy asked the Chief.

"Yes."

Indiana examined the little nook. It was empty, but an indentation at its base indicated the conical shape of the stone that once had lain there. The shape was familiar to him. "The stone, was it very smooth?"

"Yes," nodded the shaman.

"It was from the Sacred River?"

"Yes. Brought here long ago, before my father's father."

"With three lines across it." Indy could see it in his mind.

"Yes, that is right."

"Representing the three levels of the universe," Indy went on: the illusion of worldly matter; the reality of transcendental spirit; the oneness of all space, time, and substance. It was potent mythology; it vaunted potent talismans. "I've seen stones like the one you lost. But why would the Maharajah take this Sacred Stone from here?"

Willie was peering into the empty shrine over Indy's shoulder. Shorty held on to her leg.

The shaman spoke fiercely. "They say we must pray to their evil god. We say we will not." Firelight danced in the tearful mist that coated his eyes.

Willie spoke softly. "I don't understand how losing the rock could destroy the village."

The shaman was torn by the fullness of his emotion. He tried to speak, but could not find the words in English. Slowly he talked, in his own language, to give his heart some small measure of ease. "Sive linge nathi unata . . ."

Indy translated softly for the others. *"When the Sacred Stone was taken, the wells dried up. Then the river turned to sand."* He looked back at the shaman. "Idorayak?" he asked, meaning: "Drought?"

"Na!" the shaman denied. "Gos Kolan maha polawa . . ."

And again, Indiana translated the Hindi: *"Our crops were swallowed by the earth, and the animals lay down and turned to dust. One night there was a fire in the fields. The men went out to fight it. When they came back they heard the women crying in the darkness. Lamai."*

"Lamai," echoed Willie, intently following the words on Indy's lips in the light of the torches.

"The children," whispered Indy. "He said they stole their children."

The shaman walked to the edge of the torchlight and stared out into the darkness. Willie wanted to cry. Short Round felt a chill creep into his breast; he moved closer to Indy. Indy had no words.

The shaman gave a weighted sigh, returned to the circle of light, faced Indy. "You will find our children when you find Sivalinga."

Indy had to clear his throat before he could speak. "I'm sorry. But I don't know how I can help you." He didn't want to know. There was something deathly about all this. It felt like the edge of a maelstrom.

The shaman and the Chieftain stared keenly into Indiana's eyes, refusing to accept his denial. Theirs were the eyes of the village, the soul of a crumbling people.

Indy continued to protest. "The English authorities who control this area are the only ones who can help you."

"They do not listen," droned the Chieftain.

"I have friends in Delhi, and I will make sure they investigate this."

"No, you *will* go to Pankot," the shaman charged him. The old man repeated this over several times in his own tongue; with each monotone repetition, Indy felt his resistance dissolving, felt his will reforming in the way the banks of a river will change inexorably under the torrent of the monsoon and be the same river yet altered in its course.

The shaman continued speaking, still in the language of his people.

"What's he saying now?" Willie prompted.

Indy spoke hoarsely. "He says it was destined that I come here. He says I will know evil; evil already sees me here and knows I am coming. This is my destiny, and the future cannot be changed. He says he cannot see this future. It is my journey alone."

Short Round and Willie stared at Indy, in the thrall of the story.

Indy gazed, disturbed, at the shaman, each man dancing in the other man's eyes.

The three companions lay in their hut, trying to sleep, but could not sleep. Images haunted them: disappearing children, animals turning to dust, emptiness incarnate; red flames, black souls.

Indy had explored enough dark regions of the globe to know that every belief system had its own sphere of influence; every magic held sway in the provinces that spawned it. And magic was afoot here, exerting a power over him he could as yet ill define. Still, neither could he put it from his mind. He could only wrestle with it, in the shadows of his half-sleep.

Willie just wanted to leave. She hated this place—the dirt, the hungry farmers, the tense air. It was like just before a tornado, back home. Just before the roof fell in. She wished she could hail a taxi out of here.

Short Round had a bad feeling, a very bad feeling. These people were putting Indy under a spell, binding his spirit so his body would have to follow. Short Round had heard such stories from sailors who'd been to the Philippines or to Haiti; such stories rarely ended well. He would have to be constantly vigilant now, to protect Indy from inner threats as well as outer. He'd have to be more than a bodyguard now; he'd have to be a soul-guard.

Nor was the lady safe, he sensed. Ghosts nibbled her shadow. He could see them from the corner of his eyes; they vanished only if he turned his head to view them straight on. So Short Round would have to watch out for her, too. Otherwise, who would be Indy's wife in America, after they escaped this spooky, barren place?

He invoked Huan-t'ien, the Supreme Lord of the Dark Heaven, who lived in the northern sky and drove away evil spirits. Only after he'd done so could he finally go to sleep.

At last, Indiana, too, slept. In a dream, something came to him.

It came out of darkness, rushing headlong. Terror was at its core; branches tore at its face. Its breathing was heavy under the full moon. The wind moaned it along, it flew through the night out of the night's black nothing into Indy's sweating, sleeping brain. . . .

His eyes opened. What was it? He heard something; he was certain of it. Something running; crashing through the underbrush. Slowly, he sat up, listening.

Short Round and Willie slept near at hand. Something strange was happening, though. Indy sensed it. He stood, went to the door of the hut, walked outside.

The wind was rising; the moon, an ocherous coin. There: a crunch in the bushes over to the left. Indy turned. The branches rustled. Suddenly, out of the undergrowth, a child appeared, running straight toward him.

Indy squatted down; the child fell into his arms, unconscious. It was a boy of seven or eight, emaciated to the point of starvation, dressed in a few shredded rags. His back was marked by the lash.

Indiana called for help, carried the child into his hut, lay him down on the blanket. A few minutes later the elders were all crouched around. Yes, they said, this was a child of their village.

The shaman dripped a wet rag over the boy's forehead and into his mouth, then said a few words of healing. The child's eyes fluttered open. He looked around the room dazedly at all the strange and familiar faces that peered down at him—looked around the room until his gaze fell on Indiana.

The boy's arm moved weakly, lifted up, reached out to Indy and to no one else. Indy took the small hand in his own. He could see that the dark, delicate fingers were cut and bruised; they held something tightly. Gradually the child's fist relaxed; the fingers dropped something into Indy's hand.

The boy tried to whisper. Indiana leaned close to hear as the child's lips moved, almost inaudibly: "Sankara," he said.

His mother ran in; word had quickly reached her that it was her child. She kneeled down, took the boy in her arms, hugged him hard, choked back her sobs. Willie and Short Round looked on, wide-eyed and speechless.

Indy stood, staring at what the little boy had given him. It was a small, tattered piece of cloth, an old fragment of a miniature painting.

And Indiana recognized it.

"Sankara," he murmured.

FOUR

Pankot Palace

DAWN CAME EARLY.

Indy walked briskly across the village, getting last-minute instructions and pleas from the peasants who trotted alongside him to keep up with his pace. At the outskirts of town, two large elephants stood waiting.

Sajnu, the guide, was politely trying to drag Willie toward one of them. She was politely refusing.

"Damn it, Willie, get on! We've got to move out!"

Okay, okay, he's right; this is stupid, she thought. *We've got to go, and this is just a domestic animal. A large, unpredictable, occasionally ferocious, domestic animal. Besides, it's the only ride in town. Okay.* She hadn't gotten to where she'd gotten in life by being a shrinking violet. Then she wondered just where *had* she gotten. Mayapore, India. She didn't want to think about that too long, so she took a deep breath and let Sajnu help her up onto the back of the beast.

"Whoa! Easy, now. Nice elephant," she soothed, sitting rock-still on its shoulders, a cross between absolute self-control and impending terror on her face, her golden dress still in her hands.

Standing by the second elephant, Short Round watched Indy approach. He ran up to the doctor with a scrutable smile all over. "I ride with you, Indy?"

"Nope, you got a little surprise over there, Shorty."

Short Round ran behind the large lead elephant, to see a baby pachyderm being brought in. Just his size! He couldn't believe his incredible luck! What an adventure! What a nifty trunk! What a great pet!

"Oh, boy!" he shouted, and jumped up with a hand from the second guide. He knew just how to do it: he'd learned it all watching *Tarzan*. The elephants in that movie were great friends to Tarzan; so they would be to Short Round.

Jane was also a great friend to Tarzan. Short Round reflected on the ways in which Willie compared to Jane, with respect to men. He hoped Willie did better with Indy than she did with elephants.

Sajnu goaded Willie's animal over toward Short Round. She'd gotten over her initial fears, but was now twisting and shifting all over in a vain effort to find a satisfactory position on the animal's back. When her mount was even with Shorty's, the two guides began leading them out of town.

Willie relaxed enough for a moment to notice the grief-stricken look on many of the villagers' faces. Some even wept. It caught Willie short.

"This is the first time anybody ever cried when I left," she confided to Short Round.

"They don't cry about you," he assured her. "They cry about the elephants leaving." That must be it: they were such great elephants!

"Figures," Willie admitted sullenly.

"They got no food to feed them. So they taking the elephants away to sell them. Indy said so."

Willie heard the third elephant behind her just then, and swiveled completely around on her own creature's back to see Indy lumbering over on his long-tusked bull.

"Willie, stop monkeying around on that thing," he scolded her.

Short Round giggled. "Lady, your brain is backwards. That way China; this way Pankot."

Pankot? she thought.

Indiana called down to Willie's guide: "Sajnu, imanadu."

And Sajnu yelled up at Willie, "Aiyo nona, oya pata nemei!" Then he yelled at her elephant.

"Wait a minute, wait a minute, I'm not comfortable yet," she shouted back. "Indiana, I can't go all the way to Delhi like this."

"We're not going to Delhi," Indiana said more quietly.

"Not going to Delhi!" she shrieked. Panic seized her. "Hey, wait a minute!" She looked down at the villagers in supplication. "Can't somebody take me to Delhi? I don't want to go to Pankot."

"All right, let's go," Indy called down to the guides. "I want to get there before tomorrow night."

Sajnu guided Willie's elephant; the beast lurched forward. The villagers waved at her fondly, and wished her great success, and blessed her for her courage.

"Indiana!" she hollered at the mastermind of this plot. "Damn it, why'd you change your mind? What did that kid tell you last night?"

For the time being, he disregarded her. The elephants moved off through the hordes of pitiful townspeople. In their midst, Indy saw the Chieftain and the old shaman, who brought his hands up to his forehead as the entourage rode past.

The going was slow but steady, bringing the distant hills closer with each passing hour. The countryside remained sparse here, though not nearly so desolate as it had been in the areas immediately surrounding the village. Tall grass became prevalent, along with short, scrubby trees. An occasional small mammal could be seen skittering out of harm's way.

Short Round was constantly discovering new things about his elephant. The fine, fuzzy hair that stuck straight up all over the top of its head was bristly as a blowfish; its skin was coarse everywhere but the underside of its trunk, which was smooth as a cow's udder; and if he scratched the bony knobs above its eyebrow, it would honk the most pleased and funny sound. It told him its name was, coincidentally, Big Short Round.

Willie had come to terms with her brute, in a manner of speaking, although the manner of speaking was too down and dirty to be called exactly the King's English. Nonetheless, they'd reached an uneasy truce, in which the elephant moved the way it wanted to and Willie enumerated all the uses she could think of for elephant glue.

By early afternoon the sun was enormous. They trekked through areas that were increasingly verdant, replete with banyan trees, climbing fig, leafy ground cover, tepid streams. Increasingly muggy, as well.

Willie looked down at herself in disgust. She still wore Indy's baggy formal shirt, now all sticky with heat, filthy with leaves and trail dust; his tuxedo pants, nearly rubbed bare on the seat, it felt like; and his white coat, tied around her waist. How could she have sunk to this level? What had she ever done to hurt anyone? She looked at her sequinned gown, all bunched up in her hands. Just yesterday she'd been a real lady.

She pulled herself together all of a sudden. *Stop it, Willie, stop it, stop it. Being a lady is all a state of mind, and there's no reason on earth why I can't be one right here on this Godforsaken lump of animal.*

She removed a small bottle of expensive French perfume from an inner pocket of her once-beautiful dress. And with great aplomb began to dab it behind her ears.

It soon became evident, however, that she wasn't the only one suffering from this heat. She looked down at the beast between her legs and muttered, "I think you need this more than me." So she leaned forward and, with a sense of her own largesse, dabbed some of the cologne behind the elephant's ears. She had to lean close to reach down there, though; the animal's smell was so overpowering, Willie grimaced, swung around, and dumped half the contents of her bottle over its back.

The elephant was outraged. It brought its trunk back over its head, sniffed the foreign fragrance perfunctorily, and trumpeted in disgust.

Willie looked irked. "What are you complaining about? This is ritzy stuff."

The elephant only moaned, and kept on trudging.

Indy dozed recurrently throughout the day, while Short Round carried on an endless conversation with Big Short Round. By late afternoon, the terrain changed again; they passed into the lower jungles.

The surroundings here were lush, steamy. The canopy hung a hundred feet overhead, so thick that the sun barely sparkled through, making the air itself seem to take on a deep gold-green hue. Huge rubber trees abounded, draped with hanging moss and dangling lianas. Interspersed everywhere were exotic fruit trees, fern trees, palm, and willow.

A path did exist, but it was intermittent. Periodically one of the guides would have to clear away a fallen branch or cut back a tendril.

The place was full of sounds, too. Willie had never heard so many unknown calls: chirps, caws, growls, screams, and clackerings. Some of them gave her goose bumps. Once, something died out there: nothing else could have sounded so. It made her swear under her breath; she held on tighter than she liked to her elephant's rein. Sometimes, she reckoned, it was just plain hard to be a lady.

It was easy, however, to be a little boy. Short Round took in the sights and sounds as if they were all part of a grand new game, designed especially for him. He carried himself alternately like a king or a puppy dog—though he regularly looked over to check on

Indy's whereabouts, never forgetting his first responsibility was still as number-one bodyguard.

There was thunder and lightning for a short time, though no rain came. To Short Round this was a bad portent. It meant Lei-Kung (Lord of Thunders) and Tien-Mu (Mother of Lightnings) were fighting without cause. No good could come of such a quarrel. Lei-Kung was hideous to behold: owl-beaked, with talons on his blue, otherwise human body; he tended to hide in the clouds, beating his drum with a wooden mallet if anyone came near. Tien-Mu made lightning by flashing two mirrors; but when her mood was perverse, she would flash one at Lei-Kung, so he could see his own reflection and be appalled. Then he would beat his drum louder. But there was no rain to issue from the confrontation; only the dry anger of these two Ancient Ones.

Short Round made an invocation to the Celestial Ministry of Thunder and Wind, requesting a higher authority to intervene in the matter, whatever it was.

Ultimately the bickering ceased. Short Round remained cautious, however.

Once, spotting something on an overhanging branch, he stood precariously on the baby elephant's back to reach up and grab it. It was a globular fruit. He plucked it from its twig, then plopped back down onto his mount. He held it snugly between the knuckles of his first two fingers and the ball of his thumb, and gave his wrist a smart twisting motion several times. Lefty Grove.

"You come to America with me and we get job in the circus," he told Big Short. "You like that?" Ever since he'd seen the Charlie Chaplin film about the circus, Short Round had wanted to join.

The junior elephant's trunk curled back, took the fruit from Short Round's hand, and stuck it into its mouth with a joyful little slurp. Short Round understood this to mean that his elephant had appreciated the same movie.

They came to a shallow river. Sajnu called up to Indy; Indy nodded. Sajnu turned and led the procession up the wide, shin-deep stream: Shorty's elephant first, then Indy's, then Willie's. Thirty yards upstream, Shorty heard a strange noise, followed it aloft into the treetops.

"Indy, look!" he shouted.

Indy and Willie both looked up to see hundreds of huge winged creatures flapping across the dusky sky.

"What big birds," Willie commented. How interesting.

Sajnu said something to Indy, and the professor nodded. "Those aren't big birds," he told Willie. "Those are giant bats."

Short Round cringed. He'd seen *Dracula* twice, so he knew what bats could mean.

Willie shuddered too, instinctively crouching lower on her elephant. Unfortunately, this brought her closer (again) than her nose wanted to be. She made a face, mumbling, "Honey, this jungle heat is doing nothing for your allure," and poured the rest of her perfume on its neck.

The effect was instantly gratifying. It was the aroma of civilization; it evoked the memory of cabarets and rich benefactors and beautiful clothes and satin pillows. It made Willie positively glad to be alive, giant bats or no giant bats; and without another thought, she burst into loud, exuberant song:

" 'In olden days a glimpse of stocking was looked on as something shocking; now, heaven knows, anything goes!' "

It took Indy by surprise to hear her singing like that out here. Made him laugh; made him want to sing himself, suddenly, though he hardly knew any songs, and his voice was profoundly unmelodious. Nevertheless, he began to bellow: " 'Oh, give me a home, where the buffalo roam, where the deer and the antelope play.' "

Short Round thought this was hysterical. A singing game in which everyone sang their favorite song as loudly as possible. Instantly he chimed in:

" 'The golden sun is rising, shining in the green forest, shining through the city of Shanghai.' "

And Willie crooned louder: " 'Good authors, too, who once knew better words, now only use four-letter words writing prose, anything goes.' "

" 'Where seldom is heard a discouraging word, and the skies are not cloudy all day.' "

" 'The city of Shanghai, I love the city, I love the sun.' "

" 'The world's gone mad today, and good's bad today, and black's white today, and day's night today.' "

" 'Home, home on the range.' "

Then Shorty joined in with Indy, because he loved that song, too: " 'Where the deer and the antelope play.' "—except he was singing it in Chinese.

And they were all singing at the top of their cacophonous voices, to drown each other out, to celebrate the great good fortune of being alive and singing in this very moment of the universe.

Well, this was the last straw for Willie's elephant. First that horrible alien odor, now this agonizing squawking: the combination was simply intolerable. The animal stopped suddenly, dipped its trunk in the stream through which they were marching, sucked up about twenty gallons of water, curled its trunk backwards over its head, and gave Willie a sustained, pressurized hosing.

She flew off the critter's back, splashing down into the stream with an ignominious thump.

Short Round giggled uproariously, pointing down at her. "Very funny!" he said with glee. "Very funny all wet!"

It was the last straw for Willie as well, though. Like an overtired child slapped for playing too hard, she was caught between rage and tears of frustration. She was wet and dirty and hungry and taxed to the end of her rope, and this was the damn limit.

"I was happy in Shanghai," she seethed, letting her temper rise to its own level. "I had a little house, a garden; my friends were rich; I went to parties and rode in limousines. I hate being outside! I'm a singer; I'm not a camper! I could lose my voice!"

Short Round's eyes grew wide as he watched her. "Lady real mad," he concluded.

Indiana looked around where they were paused, judged the height of the declining sun, the depth of the encroaching gloom, and came to his own conclusion. "I think maybe we'll camp here."

He figured they were probably *all* getting a bit fatigued.

Sunset.

The three elephants submerged, chest deep in a wide spot in the river. Indy waded nearby, his shirt off, splashing water on the weary animals. Sajnu did the same from the other side.

Short Round played laughingly with the baby. The elephant would wrap him in its trunk, swing him in the air, flop him on its back. Then he'd dive in again, and when he resurfaced, the elephant would give him a shower. The two of them were of an age.

Thirty yards upstream, in a shady, recessed alcove, Willie was taking a leisurely swim. She dove to the cool bottom, turned slowly, went limp, resurfaced, wiped her hair from her eyes, backfloated, hummed contentedly, watched the patterns in the leaves overhead. She needed this.

Her life had turned upside down over the past two days. Things had been just peachy until this guy walked into the club, and then. . . . He wasn't so bad, really, she supposed—if you liked the type—but she didn't particularly think she wanted to elevate him to the category of Current Events.

For one thing, he was an academic, which meant, for all intents and purposes, broke. For another thing, although he was obviously infatuated with her, he never said anything nice, never went out of his way to cut her any slack, never empathized with her, and, in general, never acted like a gentleman. A thoroughly selfish, manipulative boor. So what good was he, she wondered.

Well, he *was* nice to the kid. That was one thing. Nobody had ever been nice to *her* when *she* was a kid, and it made her feel good to see this kid treated right. The starving kid in the village last night had really affected him, too; she'd seen that. So, okay, he was good with kids. What else?

Well, he *had* saved her hide when everything had gone to hell in the nightclub, and again in the crashing plane—though if he hadn't come along, it seemed unlikely any of that would have happened in the first place. Or maybe it would have. That's what karma was all about; these Indians loved to talk it to death. So did the Chinese, at some of the parties she used to go to.

Parties. They must be a thousand miles from the nearest party right now. *When every night the set that's smart is intrudin' in nudist parties in studios, anything goes.* His eyes, of course; that was his best feature. She wondered what they *really* looked like, up close.

She dove under again, letting the cool water relax her further, drain all the accumulated tension from her limbs. Oh, well, things would work out; they always did, if she just hung in there.

Imagine, though: a thousand miles away from the nearest pair of stockings.

Indiana wandered up the riverbank in his dripping trousers, checking on Willie, to make sure she was safe.

Not that she wouldn't be, of course. She was a lady with sand; that much was obvious. She'd been around the track, and she didn't always come up smelling like roses, but she always came up. She was just out of her element here, that's all. She was a city girl.

He wouldn't have ridden her so much if he hadn't thought she could take it. But he felt compelled to do it; she was such a royal pain at times. Still, you couldn't exactly blame a person for being a pain if they were so clearly hurting. Only did she have to be so vocal about it? He supposed that's why she was a singer.

Anyway, it was clear she needed to be cared for out here, and the poor thing obviously had a huge crush on him, so he thought he might as well check up on her, just make sure she didn't get carried off by mosquitoes.

He came upon her drying clothes spread out on a tree limb hanging low over the water. A moment later, he saw Willie paddling around just beyond—completely, so to speak, unencumbered. The sight made his mouth go ever so slightly dry.

"Hey, Willie," he called. "I think you better get out now."

His sudden appearance startled her, but she quickly recovered her composure: this was a scenario she'd encountered hundreds of times. "Stark naked?" she said evenly. "You wish."

"C'mon, time to dry off."

"Dry up," she countered. "Dr. Jones, if you're trying to seduce me, this is a very primitive approach."

Try to be a nice guy, and look where it gets you. "Me seduce *you*? Honey, you're the one who took your clothes off." He shrugged with monumental disinterest. "I just came over to remind you that you never know what else might be in that water."

Even though they were out in the middle of nowhere, maybe ten thousand miles from Cole Porter, Willie felt sure this was extremely familiar territory. "Somehow I feel safer in here," she smiled.

"Suit yourself," he said with a gesture of supreme indifference.

He turned and walked back to camp, just the slightest bit miffed.

While she, for all her urbane wit, found herself inexplicably peeved he hadn't stayed longer.

Night came quickly in the forest. The campfire gave a warm, orange light, but immediately outside its friendly glimmer, the shadows were black, enveloping, unyielding.

Sajnu was feeding the elephants; the other guides talked quietly among themselves. Willie, wrapped in a blanket, was wringing out her damp clothing by the fire; in this humid hothouse, it wasn't drying well. She half-intentionally dribbled water on Indy's back as he sat playing poker with Short Round, then took it all over to a peripheral low branch, to hang it out to dry overnight.

Indiana gave a look, but didn't say anything, only continued playing cards.

"What you got?" Short Round asked seriously.

"Two sixes."

"Three aces. I win." The boy grinned. "Two more games. I have all your money."

Shorty discarded; Indy dealt.

Willie looked over from unfolding her clothes along the branch. "Where'd you find your little bodyguard?" she asked Indy.

"I didn't find him. I caught him," Jones replied, picking up his cards.

"What?" she said, repositioning some of the larger pieces.

"His parents were killed when they bombed Shanghai. Shorty's been on the street since the age of four. I caught him trying to pick my pocket."

Willie went for the final piece of clothing on the branch beneath her. She unfolded a giant bat.

She let go with a scream that turned everyone's head except Indy, who simply winced. Leaping back from the flapping, clawing, hissing bat, she turned into a large fern, only to come face to face with a vicious baboon. Its snout was pink and purple; it snarled malevolently at Willie's intrusion.

She shrieked again, scaring the baboon off—and backed directly into a dark rock on which a large iguana perched. It snapped at her.

Short Round wasn't particularly worried, once the bat flew away—though he did offer a dollar (on account) to the God of the Door of Ghosts once more, as well as to Dr. Van Helsing and all the other guardians against Dracula.

Willie, unfortunately, had no such spiritual protectors. All she had were her worst suspicions about the Great Outdoors being confirmed.

In the ensuing frenzy, Indiana accidentally dealt himself a fourth card. Short Round noticed the misdeal and started doing a slow burn.

Willie began a frenetic, exhaustive examination of the environs of the campsite, punctuated by numerous squeals and yelps.

"The trouble with her," Indy grumbled, "is the noise." He tried to concentrate on his cards.

"I take two," Short Round said guardedly.

Indy nodded. "Three for me."

"Hey, you take four," Shorty protested.

"No, I did not take four." Indy was indignant.

"Dr. Jones cheat," he accused.

"I didn't take any but I think you stole a card," Indy countered.

Willie whooped at another rustling. She kicked an empty bush.

"You owe me ten cents," Shorty demanded. "You pay money. You pay now."

Indy disgustedly threw down his cards. "I don't want to play anymore."

"Me neither."

"And I'm *not* teaching you anymore."

"I don't care. You cheat. I quit." He picked up the cards and stalked off, muttering in Chinese.

Willie backed her way over to Indiana, still sitting by the fire. She was looking wildly in all directions. "We're completely surrounded!" she choked. "This whole place is crawling with living things." She shivered.

"That's why it's called the jungle," he said drolly.

"What else is out there?" she whispered.

He looked at her, smiled. *Willie.* That was a funny name. He let it roll off his tongue. "Willie. Willie. Is that short for something?"

She stiffened a bit; she would not be ridiculed. "Willie is my professional name—Indiana." She put the emphasis on the *ana*.

Short Round, still sulking near his elephant, came to Indy's defense. "Hey, lady, you call him *Dr. Jones*." She was getting a little too familiar for someone Short Round had not yet officially sanctioned to be the object of Indy's courtship.

Willie and Indy both smiled. He flicked a dime over to Shorty, to make peace, then watched Willie again. "That's *my* professional name." He turned a little toward her. "So how'd you end up in Shanghai?"

"My singing career got run over by the Depression," she moped. "Some big ape convinced me a girl could go places in the Orient."

He spread out a blanket near the fire, lay down on it. "Show business, eh? Any other ambitions?"

A terrible scream issued from the jungle. Feral, deathly. Willie tightened, drew closer to the blaze.

"Staying alive till morning," she groaned.

"And after that?"

She smiled inwardly. "I'm going to latch onto a good-looking, incredibly rich prince."

"I'd like to dig up one of those myself," he agreed. "Maybe we do have something in common."

"Huh?"

"I like my princes rich and dead, and buried for a couple of thousand years. Fortune and glory. You know what I mean." He began carefully unfolding a piece of cloth he'd removed from his pocket—the fragment the child had given him last night in Mayapore.

Willie sat beside him, staring at it. "Is that why you're dragging us off to this deserted palace? Fortune and glory?"

He showed her the relic. "This is a piece of an old manuscript. This pictograph represents Sankara, a priest. It's hundreds of years old. Gently, gently."

She took it from him to inspect more closely. It was a crude rendering, painted in faded reds, golds, blues. It was fascinating.

Willie touched its history, its arcane wisdom. Shorty wandered over to look, too; they were both getting genuinely interested, affected by Indy's tone of reverence. It even drew the baby elephant's attention; he sidled over beside Willie, placing his trunk on her shoulder.

She jumped, then brushed the trunk away impatiently, returning her attention to the pictograph. "Is this some kind of writing?"

"Yeah, it's Sanskrit," said Indy. "It's part of the legend of Sankara. He climbs Mount Kalisa, where he meets Shiva, the Hindu god."

The elephant hung its trunk on Willie's shoulder again; again, she swatted it off. "Cut it out," she snapped. Then to Indy, "That's Shiva, huh? So what's he handing the priest?"

"Rocks. He told him to go forth and combat the evil, and to help him, he gave him five sacred stones that had magical properties."

The elephant nudged Willie again. Her patience was fast running out. "Magic rocks. My grandfather spent his entire life with a rabbit in his pocket and pigeons up his sleeves, and made a lot of children happy, and died a very poor man. Magic rocks. Fortune and glory. Good night, Dr. Jones." She handed him back the cloth and walked to the edge of the clearing, where she put down her blanket.

"Where are you going?" asked Indy. "I'd sleep closer. For safety's sake." He watched her with mixed feelings. She was starting to get under his skin. He tried not looking at her, but that somehow made things worse.

Willie likewise refused to return his glance. Couldn't he be honest about his feelings, for crying out loud? She just didn't trust men who weren't straightforward about what they wanted. "Dr. Jones, I think I'd be safer sleeping with a snake."

At that moment, a giant python descended from the tree behind her; it curled over her shoulder. Short Round was aghast. Indy was more than that: Indy was frozen-stone-petrified of snakes. He didn't know why, he didn't care why. He only knew that of all the creatures that ever existed, might exist, or would never exist, snakes alone made him sweat bullets, shiver, want to run.

Willie, however, thought this was still the baby elephant. Losing all patience, she reached up behind her without looking, grabbed the snake by the neck, and hurled it backwards. "I said, cut it out!"

Indy inched a slow retreat, staring, sweating. Willie bent over to straighten her blanket. The snake slithered away.

"I hate this jungle," Willie muttered. "I hate that elephant. I hate these accommodations."

Nearby, unseen, a Bengal tiger cut a silent path through the thicket and was gone. Indy sat on a rock for a few seconds, took a couple of deep breaths; then got up and started loading more wood on the fire.

A lot more wood.

They broke camp early the next morning, to try to make time before the heat of the day. Tropical winds rippled the uppermost vines as the elephants plowed on through the thick of it. The air was teeming with sounds of animal life, though it didn't seem nearly so ominous now that night had lifted. It reminded Willie of a large, poorly kept zoo.

Short Round was back to conversing with Big Short Round, increasingly convinced that the spirit of his lost brother Chu, snagged on the Wheel of Transmigration, had been deposited in the body of this large baby. For one thing, Chu had himself been of the rotund persuasion, a proclivity well invested in an incarnation like the elephant; for another, Chu was always in excellent good humor, as was this beast. Lastly, Chu's nickname had been Buddha, not only for his portliness and disposition, but because of the substantial size of his earlobes—and of course the size of the young elephant's ears need hardly be mentioned.

So Short Round discussed things with Big Short Round that only Chu could have understood or cared about—family matters, certain toys of disputed ownership, apologies for long-dormant squabbles over such heated concerns as whether Jimmy Foxx or Lou Gehrig was the stronger clean-up batter—and to Shorty's great relief, the elephant put his mind at ease on all of these issues.

They were just on to New Business, speculating about all the things they would see in America when they joined the circus together, when they came over a rise, and saw, far in the distance, the palace.

Resplendent, almost iridescent white alabaster, it perched on the carpeted jungle crest like a carved pearl on a sea of green jade.

"Indy, look!" gasped Short Round.

"That's Pankot," he nodded.

They all stared in silence a full minute; then headed on.

It was well after lunchtime before they reached the base of the foothills that rose finally to the palace. They were about to enter the first low pass when Sajnu stopped the elephants with a command and ran forward.

"Navath thana." His voice held fear.

Indy jumped down off his mount and walked ahead to join the guide. As he approached, he could see that Sajnu was staring at something, chattering frantically: "Winasayak. Maha winasayak." *A calamity, a great calamity.*

Indy tapped him on the shoulder; he ran back to the other guides, gibbering away. Indy now saw what had affected him so.

It was a small statue guarding the path, a goddess with eight arms. A malign deity, wearing a carved necklace of small human heads. Each of her hands dangled another head by the hair. She scowled demonically.

It was further adorned with ritual objects: leaves, dead birds, rodents, turtles. Around its waist was a bandolier of real, pierced human fingers.

Indy walked back to the group as Willie and Short Round were dismounting.

"Why are we stopping here?" asked Willie.

"What you look at, Indy?" said Short Round. Some treasure, maybe, for Chao-pao to discover.

Indy was talking to the agitated guides, though. Sajnu just kept shaking his head, turning the elephants around. "Aney behe mahattaya," he was saying. The guides began quickly driving the elephants away.

This rather distressed Willie. She ran after them a few steps, shouting. "No, no, no! Indy, they're stealing our rides!"

"From here on, we walk," said Indy. It was no use forcing natives to go where they were afraid to go; inevitably, things got worse.

"No!" she pouted. After all that aggravation yesterday, she was just starting to get used to the big ugly brutes.

Short Round watched the elephants trudging away. His big round friend turned its head to look back.

"Baby elephant!" Shorty called out. Could it be that after all these years, his beloved brother Chu had returned, only to stay for two days, then leave again? Wait! No fair! What about the circus?

But maybe he'd just come back to straighten out the differences between them that had been left unresolved years before in Shanghai. Maybe now that everything was settled amicably, it was time for Chu to leave again. This was hard for Short Round to accept, or even fathom, but it seemed to be so. For wasn't the reborn Chu smiling now as he bid farewell?

Short Round waved at the lost, found soul. His little pal trumpeted, and flapped his ears, and waved his trunk and lumbered off. Short Round tried very hard not to cry.

Indy walked back up to the idol. He studied it closely.

Short Round called up to him. "Dr. Jones, what you looking at?" Treasure was small consolation for a twice-lost brother, but it was some.

"Don't come up here," Indy called back. He didn't want them

to see this, especially Short Round. It was a wicked totem, full of occult power. At best, it would cause horrible dreams; at worst . . .

Indy didn't think it served any purpose to expose Short Round to such depravity—or to expose Willie, for that matter, for he was beginning to feel a bit protective toward her, as well.

He stood and returned to his waiting friends. "We'll walk from here."

By late afternoon they came to a rock-paved road that ran along a high stone wall. Willie limped along a few yards behind the others, carrying her high heels, sweating, disheveled, grumbling, ". . . shot at, fallen out of a plane, nearly drowned, chomped at by an iguana, attacked by a bat; I smell like an elephant . . ." Suddenly, feeling as though she couldn't take another step, she shouted at their backs: "I tell you, I'm not going to make it!"

Indiana stopped, walked back to Willie, was about to make a comment—something pithy, or sarcastic, or pointed—when, as in the first moment they'd met, their eyes came together. Something he saw there—lost, quiet at the end of the noise—stopped him. And something *she* saw, at least momentarily, brought her quiet to the surface.

Without a word, he picked her up in his arms, started carrying her the remaining distance. She was surprised, and puzzled—though not displeased.

"Any more complaints?" Indiana asked.

She smiled faintly. "Yeah. I wish you'd thought of this sooner." It didn't feel so bad at all.

Short Round rolled his eyes to the heavens. He'd seen Gable do that in *It Happened One Night*. He thought it was dumb in the movie; he thought it was dumb now.

Indy carried her all the way up the road along the wall, until they reached the large front gate. Here he put her down, gently smoothed her collar back in place. "Well, no permanent damage." He smiled.

She straightened herself, turned around, and for the first time saw Pankot Palace up close. She whistled.

It was magnificent, sprawling. An extravagant mixture of Moghul and Rajput styles, it reflected the dying sun with a bloody, opalescent hue.

The three travelers started slowly across a marble bridge toward the main entrance.

FIVE

The Surprise in the Bedroom

PALACE GUARDS stood lining the bridge along both sides.

Bearded, black-turbaned, and beribboned, with scimitars in their belts and lances at their sides, they snapped to attention in sequence as the threesome passed. It made Willie jump at first, but she quickly grew to enjoy the attention. Her carriage improved; she assumed an air of grace appropriate to someone of her stature. She only wished she'd thought to put on her shoes before she'd come in.

They passed under a dark archway, into a glittering courtyard. Quartz and marble walls, lapis lazuli minarets, arching windows with gilt facades . . . like an opulent mausoleum. And just as deserted.

"Hello?" shouted Indy. His voice echoed from the somewhat foreboding walls.

Three enormous Rajput guards appeared silently at the opposite side of the courtyards. They did not look as deferential as the first platoon.

"Hi," Willie said to them, placating. The only response was her own echo.

A few moments later, between the guards, down the marble

steps of the expansive entryway, stepped a tall, bespectacled, severe-looking Indian man dressed in a white English suit. He looked courteously, but suspiciously, at the woozy beauty dressed in a man's wrinkled tuxedo who carried her shoes and gown; the dirty Chinese boy wearing the American baseball cap; the Caucasian ruffian with a squint and a bullwhip.

His name was Chattar Lal.

He walked forward with a bureaucrat's briskness, to appraise the visitors more closely. Their appearance did not improve with proximity. "I would say you look rather lost." He smiled disdainfully. "But then I cannot imagine where in the world the three of you would look at home."

Indiana smiled his best, even, I'm-right-where-I-should-be-no-matter-where-I-am, American smile. "Lost? No, we're not lost. We're on our way to Delhi. This is Miss Scott, and this is Mr. Round. My name is Indiana Jones."

Chattar Lal was taken aback. "*Dr.* Jones? The eminent archaeologist?"

Willie sneered without rancor. "Hard to believe, isn't it?"

Chattar Lal went on. "I remember first hearing your name when I was studying at Oxford. I am Chattar Lal, Prime Minister for His Highness the Maharajah of Pankot." He bowed to do them honor. "Welcome to Pankot Palace."

He accompanied them through the central foyer, down pillared marble halls, past dazzling interiors, inlaid with mirror and semi-precious stones, ivory fountains, intricate tapestries.

Willie gazed in awe at the ornate splendor. Down the next corridor they passed the portraits, hanging chronologically, of the Pankot Princes. The faces were variously dissipated, elegant, evil, vapid, aged, ageless.

Willie whispered to Short Round as they went by each one. "How'd you like to run into *him* in a dark alley? That one's kind of cute. I could see myself married to a prince like that. Princess Willie."

Ahead of them, Chattar Lal questioned Indy in a tone midway between curiosity and mistrust. "The plane crash and your journey here sound . . . most incredible."

Willie heard that. "You should've been there," she cracked.

Indy sounded earnest. "We'd appreciate it if the Maharajah would let us stay tonight. We'll be on our way in the morning." Right after a little covert inspection tour.

"I am only his humble servant"—Chattar Lal bent his head obsequiously—"but the Maharajah usually listens to my advice."

"Is that him?" Willie asked. They'd come to the last picture in the row of portraits that lined the wall. Willie stopped and stared in frank disappointment at the immensely corpulent, aged Rajput prince. "He's not exactly what we call a spring chicken," she sighed.

"No, no," advised Chattar Lal, "that is Shafi Singh, the present Maharajah's late father."

"Oh, good," Willie brightened up some. "And maybe the present Maharajah is a little *younger*? And thinner?"

Two female servants materialized from a side door and bowed.

Chattar Lal nodded to Willie. "They will escort you to your rooms now. You will be provided with fresh clothes. Tonight you will be dining with His Highness."

"Dinner?" beamed Willie. "And with a prince? Hey, my luck is changing." Until she caught sight of herself in a piece of decorative mirror. "But look at me. Oh, my God, I've got to get ready." To hook a prince, the correct bait was essential. She hurried off with one of the servants.

To Indiana, Chattar Lal offered a cool smile. "Eight o'clock in the Pleasure Pavilion, Dr. Jones."

They both bowed, each less deeply than the other.

An extraordinary golden dome rose above elaborate gardens. The night air was perfumed with jasmine, hyacinth, coriander, rose.

The strains of sitar, tambour, and flute wafted on the torchlit breeze. The Pleasure Pavilion was aglow.

Rich court ministers and Indian merchants, decked out in their formal Rajput finery, mingled on the paths, trading innuendo and promise of booty for court favor and imagined privilege. Into this net of palace intrigue strode Indiana Jones with his bodyguard, Short Round.

Indy wore his traditional professorial raiment: tweed jacket, bow tie, round eyeglasses; his pants and shirt had been freshly cleaned by palace servants. He'd decided to keep his three-day growth of beard intact: he wanted to look rough and ready to this weird Prime Minister—and besides, he didn't want Willie to think he was trying to impress her. Short Round, too, was clean, though he'd refused to change clothes or remove his cap.

"Look around, Shorty," said Indiana. "You like to have a place like this someday?"

"Sure," said Short Round.

"Wrong," said Indy. "It's beautiful, okay, but it reeks of corruption. Smell it?"

Short Round sniffed the air. "I . . . think so." There *was* a peculiar pungence to the air, like a too-sweet incense.

"Attaboy," nodded Indy. The kid had enough disadvantages without hooking him on this kind of wealth. "It looks good. I'll admit that. And it might be a nice place to visit, but you wouldn't want to live here."

"I live in America," Short Round agreed.

"Take that carved ivory sundial, over there, for example." He wished he *could* take it, all the way back to the university—it was a prime specimen of Tamil craftwork—but that wasn't the point he was trying to make. "It was clearly stolen from a different kingdom, purely for the aggrandizement of this palace."

Short Round nodded. "Just like us: they find new home for things."

Indy cleared his throat. "I don't think exactly just like us, Shorty."

Short Round was momentarily confused, but then he thought he saw what Indy was getting at. "Ah: these mans can't spell!"

"Right," said Indy. He decided to leave it at that, for the time being. "They can't spell."

"I think they know numbers pretty good, though," Short Round figured; anybody this rich had to at least be able to count money.

Indy smiled at his pal. "You got good eyes, kid."

They let their good eyes wander over the porcelain tiles, jade facades, fluted pillars.

As the hangers-on and functionaries began filing in, Chattar Lal approached. With him was a British cavalry captain, in full regalia.

Chattar Lal made the introductions. "We are fortunate tonight to have so many *unexpected* guests. This is Captain Phillip Blumburtt."

Blumburtt bowed to Shorty and Indiana. He was a proper gentleman, perhaps sixty, mustachioed, balding, wearing four medals across the chest of his dress uniform.

Indy shook his head. "Hello. I saw your troops come in at sunset."

"Just a routine inspection tour," he assured them all politely.

"The British worry so about their Empire." Chattar Lal tried to sound warm.

"Looks like you've got a pretty nice little empire here to worry about," smiled Indy.

As the four of them stood there admiring the architecture, Willie entered the gardens from a separate path. Indiana admired her architecture as well.

She looked stunning. Washed and made-up, she'd been lent a royal bone-colored silk sari, slightly westernized with a low V neckline and brocade borders. In her hair draped a diamond-and-pearl tiara; golden hoop earrings set off her face; an ornate gem-studded necklace sat, dazzling, across her chest; over her head was the finest silk veil.

It was truly a transformation.

"You look like a princess," said Indy.

As far as she could remember, this was the first nice thing he'd ever said to her. She nearly blushed.

Blumburtt and Lal made similarly complimentary remarks. The Prime Minister then noted that the dinner would soon begin, and led the way toward the dining hall. Willie was about to accompany him when Indy held her back a few steps.

"Don't look *too* anxious," he advised. "Your mouth is watering."

"I think it *is* sort of like being in heaven," she confessed. "Imagine, a real prince. My best before this was a provincial duke."

They crossed the gardens to the inner pavilion, Willie on Indy's arm. Her eyes were like a kid's at Christmas.

Short Round lagged several paces behind just to watch them. Lovely, stately, devoted, charmed. They were his idealized parents, at that moment, and he their faithful son. Pausing briefly, he sent off a simple prayer to his favorite stellar divinities—the Star of Happiness, the Star of Dignities, the Star of Longevity—asking that this moment be noted in the Celestial Archives so it could be later reproduced upon request.

Prayer finished, he caught up with them at a trot, falling quickly into step.

They entered the dining hall. Massive granite columns supported the rococo ceiling. Alabaster horses danced in bas-relief along the walls. The floor was marble and ebony. Crystal chandeliers refracted candlelight to every corner. In the center of the room a long, low table had place settings for twenty, marked by solid gold plates and cups. Bejeweled guards stood at rigid attention beside the doorway. Indy and company walked in.

Off to the side, drums and strings wove an exotic melody as a sparsely dressed dancing girl spun to the ecstasy of her muse. Indiana gave her the once-over, smiling appreciatively. "I've always had a weakness for folk dancing."

Willie nodded to the dancer, half-snide, half-encouraging. "Keep hoofin', kid; look where it got me." She gave Jones a disparaging glance, then quickened her stride to catch up to the Prime Minister. "Oh, Mr. Lal." Willie affected her most conversational tone. "What do you call the Maharajah's wife?"

"His Highness has not yet taken a wife," Chattar Lal demurred.

Willie beamed. "No? Well, I guess he just hasn't met the right woman."

As Willie entered into more intricate levels of small talk with the Prime Minister, Indiana wandered over to a far wall where numerous bronze statues and outré devotional objects were on display. One strange clay figurine attracted his attention right away. He picked it up to examine it as Blumburtt walked over to join him.

Blumburtt grimaced when he saw the small, strange doll. "Charming. What is it?"

"It's called a Krtya," said Indy. "It's like the voodoo dolls of West Africa. The Krtya represents your enemy—and gives you complete power over him."

"Lot of mumbo jumbo," Blumburtt blustered.

Indiana took an even tone. "You British think you rule India. You don't, though. The old gods still do." He'd had a sense of that when he saw the little statue that guarded the path to the palace. This Krtya doll only reinforced his impression.

Blumburtt looked sour. Indy put down the doll. Willie ran over, all excited from her chat with the Prime Minister.

"You know, the Maharajah is positively *swimming* in money." She flushed. "Maybe coming here wasn't such a bad idea after all."

Blumburtt arched his eyebrows at her with the gravest sort of misgivings. Indy merely smiled.

A drum boomed sonorously from the musicians' dais.

"I believe we're being called to dinner," Captain Blumburtt said, showing some relief.

"Finally!" Willie exclaimed. Blumburtt moved to separate himself from these people as quickly as possible.

Indiana took Willie's arm, and escorted her to the table.

As the drum continued beating, the assembled guests took their places standing beside floor pillows that surrounded the low banquet table. Only the head of the table remained empty. Indiana was placed to its right, beside Captain Blumburtt; Willie and Shorty stood opposite them, to the left of the seat of honor.

Chattar Lal strolled over to the corner, near Willie, clapped his hands twice, and made an announcement, first in Hindi, then in English: "His Supreme Highness, guardian of Rajput tradition, the Maharajah of Pankot, Zalim Singh."

All eyes focused on two detailed, solid silver doors that were closed some ten feet behind the Prime Minister. At once, the doors opened; across the threshold strode the Maharajah Zalim Singh. Everyone in the room bowed.

Indy saw Willie looking up from her obeisant position; saw her jaw literally fall open. He looked from her face to that of the entering monarch: Zalim Singh was only thirteen years old.

"That's the Maharajah?" she whispered. "That kid?" Never had disappointment weighed more heavily on a human face.

"Maybe he likes older women," suggested Indy.

Zalim Singh walked to the head of the table. He was outfitted in a long robe of gold and silver brocade, festooned with diamonds, rubies, emeralds, pearls. His turban was similarly jewel-encrusted, topped with a diadem in the shape of a spraying fountain. He was further adorned with earrings, finger rings, toe rings. His face had that pre-adolescent delicate softness about it: no wrinkles, no hair, puffed out to the barest sulk by the last vestiges of baby fat. Actually he looked quite feminine. And actually quite beautiful.

He gazed imperiously at the crowd . . . until his gaze fell upon Short Round. Short Round was not bowing.

Short Round was standing there in his baseball cap, chewing gum, glaring antagonistically at this kid who seemed to think he was some kind of bigshot.

Natural enemies.

Indy sent Short Round a withering look across the table, and though Shorty did *not* wither, he *did* bow. But he was bowing for Indy, he told himself, not for this haughty wimp.

The Maharajah finally sat down on his golden pillow. At a nod, the guests took their seats on the floor, reclining against cushions of their own.

Indy smiled sympathetically at Willie, her dreams of monarchy evaporated. "Cheer up," he consoled her. "You lost your prince, but dinner's on the way."

It was just what she needed to hear. Her crestfallen features became salivary. "I've never been so hungry in all my life."

Servants appeared with silver platters of steaming food. Willie closed her eyes a moment, savoring the aromas that filled her nostrils. When she opened them again, the first course sat before her: an entire roasted boar, arrows piercing its back and bloated stomach, tiny fetal boars impaled on the shafts, a rafter of broiled baby boars suckling on their well-cooked mother's teats.

Willie grimaced in amazement. "My God, it's sort of gruesome, isn't it?"

Indiana furrowed his brow. It seemed rather odd, at best. Hindus didn't eat meat. He glanced at Blumburtt, who seemed equally puzzled. Willie continued to stare at her food.

The young Maharajah leaned over to whisper something to Chattar Lal, on his left. The Prime Minister nodded, and addressed the group.

"His Highness wants me to welcome his visitors. Especially the renowned Dr. Jones from America."

Indy tipped his head slightly toward the little prince. "We are honored to be here."

A small pet monkey jumped up on Short Round's shoulder, stole a flower off the plate, chattered gaily. Short Round giggled. The monkey took his cap; he took it back. They shook hands, whispered secrets, played with the flower petals, like rowdy siblings at a family affair.

Willie just kept staring at the roast boar, skewered on its own children.

Indiana conversed neutrally with Chattar Lal. "I had a question, Mr. Prime Minister. I was examining some of the Maharajah's artifacts—"

"A fine collection of very old pieces, don't you think?"

"I'm not sure all the pieces are that old. Some were carved recently, I think. They look like images used by the Thuggees to worship the goddess Kali."

At the mention of the word *Thuggee*, the entire table quieted. As if a taboo had been broken, or some inexcusable social transgression committed, all the Indians stared at Jones.

Chattar Lal made an effort to be civil, though his manner was cold. "That is not possible, Dr. Jones."

"Well, I seem to remember that this province, perhaps this area, was a center of activity for the Thuggee." He seemed to have hit a nerve. From the reaction generated, he sensed it would be a useful line to pursue.

Blumburtt entered the conversation now. "Oh, the Thuggee. Marvelous brutes. Went about strangling travelers. Come to think of it, it *was* in this province. Brought to an end by a British serving officer, a major—"

"Sleeman," interjected Indiana. "Major William Sleeman."

"That's the fellow," Blumburtt concurred.

"He actually penetrated the cult and apprehended its leaders," Indy went on. "1830, I believe. Courageous man."

"You have a marvelous recall of past events." Chattar Lal spoke with growing interest.

"It's my trade," acknowledged Indy.

"Dr. Jones," the Prime Minister pressed, "you know very well that the Thuggee cult has been dead for nearly a century."

Blumburtt agreed. "Of course they have. The Thuggees were

an obscenity that worshipped Kali with human sacrifices. The British army did away with them nicely."

A second platter was placed on the table by servants: steaming poached boa constrictor, with a garnish of fried ants. One of the servants slit the huge snake down the middle, exposing a mass of squirming, live baby eels inside.

Willie turned quite pale.

The merchant to her left chortled with satisfaction. "Ah! Snake Surprise!"

"What's the surprise?" Willie drooped. She was distinctly less hungry than she had been.

Indiana was pressing his dialogue with Chattar Lal. "I suppose stories of the Thuggees die hard." Especially when they had some basis for being perpetuated.

"There are *no* stories anymore." The Prime Minister begged to differ.

"Well, I don't know about that." Indy shook his head pleasantly. "We came here from a small village, and the peasants there told us that the Pankot Palace was growing powerful again, because of some ancient evil."

"These stories are just fear and folklore," Lal sneered.

"But then," Indy continued, "as I approached the palace, I found a small shrine. It contained a statue of the goddess Kali, the goddess of death, destruction, and chaos."

Zalim Singh and his prime minister exchanged a glance. Indiana noted the exchange. Chattar Lal composed himself before answering. "Ah, yes. We played there as children. My father always warned me not to let Kali take my Atman, or soul, as you say. But I remember no evil. I only recall the luxury of being young. And the love of my family and pets. Village rumors, Dr. Jones. They're just fear and folklore. You're beginning to worry Captain Blumburtt, I expect." His face was a mask.

"Not worried, Mr. Prime Minister," denied the jovial Blumburtt. "Just interested."

Short Round went back to playing with his little monkey friend. He didn't like this scary conversation. He hoped Huan-t'ien, Supreme Lord of the Dark Heaven, was keeping an eye on things down here.

But as if the talk weren't bad enough for Willie—human sacrifices, indeed—this food was unbelievable. And just when she was wondering about eating a flower, she looked up to see a servant lean over her shoulder and place a six-inch-long baked black beetle on her plate.

She whimpered quietly as she watched the fat merchant next to her lift a similar shiny, giant, grotesque insect off his dish and crack it in two. At which point he enthusiastically sucked the gooey innards out.

Willie turned even paler. Shimmering lights wiggled in her vision.

The merchant looked at her dubiously. "But you're not eating!"

She smiled weakly. "I, uh, had bugs for lunch." Always be polite when dining with a Maharajah.

Meanwhile, the uneasy banter continued near the head of the table.

"You know," Indiana was saying, "the villagers also claimed that Pankot Palace took something from them."

"Dr. Jones." Chattar Lal's voice had become thick. "In our country a guest does not usually insult his host."

"Sorry," said Indiana. "I thought we were just talking about folklore." He kept his tone innocent, conversational, but his insinuations were clear to the people who feared them.

"What was it they claimed was stolen?" asked Blumburtt officiously. Thievery: now that was a different matter; that fell squarely within his purview.

"A sacred rock," said Indiana.

"Ha!" barked the Prime Minister. "There, you see, Captain—a rock!"

They all laughed uncomfortably.

Willie could concentrate only on the sight and sound of a dozen dinner guests breaking open these horrible mammoth beetles, then sucking out the insides. She leaned over to Short Round, who was teaching baseball signs to the monkey.

"Give me your hat," she rasped.

"What for?" he asked suspiciously.

"I'm going to puke in it."

A servant came forward to her side to offer assistance. Willie smiled at him as well as she could; she was nothing if not a trouper. "Listen, do you have something, you know, simple—like soup, or something?"

The servant bowed, left, and returned almost immediately with a covered bowl. He placed it in front of her, removed the cover. It was soup. Some kind of chicken base, it smelled like. With a dozen eyeballs floating in it.

The merchant nodded approvingly at Willie's choice. "Looks delicious!" he exclaimed.

Tears began to run down Willie's cheeks.

Indiana was still pushing Chattar Lal. "I was dubious myself, at first. Then something connected: the village's rock and the old legend of the Sankara Stone."

Chattar Lal was obviously having difficulty controlling his anger. "Dr. Jones, we are all vulnerable to vicious rumors. I seem to remember that in Honduras you were accused of being a graverobber rather than an archaeologist."

Indy shrugged. "The newspapers exaggerated the incident."

"And didn't the Sultan of Madagascar threaten to cut your head off if you ever returned to his country?" Chattar Lal suggested.

Indy remembered the Sultan well. "It wasn't my head," he mumbled.

"Then your *hands*, perhaps." By the gleam in his eye it seemed clear that the Prime Minister knew precisely what body parts had been threatened with extinction.

"No, not my hand," Indy backed off, a bit embarrassed. "It was my . . . it was my misunderstanding."

"Exactly what we have here, Dr. Jones." Lal sat back with a smile. "A misunderstanding."

The Maharajah suddenly coughed and, for the first time, spoke. "I have heard the terrible stories of the evil Thuggee cult."

His words silenced the table, as if it were a great surprise for him to offer an opinion about anything.

"I thought the stories were told to frighten children," he went on. "Later, I learned that the Thuggee cult was once real, and did unspeakable things." He looked hard at Indiana. "I am ashamed of what happened here so many years ago. We keep these objects—these dolls and idols—to remind us that this will never again happen in my kingdom." His voice had risen by the end; a fine sweat lined his upper lip.

The room was hushed.

"Have I offended?" Indiana finally said quietly. "Then I am sorry."

The room breathed again. Servants whisked away the old plates and brought in the new. Conversation resumed. Indy felt both more informed and more ignorant about the situation here.

"Ah," said the obese merchant beside Willie, "dessert!"

Short Round's monkey suddenly screeched and tore off through an open window. Willie closed her eyes: she would not look, it would be too gross, she didn't need this. She heard silverware clattering, though, and people digging in. Ultimately, curiosity prevailed, in conjunction with general lightheadedness; she opened her eyes.

It was instantly too late, though. She couldn't not see what she saw, and it was infinitely worse than she'd imagined.

Plates full of dead monkey heads.

The tops of the skulls had been cut off, and sat loose, like little lids, atop the scowling heads. Each plate sat on a small serving pedestal down which the long white monkey hair dangled from the little scalps.

Short Round looked shocked. Even Indy and Captain Blumburtt seemed somewhat unsettled, unsure.

Willie watched in utter dismay as the Maharajah and his guests removed the skull tops and began dipping small golden spoons into what was inside.

"Chilled monkey brains!" The merchant beside her could scarcely contain his delight.

Willie could scarcely contain anything else. So she dealt with the situation as honorably as she could, and fainted dead away.

"Rather bizarre menu, wouldn't you say?" Blumburtt remarked to Indiana as they strolled out of the pavilion, through the gardens. Short Round walked alongside. Hundreds of lanterns illuminated the after-dinner hour; the scent of the hookah mingled with the natural fragrances of the garden.

"Even if they were trying to scare us away, a devout Hindu would never touch meat," Indiana nodded. "Makes you wonder what these people are."

"Well," gruffed Blumburtt, "I hardly think they were trying to scare us."

Indy made a noncommittal expression. "Maybe not."

"Well, I must be off. Retire the troops and all that. Terribly nice to have met you, Doctor."

"Same here, Captain."

They shook hands once more; Blumburtt retreated.

Indy looked down at Shorty. "C'mon," he said. "Let's see what we can come up with."

They made their way around to the kitchen. Indy firmly believed that if you *really* wanted to learn something about a place, you talked to the servants.

A dozen people were back there cleaning up, washing dishes, putting things away. Indy spoke to the man who looked like the cook, but the man remained silent. Indy switched dialects. No response. He approached several others, all with the same results.

He saw a bowl of fruit on a sideboard, picked it up, asked if he could eat some. No one seemed to care.

"See, Shorty, it's just like I always say, you want to know about a household, you ask the help."

Short Round yawned.

Indy seconded the motion.

One young lady did look like she was winking at Indy—at least that's what he thought—but an older man immediately ushered her from the room. She left with a motion that Indy seconded even more heartily, a certain subtle motion of the hips that gave him a sudden wistful pang for a certain lady-in-waiting who was recently occupying a few of his thoughts.

He looked at the dour servants bustling about; he looked at the fruit bowl on the table; he looked at Shorty, dozing upright. He decided they *all* needed to relax a little.

Five minutes later, they were walking down the shadowy corridor to their bedroom. Short Round carried a covered plate, and yawned every ten seconds.

Indy patted him on the head, took the plate from him, stopped at their bedroom door. "Umm, I think I'd better check on Willie," he told the boy.

"That's all you better do," Shorty joked. He backed into their room as Indy continued on down the hall; then whispered loudly: "Tell me later what happen."

Indy stopped short. "Amscray," he ordered. Shorty shut the door.

But he opened it a crack, just to watch, just for a minute. This was the beginning of the big love scene, after all, a union with potentially grave import for Short Round.

Just like the great Babe Ruth, Indy was about to score a home run—if he didn't strike out first.

Nothing would go wrong, though. Shorty was increasingly

convinced that Indy and Willie were, in fact, the legendary lovers Hsienpo and Ying-t'ai, descended from the sky. Originally, they'd died in each other's arms, whereupon the Jade Emperor had sent them to live in all rainbows, Hsienpo being the red, Ying-t'ai the blue. And weren't Willie's eyes just that shade of blue? And didn't Indy's contain that reddish tinge? So now hadn't they obviously returned to join once more on earth and claim Short Round as the violet product of their fusion?

Short Round felt certain that they had.

For weren't his own brown eyes flecked with violet?

He could hardly keep his violet-flecked eyes open now, he was so sleepy. It made him wonder if Willie, like The Shadow, had the power to cloud men's minds. But Shorty would not sleep yet; he would at least witness the first coy twinings of this mythic pair.

Indy walked a few more steps to Willie's suite. The door was closed. He was about to knock, when it opened. Willie stood there, still in princess garb, looking mildly startled.

"My, what a surprise," she said.

"I've got something for you." Indy spoke from his throat. He was trying to be suave, though his face wasn't entirely in control.

"There's nothing you have that I could possibly want." She said it to tease, but even as she said it she knew she didn't really mean it.

"Right," nodded Indy. No point in sticking around where you weren't wanted. He turned to go, pulling an apple out from under the covered tray he carried. He bit down on it. Willie heard the crunch.

She grabbed the apple from him and took a bite. Apple never tasted so good. She closed her eyes, savoring the tart juices, the crisp texture. Heaven. As she opened her eyes, he took the cover off the tray, holding it up to her: bananas, oranges, pomegranates, figs, grapes.

Willie gasped. She took the tray into her room. He followed.

Short Round smiled wisely and went to bed.

Jones wasn't such a bad guy, really, Willie mused, if he were only a little less conceited. He *had* helped her out, though, and people *did* seem to have heard of him, so maybe he was actually sort of famous, and now this divine food, and you know, really he was very cute, and here they were thousands of miles from a radio or a car. . . .

She stuffed a few more grapes in her mouth and smiled at him, standing there like a busboy in the doorway. *If driving fast cars you like, If low bars you like, If old hymns you like, If bare limbs you like* . . . She rolled up her sleeves and peeled a banana. *If Mae West you like, Or me undressed you like, Why, nobody will oppose* . . .

He smiled back at her. The desperate girl. She obviously wanted him badly. Well, he didn't mind. She had what it took, and he certainly wouldn't refuse a little pick-me-up. He inched a step toward her.

"You're a nice man," she purred. "You could be my palace slave."

In fact, she'd been looking better each day. Gave him that old funny flutter to watch her now. "You wearing your jewels to bed, princess?"

"Yeah, and nothing else," she countered. "That shock you?" Anything goes.

"No." He moved up to her. "Nothing shocks me. I'm a scientist." He took the apple from her, chomped down on a mouthful.

"So," she said, "as a scientist, do you do a lot of research?"

"Always," he intimated.

"Oh, you mean like what kind of cream I put on my face at night, what position I like to sleep in, how I look in the morning?" This was getting kind of randy; she hoped he made his move soon.

Indy nodded as if he'd heard her thoughts. "Mating customs."

"Love rituals."

"Primitive sexual practices."

"So you're an authority in that area," she concluded, untying his tie. He was looking better all the time.

"Years of fieldwork," he admitted. Love in the tropics.

They kissed. Long, soft; controlled, but picking up speed.

They came up for air. "I don't blame you for being sore at me," she half-apologized. "I can be a real handful."

"I've had worse," he replied with *noblesse oblige*.

"You'll never have better," she promised.

"I don't know," he smirked, starting to close her door behind him. "As a scientist I hate to prejudice my experiment. I'll let you know in the morning."

Experiment! she thought, turning livid. *Like I'm his performing rat or something!* "What!" she hissed. She would be a lover, with pleasure; she would not be a conquest.

She opened the door he'd just shut. "Why, you conceited ape! I'm not that easy."

"Neither am I," he said, puzzled, then riled. "The trouble with you, Willie, is you're too used to getting your own way." He stalked out, to his own door across the hall.

"You're just too proud to admit you're crazy about me, Dr. Jones." *That* was *really* his problem: he had to be in control all the time, and being passionately in love with her made him feel too vulnerable, too much at her mercy. Well, she would show mercy—if he acted more like a gent.

"Willie, if you want me, you know where to find me." He stood in the doorway to his suite, trying to sound cool. She'd be around, soon enough.

"Five minutes," she predicted. "You'll be back here in five minutes." He wanted her more than he cared to admit; that was clear. He wouldn't last long in that state, poor boy.

Indy made a big show of yawning. "Sweetheart, I'll be *asleep* in five minutes." He closed the door.

"Five minutes," she repeated. "You know it, and I know it."

Indy opened his door a crack and peeped out, then closed it again. Willie slammed hers like the last word.

Indy stood in his room, leaning with his back against the door. No footfalls outside; no apologies forthcoming. Well, the hell with it. He walked over to his bed and sat down. Really steamed, and with good reason.

Willie marched away from her door, sat on the bed. She sank into the down mattress, muttering grimly. He'd be back. He wasn't all that smart, but he was a man—and she was a lot of woman. She picked up the clock by the bed and challenged it: "Five minutes." She took off her robe.

Indy took off his jacket. He glowered at the bedside clock. "Four and a half minutes," he grunted. Ridiculous. She was a ridiculous woman, this was a ridiculous palace, they were in a ridiculous situation, and he felt simply . . . put-upon.

Willie paced around her lavish suite. She blew out candles, turned down lamps, paused in front of the full-length mirror, began to primp. Her hair was really kind of a mess in all this dampness; could that have been the problem? She wished he hadn't stormed out *quite* so abruptly. But he'd be back.

Indy looked in his bureau mirror. So what was wrong with how he looked? Nothing, that's what. Of course she was a handsome woman, there was no denying that—but that was no reason to expect him to come groveling.

He walked over and tucked Shorty in on the couch. Ah, to be twelve again. Along the wall there were full-scale portraits of Rajput princes on prancing horses, palace landscapes, dancing girls. Dancing girls. Dancing girls.

Willie reclined on her four-poster bed, assuming various seductive poses. Periodically, she would look up, sweetly surprised at her contrite, imaginary visitor: "Why, Dr. Jones . . ." or, "Oh, Indiana . . ."

Her bedside clock said 10:18.

Indy lay on his bed, staring at the ceiling. How was he supposed to go to sleep now? Did she think he was made of steel? Could any man stand this kind of torture?

His bedside clock said 10:21.

Willie grabbed her clock, put it to her ear, shook it to see if it was working. Tick, tock, tick. She tapped her fingers irritably on the bedpost. Could her charms have failed? Was she losing her touch? How could he not be scratching at her door by now? How could he not?

Indy wanted to get up, but he refused to get up. The clock ticked beside him. He could wait her out; archaeology had trained him in the waiting game. Sooner or later she'd break down, give in, come around, hurry over. He just hoped it was sooner.

He looked toward the door. "Willie!" He smiled. The door remained closed. He tried a different voice. "Willie?" No. He tried nonchalance. "Willie. Oh, hi."

The door remained closed. Short Round kept sleeping.

In her room, Willie was trying new poses, new greetings. "Jones. Dr. Jones. Why, Indiana, hello."

Indiana's clock read 10:35. He smashed it to the floor and began to pace.

Willie slid to the foot of her bed, stretched out along the satin coverlet, arms akimbo. She slid off the end of the bed to the floor.

Indy paced back and forth along his row of wall paintings of princes, prancing horses, and dancing girls.

Willie paced back and forth along her row of wall paintings, muttering. "Nocturnal activities, crap! Primitive sexual practices! 'I'll tell you in the morning.' "

Indy began muttering too, in his truncated promenade. "Palace slave. I'm a conceited ape. Five minutes."

Willie stopped pacing. She stared at herself in the mirror, dumbfounded, frustrated, bewildered. "I can't believe it: he's not coming."

Indy stopped pacing, stared into space. "I can't believe it: she's not coming. I can't believe it: I'm not going."

From behind the last wall painting stepped a darkly clothed guard, who slipped a strangling cord around Indiana's neck.

Jones managed to get a few fingers around the garrote, but even so, he could feel his larynx nearly crushed within a matter of seconds. Gasping futilely for air, he sank slowly to his knees. His eyes bulged as he stared at the tiny, smiling skulls on the ends of the death-cord clutched in the assassin's fists. With a last, lunging effort, Indiana bent forward sharply: the guard spilled over his back onto the floor.

The guard pulled a knife, but Indiana smashed him in the head with a pot; the dagger clattered to the ground. Short Round began to stir. Indy heard something in the hall and looked up at the door. The guard jumped him again.

In the hall, Willie stood shouting at Indiana's closed door. "This is one night you'll never forget! It's the night I slipped right through your fingers! Sleep tight, Dr. Jones. Pleasant dreams. I could've been your greatest adventure."

Indy flipped back over the guard; the two of them tumbled across the tiles. Short Round woke up with a start. As Indy stood shakily, Shorty grabbed the whip, tossed it over. Indy caught it.

He whipped the assassin's arm, but the man unleashed himself and ran toward the door. Indy lashed out again, this time catching the guard around the neck. The thug yanked on it; the handle flew out of Indy's hand, up to the ceiling fan.

The whip twisted around the revolving blades like fishing line around a reel. And like a doomed flounder, the assassin was slowly dragged toward the ceiling. His toes lifted off the marble floor. He let out a short, choked scream. . . . His legs twitched . . . and he was hanged.

"Shorty, turn off the fan!" Indy shouted. "I'm gonna check Willie."

Shorty hit the wall switch; the fan stopped as Indy ran from the room.

He burst into Willie's suite, wild-eyed.

She lay on the bed, heart a-flutter. "Oh, Indy." He'd come after all. Sweet man. Maybe he just didn't know how to tell time.

He dove onto the bed.

"Be gentle with me," she whispered.

He scrambled across the bed, looked underneath it. Empty. He got up and began a furious search of the room.

"I'm *here*," Willie called.

Indy continued his frantic examination. Willie drew aside the bed curtains. His eyes had doubtless misted with love: he wasn't seeing clearly.

Indy walked around the end of the bed, stood in front of the doors. "Nobody here," he muttered.

"No, I'm here," cooed Willie, drawing the last curtain.

Indy moved over to the mirror. Willie jumped off the bed and followed him. He felt a draft by the vase of flowers, coming from somewhere over to the left. The assassin had entered through a secret passage in his room; there had to be one in this chamber as well.

He walked over to a pillar. The draft was stronger here.

Willie still followed him. "Indy, you're acting awfully strange."

Indy looked at the pillar: a naked dancing-girl was carved into the stone. He began feeling around the carving's protuberances: shoes, baubles, hips, breasts.

Willie thought this was *exceedingly* strange. "Hey, I'm right *here*."

The lever was in the breasts. Suddenly the entire pillar disappeared into the wall with a grinding creak, forming an entrance-way into a tunnel.

Indy walked in. He struck a match, read the inscription on the wall: " 'Follow in the footsteps of Shiva.' "

"What does that mean?" whispered Willie excitedly. She was right behind him now.

" 'Do not betray . . .' " He stopped, removed the small fragment of ancient cloth from his pocket, compared it with the inscription on the wall.

Shorty appeared in the doorway now, and approached the niche.

Indy read the Sanskrit on the piece of cloth. " 'Do not betray his truth.' " He turned to the boy. "Shorty, get our stuff."

Short Round ran back to the bedroom as Indy turned into the tunnel.

SIX

The Temple of Doom

"**W**HAT'S DOWN THERE?" quaked Willie.

"That's what I'm going to find out. You wait here. If we're not back in an hour, I want you to wake Captain Blumburtt and come after us."

She nodded. Short Round returned with Indy's bag, whip, and hat, and the two of them started down the secret passage.

Shorty led the way around the first corner, to make sure it was safe for Indy. The shadows looked pretty ominous, though. "Dr. Jones, I don't think we supposed to be here."

Indy grabbed him by the collar, planted him to the rear. "Stay behind me, Short Round. Step where I step. And don't touch anything."

As Indy moved forward, however, Short Round noticed a door off to the side, a door Indy had missed. Short Round put his hand on the knob and pulled: the door collapsed: two skeletons fell forward on top of him.

Shorty yelled, sitting down hard. He'd seen these guys before—in *The Mummy*. He thought he'd made it quite clear then, to Whoever was in charge, that he never wanted to run into anyone in this condition, especially not in a dark tunnel. Someone must be trying to teach him a lesson.

Indy pulled him erect, half-carried him around the next turn. A hollow wind sprang up here, blowing flayed skins in their faces—human skins, they looked like.

Short Round drew his knife. "I step where you step. I touch nothing."

More skins flapped in their faces. Shorty broke into a voluble string of Chinese prayers, epithets, and warnings about ghosts. More like *The Invisible Man*, here: tattered coverings falling away from an empty presence. Shorty was glad he'd seen such creatures before, so he wouldn't be undone now.

"Relax, kid." Indy smiled grimly. "They're just trying to scare us."

They kept walking. The tunnel was stone—cool, moist, solid. The farther they went, the more it seemed to twist downwards into the earth, and the darker it got.

Soon it became too black to see.

"All right, it all gets dark now," said Indy. "Stick close."

A few more paces, and Shorty felt something crunchy underfoot. "I step on something," he whispered.

"Yeah, there's something on the ground."

"Feel like I step on fortune cookies."

"Not fortune cookies." Indy shook his head. It was moving, whatever it was. He struck a match; they looked around. Before them was a wall with two holes in it. Out of one of the holes exuded an effluent of gooey mung, and millions of squirming, wriggling bugs. The bugs poured out onto the floor, covering it completely: a living carpet of shiny beetles, scurrying roaches, wriggling larvae.

Short Round looked down to see a few of them start to crawl up his leg. "That no cookie." He winced.

Indy brushed the bugs off. At the same moment, the match he

was holding burned down to his fingertip and went out. "Ow! Go!" he shouted, pushing his small friend ahead of him. They ran quickly, dashing directly into the next chamber.

Just past the threshold, Shorty stepped on a small button in the floor. This triggered the mechanism that started a great stone door rolling shut behind them.

"Oh, no," breathed Indy. He dove back, tried to hold it open.

But it closed.

As he turned, he saw the door on the opposite side of the cave slide down: the dim light emanating from beyond it was extinguished. Indy dove toward the portal—but again, he was too late.

He sat on the floor a moment, collecting his thoughts.

"Are you mad at me?" Shorty asked in a small voice out of the darkness. He felt like one of the Little Thunders—children of My Lord the Thunder and the Mother of Lightnings, who, through well-intentioned inexperience, were always having misadventures.

"Indy, you mad at me?"

"No," Indiana mumbled. And then, more softly: "Not exactly." Mad at *himself* was more like it. He never should have brought the kid down here; it was too dangerous.

"Oh, you just angry?"

"Right," said Indy, striking a match. He found a piece of oily rag on the floor and lit it. Human skeletons littered the ground. Shorty moved toward him. Indiana didn't want the boy inadvertently stumbling into any other trigger mechanisms, though. "Stop right there," he warned Shorty. "Look, go stand up against the wall."

Short Round did as he was told. He flattened his back against a block protruding from the stone wall. The block slid into the wall, triggering another device.

From the ceiling, spikes began to lower.

"Oh, no," groaned Indiana.

The burning rag illuminated the spikes as if they were the fiery teeth of hell.

Short Round shouted angrily at Indy, "You say stand against wall, I listen to what you say. Not my fault, not my fault!"

Indy wasn't listening, though. He was shouting through the door at the top of his voice. "Willie, get down here!"

Back in her room, Willie heard Indy call. She pulled on her robe, stepped into the drafty tunnel. "Indy!" she yelled back. There was no answer. She grabbed a small oil lamp from the table, began walking down the corridor. "I bet I get all dirty again," she muttered, rounding the first turn.

The two skeletons leapt out at her. "Indy!" she screamed. "There's two dead people in here!"

"There's going to be two dead people in *here* if you don't hurry up!" he shouted back.

She ran past the disgusting, flapping skins, down the steep grade, into the deepening dark, the rising wind. The wind blew out her lamp. Then came the foul odor.

"Ooh, it stinks in here," she moaned.

"Willie, get down here!"

"I've had almost enough of you two," she barked. What did they think, she did this for a living?

"Willie!"

The ceiling spikes were coming lower, getting closer. They looked more like sword blades now, with razor cutting edges.

"I'm coming," she hollered.

"C'mon, we're in trouble!" he roared. Then to Short Round: "Give me your knife." He took the dagger from Shorty, began digging frantically at the inset block of stone.

"What sort of trouble?" she called.

Spikes were rising from the floor now as well. "Deep trouble."

"Indy?" She kept walking. The smell got worse as his voice got louder.

"This is serious," he urged her on.

"What's the rush?"

"It's a long story. Hurry or you won't get to hear it."

"Oh, God, what is this?" She stopped at the new sensation underfoot. "There's stuff all over the floor. It's kind of crispy . . . and then it goes kind of creamy. Indy, what is it? I can't see a thing."

She struck a match.

All over: bugs.

Skittering beetles with black carapaces, long-legged arthropods, puffy translucent things that resembled scorpions, squirming wormy things, hopping locusts, segmented cave things . . .

It made her too sick to scream; all she could do was gag. "Indy, let me in. There's bugs all over here, Indy."

"Willie," Indy explained to her from the other side of the stone door that separated them, "there are no bugs in here."

"Open the door and let me in," she begged.

"Open the door and let us out," wailed Shorty. "Let us out, let us out!"

"Let me in, Indy, please," she squeaked.

"Right. Workin' on it."

"Indy, they're in my hair." Making nests there, burrowing in, spinning webs, clicking their pincers.

"Willie, shut up and listen. There's got to be a fulcrum release lever."

"A what?"

"A handle that opens the door."

"Oh, God, Indy. They're in my hair." Scratching, nibbling.

The tips of the spikes were now at head level.

"Open your eyes, Willie. Look around. There's got to be a lever hidden somewhere. Go on, look."

"There's two holes," she whimpered. "I see two square holes."

"Right. Now go to the right hole."

Sure. The one with all the mung and bugs oozing out of it. This was a joke, right?

Tentatively, she stretched her hand toward the left-sided hole, the relatively clean one. Not clean, exactly, of course, but at least not that disgusting slime-infested . . .

A hand reached through the left hole and grabbed hers. Indy's hand.

"No, not that hole, the other one!" he shouted. "The hole on your right!"

"It looks alive inside. I can't do it," she protested.

"You can do it. Feel inside," he guided her. Come on, kiddo, I need your help.

"*You* feel inside." Big wheel, telling her what to do.

"You've got to do it now!" he yelled. He was scrunched way down already; the spikes were pressing his flesh.

Willie eased her hand into the mess. "Oh, God, it's soft. It's moving. It's like a bowl of rotten peaches."

"Willie, we are going to die."

"I got it." She found a lever and yanked. The door rolled back.

Indy sat there beside Shorty, inside the doorway, as the spikes slowly started to recede.

Willie ran in tearing the bugs from her hair, shivering at the feel of their little feet all over her skin.

Shorty ran to the opposite door, which was sliding up, and took a long slide across the threshold—just like the immortal Ty Cobb stealing second. He wanted out of there, before anything else went wrong.

Willie stomped and shook. "Get them off me. They're all over me, get them off, I hate bugs, they're in my hair."

As she bent down to comb them out, she pushed in the block that was the trigger mechanism for the whole thing to start over again.

The first door commenced to roll shut.

Short Round called from the opposite door: "I didn't do it. She did it. Come on, get out!"

He began burbling in his native language as the far door, and the spikes, began once more descending. Like a Cantonese Little League third-base coach, he shouted in Chinese: "Slide, Indy, slide!"

Indy took hold of Willie; they sprinted across the room. He pushed her under the falling door, then dove under himself, just knocking his hat off on the way out.

And then, with inches to spare, he reached back in under the descending door, grabbed his hat, and pulled it out moments before the door crashed into place.

You should never go on an adventure without your hat.

They found themselves in a large, eerily lit tunnel through which blew a strange and forlorn wind, howling like a dirge from the earth's own core.

The light came from up ahead, around a curve in the tunnel. Reddish light; brooding, spectral. Indy, Willie, and Short Round walked slowly to the mouth of the tunnel; then stared, astonished, at the sight below them.

It was a cavern, staggeringly vast, carved over every inch of its surface, as if it had been carved out of the solid mass of the rock, carved with a vaulted, cathedral-like ceiling supported by rows of stone columns, carved into a colossal, subterranean temple. A temple of death.

Stone balconies overhung the granite floor, supported by pillars and arches that led off to dark side chambers. From these grottos poured worshippers, hundreds of them, chanting as they entered the temple. They chanted in unison, in response to the bizarre, lonely winds that howled out of the tunnels that pierced the upper levels of the cavern.

This strange tunnel-music created its own harmonics, its own dynamics, rising and falling in pitch and volume, echoing off all of the resonant hollows. And as these winds galed or died, the worshippers droned in answer, loud, or discordant, or muted, or keening: "Gho-ram gho-ram gho-ram sundaram, gho-ram gho-ram gho-ram sundaram . . ."

Mammoth stone statues loomed around the swelling congregation, rock, fashioned into elephants, lions, demigods and demons; ornate monstrosities, half-human, half-animal, some surely erupted from the mind of madness.

Torches were lit over the balconies, affording a clearer view to the three onlookers who stared, transfixed, from their tiny perch high above and to the rear of the scene. Below them, the mystery cult began bowing toward an enormous altar at the far end of the temple. Separating them from this altar was a crevasse—it looked partly natural, partly carved and shaped—from which the dull red light emanated, out of which sulfurous wisps of smoke and steam rose until they were sucked away up some nether tunnel by the moaning, baying winds.

The altar itself, on the far side of the crevasse, was roiled in smoke, obscuring its precise shape. As the ceremony continued, robed priests emerged from this miasma, carrying pots of incense, clearing the air around the altar as they came forward to the far edge of the crevasse. Soon, the incense dissipated; a giant stone statue appeared on the altar, its back to the far wall, standing partly within an enormous, domed niche carved into the stuff of the rock.

It was Kali—the hideous protectress of the temple, the malevolent, bloodthirsty goddess who was the object of all this devotion.

She stood twenty feet tall. Carved snakes curled up her legs, while girdling her hips was a skirt of hanging human arms. The statue itself had six arms: one held a saber; one grasped the severed head of a giant victim by the hair; two supported her on the altar; two, outstretched, dangled a flat, iron-mesh basket on chains.

Around her shoulders were draped necklaces of human skulls.

Her face was vile, half mask, half ghoul: a loathsome miscreant. Her eyes and mouth glowed with molten lava from the pit below, scorching her stony fangs black; there was no nose, only a deformed hole; her headdress was carved with ancient markings that bespoke great evil.

The priests gazed up at the deity reverently. The worshippers chanted louder, in a growing passion of foul cravings.

Up in the wind tunnel, Willie shivered. "What's happening?" she whispered. It made her feel cold, hollow; shaken.

"It's a Thuggee ceremony," said Indy. "They're worshipping Kali."

"Ever seen this before?"

"Nobody's seen this for over a hundred years." He was excited, on edge. What an incredible discovery he'd stumbled upon! An extinct religion, its rituals and totems as alive now as they'd ever been. It was as if he were viewing the reanimated bones of a lost tribe.

Suddenly they heard a wailing from behind the altar—inhuman, but all too human.

"Baachao; muze baachao. Baachao koi muze-baachao."

"What's that?" muttered Willie.

"Sounds like the main event," Indy replied. "He's calling 'Save me, someone please save me.' "

Grimly they watched as the ritual continued.

A huge drum sounded three times; the chanting stopped. Only the wind sustained a relentless groan. In the chill of its echo, another figure stepped forward onto the altar. This was the High Priest, Mola Ram.

His robes were black, his eyes red and sunken. He wore a necklace of teeth. On his head sat the upper skull of a bison, its horns curling out like those of the devil incarnate.

He walked to the edge of the crevasse, facing the crowd. Just on the other side of the pit, facing the High Priest, Indy noticed a familiar figure sitting. "Look," he said quietly to Willie. "Our host, the Maharajah."

"Who's the guy he's lookin' at?" Willie nodded.

"Looks like the High Priest."

To Short Round, he looked like Frankenstein.

Mola Ram lifted his arms above his head. Again, a pitiful scream rose from behind the altar, as if it were coming from the statue of Kali herself. Quickly the true sound of the scream became identifiable: a struggling, ragged Indian was dragged out onto the altar by priests and tied to the rectangular iron frame basket that hung from Kali's arms, just above the stone floor.

All watched in silence.

Mola Ram walked over to the bound victim, who was writhing helplessly, spread-eagled on his back atop the hanging frame. The man wailed. Mola Ram uttered an incantation. The man sobbed. Mola Ram extended his hand towards the bound man; his hand pierced the victim's chest.

Pierced it, sank into the poor, squirming torso . . . and ripped out the Indian's living heart.

Willie covered her mouth.

Short Round's eyes opened wide. "He pulled his heart out. He's dead." Emperor Shou-sin used to remove the hearts of sages, Short Round had heard, to see if it was true that the heart of a sage is pierced with seven holes. This man's heart had no holes, though, and that priest wasn't Shou-sin. To Short Round, it looked like they'd fallen into hell.

There were ten hells, ruled by the Yama Kings. At various levels, a person might be buried in a lake of ice, bound to a red-hot pillar, drowned in a pool of fetid blood, reincarnated as a Famished Demon; many tortures were there.

This was certainly the fifth hell, in which the dead soul's heart was repeatedly plucked out.

Short Round did not want to be here.

Indy didn't believe in hell. But he believed in what he saw. And what he saw now was more unbelievable than any hell he'd ever imagined. He stared, rapt, at the man being sacrificed.

"He's still alive," murmured Indiana.

Indeed, the man still screamed, and his bloody heart maintained a steady beat in Mola Ram's hand. Mola Ram lifted the heart above his head. Once again, the worshippers began to chant:

"Jai ma Kali, jai ma Kali, jai ma Kali . . ."

The sacrificial victim kept wailing, very much alive. There was no evidence of a gash on his chest, only a reddish mark where Mola Ram's hand had entered.

The priests added chains to the iron frame, upended it, then reversed its orientation so that the man was suspended face-down, suspended above a massive stone door in the floor—a door that began rolling away with a sonorous rumble, to reveal the same pit below him as the one at the bottom of the crevasse: bubbling, crimson lava.

And then the iron frame was lowered into the pit.

The victim saw the fiery magma slowly rise to meet him. His heart continued to beat in Mola Ram's hand. The crowd kept chanting, the wind continued to howl: these were the last sounds he heard on this earth.

His face began to smoke and blister as the lava flared closer to his lowering body. His flesh sizzled, peeled, charred. He tried to scream, but the noxious fumes filled his lungs; the superheated vapors seared his throat.

His hair burst into flame.

Finally, the frame submerged into the boiling molten ore.

Up in the tunnel, Willie closed her eyes; Indy watched in horror; Short Round looked, and turned away, and looked again. He appealed to the Celestial Ministry of Fire to deliver them from this hellish domain.

Beside the altar, Mola Ram held the heart high: still beating, dripping blood, it began to smoke. Then it, too, burst into flame. And then it disappeared.

The iron frame was raised, on its winches, out of the chasm by priests who turned a great wheel at the side of the altar. The metal glowed red, like a brand, but there was no trace of the sacrificed victim. He'd been completely incinerated.

The multitudes chanted. "Jai ma Kali, Jai ma Kali, gho-ram, sundaram . . ."

The wind railed.

Indy, Willie, and Short Round stared, glassy-eyed, at this thing they'd just witnessed.

Mola Ram left, behind the altar. Three priests emerged from the shadows, carrying cloth-wrapped objects toward the altar.

Willie began to cry.

"Quiet," whispered Indy; but Short Round looked on the verge himself, and hugged Willie close.

The priests carefully unwrapped three conical pieces of crystallized quartz, bringing these tokens to the base of the statue of Kali. Mounted between the statue's legs was a four-foot-tall stone skull, its eyes and nose hollow. The priests brought the three crystals together in front of the skull. The stones began to glow with a burning, incandescent radiance. The priests pulled the stones apart; the glowing stopped. They brought them together once more, nestling them in the three waiting skull sockets. The stones glowed brightly.

Indiana watched in mounting fascination. "They knew their rock was magic. But they didn't know it was one of the lost Sankara Stones."

"Why does it glow in the dark?" Short Round trembled.

"Legend says that when the stones are brought together, the diamonds inside them will glow."

Willie wiped her eyes, pulled herself together. She almost laughed, from fatigue and tension. "Diamonds?" She nudged him with renewed interest.

The Sankara Stones shimmered brilliantly, seducing all caught in the web of their luminescent power. The three bearer priests bowed repeatedly to the crystals, finally backing out on their knees, into the dark space behind the altar.

The other priests followed. Then the entire crowd started dispersing. In a couple of minutes, the cavern was empty once more. Only the wind cried at the horror.

Indiana turned to his friends. "All right, now listen: you two wait here and keep quiet."

Short Round nodded. He was in no hurry to go any closer. He handed Indy the bullwhip and shoulder bag. Willie didn't look so sure.

"Wait. What're you doing?" she demanded. She just wanted to get out of here.

Indy peered down the sheer drop from the mouth of the wind tunnel to the stone floor far below. "Going down there," he advised her.

"Down there? Are you crazy?"

"I'm not leaving without those stones." They were the find of the century; they'd touched him with their glow; he had to have them.

She was suddenly furious. "You're gonna get killed chasing after your damn fortune and glory!"

He looked at her with real warmth in this dank place: she cared for what happened to him. "Maybe, someday," he smiled affectionately. "Not today." Today, he was going to own those magic stones.

Without waiting for her reply, he lowered himself meticulously out the mouth of the tunnel.

There were plenty of footholds and handholds in the pocked stone. With skill, Indy was able to maneuver himself over and down to one of the monumental supporting columns near the rear of the cavern. Once there, he inched down the pillar, hanging on to stone cobras, sculpted lions, carved dancing maidens. After what seemed a long time, he made it all the way to the bottom.

Quietly he ran across the length of the chamber, stopping when he came to the crevasse. He looked down. Fire bubbled there, like the liquid soul of the temple. Its fumes stung his eyes and nostrils; he had to step back.

Across the gulf stood the statue of Kali, and, before her, the three Sankara Stones. It was too wide to jump across. Indiana looked from side to side; no way around, either.

Then he noticed two columns on the far side of the abyss, on top of which stone elephants perched, flanking the altar. Indy uncurled his whip and, with master precision, let it fly.

The bullwhip cracked. Its end wrapped tightly around the tusk of the closer stone elephant. Indy tugged on the whip handle, pulled the thong taut, took a deep breath . . . and ran.

At the edge, he leaped. The whip snapped tight as he cleared the lip. Then he was arching down, then up, across the fiery breach.

He landed on his feet, near the towering goddess. The wind rose, in a mocking warble. Indy released the whip end from the elephant's tusk.

Short Round waved to him from the elevated wind tunnel: all clear. It was hard being a bodyguard long-distance, but Shorty took the job seriously even at the outposts. Indy nodded, recoiling the whip onto his belt. He turned toward the altar. There the three stones continued to glow. Cautiously, Indiana approached.

He stooped to examine them closely. The middle stone—the one stolen from Mayapore village—had three lines painted across it. They glimmered intensely. Indy touched it: it didn't burn. Carefully, he lifted it to his face, peered into its glowing matter.

A magical diamond sparkled within the substance of the rock. Its light was ethereal, hypnotic. Beautiful. Rainbow light. Star light. But as soon as it was away from its niche a few moments, its light dwindled and died. Indy brought it near the other two again; again, they all glowed intensely. Apart, dark; together, bright.

He put the jewels in his pouch.

All of them touching, in the sack—it was like a tiny, cool sun.

Willie and Short Round apprehensively watched Indy bag the three Sankara Stones. He pulled the drawstrings tight, sealing off the emanation.

Kali, too, watched.

Indiana backed off, looked up at the horrific statue. Kali looked down on the puny mortal . . . and spoke.

Indiana jumped back. The demonic face seemed to laugh at him, to echo, to mumble, accuse . . .

Wait. The sounds were coming from behind the altar, not from the mouth of the statue. Indy chuckled at himself—though not too loudly—and walked around behind the altar to see what the noises were.

Willie and Short Round grew immediately concerned as Indy disappeared from sight beyond the altar.

"Oh, hell, *now* where's he going?" she whispered harshly. She did not like being left alone.

The wind was moaning again. The note in their tunnel began to quaver slightly, though, to shift its pitch in a series of funny staccato modulations. Short Round turned to see two shadowy figures moving down the tunnel toward him: their bodies moving through the wind tunnel altered the tone, creating the eerie harmonics.

Short Round froze.

"What're you—" Willie began—but then she saw.

In another second the two huge Thuggee guards were lunging at them. Short Round drew his dagger in time to slash the closer Thug's hand. The man fell back, in surprise and pain. The other guard grabbed Willie.

She'd been wrestling with goons like this one for as long as she'd worn lipstick, though. With a well-practiced move, she brought her knee up sharply into his groin. He groaned, and sank to his haunches.

The other guard was now cautiously closing in on Short Round. Willie jumped up on the lug's back, wrapping her hands around his face, going for the eyes. He swung around, slamming her into the wall. She slumped to the ground, the wind knocked out of her. In that moment Shorty stuck the guard in the leg, then backed off again. He and the wounded guard circled.

The other Thug started crawling toward Willie. When he was a few feet away, she scooped up a big handful of dirt and hurled it into his face. The man clawed blindly at his eyes as Willie stood up.

"Run, Willie! Run!" Short Round called. He still kept the other guard at bay: like Dizzy Dean, holding the runner at first.

Willie ran ten yards up the tunnel, then stopped and turned.

Shorty swung his dagger in tight arcs, keeping his distance from the assassin. Suddenly the guard shouted something in Hindi, and dove, knocking Short Round off his feet. The knife clattered to the dirt. He grabbed Shorty by the ankle, and dragged the boy, kicking, to him.

Willie hesitated. The other guard was stumbling to his feet. This wasn't working.

"Run!" screamed Short Round. "Go get help!"

Willie ran back up the tunnel. The last thing she saw was Short Round being lifted bodily by the throat, until his little feet dangled helplessly above the ground.

Meanwhile, Indiana entered the darkened chamber behind the altar. The only illumination came from two places: the smoky red light from the inferno in the temple, streaming in here around the gigantic silhouetted statue of Kali; and, up ahead, a dim cylindrical shaft of yellowish light rising from what appeared to be an enormous hole in the ground.

Indy slowly crossed a narrow stone bridge toward the hole—a bridge over what, it was too dark to tell. Presently he reached the other side, though. As he neared the great cavity, he began to hear voices, and the clink of metal against rock. The ground was inordinately dark; he crept toward the precipice with extreme uncertainty, ready to run on short notice. He reached the edge, and looked down.

What he saw was a wide, deep pit, around the sides of which concentric paths spiraled leading off into numerous narrow tunnels. Crawling in and out of the burrows, scrawny children lugged sacks of dirt and rock. Other hollow-eyed kids, mostly chained, pulled these sacks to mine cars parked on rails that crisscrossed the excavation.

It was a mine.

Torchlight cast weird dancing shadows across the walls. Beyond the farthest tracks in the main excavation site, a vertical stream of water hugged the cavern wall, filling a massive cistern that overflowed into a sparkling dark pool. Machines whined; exhaust fumes hung in the stagnant air; black fires erupted from vents in the rock; sparks billowed out of holes where iron grated on stone.

Children were whimpering or silent, according to inclination; none were other than miserable, though. Sadistic Thuggee guards lashed at them, or beat them mercilessly. Some laughed.

Indy saw several children slip and fall while straining to lift a bag of rocks into one of the mine cars. Guards kicked them. One child didn't get up; fortunate soul, he had finally found his only escape from this travail in hell.

Indiana edged around the pit. It was ghastly, a scene so grotesque as to defy comprehension. He couldn't fathom what to do. This was beyond anything involved with even the most ghoulish rites of the most pagan religion.

He hefted the bag of stones on his shoulder. They burdened him now with choices: he could leave, if he wanted, with the Sankara Stones in his possession, priceless artifacts to be studied and prized for centuries yet to come.

But he could hear the pleading of a child. He looked down to see a huge, burly, bare-chested guard cruelly beating the pitiful little slave. The fury welled up in Indiana without release. He clenched his fists; he ground his teeth.

The guard seemed to feel the intense pressure of Indy's stare on his back. He stopped beating the child; looked up at Indy looking down. Their gazes met, locked, wrestled. Slackly, the guard smiled: he was enjoying himself.

The brute was far below him. Indy could still leave, if he chose. His choice wasn't hard.

He bent down, picked up a rock, stood, held it over his head, took aim, and flung it down into the mine.

By the time it hit bottom, it must have been going at a pretty good clip, but the guard just caught it. Just plain caught it. It bent him over some; then he straightened up, looked back at Indy. Their eyes met again; again the guard smiled—only this time he was memorizing Indy's face: imprinting every last detail on his brain, so he would not forget this puny insurgent who had dared annoy him.

Indy returned the smile, though he knew this wasn't a real good first round. The startled slave children looked up at him in shock. He postured victoriously and doffed his hat at the bewildered Thuggee guards who ran over to see what the commotion was.

This is just the beginning, you bastards, he thought. He began to look for a boulder, when something unnerving happened: dirt started crumbling away from the rim of the pit. A small landslide, in fact.

And then, as luck would have it, a big landslide.

In the space of a backstep, the entire floor gave way; that section of the rim sheared off, and Indy toppled with it. Debris and Indiana went plunging into the mine, bouncing off dirt ledges and loose clay, until he lay in a pile of rubble at the bottom of the shaft.

Bruised and cut, he looked up. Thuggee guards surrounded him, appearing much larger and angrier than they had just a few moments before.

He smiled at the big one, shaking his head. "How did you get so ugly?"

SEVEN

. . . And into the Fire

THE GUARDS grabbed him, clubbed him, dragged him into a small holding cell. There they chained his wrists to the low roof. The pain of the manacles cutting into his arms woke him in time to see the barred door slam shut. As it was being padlocked, three other prisoners who'd been cowering in the corner of the cell ran up to him. Two of them were Indian slave children; one was Short Round.

Tearfully the boy hugged Indy. Shackled as he was, Indiana could not return the embrace. Below them, in the quarry, he heard children being whipped. It was the foulest sound he'd ever heard. He had to get out of here.

Shorty stepped back and began scolding him. "You promise to take me to America. This doesn't happen in America. I keep telling you: you listen to me more, you live longer." It was outrageous! Indy, caught like a Little Thunder.

Indy nodded, smiling. He wondered if Shorty could talk him out of his irons. If Willie were here, she could for sure.

Short Round pointed to one of the boys beside him. "This is Nainsukh, from that village. He speak pretty good English for a foreigner. He say they bring him here to dig in the mines."

"But why?" Indy asked.

"Children are small," said Nainsukh. "We can work in tunnels."

"Why are you two locked up, then?"

"Now we are too old—too big to crawl into the little tunnels—" The boy's throat choked with emotion; he had to stop speaking.

"What they do to you now?" Short Round asked, his pupils dilated in fear of the answer.

"I pray to Shiva to let me die," wavered Nainsukh, "but I do not. Now the evil of Kali will take me."

"How?"

"They will make me drink the blood of Kali. Then I fall into black sleep of Kali Ma."

"What's that?" Indy stopped him.

The boy steeled himself against the vision of what he was going to be forced to do. "We become like them. We be alive, but like in nightmare. You drink the blood, you not wake up from nightmare of Kali Ma."

Indy and Short Round saw the terror on the child's face. Shorty fervently spoke the name of the God of the Door of Ghosts. Indy vowed revenge, in the name of these nameless children. Suddenly there was a clanking noise. Indy saw two guards unlocking the door to the cell.

Nainsukh and the other boy yelped, ran to the back of their cage, trembled in the darkness like trapped animals awaiting the inevitable.

The guards weren't there for the children, though; they were there for Indy and Short Round. They unchained Indiana, marched the two friends out of the cell, up the winding path that curved around the sides of the mine pit, down a long dark tunnel. At the end of the tunnel, a thick wooden door opened. The prisoners were shoved inside.

They stumbled into the chamber. It was the chamber of the High Priest, Mola Ram.

The place was a gallery of terror. Ritualistic statues and grisly icons covered the walls, staring down like all the eyes of Evil. The rock itself seemed somehow deformed. Small fissures perforated the floor, leaking red steam, filling the cave with a putrid essence. It made Indy want to choke.

In one corner, an iron pot was filled to overflowing with burning coals and strange incense. It was tended by an androgynous man with painted lips, thin arms, delicate hands, a face rank with madness. He stirred the coals, humming a twilight melody.

Across the room stood the most grotesque statue Indiana had ever seen. It could only have been nightmare-spawned; it was the stone effigy of Death.

Twice human size, its head was formed into the shape of a skull—but a skull too big in back, as if malformed, or hydrocephalic, with its jawbone dangling open too wide, in a demented grimace. A candle burned in each eyesocket, and atop its forehead.

Its body was no skeleton body, however. It was a woman's body, but also mutant: no neck, no arms, asymmetric breasts, legs that fused into a morbid, lumpy base.

Candlewax ran down its stone head, out of its eyes into its nasal cavity, down its hanging jaw, like drool, over its stumpy shoulders, down its swollen breasts—candlewax, and, Indy could see now, just beginning to congeal: fresh blood.

Beside the foul thing stood a giant, bearded Thuggee guard, grinning insanely, wearing bracelets of human hair. It was the same guard Indy had thrown the rock at, the one who'd caught it. Now he'd caught Indy; now he was going to get even.

And in the center of the room, crosslegged, his eyes closed, sat Mola Ram.

This was the first opportunity Indy had to see him up close. He was a loathsome sight. His bison-skull headdress cradled his brow; affixed to its center was a shrunken human head. His face was hideously painted in some occult design. His teeth were bad; his eyes were sunken. His sweat smelled of rotting flesh.

His eyes opened; he smiled. "I am Mola Ram. You were caught trying to steal the Sankara Stones."

"Nobody's perfect." Indy smiled in return.

The stones began to glow. He hadn't seen them before, but there they were, near the base of the statue—glowing, seemingly in response to the High Priest's state of agitation.

Mola Ram's eyes glazed over as he stared, absorbed, at the pulsing crystals. "There were five stones in the beginning," he said. "Over the centuries they were dispersed by wars, sold off by thieves like you."

"Better thieves than me," Indiana said modestly. "You're still missing two."

"No, they are here," Mola Ram protested. "Somewhere, they are here. A century ago, when the British raided this temple and butchered my people," he decried, "a loyal priest hid the last two stones down here in the catacombs."

Suddenly Indy realized what this treachery was all about. "That's what you've got these slaves digging for, these children." The anger started to churn within him again.

"They dig for gems to support our cause," Mola Ram assented, "and yes, they also search for the last two stones. Soon we will have all five Sankara Stones, and then the Thuggee will be all-powerful."

"Can't accuse you of having a vivid imagination," Indiana jibed.

"You do not believe me." The High Priest focused on Indy now. "You will, Dr. Jones. You will become a *true* believer."

He gave a sign. The guards clamped an iron collar around Indiana's neck, dragged him over to the Death statue, and chained him to it, his back pressing into its front, the chains stretching from his neck and wrists around behind the idol's backside. He could smell the blood that stained its chin.

He was afraid. This fevered air, these maniac priests—anything could happen. He wouldn't show his fear, though; he wouldn't give them the satisfaction. These fanatics thrived on fear, fear and suffering. He would not sate their lusts. And he would not give Short Round cause to despair, for the boy still stood, trembling, near the front of the room. He would set an example for Short Round, show him dignity could rise above defilement, even in a place as degraded as this . . . if you were strong of heart.

The giant guard strode forward, up to Indy.

Indy grinned ferociously. "Hi. I hate a bully."

The guard also smiled. He'd witnessed such bravado many times; he knew it was futile.

The door opened. In walked the young Maharajah. Behind him came the boy Nainsukh, who'd recently shared Indiana's cell. The child looked different now, Indy noticed, becalmed as a ship on a windless sea. In his hands he carried a human skull.

Mola Ram turned to the Maharajah Zalim Singh. "Your Highness will witness the thief's conversion."

The Maharajah stood before Indiana with a look of concern. "You will not suffer," he reassured the thief. "I recently became of age and tasted the blood of Kali."

Indiana was not reassured. He saw Mola Ram take the skull from Nainsukh. It was a laughing skull, still covered with frayed skin, its nose half-rotted away, eyes nearly gutted, leathery tongue flapping out askew. Mola Ram brought the skull over to Indy.

The huge guard grabbed Indy's face, forced his head back against the slope of Death's breast, and forced his mouth open.

Before Indiana knew what was happening, or had a chance to react, the High Priest was tipping the gruesome skull forward, pouring blood from its mouth, cascading down the sluice of its tongue . . . into Indy's mouth.

Shorty screamed from across the room. "Don't drink, Indy! Spit it out!" He cried with all his spirit to Huan-t'ien, Supreme Lord of the Dark Heaven, who lived in the northern sky, to drive the evil winds from this room; he cried to The Shadow, who knew what lurked in hearts like these; he cried for immediate deliverance; and he just cried.

Indy was disoriented for a moment. He'd been expecting torture, or magic spells, but not drinking. He gagged on the foul liquid before he spat it out all over Mola Ram.

The High Priest backed off in anger. Warm blood dripped down his face, over his mouth. He licked his lips. He spoke to the Maharajah in Hindi.

Zalim Singh took a small doll from his pocket. The figurine wore pants, and a tiny rough-hewn hat. Its skin was lighter than the skin of most local dolls; the features painted carefully on its face appeared decidedly Western. It looked arguably like Indiana Jones.

The Maharajah held it up to Indy's face, to show him, then wiped the doll over Indy's body, where it soaked up his sweat and dirt and fleshy oils. And then the Maharajah began to dip the doll in and out of the flames that rose from the pot of coals in the corner.

Into the fire went the doll . . . and into spasms of pain went Indy. His body felt aflame, as if his very brain were being consumed. He screamed, he screamed.

"Dr. Jones!" wailed Shorty. Just to watch such a horror contorted the boy's heart nearly to stopping. He let out a series of Chinese invectives, ran up, kicked the Maharajah hard. The little monarch fell, dropping the doll. Indy slumped forward.

Short Round dove for Indy's whip, but was thrown down to the floor by one of the guards. Mola Ram gave commands. The chief guard picked up Indy's whip.

Indiana was unchained momentarily, then was turned around and rechained facing the statue, pressed to it, his cheek pushed down on its horrid, bloodsticky breast, his gaze staring directly up into its gargoyle face.

He felt a cold noise garble through his chest.

Nainsukh went to refill the skull with fresh blood. Mola Ram began to chant. Shorty picked himself up, ran at his guard, punching, but he was quickly subdued by priests, quickly strung up against the far wall, in chains.

And then the two of them were whipped. First Indy—Shorty cried to watch it. Then Shorty.

"Leave him alone, you bastards," Indiana muttered through his haze. This was the lowest. For this, he would exact a proper price.

So they left Short Round alone; went back to whipping Indy. The leather ripped through his shirt, tore open his skin. Blood was soon soaking the splayed tatters of cloth and flesh. Indy tried to keep his mind closed. He breathed harder—the candles in Death's eyes blew out. This seemed to infuriate Mola Ram even more.

"You dare not do that," the High Priest intoned. Nainsukh returned with the second skull full of blood, gave it to Mola Ram.

Indy was turned around again, once more with his back to the idol. The giant guard pried open his slack and weary mouth, and pinched shut his nose. Once again, Mola Ram poured the bloody elixir from the laughing skull into Indiana's mouth.

"The British in India will be slaughtered," said the High Priest as he poured. "Then we will overrun the Moslems and force their Allah to bow to Kali. And then the Hebrew God will fall. And finally the Christian God will be cast down and forgotten."

He finished pouring. The guard clasped down Indy's mouth. Indy gagged, sputtered, choked, held his breath . . . and finally swallowed.

"Soon Kali Ma will rule the world," pronounced Mola Ram.

Willie stumbled through the secret tunnel entrance, back into her room. Insects covered her totally, from her flight down the caves. She knocked them off, holding her breath, doing what she had to do to save herself. And to save Indy. She'd have plenty of time later to break down—she hoped.

She managed to stagger to her feet, headed for the door, rushed out of her room. Down the corridors of the deserted palace she flew, looking for help in the lightening shadows; the dawn was not far off.

In the first open courtyard, she stopped, panting heavily. She called out. Nobody answered. Desperately, she backed down the next hallway, stifling sobs. Paintings lined the walls here; the grand portraits of the Maharajah's forebears. They seemed to be lurking, now: spying on her from another time, in this cold hour of the late night. Slowly she paraded through this sinister gauntlet. At the end, something moved in the corner of her eye. She turned . . . one of the faces! She gasped—it was a mirror.

But then the face was behind her in the mirror, moving again. She whirled once more, her hand ready to strike. It was only Chattar Lal, the Prime Minister.

"Oh, my God, you scared me!" Willie exhaled with relief. "Listen, you've got to help. We found this tunnel—" She grabbed his shoulder, for support, and to try to communicate the urgency of the situation to him.

Captain Blumburtt rounded the corner at that moment. He nodded politely to Willie, but spoke to Chattar Lal. "Jones isn't in his room." Then, to Willie, "Miss Scott, my troops are leaving at dawn, if you'd like us to escort you as far as Delhi."

Willie felt pale. "No, you can't go! Something awful's happened. They've got Short Round and I think Indy's been—"

"What?" blurted Blumburtt.

Willie nodded excitedly. "We found a tunnel that leads to a temple below the palace! Please, come with me, I'll show you!"

The two men exchanged dubious looks. Outraged, frustrated, unraveling, Willie clutched Blumburtt by the arm and began running down the hall to her room.

Chattar Lal accompanied them. "Miss Scott, you're not making any sense," he said condescendingly.

Her teeth started chattering. "Hurry. I'm afraid they'll kill them. We saw horrible things down there—a human sacrifice. They dragged in this poor man, and this other man reached into his chest and ripped out his heart." She covered her face with her hand, to make the image go away. The two men looked at each other even more skeptically.

"Who?" pursued Blumburtt with the utmost tact.

"The priest," she rasped. "They've taken Short Round, and Indy's gone—I don't know where Indy's gone. Right beneath my bedroom there's this gigantic cathedral—a temple of death. There's some kind of cult down there, with the sacred stones Indy was searching for."

Chattar Lal smiled indulgently. "I sense the fumes of opium in all this. Perhaps Miss Scott picked up the habit in Shanghai?"

She became furious. "What're you talking about? I'm not a dope fiend! I saw it! I'll show you!"

She pulled them into her suite. "There—it's still there!" She pointed to the dark opening in her wall. "There: I told you!" she hissed in triumph.

Blumburtt picked up an oil lamp, held it toward the covert entryway . . . when suddenly Indiana emerged, flicking a beetle from his lapel.

Indy smiled faintly. "What's this, hide and seek?"

They were all a bit startled by his unexpected presence. Willie's shock melted instantly to relief, though. She ran to Indy, put her arms around him, felt ready to collapse.

"Oh, Indy, you got away," she wept. "Tell them what happened, they won't believe me."

She trembled in his powerful arms. He walked her to the bed, sat down there with her. Physically and emotionally exhausted, she let him take over without an argument.

"It's okay," he whispered into her hair. "You're all right now."

"They think I'm insane," she sniffled. "Tell them I'm not, Indy. Please, help me."

The awful events of the night had taken their toll. Willie sobbed into Indiana's chest, quaking, desolate.

Indy laid her down on the satin covers, stroked her cheek, brushed the hair from her face. "Hey, I thought you were supposed to be a real trouper, Willie?" He wiped the tears away.

She held his hand. "What?" she whispered. He was here now; she was safe. She could let go.

"You've got to go to sleep now."

"I want to go home," she answered, letting her eyes close. The mattress felt so soft, his voice so deep, his hand . . .

"I don't blame you," he soothed. "This hasn't been what you'd call a fun vacation."

She smiled despite herself, as he continued caressing her cheek. She could feel herself sliding effortlessly to sleep. It was almost . . . a miracle: Indy was saving her. She'd never had such a sense of total well-being, unencumbered tranquility. It was as if she were floating placidly down, on the sound of his voice: like a child, lost in an enchantment. She felt wrapped in the safety of his nearness. She felt blissful. Serene.

Entranced.

Indiana stood. He joined Blumburtt and Chattar Lal in the hallway outside Willie's room. The Prime Minister led the way to the verandah.

First light was breaking over the mountain peaks. Orange rays highlighted the low-lying clouds; the air was crisp, expectant. In the valley below, they could see the cavalry troops readying their horses and trucks.

Indy breathed deeply the rare spirit of dawn. "I've spent my life crawling around in caves and tunnels." He shook his head, remonstrating himself. "I shouldn't have let somebody like Willie go in there with me."

Blumburtt nodded, as if he'd suspected this all along. "Miss Scott panicked?"

Indy shrugged. "When she saw the insects, she passed out cold. I carried her back to her room. She was sound asleep when I reentered the tunnel to look around some more."

"And as she slept," suggested Chattar Lal, "she undoubtedly had nightmares."

Indy looked at the Prime Minister and nodded, speaking with complete understanding in his voice. "Nightmares, yes."

"The poor child," commiserated Lal.

Indy went on nodding. "Then she must have jumped awake, not realized she was dreaming, and run out of her room. And you found her."

Blumburtt squinted at the sun rising gently over his little corner of the British Empire. "Did you discover anything in that tunnel, Dr. Jones?"

Indiana stared into the same sun, but it rose over a different quadrant of the universe for him now. "Nothing," he replied. "Just a dead end. That tunnel's been deserted for years."

From far below them a sergeant-major shouted up that the troops were ready for departure. Blumburtt waved acknowledgment.

"Well, Mr. Prime Minister," the Captain assured, "my report will duly note that we found nothing unusual here in Pankot."

Chattar Lal bowed with respect for the Crown's wise decision. "I'm sure that will please the Maharajah, Captain."

Blumburtt turned one last time to Indy. "As I said before, Dr. Jones, we'd be happy to escort you to Delhi."

Indiana smiled serenely. "Thanks, but I don't think Willie is ready to travel yet."

Dust swirled in the valley as the British army moved out, across the lowest pass. Foot soldiers, horse cavalry, supply trucks. Captain Blumburtt headed the ranks, seated in an open car. Bringing up the rear was a troop of Highland Pipers beating out a stately tattoo on the pipes and drums.

In a short time they were winding slowly down the other side of the mountain, leaving Pankot Palace to its own.

Willie half woke to the dirgelike whine of the fading bagpipes. She wasn't certain if she was dreaming or not; it was such a muted, eerie sound.

Through the mosquito netting that hung all around the bed, she saw the door to her room open. It was still dim, with the curtain drawn, but she could make out Indiana's form softly approach. She smiled. He'd come for her at last.

She shifted her position slightly as he sat down on the edge of the mattress. He remained that way, his back to her, shoulders slumped. Poor man; he must be exhausted.

She stared through the gauzy netting at the back of his head, his tousled hair. "Indy? Did you talk to them?"

"Yes," he said.

"So now they believe me," she filled in the blank.

"Yes, they believe you," he echoed.

His voice registered in a strange monotone. *He must be more ragged out than I thought*, she thought. *My turn to be gentle with him.* "Then they'll send the soldiers down into the temple," she said aloud.

He didn't say anything. She hoped he hadn't just fallen asleep right there where he was sitting; though if he had, she'd understand. She'd just pull him right down where he belonged. "I was scared to death last night," she admitted, "when I thought they were going to kill you."

"No, they won't kill me."

She laid her hand on his back. It felt moist, through his shirt, through the netting. She smiled, lovingly reproachful. "You know, you've been nothing but trouble since I hooked up with you. But I have to admit, I'd miss you if I lost you."

Slowly, Indiana started to turn. "You won't lose me, Willie."

She pulled her hand back; her fingers were viscid with blood.

His face came around until it was staring straight at her. The netting hung between them, a diaphanous veil, but even so, she could see the change in his eyes.

His eyes, normally so deep, so clear, flecked with coppery gold, crystal-pure—his eyes had undergone some indescribable transformation. Something about them was opaque now. Tarnished. It made her cold. Viscerally ill. She shuddered.

She had lost him.

Morning services began in the temple of death. A sea of lurid faces swayed to the droning of the winds in the subterranean cathedral. The sacrificial chant grew slowly, organically, feeding on its own rumble and wail.

Among the worshippers the young Maharajah sat on a low, raised platform at the edge of the crevasse, staring across the fuming chasm toward the altar of Kali Ma.

"Jai ma Kali, jai ma Kali . . ."

Once again, the three Sankara Stones glowed magically at the feet of the demon goddess. Mola Ram materialized out of the swirling smokes that shrouded the altar; he, too, was chanting.

"Jai ma Kali, jai ma Kali . . ."

Female acolytes appeared from side chambers, swathed in red tunics. They passed along the row of somber priests, and painted lines on their foreheads, as Mola Ram began addressing the audience in Sanskirt.

Chattar Lal, dressed in robes, stood beside Indiana, to the left of the altar. An acolyte drew the devotional markings on Lal's forehead. Indiana stared vacantly into the liquid flames at the bottom of the pit. He was living the Nightmare now.

Liquid flames at the bottom of the pit scudded across the surface, leapt up twisting, turned into dark birds that fluttered insanely, looking for somewhere to roost. Higher, they flew, flapping against each other and the stone walls, screeching out of the pit . . . and into his head.

No brainstuff in there now, only a vast, umbrageous cavern: murky, with these large birds flapping. They didn't seem to be able to land, they just kept beating their wings against the inside of his skull.

Shadows whispered in this lingering midnight.

Somewhere, a nocturne dawdled over the lower registers, nearly off-key.

Somewhere, a candle guttered.

He moved, without moving: back, in time, in space, an hour, a dun-

geon, a bloodthirst, a blacksong, turning through pitchy tunnels brilliant with death, painlit and tomb-ridden, emerging into Willie's chamber, spilling from the stony wound. What's this, hide and seek?

Willie was there, the sorceress, entwining her tendrils around his back; her fingers were flaming talons gouging his flesh. Oh Indy you got away, she said, tell them what happened they won't believe me. Her hair was afire, her mouth a treacherous cavity without bottom, her tongue a salamander, her eyes icy mirrors reflecting the face of his own dusky soul.

He walked her to the bed, her flaming hair spattered his cheek. The birds in his head fluttered wildly, scraping the inner table of skull with their craggy beaks.

It's okay you're all right now.

They think I'm insane tell them I'm not Indy please help me.

Her salamander tongue lashed out as she leaned her head down against his body. Her sobs covered the sound of its gnawing: the lizard was taking great bites from his flesh, chewing open his chest.

He laid her down on the covers, hey I thought you were supposed to be a real trouper Willie, tears streamed down her cheeks, tears of blood, he touched them and they turned to lava, burning through his fingers to the bone, white bone gaping in the somber wind.

What? she whispered.

You've got to go to sleep now.

The serpent in her mouth had chewed down to his ribs now, crunching on his breastbone. I want to go home, the serpent was saying.

Its home was in his chest.

I don't blame you this hasn't been what you'd call a fun vacation. The snake slithered into his chest, curled up, slept there.

The sorceress slept.

The birds fluttered.

He joined Blumburtt and Chattar Lal on the verandah. Blumburtt had no face. The sun broke over the peaks in a bloody mist. Lal spoke, but the words came out of Indy's mouth, like a gaseous exhalation.

I've spent my life crawling around in caves and tunnels I shouldn't have let somebody like Willie go in there with me.

The faceless captain nodded.

When she saw the insects she passed out cold I carried her back to her room she was sound asleep when I re-entered the tunnel to look around some more.

The serpent shifted positions in his chest, recurled, settled back into uneasy slumber.

And as she slept she undoubtedly had nightmares.

Nightmares. Yes.

The poor child.

Two of the lightless birds tangled, brawled, tumbled to the base of his skull, lay there flapping on their backs, wounded, terrified.

Did you discover anything in that tunnel Dr. Jones?

Nothing.

Just a dead end.

Deserted.

The deserted hollows in his skull echoed; the echoes of broken feathers, scratching the stone. Empty, obscure. The birds had left.

But I don't think Willie is ready to travel yet.

He returned to her room. She still slept there, the sorceress, curled in her bed.

In his chest, the serpent stirred.

The sorceress awoke. He sat beside her. He faced away, that she could not see the shredded tissue of his breast, the ragged hole through which the reptile had crawled to nestle by his heart.

Indy?

Yes.

So now they believe me.

Yes they believe you. You leave us no doubt. Sorceress with flaming hair you will die before I let you rouse the beast within my chest.

I thought they were going to kill you.

No they won't kill me.

She drew her talons down his back, tearing skin, calling forth blood.

You won't lose me.

He turned, stared into her mirror eyes, saw himself: man of smoke,

laced with horror, oozing blood, trying to still the serpent, listening for
echoes in the dusk, waiting for the shattering scream.

The serpent twisted.

From the distance came a flapping.

Indiana continued to stare into the liquid flames at the bottom
of the pit as Mola Ram spoke. Chattar Lal translated the High
Priest's speech to Indiana. "Mola Ram is telling the faithful of our
victory. He says the British have left the palace, which proves Kali
Ma's new power."

Indy nodded hypnotically. "Yes, I understand." He understood
well.

Mola Ram finished orating. The intonations resumed. The
wind howled, the sulfuric fumes billowed and thinned.

Indiana rocked on his heels, staring up at the divinely inspired
idol beside him.

Beneath the temple, in the dark of the mine, children dug at the
earth with bleeding fingers. Fat guards flogged malingerers, or
those too sickly to go on, with leather straps. The earth crumbled
sometimes; children were buried alive or crushed in the rubble or
maimed or suffocated.

Short Round worked here now. He sweated next to the others,
the lost children, clawing at the rocks, seeking the last two Sankara
Stones. Chained at the ankles, they toiled, praying to die; doomed.

Short Round and five others were starting a new tunnel when
the finality of the situation began to sink in. The weight of this
knowledge—the agony of the remainder of the short life of Short
Round—hit him squarely, sat him down in the dirt. What could it
all mean? Had he offended some god or ancestor? What would
Indy do now? But he couldn't count on Indy anymore. Indy had
drunk the evil potion that had turned him from Dr. Jones to Mr.
Hyde. Indy was lost.

Shorty appealed to the Celestial Ministry of Time, to contract the length of his stay here. He sat on the ground, near tears; picked up a handful of dirt, let it sift through his fingers. "Grounded out," he whispered.

He didn't sit for long. A leather thong flayed his back; only the hot shock of it prevented him from screaming in pain. The guard moved on; Shorty got back to work.

He and two others strained at a large rock wedged in the wall, blocking the way the tunnel was to go. They pulled, they levered it; finally it gave. It came loose, rolled down a short incline—and Short Round gave an involuntary shout.

They'd exposed a vein of molten lava. Thick with itself, barely moving, it hissed like a wary cobra.

The children shouted, pointing until the guard came; then he whipped them brutally for being so stupid and noisy. His eyes reflected the glowing venom of the nearby vein.

Suddenly the small fissure spurted out a tiny bubble of steam, spewing a fine spray of lava over the guard's legs.

He shrieked, fell to the ground, tried to rub the melting ore off his skin. The odor of burning flesh filled the tunnel.

As the children watched him, a strange thing happened. His face actually relaxed, shed its hardened edges. His eyes, which had so easily reflected the blood-tones in the lava just a moment before, now dimmed with human frailty, and seemed to come alive. To remember.

He stopped moaning; his eyes came to focus on Short Round. The man looked almost thankful; he seemed on the verge of tears, as if realizing he'd only been having a nightmare and now he was awake.

He pleaded forgiveness to Short Round—in Hindi, then in English.

Other guards appeared suddenly. They grabbed this fallen comrade, dragged him out of the tunnel. He struggled against them, though, trying to break away. Trying to stay awake.

He didn't want to return to the nightmare of Kali.

Short Round watched with dawning comprehension as the wretched guard was pulled out of sight by his brethren mindslaves. "The fire," Short Round whispered to himself. "The fire makes him wake up! I can make Dr. Jones—"

Before he finished articulating his discovery, he lifted a heavy rock. The other children observed him fearfully as he hefted it with defiance, afraid he was going to lob it at the last retreating guard, thereby earning them all more lashes. He didn't heave it at the guard, though; rather, he smashed the rock down on the leg-chains that bound him to the other kids.

The ankle-iron was rusty, he figured; it couldn't withstand all that much battering. None of the guards really expected any of the children to actually *try* to escape—after all, where could they go? Short Round smiled grimly with his newfound knowledge. Knowledge was power, Dr. Jones had always told him.

With this power, he would free Dr. Jones.

Repeatedly he brought the rock down on his rusting shackles as the other children stared nervously.

Short Round was determined to escape. And unbeknownst to the guards, he had somewhere to go.

The wind thrummed over the cavernous ceiling, joining the atonal incantations of the multitude gathered in the temple. Mola Ram warbled in counterpoint to the tumultuous chanting. The Maharajah sat upon his dais, weaving, transfixed in the smoke and fervor.

Chattar Lal still stood beside Indiana. "Do you understand what he tells us?" he prodded the neophyte.

Indiana nodded dully. "Kali Ma protects us. We are her children. We pledge devotion by worshipping her with offerings of flesh and blood."

Chattar Lal seemed pleased. His student was coming along so quickly.

A scream prevented his response though—heartrending, terrified, rising out of the fume-clogged shadows.

Indiana watched emotionlessly as Willie was brought out. She was dressed now in the skirt and halter top of a Rajput maiden, draped with jewels and flowers; held fast by two priests, she wailed, struggling to break free, sweating, crying, swearing, spitting: she knew the fate that awaited.

Chattar Lal motioned toward her to Indy. "Your friend has *seen*, and she had *heard*. Now she will not *talk*."

As she was dragged before the statue of Kali, she saw Indiana. "Indy! Help me! For God's sake what's the matter with you!"

Indy stared at her impassively while her wrists were manacled to the square iron frame that hung from the tireless arms of the fearsome stone goddess.

The sorceress hissed at him Indy help me for god's sake what's the matter with you, but he could only smile at her treachery. Everything was red now, but in negative, so what was dark was light and what was light was dark; but all red. Except the sorceress: she was black.

Black and buzzing, as if ten thousand hornets comprised her substance. Zzzzzzzzhhhh, she screamed at him.

Ssshhh, he thought, you'll wake the serpent. But Kali was here, now. Kali's inspiration alone would quiet the buzzing, still the serpent in his chest. Only through pain and torture and sacrifice to Kali Ma would the buzzing cease, would the serpent sleep.

Indy looked down at his feet. A live boa constrictor slithered over the stone floor, heading for someplace dark. Indy stooped, picked it up, caressed its head: they were spiritbrothers, now. He held the snake to his chest, near its cousin who slept there—held it so Willie could see him with his new family.

She couldn't believe what was happening. "Indy," she begged. "Don't let them do this to me. Don't do this." But he didn't move a muscle to help her. He just kept petting the damn snake.

She was going to die.

She was going to die horribly. Painfully. Alone.

They had taken hold of him somehow; she could see that clearly enough. But how? He'd always been too arrogant for his own good, but she'd actually found that kind of cute—sometimes, at least. Could arrogance account for this . . . possession? Possessed, that's how he looked.

Or maybe this was just the final stage of a powerful seduction, seduced by the fortune and glory he was always after. She could understand seduction—those diamonds were certainly alluring—but this seemed a little over the edge.

Magic?

She didn't know, or care. She only knew she was about to die, and she didn't know why and didn't want to, and hated him for it, and was afraid.

The priests shackled her ankles to the basket.

"Stop it, you're hurting me!" she screamed. "You big lousy dirty ape." Rage foamed at her lips, then dissolved again into supplication. "Be nice, fellas. Come on." And when this had no effect, the distress call again: "Indy!"

Mola Ram circled her as the front of the frame was closed, wedging her, spread-eagled, in the wafer-thin cage. Indiana looked away from her, to gaze adoringly at the face of the monstrous goddess above them. He dropped his snake to the floor; it crawled into a corner.

The priests tore off Willie's necklaces.

"You got some kind of nerve!" she roared. "I knew you thugs were just a bunch of cheapskates! You're saving these trinkets for someone—well, she'll never look as good as me!" She was defiant now, contemptuous.

Mola Ram came before her. He seemed pleased with her insolence. He bowed slightly, then raised his hand, tauntingly, toward her heart.

Icy chills coursed through her, to watch the High Priest's fingers approach her chest. She'd seen this part before; it terrorized her to envision it now. Her knees turned to water. If she hadn't been held up by shackles and meshing she'd have crumpled to the ground. All her fine brazen boldness shriveled in the face of this wizard's advancing hand. She fell to bargaining. "Wait. Not yet. Please. I'll do anything. I know a lot of politicians and important industrialists. I was a personal dinner guest of Chiang Kai Shek. I know people who work for Al Capone." A surrealistic thought struck her, and she laughed absurdly. "In fact, do you have a cousin named Frank Nitti, he lives in Chicago, you know you could be his brother."

Mola Ram sneered at her rantings. Heinously, he brought his hand closer. She felt his icicle fingers touch the cloth over her breast. There was a sickening pressure, like a finger pushing into a throat, or a thumb over an eye: nauseating pressure, intrusive, unexpected, violating.

She swooned.

In the half-lit tunnel, Short Round set a measured beat, stone against iron, trying to crack his bonds. He'd seen it done just this way in *I Am a Fugitive from a Chain Gang*, except it was harder to do than to watch. His arm was growing tired, his despair strong. What would Indy and Willie do without him? What if the Wheel of Transmigration separated them in the next life? It well might; there was no predicting the roll of the Wheel.

The other children continued to watch him. He wouldn't have minded some help, but they looked so weird standing there—like ghosts, or worse—that he decided concentrating on his task was the best bet. He thrust his fatigued arm down one more time, knocking stone against iron. And the clasp broke. Just like that: he was free.

The other children stared darkly at him, in wonder, in disbelief, in unanticipated *new* belief. This was freedom, here, in their midst.

Furtively, Short Round peered about. He was out of bondage none too soon, it seemed. At the tunnel mouth, a guard was approaching. In the torch-lit shadows, Short Round took a chance. He dove, rolled across the tunnel to a mine car full of rocks being pushed along the rails by two chained slaves.

The guard lumbered past, unsuspecting. Using the mine car as cover, Short Round crouched, walking along with it, up and out of the pit.

The other children from his chain gang watched him escape, but said nothing.

Up in the temple, Willie came out of her swoon to see Mola Ram walking away. He hadn't plucked out her heart; he'd just been toying with her! Tears of hope sprang to her eyes. Maybe all wasn't lost yet.

She struggled fiercely to break her bonds, pulled and tugged at her wrists—and good God, it happened: with all the lubricating sweat, she managed to extricate one slender wrist from the manacle that strapped her to the sacrificial frame.

She reached out her free left arm imploringly to Indiana. "Indy, help us! Snap out of it. You're not one of them. Please. Please come back to me. Please, come back to me."

Indy walked over to her cage, reached out slowly, took her hand in his. She grasped his fingers tightly. He brought her hand up to his lips, kissed it. They stared deeply into each other's eyes. *Yes, yes,* Willie thought, *he's come for me.*

Resolutely he lifted her hand back to the iron frame, wrapped the shackle around her wrist, snapped it shut, locked the cage door in place. Then he bestowed a knowing look upon Mola Ram, who smiled, nodded, began chanting again.

Willie was aghast. "No. What're you doing? Are you mad?"

He just stared at her, as if from a long way away.

She spat at him. She had never hated anyone so much. She would not beg again. She hoped he burned in hell.

The sorceress-demon spat: from her black mouth, it sparked and flared. The buzzing was intensely loud now. It almost drowned out the fluttering, which had returned. The spit seared like fire, hissing in the flesh of his face, hissing with the serpent in his chest, the serpent awake now, uncoiling . . .

But Kali would put it to rest. If he only gave himself to Kali, lost himself in Kali, quelled the buzzing fluttering hissing with the soporific drone of the name of Kali Ma.

Calmly, hollowly, he wiped her spittle from his face; walked away from her, joined the congregation in its febrile chanting: "Mola Ram, Sunda Ram, jai ma Kali, jai ma Kali . . ."

Chattar Lal and Mola Ram exchanged a satisfied glance, gladdened at the sight of the cold-hearted betrayal.

The chanting grew louder.

The wind blasted on, its abominable yowl.

Short Round raced up the next tunnel, then flattened himself against a wall, panting. He peeked around the corner. Just as he'd remembered: this was one of the holding caves. There on the floor in one corner were Indy's whip, hat, and bag. He ran in, picked the things up; put the hat on his head, the bullwhip on his belt, the bag over his shoulder . . . and felt, for all the world, like a miniature Indiana Jones. He pulled himself erect and marched upright into the adjacent tunnel. There, two guards saw him. They immediately gave chase.

Now he *really* felt like Indiana Jones. He tore out into this level of the excavation, running full throttle, dodging guards, outdistancing his lumbering pursuers, weaving among the scores of slave children who watched this elusive boy in amazement.

He darted in a narrow side tunnel, losing the guards on his tail. Up a twisting shaft, Short Round climbed, coming out on another level. Stealthily he crawled through an access tunnel; warily he peered back into the main pit.

Twenty yards away, he saw a tall, wooden ladder leaning against the wall, its top perched against a ledge that fronted a warren of burrows. Other tunnels pierced the rockface up and down the length of the ladder. From the lowest of these, a child emerged, carrying a sack of rocks. He stepped out onto the ladder, climbed down carrying his load.

When the boy reached the bottom, he nearly collapsed from exhaustion—then jumped in shock to see Short Round running toward him at top speed. Shorty motioned him to keep quiet. Incredulous, the boy simply gaped at Short Round as the furtive escapee leapt to the ladder and began to scramble up. Just like James Cagney in the last scene of *Public Enemy*. Short Round hoped it wasn't going to be his own last scene, as well.

He was already fairly high when the guard spotted him. The guard chased him up the ladder. Children in nearby alcoves stopped working to watch as Short Round ascended higher and higher, the angry guard closing the distance between them.

Twenty feet above the top of the ladder, a wide overhang of rock jutted out far into the center of the great pit. Twenty feet out from the wall against which the ladder teetered, a rope hung in space, straight down from the overlying shelf, dangling from a small hole in that partial ceiling.

Dirty faces stared up at Short Round from every nook and burrow as he reached the top of the ladder. The guard was barely ten feet behind him. Shorty climbed off the ladder into the tunnel at the top . . . then a moment later, with a running jump, leapt back onto it, kicking it away from the wall.

He held on tightly—so did the guard, several rungs lower—as the ladder tipped in a gentle arc, away from the wall, out into the open pit. Certain suicide. At least that was the thought of the mesmerized children who watched the scene being played out. They wished him well in his final escape from this place.

But as the top of the ladder passed the bottom of the hanging rope, Short Round grabbed onto it. The ladder, with the guard, continued on over, crashing thunderously to the earth far below—

while Short Round dangled precariously in space for a moment, then steadily pulled himself up the rope, through the roof hole, into the overhead chamber.

He rolled a few feet across the floor; he lay still. It was empty in here, and quiet, though in the next room he could hear the muffled droning of a thousand narcotized voices. It was a disturbing sound.

He got up, went to the far door, pushed it open a crack.

Red light flared around the black statue of Kali, into the small room behind the altar of the temple of death.

In the temple, chains clanked, gears ground, as the sacrificial frame was raised, then supinated, then up-ended, and flipped over, until Willie, stretched out on the iron bracing, found herself staring facedown into the bubbling lava pit.

Staring at her own death. How excruciating it would be; how meaningless. How alone: that was the worst. Periodically she caught an image of herself in the glistening curvatures of the red bubbles far below, forming, breaking, distorting her reflection until it burst. Reflections of her life: contorted, overheated, now about to explode, like a droplet of water in a vat of acid. She wished she could do it over; she'd do it differently next time.

But there wouldn't be a next time. She didn't believe in karma, or reincarnation, or heaven, or miracles. It would take a miracle now to save her.

She held her breath. She hoped she passed out before it got too painful.

Mola Ram gave orders to the executioner, who slowly turned the giant wooden wheel that lowered the basket. The crowd chanted. Willie screamed. Indy turned to watch.

The sorceress hung above the pit in her true form, that of giant raven, suspended floating on the hot-air currents above the hole of fire. She was not flapping or fluttering now, as she had against the inside of his skull. She only floated, now: smiling, buzzing softly, knowing. Knowing the horror. The emptiness of his skull. The poison in his chest. She knew. She knew it all.

She had to die.

Mola Ram joined in the chanting now; the chanting got wilder. Indiana lent his voice to the masses.

Willie hung, suspended on the iron frame, watching the boiling magma draw nearer to her body, as it was lowered, inch by inch, into the sacrificial pit. Into the fire.

EIGHT
Break for Freedom

SHORT ROUND peered from behind the altar, into the cavernous temple, just in time to see Willie being dipped. And there, at the crater's edge, stood Indiana, impassively watching her disappear.

Shorty whispered to himself. "Indy, no."

The chanting was so loud it almost drowned out his thought. But he knew what he had to do. He had to be Indy's pinchhitter. He had to wake Indy up. He had to pull Willie out. He had to get to America, and that was no big joke.

But first things first. He promised the Three Star-Gods a shrine in his heart forever, in return for success on this mission. He promised Lou Gehrig never to doubt the great slugger's batting average again, even if his brother Chu came back as a whole herd of baby elephants.

He laid Indy's accessories down on the shadow of an archway; he turned his baseball cap brim-backwards for action; and he jumped out onto the altar.

He waved at Indy. Chattar Lal saw him first, though. The

Prime Minister shouted at two guards to grab the kid, but the kid was too fast. As the guards tried to apprehend him, he scooted off the altar toward Indiana.

One of the priests intervened, grabbing Short Round by the arm. Shorty bit the man's hand; the priest let go. Another priest got in the way. Short Round kicked him hard, then skirted his crippled lunge.

In another second, he made it to Indy. He smiled up hopefully: maybe the good doctor was already awake, was just putting on a good act as part of a clever con game, to fool these fools into something foolhardy.

Indy brutally backhanded Short Round across the face. He fell to the ground, his hat knocked off.

Tears coated his eyes. "Wake *up*, Dr. Jones."

Blood trickled from the corner of Short Round's mouth as he stared at his hero in wounded disbelief. The moment didn't last long, however; it only forged, for Shorty, the notion of what he had to do. It would be hard for him, but what, in this life, was not hard?

He sprang up, ran toward the wall. Another guard was quickly on his heels.

Chattar Lal had observed this entire transaction with distinct approval: the great Indiana Jones was now an obvious convert and devout believer. Satisfaction filled the Prime Minister's eyes as he watched the guard chase down the annoying child, and as he watched Willie creak down to her final consummation.

Willie continued to try holding her breath on the descending frame, but it was no use. It was impossibly hot, immeasurably bright. Waves of heat rose to scald her face; the acid fumes burned her eyes, her lungs, her skin. She was going to die.

It was lonely. And scary. She tried to think of a prayer, but couldn't think. She tried to twist away from the searing pain, but couldn't move. Except she kept moving closer.

Short Round, meanwhile, reached the wall, where he yanked a

flaming torch out of its bracket, and swiveled on his attacker. The firebrand whisked past the guard's face, backing him off. Shorty ran up to the executioner, swinging the torch fiercely. The executioner retreated from his wheel; Willie hung, suspended where she was, temporarily unmoving.

Mola Ram was not as sanguine about these events as Chattar Lal seemed to be. This little monster was defiling the rites of Kali: he had to be punished. "Catch him! Kill him!" the High Priest shouted in Hindi, enraged.

Two more guards went after Short Round, who was once more running straight at Indy.

"Indy, wake up!" he yelled again. No response. At the last second he turned on the two guards about to catch him, forcing them back with his torch. In that second, Indy grabbed him from behind and began to strangle him.

Indy held Shorty by the neck, lifting and turning the boy in the air until they were facing each other, at Indy's arm's length. Short Round gasped for breath, turning blue, as Indiana choked the life out of him.

The serpent hissed and rattled in his chest, angered at the rude awakening. It had sensed the demon-child's attack before Indy had actually seen him. By the time the demon approached with the torch, Indy was ready, the serpent was ready. Ready to strike.

Indy wake up! the demon-child screamed, the words etched in the torchlight he cradled. The serpent recoiled. The demon was protean: he transformed into a ruby clot of blood, thick with purpose, gelid and steaming in the cold cave air, smelling juicy with death.

Spinning, sputtering . . . Indy grabbed it, this clot-thing demon-child. Grabbed it and squeezed, tried to squeeze the dark squirting gob into something of a more pleasing shape, something the shape of Kali, something the size of his fist. Twisting, molding, forming, he turned the thing in his hands, turned it around and around until it faced him, its ghastly eyes bulging out of the gelatinous mass, waving its fire, facing his screaming, calling to the serpent.

With his last breath the boy croaked, "Indy, I love you," uttered the name of the Caretaker of the Celestial Ministry of Exorcism, and thrust the flaming torch into Indy's side.

Indiana went down, the fire roasting his flesh. He wailed in pain, letting go of Short Round.

Fire filled his head, raging out of control in the empty caverns. The serpent shrieked, uncoiling, writhing. The demon-child called to it: it called back, angry with new memory.

Short Round held the torch fast against Indiana's flank, until a guard finally grabbed him, knocking the torch away.

Indiana writhed in pain on the ground. *The light was blinding.* The chanting started to crescendo. The executioner returned to his wheel, began lowering Willie once more. Chattar Lal smiled. Mola Ram praised Kali. The guard drew a knife, brought it up to Short Round's throat. "Hold it," said Indiana, rising. "He's mine." Indy took Shorty from the assassin, carried him a few steps away, lifted him into the air, held him high over the pit. Short Round looked down into the boiling furnace in terror; then into Indy's eyes, for the last time.

Indy winked.

"I'm all right," he whispered. "You ready?"

Shorty winked back.

He threw Short Round to a clear area, turned, and punched the nearest priest in the face; then punched another in the belly. Short Round gave one nearby guard a whirling karate kick to the side. At the same moment, a priest attacked. Shorty grabbed the cleric's belt, rolled onto his own back, and flipped the man onto his head. The crowd beyond the crevasse was all wrapped up in the ecstasy of the ritual; they had no idea what was going on around the stone goddess. Chattar Lal knew well; he quickly exited behind the altar as the fighting increased.

Two priests converged on Indy, but Short Round threw himself in front of one, who consequently flipped into the other. Indy threw another priest into the executioner. Both went flying down off the platform. Unfortunately, the executioner disengaged the handbrake. The iron cage containing Willie started plummeting down the pit.

Indy jumped on the platform, clamping the brake on the spinning wheel. Again Willie stopped in her deathly plunge.

Mola Ram was growing more disturbed. He moved carefully through the disorder, toward the Sankara Stones on the altar.

Another priest attacked Indy, swinging his incense burner. Indy doubled over, then stood up under the priest, letting the man's own momentum carry him over, and into the crevasse. There was a hissing flash; the priest was no more.

Short Round stood with his back to a wall, holding several guards at bay with a torch in one hand, a knife in the other.

The executioner crawled to his wheel, went back to lowering Willie. She was only yards away from the spumes of fulminating lava now. The heat was so intense, her clothes began to smoke; her eyelashes began to singe. Her consciousness reached the limits of its strength; her life began to shimmer. Random images flitted through her cooking brain; ancient memories, silvered feelings. The last thought that trickled by before she blacked out entirely was, *In olden days a glimpse* . . .

Indy knocked the executioner off the platform once more. As he was beginning to crank the cage up out of the brew, a priest attacked him with a pole. He grabbed the pole, threw the priest off its other end, into the pit.

He fenced a guard with the pole, finally bashing him unconscious. This brought him near the altar, where he noticed Mola Ram bending over the stones. Indy broke the stick over Ram's back.

Mola Ram fell forward. Indy raised his half-stick to finish the job on Ram, when the High Priest looked up, smiled . . . and disappeared through a secret trapdoor at the base of the altar.

Indy swore, threw the stick away, raced back to the wheel, and began to crank it, once more slowly raising the cage in which Willie's unconscious body was still trapped, still smoking.

Chattar Lal appeared behind him, dagger upraised.

"Indy, look out!" shouted Short Round, still swinging his torch.

Indy turned in time to dodge Lal's dagger thrust; the two men struggled beside the wheel. Below, the iron frame creaked lower; the brake was on, but worn thin.

By now the congregation across the crevasse could see something was awry. They stopped chanting, began dispersing in increasing panic. The little Maharajah was one of the first to leave, surrounded by a cadre of his bodyguards.

Indy, breaking free from Chattar Lal, managed to hold the wheel steady. Lal attacked him again. Indy blocked the knife, stunning Lal, knocking him against the wheel.

The wheel turned; Chattar Lal was caught in its spokes. His leg was partially crushed in the gears; but he managed to free himself, and crawled away.

Shorty jumped up on the platform, holding the last guard back with his torch as Indy once more put the brake on—though it didn't feel like it would hold for long. Then Indy stood up, but the guard ran away. Indy and Shorty frantically began turning the wheel, raising the cage.

When the iron frame was out of the pit, suspended at floor level, Short Round stayed at the wheel, holding it with all his strength, while Indy ran to the edge of the pit and pulled the basket over solid ground.

"Give me some slack," he called to Shorty. Short Round turned the wheel a bit; Indy lowered the cage to the earth.

He released Willie's bindings, stared anxiously at her unconscious form. "Willie, Willie. Wake up, Willie." He could hardly remember the specifics of the Nightmare anymore, only the feeling of sickening terror, and a few flitting images: huge scavenger birds, hungry snakes (ugh! snakes!), a demon-child who was Shorty but wasn't, and Willie as a malignant sorceress bent on eating his soul. And he'd tried to kill her, he remembered, had laughed to see her lowered into the pit for Kali's pleasure. Thank God it was over; over, awake, back among the living.

Willie moaned, moved her head, fluttered her eyes.

"Willie!" he said happily.

She opened her eyes, saw him over her . . . and slapped him. Tried to, anyway; her hand was so weak, it barely grazed his cheek.

Shorty flinched all the same.

Indy just grinned. "Willie, it's me. I'm back, I'm back, Willie." And then he sang: " 'Home, home on the range, where the deer and the antelope play.' "

Willie had never been so glad to hear such bad singing in her life. As the fresh air and foul voice revived her, she was crying, coughing, laughing, all at once. She didn't see Chattar Lal with the knife until it was almost too late.

"Look out," she choked.

Indy whirled. Falling backwards, he kicked the dagger from Lal's hand. Lal was on him in an instant.

They rolled around the floor. Willie was too weak to move; Shorty stayed by his post at the wheel.

The antagonists scuttled near the edge, then away. They pushed apart; both men stood, Indy between Lal and the pit. Willie inched away from them, toward the wheel.

Lal began wailing in Hindi: "Betray, betray, you betray Kali Ma. Kali Ma shall destroy you."

Then he lunged.

With the strength of madness, he flew into Indiana, attempting to take Indy with him in a glorious suicidal plunge.

He knocked both of them back onto the sacrificial frame. Their combined momentum scraped it along the floor, swung it out over the pit, where it dangled precariously.

Indy broke from Lal's grip, leaping away, slamming against the inner upper lip of the shaft, hanging on to the precipice . . . as Willie threw off the brake with all her returning strength. The crankwheel whined, and the frame sank like pig iron.

Fell and tumbled, with Chattar Lal riding it all the way.

The splash of molten lava. To Willie, it sounded like sweet revenge.

Indy looked down. Chattar Lal's body briefly exploded into

flame. The flesh was gone in an instant; there was a momentary glimpse of skeleton; and then all was consumed and obliterated by the broil.

Indiana pulled himself back to safety. Willie sat up; Shorty ran over. They huddled there a moment, quiet, in each other's arms. Glad to rest, to be together, to be alive.

The temple was empty now, and silent, except for the bodies of unconscious priests and the hissing of the liquid fires.

Indy walked over to the three Sankara Stones at the base of the altar. They weren't glowing anymore. Shorty brought his bundle over to him: hat, whip, bag, shirt. Indy put the stones in his bag, the bag over his shoulder; the whip on his belt; the shirt on his wounded back.

Then he walked over to where Short Round's cap still lay on the floor. He picked it up, dusted it off, set it ceremoniously on Short Round's head.

Then he put on his own hat.

And all was right with the world.

Shorty smiled loudly at his old pal. "Indy, my friend." No matter what else happened now, that existed still, and would forever exist, like the stars.

Willie got her legs back and walked over to them. "Indy, you've got to get us out of here."

Indy looked around this place of evil, heard the distant rumblings of the mine cars full of rocks, the clandestine tortures, the whimpering of innocents. . . .

"Right. All of us," he muttered.

They moved off, toward the chamber behind the altar.

In the mines, a remarkable thing had begun to happen. The children had seen the face of freedom.

Dozens of children had actually witnessed Short Round's miraculous exploit. Then rumor of the feat had spread to scores of others:

One had escaped.

One had escaped.

One could escape.

It put an edge to their work now. They watched their guards through lowered lids, instead of lowering their heads altogether. They shuffled their feet from surliness or indecision, rather than from exhaustion. Some even counted their numbers, and the number of the guard.

When Mola Ram fled the fighting at the altar, he hurried down to the mines. He told the chief guards what was taking place. He directed some of them back up to the temple, to help with the battle; he told the rest to be on the alert for the three heathens, who might try to escape by fleeing this way, through the mines.

He told no one to be on the alert for a slave rebellion.

A chain gang of five children trudged with effort down a dark tunnel toward an empty mine car. The little girl at the end of the line fell.

The guard at the tunnel mouth saw this as an obvious case of malingering. He stormed in furiously, yanked her to her feet, raised his strap to beat her. At the top of his swing, he saw Indy rise out of a shadow. Indy crashed his fist into the guard's jaw; the guard went down and out.

Short Round took the key from the guard's belt and quickly unlocked the leg-irons on the slave children as they stared in silent awe at these proceedings. When they were free, Indy showed them how to shackle the guard to the mine car.

That's how it began.

These five jumped another guard in another tunnel—he was so surprised he didn't even shout before he was knocked unconscious with rocks—liberating five more. And then there were ten.

It was like a chain reaction. Dozens were roaming the tunnels at will before the remaining guards even knew anything was amiss. Then it was a free-for-all.

The alarm was given. Guards tried to herd the manacled kids to a central cell. Indy stopped many, though; he'd bring one down with his whip and the free children would pelt him with stones, or he'd punch one cold and Willie or Shorty would take his keys.

Every guard that fell freed more children.

The power was infectious. Guards were on the run. Willie would crack them senseless with a spade; Shorty tripped them with chains; bands of ex-slaves pushed them from ledges or off ladders; baskets full of rocks were emptied onto the heads of fleeing guards.

Finally, the guards were just massively outnumbered by their prisoners. And, of course, outclassed.

When all were free, with the mine guards routed, the children stood in a great pack, looking around with a lot of exhilaration, and not a little surprise.

Short Round stood before them, the true inspiration for this revolt in the first place. "Come on, follow me!" he called out, leading them, cheering, toward the exit. It was a children's crusade.

Indy and Willie followed. The troop encountered an occasional guard on the way—either trying to stop them or trying to flee—but the children stormed right over them, overwhelming any opposition by sheer weight of numbers and momentum.

Up the winding path they marched, their own masters at last. Through the last tunnel, up to the top of the excavation, into the room behind the altar . . .

Into the temple.

Deserted now. Only the wind hummed its lonely melody; only Kali stood there to watch.

Indy, Willie, and some of the bigger children tore down a long wooden plank from the altar, one of the decorative elements flanking the giant statue, carved with myriad hideous figures of Kali and her atrocities. When it had fallen to the ground, they carried it to the edge of the natural chasm separating the altar from the rest of the temple, the last barrier to freedom.

They planted one end firmly on the edge, upended it—for a moment it looked as if they were erecting a flagstaff—then let it arc down across the crevasse, until its other end rested on the far precipice.

It formed a narrow plank over the churning lava.

Children kept arriving. The altar side was already filled to overflowing; kids were teetering on the brink.

Indy started them running across the plank to the other side. Below them fire bubbled, flaring with occasional outbursts of molten spray. But none of the children faltered. One by one they ran to the far side of the temple, toward the palace, toward freedom.

After a while, though, Indy noticed the plank beginning to smoke, from the constant, intense heat that rose. The children were yelping as they ran, now, the hot, dry wood scorching their bare feet. Indy sent them packing faster and faster; the wood smoldered progressively, white smoke turning black.

Finally the plank burst into flame at two points. Indy urged the last kids on, shouting them across as they leapt over the flames. The plank cracked as the last child scrambled to the other side. When Shorty stepped out onto it, it burned through completely, flaming into the pit. Indy and Willie caught him by the collar at the last moment and dragged him back from the fall.

On the other side, some children turned to wait for their deliverers.

"Go! Go!" Indy called to them.

So they went.

Out the rear exit of the temple, up a hundred twisting stairs, through a dozen secret passages, out a dozen secret entrances to the palace.

Through the palace corridors they ran, hundreds of fleeing children, wearing hundreds of unchained smiles. They crossed courtyards, crossed bridges when they came to them, crossed foyers and exterior portals and entrance ramps and gateways.

And then it was the open road, the jungle, the mountain passes.

They were free.

"Now what are we going to do?" asked Shorty as the last liberated slave child disappeared out of the temple.

"Go the long way," Indiana suggested. As always, just making it up as he went along.

They trotted back into the room behind the altar, then on to the top of the quarry. Indy looked at one of the small, empty gondolas sitting unattended on its rails.

"Those tracks have got to lead out of the mines," he reasoned.

He moved forward, to the top of a circular path.

"Where are you going?" Willie asked suspiciously.

"To get us a ride."

About half of the mine cars were moving at various speeds along the rails, pulled along by underground cables. Some were full of rocks; some were empty. Indy went for an empty one.

As the trolley rolled in to the central collection terminal, Indiana ran alongside it, holding on, trying to stop it, getting half-dragged. All at once the car stopped, seemingly of its own accord.

It wasn't of its own accord.

Indy jerked to a halt and looked up to see a giant guard stopping the cart with his arm. A really giant guard. The same guard he'd tangled with twice before. He hadn't done too well either time. Okay, then, so it was a grudge match.

Indy started to throw a punch, then thought better of it. Instead, he stooped for a piece of timber and smashed the guard in the head. The timber splintered. The guard didn't move. This looked serious.

He grabbed a sledgehammer out of the truck, swung it into the giant's left ribs. The titan only smiled, belched, tore the hammer out of Indy's hand, tossed it aside. Then he wrapped his left arm around Indy's waist. Then he punched Indy's belly in.

Indy hit the dirt. He bounced right back up, kicking the giant in the face, but the colossus barely rocked. This looked really serious.

The guard seized Indy again, punched him twice in the chest, once in the throat, dragged his head along the side of the mine car, then lifted the unfortunate adventurer into the air.

Shorty lashed the big ape with Indy's fallen bullwhip. There was a CRACK and a yowl: the lummox dropped Indy into the mine car. Shorty flayed the giant again, but the brute just grabbed him and flung him far away.

The mine car started moving, pulled up a long slope by its cable. The giant jumped in. In a moment, the two men were bashing away at each other, riding up the hill.

Willie followed the cart along at a distance, sometimes watching the fight, sometimes throwing rocks at the guard (when she could get a clear shot), sometimes looking for an empty, freely moving car on a rail that didn't dead-end.

Indy had found a weak spot at the giant's neck and was doing his best to batter it with an iron bar. But every time he started pressing his advantage, horrible pain would wrack his body and he'd crumple again to the guard's pummeling.

"What's the matter with him?" Willie shouted to Short Round.

Short Round saw the problem; he pointed up. There, on the next ledge higher, stood the Maharajah. He was jabbing his turban pin into his Indiana Jones doll.

The mine car reached the top of the slope and tipped over, dumping Indy and the giant out with a pile of rocks onto a moving conveyer belt. The giant picked up a spade. Indy raised a pickax to parry, but dropped it as the agony seared through his face. He rolled over just in time to avoid being brained by the giant's blow.

On the shelf high above, the Maharajah twisted his pin in the face of the little figurine.

Willie found an empty car that appeared to lead out to one of the exit tunnels. "I got one, Indy, I got one! We can go home now!"

Indy wasn't listening, though. He was alternately dodging punches or swinging a kerosene can against the guard's head.

Shorty, meanwhile, had made his way to a thin waterfall that cascaded down from the Maharajah's level. It poured into a revolving wheel of buckets, the function of which was to bring full buckets of water up to the top tier. Shorty jumped onto a full bucket at the bottom, rode it up to the higher level, jumped off again. He ran across the ledge; moments later, he was battling the evil Prince. The doll skittered across the ground.

Indiana skittered across the conveyor belt, wrestling with the guard. He could see the end of the line now: a great iron wheel that crushed every rock and boulder that passed under its momentous turning. The conveyor fed the crusher endlessly; it was insatiable.

Willie threw rocks at the giant. The giant pounded Indy and sometimes threw rocks back at Willie. Indy kicked at the giant or blasted him with the kerosene can as Short Round struggled with the Maharajah in mortal, twelve-year-old combat. With each passing second Indy was conveyed nearer to the jaws of the stone-crusher.

Shorty got the Maharajah by the throat. The Maharajah stabbed the turban pin deeply into Short Round's leg. Shorty winced in pain, rolling away, holding his leg. This prince was more of a streetfighter than he looked. But that was fine; Short Round was no debutante.

The giant grabbed Indy's arm, but the sleeve tore off. As he twisted back off-balance, the huge man's sash got snagged by the iron roller. He desperately tried to crawl away against the relentless tugging. But it had him. He screamed hideously as his body was pulled under the crusher, feet first, and pulverized.

Bloody rock dust crunched out the other side.

Up on the high level, Short Round stumbled to a near wall, grabbed a torch; he turned as Zalim Singh rushed him with a knife. Shorty crouched and extended his arm; the Maharajah impacted himself on the burning tar.

He wailed, fell back, sat down hard. Short Round threw dirt on a flap of burning cloth, prepared to leap on the young monarch again . . . but there was no need.

The Maharajah looked as if he'd just awakened from a bad dream. And so he had.

Short Round sat before him. He'd seen this transformation before. "It was the black nightmare of Kali," he explained to Zalim Singh. Short Round, like The Shadow, knew what evil lurked in the hearts of some men; some boys, too.

The Maharajah nodded. His eyes were full of grief. "They made me do evil things. May Lord Krishna forgive me." It was only fragmented visions now, but they stabbed at his conscience like broken shards.

Indiana, in the meantime, had jumped up to a catwalk above the conveyor belt, leading near where Willie waited with the empty trolley. Time was running out, though. Mola Ram arrived, with reinforcements.

In seconds, they were encircling the place.

"Get down here, Shorty!" yelled Willie. "I got us a ride!"

A guard rushed her. She yanked the iron brake handle off the mine car and bashed his head in—then held another, more leery, at bay.

Short Round lowered himself down the rocky balcony. The Maharajah leaned over to see him off. "Please, listen. To go out you must take the left tunnel," he warned.

Shorty stared at him uncertainly a moment, then knew he was telling the truth. "Thanks," he said, and scooted down the rock.

Indy was having trouble. Three guards jumped down to the catwalk, forcing him back. He shinnied up a short ladder, knocked it away, ran along a parallel ledge. The guards opened fire with pistols. Indy shielded himself behind a cart, wheeling it to the next catwalk.

Willie started her car rolling down the track; climbed in. The guard who'd been watching her took his chance now and grabbed her leg. Short Round was there, though. He picked up a perfect rock, took his stance, checked the runner at first, shouted, "Lefty Grove!" and let fly with a sliding pitch that caught the guard hard behind the ear. The man went down.

Another guard grabbed Shorty from behind as Willie's car slowly started gathering momentum. Shorty slithered out of his assailant's grip and karate-kicked him in the stomach.

A wild-looking priest now began chasing Willie's truck. Shorty raced up to intersect the man, rolled into a little ball, threw himself in the attacker's path. They both went spilling in different directions. Short Round got right up again, pursued the mine car another fifty feet, and finally managed to jump on, just as it was really picking up speed. Willie pulled him in.

They looked around quickly until they spotted Indiana, still dodging guards up in the catwalks and scaffolds.

"Indy, come on, hurry!" they bellowed together.

Indy looked down at them, saw where he was in relation to them, saw where they were heading: into a large exit tunnel at the near end of the quarry.

He ran hard, jumping from ledge to ladder to catwalk to beam. Guards were shooting at him from all sides now, splintering wood, chipping rock. Mola Ram stood on high ground, shouting orders, pointing to the departing commandoes.

"They are escaping! Kill them!" he commanded in Hindi. The guards doubled their efforts.

Indy came to the end of the scaffolding. Guards rallied behind him; below and above. He leapt into dim air, caught hold of a block and tackle that carried him at dizzying speed, down, on a line coverging with the accelerating mine car.

"Follow them! Kill them!" Mola Ram roared.

Bullets whizzed and exploded. The car sailed on toward the tunnel; Indy sailed on toward the car. When he was a few yards above it, a few to the side, he let go—and flew, in a not-so-gentle arc, into the speeding gondola.

They whooped, crouching down to avoid the caroming bullets.

Indy noticed an unconscious thug at the bottom of the car. He took the man's gun, then dumped him out over the edge, just as the car tore into the blackness of the tunnel.

Suddenly it was totally dark; no more bullets shattered the air; and they were barreling down the tracks at the bottom of the cab. And they were going to make it.

Back in the quarry, Mola Ram watched the cart zip into the first leg of the escape route to vanish from sight. Fury darkened his eye as he whispered to his aide. "They've stolen the Sankara Stones. They must be stopped."

NINE
Cliffhangers

Torches lighted the way for the careening trolley. Indy quickly saw the tracks separate in two directions, one back around toward the quarry again, one straight out. He lifted a shovel from the floor of the car, swung it down the side just in time to hit a switch on the tracks that hunted them, with a CLANG, onto the exit rail.

This line soon entered another cavern, and branched into two more. Before any action could be taken, it tore down the right fork, into that tunnel.

Short Round looked worried. "No, Indy, big mistake. *Left* tunnel."

But it was too late. They all just held on as the mine car shot down into the darkness of the echoing caves.

There were long descents, short rises; Indiana had a sense they were going even deeper into the mountain. The wind rushed past his face as he stuck his head up on the wide curves, still picking up speed. Willie huddled in the bottom of the cart, trying to catch her breath. Short Round had seen roller coasters in a couple of movies, but nothing as good as this. Except maybe the one in *King Kong*, at the end of the film, when the ape derailed it. But Short Round wasn't scared of monkeys, no matter how big: he'd been born in the Year of the Monkey—which he now took for a good sign that this ride would end well.

Back in the quarry, Mola Ram organized pursuit cars. Guards carrying Khyber rifles filled two wagons and pushed off, rolling into the tunnel the infidels had taken.

Ram stopped a third car from joining the chase, though. He had a more foolproof plan for destroying the thieves of the Sankara Stones, a plan that didn't involve losing more loyal guards in rail-to-rail combat.

Resolutely he walked toward the large side cavern where the main waterfall tumbled into the black crystal of the underground lake.

Indy reaffixed the brake handle to the front of the car, the one Willie had pulled off during the fight, and applied variable pressure to it as they hurtled around, trying to control their speed. Even so, once or twice they took a corner on two wheels. Indy scrunched down, to lower their center of gravity and prevent derailment.

Short Round peered over the back end, expecting trouble. He'd been a thief half his life; it was second nature to him to keep an eye over his shoulder when he was running with the goods.

Willie stayed low. She could see the horizontal support beams of the tunnel racing overhead. They seemed to flash by closer to the car with each successive turn: the tunnel was getting lower.

She was about to mention this, when all at once the car plunged downward—at what felt to Willie like a vertical drop, but was probably just a rather steep incline—throwing them all against the back of the cab; leaving Willie's stomach somewhere back up in the neighborhood of the top of the grade.

They leveled out. Indy returned to the brake lever. Shorty returned to his rear-end lookout post. He was soon rewarded.

A gunshot rang out. Short Round saw the first Thugee car take a curve far behind them. On the straightaway, the riflemen began blasting.

Bullets richocheted off the back of their car, all around the tunnel. They ducked low, until the next bend. Then Indy shouted over the din of the clackering wheels.

"Shorty, come here and take the brake!"

"Read you loud and clear, Indy!" Short Round scurried forward to take the wildly vibrating handle from Indy.

Indiana slid back to the rear. "Slow on the curves," he shouted up, "or we'll fly off the tracks!"

"Read you loud and clear, Indy!" the boy shouted back. He gripped the brake with every muscle in his little hands; he grinned with every muscle in his little face.

With yet one more sinking feeling, Willie realized that this catastrophe was Short Round's idea of a good time. She yelled up at him in a panic of anger: "I hope you're better at this than driving a car!"

His grin grew even more ferocious. "We could let you off right here, lady!" She wasn't his mother *yet*.

Willie closed her eyes, counted to ten. Dear God, the child was turning into another Indiana Jones.

Mola Ram directed a detail of men to the waterfall—more precisely, to the gargantuan cistern that took the run-off from the falls. Like a great round iron pot, it rested on timber and rock supports that wedged it in place, poised there, almost delicately.

Mola Ram had his men get sledgehammers.

The lead chase car was gaining on the escaping vehicle. Indy, Willie, and Shorty spent more time crouching as rifle bullets flared

in the iron-rich ore that filled the tunnels around them. Sporadi-
cally Short Round would pop up to brake on a curve; Indy would
do the same to shoot. He only had six shells in his gun, though, so
he was judicious in his firing.

He actually hit one rifleman, but another immediately took his
place. They seemed unstoppable; they were getting closer.

At the next hard turn, Short Round rode the brake with all his
weight. The brake pad screeched on the metal wheel; sparks flew
like a comet tail.

The ceiling was getting lower again as well. The support beams
rushed over their heads so closely, Indy could barely look over the
top of the car to shoot. His last bullet buried itself in a length of
timber.

One of the thugs sat up to take proper aim and died a hero to
his cause: his head struck an onrushing beam; he was knocked
from the car in two directions. This lightened the load of the pursuit car considerably; it increased its speed.

Indy crouched low, his knees touching Willie's. "Get down,
everybody," he barked. "Get down. They're coming."

Mola Ram's men rhythmically swung their sledgehammers against
the wedges under the huge water-filled cistern. Several tons of
weight pressed down, holding the struts in place. Mola Ram was
not worried, though. They would give with each blow, a millime-
ter at a time, until they finally gave way completely.

And then the cistern would roll over, spill.

"Faster," he ordered.

The sledgehammer rhythm picked up its pace.

Indy yelled at Short Round. "Let up on the brake!"

"What!" shouted the kid. They were already hurtling along like
a train in a silent movie.

"Let her go! Our only chance is outrunning them."

"What about the curves?" Willie pointed out.

"To hell with the curves." He pulled Short Round's hands off the brake. They tore around the bend half an inch airborne, then settled back down on the tracks with a thunderous rattle.

"We're going too fast!" cried Willie.

The guards in the pursuit car were thrown from side to side; they almost went over. Indy's car hit the next curve on two wheels. "Get over on the other side!"

They all hugged the inside, low, as the car whipped around.

The Thuggee car, just behind, also took the curve at full speed. They were heavier, though—big men, long guns. They derailed.

The car flew off the tracks sideways. The guards' heads peered over the top like worried fledglings. They weren't worried long, though. They crashed into a stone wall with an explosion that shook the cavern.

Indy's cart rocketed away. The second Thuggee car was pummeled with debris from the wreck; the driver grabbed for his brake, to avoid the same fate.

Indy smiled boyishly. "One down, one to go."

Mola Ram's guards continued to hammer away at the supports under the mammoth cistern. Finally one of the lateral rocks began to crumble, then quickly shattered under the redistributed pressure.

High above the workers, the cistern listed fractionally. Water lapped over the edge, sloshed around the rim, as the huge tank creaked into this new, slightly tilted position.

Indiana hefted a railroad tie out of the bottom of the car. He leaned it against the rear wall and, after the next burst of gunfire, teetered it over the back, onto the tracks.

It bounced along the rails a few seconds—long enough for the pursuers to spot it and scream, before crashing into it. They weren't demolished, though; the tie just skidded, tumbled, bounced out of the way like a large, useless matchstick.

The guards looked overjoyed. Indy looked sick.

"Any more ideas?" Willie moped. She'd largely decided to forget about getting out of this place alive. That way, maybe she'd be pleasantly surprised. It seemed pretty much out of her hands, in any case.

"Yeah. Short cut," said Indy. He swung at another set of points on the track; the car veered off into a side tunnel. A moment later, the second car forked off in a different direction and disappeared.

"Bad guys go away," noted Short Round with some suspicion. "Where they going?" It couldn't be that easy.

It wasn't. The Thuggee cart suddenly reappeared out of another tunnel—on a parallel track, directly beside them.

One of the guards fired point blank at them, but, in all the jostling, missed. Indy grabbed the muzzle of the rifle, wrenching it from the thug's hands. He swung it around, catching one guard on the jaw.

Another snatched Shorty by the arm.

"Indy, help!"

Indy grabbed his other arm. The two men had a tug-of-war with the boy while Willie jabbed at the others with the Khyber rifle.

Indy won the pulling contest; Shorty lurched into their car, falling to the bottom. In the same second, another guard leapt across onto the rear of Indy's truck. He got his arm around Indy from behind.

Indiana swiveled around and leaned back, scraping the thug against the stone wall flying by. This stunned the man enough so that Indy was able to break his grip. He whirled in a crouch, then came up punching—and knocked the guard over the end of the car.

He turned to help Willie, who'd just slammed another thug down with the gun butt. Before he took a step, the guard he'd just dispatched climbed over the back of the truck again, though; he bashed Indy on the head with a rock. Indy went down.

Willie stepped up instantly. She took aim, gave the man a good right hook to the face, and sent him sailing down onto the tracks for the count. She hadn't spent time in Shanghai without learning *something*.

Indy stood up wobbily. "My mistake." He smiled.

She handed him his hat.

In the car alongside, the guards were picking up their guns. They'd dropped behind about five yards during the last interchange.

"Get down!" shouted Indy. He saw something useful.

He grabbed the shovel, swung it hard at an overhead dumper release; then hit the deck.

A barrage of rocks, dirt, and gravel pelted both cars from the dumper. The following car took it full bore: one guard was crushed outright, then the whole trolley was derailed by debris on the tracks. They went over in a cloud of rock dust as Indy's group, bruised and dirty, roared on.

Roared on into a tunnel studded with stalactites. Indy stuck his head up, but scarcely had time to say "Duck!" The car crashed through the rocky projections, breaking off tips that hung too low from the ceiling, then careening out again with only a minimal loss of speed.

Willie looked up this time. There was once again nothing to do but close her eyes: twenty feet ahead was a break in the track.

They hit the break at sixty. The *good* news was there was a five-foot drop-off beyond it. The car went sailing over the edge, dropped the distance, landed with a CRUNCH on the lower section of track . . . and kept going.

Willie giggled lightly. Anything goes.

———

The sledgehammers kept beating. Two more rock supports gave way; then a third. Almost in slow motion, the enormous pot began to tip.

There were shouts as the guards ran for cover.

Mola Ram stood, removed, on a platform overlooking the event. The noise alone was incredible—the sound of the earth's own engines—as the huge vessel rolled, keeled over, crashed to its side.

With a deafening roar, a million gallons of water burst across the cavern in a surging tidal wave.

Into the tunnels.

This new length of track was straight; the tunnel, high.

Indy smiled with that air of nonchalance Willie both loved and hated. "Brake, Shorty, brake," he said.

Short Round was a little sorry the ride was over already, but figured there'd be other rides. He pulled casually on the brake lever.

It didn't work.

He pulled harder.

It came off in his hands.

"Oh, oh. Big mistake," he said, wide-eyed.

Willie only nodded. "Figures."

It also figured that they were just heading into a long, gentle slope that didn't seem to go anywhere but down.

They, of course, began moving faster still.

Indy bent over the front of the car to look underneath. The entire braking apparatus was hanging loose from the pad. Indiana pulled himself back in.

The three of them looked at each other with complete understanding of what had to be done. They'd been through a lot together. Here was half a moment to remember it.

Willie thought: *You're a good man, Indiana Jones. Wish I'd known you somewhere else.*

Indy thought: *Hope you two guys stick together, 'cause I sure haven't been much help to either one of you.*

Shorty thought: *If this lady is the last treasure Chao-pao discovered before he leaves me in this life, she must be pretty big fine treasure. Better I keep her.*

Willie and Shorty each squeezed one of Indy's hands. Then Indy climbed out over the front of the racing car.

Facing backwards, he lowered himself down. Willie and Short Round held on to his arms and jacket, to give him extra bracing. When his bottom was inches from the rails, he swung a leg underneath the car, trying to kick at the brake pad. The ground was a blur beneath him. His feet fell momentarily—he bumped along, in danger of being dragged under the iron wheels—but he regained his grip.

With one leg he managed to find a foothold on the undercarriage of the car; with his other, he located the brake pad. Slowly, firmly, he applied pressure with his foot; the pad closed against the spinning disk.

"We're going too fast," noted Willie with a feverish grin. She was sweating; her hands were cramping, holding on to Indy for all of their dear lives.

Then she looked up, for one last laugh: the tunnel was ending; the tracks stopped dead at a not too distant stone wall.

Shorty saw it too. "We're gonna crash!" he shouted. The ride was not supposed to end this way at all.

Indiana looked around behind him. No doubt about it: they were flying at top speed into a wall the size of a mountain, and the first thing to hit was going to be Indiana Jones.

He slammed his foot into the brake pad with every ounce of strength he could muster. The pad screamed against the angry iron. Sparks shot out in skyrockets. Indiana's sole was getting hotter, but he closed his mind to the pain, concentrated only on the force his leg could exert, didn't waste energy thinking about the wall.

The wall drew nearer.

But not quite as quickly. Indy groaned with pushing; the brake pad began to smoke. The car slowed even further. The wall approached. Indy jammed down with his whole body. The car slowed more. Indy pressed.

It slowed until it ran down the last few yards to the dead end; rolled gently to a stop, and just nudged Indy's back against the wall.

He stood, limped a few steps away, his boot smoking. "Water," he rasped.

The others got out of the cab, stood there shakily, smiling tentatively.

They could see that the tunnel continued on, somewhat to the left, without any more tracks. So they started to walk.

No one spoke. They were all too full of what had just happened.

Soon, a wind rose quickly to a stiff blow. Then a strange rumbling sound echoed down the tunnel from behind. The walls seemed to be reverberating.

It felt . . . worrisome.

They exchanged uncertain looks, shrugged, walked a little faster. The wind, in particular, disturbed Indy. There shouldn't be so high a wind so low in the earth.

The noise grew louder. They glanced over their shoulders. Nothing. "Indy?" said Willie.

He wasn't sure, but he grasped Willie by the hand; all three of them started jogging.

The rumbling increased. Small debris began to fall from the ceiling; the ground was almost quaking. It made Short Round remember a volcano movie he didn't want to remember just now. He wondered if The Lord of Thunder was angry about something.

They ran. Ran fast, though they didn't know why. Yet.

The noise was stunning now. Willie looked around again. Suddenly she slowed; stopped. Stopped dead in mid-stride, paralyzed with disbelief, awe. Doom.

It was a monster wall of water, crashing spectacularly into the opposite embankment of a cross tunnel far behind them.

But not far enough.

Willie whispered. "Oh, shit."

Short Round and Indiana stopped to see what was keeping Willie. What they saw was a watery cataclysm spewing forward, soon to overtake them. For a long moment, they just stared.

Then Indy grabbed Willie, and they all ran like hell.

The tidal wave smashed furiously down, booming closer every second. At its foaming muzzle it carried the debris of a hundred cluttered tunnels: boulders, branches, animals.

They weren't going to make it.

Except just maybe, at that small side tunnel in the bend ahead . . .

"There!" Indy screamed above the roar. "Dive!"

They sprang toward the hole. Short Round dove through first, just like stealing home. Indy shoved Willie in, then followed himself—just as the tsunami exploded past in the main shaft.

This narrow tunnel dropped precipitously. They slid at a tumble, showered by the small side current of water diverted from the central stream.

They rolled down the chute to a larger tunnel. Shorty looked particularly lighthearted. "That was fun. Wait a minute, I do it again."

Indy collared him before he could take a step, however, pointing him in a more proper direction. Where did these kids learn this stuff? he wondered.

The growl of the tidal wave receded as they caught their breath.

Up ahead, Willie dared to believe she could actually see light, yes, at the end of the tunnel. She was about to mention it when a new explosion boomed behind them. They turned to see another arm of the same wave cascading down now this tunnel, with an alarming force.

They all hollered in unison, started running full tilt toward the daylight. The towering wall of water surged mirthlessly after them.

They raced to the mouth of the tunnel; the first tongues of water were on their backs. Out into sunshine, they emerged . . .

And teetered on the brink. The tunnel exited midway up a cliff: they were looking at a three-hundred-foot sheer drop straight down to a rocky gorge.

Arms flailing to keep their balance, they hovered there a lifetime. Then Indy swung Willie to a narrow ledge on one side of the tunnel-mouth cliff-face, pushing Short Round after her; he jumped to the other side—just as the tidal wave crashed between them, out this gutterspout in the rock. At the forefront was the wreckage: rail ties shot out, and barrels, and all manner of detritus; even a mine car rocketed past. All surging in the water.

It was a massive gusher, spurting out of this and multiple other tunnels all around them in the cliffside. Short Round and Willie stayed balanced on their little ledge; Indy remained perched on his, on the opposite side of the erupting geyser.

Willie looked down for a second, but vertigo nearly overcame her. Water thundered into the gorge below; crocodiles slithered angrily in the shallow streambed there, disturbed out of their afternoon slumber.

Indy looked around. The gorge was maybe a hundred yards across; craggy bluffs rose on the other side to an expanse of flat plain that resembled the way home, as far as Indy could tell from this distance. Then he saw the bridge.

It was a thin rope bridge, swinging between the two plateaus. On this side it emerged about twenty feet above and another twenty beyond where Willie and Shorty were clutching the rocks. Indiana shouted to them across the blasting waterspout.

"Willie, head for the bridge!" He pointed up.

She looked. She looked away. Would this never end?

"Nothing to it," Short Round encouraged. "Follow me."

He edged along the narrow precipice on which they were balanced, toward the outcropping that lay directly beneath the bridge. Reluctantly, Willie followed. Once under the bridge, they began climbing up the rocks.

Rockclimbing is an activity at which twelve-year-olds are known to excel; this instance was exemplary of that fact. Short Round scrabbled like a mountain goat, finding nooks and handholds that seemed to have been awaiting his arrival all these centuries. Willie was somewhat less agile in this endeavor. Still, she was a dancer; moreover, she was running for her life—and she hadn't gotten as far as she *had* gotten without being light on her feet. So she wasn't all that far behind Shorty.

Indiana was having a bit more difficulty. For one thing, his foot was still painfully numb from braking the runaway mine car. For another, he had to scale the cliff up, over, and around the several geysers between him and the bridge. The rockface here was wet, slippery, perilous.

He grabbed at the sparse scrubbrush for support; he inched along, crab-wise, slowly. With one unfeeling foot, his size was a distinct disadvantage.

Willie and Short Round pulled themselves up at the end of the bridge. Behind them in the cliff, a dark tunnel ran back into the mines. In front of them, the rope bridge looked more like taunt than hope.

It spanned the gorge like the last strands of a spiderweb at the end of the summer. It was at least a century old. It had not been built by the army corps of engineers.

It consisted of two thick lines at its base, connected by hundreds of worm-eaten, moldy wooden slats—and hundreds of empty spaces where slats used to be. Along the length of this catwalk, vertical side ropes linked the foot-span to two thin upper ropes that crossed the gorge, constituting flimsy hand railings.

Willie balked.

Short Round, though, it should be remembered, had had lots of experience running hell-bent along Shanghai rooftops, not to mention scatting across the clotheslines that connected tenement windows, to elude pursuit. So he was less deterred by the sight that confronted them now.

Tentatively, he stepped out onto the bridge. It held. He turned, smiling to Willie. "Easy like pie! Kid's stuff!"

Suddenly the board under him broke. Disintegrated, actually. Had Willie not been expecting such an eventuality, the boy would have tumbled into the abyss. But she grabbed him by the scruff, yanked him back to safety.

He looked a little pale, less cocky now. Yet there was nowhere to go but onward. Once more, he stepped onto the risky footing, concentrating very hard on being much more yin than yang. This time, it held. After weighing the alternatives, Willie followed. She tried to imagine this was a solo performance for a big producer: there could be no wrong moves; there was no starting over.

Cautiously, step by step, they made their way along the span, walking gingerly over the missing or obviously rotten slats. They had to cling to the rope hand rails, too, for the bridge swayed constantly in the wind, as well as bouncing up and down in synchronized resonance to their footfalls. Short Round begged Madame Wind, Feng-p'o, to go play somewhere else.

It was the longest, slowest promenade Willie had ever taken.

Behind them, Indy finally pulled himself up from under the bridge. Almost free. He paused for a moment, catching his breath. Willie and Short Round, he could see, were halfway across, wavering every step. Maybe he ought to wait until they were over so his additional weight didn't rock the crossing too much.

Behind him, there were footsteps. He ducked to the side of the tunnel mouth, disengaging his whip from his belt as he did so. All at once, two Thuggee guards rushed out.

Indy cracked the whip, catching the first guard around the neck. He spilled forward, tripping the second guard. As the first Thug tried to stand, Indy kicked him in the head.

The second man stood, swinging his sword. Indy ducked and came up with his fist in the assailant's belly. The guard doubled over as Indy dove for the unconscious man's saber. Then Indy rolled to avoid a downthrust from the recovering guard's blade. He stood quickly; the two men faced each other, ready to duel.

Indy suddenly realized he didn't know a thing about this kind of sword. He hefted the flat, curved blade, held it out, up, over, trying to decide the best way to use it, when the enraged Thuggee guard shouted and charged.

Indy decided quickly that shouting was the way to go, so he made his own rather voluble, inarticulate noise and raised his scimitar to parry the attacker's first slash.

The duel was on. Sparks erupted with each CLANG as the Thuggee swordsman lunged and feinted, and lunged again. Indy's moves were more in the nature of blocks and flails, and then blocks and tackles: Indy took his opponent flying at the waist: the two of them rolled, *corps à corps*, along the rocky slope.

Indy came out on top when the tumble ended in some scrub. He punched the guard once with the iron knuckles of the sword-handle, and the fight was over.

He rose, ran back to the bridge, keeping the saber. Willie and Short Round were just about across. Indiana started out onto the rickety span.

He walked quickly, hanging on to the twine rails. Every few steps his boot would break through; he'd have to catch himself on these upper ropes. Consequently, he kept his eyes turned downward most of the way, looking to step over the weak boards. When he was nearing the middle, he heard shouting ahead. He looked up to see temple guards appear at the far end of the bridge.

Willie and Short Round were caught as soon as they stepped onto hard ground. They struggled with their captors, but it was futile. There were too many.

Indy paused, uncertain what to do next. Suddenly Willie called, "Indy, look out behind you!"

Indy turned. More guards rushed out of the tunnel behind him.

He turned again. Two of the Thugs who'd captured Willie and Shorty were stepping onto the bridge ahead of him.

Indiana stood helpless in the center of the swaying bridge, with guards approaching from both sides, nothing but the crocodile-infested, rocky gorge far below, and the glorious heavens above.

Well, almost helpless. This was, after all, Indiana Jones.

The wind came up like an omen. Mola Ram, the High Priest, appeared on the far end of the bridge. He stood there in his priestly robes, smiling the smile of the man who holds all the cards. Beside him, Willie and Short Round were held fast by guards.

Indy staggered unsteadily in the buffeting wind. Bracing himself on the rope rails, he shouted to Ram. "Let my friends go!"

Mola Ram yelled to his men in Hindi. They started moving toward Indy from both sides of the bridge.

"That's far enough!" Indiana commanded.

"You are in no position to give orders, Dr. Jones," the High Priest remarked.

Indy pointed to the bag over his shoulder. "You want the stones, let them go and call off your guards! Or I'll drop the stones!"

"Drop them, Dr. Jones," said Mola Ram. "They will be easily found. But you won't!" He called out to his henchmen: "Yanne!"— and made a short hand-motion. They moved farther along the swaying bridge, closer to the madman in the middle.

Why is nothing easy? Indy wondered. Without further warning, he swung the sword he still held, cutting halfway through one of the bottom rope spans. The bridge reeled violently under the assault; the partially severed rope frayed, fiber by fiber, under the tension. The guards all stopped in their tracks.

Mola Ram nodded appreciatively. "Impressive, Dr. Jones," he congratulated his adversary. "But I don't believe you would kill yourself." He motioned again. Somewhat more reluctant now, his guards stepped farther onto the bridge, moving closer to Indy from both ends.

Indy slashed his blade again, this time into the opposing lower rope span. It, too, partly severed, continued fraying slowly: slow, like an alarm clock.

The bridge jolted; again, the guards stopped, swaying, with Indy, in the jostling wind.

Mola Ram lost his smile. He shoved Willie and Short Round out onto the bridge, then followed with his dagger drawn. He put the knife to Willie's back. "Your friends will die with you!" he bellowed.

Indiana looked at the guards in front and behind. He looked at Willie and Short Round ten feet out on the bridge, and at Mola Ram standing determined, at their backs. He looked at the land; he looked at the sky. And he shouted to all, in a voice meant to leave no doubt: "Then I guess we're all going to take a big dive!"

Indy's eyes met Short Round's. Much transpired in that meeting: memories, regrets, promises, graces; and a real clear message: this ain't no joke.

Willie saw it too. She looked wistfully at Indy: it might have been different, chum. She looked anxiously at Short Round . . . and noticed he was surreptitiously wrapping his foot around a loose rope support. Petrified—but also excited—Willie secretly did the same, twining an arm around one of the ropes as well.

Mola Ram roared like an angry priest: "Give me the stones!"

"Mola Ram," called Indiana, "you're about to meet Kali—in Hell!"

He swung the sword defiantly down. It swooshed through the air, then cut cleanly through top and bottom ropes on one side of the bridge.

Two guards fell off immediately, screaming all the way to their deaths. The rest began to flee in panic. Not quickly enough, though, for Indy slashed his sword down the other side, cleaving the span completely in two. The two halves separated, seemed to hang suspended in midair for a long, strange moment . . . and then fell apart.

Guards wailed horribly as they plunged three hundred feet to the valley. All tried desperately to cling to the remnants of rope bridge that were falling back to the cliffs; only some made it.

On the side that Indy was holding on to, three guards fell away in the first lurch. By the time the bridge finally crashed into the side of the cliff wall from which it now continued to dangle, only six people remained, grasping the fragile rope and slats: Mola Ram at the top, just several feet below the cliff-edge to which the bridge was attached; below him a guard; Willie; Short Round; another guard; and, at the very bottom, swinging precariously in space beyond an outswelling of rock, Indiana.

Willie and Shorty clung to their established footholds in the now vertical bridge. Everyone was motionless for a few seconds, realizing they were still among the living, swaying slightly, waiting to see if the ropes would hold, or settle.

Then Mola Ram began to climb. He reached very near the moorings of the rope ladder, when he grabbed a dry-rotted rung, which splintered in two. He skittered down ten feet, coming to rest finally between Willie and Short Round. In the process, he knocked off one of the guards, who fell past them all to the depth of the gully.

The ladder swung. Nobody moved.

Then Indy began to climb. He climbed past the guard, whose eyes and hands were tightly closed; he grabbed at Mola Ram's legs, to try to throw the fanatic to his death. Ram kicked him in the face, though, and resumed his own ascent.

Indy went up after him, got his foot again. He jerked hard. Mola Ram lost his grip, crashing down to Indy's level. They clutched each other and the ropes, nearly deranged with hatred. There they did battle.

Indy butted Ram in the chin with his head. Ram kneed Indy, then elbowed his neck back, then reached for his chest.

From above, Willie screamed, "Oh, my God! Indy, cover your heart!"

With sudden cold terror, Indy looked down to see Mola Ram's

hand starting to enter his chest—as he'd watched the priest once do to the sacrificial victim.

He grappled with Ram's wrist, desperately holding the probing hand at bay. But slowly, fiendishly, the sorcerer's fingers began to inch through Indy's skin—into his body.

It was an icy, nauseating feeling. Not painful, really, just horribly violating his innermost spirit. It was rapacious, vile, lacerating. It made his forehead sweat; iridescent spots fluttered before his eyes. He swooned, almost fell.

But his sense of self-preservation was strong; he kept his nerve, and he forced Ram's piercing fingers away from his heart, pushed them out of his chest. Knocked the hand back against Ram's own face.

Furious, the High Priest climbed once more, while Indy took a moment to recuperate. Ram climbed only a few feet, though, to the level of his own last guard. He got an arm around the man's throat, dislodged him from the ropes, and cast him down upon Indiana, in an attempt to knock Indy from the dangling ladder.

Willie and Shorty, near the top, shouted in unison. "Look out, Indy!"

The falling guard hit him square across the shoulders. Indy clung tightly; the hapless guard bounced, fell end over end, screaming all the way to his Maker.

Mola Ram laughed.

There were noises from across the gorge. Indy looked over to see a dozen more Thuggee guards streaming out of the tunnel on the other side, stranded there for lack of a bridge.

Mola Ram's voice sailed across the chasm to his men: "Kill them! Shoot them!"

The Thuggees ran up a path to a small grove of trees on a plateau above where the crossing had been. They unslung bows and arrows and took up firing positions.

Indy pulled himself higher, managing to grab on to the bottom of the High Priest's robe. Arrows began hitting all around him, though; one buried itself in the rung he was hanging on, grazing his hand. He had to let go of Ram.

Mola Ram took the opportunity to clamber up a few more steps. Shorty and Willie were waiting for him this time, however: they stomped on his hands as soon as he reached the slat they balanced on.

He let go, and fell.

Fell on top of Indy, breaking *him* loose of his hold. The two of them toppled another ten feet before catching on one of the bottom rungs.

Indy held on by his hands only. Ram didn't waste any more time struggling with the infidel. Priestly duties had not prepared him for such acrobatics; he was beginning to tire. He just wanted to get to safety.

Pushing off from Indy's head, he once again started his ascent.

Shorty finally made it to the top. He heaved himself up onto rocky ground, then turned and gave Willie a hand. They lay there panting a moment, hugging the earth, while arrows continued to fly all around them. Fortunately, all the guards on this side of the gorge had taken the plunge, so for the moment, at least, dodging arrows was all they had to worry about.

That wasn't all Indiana had to worry about. He started to mount the rope ladder yet again, when his wounded hand cramped. He crooked one elbow over a rung and for a few seconds just oscillated in the breeze. What a way to earn a living.

Indy got that old sinking feeling. Across the canyon he could see the dozen archers loosing volleys of shafts toward him. He looked down. The frayed ropes released another lower slat, which flipped in the wind like a broken propeller. It took a long time to spiral all the way to the base of the cliff.

Resolutely, Indiana renewed his climb.

Mola Ram reached the top. He extended a hand over the edge, feeling for a stable hold . . . and Willie smashed his fingers with the meanest rock she could find.

The High Priest yelped in pain, slipping out of control down the ropes, until he was once again stopped by Indiana's bulky form. They locked grips there, punching and wrestling and pivoting in the void.

On the cliff ledge above, Short Round and Willie watched the combatants powerlessly. Off to the right, Short Round heard a noise. He tensed, ready to run or fight.

"Willie, look!" he shouted.

She followed his gaze. There, horses were galloping through a narrow pass toward them. The British cavalry was returning.

"Well, come on. It's about time," she fumed.

Captain Blumburtt and the first troops drew up their horses, dismounting quickly. A fusillade of arrows forced everyone to take cover, but they immediately leveled their long rifles at the Thuggees across the gorge, and returned fire.

Willie and Short Round crawled back to the edge, to see if they could give Indy any help.

Indy and the priest were clearly in a death struggle now. They seemed to be giving no thought to the barrage of arrows or the danger of the swinging ropes. Their only concern was to destroy each other.

Indy slugged; Ram gouged. The bag holding the stones broke loose from Indy's shoulder. He held on to the strap; but Mola Ram, remembering his treasure, grabbed the bag itself.

"No, the stones are mine!" charged the High Priest.

Indy uttered fiercely, "You have betrayed Shiva." Then, his face just inches from Mola Ram's, he began to chant Sankara's warning in Hindi, over and over: "Shive ke vishwas kate ho. Vishwas kate ho. Vishwas kate ho."

And then a remarkable thing happened. As Indy repeated the magical words, the stones began to glow through the bag.

They were painfully bright; they burned through the sack. They started falling.

Desperately, Mola Ram reached for them.

Indy kept pronouncing the incantation: "Vishwas kate ho. Vishwas kate ho."

Ram caught one of the stones, but it burned intensely hot now, searing his hand. He dropped it, letting go with his other hand as well. Indy snatched the radiant Stone out of midair as Ram released it. But to Indiana's hand, it felt cool.

For a protracted instant their eyes made contact—these last two cliffhangers—and Mola Ram looked, to Indy, as if he'd just awakened from a nightmare. Though it was a nightmare Indiana remembered only dimly, its images would haunt him forever. He felt a pang of sympathy for Mola Ram, who was balanced on the cusp of awareness of both worlds, with no future, and memories of his past sodden with horror.

The High Priest tipped backwards, his hand savagely burned. His feet broke through the splintered rung he'd been bobbling on; he pitched over, soaring down in his robes like a runaway kite, crunching at last into the jagged rocks at the bottom.

The crocodiles rapidly tore apart his lifeless corpse. Their hunger knew nothing of his abominations.

Two of the Sankara Stones hit the shallow water, sank into the murky current, and were carried downriver . . . somewhere.

And then there was one.

Indy put the last Sankara Stone, now dark again, into his pocket. He climbed up the hanging bridge to the top, where he was pulled over the edge by Willie, Shorty, and Blumburtt.

Across the gorge, more British troops emerged from the mine tunnels to subdue the remaining Thuggee guards on that side. At their rear, the young Maharajah came out with the soldiers. He saw Short Round, standing with Indy; he bowed from across the chasm, to thank Shorty for saving him from the black nightmares of his own soul.

Short Round waved his cap at the Maharajah, returning the salute in thanks for bringing back the troops. The prince was obviously a born relief pitcher.

Willie stood at the lip of the gorge, looking down into the river far below. "I guess Mola Ram got what he wanted."

"Not quite," said Indy. He pulled the coveted object out of his pocket. "The last Sankara Stone."

Willie took it carefully from Indiana. She held it up to the sun. It sparkled and flashed from deep within its core, like a thing of the earth, with a secret heart.

For just a moment, they all shared its secret.

They rested a few days at the palace. The army collected many of the children, still hiding in the woods nearby, and fed them and tended their injuries. When all were strong enough to travel, Blumburtt sent a small contingent of soldiers, with Willie, Indy, and Shorty, to take the children home.

Short Round felt like King of the Children. He spent his time with them being fatherly, instructive, responsible.

He taught them never to steal, as Mola Ram had stolen them. (Except to steal bases.)

He instructed them to keep the Stars of Happiness, of Dignities, and of Longevity always near their hearts.

He taught them how to hit and pitch—with sticks and fruits.

He taught them how to distinguish mummies from draculas, and how to flip a coin, and how to look tough, but still be nice.

He sent them to Willie for tutorials in how to cloud men's minds.

He taught them the names of all the important deities, who had always responded to his prayers—though by this time, Short Round had made so many promises to so many gods, he had his doubt about any of them answering him in the future.

But Indy had answered; Indy was here. And Indy was still taking him to America.

Willie spent the time in a daze. She'd never been through anything like this before. Now that it was over, she couldn't quite believe it was over. She kept touching trees, touching Short Round, touching Indy, to make sure that it was real, that it wasn't a dream. It was still a little hard to tell.

Indy was somewhat disgruntled about losing two of the Sankara Stones—he'd held them in his hands!—but he had one. This one was his, for the time being. Besides, the children were free; that was the main thing. And the Thuggee were once again extinct.

Two days later, the troops dropped off one bunch of kids outside Mayapore village, then went on to escort the remainder to other outlying towns.

Indiana and his companions walked back down the dirt road into Mayapore, followed by the village's youngsters. They were astonished to view the landscape: what had been barren countryside was being reborn.

Trees budded beside streams that flowed clear and vital. Flowers were trying to bloom; the hills had turned from brown to green. Peasants were tilling the fields.

In the village itself, people were rebuilding their primitive dwellings. Fine crafts hung from the walls; the villagers worked on the details of their lives with a vigor that spread to all the land.

Shouts of joy arose as the peasants saw their own returning. They dropped what they were doing and ran out to meet the children, who rushed on ahead to this jubilant reunion.

There were tears, and laughter, and all manner of grateful tidings. The shaman approached Indiana, touched his fingers to his forehead, bowed. The three travelers returned his greeting.

He was profoundly moved as he spoke to Indy. "We know you are coming back"—he indicated the surrounding landscape—"when life returns to our village."

Willie nodded. "I've never seen a miracle before." But this was a miracle, plain and simple. It made her grin brightly. Miracles not only *could* happen; they sometimes *did*.

The shaman smiled. "Now you see the magic of the 'rock' you bring back."

Indy took the stone from his pocket, unwrapped it from the bit of Sankara cloth he still had. "Yes, I've seen its power."

The shaman reverently took the stone from Indy, bowed to them again; then walked, with the other elders, to the sacred shrine. Willie, Indy, and Shorty stayed back.

The shaman knelt before the small altar, placed the Sankara Stone in its niche, chanted: "Om sivaya namah om . . ."

Indy and Willie walked away.

"You could've kept it," she said to him.

"What for? They'd put it in a museum, where it'd be another rock collecting dust."

"It would've gotten you your fortune and glory."

Indy shrugged, then smiled slyly. "Well, it's a long way to Delhi. Anything could still happen."

She looked at him as if he were crazy. "Oh, no. No, thanks. No more adventures for me, Dr. Jones."

"Sweetheart, after all the fun we've had . . ."

A big purple cloud began welling up inside her. What was he, nuts? They were alive—quite accidentally, she thought. Wasn't that good enough for him? Fuming, frustrated ire rose in her craw.

"If you think I'd go with you to Delhi or anyplace else after all the trouble you've gotten me into, think again, buster," she started, and then she got rolling. "I'm going home to Missouri, where they never ever feed you snake before ripping your heart out and lowering you into hot pits. This is not my idea of a swell time! No more Anything Goes! No more—"

She stopped before she started frothing; turned, walked toward a villager with a bundle on his back. "Excuse me, sir?" she called to him. "I need a guide to Delhi. I'm really very good on an elephant."

The whip cracked, wrapping around Willie's waist. With a gentle insistence, Indy pulled her in to his arms.

She resisted only briefly. No use fighting karma: this clinch was meant to be since the second he'd walked into the club, and their eyes had closed the deal.

They kissed.

It was warm, glad, giving as a summer rain.

Water rained down on them in a brief, torrential shower. They separated, looked up. There was Short Round, sitting on the back of his baby elephant, which was spraying them gleefully with its trunk.

Short Round laughed. Indy and Willie laughed. The baby elephant laughed.

"Very funny," said Short Round. "Very funny big joke."

They did eventually all make it to America. But that is another story.

INDIANA JONES
AND THE
LAST CRUSADE™

"The problem of the hero going to meet the father is to open his soul beyond terror to such a degree that he will be ripe to understand how the sickening and insane tragedies of his vast and ruthless cosmos are completely validated in the majesty of Being. The hero transcends life with its peculiar blind spot and for a moment rises to a glimpse of the source. He beholds the face of the father, understands—and the two are atoned."

—JOSEPH CAMPBELL
The Hero with a Thousand Faces

"One can easily imagine how I felt: suddenly to see in a modern city, during the noonday rush hour, a crusader coming toward me."

—CARL JUNG
Memories, Dreams, Reflections

UTAH:
1912

ONE
Desert Chase

THE TROOP CHARGED across the desert, their horses thundering beneath them, a cloud of dust billowing in their tracks. They rode hard and fast, as if to escape the sun, which had peaked over a barren mountain. It was already casting harsh beams of light across the arid landscape, and soon the desert would be baking.

Just ahead was a rock formation, and under it was a labyrinth of caves. The uniformed riders reined in their horses as they saw their commander raise a hand.

"Dis-mount," he shouted.

A rider with a thatch of straw-colored hair was the first one off his mount. He glanced around at the troop members. From a distance, he thought, they probably looked like a company of army cavalry soldiers. Up close, he conceded, it was another matter. Even his best effort to imagine them as soldiers failed. It was pretty obvious they were just a scout troop. Except for Mr. Havelock, none of them was over thirteen.

He watched as a pudgy kid tottered away from his horse. He knew the kid's name was Herman but didn't know him well. He had heard a couple of the other kids say that Herman had trouble at home. He wasn't sure what kind of trouble, but it was obvious that he was also having problems right here. He bent over, wobbled, and looked as if he was going to pitch forward onto his face. Finally he stopped, braced his hands on his knees, gagged, and vomited.

Everyone around him roared. They elbowed each other and pointed at the pathetic scout.

"Herman's horsesick," one of them yelled.

"Yeah, and he wet his saddle, too," another howled gleefully.

The blond scout, whose uniform was dressed with a Hopi woven belt, walked up to Herman and asked if he was okay. There was a look of concern and understanding on his face and not a trace of ridicule. It was obvious that he was more mature than the others, and no one dared say a word as he led Herman away.

Mr. Havelock yelled for the boys to follow him with their horses. They led their mounts toward the rocks and left them in the shade of a massive boulder. The boys grouped around the scoutmaster as he explained that the original caves were natural formations and were the home of a primitive people. There was also a legend that Spanish conquistadores explored the caves, and it was well known that during the last century miners had opened new passages in their quest for gold. "Now, don't anybody wander off. Some of the passages in here run on for miles." As the troop fell into step behind their leader, the scouts mumbled under their breath. "This better be good," one said.

"Yeah, the circus arrives today," another murmured. "We could be watching them pitch the tents."

They climbed a trail leading up the rocks. It was hot, dusty, and steep. Everyone was too caught up in the ascent to pay any attention to Herman or the blond kid who brought up the rear of the line.

A minute or so later they stepped inside the mouth of the cave. It was cool and dark, and the boys complained they couldn't see.

Mr. Havelock lit his lantern and assured the scouts their eyes would quickly adjust to the dim light. They continued on, following a well-traveled route.

Even though he was at the tail end, the blond scout was the most attentive of the troop. It almost seemed as if he were sensing what the place was like when it was inhabited by an ancient people. As the troop turned a corner, he suddenly gripped Herman by the arm.

"Ssh. Listen."

Herman caught his breath. He glanced around uneasily, wondering what had caught his new friend's attention.

Another trail branched off from the one they were on, and from deep within the dark passage they heard voices. They were faint, but distinct. The blond boy signaled Herman to follow him.

"Come on. Let's take a look."

Herman glanced back in the direction the troop had gone. He seemed uncertain about what he should do, then made up his mind and scrambled ahead.

"Okay, Junior, I'm coming."

Spiderwebs tangled in their hair. The passageway was darker and cooler and obviously not well used. "Where are we going?" Herman called out.

The blond kid—Junior—turned, touched his index finger to his lips. The voices were louder now. The walls ahead were suddenly illuminated, and hulking, ghostly shadows danced across them. The two boys pressed against the wall. They held their breaths as they edged slowly forward.

Then Junior spotted four figures digging with shovels and pickaxes. He knew immediately that these were no ghosts. He was sure they were thieves, and he knew what they were doing. According to legend, the Spanish had buried treasure here.

His father was a medieval scholar who taught at the university. He knew all about the legend, and a lot of other things, too. He had tried to get his father to come along today and tell the scouts about the history of the caves and the ancient people who used to live there. But, as usual, his father was too busy to be bothered with a bunch of kids. Besides, he said, North American archaeology wasn't his field of expertise.

Junior looked over the four men as well as he could. One of the men was smaller than the others, and now he could see that he wasn't a man at all. He was a kid, and he wasn't much older than they were. But he looked pretty tough.

"Roscoe, hold the lantern up," one of the men snapped at him.

The man who had spoken was dressed in a leather jacket with fringes. He wore a hat with the rim turned up on one side, and he looked like a Rough Rider. The man on the other side of Roscoe had thick black hair that cascaded over his shoulders. An Indian. No. A half-breed.

The last man was on the far side of the other three, and in shadows. He wore a leather waist jacket and a brown felt fedora.

Junior moved soundlessly ahead a couple of steps to get a better look. He signaled Herman. He heard him breathing loudly and glanced back to quiet him. Herman's mouth was open, and sweat was pouring down his forehead.

I hope he doesn't puke again. Not here.

Herman's foot slipped on a loose stone. It made a soft, crunching noise, and Herman slapped the wall to regain his footing.

Junior hunkered down low, trying to make himself as small as possible, trying to blend in with the shadows. Herman followed his example.

"Sorry," he whispered.

Junior winced and shushed Herman with a wave of his hand.

The man with the fedora turned slowly, raised a lantern, and looked their way. They could see his face now for the first time. "Thought I heard something," he muttered, then turned his back again.

The boys were frightened, yet mesmerized. They watched with rapt attention as Fedora poured water from his canteen over a mud-shrouded object. In the light of the lantern Junior could see that it was a gold cross encrusted with precious jewels.

Fedora's buddies leaned close. "Look at that! We're rich!" Roscoe shouted.

"Pipe down. Not so loud," Half-breed chastised.

"You wait. Soon enough. That little darling is gonna fetch top dollar," Rough Rider said in a hoarse whisper.

Fedora turned the cross in his hand, silently appraising its beauty and value. He seemed aloof from the others, somehow superior to them.

Junior touched Herman on the shoulder, unable to contain his excitement and concern. "It's the Cross of Coronado!" he whispered. "Hernando Cortés gave it to him in 1520! It proves that Cortés sent Francisco Coronado in search of the Seven Cities of Gold."

Herman looked baffled. "How do you know all this stuff anyhow, Junior?"

Junior shifted his gaze toward the men and watched them a moment longer. "That cross is an important artifact. It belongs in a museum. And, do me a favor, don't call me Junior."

"That's what Mr. Havelock calls you."

"My name's Indy."

He hated being called Junior. It made him sound like a kid in short pants. But his father just ignored him whenever he mentioned the matter of his name.

They watched a minute longer, and Indy's demeanor hardened into a look of resolve as he reached a decision. He turned to Herman. "Listen, run back and find the others. Tell Mr. Havelock that men are looting the Spanish treasure. Have him bring the sheriff."

Herman didn't look as if he was listening. His mouth was moving, but no words came out as he stared wide-eyed and horror-struck at a snake that was slithering across his lap.

"It's only a snake," Indy said as he matter-of-factly picked it up and tossed it aside. "Did you hear what I said, Herman? It's important."

"Right. Run back. Mr. Havelock. The sheriff." He nodded and gazed past Indy toward the men. "What are you going to do, Jun . . . Indy?"

"I don't know. I'll think of something. You better get going."

Herman dashed along the passageway, retracing his steps, as Indy returned his attention to the thieves. They had set the cross aside and were busy searching for more artifacts. Slowly Indy worked his way along the wall until he was within an arm's length of the cross. Even in its tarnished state, its jewels sparkled in the lantern light and captured his attention.

He reached out, grasped it, and as he did, saw a scorpion clinging to the cross. He tried to shake it off, but the deadly creature seemed to be glued to the cross. He cursed under his breath, still shaking his hand. The scorpion dropped off, but he'd given himself away.

The thieves turned as one, spotting him. "Hey, that's our thing," Roscoe shouted. "He's got our thing."

"Get 'im," Half-breed yelled.

Indy hurtled blindly down the passageway, clutching the cross, his heart hammering against his ribs. He glanced back once, to see one of the thieves stumble and fall and two others crash into each other as they tripped over him. He stopped a moment as he reached a chimney the gold miners had cut into the ceiling. Faint rays of light filtered down through it, and a rope hung down to within a couple of feet of his head. He looked back to see if they were going to let him go. But no such luck. He saw Fedora cast a disgusted glance at his companions and bolt down the tunnel after him.

Oh, damn. He tucked the cross under his belt and leaped for the rope. He missed, tried again, and grasped it with one hand, then the other. He worked his way up the chimney, hand over hand along the rope, and from one foothold to the next. He saw

Fedora and the others race by, and felt relieved. He could take his time. A moment later, he felt a tug on the rope and looked down. Fedora had backtracked and was deftly scaling the chimney.

If only his father were here, Indy thought as he struggled to reach the top. Dad would take care of those guys. He imagined his father pointing an accusatory finger at the thieves and the men shrinking away. Yeah, he'd do something like that.

The light was getting brighter, and finally Indy reached the top. He gasped for air as he crawled from the chimney into brilliant daylight. He paused, squinted, and shielded his eyes as he caught his breath. He glanced about in every direction. He realized he was standing on a boulder not far from where they had entered the cave.

"Herman! Mr. Havelock! Anybody! Where are you?" He shook his head. "Damn, everybody's lost but me."

"Here we are, kid."

Indy turned and saw Rough Rider, Half-breed, and Roscoe scrambling up a rocky trail toward him. He ran toward the edge of the rock and spotted a ladder sticking up. Instead of climbing down, he quickly calculated the distance to the next boulder. He charged the ladder, pushed off, and vaulted the gap.

The three thieves raced to the edge of the rock and stopped abruptly. They glanced around in confusion, wondering how to catch him.

Indy, meanwhile, had reached the far side of the next boulder and was uncertain what to do. This time there wasn't any ladder, and the ground was twenty feet below him. Then he saw the horses resting in the shade, where the scout troop had left them. He placed two fingers in his mouth and whistled for his steed. The horse shook its mane and trotted over.

Indy glanced back and saw Fedora charge past his companions and leap the chasm. Once he was on the other side, he paused long enough to look back at the others with obvious disdain. Then, shaking his head, he pushed the ladder over to them.

Indy crouched, preparing to drop into the saddle, but the horse wouldn't stand still. He hesitated, but heard footsteps. "Stand still, boy," he yelled. "Don't move. Good boy."

He leapt, and at that moment the horse pranced ahead, and Indy missed the saddle. He landed on his feet and rolled over, breaking his fall. The impact jolted his body, rattling him from his heels to his teeth. The cross dropped from his belt into the dust. He scooped it up, shoved it in the saddlebag, and mounted the horse.

As Indy galloped off, he glanced back to see Fedora standing at the edge of the boulder watching him. He grinned, kicked the side of the horse, urging him on. He had to get to the sheriff as quickly as he could so the thieves wouldn't get away.

Fedora put two fingers in his mouth and whistled. None of the horses moved. Instead, two automobiles roared out from behind the next rock outcropping. One of the autos, a convertible, circled around and skidded to an abrupt stop beneath Fedora, who immediately vaulted from the boulder into a cloud of dust. As the air cleared, the car pulled away with Fedora perched on the top of the backseat.

He adjusted his hat with an expression of satisfaction, and yelled, "Giddyup!"

The driver prodded the gas pedal, and the car surged rapidly ahead. The second car lagged behind, as the driver waited for Roscoe, Rough Rider, and Half-breed to catch up.

Indy raced across the desert, cutting through the dry air as cleanly as a blade through butter. The sun blazed down without sympathy, scorching the earth, baking him into the saddle. Behind him the two automobiles were rapidly closing the gap.

The desolate mountain in front of him wasn't getting a bit closer. It seemed as if the horse were galloping in place. The only things moving were the cars, which were pulling up on either side of him. He felt like a sandwich, and he and the horse were the meat.

Indy glanced to his right and saw a man in a Panama hat behind the wheel of a cream-colored luxury sedan. He wore an expensive white linen suit, and his face was concealed by the wide brim of his hat. In the window of the backseat Roscoe grimaced and shook his fist at Indy. As the driver reached toward his leg, Indy spurred his mount and for a moment gained a few feet.

His extraordinary effort was useless, though. The autos quickly regained the slight margin he had achieved. They were not only keeping pace with him, but were squeezing in on him like a giant vise on wheels. Only the hot wind and the dust separated him from the speeding vehicles. Indy crouched low and leaned forward in the saddle, intent on escaping. His heart pounded, his adrenaline pumped, and he flew forward.

On his left, Fedora climbed over the side of the convertible and stepped onto the running board. Indy looked down into his face. The man grinned up at him as if to let him know he was enjoying the chase. Then, he sprang gracefully onto Indy's horse.

But Indy was just as quick and equally as daring. Before Fedora could reach him, he hurled himself onto the hood of the sedan to his right. He landed on his knees, braced himself by hanging on to the edge of the roof. Rough Rider and Roscoe crawled out the windows and were reaching for him when Indy suddenly realized that he no longer had the cross. His head snapped toward the horse; he spotted the cross hanging half-out of the saddlebag.

Fedora, however, was unaware that the cross was within inches of his hand. He looked irritated and leapt on top of the sedan. He thrust an arm toward Indy, but Indy bounded back onto the horse, avoiding his grasp and slipping away from Rough Rider and Roscoe, who knocked heads as they lunged for him.

Indy pulled back hard on the reins, slowing the horse as the two automobiles sped past. Inside the shroud of dust, he veered in a new direction and galloped toward the railroad tracks, where a train was quickly approaching. Behind him the autos swung into wide turns and resumed the chase.

As Indy reached the tracks, the train was barreling alongside him. There was something odd about the train, he thought. The railcars were a blur of color rather than the usual brown and gray. But he didn't have time to consider it because the two autos were catching up to him. He had only one choice.

He tucked the cross into his belt, rose up in his saddle, and grabbed on to the ladder of the nearest railcar. He started to climb to the top, but changed his mind when he spotted a nearby window that was open. He clutched the side of the car like a spider and worked his way toward it. He glanced once over his shoulder, to see the autos pulling up to the train.

Indy reached the open window and tumbled through it. He landed on something soft, voluminous, like a bed of marshmallows. But it was a human marshmallow. He sank into rippling, undulating folds of flesh. He pulled away and realized his head had landed in the copious cleavage of an immensely overweight woman.

Startled and embarrassed, Indy jumped up. The massive woman was seated on a wide bench large enough to accommodate her four hundred–plus pounds. He backed away, smiling. He heard someone laughing and spun around. His jaw dropped open.

Gawking at him were a host of the strangest looking people Indy had ever seen in his thirteen years. There were pinheads, a bearded lady, dwarfs, a rubber man, a boy with flipper feet.

Of course. It was the circus train headed for town.

"Ah, hello. I hope you don't mind me dropping in like this." He kept turning around as he spoke. "I couldn't really help it. I had a horse, but ah . . ."

He stopped as a dwarf approached him. "You mean you jumped on the train from a horse—like a circus trick?" The man spoke in a tiny voice that matched his size.

Indy smiled. "Yeah, I did."

"I didn't see any horse."

"He's lying," someone else said.

"I bet you want to join the circus," the dwarf said, poking him in the stomach.

"He's too normal looking," the rubber man groused.

"Leave the kid alone," said the bearded lady, running her fingers through the hair on her face.

The dwarf, who was eye level with Indy's belt, leaned forward and examined the cross.

"What's that?" he asked, frowning a little.

"Oh, nothing."

"Can I have it?"

"No." He said it too quickly, too loudly. "I'm taking it to a museum. That's where it belongs."

"A museum," the dwarf repeated. "Uh-huh. I bet."

Indy sat down on a box so the dwarf would stop eyeing the cross. He figured he would slip off the train when it passed near his home. Once they were in town, the thieves wouldn't dare bother him. They would be too afraid of getting caught. If they tried anything, he would just yell for help. And once he got to the house, he would explain everything to his father.

It was going to be okay, he told himself. His father would be proud of him. He was always complaining about people who looted archaeological sites. And now his son, Junior—Indy, I'm Indy—had caught four of them red-handed.

He felt someone tapping him on the shoulder, and he turned to see the dwarf, who was now nose to nose with him. "I've got another question."

"What's that?" Indy asked.

The dwarf pointed past him. "Did he come on a horse, too?"

Indy jerked around and saw Fedora staring at him through the window.

TWO

Circus Tricks

"MAKING NEW FRIENDS?" Fedora asked with a grin.

Indy stood up and started backing away. "Yeah, sure am."
He kept his eyes on Fedora but spoke to the others. "Watch out for
this man. He's a thief."

Fedora climbed in through the window and tried to squeeze
around the fat lady.

"Now just a minute," she said, pushing herself to her feet and
blocking Fedora's way. "We don't want your kind on this train."

Indy seized the opportunity and charged for the door at the end
of the car. He pushed through it and leapt onto a flatcar. In the
center of it was an impressive calliope with rows of shiny steam
whistles rising behind a pearly keyboard. He ducked around it and
glanced back to see Fedora crashing through the door with the
bearded lady clinging to his throat. Fedora threw her off and
vaulted onto the flatcar.

Indy grasped a lever on the side of the calliope for support, but
the lever moved and the calliope burst into life. Steam and noise
blasted from the pipes. Fedora's companions, who had boarded the

flatcar from the auto, stopped in their tracks and covered their ears against the horrendous off-key honks and squeaks. They staggered back and were nearly blown from the train by an explosion of steam.

Indy, meanwhile, scrambled to the roof of the next car and clambered along it until he reached a trapdoor. He threw open the lid and lowered himself onto a catwalk suspended from the ceiling of the car. Several feet below were numerous vats that looked as though they contained every species of snake, lizard, alligator, and crocodile. It was a virtual Noah's Ark of the reptile world.

Indy stared into the vats, fascinated and horrified. The last thing he wanted to do was end up down there. His only hope was that the others would somehow miss seeing the trapdoor and would keep going to the next car. But the moment he thought it, the door flew open and Half-breed and Roscoe dropped down onto the catwalk.

Now what?

Indy scurried toward the rear of the car, wondering what he was going to do when he reached the end of the catwalk. No matter how brave and strong he thought he might be, he knew he wouldn't be able to handle both of them. Hell, Roscoe alone could be trouble. He was the sort of kid who would fight dirty, would do things like give up and then jump on you when your back was turned.

He noticed a second trapdoor above him at the end of the catwalk. Great. He'd slip out before they cornered him. Sure. It'd be a cinch. But before he could take another step, a metallic screeching sound pierced the air. The catwalk started shaking. He looked up, and dread filled him like a poison gas. Their combined weight was too much for the structure, and one of the bolts holding it to the ceiling had begun to pull loose. The catwalk was slipping and swaying, threatening to dump them into the vats of slithering reptiles.

The three of them froze in place, fearing that a single step would send them tumbling. Indy glanced up at the trapdoor. It was a step away, and there was a handle next to it. He could grab it, swing up, kick open the door, and swing out onto the top of the car.

And then what, hotshot? The other two thieves are probably waiting up there, Indy said to himself.

He didn't know what he would do, but there wasn't time to think about it.

He crouched and leapt for the door handle. His fingers grazed it, but he couldn't get hold of it. He landed off balance on one foot and grasped the railing. The catwalk swayed beneath him, and he heard a series of loud cracks as several bolts suddenly tore free. Roscoe and Half-breed screamed, but it was Indy's side of the catwalk that dropped. He plunged to the floor of the car, landing with a heavy thud on a raised wooden platform.

For a moment he didn't move. He was afraid he had broken something—his legs, maybe his arms, maybe even his neck. But worse than the fear that he had broken a limb was the darkness. He couldn't see. Panic bubbled in his throat, and a scream slid down his tongue—but then he realized he'd squeezed his eyes shut when he fell. He laughed softly to himself, but as he opened his eyes, his laughter turned weird, desperate, almost a cackle. He was eye to eye with an enormous anaconda.

The head of the snake was so huge that it looked more like Tyrannosaurus Rex than a snake. Its tongue darted out and flicked against his cheek. An icy chill raced down his spine, his eyes widened in horror. He rolled over, bolted to his feet, and edged backward.

He was afraid that if he looked away from the anaconda, it would attack him. He wasn't watching where he was going, and one foot stepped off the edge of the platform. He wobbled a moment, then tumbled backward. He landed softly; he wasn't hurt. But then he realized where he was—he had fallen into a vat of snakes.

Hundreds of writhing reptiles were suddenly sliding under and over him. The roiling mass engulfed him like quicksand. Only it was worse than quicksand, much worse. He was smothering. The snakes were sucking away his breath, his life. Once, when he lifted his head from the wiggling nightmare, he glimpsed Half-breed and Roscoe struggling to stay on the dangling catwalk above him.

Roscoe clung to Half-breed's leg, but the dark-haired thief wanted no part of the kid. He reached for the trapdoor and shook his leg, attempting to rid himself of Roscoe, who cried out, terrified that he would plummet into the jaws of one of the carnivorous crocodiles snapping below them.

Then the snakes covered Indy again, and he lost sight of everything. But he didn't give up. He was fighting for his life. Snakes were piled below him as well as on top of him, and that kept him from regaining his footing. So he did the only thing he could do: he kicked against the wall of the vat.

After several kicks at the same spot, the side of the vat cracked open. With all the energy he had left in him he kicked again. This time the wall gave way, and the wiggling mass of snakes suddenly slid out the side, taking Indy along for the ride.

He leapt up, gasping for breath. He jerked snakes off his shoulders, his legs. He would never feel the same about snakes again. Above him he heard the screech of metal and curses, as the two thieves struggled to get through the trapdoor. But his focus now was on a door in the floor that was probably used when the car was cleaned out.

Indy snapped open the door and was immediately bombarded by the pounding din of the cars speeding over the rails. The tie beams of the tracks blurred below him. He hesitated—his father would kill him if he knew what he was about to attempt. Bad enough that he'd leapt onto a moving train from a horse and had fallen into a vat of snakes, but now he was going to attempt the impossible.

But he wasn't about to stay in the car with snakes and gators.

And there was no other way out. Besides, he had to get away from these thieves.

He took a deep breath and lowered his head through the door. A steel bar ran the length of the car. He reached down and touched it with his hand. It was warm but not hot, and it was just high enough above the tracks to accommodate him as long as he kept the bar close to his chest.

Only ten feet. That was all the distance he had to crawl.

And ten feet isn't impossible, is it? I can crawl ten feet. I know I can, Indy told himself.

Carefully he lowered himself through the door, gripping the steel bar first with his hands, then with his arms and legs. He inched forward; the clatter of the train vibrated through his body, threatening to shake him from it.

Oh, shit. What did I do this for?

He told himself to concentrate. He knew that as long as he concentrated and used every ounce of his strength, he could do it.

I'm going to make it. I'm going to make it. He said it over and over again as he pulled himself forward.

Finally he reached the end and realized he hadn't figured out how he was going to get off the bar. The front of the car extended a foot or so beyond the end of it. Maybe if he just stayed where he was, he'd be okay.

But how long could he hold on before his arms would tire? The vibration was already jolting him to his bones.

He thought a moment about the cross tucked beneath his belt. If it slipped out and smashed on the tracks, all his efforts would be useless. He let go with one hand, and carefully reached forward to the end of the car. His fingers patted the lower edge of the front wall, feeling for something to grasp. But he didn't find anything.

Then he remembered the safety cable that connected the cars below the coupling. Where was it? He extended his arm as far as he could reach. His fingers touched something, then slipped off. He tried again, and this time he grabbed the cable.

Now what?

He was stretched between the cable and the bar and he had to go one way or the other. He was momentarily paralyzed by indecision. Which way? Does it matter? He closed his eyes, let go of the bar with his other hand, and reached blindly for the cable. He grasped it and slid his feet along the last inches of the bar. Then his legs were dangling in midair, and he was pulling himself forward, hand over hand. He opened his eyes and saw the coupling above him. He hooked his arm over it, then swung a leg up as if he were mounting a horse. He had done it! He was riding atop the coupling between two cars.

He pulled himself forward toward the next car. It was virtually a cage on wheels. Inside, behind the bars, was a huge Bengal tiger. He reached up to the nearest bar, stood up on the coupling, balancing himself. Then he climbed to the outside of the cage.

He edged his way along the narrow outer skirt of the car by holding on to the cage. He stopped once as he felt something crawling along his leg. He wriggled his nose as he reached into his pants and pulled out a snake. He readjusted the cross under his belt and moved ahead.

The tiger paced back and forth inside the cage, watching him. Indy stared back. As he neared the front of the cage, the tiger paced closer and closer. He crouched down to rest, hoping the massive cat would ignore him. Even though the bars were between him and the tiger, a swipe from the creature's paw through the space between the bars would be deadly.

What he didn't realize, though, was that another sort of danger was literally around the corner. Rough Rider had worked his way along the opposite side of the cage and was inching across the front now. Like the tiger, the thief had fixed his eye on his prey.

Indy was staring at the tiger, mentally telling it to back off, when a hand clamped on his neck.

"Gotcha!" Rough Rider shouted.

At that moment the tiger lunged at the bars. He thrust his paws out, raking his claws across Rough Rider's shoulder and back, shredding his jacket. The thief yelled out in pain and surprise and grabbed his shoulder. He tottered a moment, then fell from the train.

Indy glanced back, to see Rough Rider rolling along the railroad bed. He turned toward the front of the car, and a fist sank into his stomach, knocking the wind out of him. He doubled over, gasping for breath, certain he was dying. He looked up, to see Roscoe hovering over him.

"Girl Scout." The kid sneered and drew back his fist to punch him again.

But Indy slammed the heel of his boot down onto Roscoe's foot. He poked him in the eye and bit his hand. The kid yelped in pain, and Indy scooted past him. He fled to a neighboring stockcar and climbed up a ladder to its roof.

Roscoe quickly recovered and cursed Indy as he climbed behind him. Indy had just reached the top when Roscoe grabbed his ankle. He fell to the roof, and the two boys grappled, rolling perilously close to the edge.

The rattle of the rails pounded in Indy's ears as he saw Roscoe raise a knife in the air. The tip of the blade glinted as Roscoe thrust. Indy rolled over just in time to avoid the plunging blade. He crawled away, but Roscoe scrambled after him, tackling him as he tried to rise to his feet.

Whatever was in the boxcar beneath them must have been huge, Indy thought, because every time he or Roscoe moved, something pounded against the side of the boxcar, shaking it. But he didn't have time to ponder that matter. He was too busy trying to stay alive.

"Gimme that cross!" Roscoe shouted, flashing the blade in the air over Indy. "Right now!"

Indy grabbed Roscoe's wrist, bending it back, trying to get him to drop the knife.

Suddenly a rhino horn slammed through the roof's wooden

slats, missing Indy's head by inches. He rolled to one side, and Roscoe's wrist slipped free. Indy pushed him away, but Roscoe lunged for him, stabbing the knife at his throat. Indy jerked his head, and the blade slammed into the wood, just missing his ear.

As Roscoe struggled to loosen it, the rhino struck again and this time his horn went right between Indy's legs. Roscoe pulled out the knife and thrust it at Indy's midsection. Indy saw it coming down, saw the blade gleaming in the light. His legs shot out and slammed into Roscoe's chest, throwing him back. Roscoe faltered a moment, arms pinwheeling for balance, and barely avoided falling off the car.

Indy rolled over onto his stomach and looked back just in time to see Roscoe hurtle the knife at him. It probably would have slammed into his face, but at that instant the rhino horn burst through the roof next to Indy's head and the blade struck it.

Indy stumbled to his feet and saw a water tank alongside the tracks directly ahead. Its spout was facing the tracks and protruded above the train. He suddenly knew how he could get away. He ran to the side of the car, calculated the distance, and timed his leap.

He caught the spout perfectly, but the train's velocity caused the spout to swing rapidly around the water tank. He hung on, closed his eyes, and finally, as the spout slowed, he let go. He only dropped a couple of feet and realized he had spun completely around. He was back on the train! This time he landed on the roof of another stockcar and immediately collided with Half-breed, who was knocked off his feet.

Indy reeled backward, dazed by what had happened. But what happened next confused him even more: he fell through an opening in the roof.

Dust flew up around him as he struck the floor. Rays of sunlight leaked through the cracks in the boards, but it took a moment for his eyes to adjust to the dim light. He smelled a heady animal scent in the air, and his nose twitched. Then he saw the source of the odor. In the opposite end of the car an African lion was slowly rising to its feet. Obviously it was intent on investigating the creature who had dropped into its den.

The lion roared, and the stockcar walls seemed to shudder. Dust swirled in shafts of sunlight around the lion as it stalked him like prey.

"Oh, boy." Indy gulped as he backed away toward the corner of the car.

He saw a glint of light reflect off something on the floor and suddenly realized what it was. The cross had dislodged from his belt when he fell, and now it lay at the lion's feet.

He glanced around and continued stepping back until he felt the rear wall of the car against his spine. He pressed his hands against the wall as the lion continued stalking him, preparing to make a deadly pounce. His right hand struck a nail. Under it he felt something leathery. He snapped his head around, thinking it was another snake. Instead, it was a whip—a lion tamer's whip.

He carefully took it down by its handle. The lion recognized the whip and growled softly. Indy swallowed hard and gave the whip a snap. It unraveled awkwardly, its tip flying back and striking him across the face, cutting his chin.

The lion growled louder.

Indy quickly gathered up the whip, wet his lips, and tried again. This time it cracked sharply, as it was supposed to, as he'd heard it crack at the circus when the lion tamer circled the king of beasts, whip in hand.

The lion bellowed, swatted the air, and snarled, then backed off. He knew from experience what the crack of the whip meant.

Indy grinned, amazed and delighted by his feat. He cracked the whip again, and the lion backed away even more. Indy inched forward until the cross was just in front of him. The lion stood its ground about ten feet away. Slowly, Indy bent over. Never taking his eyes off the lion, he picked up the cross.

Then he stepped back and realized his hands were shaking and sweat was pouring down his face. He took a deep breath of musty air, exhaled, gathering his wits. Now, how was he going to get out of here?

He looked up at the opening he had fallen through and saw Fedora looking down at him. Fedora nodded to him, smiled, and extended a hand.

That was all it took. Indy decided he would rather face Fedora than remain a minute longer caged with the lion. He tossed one end of the whip toward the hole, and Fedora snagged it.

Fedora slowly reeled him in as Indy walked up the side of the wall. He looked back once, to see the lion crouched and ready to pounce if he fell. He quickly turned back and concentrated on getting out.

When he reached the edge of the hole, Fedora clasped his arm and pulled him out, depositing him on the roof. Indy dropped to his hands and knees. He was breathing hard; he was exhausted. The lion had finally taken the fight out of him.

"You've got heart, kid. I'll say that much," Fedora said. He pointed at the cross. "But that belongs to me."

Indy looked up to see that he had more company. Half-breed and Roscoe were also there. He stared at Fedora. "It belongs to Coronado."

"Coronado is dead. And so are all his grandchildren." Fedora reached out, turning up his palm. "Come on, kid. There's no way out of this."

"Yeah, fork it over," Roscoe barked, then grabbed at the cross. Indy clung to one end of it, refusing to let go. A tug-of-war ensued. In the middle of it, a snake slithered out from Indy's shirtsleeve and wrapped around Roscoe's hand.

"Get it off me," he screamed. He let go of the cross and shook his arm until the snake was flung away. The lion roared beneath them. Indy took advantage of the momentary diversion and darted between Half-breed's legs and bounded onto the next car. Half-breed was about to give chase, but Fedora motioned him to wait.

"Stay put! Don't let him double back." He turned and headed after him.

Indy scurried down the ladder between two cars and entered the caboose. The car was full of costumes and magic equipment. He looked around for a place to hide. He heard Fedora coming down the ladder and slipped out of sight.

Fedora walked calmly into the caboose and surveyed the car. He strolled over to a large black box and casually pulled off the cover. One by one the four sides of the box flopped away, revealing nothing.

He smiled confidently when he saw the top of another smaller box move slightly. "Okay, kid. It's all over. Come on out."

He opened the box, and several pigeons flew out, scattering about the caboose. He was getting fed up with this elusive boy. He pawed his way through the costumes and magic gear. He picked up a cane and prodded into the corners, but the cane wobbled and turned into a handkerchief. "Damn it. Where the hell . . ."

Then he saw a couple of the pigeons fly out the rear door of the caboose, which was swinging in the breeze. Realizing what had happened, he rushed out onto the rear balcony. The train was slowing as it neared its destination, and in the distance he saw Indy disappearing down a street of modest clapboard houses.

THREE
The Home Front

OUT OF BREATH but still carrying the Cross of Coronado, Indy charged into his house. He quickly locked the doors and raced from the kitchen to the living room, peering out windows. The street was clear.

He hurried through the hallway and ducked into another room to check outside again. He squinted into the sunlight. He could still taste dust in his mouth. Water, he thought. He wanted a big, tall glass of ice water. But first things first. His father. He needed to talk to his father.

"Dad?"

There was no answer, but Indy knew his father was in his study. Ever since Indy's mother had died, it seemed his father lived in his study, forever hunched over old books and parchments. The ancient past was more real to him than the present.

Just look at the house, Indy thought. The rooms said it all: no feminine touches, nothing soft, no color, just books and old things everywhere. He was the only one who cleaned the house. Sometimes Indy felt as if his father had abandoned life beyond his study. That was the only place his father's presence was real to him.

He opened the door to the study. Books spilled off shelves and were piled on the floor. The walls were covered with maps of ancient lands and pictures of wonderful old castles and cathedrals. In one corner was a rusting helmet that a knight had once worn. Everything in the room seemed to possess meaning, even if Indy didn't know what it was. All of it reflected a passion for medieval European studies.

Indy cleared his throat. "Dad?"

Behind a heavy, dark mahogany desk, his father, Professor Henry Jones, was absorbed in his work. Papers and books were strewn around him. Indy stared at the curve of his father's back, willing him to speak, to nod, to acknowledge him in some way. He knew his father had heard him, but the fact that he didn't greet Indy, didn't even turn around, meant he didn't want to be disturbed.

He never wanted to be disturbed.

Still, this was important. He neared the desk, glimpsed the ancient parchment his father was working on, and said, "Dad, I've got to talk to you."

"Out!" Henry snapped at his son without even turning to look at him.

"But this is really important!"

Henry continued with his work. "Then wait. Count to twenty."

"No, listen. . . ."

"Junior," Henry warned, his voice low and threatening and stern.

Indy gulped, nodded, and took a deferential step back. He knew his father was annoyed with him. There was little he could do. He started counting in a faint voice and, as he did, looked over his father's shoulder.

He saw that the top page of the parchment revealed an illustration of what looked like a stained glass window containing several Roman numerals. His father was busy copying the drawing in his notebook.

"This is also important . . . and it can't be hurried . . . it's taken nine hundred years to find its way from a forgotten box of parchment in the Sepulchre of Saint Sophia in Constantinople to the desk of the one man left in the world who might make sense of it."

". . . nineteen . . . twenty." *This is really important. Pay attention to me.*

Indy pulled the Cross of Coronado out of his shirt and started talking fast and loud again. "I was in the cave with the scout troop and . . ."

"Now do it in Greek," Henry commanded, still not turning from his work or listening to his son.

He never listens to me.

Indy hated him for that.

In a louder, angry voice, Indy began counting in Greek. He imagined each number was a curse word that he hurled at his obstinate father.

He heard a car stop in front of the house. He backed out of the study, still counting, and spotted a police car.

Now what should I do? He realized that if his father saw the police there, he'd think Indy had gotten into trouble again. He wouldn't even give him a chance to explain. He knew that from experience.

He glanced back into the study at his father, who was still working on his sketch. He listened as his father spoke softly to himself.

"May he who illuminated this, illuminate me."

Indy held his breath as he carefully closed the study door and stepped into the hall. He jammed the cross back under his shirt as the front door swung open, and Herman stumbled, out of breath, into the living room.

"I brought him, Indy! I brought him!"

The door opened again, and the sheriff entered the house and looked around.

"Sheriff, sir! There were five or six of them! They almost got me, but . . ."

"All right, son." The sheriff held up a hand. "Do you still have it?"

"Yes, sir. Right here."

Indy pulled out the cross again and handed it to the sheriff, who casually took it without even bothering to look closely at it. As the cross left his hand, Indy sensed something was wrong about the way the sheriff was acting. If he only knew what he had gone through.

"That's good, boy. That's good . . . because the rightful owner of this cross said he wouldn't press charges against you if you co-operated."

Indy did a double take. His jaw dropped. His fingers curled into fists. "Press charges . . . What are you talking about?"

Fedora walked into the house and removed his hat. He nodded to Indy in a friendly manner and patted Herman on the head.

"Theft," the sheriff said. "He's got witnesses, five or six of them."

The sheriff and Fedora were in cahoots. What else could it be? The lawman wasn't even going to listen to him. He didn't care about what really had happened.

"And we wouldn't want your mama turning in her grave, would we now?"

The sheriff handed the cross to Fedora, who put it into the leather pouch that hung from his hip. As the sheriff walked away, Indy glanced through the screen door and saw a cream-colored sedan, the one that had chased him through the desert. It was parked behind the sheriff's vehicle and was coated with a thin layer of desert dust. Behind the wheel, waiting patiently, was the man in the Panama hat.

Fedora lingered behind after the sheriff was gone. When he spoke, it was in a man-to-man tone that was laced with irony. "Well, you lost today, kid, but that doesn't mean you have to like it."

He took off his fedora, held it a moment by the crown. Then he took a step forward and extended it as if he were about to place it on Indy's head as a show of respect and admiration. But he checked himself as Indy spoke up.

"The Cross of Coronado is four hundred years old, and it still has a long way to go. I aim to be around. You can count on it."

Fedora grinned, dropped the hat on Indy's head, and turned away. "I'll tell the boss," he said, and laughed.

He stopped a moment at the door and looked back at Indy. "You were good with that whip today, kid. I like your spunk."

Indy kicked the door, slamming it behind Fedora.

He heard Fedora chuckling as he walked down the sidewalk.

He ran to the window and saw Fedora slide into the cream-colored sedan, the cross in his hand. He saw him pass the precious artifact to the man behind the wheel and watched them drive away.

He would get that cross back, he swore to himself as he touched the brim of the felt hat. He would do it no matter how long it took.

AT SEA:
1938

FOUR
Atlantic Crossing

THIRTY-FOOT WAVES CRASHED across the deck of the old cargo ship, washing away everything that wasn't tied down. Rain whipped it from every side. Wind howled. The old cargo boat's wood shrieked as though it were being yanked apart at the seams. It was a hideous sound, the sound of a thing in pain, and Indy couldn't block it out.

He clung to the edge of his bunk, certain that in the next second, or the one after that, a wave would slam through the wood, crushing it, and sweep him away. He squeezed his eyes shut as the storm hurled the ship to the right, the left, the right again. Now it was slammed down at the stern. Now it was flung backward. Now it rolled, it rocked, it rose and fell.

I'm going to puke.

But when his eyes flew open, the press of the dark against his porthole took his breath away. Then a wall of water crashed against the side of the ship, smeared against the glass, and the impact threw him out of his bunk. He smacked the floor and for a second or two just lay there groaning.

Get up, man. Make your move now.

Right. His plan. He had a plan, didn't he?

He lifted himself up on his hands, shook his head to clear it, and grappled for a hold on anything that wasn't moving. On your feet, mate. Now. Make your move now while the captain's on the bridge.

Yeah, the captain. The captain and the cross. Got it.

He gripped the edge of his bunk and pulled himself to his feet. He buttoned his leather jacket with one hand, tugged his fedora down tightly over his head, made sure his bullwhip was secure at his waist, and reeled toward the door.

Forward, mate.

Right foot, left, right foot again. Good, real good. He was going to make it to the door and then outside onto the deck and then down the deck to the captain's quarters. Where the cross was.

Indy had booked passage on this cargo ship after receiving a tip on the location of the Cross of Coronado. A man had called his office at the university and told him that if he was interested in the cross, he should meet him in Lisbon, Portugal. When he had questioned the caller, he had accurately described the man Indy had seen only once when he was a child—the man who had taken possession of the cross, the man he had pursued for years.

When Indy asked what he wanted for the information, the caller had said he was only after revenge. The man with the cross was his boss, and only recently he had found out the man was having an affair with his wife. The tip—and the justification—seemed reasonable to Indy, and he had a few days available. He had followed leads that were far less substantial, and this one sounded like the break he needed. He had narrowly missed catching the man whose trademark was his Panama hat several times, but he hadn't had a lead for a couple of years.

When he arrived in Lisbon, his informant told him the cross had been moved and that he should wait until further notice. Eight days passed, and he was ready to give up and return to the States.

He was already late for the new semester of classes. That day his informant contacted him and told him the cross was being sent on a cargo ship to the United States the next day, and the captain of the vessel had been entrusted with it.

Now Indy was on the ship, and this was the first chance he'd had to search the captain's quarters. With weather like this, he was certain the captain would be on the bridge.

First and maybe the only chance, mate.

He flung the door open, and the wind lashed him. He moved against it, one hand holding the fedora down on his head, the other gripping the doorjamb.

The ship rolled to the left; Indy rolled with it and nearly lost his footing. He had to let go of the fedora to grab on to the other jamb, and the wind whipped up under the hat's brim and swept it off his head, back into his room. He left it. He leaned into the wind, into the thickness of it, and made his way out onto the deck, slamming his door shut behind him.

The ship lifted onto the crest of a wave, its tired wood moaning and screeching, and Indy grabbed on to the railing, waiting for the boat to slam down. When it did, water rushed across the deck, almost jerking his hands from the railing. It was over in seconds, and he thrust himself forward, hand over hand, pulling himself through the violence. The wind howled around him. The taste of salt coated his lips and stung his eyes until they were barely slits.

The captain's on the bridge, and it's now or never.

He kept moving. The storm tossed the ship around like a piece of driftwood. He thought of the cross. The cross burned through his mind, brighter than mercury, hotter than the sun. After a while he no longer felt the wind or the storm or the rolling of the sea. He moved as the ship moved, as though he were a part of it, one with it. His legs seemed sturdier, more certain. He found new strength. The image of the cross in his head burned and burned.

By the time he made it to the captain's quarters, he was soaked to the bone. Water ran in rivulets down the sides of his face. Salt was thick against his lips, his tongue. He took out a long, slender tool, like an ice pick but made of a more malleable metal. It was a tool used by thieves, not archaeologists. He gripped the doorknob and held his hand as steadily as possible. He pushed the tip of the tool toward the lock, but the boat swayed, and his arm lurched about like a symphony conductor waving a baton. He tried again, and this time stabbed himself in the wrist.

Damn it. He shook his hand. Steady. Steady.

He made two more efforts before finally inserting the tool in the keyhole. He eased it into the lock, gingerly prodding and jiggling it until it was fully inserted. He took a deep breath and carefully turned the doorknob. He smiled as it opened.

The moment he was inside, the door slammed shut, blocking the din of the storm. He looked around, making sure he was alone. Then he headed straight for the captain's bunk. The lamp on the wall flickered, blinked out, on, and the ship rolled onto its side. He grabbed on to the edge of the bunk and held on until the vessel righted itself again.

His informant had assured him that the captain would keep the cross in the ship's safe. He had not only told him where the safe was located but had even handed him a scrap of paper with the safe's combination. When Indy asked him how he'd gotten it, the man smiled and told him not to question his good fortune.

He was wary about the guy. He didn't like him. But this was the best lead he'd had in years, and who said you had to like everyone you work with?

Now he would see just how good his fortune was. Maybe the whole thing was a hoax.

He dug his hands under the mattress and lifted it. The safe was there, all right, built into the floor, beneath the bed. He grasped the bed frame and shoved it aside.

So far, so good.

The next question was whether he could open it. If the combination didn't work, he wouldn't be any closer to the cross than if he'd stayed home. He twitched the dial back and forth, getting the feel of it. He had memorized the combination—he turned to the first number, then followed the sequence of five more numbers.

He paused a moment when he was finished, then slowly turned the arm. The safe opened. It was dark inside. He reached blindly into it. He felt a couple of boxes, jewelry boxes no doubt. His fingers ran across a packet of papers. He reached beneath them and felt an object wrapped in cloth—in the shape of a cross.

He pulled it out, growing increasingly excited. He untied the knot in the string that bound it, then unraveled the cloth. It was the Cross of Coronado. He hadn't forgotten its beauty, but the sight of the precious artifact still stunned him.

It felt cool and heavy in his hands. It felt right. He tucked it under his jacket, inside his belt, in almost the exact same spot where he had hidden it twenty-six years ago.

He closed the safe, spun the dial, and pushed the bed back into place. Once he was outside again, the place where the cross rested against his wet shirt seemed warm, thick, protected. He was giddy with relief and fatigue and a sense of triumph. Twenty-six years, you bastard, he thought. Twenty-six years.

Something gnawed at the back of his mind, something he couldn't focus on, something important. He tried to seize it, to scrutinize it, but he was so tired and the wind was so loud and . . . later, it'll come to you later.

Then he looked up and saw a burly sailor staring sullenly at him from the end of the corridor. He turned and saw another at the other end. Suddenly he understood.

A setup. No wonder it was so damn easy. No wonder the informant had the combination. It was all too easy. That's what had bothered him.

The sailors rushed forward from either side. He was about to throw a punch, but the boat swayed, and he stumbled back right into the arms of the second sailor. They pinned his arms behind him and dragged him to the end of the corridor and onto the deck.

Then a third figure stepped out of the wet shadows and punched him in the gut.

Indy gasped. He felt his legs crumpling. One of the sailors held him up and jerked him to the right, under an awning that offered some protection from the storm. And that was when Indy saw him, the bastard who had punched him. It was a man clutching a Panama hat to his head, the same man behind the original theft, and the one no doubt behind the setup. He was older, but even in the dark Indy could see his icy blue eyes glowing like twin moons.

"Small world, Dr. Jones."

"Too small for both of us. I see you haven't changed your style a bit," he commented, glancing up at the Panama hat.

"How observant. I seem to have seen your favorite attire somewhere myself. But let's get down to business."

The man grabbed his jacket with such force that Indy thought the leather would rip. He reached into Indy's belt and removed the cross. "As you know, this is the second time I've had to reclaim my property from you, but it's no coincidence that we meet here tonight."

"I know. You set me up."

"You're the fall guy, Dr. Jones."

He told Indy that he was well aware of his persistent search for the cross, the prize of his collection. Ever since the Depression had weakened his financial base, he had been attempting to sell it. Finally he had been offered a sizable sum that would end his economic woes. The catch: the arrangement included a stipulation that the pesky Dr. Indiana Jones must be disposed of before the transaction was completed.

"So I decided to arrange for you to come to me. I played fair. I even gave you one more chance to steal the cross." He grinned at Indy. "Too bad you were caught again."

"That cross belongs in a museum."

"So do you." He glanced at the sailors. "Throw him over the side."

Indy was propelled across the rolling deck toward the rail. As they passed a bundle of fuel drums, he saw his chance to take advantage of the storm. Using the sailors as leverage, he kicked up his feet and broke the clamp on the metal bands that held the drums together.

Suddenly the drums were loose and careened wildly across the deck. Indy jabbed his elbows into the stomachs of the startled sailors and rushed toward his nemesis.

Panama Hat saw him coming and lurched toward a ladder that led up to the bridge. But before he could reach it, a huge fuel drum crashed against the ladder, blocking his path. The drum started to roll back toward him. He leaped to the side, and as he did, the cross flew out of his grasp and skittered across the deck.

Indy pitched forward toward the cross, but one of the sailors blocked his way, then swung a crowbar at his head. He ducked just in time, then let loose a powerful uppercut that caught the sailor under the jaw. The man reeled backward just as a wave slammed against the deck.

Indy looked around frantically for the cross, and spotted it several feet away. He threw himself at it and slid across the deck on his stomach, arms extended like wings. He snatched up the cross just as another wave crashed against the deck, burying him in water.

He slid a few more feet and saw a giant fuel drum rolling toward him. He pushed off from the deck, but lost his footing. An instant before he would have been crushed, he dived and rolled, and the drum thundered past.

He looked up to see several more drums rolling his way. He leapt to his feet and sidestepped them all. That was close. Just then, he turned and saw another sailor brandishing a stevedore's hook and moving his way.

He unhitched the bullwhip from his hip and flung his arm forward. The whip cracked. It struck its mark, wrapping around the sailor's ankle. He jerked on the whip, and the rolling ship did the rest: the sailor crashed to the deck.

Indy paused to admire his nifty work. At that moment a net dropped over his head, and Panama Hat pummeled him with his fists. The man took pleasure in his work, beating him hard and fast, again and again. Indy tried to dodge the punches, to ward them off with his arms, and to escape the net, but it was no use.

All the drums that Indy had dodged when they rolled from port to starboard changed direction as the ship began to list the other way. Now they trundled back in his direction, and this time they were also headed for a large stack of crates near him marked TNT— DANGEROUS.

Indy shouted as one of the drums bore down on him. Panama Hat turned, saw the drum, and tumbled across the deck. Indy jerked away in the other direction, barely avoiding the drum.

He struggled to pull the net away from him, but the cross was tangled in it. The only way to escape it would be to drop the cross, and he wasn't about to do that. He looked up just in time to see another fuel drum rolling directly toward the explosives.

There was only one thing to do, and he did it. He hurtled himself over the side into the stormy seas.

The moment he hit the water, the ship split apart in a fiery blast. Bits of debris rained from the sky as if they were part of the storm, and what remained of the ship quickly sank beneath the waves.

The concussion of the water and the blast tore the net away from him. He tumbled about in the water and finally bobbed to the surface like a piece of cork, still clutching the cross. His legs kicked frantically as he tried to keep his head above water.

He grabbed for something to hold on to, went under, surfaced again, coughing and spitting out water. His hand found something—a preserver, one of the ship's doughnut-shaped life preservers. He hooked one arm, then the other, through it.

Then he saw something else floating by that looked familiar. He reached out and snatched it and held it up to his face. He recognized it as the shredded remains of a Panama hat.

In the distance an American freighter sounded its horn. Indy waved his arm, hoping to get the ship's attention, and realized he was waving the cross in the air. He wondered how the hell he would explain it. I'm a priest. I saved the cross. The cross saved me.

What the hell did it matter? He wanted to laugh and to cry at the same time. He knew, damn it, that he was going to make it. And, hey, he had the cross.

NEW YORK:
A FEW DAYS LATER

FIVE

On Campus

THE WARM SPRING AFTERNOON had drawn students outside in droves. Young women in calf-length dresses and men in ties strolled along the tree-shrouded brick paths that twisted through the campus, past ivy-covered brick buildings. Books were bundled under their arms, pencils rested behind their ears, and none of the young people seemed to be in any hurry.

A black raven soared silently above the students and landed on a window ledge on the second floor of one of the ivy-covered buildings. Inside, a professor wearing a tweed jacket and wire-rim glasses glanced toward the window, momentarily distracted by the bird, then turned back to his class. The students stared attentively, waiting for him to continue.

Despite his professorial attire, there was an underlying ruggedness about him, a sense that when he took off his coat and tie and ventured out into the field in search of ancient artifacts, anything could happen and probably did. It was this mysterious air about him—as well as a certain shyness—that appealed to the coeds who seemed to dominate his classes. For his part he never complained about the profusion of attractive young women who showed up for his lectures.

Those who knew him well were aware that he tended to understate his own experiences. Maybe it was because he felt he lived in the shadow of his famous father, the renowned medieval scholar, Dr. Henry Jones. Whatever the reason, he tended to say one thing about himself and his career but at the same time told you in other ways—gestures, sly looks, and hidden smiles—that what he was saying was only part of the story.

He looked out over his class, hands jammed in the pockets of his pants. ". . . So, forget any ideas about lost cities, exotic travel, and digging up the world. Seventy percent of all archaeology is done in the local library. Research and reading—that's the key. We don't take mythology at face value, nor do we follow maps to buried treasure and *never* does *X* mark the spot! The Lost Continent of Atlantis! Knights of the Round Table! Nothing more than charming, romantic nonsense."

He paused a moment, feeling the weight of the jewel-encrusted gold cross that was resting in his coat pocket. He looked down, scratched behind his ear, and continued. "Archaeology is our search for *fact* . . . not *truth*. If it's truth you're interested in, ladies and gentlemen, Dr. Peterman's philosophy classes are a good start."

The class laughed, and Professor Indiana Jones glanced at a pretty coed seated in the front row and smiled. He cleared his throat. "Next week: Egyptology. Beginning with the excavation of Naukratis by Flinders Petrie in 1885. Irene, my secretary, has the list of assigned reading for the semester." Expecting a rush of students to the podium, he added: "If you have any questions, please see me in my office."

As the students filed out, Indy gazed toward the back of the lecture hall, where Marcus Brody, director of a prestigious archaeological museum and longtime friend of his father, waited for him. He stepped around the podium and headed down the aisle.

Brody, who was discernibly English, was about sixty, a man who was incessantly caught between the tallies of the museum's accountants and the whims of wealthy contributors. He had told Indy more than once that he saw him as a light in the darkness, a man with conviction who was willing to stand toe-to-toe with those who only saw quick profit in ancient artifacts.

He had an expressive face that was filled with deep furrows and lines, each of which told a story. He nearly always looked worried, too, and Indy felt his usual compulsion to pat Brody on the back and assure him things were going to turn out just fine, really.

"Marcus!" Indy slapped his pocket. "I did it."

Brody's eyes lit up. "I want to hear all about it."

"Come on."

As they left the room and headed down the hall, Indy slipped the Cross of Coronado out of his jacket pocket and held it out for Brody to see.

"You've really got it. Bravo. I'm elated. I'm more than elated. I'm overjoyed."

"How do you think I feel? Do you know how long I've been after this?"

"All your life."

"All my life."

They had spoken at the same time, and both of them laughed. "Well done, Indy. Very well done, indeed. Now tell me how you did it."

Indy shrugged. "It wasn't much. It just took a little friendly persuasion, that's all."

"That's all?" Brody asked skeptically.

"Well, when the cordialities wore out, it took a bit of diplomatic arm twisting."

"I see." Brody nodded. It was obvious he was interested in hearing more. But he was also worried that he would hear something that wasn't up to the standards of the museum he represented.

Before Indy could even begin his story, though, two of his colleagues approached them in the hallway. "Where you been, Jones?" asked the taller man. "Semester break ended a week ago."

The second colleague shoved a ceramic fertility goddess toward Indy. "Have a look at this, Jonesy. I picked it up on a trip down to Mexico. Possibly you could date it for me. What do you say?"

Indy turned the piece of pottery over in his hands. A wry smile crossed his lips. "Date it?"

The man adjusted his tie and looked uneasily at Indy. Then, with a false tone of self-assurance, he added: "I paid almost two hundred dollars for it. The man assured me it was pre-Columbian."

"Pre-October or November. Hard to say. But let's take a look." Before the startled professor could say a word, Indy snapped the figurine in two. "See, you can tell by the cross section. It's worthless."

"Worthless?"

"You got it." He handed both pieces of the figurine back to the professor and walked off with Brody.

"I should have showed them what a real artifact looks like," Brody said, holding up the cross.

Indy shrugged. "Why bother?"

A moment later they stopped in front of Indy's office. "This piece will find a place of honor among our Spanish acquisitions," Brody assured him.

"Good. We can discuss my honorarium later on over champagne."

"When can I expect you?"

Indy thought a moment. He hadn't been to his office yet and wasn't looking forward to the stack of paperwork that was probably awaiting him as a result of missing the first week of the semester. "Let's make it in half an hour."

Brody smiled, slipped the cross into his briefcase, and was still beaming as he walked off.

Indy opened the door of his office and winced. The outer office was bursting with students, who immediately surrounded him.

"Professor Jones, could you . . ."

"Dr. Jones, I need . . ."

"Hey, I was here first. Professor . . ."

Indy shouldered his way to his secretary's desk. The woman, a teaching assistant named Irene, looked as if she was suffering from shell shock. She sat transfixed, ignoring the bombardment of students. Then she saw Indy and was suddenly reactivated.

"Dr. Jones! For God's sake, I'm so glad you're back. Your mail is on your desk. Here are your phone messages. This is your appointment schedule. And these term papers still haven't been graded."

Indy nodded and took the papers, then turned to enter his private office. The students were still clamoring for his attention.

"Dr. Jones."

"Wait, Dr. Jones. My grade."

"Sign my registration card."

"Listen, Dr. Jones. If I could just have . . ."

Indy held up a hand, and suddenly the mob was silent and attentive. "Irene . . . put everyone's name down on a list in the order they arrived. I'll see each and every one of them in turn."

Irene glanced from Indy to the students. The horde immediately descended on her like a swarm of mosquitos. "Well, I'll try," she muttered.

"I was first. . . ."

"No, I was here before you. . . ."

"I'm sure I was second. . . ."

"Hey, watch where you're stepping there."

Indy slipped into his office and impatiently sorted through his mail: an assortment of college bulletins, archaeological newsletters, the current issues of *Esquire* and *Collier's*, and a thick envelope with a foreign postmark on it.

He stared at it a moment. "Hmm . . . Venice." He tried to think of whom he knew in Venice and came up with a blank. Before he had a chance to open the envelope, Irene's distraught voice squawked over the intercom.

"Dr. Jones . . . there seems to be some disagreement out here about who arrived first, and I—"

"Fine, fine," Indy cut in. "Do the best you can. I'll be ready in a moment."

Like hell I will.

Indy stuffed his mail into his coat pockets, took a quick look around, then opened his window and crawled through it. He took a deep breath of the late-afternoon spring air as he stepped out into the adjoining garden. Roses, gardenias, grass. It was marvelous.

"A fine day," he said to himself, and headed across the garden away from his office. He walked swiftly and confidently. He was smiling, enjoying his freedom, and ignoring any thoughts about responsibilities. After what he had been through to recover the cross, he deserved a little break.

If anyone complained, well, he never said he was as conscientious as his father. He was well aware that his father's reputation was a double-edged blade. When it cut one way, it served to secure his position at the university. When it cut the other way, it made him feel like a second-rate scholar who never would measure up to the old man.

Maybe that was why he was irresponsible and why he took chances. In his own way he wanted attention. What he couldn't equal in scholarship, he could master in the field. And the field was forever a wide-open space full of adventure.

As he reached the curb outside the building on the edge of campus, a long, black Packard sedan pulled up to him. Indy glanced inside and was about to continue on his way when the back door swung open and a man stepped out. He was dressed in a dark three-piece suit, with the brim of his hat pulled low enough so that his eyes were in shadow. There was a no-nonsense look about him. Everything he saw told Indy that he was a G-man.

"Dr. Jones?"

Indy met his gaze. "Yes? Is there something I can help you with?"

"We have something rather important to talk to you about. We'd like you to come with us."

Indy hesitated, looking the man over closely. A bulge in the coat. *Terrific. I need this.* As if to justify his suspicion, the man let his coat fall open, revealing a shoulder holster. Indy eyed the gun, then the three men in the car. Each of them was cut from the same mold as the guy in front of him.

He didn't know what they wanted, and he didn't care to find out. "I'm not sure I have the time at the moment," he said in a halting voice as he tried to think of an easy way out.

"There's nothing to think over, Dr. Jones. I'm afraid we insist you come with us."

For the next half hour Indy was ensconced in the backseat of the Packard between two of his burly escorts. A couple of times he attempted to find out what was going on, but they said he'd find out soon enough. When he commented about the spring weather, the man to his left grunted. The one on his right just looked ahead.

Real friendly bunch.

It occurred to him that none of them had shown him any identification. He turned to the guy next to him and asked for his ID. The man acted as if he hadn't heard him.

"You guys are feds, right?"

"We're delivery boys," one of them said, and all of them laughed.

Indy laughed, too, and squirmed uncomfortably. Things were getting very funny.

SIX

The Crusader Tablet

I T WAS NEARLY DUSK when the Packard pulled up to an exclusive
Fifth Avenue building overlooking Central Park. Indy climbed
out and was accompanied into the building by two of the men. He
was whisked through the lobby and into a private elevator. When
the door opened to a penthouse, he stepped out and looked
around, impressed by the luxurious surroundings.

"Come on," one of the men muttered. "You can do your sight-
seeing inside."

They ushered him into a plush art deco penthouse and disappeared, leaving him in a room furnished with numerous museum-
quality artifacts on display. Indy walked around, examining one
after another. Whoever owned this place had money and taste,
with a considerable amount of the former. He picked up a ceramic
pot with a painting of a peacock on one side. He recognized it as
Greek in origin, and even though it was over twenty-five hundred
years old, the luster of its colors was incredibly well preserved.

Indy's inspection was interrupted when a door opened in front
of him. He heard soft piano music and voices, and momentarily

glimpsed a cocktail party inside before the doorway was filled by a tall, broad-shouldered man in a tuxedo. His jaw was square, his blond hair thinning. Even though he appeared to be well into his fifties, his physique was trim and muscular, like that of a much younger man. There was something regal about him as he strode across the room, and Indy had no doubt that he was about to meet the owner of the penthouse.

He looked familiar, but why? Then he knew. He was one of the major contributors to the archaeology museum. He'd seen him a couple of times at social events associated with the museum, and he had heard Brody fussing about him more than once. His name was Walter . . . Walter Donovan. That was it.

"Notice the eyes in the tail feathers," Donovan said, nodding to the pot that Indy was still holding.

He carefully set the precious artifact back in place. "Yeah. Nice eyes."

"You know whose eyes they are?"

Indy smiled. "Sure. They're Argus's eyes. He was a giant with a hundred eyes. Hermes killed him, and Hera put his eyes in the peacock's tail."

Donovan regarded him a moment. "I should have guessed you knew a bit about Greek mythology."

Indy shrugged. "A bit."

The study of Greek myths was an aberration of his childhood, one that he had undertaken at the insistence of his father. He had grudgingly enjoyed some of the tales, especially the ones about Heracles and his feats, but all the while he had despised his father for forcing him to read and learn them. Now, however, he was amazed that thirty years later the heroes and their stories returned so easily to him; it was as if he'd read them last week.

"I trust your trip down was comfortable, Dr. Jones." Donovan smiled, exuding confidence and power. "My assistants didn't alarm you, I hope."

Indy was about to make a crack about the fascinating discussions en route, but Donovan extended a hand and introduced himself.

"I know who you are, Mr. Donovan," Indy said as Donovan released the firm grip on his hand. "Your contributions to the Old World Museum over the years have been extremely generous."

"Why, thank you."

"Some of the pieces in your collection here are very impressive," Indy added, looking around.

Now what the hell do you want with me?

"I'm glad you noticed."

Donovan walked over to a table where an object was covered by a cloth shroud. It was one of the pieces Indy hadn't examined. Donovan pulled back the cloth, revealing a flat stone tablet about two feet square. "I'd like you to take a look at this one in particular, Dr. Jones."

Indy moved closer and saw letters and symbols inscribed on the tablet. He removed his wire-framed glasses from his pocket, slipped them on, and leaned over for a closer examination of the ancient artifact.

"Early Christian symbols. Gothic characters. Byzantine carvings. Middle twelfth century, I'd say."

Donovan crossed his arms. "That was our assessment as well."

"Where did you find this?"

"My engineers unearthed it in the mountain regions north of Ankara while excavating for copper." He paused a beat, studying Indy out of the corner of his eye. "Can you translate the inscription, Dr. Jones?"

Indy took a step back. His eyes were still fixed on the tablet. He explained that translating the inscriptions wouldn't be easy, even for someone like himself, who was knowledgeable of the period and languages.

"Why don't you try, anyhow?" Donovan said in his most persuasive voice.

Why the hell should I?

"I'd appreciate it," Donovan added.

Yeah, I bet you would.

Indy frowned as he stared at the inscription. Finally he cleared his throat and spoke in a slow, halting voice, like a child who was just learning to read.

". . . drinks the water that I shall give him, says the Lord, will have a spring inside him . . . welling up for eternal life. Let them bring me to your holy mountain . . . in the place where you dwell. Across the desert and through the mountain . . . to the Canyon of the Crescent Moon, broad enough only for one man. To the Temple of the Sun, holy enough for all men. . . ."

Indy stopped, looked up at Donovan with a startled expression, saw no reaction on the other man's face, and continued with the final line. ". . . Where the cup that holds the blood of Jesus Christ our Lord resides forever."

"The Holy Grail, Dr. Jones." Donovan's voice was hushed, reverent. He was obviously impressed by what Indy had read. "The chalice used by Christ during the Last Supper. The cup that caught His blood at the Crucifixion and was entrusted to Joseph of Arimathaea. A cup of great power to the one who finds it."

Indy rubbed his chin and looked dubiously at Donovan. "I've heard that bedtime story before."

"Eternal life, Dr. Jones." He emphasized the words, as if Indy hadn't heard him. "The gift of youth to whoever drinks from the Grail."

Donovan, it seemed, was taking the inscription at face value rather than considering it in a mythological context. Indy nodded but didn't say anything, not wanting to encourage the man in a pursuit that had consumed countless lives. He was too well aware how the search for the Grail Cup had become an obsession for even the most rational scholars.

"Now, that's a bedtime story that I'd like to wake up to," Donovan continued.

"An old man's dream."

"*Every* man's dream," Donovan countered. "Including your father's, I believe."

Indy stiffened slightly at the mention of his father. "Grail lore is his hobby." He spoke evenly, covering the discomfort he always felt when the Grail and his father were mentioned in tandem, like parts of a rhyme or a riddle.

"More than simply a hobby," Donovan persisted. "He's occupied the chair of medieval literature at Princeton for nearly two decades."

"He's a professor of medieval literature. The one students hope they don't get."

"Give the man his due. He's the foremost Grail scholar in the world."

Indy gave Donovan a sour look and was about to say something when the door opened. The music and sound of chatter suddenly pumped into the room, and both men turned as a matronly woman in an expensive evening gown stepped through the door.

"Walter, you're neglecting your guests," the woman said in a tone that didn't hide her annoyance. Her eyes shifted from her husband to Indy and back again.

"Be along in a moment, dear."

Indy turned his attention to the tablet once more when it became evident that Donovan wasn't going to introduce him to his wife.

Mrs. Donovan sighed, a sigh that said she was accustomed to this, and returned to the party, her gown rustling as she walked away.

In spite of his skeptical comments, Indy was fascinated by the Grail tablet. He wouldn't swear to it, but he was almost certain the tablet was what it appeared to be. The fact that it existed was an important discovery. What it could lead to was something he didn't even want to consider right now.

He had forgotten all about the way he had been picked off the street. It was inconsequential. The tablet, and what it said, was what mattered.

"Hard to resist, isn't it?" Donovan commented, acutely aware of Indy's interest. "The Holy Grail's final resting place described in detail. Simply astounding."

Indy shrugged and recovered his skeptical, scientific attitude, the one that dominated his classroom persona. "What good is it? The tablet speaks of desert and mountains and canyons. There are a lot of deserts in the world—the Sahara, the Arabian, the Kalahari. And the mountain ranges—the Urals, Alps, Atlas . . . Where do you start looking?"

Then he pointed out the obvious flaw in the discovery. "Maybe if this tablet was completely intact, you'd have more to go on. But the entire top portion is missing."

Donovan wasn't about to be easily discouraged. He acted, Indy thought, like a man who knew something he wasn't telling—a *big* something.

"Just the same, Dr. Jones, an attempt to recover the Grail is currently under way."

Indy frowned and shook his head. "Are you saying the tablet has already been translated?"

Donovan nodded.

"Then why drag me here, just for a second opinion? I could charge you with kidnapping." His tone was deliberately gruff.

Donovan held up a hand. "You could, but I don't think you will. I'm getting to the reason. But first let me tell you another 'bedtime story,' Dr. Jones. After the Grail was entrusted to Joseph of Arimathaea, it disappeared and was lost for a thousand years before being found again by three knights of the First Crusade. Three brothers, to be exact."

"I've heard this one, too," Indy interrupted, and finished the story himself. "One hundred and fifty years *after* finding the Grail, two of these brothers walked out of the desert and began their long journey home. But only one made it back, and before dying of *extreme* old age, he imparted his tale to a Franciscan friar."

Donovan nodded, clearly pleased that Indy knew the story. "Good. Now, let me show you something." He walked across the room and returned with an ancient leather-bound volume. He opened it carefully. It was obvious that the pages were extremely brittle.

"This is the manuscript of the Franciscan friar." He paused a moment, letting that fact fully register. "It doesn't reveal the location of the Grail, but the knight promised that two 'markers' had been left behind that would lead the way."

Donovan pointed at the stone tablet. "This, Dr. Jones, is one of those 'markers.' This tablet proves the story is true. But as you pointed out—it's incomplete."

Seconds passed. Indy could almost feel them filling the room and felt his own body tense, waiting for Donovan to continue. "The second 'marker' is entombed with the remains of the knight's brother. Our project leader—who has brought years of study to this search—believes that tomb is located within the city of Venice, Italy."

"What about the third brother, the one who was left behind in the desert? Does the friar say anything about him in his manuscript?"

"The third brother stayed behind to become the keeper of the Grail." Donovan carefully closed the ancient manuscript. "As you can now see, Dr. Jones, we're about to complete a great quest that began almost two thousand years ago. We're only one step away from actually finding the Grail."

Indy smiled. "And that's usually when the ground disappears from under your feet."

Donovan sucked air in through his teeth and expelled it, a sigh that spoke of some minor inconvenience that had somehow become a burden. "You may be more right than you know."

"How so?"

"We've hit a snag. Our project leader has vanished. So has his research. We received a cable from Dr. Schneider, his colleague. Schneider has no idea of his whereabouts or what's become of him."

Donovan looked down at the ancient manuscript, then back at Indy. His eyes seemed distant now, almost glazed, as though a part of him were as lost as Schneider's colleague. "I want you to pick up the trail where he left off. Find the man and you will find the Grail. Can you think of any greater challenge?"

Indy held up both his hands, patting the air and shaking his head. He gave a small, uncertain laugh. Challenges were one thing; stupidity was quite another. Besides, he rationalized, he had a commitment to the university to fulfill. He couldn't just run off, especially since he had just returned late from another little field trip.

"You've got the wrong Jones, Mr. Donovan. Why don't you try my father? I'm sure he'd be fascinated by the tablet and ready to help out in any way."

"We already have. Your father is the man who's disappeared."

SEVEN

The Grail Diary

INDY SPED ALONG a tree-lined boulevard through an old neighborhood. He cranked the wheel of his Ford coupe, skidded around the corner, and almost hit a man who had stepped into the street.

"Indy, for the Lord's sake and my poor heart, slow down," Brody yelled, from the passenger seat.

A block later Indy pulled over, screeching to a halt at the curb. He gazed for a moment through the windshield toward the house partially hidden by a hedge and trees.

It was two stories, with numerous windows and a nicely landscaped front yard. It might have belonged to an ordinary family with kids and pets, the sort of family that had barbecues on weekends, the family Indy had never had. It didn't look anything like the place where he and his father had lived when he was younger. But it elicited the same feelings of unease, of awkwardness, even though he hadn't set foot here in at least two years.

But none of what had happened between him and his father mattered now.

He hopped out of the Ford and was halfway to the front door

when Brody caught up to him. He was breathing hard from the burst of exertion; a frown creased his forehead.

"Your father and I have been friends since time began. I've watched you grow up, Indy. And I've watched the two of you grow apart." He climbed the stairs to the porch a step behind Indy. "I've never seen you this concerned about him before."

Indy strode across the porch. "He's an academic. A bookworm, not a field man, Marcus. Of course I'm concerned about . . ."

The front door was ajar, and it silenced him. He and Brody glanced at each other, and Indy stepped cautiously closer, muscles tight, expectant. He touched his hand to the door and nudged it open. It creaked. The air that struck his face was cool—and empty.

"Dad?"

"Henry?" Brody called out as he followed Indy inside.

Their voices echoed hollowly. Indy's dread bit more deeply. He called for his father again and moved quickly down the hall, peering into empty rooms, rooms that hadn't changed all that much since they moved here from Utah when he was fifteen. The furniture was nicer, there was *more* of everything, but the air here was just as barren and devoid of character as it had been in the other house after his mother had died.

A clock ticked in the silence. The refrigerator hummed. The quiet mocked him. Gone, Indy thought, and flung back the curtain that separated the hall from the sitting room.

He grimaced, and Brody whispered, "Dear God."

The room hadn't just been ransacked; it had been decimated. Drawers had been pulled out and dumped on the floor. Shelves had been swept clean. The couch cushions had been torn away and hurled across the room. Books, letters, and envelopes were strewn through the mess.

For several long moments Indy just stood there, his eyes flicking this way and that, seeking something, anything, that would provide a clue.

He bent down and picked up a photo album that had been cast

aside. Several pictures fell out, and he plucked them from the ruin and stared at the top photograph. A young boy stood with an unsmiling older man whose beard had not yet turned completely gray. Both the man and the boy were stiff, obviously uncomfortable, and they both looked as though they wanted to be anywhere other than where they were. And that, he thought, had always been the point with him and his father, even as far back as when this picture had been taken. They had never felt comfortable around each other, and now, as all the old feelings flooded back, something hitched in Indy's chest.

The picture had been taken the year after his mother's death. His father had been sullen that year, and Indy knew he thought a lot about the woman who had formed a bridge between father and son. When she died, the bridge vanished. His father had never talked to Indy about her. If he mentioned his mother or anything related to her, his father would cast a frigid glance at him and change the subject or give him a chore to do.

Then there was the intimidation. He remembered the constant reminders that he would never measure up to the old man. He didn't have the discipline, the determination, the intellect. Sure, he had a sense of curiosity, his father had conceded. But what good did it do him? All he did was get into trouble.

As Indy grew older, all the anger and resentment he felt only grew worse. One day, he told his father that he would show him. He would be an archaeologist, too, and a good one. His determination to be as knowledgeable as his father seemed to have grown in direct proportion to his old man's stubbornness and insistence that he would never amount to anything.

The sound of Brody's footfalls on the stairs snapped him back to the present. His misgivings about his father were quickly replaced by a huge and terrible guilt for the times he had wished he would never have to see him again. And for the times he had wished him dead. In spite of his father's toughness and unwillingness to grant him an inch, the texture of everything was different now that he was missing. Right this second there was no one in the world whom Indy wanted to see more desperately.

"He isn't anywhere in the house," Brody said.

"I didn't think he would be."

Brody's face skewed with concern and worry. "What's that old fool gotten himself into, anyway?"

"I don't know. But whatever it is, he's in over his head."

"I just can't imagine Henry getting involved with people he couldn't trust. Look, they've even gone through his mail."

Indy stared at the clutter of torn papers and envelopes and suddenly realized he had forgotten about his own mail.

"The mail. That's it, Marcus!"

He immediately rifled through his pockets and pulled out the overstuffed envelope he had been carrying around since he left his office. He looked at the foreign postmark again and shook his head.

"Venice, Italy. How could I be so stupid?"

Brody looked baffled. "What are you talking about, Indy?"

He tore open the envelope and pulled out a small notebook. He quickly flipped through several pages. It looked like a journal or diary. Page after page was covered with handwritten notes and drawings.

Brody glanced over Indy's shoulder at it. "Is it from Henry?"

"That's right. It's Dad's Grail diary."

"But why did he send it to you?"

"I don't know." He looked around at the room again and back to the diary. "I've got the feeling this is what they were after. It looks like somebody wanted it pretty badly, too."

He lightly stroked the leather cover of the diary. He trusted me. He finally did something to show that he trusted and believed in me.

"Can I see it?" Brody asked.

"Of course. It's all in there. A lifetime's worth of research and knowledge."

As Brody paged through the diary, the lines on his face deepened by the second. "The search was his passion, Indy."

"I know. But do you believe in that fairy tale, Marcus? Do you believe the Grail actually exists?"

Brody stopped turning pages as he came to a picture pasted into the diary. It was a depiction of Christ on the cross, his blood being captured in a golden chalice by Joseph of Arimathaea.

He glanced up and spoke with conviction. "The search for the cup of Christ is the search for the divine in all of us."

Indy nodded and tried to disguise his skepticism. But his indulgent smile wasn't lost on Brody.

"I know. You want facts. But I don't have any for you, Indy. At my age, I'm willing to accept a few things on faith. I can feel it more than I can prove it."

Indy didn't say anything. His gaze flicked to a painting on the wall. It portrayed eleventh-century crusaders plummeting to their deaths over a high cliff. One crusader, however, floated safely in midair because he was holding the Grail in his hands.

He remembered how his father had forced him to read Wolfram von Eschenbach's *Parzival*—the Grail story. He was only thirteen and couldn't think of a drearier way of spending his summer afternoons. At least not until the next year, when Dad made him read it again, this time in the early German version. That was followed by Richard Wagner's opera, *Parsifal*, based on Eschenbach's work.

Each day his father would ask him about the story, to make sure that he was understanding it. If he didn't know the answer to one of the questions, he was required to go back and reread the related section. As an incentive his father promised him that he would be rewarded when he had satisfactorily completed Wagner's work.

He had thought about what kind of reward his father might give him and hoped it would be a trip to Egypt to see the pyramids, or maybe to Athens to see the Parthenon, or Mexico to the Yucatan to see the Mayan ruins. At the very least he figured he deserved a trip to the museum in the state capitol to see the mummies.

As it turned out, his reward was the Arthurian Grail legends. First came *Le Morte d'Arthur* by Sir Thomas Malory, and he had to read it in French first, then English. After that was Lord Tennyson's *Idylls of the King*. Some reward, he glumly thought. In spite of his hatred of the difficult books and his silent anger about his reward, he had never forgotten the adventures of the knights Parzival, Gawain, and Feirifs—the heroes of *Parzival*—or Arthur, Lancelot, and Merlin from the Arthurian legends. In fact, now that he thought of it, those books probably had considerable bearing on how he lived his life.

When Indy didn't speak, Brody cleared his throat, and continued: "If your father believes the Grail is real, so do I."

Indy wasn't sure what to believe, except that he needed to act, to do something, to begin searching. "Call Donovan, Marcus. Tell him I'll take that ticket to Venice now. I'm going to find Dad."

"Good. I'll tell him we want two tickets. I'm going with you."

They motored to the airport in style, seated in the rear of an opulent limousine, accompanied by its owner, Walter Donovan. Indy had taken an emergency leave of absence from the university. At first, when he had made the request, the dean had stared at him askance. How could he even think about petitioning for a leave when he'd just missed the first week of the semester? Then Indy had informed him of the details, and the dean's attitude immediately changed at the mention of his father's name.

He had nodded solemnly, glanced out the window, and told Indy a story about his father. Indy had heard it before, but this time the story had a different twist at the end. It dealt with an incident in which a particularly arrogant colleague of Dr. Jones held an exhibition of his latest archaeological finds. Because of his prominence and his power in academic circles, the reception was attended by scholars and archaeologists from several eastern universities. They had attended not because they admired the man but because they feared him.

When the moment came to unveil the most significant find of the collection, Dr. Jones had stridden to the front of the room, ripped the covering from a piece of pottery that supposedly predated anything ever discovered in the New World. He then smashed it on the podium and declared it fraudulent. He had been quickly ushered away by guards, but the evidence left behind proved him right, and the professor's reign of terror ended.

The dean had turned from the window and looked Indy in the eye. "That professor had been my adviser and had been on the verge of having me expelled because I'd disagreed with him on the dating of an artifact. What your father did inadvertently saved my career. Yes, by all means, go and find Dr. Jones. The world needs men like him."

Indy spent the trip to the airport quietly mulling over what he knew about his father's disappearance. The problem was that there were still too few facts. What he suspected was that the man's passionate interest in the Grail Cup could very well have led him to undertake an uncharacteristic expedition. Considering his age, he had probably felt this would be his one and only opportunity to find the Grail and to complete his life's quest.

Damn that old man and his obsession.

If only they had been on better terms, this never would have happened. He blamed himself. He always had a bad attitude about anything that dealt with his father. But now, somehow, he was going to make up for his past shortcomings and rectify things.

As the limo pulled over to the curb outside the airport entrance, Donovan shook Brody's hand. "Well, Marcus. Good luck."

Like luck's got anything to do with it, Indy thought.

"Thank you, Walter." Brody nodded nervously. "Now, when we arrive in Venice . . ."

"Don't worry," Donovan assured him. "Dr. Schneider will be there to meet you. I maintain an apartment in Venice. It's at your disposal."

"I appreciate that, Walter."

Brody climbed out of the car, and Indy was about to follow, when Donovan touched his shoulder. "Be careful, Dr. Jones. Don't trust *anybody*. You understand?"

Indy met his gaze. "I'm going to do whatever is necessary in order to find my father."

The plane soared through bright sunlight, past clouds that clung to the sky like tiny white commas. The Atlantic stretched below them, an endless stretch of blue, a desert of blue, brilliant and blinding. But Indy saw none of it. For most of the trip he was pre-occupied with his father's Grail diary.

He went through it, carefully reading each entry, each page, seeking clues. " 'The word *Grail* is derived from *graduale*, which means step-by-step, degree by degree,' " he read on a page near the beginning. " 'There are six degrees or levels of awareness in the Grail quest, and each one is represented by an animal.' "

The raven was the symbol of the first degree and represented the messenger of the Grail and "the finger of fate" that initiated the quest.

The peacock signified the second degree and symbolized the search for immortality. It also suggested the colorful and imaginative nature of the quest.

The sign for the third degree was the swan, because the one who took up the Grail quest sang a swan song to selfish and indulgent ways. In order to succeed in the quest, one must overcome weaknesses of the mind and heart and move beyond petty likes and dislikes.

The fourth degree was signified by the pelican, a bird willing to nurture its young by wounding its own breast. It symbolized the quality of self-sacrifice and the willingness to endanger self for the sake of saving one's own people.

The lion was the sign of the fifth degree. It stood for leadership, conquest, and the attainment of high goals.

The sixth and highest level, represented by the eagle, was achieved at the end of the quest. At that time the seeker of the Grail would have gained the power and knowledge necessary to understand fully the significance of the search.

Indy looked up from the book and shifted his position in the tight quarters of his seat. It was typical of his father to couch things in symbols and metaphors. As a scholar, he worked in the abstract. He suspected that the Grail diary was almost as mystifying as the Grail Cup itself.

The mention of the animals reminded him of something he hadn't thought about for a while. When he was eighteen, he had returned to the Southwest and undertaken a vision quest under the guidance of an old Navajo Indian. He had climbed a mesa in New Mexico alone and without food. There he had built a shelter and waited.

The Indian had told him that he must wait until an animal approached him, and from that time on it would be his protector, his spiritual guardian. Two days passed, and his stomach was empty, his throat dry. He wanted more than anything to climb down and find water. He stood up and walked to the edge of the mesa and stared down. Whatever had possessed him to do something so crazy?

He was about to start his descent when he thought he heard the voice of the old Indian telling him to wait. Startled, he turned around. No one was there. His hunger and thirst were causing him to hear voices, he thought. But instead of climbing down the mesa, he headed back to his shelter.

He had taken no more than a dozen steps when suddenly an eagle swooped out of the sky, skimming low over the flat, rocky surface. The majestic creature landed on the wall of his shelter. He had found his protector. When he had told his story, the old Navajo nodded and said that the eagle would always guide him on his journeys.

Indy snapped out of his reverie as the steward tapped him on the shoulder and asked if he'd like a drink. He nodded, and as he adjusted himself in the seat, a folded piece of paper fell from the diary into the aisle. The steward picked it up and handed it to him along with a drink. He set the glass down on the tray in front of him and unfolded the paper.

It was a rubbing that he immediately recognized as an impression of Donovan's Grail tablet. The top part of it was blank, as if space had been left for the missing section of the tablet.

"Look at this, Marcus."

He held it out to Brody, then realized his traveling partner was fast asleep.

He refolded the paper and was about to slip it into the diary when he noticed the drawing on the page that had fallen open.

It was a sketch of what appeared to be a stained glass window of a knight. Below it was one word: Venice. He wondered about its significance.

It wouldn't be long before he would find out.

VENICE

EIGHT
Roman Numerals

"**A**H, VENICE." Indy sighed, looking around, nodding to himself, drawing a kind of sustenance from his surroundings. Venice was like no other city on earth and was a perfect balm for his dark mood. As he and Brody traversed the city by water bus, the gloom that had hovered over him ever since he found out about his father's disappearance lifted.

The air smelled sweetly of water, the sky overhead was a soft cushion of blue, and Indy's spirit soared. It's going to be all right, he told himself. He would find his father. He had to believe that.

"Think of it," Brody said, "a city built in a lagoon on a hundred and eighteen islands."

Indy nodded. "And look what they built."

Venice's heritage was visible along virtually every street and waterway. The city was a harbor of culture and knowledge, of history and romance, and no doubt intrigue and adventure as well.

As he and Brody disembarked from the water bus at a boat landing, Indy's sense of euphoria abruptly evaporated. A band of Fascist militiamen passed by with a civilian suspect in tow. At the sight of the boat, the civilian started struggling to escape. The militiamen reacted swiftly and harshly. They struck the man with their clubs, kicked him with their heavy boots, and the man whimpered and cried out and tried to get away. He finally collapsed against the cobblestones, his face bloody, his body as still as a dead man's.

It disturbed Indy at a level too deep for words. He sensed a vengefulness in the militiamen's attitude that far exceeded military code. They obviously enjoyed their work, and reminded him of the sailors he had tangled with on the cargo ship.

"Ah, Venice," he said again. But this time his voice was heavier, thicker, reflecting his concern for what was taking place in Italy and throughout Europe. Fascists and Nazis had thrown the continent into havoc. Who the hell knew where it would all end? Or when? Or how? Or if?

Some of his earlier gloom returned.

"I find that sort of thing very disturbing," Brody remarked as they made their way across the dock. "I hope we don't encounter any more violence on this trip."

Indy glanced at him; Brody wore his fretful expression again. "Yeah, me, too." But he had the feeling that wouldn't be the case.

As they looked around, Indy wondered aloud how they would recognize Dr. Schneider when they saw him. Donovan hadn't given them any description of his father's colleague. He just said he'd be there waiting.

"Maybe he'll be holding a sign," Brody suggested hopefully.

A woman suddenly approached them from the crowd, and smiled. She was an attractive blonde with high cheekbones and a slender figure. Her lapis-colored eyes were bright and intelligent.

"Dr. Jones?"

"Yes." Indy smiled. Schneider must have sent his secretary to pick them up, and he didn't mind one bit.

"I knew it was you." Her manner was brazenly flirtatious. "You have your father's eyes."

Indy was instantly attracted to her. "And my mother's ears. But the rest belongs to you."

He expected her to be flustered. Instead, she laughed. It was a light, beautiful sound, full of life, and for a second, he thought she was laughing at him. What the hell, he thought. So it wasn't the most original line. Who cared? He would have said it again just to hear her laugh once more.

"Looks like the best parts have already been spoken for," she said.

Indy grinned, enjoying the repartee.

The woman turned to Brody. "Marcus Brody?"

"That's right."

"My name is Elsa Schneider."

Indy's grin faded.

Brody tried to cover his surprise but without success. "Ah, Dr. Schneider. I see."

He shook her hand as she extended it. He cleared his throat, glanced at Indy as if hoping he would pick up the conversation, then looked back at the woman. "It's nice to meet you. Walter didn't, ah . . ."

She smiled and turned. "I thought as much. I guess Walter likes to surprise people. This way, gentlemen."

They entered the vast Piazza San Marco, and she directed the conversation immediately to the matter at hand. "The last time I saw your father we were in the Marciana Library. That's where I'm taking you now. He was very close to tracking down the knight's tomb. I've never seen him so excited. He was as giddy as a school-boy. He was certain the tomb would contain the map leading to the Grail."

Dr. Henry Jones—Attila the professor—giddy as a schoolboy? That was a side of him he'd never seen, Indy thought. "He was never giddy, even when he *was* a schoolboy."

Maybe working with Elsa Schneider had deranged the old man, Indy thought. Indy couldn't take his eyes off her, and he had to admit he felt a bit giddy himself. As they strolled along, he noticed a vendor selling flowers from a cart. He reached back and pulled out a red carnation from a corner bouquet. The vendor was busy with a customer and missed his quick fingers.

He held out the flower to Elsa and smiled. "Fräulein, will you permit me?"

She eyed the flower, then glanced up at Indy. "Well, I usually don't."

"I usually don't, either."

She regarded him a moment longer. "In that case, I permit you."

"It would make me happy."

She took the carnation from Indy. "I'm already sad. By tomorrow it will have faded."

"Then tomorrow I'll steal you another. That's all that I can promise."

She laughed again, that beautiful laugh, that laugh Indy suddenly craved. He started to say something else, but Brody spoke up. "Look here, I hate to interrupt, but the reason we are here . . ."

"Yes, of course," Elsa said in a serious voice, and reached into her purse. "I have something to show both of you. As I was saying, I left Dr. Jones working in the library. He sent me to the map section to fetch an ancient plan of the city. When I got back to his table, he was gone, and so were all of his papers. Except for one thing."

She held up a scrap of paper and looked from Brody to Indy. "I found this near his chair."

Indy took the paper from her and unfolded it. The only thing that was written on it were the Roman numerals III, VII, and X.

Indy contemplated that bit of information.

Elsa pointed her gloved hand to her right. "Here's the library."

They climbed the front steps, and Elsa led the way inside. Their shoes clicked against the polished marble floor. It was the sort of place, Indy thought, that encouraged you to speak in hushed, almost reverent tones. "I've been trying to figure out those numbers all week," Elsa whispered. "Three, seven, and ten. They don't appear to be a Biblical reference. I've checked every combination of chapter and verse in the gospels."

Indy glanced up at the ceiling fifty feet overhead and at the stone walls interspersed with towering stained glass windows. The library was immense and shadowy, huge enough to get lost in.

Maybe his father was still here, he mused, absorbed in some ancient manuscript. He wouldn't even know he was missing.

"Now I'm looking into the Medieval *Chronicles* of Jean Froissart," Elsa continued. "This library has copies of the original text. Perhaps three, seven, and ten represent volume numbers."

Indy nodded. He was impressed with the library, but he also felt uneasy here, knowing this was where his father vanished.

It was ironic in a way. He recalled Professor Henry Jones lecturing him about libraries. Storehouses of knowledge, Junior. Spend more time in libraries, and you'll be the wiser for it. His father thrived in libraries, immersed himself in books, but he didn't lose himself. Indy was sure of that. He had disappeared under duress, not voluntarily. He wasn't the type who ran from trouble. He was too stubborn for that.

They walked between two massive granite pillars and entered a room with tall rows of bookshelves. Elsa led them to the corner of the room and stopped by a table, where she ran her hand lovingly over a couple of precious leather-bound books.

"Your eyes are shining," Indy commented.

"A great library almost makes me cry. Even a single book. It's almost sacred, like a brick in the temple of all our history."

"Yeah. I like a good book," Indy quipped.

"Like being in a church, I'd say," Brody chimed sympathetically.

"In this case it's almost the literal truth. We're on holy ground. This used to be the chapel of a Franciscan monastery." Elsa pointed toward several marble pillars. "Those columns were brought back as spoils of war after the sacking of Byzantium during the Crusades."

Indy noted the columns, but at the moment he was more interested in the window above the table. It was stained glass and depicted a knight of the Crusades. He walked around the table to take a closer look at it, then turned to Elsa. "Is this the table where you last saw my father?"

She nodded, moved her fingertips over the edge of it. "He was working right here. That reminds me. I have to check with the reference counter. I left a picture of Henry. They said they'd be watching in case he showed up again."

The moment Elsa was out of sight, Indy grabbed Brody by the arm and pointed at the stained glass window. "Marcus, I've seen this window before."

Brody frowned. "Where?"

Indy took out the Grail diary and opened it to the sketch he had noticed during the plane flight. He tapped the diary. "Right here."

Brody studied the sketch, looked up at the window, down at the sketch again, and nodded slowly. "Good God, Indy. It's the same."

"Do you see it?"

"Yes, the Roman numerals are part of the window's design."

"Dad was onto something here."

Brody handed the diary back to Indy. "Yes, but what? We know where the numbers came from, but we still don't know what they mean."

Indy saw Elsa approaching and quickly tucked the diary back into his pocket. "Dad sent me this diary for a reason. So until we find out why, I think we should keep it to ourselves."

"Agreed," Brody said.

Elsa shook her head. "No sign of him." She frowned slightly, looking from Indy to Brody and back again. "You two look like you've found something. What is it?"

"Is it that obvious?" Indy asked.

He was scanning the walls and the ceiling. Somewhere around

here there had to be a clue; he was sure of it. He had never been as sure of anything in his life.

Brody pointed to the window. "Three, seven, and ten. There it is, the source of the Roman numerals."

"My God, you're right."

"Dad wasn't looking for a *book*, but the knight's tomb. He was looking for the tomb itself."

Elsa's expression was utterly blank. She finally shook her head. "What do you mean?"

"Don't you get it, Elsa? The tomb is somewhere in the library. You said yourself that this place used to be a church."

Indy's eyes rested on one of the marble columns. "There." He jabbed his finger at it and strode across the room as Elsa and Brody hurried after him.

"Three." Indy pointed at the Roman numerals embedded in the column and smiled triumphantly. "I bet they're all numbered. Spread out. Let's find the others—seven and ten."

They headed off in separate directions, each one making a beeline toward a column. A moment later, Brody motioned to Indy. He found VII.

They kept looking, but none of them could find the last one—X.

They regrouped in the center of the room, about halfway between the III and VII columns. "Damn, it has to be here," Indy muttered. "It's got to be. I'm sure of it."

He walked over to a ladder leading to a loft, climbed up it, and looked down, hoping that his new perspective would offer a clue. It took only a moment to see it, it was that obvious. The floor where Brody and Elsa stood was an elaborate tile design that contained a huge X that was visible only if you were above it.

"X marks the spot," he said aloud, and grinned. He rushed down the ladder and found the center tile where the X intersected. He bent down on one knee and started prying the tile with his knife.

"What're you doing?" Elsa whispered, and looked about anxiously to see who might be watching the crazy foreigner who was ripping up the floor.

"I'm going to find the knight's tomb." The words hissed through his gritted teeth as he struggled with the tile. "What do you think?"

After several moments the tile popped free, revealing a two-foot square hole and proving him right. Cold air and a wet, rancid smell escaped from the dark cavity.

Indy looked up at Elsa and Brody and smiled broadly. "Bingo."

NINE

The Crusader's Tomb

"You don't disappoint, Dr. Jones," Elsa said, brushing a strand of blond hair back in place. "You're a great deal like your father."

"Except he's lost, and I'm not."

Indy peered down into the blackness of the hole, then took a coin from his pocket and dropped it. He heard a soft plop a second later. The bottom was about six feet down. "Be back soon."

He was about to climb into the hole when Elsa touched him on the shoulder. "Ladies first, Indiana Jones. Please lower me down."

Indy tipped his fedora, impressed by the woman's spirit. She sat down, swung her legs over the lip of the hole, then dropped her head back and looked up at him. "Ready?" she asked.

"Ready," he said.

She lifted her arms above her head. He gripped her hands, and she pushed away from the edge. For a second or two she hung in the center of the blackness; then Indy slowly lowered her until she told him to let go. He did and heard her drop to the floor an instant later.

Indy glanced over his shoulder at Brody. "Keep an eye on things, Marcus."

Brody nodded. "I'll put the tile back in place so we don't attract any attention."

"Good idea." He reached in his pocket for the Grail diary and removed the folded piece of paper. He stuffed it in his shirt, then passed the diary to Brody. "Take care of this for me."

"Will do."

Indy glanced down the hole, then back to Brody. "Be back soon. I hope."

He dropped down into the hole, and the tile slid back in place. Instantly the darkness collapsed around him. Overhead, he heard a clatter of footsteps. What the hell was Brody doing, taking dance lessons?

"Elsa?" he whispered.

Her cigarette lighter flicked on; the tiny yellow flame looked like some sort of weird, glowing insect. He blinked and saw her peering at him.

"Did you hear that?" he asked.

"What?"

He glanced up, torn between going back and moving on. Maybe a librarian or the police had found Brody messing around with the tile. If they went back up now, they might never get another chance to look for the knight and the second marker. "Nothing, I guess."

He took the lighter from Elsa. "Come on. Let's get this over with."

It was cool and still, and the air smelled like wet socks. They moved along a stone-walled corridor as Indy sheltered the lighter's flame with his palm. It didn't offer much light, and every now and then he had to look slightly to the right or the left of the flame to see what lay ahead of them.

He stopped and gazed a moment toward a niche carved in the wall. He took a couple steps closer, at first not believing what he saw in the flickering light. He held the lighter slightly to one side and peered ahead, directly at a leering skull attached to blackened skeletal remains that were covered in rotting strips of linen.

"I think we've found a catacomb," Elsa said from behind him. "There's another one of these guys on the other wall."

Indy looked over his shoulder. "Nice. Let's keep going. I don't think either of these fine fellows is our fabled knight."

They moved on, passing several similar burial sites before Elsa pointed to symbols carved on the wall near one of the skeletons.

"Look at this," she said. "Pagan symbols. Fourth or fifth century."

Indy held the lighter up and stepped closer to examine the markings. "Right. About six hundred years before the Crusades."

"The Christians would have dug their own passages and burial chambers centuries later," Elsa added.

He knew she was right and told her so. "If a knight from the First Crusade is entombed down here, that's where we'll find him."

They moved on down the tunnel. "We're on a crusade, too, aren't we?" Elsa's voice was hushed and sincere.

Funny, he thought. She took this Grail stuff as seriously as his father did. "I guess we are. You could say that." He paused. "Hold my hand."

"Why?"

She didn't sound very enthusiastic, he thought, but what the hell. "I don't want to fall."

She laughed, and her fingers brushed his, and Indy clasped her hand.

The passageway wound to their left for another hundred yards or so, then opened into a section of the catacombs that was wider and wetter. They were soon slogging through ankle-deep water that was dark and slimy.

Indy noticed the water percolating in spots. He dipped his fingers into it and rubbed them together. "Petroleum. I could sink a well down here and retire."

"Indy, look." Elsa pointed to another marking on the wall. "A menorah. During the tenth century a large Jewish ghetto formed in Venice."

"I guess that means we're headed in the right direction."

Elsa stopped in front of another carved symbol. "I don't recognize this one."

Indy perused the wall and knew instantly what the etching depicted. He had not only seen it before but had pursued what it represented halfway around the globe, barely escaping death a handful of times.

"That's the Ark of the Covenant."

"Are you sure?"

He glanced over at her, a slight smile forming on his lips. "Pretty sure."

They continued deeper into the catacombs. The passageway narrowed. The water rose to their knees. Indy stopped. He heard a thrashing in the water and a squealing sound. He held up the lighter.

"Rats."

Two, three, four of them. No big deal. As soon as he had discounted them, he saw a couple more, then others. There were dozens of them diving from ledges into the water. He cautiously stepped ahead and saw the water churning with rats. He recalculated. There were hundreds, maybe thousands, of them pouring into the passageway.

He was getting worried.

He looked over at Elsa. Shadows and light danced across her face; her expression was one of disgust, not squeamishness, for which he was grateful. The last thing he needed was a woman who would faint at the sight of a rat. He suggested they climb up onto the ledge, and she readily agreed.

The outcropping of rock was just wide enough for them to gain footing. It was wet and slippery, and they inched forward holding hands, their backs flat against the wall. Below them the river of squealing rats rushed by, and occasionally Indy booted a few from the ledge. At least it wasn't snakes. Ever since he had fallen into a vat of snakes as a kid, he had had an aversion to them. A couple of years ago, during his search for the Ark of the Covenant, he had been trapped in a den of snakes and still had nightmares about that experience.

Adrenaline surged through him as he sidled along the ledge. Danger was a two-sided experience: apprehension on one side, thrills on the other. He squeezed Elsa's hand and smiled to himself. If he had to be prowling through slimy, rat-infested catacombs, he couldn't think of a better choice of companion than Elsa Schneider. She was bright, lovely, and didn't seem to be any more disturbed about their tenuous circumstances than he was. He liked that. Besides, he knew the shared experience was bonding them together, and he thoroughly enjoyed the thought of what might develop—provided they survived the excursion.

Encounters with beautiful women in exotic, dangerous circumstances were hardly everyday experiences in his profession. They never rated mention in his university lectures. But maybe someday he'd write a book and turn his more interesting encounters in the field into an eye-opening adventure tale.

The passageway turned and opened into an expansive chamber that was flooded with black, briny water but appeared devoid of rats. Their eyes had adjusted to the darkness, and Indy no longer needed the lighter. They paused a moment, gazing in silence toward the center of the cavern. Jutting up above the water on a stone platform were several ancient caskets. An "island altar," Indy thought.

They waded toward the coffins, the putrid water deepening with every step. It was up to their knees, and they were still fifty feet away.

"Be careful," Indy said. "Stay behind me. The bottom's slippery."

As soon as he said it, he lost his footing and fell to his knees.

"See what I mean?" He stood up, smiled sheepishly, then took another step forward, and instantly the water rose to his chest.

"It's only water. C'mon."

They carefully moved ahead, the water remaining at Indy's chest and Elsa's shoulders. "If this gets any deeper," Elsa warned him, "I'm climbing on your back."

"Yeah. Fine. But whose back am I going to climb on?"

When they reached the center of the chamber, they crawled onto the elevated platform and immediately forgot about the water and the rats. The two scholars began examining the ancient, ornately carved caskets, which were made of oak and held together by straps of etched brass.

"It must be one of these," Indy said.

"This one," Elsa said.

Indy nodded. He wasn't sure she was right, but she seemed confident about her choice.

"Do you doubt me? Look at the artistry of the carvings and the scrollwork. This is the work of men who believed that devotion to God and to beauty were one and the same," she said, placing her hands gently on the coffin.

Indy leaned over and strained to open the lid. Elsa joined him. The top groaned as it slowly rose. Then suddenly it slid away from the coffin and banged against the stone platform.

He peered down and saw a rusted suit of armor and an intricately carved shield. The hood of the helmet was turned up, and inside it, the hollow eyes of a skull stared up at him.

"This is the knight," Elsa proclaimed. "Look at the engraving on the shield. It's the same as Donovan's Grail tablet."

Indy was elated. He clasped her arm, and the words spilled out of him. "The shield is the second marker. We found it."

"I just wish he was here now to see this."

"Who, Donovan?"

"No, of course not. Your father. He would be so thrilled."

He glanced around the chamber and tried to imagine his father here. He couldn't. Libraries were his idea of an excursion.

"Yeah, thrilled to death."

He leaned over the coffin and brushed away the dust and corrosion from the knight's shield. Despite Indy's enthusiasm, the past and his difficult relationship with his father were never far from his mind.

"He never would have made it by those rats. He hates rats. He's scared to death of 'em." He recalled an incident from his childhood. "Believe me, I know. We had one in the basement once, and guess who had to go down there and kill it? Yours truly, and I was only six."

Indy reached into his shirt and took out the paper impression of the Grail tablet. He unfolded it and laid it over the shield. The portion missing from the tablet was there on the shield. "A perfect match. We've got it."

"Where did that come from?"

"Trade secret."

"Oh, I thought we were partners."

She sounded miffed, and Indy, who had started making a rubbing of the missing portion of the Grail tablet, paused long enough to glance up and smile.

"No offense, Elsa. But we just met." He went back to work on the rubbing.

"This is no time for professional rivalry, Dr. Jones. Your father is missing. Quite possibly in serious danger, and here . . ."

Indy's head snapped up. "Hold it." It wasn't what she said that had made him shout at her.

He looked around, tilted his head, listening. Something was wrong. He heard a distant squealing. It was getting louder, closer. Rats again.

Then he saw the glow of firelight dancing across the walls of the catacombs. A moment later he saw the rats. Thousands of them squirmed through the narrow passage, stampeded into the chamber, and headed toward the stone platform.

Within seconds the rats washed over the platform and caskets, a squirming, squealing tidal wave. Then Indy saw what they were scurrying to escape. An enormous fireball roared around the corner—it was feeding on the oil slick and depleting the oxygen, an elemental monster devouring everything in its path. It was spreading across the chamber and heading toward them.

Elsa screamed.

Indy stuffed the rubbing from the shield inside his shirt, then braced his back against the altar and toppled the coffin with his feet. It crashed against the stone platform and splashed into the water. It sank, then bobbed to the surface.

"Jump," Indy shouted.

For a second Elsa didn't move. Indy grabbed her hand and yanked her along after him. They struck the water, inches from the bobbing, overturned coffin. Fingers of flame licked across the surface, sizzling masses of shrieking rats.

Indy grabbed on to the coffin. "Get under it. Quick. Air pockets."

When Elsa hesitated, Indy fit his palm over her head, dunked her, and dragged her under the coffin. She surfaced in the air pocket, sputtering and coughing, clawing her hair from her eyes so she could see. She gasped as she found herself face-to-face with the ghastly, decomposed skull of the Grail knight, whose armor had remained attached to the coffin.

Indy popped up next to her, grimaced at the skull, then struggled to detach the corpse. He jerked it from the coffin, pushed it down. However, there were air pockets in the armor, and the grisly skull popped to the surface and stared blindly at them.

"Get lost." Indy struck the top of the head with his fist, like a hammer, and pounded it back down. This time it slowly sank beneath them. He kicked the armor and it drifted away.

The heat rose. Hundreds of rats scrambled across the top of the coffin. The scratching of their claws and their relentless squealing created a deafening din. The coffin rocked back and forth and started to sink beneath the weight of the rats. Some of them surfaced inside the coffin, still chattering, squealing.

"Indy. My God."

Elsa swatted at a rat that was swimming toward her, then swatted another that had scrambled onto her shoulder from behind. The rats seemed to be everywhere, and there was no end to them. They were panicked and biting at anything near them.

Indy punched one rat after another on the snout as they neared him. Above them, sawdust rained as the rats above desperately tried to burrow through the top of the coffin. One rat dropped through a hole. Several more followed, plopping down on them.

Some of the rats were on fire and hissed as they struck the water. The stench of burned hair and flesh filled the coffin. The heat of the fire pressed down on them, sucking greedily at the air, gobbling it up. Indy coughed and knuckled an eye.

Elsa screamed as she was bitten.

It can't last much longer. It can't, Indy was trying to convince himself.

"The coffin's on fire," Elsa yelled above the shriek of rats.

"There go the rats," Indy said as nonchalantly as possible. But he knew their situation was desperate. "Can you swim?"

"Austrian swim team. 1932 Summer Olympics. Silver medal in the fifty-meter freestyle."

"A simple yes or no would've sufficed. Take a deep breath. We'll have to swim under the fire."

They filled their lungs and dove under. As he swam, Indy wondered why the fire had started. Maybe a spark from the lighter had ignited it. But they would have noticed it much sooner.

Thirty seconds. What if someone had followed them? If so, then what happened to Brody?

Forty-five seconds. Indy felt the side of the chamber. He saw a faint light to his left and headed toward it.

One minute. The light was filtering through a storm drain that opened into the wall.

Indy paused and looked back to Elsa. The source of light must lead outside. But would they fit through the opening? He swam into the drain and had gone less than fifty feet when he reached a hole in the top of it. A spindle of light pierced down through it, and the opening was just large enough for his shoulders.

He took one more look back for Elsa, pointed at the hole, and urged her to go up. She shook her head, and motioned him to go first.

Indy wasn't about to argue. He had been underwater at least a minute and a half, maybe longer, and his lungs were ready to burst. He kicked hard, shot up, and his head broke the surface. He gulped at the air. Nothing had ever tasted so sweet.

A moment later, Elsa surfaced next to him. To his surprise, she didn't even seem out of breath.

He looked up. A shaft rose twenty feet up to daylight. Indy pressed his back against one side of it, his feet against the other and worked his way up.

Elsa mimicked his style. "Don't fall on me, Indy," she yelled.

"Wouldn't think of it."

He glanced down only once. Elsa looked like a crab of some kind, working her way up the shaft beneath him, her blond hair wet and tangled. She sensed his eyes and tipped her head back. She grinned, and Indy chuckled and kept on climbing.

When he reached the top, he pushed up on one side of the grating. It lifted a couple of inches, then fell back. He tried again with no better success. He could see feet walking by, and yelled. Someone looked down, and he called for the man to pull off the grating.

The stranger complied and gave him a hand.

As soon as he was out, he swiveled around and reached down inside the sewer, shouting for Elsa to grab his hand. She did, and he hoisted her up onto the sidewalk.

The man looked at them and asked in Italian if they were all right.

Elsa answered in a reassuring voice, telling him everything was fine.

Indy glanced around. They were in the corner of Piazza San

Marco a few feet from a sidewalk café, where the people were gawking and talking excitedly among themselves.

Indy smiled broadly as he gazed at the postcard-perfect scene. "Ah, Venice."

His good humor, however, was short-lived.

TEN

Lethal Agents

INDY TURNED from the gawking patrons of the café to the man who had helped him from the sewer. He was about to thank him when he realized something was wrong. Unlike everyone else nearby, the man's attention was turned away from them. He was staring across the plaza toward the library. Indy followed his gaze and saw four men running in their direction. He noticed the one in front wore a fez. Then he saw something else. One of them was sporting a machine gun.

"Oh, oh."

Suddenly several things clicked together: the clatter he had heard after Brody had lowered the tile; his question about the source of the fire; and the direction from which the men were running. Indy had the distinct impression that they were being hunted. He grabbed Elsa by the hand and ran in the opposite direction toward the Grand Canal.

Elsa lagged behind him, confused by Indy's abrupt sprint toward the water. "What are we doing now? Are you crazy?"

He tugged on her hand. "We've got some company on our trail."

She glanced back, then suddenly surged ahead of him. "You're right."

Indy leaped into a motorboat. He fired the engine. It sputtered and died.

"Hurry, Indy. They're almost . . ."

He pulled again and the engine fired. He shoved it into gear, and at that moment the boat rocked violently and Elsa shouted.

Indy pulled down on the throttle and glanced back just in time to block a punch. One of the men had boarded just as he pulled away. The boat veered wildly as the two men exchanged punches. Elsa crawled past them, grabbed the wheel, and turned sharply, barely missing several gondolas. Gondoliers stopped singing and shook their fists as they careened along the canal. One of the gondolas flipped over in the sudden backwash of the speedboat.

"Sorry," Elsa called out.

Indy, meanwhile, battled as best he could on the bouncing speedboat. He took a savage punch to his stomach and doubled over, holding a rib. The attacker rose up, pulled his arm back for the finishing blow, but Indy struck first. He caught him squarely in the jaw, hurtling him over the side.

He brushed his hands off, wiping them clean of the ordeal. He wished the man had stayed around so he could question him, but then again he hadn't seemed very cooperative.

"I guess that takes care of that," he yelled forward to Elsa.

"Think again."

Behind them a pair of speedboats was giving chase and gaining rapidly on them. He crawled toward the wheel. "Let me handle this."

"Wait until I . . ."

He looked up, and his jaw dropped. They were moving toward an enormous steamship straight ahead. The hull of the ship was drifting toward the dock, and the gap ahead of them was narrowing.

"Are you crazy?" he shouted. "Don't go between them. We'll never . . ."

But Elsa only caught snatches of what he'd said. "Go between them? Are you nuts?"

Indy shook his head, confused. He took another step toward the wheel, but Elsa had already committed the speedboat to the perilous course between the steamship and the dock. He frantically waved his hands. "No. Elsa, I said go *around* them!"

"You said go *between* them."

"I did not."

At this point it no longer mattered. The hull of the ship and the side of the dock loomed on either side of them like cavern walls. Indy crouched down, grabbed the side of the boat, and squeezed his eyes closed, waiting for the impact.

He heard a piercing screech of metal. But they were still in one piece. He opened his eyes and looked back. Just behind them one of the other boats had smashed into the hull.

Indy breathed a sigh of relief. But a moment later he saw the other boat emerge from the far side of the steamboat. "Let me handle this," he said, taking over the steering. "You scare me."

That said, he jammed the wheel to the right in a diversionary move. The boat swerved sharply, but the one pursuing them smoothly matched the turn. It was still gaining on them, moving up on their left side.

"All right, guys," Indy said through gritted teeth. "Let's see what you're made of."

He jerked the wheel to his left, hoping to drive the other boat into the side of the canal. Suddenly a machine gun chattered, and splinters flew away from the side of the boat.

"Okay. I get your point."

He quickly changed his course, zigzagging ahead of his pursuers. But the machine-gun blasts battered the engine. It coughed, sputtered, and then it died.

Indy grabbed his pistol and fired at the other boat until he was out of bullets.

"Indy, look!"

"What?"

Elsa was pointing to the side of the boat. They were drifting and heading right toward the rotating blades of an enormous propeller on the stern of another steamship.

The other boat drew close to them. One of the men held a machine gun on them. The other, who was behind the wheel, stood up and smiled at Indy. He was swarthy, in his late thirties, with a mustache and black, wavy hair protruding from beneath his fez. His dark, compelling eyes seemed to bore right through Indy. The boat bumped against them, pushing them closer to the churning propeller.

Indy was almost too exhausted to think. He had unraveled the ancient code, battled rats in slimy water, found the Grail knight, and narrowly escaped a fire. Then the flight and battle on the water had followed in rapid succession. Now, as he stared eye to eye at the man, he just wanted to know what the hell was going on.

Then he remembered Brody. "What did you do to my friend back in the library?"

The man laughed; his eyes were now dark pools that revealed nothing. "Your friend will be okay. You better worry about yourself."

Indy glanced over his shoulder and saw they had drifted closer to the propellers. "Who are you, and what do you want anyhow?"

"My name is Kazim, and I'm after the same thing you are, my friend."

"Your kind of friends I don't need. I don't know what you're talking about."

"Oh, I think you do, Dr. Jones."

The boat rocked in the turbulent waters near the propeller. Indy turned to Elsa and signaled her with his eyes that it was time to act.

"Enough talk," Kazim yelled over the noise of the propeller as it slapped against the water. "Better luck in the next world." He motioned for the man with the machine gun to shoot them.

Elsa jumped to the other boat, momentarily distracting the man with the gun. Indy leaped the gap, and his forearm came up under the machine gun, which fired harmlessly into the air. As they battled for control of the gun, the engine started.

The boat sped forward, and Indy lost his balance. He fell over the side, pulling the man with the machine gun with him. He let go of the man and swam as fast as he could away from the pull of the propeller. The gunman, desperate and panicking, yelled for help.

Behind him Indy heard a loud crunch as the other boat was dragged underwater. With a deafening crash the propeller blades of the steamship violently tore it apart like a piece of balsa wood, scattering shredded bits of the boat across the surface of the water.

Kazim swung the boat about and edged as close as he could to the steamship. Indy swam for it as Elsa leaned over the side, stretching her hand until he grasped it.

The gunman wasn't so lucky. He was already floundering in the bubbling maelstrom a few feet from the slicing blades. He screamed again to Kazim, but it was too late. Indy looked back just as the man was sucked into the blades.

The water abruptly foamed red.

Kazim shoved the motor into gear, and the boat tore away from the pull of the steamship. He zigzagged, trying to shake Indy from the side. But Elsa clutched his arm, dragging him until he grabbed the side of the boat. Then, with a final burst of energy, he pulled himself out of the water and flopped onto the floor of the boat gasping for breath.

He looked up and saw Kazim trying to load his gun and steer the boat at the same time. He crawled forward and shoved him against the wheel, causing the boat to spin a hundred and eighty degrees back to the direction of the steamboat.

"Indy, we're going back toward . . ."

Before Elsa could finish, he switched off the ignition, and pulled out the key. He pressed his thumb against the man's throat.

"Okay, Kazim, you and I are going to have a little chat."

Kazim stammered as Indy let up on his throat. "You foolish man." He tried to sound calm and dignified. "What are you doing, Dr. Jones? Are you crazy?"

"Where's my father?"

"Let go of me, please."

"Where . . . is . . . my . . . father?"

"If you don't let go, Dr. Jones, we'll both die. We're drifting back toward the steamship."

Indy heard the chop of the blades cutting through the water. He didn't even bother to look back. His eyes were wide and his voice sounded hysterical. "Good. Then we'll die."

"My soul is prepared, Dr. Jones." Kazim's voice was even, smooth as cream. "How about yours? Is *your* soul ready, Doctor?"

Indy grabbed the front of Kazim's shirt. "This is your last chance, damn it." Kazim's shirt ripped open, revealing a tattoo on his chest in the shape of a Christian cross that tapered down like the blades of a broadsword.

He stared placidly back at Indy, undisturbed.

"What's that supposed to be?" Indy asked.

Kazim raised his head high. "It's an ancient family symbol. My forebears were princes of an empire that stretched from Morocco to the Caspian Sea."

"Allah be praised," Indy said quietly.

"Thank you, and God save *you* too. But I was referring to the Christian empire of Byzantium."

Indy smiled gamely. "Of course. And why were you trying to kill me?"

Elsa tapped him on the shoulder. "Indy, you're going to kill all of us if we don't get out of here."

"Hold on." Indy sounded irritated. "Keep talking, Kazim. It's just getting interesting."

"The secret of the Grail has been safe for a thousand years. And for all that time the Brotherhood of the Cruciform Sword has been prepared to do anything to keep it safe."

"The Brotherhood of the Cruciform Sword?" Elsa seemed to

have forgotten about their precarious situation, her curiosity whetted.

Indy's eyes narrowed as he looked again at the tattoo on Kazim's chest. Then he met the man's gaze, held it for a long moment. The roar of the blades was as loud now as it had been when he was treading water. The boat rocked violently beneath them.

"Ask yourself why you seek the cup of Christ, for his glory or yours," Kazim said.

"I didn't come for the cup of Christ. I came to find my father."

Kazim nodded, glanced over Indy's shoulder toward the steamship. "In that case, God be with you in your quest. Your father is being held in the Brunwald Castle on the Austrian-German border."

Indy suddenly pushed Kazim aside, jammed the key into the ignition. He felt the spray from the steamship's giant propeller on his back as he turned the key. The engine sputtered and died.

"C'mon. Start."

He tried again. This time the engine revved to life, and they pulled away just seconds before the blades would have chewed into the hull.

"You're dangerous!" Elsa shouted at him, her pretty face flushed red, as though she were sunburned. "You could've gotten us killed."

He smiled. "I know. But I got what I wanted. Ask Kazim where we can drop him off."

Indy's thoughts were already miles ahead of him.

Donovan's Place

AFTER A HOT SHOWER, food, and nine hours of sleep, Indy was ready to explore the apartment Donovan had allowed them to use during their stay in Venice. "Apartment," however, was something of a misnomer: the place was a virtual palace.

The ceilings were vaulted, and the floors were made of thick slabs of marble. The antique furnishings were worth a fortune. There was a courtyard and balconies and at least a dozen rooms altogether. Covering the walls were some of the finest paintings of sixteenth-century Venetian artists: Veroneses, Tintorettos, and Titians as well as a variety of works that were mostly of historical importance.

It was obvious to Indy that most of the paintings were designed to bolster the egos of the sixteenth-century aristocracy, who spent most of their time showing off the riches of their independent state for visiting dignitaries. He smiled, thinking that Donovan was cut from the same mold, a twentieth-century patrician.

Indy was impressed by it all, but at the same time found it too pretentious for a private home. Some of the works should have been in museums, where they could be appreciated by more people. In some ways it was even a little obscene that so much beauty should be enjoyed only by the people who came into these rooms.

He wandered into the library. Shelves climbed from the floor to the ceiling on each of the four walls. Impressive, he thought. His father would've loved it. He perused the books and picked up a volume called *The Common-wealth of Oceana*, by James Harrington. It was an original edition and had been published in 1656. He flipped it open to a marked page and read a sentence describing Venice. "There never happened unto any other Common-wealth, so undisturbed and constant a tranquillity and peace in her self, as is that of Venice."

"Right." Indy chuckled. Tranquillity, peace: things had changed a bit in three centuries. An image of the brutal Fascists he had seen flashed into his head. He rubbed absently one of his bruised ribs and tried not to think too much about his own less than tranquil experiences in the city.

Maybe the city was still undisturbed for some people, but he wasn't one of them.

It was his second day in Venice, and he, Elsa, and Brody were all still recovering from the incidents of yesterday. An egg-size lump had risen on the back of Brody's head where he had been struck. Indy was recovering from an odd combination of combat and travel fatigue. His jaw was tender, and two of his ribs were sore from a couple of punches that had connected. Elsa, meanwhile, was suffering from minor rat bites and a slight burn on one arm from the fire in the catacombs.

Indy had been impressed that she hadn't even mentioned the burns or bites until after they had found Brody wandering about the library in a daze and had made their way to the apartment. She was pensive today and kept looking at him as if she wanted to say something. But every time he tried to start a conversation, she abruptly found an excuse to do something else.

"Indy!"

Brody stood in the doorway of the library. He held an ice pack to his head with one hand and had a sheet of rumpled paper in the other.

"How's the head, Marcus?"

"Better, now that I've seen this. It finally dried. You've got to take a look."

In spite of the ice pack, Brody sounded as excited as Indy had ever seen him. He hurried into the library and dropped the piece of paper on the massive mahogany table that dominated the room. The paper was what remained of the rubbing from the knight's shield. It was smeared and faded from the soaking in the tunnel, but was still in one piece. Now that it was dry, Indy could see that it was fairly legible.

"We know that what was missing from Donovan's Grail tablet was the name of the city, right?"

Indy nodded.

Brody pointed at the ancient lettering, and Indy leaned close. But Brody couldn't contain himself. "You see, it's Alexandretta."

"You sure?"

"Positive."

Indy walked to a shelf and searched until he found an atlas.

"What are you doing?" Brody asked.

"Looking for a map of Hatay."

Indy knew that the knights of the First Crusade had laid siege to Alexandretta for more than a year, and the entire city had been destroyed. Today, the city of Iskenderun on Hatay's Mediterranean coast was built on its ruins.

He found the page he wanted and stabbed at it. "Here. Look, Marcus, this is the desert, and this is the mountain range. Just the way the Grail tablet described it. Somewhere in these mountains must be the Canyon of the Crescent Moon." He paused, studying it. "But where? *Where* in these mountains?"

"Your father would know," Brody said quietly.

"He would?"

"Let me take a look at the diary."

Indy passed it to him.

"Your father *did* know. He knew everything except the city from which to start. He drew a map with no names. Here it is."

He set the diary on the table and opened it to a pencil-drawn map that covered two pages. Indy had looked at it briefly on the airplane, but since there were no names, it hadn't meant anything to him.

Brody's fingers moved across it. "Henry probably pieced this together from a hundred different sources over the last forty years."

"What is it?" Indy asked, even though he had a fairly good idea.

"It describes a course due east, away from the city, across the desert, to an oasis. Then turning south to a river which leads to a mountain range, here, and into a canyon. But because he had no names, he didn't know *what* city. Or *which* desert. Or *which* river."

And now they knew, for all the good it would do his father.

"I'm sure there're enough details here to find it. Indy, I'm going after it." Brody looked up at him, his spirits soaring after his discovery. "I hope you'll come with me."

Indy shook his head and closed the Grail diary. "I'm going after Dad. I'm leaving first thing in the morning for Austria."

Brody nodded, understanding. "Of course. What was I thinking. I'd better . . ."

"No. You go ahead, Marcus. I'll . . . We'll catch up to you."

"Are you sure?"

"Yes."

Brody was quiet a moment, as if he was wondering if he had made the right choice. Then he brightened. "Well, we've got a few more hours in Venice. Let's make the most of it. I'd love to visit the Galleria dell'Accademia. It has the best collection of Venetian paintings in existence. Let's go, okay?"

"You sure you feel up to it?"

Brody took the ice pack from his head. "I'm feeling fine. Do you know that collection has Giorgione's *Tempest*, Carpaccio's *Saint Ursula Legend*, and Titian's *Presentation of the Virgin*? Everything is there," Brody gushed, "from the first masters of the fourteenth century to the great pieces of the mid-eighteenth century."

Indy shrugged. "Let's go. I'll ask Elsa if she wants to join us."

Elsa couldn't seem to make up her mind about joining them. It was as if she were suffering from delayed shock or something, the aftereffects of their tumultuous experiences. Or maybe it was depression, as if their survival were a letdown somehow.

"I think I'll skip the galleries," she finally said. "I'm going out to buy a few groceries for dinner. I hope that's okay."

"You want company?" He wouldn't mind one bit spending the rest of the afternoon alone with her while Brody toured the museum. Hell, he'd even help make dinner.

She shook her head. "You and Marcus go on. I'll meet you back at the apartment."

So much for a romantic dinner, he thought, and went off to get dressed.

After a five-minute walk from the apartment, Indy and Brody reached the Ponte dell'Accademia, a wooden bridge crossing the Grand Canal. There were four hundred bridges in Venice, but only three crossed the Grand Canal. The bridge had been built five years earlier, during the Depression, and supposedly was a temporary structure.

They stopped at the summit to take in the view. On their left, they could see as far as Basilica di San Marco—a Byzantine monument from the eleventh century. The exterior of the church dated back to the thirteenth century and the sacking of Byzantium during the Fourth Crusade. On the right was the Palazzo Balbi, a palace with obelisks on its roof.

"I've been thinking, Marcus. I don't like the idea of you going off on your own."

"Indy, I'm sure your father would approve. If we wait any longer, those violent people from that strange brotherhood might find it, and who knows what would happen to the Grail Cup."

"I won't stop you. But before you leave, contact Sallah. Have him meet you in Iskenderun."

Brody nodded in agreement. Sallah was an old friend of both men. When Indy had pursued the Ark of the Covenant in Egypt, Sallah had saved his life more than once. He would feel a lot better about Brody chasing after the Grail Cup if he knew that Sallah was with him.

The two men spent the next hour wandering about the rooms of the Accademia. Brody was an enthusiastic and knowledgeable tour guide, pointing out the significance of one painting after another. He noted that the Renaissance for Venetians was something of a paradox. Unlike the rest of Italy, they had no Roman heritage. Founded on the cusp between East and West, antiquity and the Middle Ages, the city had preserved its traditions from the early Christian era. As a result, the Renaissance was more an adaptation of style and intention than a rebirth. Yet, Venice produced some of the best works of the Italian Renaissance.

Indy found them interesting but was less enthralled than Brody. He always told his students that there was an overlap between art and archaeology, but with the latter the remains of preserved feces could be as interesting and notable as painted ceramics or finely crafted gold.

Near the end of the hour Indy could tell that Brody was tiring and reminded him that his head injury was still fresh and he had better take it easy.

"I'm all right, Indy. Just a minor concussion and a bit of a headache. I'll be fit in the morning."

But he agreed that it was time to leave.

As they neared the apartment, Indy felt increasingly anxious. It was as if dozens of tiny needles were poking the back of his neck. Over the years he had learned to pay attention to that sensation. It was a sort of inbred warning signal, one that had given him a helpful edge more than once.

As soon as they reached the apartment, he knew the intuitive sensation had proved itself again. The door was slightly ajar. He peered inside, then cautiously entered the apartment and looked around.

"Elsa?" he called out tentatively.

The silence threw his own voice back to him, an empty echo.

"Elsa?" He raised his voice this time. Again there was no answer.

Just like Dad. A chill sped down his spine.

"I'll check the kitchen," Brody said.

Indy rushed over to his bedroom and swung open the door. The room had been ransacked. The mattress was on the floor, and the drawers had been dumped.

Oh, God. What happened to her?

He hurried down the hall to Elsa's room. He paused, took a breath, and slowly turned the doorknob. Someone had rifled through her room as well. The intruder had tossed things from her drawers, jerked clothes from the hangers, torn the sheets away from the mattress.

But where the hell was she?

He backed out of the room and heard a distant, muffled voice. He crept down the hallway. The voice grew louder, more distinct. It was a woman's voice, singing, and coming from the bathroom.

He opened the door a crack. "Elsa?"

"Hello, Indy."

She was in a bathtub full of bubbles, smiling brightly at him. Bubbles encircled her throat like a necklace of translucent pearls. A smooth white shoulder lifted from the foam.

"Listen, kid. People are trying to sleep." He backed out, relieved she was okay. He'd let her enjoy her bath.

"I'll be right out," she called after him.

He returned to his room and looked over the mess. Whoever

had rummaged through the place must have been hiding when Elsa returned from her shopping trip. The intruder probably fled when she went into the bathroom.

He waited as he heard Elsa singing in the hallway en route to her room. He looked at his watch, estimating how long it would take her to change her tune.

She shrieked, and he smiled. He waited for her to run to his room. He heard footsteps. She swung open his door. She was dressed in a bathrobe; her hair was still wet.

Her jaw looked as though it had come unhinged. "Indy, my room . . ."

"Yeah, mine, too."

She shook her head. "What were they looking for, anyway?"

"This."

He took the Grail diary out of his pocket and tossed it onto the table.

"Your father's Grail diary. You had it."

"Uh-huh."

"You didn't tell me." She shook her head. "You don't trust me."

Over Elsa's shoulder Indy saw Brody peeking into the room and signaled that everything was okay. Brody, sensing that matters were turning personal, quickly backed away, slipping out of sight.

"I didn't know you." He looked into her soft blue eyes; his thumb ached to trace the pout on her mouth. Christ, but she was hard to resist. "Or maybe I wanted to know you better."

"It was the same for me." Her voice was breathy now. "From the moment I saw you."

"Does this sort of thing happen to you all the time?"

"No. Never. It's a nice feeling."

He moved closer to her, touched her face. "Don't trust it, Elsa."

"What do you mean?"

"Shared danger. Coming out of it alive. That's what did it."

"Yeah?" She smiled coyly, and Indy moved toward her, touched her chin, lifting it, and kissed her gently. Her mouth tasted faintly of toothpaste. He loved the scent of soap on her skin. She moved up against him, and suddenly he was kissing her harder, and she responded passionately, letting herself go.

"Look after me, Indy," she whispered, her breath warm against his ear.

His hands worked at the belt of her robe. "You looked after yourself pretty well yesterday. For an art historian."

"You don't know anything about art historians, Dr. Jones? Do you?"

"I know what I like."

"I'm glad you do, Indiana Jones."

She grabbed the hair on the back of his head and pulled his face toward hers. She kissed him long and deep, holding him close to her. Her kiss was so hard that Indy cut his lip on his own tooth.

He rubbed away a drop of blood with the back of his hand. "You're dangerous."

"Maybe I am. Just like you."

Her eyes flashed. She was breathing hard, waiting for him to move. A smile changed the shape of her mouth. Her hair lifted gently in the evening breeze that blew through the open window. Outside, a gondolier was singing.

"Ah, Venice," Indy said half-aloud and closed the bedroom door.

AUSTRIA /
GERMANY

TWELVE

The Brunwald Castle

THE MERCEDES-BENZ Indy had rented glided smoothly around the sharp mountain curves of the Austrian Alps. When they started out, the sky had been crisp, clear, a smooth, even blue. But by late afternoon, as he and Elsa neared the German border and the grounds of the Brunwald Castle, storm clouds climbed the horizon, and thunder rumbled in the distance.

A perfect day for a friendly visit, Indy thought, casting an eye toward Elsa.

She was staring straight ahead along the curving road. Her blond hair was tied back, and the waning light struck the sharp promontories of her face—high cheekbones, that pouty mouth, a straight nose, which was, at the moment, pink at the tip from the cold. He thought back to their passionate lovemaking in Venice and reached out, touching the back of her neck. The skin was cool and dry, and she turned her head, smiling absently, as if she had a lot on her mind.

When this was over, he thought, he and Elsa would . . . well, he didn't know. He would think of something. She had asked him about the university, its archaeology and art history programs, and hinted that she might like to visit him—who knew what might happen.

He pulled into the courtyard. The place loomed in the windshield, menacing and impregnable. The dark windows on the upper levels revealed nothing; the castle was as impregnable as a block of stone. He wondered which one was his father's room. Did he even have a room? Maybe he was in chains in a dungeon. Maybe he wasn't even alive.

No. Bad thought.

This wasn't the time for bad thoughts. He had no idea how he was going to find out where his father was being held, much less how he was going to rescue him. Maybe he wasn't even here. Maybe it had simply been a ploy by Kazim to turn him away from the trail of the Grail Cup.

"Here we are," he said quietly. He felt an all too familiar tingling on the back of his neck, alerting him to danger. Yes, his father was here. He was sure of it.

"Imposing, isn't it?" she said.

"You know anything about the place?"

"It's been in the Brunwald family for generations. They're very powerful in this region, but not particularly well liked."

He noticed a pond next to the castle; gliding across its surface was a solitary swan. Its long neck was gracefully arched, and its snowflake-white feathers seemed luminous against the pond's dark waters. He was reminded of the swan in his father's Grail diary. It represented one of the levels of awareness in the search for the Grail and meant something about overcoming weaknesses of the mind and heart.

Elsa was his weakness. He had quenched his desires like a man who had found an oasis after days in the desert without water. He had taken her greedily, and she had fulfilled his every wish. Why would he, or anyone, want to overcome such pleasures?

"What are you thinking?" she asked.

"Oh, nothing."

"Yeah, I bet," she said softly.

He frowned, hating the idea that his feelings were so obvious.

Elsa brought her hand up under her hair and flicked it off her collar. Indy sensed it was a dismissal of some sort or maybe a signal to just get on with things. He reached into the backseat for his bullwhip, focusing his thoughts on the matter at hand. He attached it to his belt as he got out of the car.

"What're you going to do?" she asked as they headed toward the castle.

"I don't know. I'll think of something."

Indy knocked on the door and waited. Fingers of lightning blazed and sutured the sky. Thunder grumbled almost instantly, and it started to rain. The drops beaded on Elsa's long, well-tailored coat and glistened.

"Let me borrow your coat, okay?"

"You're cold?" she drolled.

"Got an idea."

She shrugged off the coat, and he quickly draped it over his shoulders, covering his leather jacket and bullwhip, just as the heavy wooden door swung open.

A uniformed butler said, "Yes?" in a voice that would have chilled Jell-O.

Indy adopted the haughty manner of an upper-class English barrister and regarded the butler with a properly arrogant expression. "And not before time. Did you intend to leave us standing on the doorstep all day? We're absolutely drenched."

As Indy spoke, he pushed his way past the startled butler, pulling Elsa with him. He sneezed. "Now look. I've caught a sniffle."

He dabbed at his nose with a handkerchief as Elsa looked on in amazement.

"Are you expected?" The butler's voice remained frosty and terse.

"Don't take that tone with *me*, my good man, just buttle off and tell Baron Brunwald that Lord Clarence Chumley and his assistant are here to view the tapestries."

"Tapestries?"

Indy looked over at Elsa. "Dear me, the man is dense. Do you think he heard me?"

He looked back at the butler and continued. "This is a castle, isn't it? You have tapestries?"

"This is a castle, yes. We have tapestries, and if you're an English lord, I'm Jesse Owens."

"How dare you!" Indy responded in a stilted, English falsetto, and knocked the man cold with one powerful punch to the jaw.

The butler crumpled to the stone floor like a windup toy that had suddenly run down. Indy brushed his hands together. "The nerve of it!" He was still chattering in his stilted English voice. "Did you hear him speaking to me like that, impugning my breeding, my honor, my gift for impression?"

Elsa laughed and shook her head as she helped him drag the butler to a corner closet. "Unbelievable. Very convincing, my lord."

Indy dropped his pose, grabbed Elsa's hand, and tugged her along toward a wide, vaulted hallway. "Okay, let's get down to business." He slipped off her coat as they hurried across the foyer. She pulled it on and started to whisper something, but he touched a finger to his mouth.

Voices.

They stopped. He glanced around quickly, and they ducked into an alcove behind a large piece of statuary. They watched as a pair of uniformed Nazi soldiers walked by. One of them laughed loudly at something the other said, and his voice echoed down the hallway.

"S.S., I should have known," Indy whispered to Elsa as the men disappeared.

They slipped out of their hiding place and continued down the hallway. "Now, where do you suppose they're holding Dad?"

"The dungeon?"

"Very funny." Just a little too close to what he'd been thinking.

A servant appeared in the corridor, wheeling a large trolley that contained the remains of a feast. Indy and Elsa ducked behind a staircase and watched. They hadn't eaten in a few hours, and their eyes widened at the extent of the leftovers. Indy placed a hand over his stomach to keep it from growling. He wondered if it had been his father's dinner. He hoped so; at least he wouldn't be starving in his captivity.

They hid for a long time under the stairs. Indy wanted to get a feel for the place. He needed to have some idea of how many people were on the staff, what the routines were, or if there *were* any routines, and if so, how he might use them to his advantage.

He heard thunder rumbling, and rain thrashed against a window above their heads.

Elsa's stomach growled with hunger.

His own responded.

They looked at each other and laughed silently.

Footsteps on the stairs above them caught Indy's attention. A servant, escorted by an armed German soldier, descended with a cheap tray. On it was a tin bowl with a metal spoon chained to the bowl. *Dad's lunch just sailed past.*

"Now *that* looked more like a prisoner's meal," he whispered as soon as the two were out of sight.

"Yeah, I'm afraid so."

It was time to act. They stepped out from their hiding place and began to ascend the stairs. But just as they reached the first landing, more Nazis approached. This time they concealed themselves behind a massive pillar and waited until the sharp click of the soldiers' boots faded away.

They hurried along and, when they reached the next floor, paused and looked both ways. A door stood ajar nearby; Indy heard voices from inside the room. He peeked through the crack; Nazis were busy examining works of art. Looted booty, he thought.

Hitler was interested in amassing as many of Europe's works of art and primitive artifacts as he could, but not solely for the value of the ancient treasures. Indy was well aware that Hitler had a special interest in obtaining ancient mystical objects that he believed would enhance his power and thus expand his empire.

It was Nazis who had opposed Indy in his pursuit of the Ark of the Covenant. In fact, he had found the Ark only to discover the Führer's goons waiting to take it away from him. He never understood Hitler's motives until he experienced the power of the Ark, something he still couldn't explain. Although he had finally succeeded in getting the Ark to the States, bureaucrats had confiscated the priceless and mysterious artifact. By now he figured it was stored away in a dusty warehouse somewhere, waiting.

He had also heard that Hitler was after the ancient spear that had pierced the side of Jesus Christ. And, no doubt, the leader of the Third Reich would also like to get his hands on the Grail Cup that had held the blood of Jesus. And that, he knew, was why his father was being held captive here.

He backed away from the crack, and he and Elsa moved silently down the corridor. At the end of it were three doors. Indy looked from one to the next, then jabbed his forefinger at the door on the left.

"This one."

"How do you know?" Elsa whispered.

He pointed to an electrical wire. "Because this one's wired. I'll have to find another way in." He stepped back, studied the situation a moment, then decided to try the adjoining door.

He turned the knob; the door was locked. He reached into the pouch on his belt and took out his lock-picking tool. It seemed a lifetime had passed since he had used it on the captain's door to get to the safe with the Cross of Coronado. Yet, it had been less than two weeks ago. He slipped the long, slender tool into the lock, fiddled with it a moment, then turned the knob. The door creaked open.

The room was dimly lit and empty except for a bed and dresser. He closed the door again as soon as Elsa was inside.

"What was that?" she asked as he slipped his burglar's tool back into his pouch.

"A trade secret."

"Oh, you mean you don't tell your students about it?" she asked in mock surprise.

"Only the advanced ones," he said, and walked over to the window.

The rain pounded furiously against the pane. He raised the shade, then the window, and stuck his head out. It was almost dark. The rain splattered against his face, soaking his head. He blinked, clearing his vision. Beneath the window of the next room was a narrow ledge. It ended abruptly several feet away.

Indy pulled his head back into the room and loosened his bullwhip.

"What are you going to do?" Elsa asked.

"Take a shower."

Elsa looked out the window a moment. "You can't mean you're going to . . ." She saw Indy uncoiling the bullwhip from his belt. "I don't believe it."

"Watch me. It's a snap."

He leaned out the window and flicked the bullwhip at the gargoyle that protruded from the castle wall above the adjoining window. It was a perfect shot; the whip wrapped around the gargoyle's thick neck. He tugged hard, making sure it would hold his weight.

He swung his leg over the window frame and looked back through the window at Elsa. "Stay there. I won't be long."

"Indy, this is crazy. You can't . . ."

He held up a hand. "Don't worry. This is kid's stuff. Be right back."

Indy swung out from the window, his legs dangling in midair. He was right. It was an easy swing for him, but he hadn't taken one thing into account. The rain had soaked the ledge, and his feet skidded on the slick surface as he landed. One slipped over the ledge, his knee bent, and he wobbled precariously for an instant. Then he pulled on the whip, and recovered his footing.

Next, he had to figure out a way to open the shutters, which were closed over the window. He jerked on them, but they held tight. He was about to try again when he heard a noise. He looked down and saw two Nazi guards prowling with their dogs and flashlights.

They found the butler.

One of the beams bounced along the castle wall, heading in his direction. He pressed himself into the recess of the window and stood perfectly still. *The bullwhip*. He should have loosened it, but it was too late now. The beam skipped over him. He waited, holding his breath. Then he heard the Nazis moving on. They had missed him and the whip.

He turned his attention back to the shutters. He slid his fingers into the opening between them and tugged as hard as he could. They still wouldn't budge. He tried to use his shoulder, but he couldn't get the proper leverage.

Okay, he thought. More drastic measures were in order. But his timing had to be perfect. He watched for a bolt of lightning and noted that the rain was not quite so hard. When he saw the flash, he counted the seconds until he heard the clap of thunder.

He waited until the next bolt lit the sky. He grasped the bullwhip with both hands, counted to himself, then pushed off from the castle wall. He added an extra number in his calculation, figuring the storm was starting to recede. He curled in his legs as he swung back, and crashed through the shutters with both feet. The impact was timed precisely with the thunder.

He tumbled into the room, falling on his hands and knees. Rain and cold air whipped into the room through the broken shutters. He rose to his feet, looked around to get his bearings. Just as he realized his father was nowhere in sight, something heavy crashed down on the back of his head and shattered.

Indy stumbled, sank to one knee. Stunned, his vision blurred, he looked up helplessly as someone stepped out from the shadows.

"Junior!"

"Yes, sir," he said, responding with a reflex reaction left over from his childhood. He rubbed his head, focusing on his father.

"It's you! Junior!"

Indy's head cleared. Now he was annoyed. "Stop calling me that."

"What the devil are you doing here?"

He wondered if the Nazis had done something to his father's mind. "What do you think? I've come to get you out of here."

Henry looked down at his hand, suddenly distracted and alarmed by what he saw. "Wait a minute."

Indy sucked in his breath, tensed, glanced around. "What's wrong?"

"Late fourteenth century, Ming dynasty," he muttered to himself.

Indy frowned as he realized the fuss was about the broken vase his father was holding.

"It breaks the heart," Henry exclaimed.

"Also the head," Indy interrupted. "You hit me with it, Dad."

Still looking at the vase, Henry continued. "I'll never forgive myself."

Indy misunderstood his father, who was still talking about the vase. "Forget it. I'm fine."

"Thank God."

Henry looked relieved as he examined the broken end of the vase. "It's fake. You see, take a look, you can tell by the . . ."

". . . cross sections," Indy and Henry said simultaneously.

They looked at each other, and both of them grinned. "Sorry about your head," Henry said, frowning a little, as if noticing his son for the first time. "I thought you were one of them."

"*They* come in through the door," Indy said. "They don't need to use the window."

"Good point, but better safe than sorry. This time I was wrong. But by God I was right when I mailed you the diary. I felt something was going to happen. Did you get it?"

Indy nodded. "I got it, and I used it. I found the entrance to the catacombs."

Henry was suddenly excited. "Through the library. You found it?"

"That's right." Indy smiled, pleased to see his father impressed with something he had done.

"I knew it." He stabbed at the air with his fist. "I just knew it! And the tomb of Sir Richard?"

"Found it."

Henry was breathless. "He was actually there. You saw him?"

"What was left of him."

Henry's voice fell to an excited whisper and trembled with expectation. "And the shield . . . the inscription on Sir Richard's shield?"

Indy nodded again, paused a beat, then answered in one word. "Alexandretta."

Henry's mouth came unhinged. He stepped back, rubbing a hand over his beard, considering everything he'd just been told. Lost in thought, he mumbled to himself. "Alexandretta, of course. It was on the pilgrim trail from the Eastern Empire." He turned back to Indy, a jubilant expression on his face. "Junior . . ."

Indy winced. He would have chided his father for calling him by his childhood name again, but he knew this wasn't the moment.

Henry continued: ". . . You did it."

"No, you did, Dad. Forty years of scholarship and research."

Henry's eyes glazed; he stared at a spot just over Indy's shoulder. "If I only could have been there." His eyes flicked back to his son. "What was it like?"

"There were rats."

"Rats?" He suddenly didn't look so interested in hearing details of the adventure.

"Yeah. Big ones."

"I see."

"Speaking of rats . . . how have the Nazis treated you here?"

"Okay, so far. They've given me one more day to talk, then they get tough. But I wasn't going to say a word, Junior. I figured if I died, you would take over the search. I knew I could count on you keeping that book as far away from the Nazis as possible."

Indy's hand twitched toward his pocket. His fingers traced the outline of the diary. *Guess what, Dad. It's not too far away.*

"Yeah, I suppose." He suddenly felt uneasy. "We'd better get out. . . ."

A resounding thud silenced him. His head snapped toward the door just as it burst open, and three Nazis marched into the room. Two of them held machine guns aimed at them. The third was an S.S. officer.

"Dr. Jones!" the officer shouted.

"Yes." Indy and Henry answered at the same time.

"I'll take that book now."

"What book?" they both said simultaneously.

The officer turned to Indy and sneered. "You have the diary in your pocket."

Henry's laugh was straight from the belly, and Indy thought, Aw, God, I'm going to be sick.

"You dolt! Do you really think that my son would be stupid enough to bring the diary all the way back to the very place from where . . ."

Henry stopped and slowly turned to Indy. "You didn't, did you, Junior?"

Indy smiled uneasily. "Uh . . . well."

"Did you?" Henry thundered.

"The thing is . . ."

"You did! My God."

"Can we discuss this later, Dad? I don't think that right now is . . ."

"I should have mailed it to the Marx Brothers," he fumed.

Indy held up a hand, patted the air. "Dad, please, take it easy."

"Why do you think I sent it home in the first place?" He pointed toward the Nazis. "To keep it out of *their* hands!"

"I came here to save you," Indy said lamely, then glanced at the machine guns.

"And who is coming to save you, Junior!" Henry roared, his face turning red.

What happened next took place so fast that when it was over, Indy hardly believed what he'd done. His eyes blazed; his nostrils flared with anger. He looked as if he was about to punch his father and was so convincing, Henry drew back, anticipating the blow. But instead, Indy's arm shot out and ripped one of the machine guns from a startled guard. With a quick kick, he knocked the barrel of the second machine gun in the air. Bullets sprayed the ceiling.

An instant later Indy's finger squeezed the trigger of the machine gun. "I told you before," he yelled as the three Nazis stumbled back under the impact and crumpled to the floor, "don't call me Junior."

Henry stared in disbelief as the three Nazis bled and died. He was shocked and horrified. "Look what you did! You killed them!"

Indy grabbed him by the arm and pulled him out of the room. He placed his hand on the knob of the adjoining room, where Elsa was waiting, and turned it.

"I can't believe what you did," Henry whispered hoarsely, his eyes wide with astonishment. "You killed those men!"

Indy paused in the doorway. "What the hell do you think *they* were going to do to *us*?"

His father frowned, as if he was trying to justify his son's violence in his mind.

Indy swung the door open and raised his hand to signal Elsa that it was time to flee. His hand froze. He was staring into the face of a Nazi. One of the man's muscular arms was coiled around Elsa's waist like a thick snake. His other hand held a Luger, its muzzle pressed behind her ear.

"That's far enough, Dr. Jones."

A big man. A colonel. Lantern jaw, small, dark eyes, an insect's eyes. He redefined the word *brute*, no doubt about it.

"Put down the gun. Right now," the colonel ordered, his accent thick, but not awkward. "Unless you want to see your lady friend die."

"Don't listen to him," Henry said.

"Drop it now," the colonel demanded.

"No," Henry shouted. "She's with them."

"Indy, please," Elsa pleaded, her eyes wide with fear.

"She's a Nazi!" Henry countered.

"What?" Indy shook his head, confused. He didn't know what to do. He looked at Elsa, then back to his father. Everyone was yelling at once.

"Trust me," Henry shouted.

"Indy, no," Elsa begged.

"I'll kill the Fräulein," the colonel spat through clenched teeth.

"Go ahead," Henry told him.

"Don't shoot her," Indy yelled.

"He won't," Henry answered.

"Indy, please!" Elsa implored. "Please do what he says."

"For God's sake, do not listen to her!" Henry roared at his son.

"Enough. She dies." The colonel jammed the barrel of his Luger into Elsa's neck.

She screamed in pain.

"Wait." Indy dropped the machine gun to the floor and kicked it away.

Henry groaned.

The colonel released his grip on Elsa and shoved her toward Indy. He caught her in his arms, and he held her tightly as she buried her face in his chest.

"I'm sorry, Indy."

He comforted her. "It's okay."

"I'm so sorry."

Her hand slipped into his coat pocket and removed the Grail diary.

She smiled sadly at him. "But you should have listened to your father."

"He never did," Henry uttered in an exasperated tone. "He never did."

THIRTEEN

Betrayed

ELSA MOVED AWAY from him and over to the Nazi colonel. Indy just stood there, stunned, speechless, hating the smirk on the Nazi's face and the sweet innocence in Elsa's eyes. He wanted to grab her by the shoulders and shake her until she explained everything to him. He had to know why.

But the colonel raised his Luger threateningly, and Indy stayed where he was and simply stared. How could you do this to me? he thought at her.

She smiled a little, almost as if she had heard the thought. Indy finally averted his eyes and glanced at his father.

He wished he hadn't.

The expression on Henry's face could have turned stone to dust. No wonder he still calls me Junior. Indy was as astonished by the shift of events as his father had been a few minutes earlier when Indy decimated the opposition in the adjoining room.

"You two better come along with Colonel Vogel and me. Now."

Elsa's voice was hard and cold, the voice of a woman he didn't know. Even her face looked different now, not as he remembered it. Her jaw seemed more square, more stubborn, her skin whiter, bloodless, like china, and her eyes were cubes of ice that would never melt.

The colonel stabbed at the air with his weapon, and Indy said, "Yeah, I guess we better."

"Like we have a choice," muttered his father, his voice laced with blame.

As they were marched through the castle at gunpoint, Indy could feel his father's disgust. It radiated from him like heat or an odor, strong enough to track. It didn't diminish until they entered a large baronial room at the other end of the same floor.

Here the walls were decorated with ancient tapestries and suits of armor. A fire crackled and hissed in an enormous fireplace, casting shadows that eddied across the walls and ceiling. He caught a whiff of Elsa's skin as she fluttered past, making way for the two Nazi guards who joined them.

The guards tied their hands behind their backs. They definitely meant business, Indy thought, wincing as the ropes cut painfully into his wrists. While the guards worked on the ropes and Elsa conferred quietly with Vogel, Indy looked around furtively. There were several windows, but they were on the third floor. Besides, as long as their hands were bound and the goons were guarding them, their chances of escaping were minimal. Still, he thought, it never hurt to exercise the imagination.

When he ran out of ideas, he thought about Elsa and what he'd like to do to her if he got free. He watched her as she crossed the room toward a high-backed chair that faced the fireplace. She stopped next to the chair and held out the Grail diary. As a hand reached for it, Indy realized the chair was occupied. His eyes slid over to Henry, and he edged closer to him.

"How did you know she was a Nazi?" he asked in a whisper.

"She talks in her sleep."

"*What?*" His head snapped toward his father. "You mean you— you and that, that woman—were . . ."

"Silence!" Vogel bellowed.

Elsa and my old man . . .

The pieces fell into place. Elsa had ransacked his room in Venice, looking for the diary, then had torn through her own room, making it look as though someone had broken into the apartment.

And I fell for it.

"I didn't trust her. Why did you?" Henry muttered, tilting his head toward Indy.

The man in the chair rose to his feet and answered Henry's question. "Because he didn't take my advice. That's why."

Indy gaped as Walter Donovan strolled over to them, his bearing as regal and aristocratic as the room. Jesus. He couldn't believe it.

"Didn't I tell you not to trust anyone, Dr. Jones?" Donovan smiled benignly as he flipped casually through the Grail diary.

Indy had no snappy response; he didn't say anything at all. This was the man who had told him his father was missing, the man who had told him to meet Dr. Schneider in Venice, the bastard behind the whole scheme. What could he possibly say that would make any difference?

Everything was moving too fast. In the past few minutes, he had been betrayed by Elsa and by Donovan. To top it off, he had found out Elsa had gone to bed with his father, who had inadvertently clobbered him over the head with a vase.

Henry gave an indignant snort, but when he spoke, his voice was old and tired. "I misjudged you, Walter. I knew you'd sell your mother for an Etruscan vase; I didn't know you'd sell your country and your soul to this bunch of madmen."

Donovan ignored Henry. The crease in his forehead deepened as he paged through the diary faster and faster. Something was obviously wrong.

"Dr. Schneider!" he stammered.

Elsa rushed over to him. "What is it?"

Donovan held up the Grail diary and shook it in her face. "This book contained a map—a map with no names—but with precise directions from the unknown city to the secret canyon of the Holy Grail."

"Yes," she said. "It's known as the Canyon of the Crescent Moon."

"Where *is* the map?"

Elsa shrugged and looked a little uneasy. She said she didn't know, she thought it was in the diary. Donovan, his face pink with anger, looked from Elsa to Indy. "Well, where are the missing pages? We must have them."

Henry glanced at Indy, looking surprised and quite pleased.

Indy smirked.

"You're wasting your breath asking him," Elsa said. "He won't tell us. And he doesn't have to. It's perfectly obvious where the pages are."

She flashed a triumphant smile at Indy and turned to Donovan. "He gave them to Marcus Brody."

Henry squeezed his eyes closed as if to shut out what he had just heard. When he opened them again, he turned them on Indy. "Marcus? You dragged poor Marcus along? My God, Junior, he's not up to the challenge."

"We'll find him," Donovan said, and turned away, dismissing them.

"Don't be so sure," Indy called after him. "He's got a two-day start on you, which is more than he needs."

Donovan paused, considering what he had just heard. Indy rushed on. "Brody has friends in every town and village between here and the Sudan. He knows a dozen languages and every local custom. He'll be protected. He'll disappear. You'll never see him again. With a little luck on his side, he's probably found the Grail Cup already."

Henry grinned. "That's very impressive," he muttered. "I hope you're right."

Donovan walked up to Indy and studied the man as if he were looking for flaws in a work of art. "Dr. Jones, it's too bad you won't live to find out what happens. Neither of you will."

The way he looked at him made Indy feel as if Donovan knew more about him than he was letting on. Maybe he did. He suddenly wondered if Donovan had anything to do with the Cross of Coronado. He recalled that the man in the Panama hat had said the buyer wanted him dead. Maybe the reason had not only been to stop him from looking for the cross but to keep him from looking for his father. Then, when things had gone wrong—when the diary had disappeared, when Indy survived—everything had changed.

But that was just speculation. He was certain, if he asked, Donovan would deny knowing what he was talking about. The man was too arrogant ever to admit that anyone could outwit him.

"Something on your mind, Dr. Jones?"

Indy stared back and remained silent.

Donovan turned to the guards. "Take them away."

Indy and Henry were tied back-to-back in a pair of chairs and watched over by two hulking Nazi guards. They had been moved to another room in the castle, one in which heavy, floor-length drapes hung from all the windows blocking out the wet night. As in the room in which Donovan had condemned them, an immense fireplace dominated one wall. But here there was no cheery fire; the room was dark and cold.

They had been bound for several hours when Elsa and Donovan entered the room. Donovan addressed the guards in German and asked if the captives had behaved themselves.

"Must we be tied up like this?" Henry complained after one of the guards told Donovan that the prisoners weren't going anywhere. "We're gentlemen, not common criminals."

Donovan laughed. "I've seen your son's handiwork upstairs,

and so have these guards. I wouldn't call that the behavior of gentlemen. Would you, Henry?"

"You're hardly one to comment, Walter, considering your associates."

Donovan crossed his arms. "It won't be long now, and neither of you will be tied any longer. Everything will be all over."

Indy didn't like the sound of that. Nor did he like Donovan's gleeful chuckle, a kind of rolling, mad sound that made him realize Donovan, in his own way, fit in well with the Nazis. It wasn't hard for him to imagine the man chatting with Hitler as they talked about relics and antiquities, their values and uses.

Indy turned his attention to Elsa. She stood in the shadows, off to one side. There was just enough light for him to see her eyes, which were fixed on him. He thought she seemed sad, withdrawn, introspective, but maybe that was just wishful thinking. Besides, why should *he* care what she felt? She had tricked him. Used him. Betrayed him. And slept with his father.

So maybe she doesn't like herself for it.

A door swung open, and Indy heard the voice of Colonel Vogel. "Dr. Schneider, a message from Berlin. You are to return immediately—a rally tomorrow at the Institute of Aryan Culture."

"So?"

"Your presence on the platform has been requested." He cleared his throat. "At the highest level."

"Thank you, Herr Colonel."

Her eyes slid toward Indy, then away from him as she addressed Donovan. "I'll meet you at Iskenderun as soon as I can get away."

Donovan handed her the Grail diary. "Take this with you. It's no use to us without the map, but it will show them we're making progress. Take it to the Reich Museum. It'll be a nice souvenir."

Vogel stepped between Donovan and the captives. "Allow me to kill them. Then we'll have no more accidents like upstairs."

"No," Elsa said. "If we fail to recover the pages from Brody, we will need them alive."

Donovan hesitated, uncertain. He regarded Indy and his father as though they were interesting and possibly valuable artifacts. To Vogel, he said: "Always do what the doctor orders. We'll wait. Then they are yours."

The colonel frowned, stared coldly at Indy, then nodded to Donovan without comment. It was obvious to Indy that he thought they should be executed immediately. He was probably more concerned about punishing the ones who were responsible for the deaths of his men than with finding the Grail Cup.

"Come along," Donovan said, and walked over to the fireplace. He stepped into it and opened a hidden door. Vogel and the guards followed him. Donovan allowed them to go on through and glanced back at Elsa.

"You coming?"

"I have a couple of things to take care of before I leave. I'll be ready in a few minutes."

Donovan nodded, and smiled at Indy and his father as if they were simply friends or business partners. He's a madman, Indy thought, as Donovan disappeared through the fireplace.

Elsa watched the fireplace until she was sure they were gone. Then she turned to Indy, her expression a perfect duplicate of their most intimate moments together in Venice. *What the hell was she up to now?*

He looked away.

"Indy, that wasn't my real reason for keeping the colonel from killing you."

He raised his eyes and grinned. "Yeah? You must be the good Nazi I keep hearing about."

"Don't look at me like that. We both wanted the Grail Cup. I would have done anything, and you would have done the same."

"Too bad you think that way, Doctor." His voice was as flat as stale soda water.

She ran a hand down the side of his face, but Indy jerked his head away. Elsa bent closer to him and spoke quietly, her breath warm against his ear, and the side of his face. Her skin smelled faintly of soap and perfume and stirred memories he preferred not to think about.

"I know you're angry, and I'm sorry. But I want to tell you, I'll never forget how wonderful it was."

Henry, who could see none of Elsa's actions, but could hear the voice, responded as if she were talking to him. "Yes, it was wonderful. Thank you."

Elsa ignored him. "Indy, you've got to understand my situation."

Indy wanted to spit in her face, but instead, he nodded, playing along with her in the hope that she would loosen the knots and give them a chance to get away.

She leaned forward and kissed him passionately, stroking his head with her hand.

"Dr. Schneider!"

Elsa abruptly stood up, and turned toward the fireplace. Vogel had returned through the hidden entrance.

"Yes, Herr Colonel?" She turned her head but kept her back to the Nazi.

"Your car is waiting."

"Thank you."

She smiled at Indy and brushed strands of her hair from her cheek. "That's the way Austrians say good-bye."

Elsa walked over to Vogel. "I'm ready now." She slipped through the door behind the fireplace.

This time the colonel stayed behind. He marched over to Indy, a good soldier, his rhythm perfect. His mouth slid into a sneer. "And this is how we say good-bye in Germany, Dr. Jones."

He jerked his arm back and punched Indy in the jaw. Hard. His head snapped back, blood trickled from the corner of his mouth, from his nose. Vogel turned and vanished through the fireplace.

Indy blinked his eyes, clearing his head. "I like the Austrian way better," he muttered to himself.

INDIANA JONES AND THE LAST CRUSADE   497

"Stop chattering!" Henry admonished. "I need time to think."

"Oh, that's great. And while you're thinking, let's try to loosen these knots again. We've got to get to Marcus before the Nazis do."

"I thought you said Marcus had a two-day start, and that he would blend in—disappear."

"Are you kidding? I made that up. You know Marcus. He got lost once in his own museum."

Henry swore under his breath. "That's just great. Bad enough that monster Vogel is itching to kill us, but now we're going to get Marcus killed and lose the Grail Cup to the Nazis."

"Something to think about, isn't it?" Indy said as he struggled with the ropes.

Now his father started pulling from his side. But the harder they pulled, the tighter the knots got, and the deeper the rope sliced into their wrists.

Finally, they let their arms relax. That was better. Less pain. But just sitting there like a couple of mummies wasn't going to get them out.

Blood oozed over Indy's upper lip from his nose and over his chin from his mouth. One side of his jaw was numb. His nose itched, and his wrists throbbed. His head felt as if it were tied in knots.

Think. Think.

There were probably Nazi guards posted outside the door and others beyond the fireplace. But right now that didn't matter. He knew there had to be a way to get free of the ropes. So why couldn't he think of it?

The silence in the room seemed to stretch toward tomorrow. He wondered if his father had fallen asleep. Then Henry shifted on his chair and tilted his head back until it hit Indy's.

"Junior, what ever happened to that cross you were chasing after?" Henry asked.

The Cross of Coronado had been a sore point between father

and son since Indy was a kid. Henry had refused to believe Indy's story that he had recovered the fabled cross from thieves and had actually brought it home, then lost it again. Indy had vowed to his father that he would recover the cross if it took a lifetime. Over the years, his father had treated the subject like a joke. If he wanted to annoy Indy, he'd ask him where the cross was.

Usually Indy just simmered and said it wasn't any more humorous than his father's search for the Grail Cup. This time he had an answer. "I gave it to Marcus for the museum before we left New York. I finally got it back," he said evenly. "Just like I said I would."

Henry was silent a moment. When he spoke, he sounded conciliatory. "Marcus was very interested in your search for that cross. I can imagine how excited he must have been. But now . . . now if Donovan catches him, he'll never even have a chance to see it on display."

"That's the least of his worries."

And the least of my worries. He thought about telling his father his theory about Donovan and the cross. But that could wait. Right now, he needed to find a way out of their predicament.

Donovan and Colonel Vogel stood near a causeway in an underground storage depot in the bowels of the mountain beneath the castle. They watched as Elsa was driven away in a Nazi staff car. A second staff car pulled up, and Donovan was about to climb into the backseat when he paused momentarily to exchange a final word with Vogel.

"We'll find Brody. No problem. Go ahead and kill them now."

FOURTEEN

Burning Desires

INDY'S HEAD JERKED UP. He suddenly knew how to get the ropes undone.

Damn. And all along, it was right there and I just didn't realize it.

How could he have been so thick-skulled? If his hands hadn't been tied, he would have pounded his fists against his head.

"Dad, can you reach into my coat pocket?"

Henry came alert. "What for?"

"Just do it."

"All right, all right."

Indy squirmed against his restraints to shift his right hip as close to his father's hand as he could. It took a couple of minutes before Henry could touch the top of the pocket. Finally, after more shifting around, his fingers slipped inside it.

"What am I looking for?"

"My good luck charm."

"Feels like a cigarette lighter to me."

Indy didn't answer, waiting for his father to figure out his plan.

"That's it. Junior, you're a pip!"

Indy's impatience burned through him. "Dad, just try to burn through the ropes, will you?"

Henry fumbled to open the lighter, cursed as the top remained closed, and tried again.

Exasperated, Indy said, "Just don't drop it, Dad. Please."

"Confidence, Junior. Where did you get a lighter? You don't smoke."

"It's Elsa's. I forgot to give it back to her after we were in the catacombs."

On the next try, the lighter's top sprang open. Henry's thumb flicked at the wheel. Indy felt sparks, but the lighter didn't ignite. "Damn thing," Henry grumbled. "I think it needs fluid."

Wonderful.

"C'mon, *work*." Henry shook the lighter, tried again. "There we go. I got it."

Instantly, Indy felt the flame on his fingers. "Dad, burn the rope, not my hand."

For the next few minutes, Henry held the lighter against the rope. Once, the flame went out, and he fumbled again until he reignited it.

Indy's back ached from holding the awkward position. He gritted his teeth and tried to hold his hands steady. The stink of the burning rope saturated the air and made his nose itch again.

As the rope finally began to smolder and burn, Indy heard Henry curse.

"What happened?" Indy asked.

"I dropped it."

Indy craned his neck, but couldn't see where the lighter had fallen. He knew the only way to retrieve it was for them to tip the chairs over. Then they'd have to work on their sides. He said as much. "You ready to try it?"

Henry didn't answer him.

"Dad?"

"Junior, there's something you ought to know."

Indy misinterpreted his father's apologetic tone. "Don't get sentimental now, Dad. Save it until we're out of here. Okay?"

Indy smelled something. "Hey, what the hell's burning?"

"That's what I was going to say. The, uh, floor is on fire."

"What?" Indy cranked his head as far as he could and saw the tongues of fire. "All right, let's move. Rock your chair. Do what I do."

They inched their way slowly across the room and away from the burning carpet. The chairs scraped against the floor and nearly toppled.

"Head for the fireplace."

They rocked and hopped in their chairs, moving toward the only safe place in the room. Behind them the fire seemed to feed itself, spreading fast, racing across the rug.

Indy rubbed his hands up and down, trying to get them free of the rope. As they wobbled into the fireplace, nearly toppling their chairs, Indy's foot kicked out and accidently hit the lever that opened the hidden door. The fireplace floor rotated like a lazy Susan, and they found themselves in a communications room. Four Nazi radiomen wearing headphones sat behind an elaborate panel of dials, switches, and meters. Their backs were turned to them, and for a moment they didn't see Indy or Henry.

"Our situation has not improved." Henry whispered his sentiments, but his voice was still too loud.

One of the radiomen glanced over his shoulder and was startled to see the two men tied back-to-back in their respective chairs.

Henry groaned. "Now what, Junior? Got any more good ideas?"

Indy looked around frantically for the lever that would turn them back. The radioman was already rising from his chair and alerting his partners. Indy spotted the lever directly in front of them and kicked out a leg. It was too high to reach with his foot. There was only one other way that he could think of to activate it.

"Push off with your feet," he yelled. He rocked forward as hard and fast as he could. His head struck the lever, and the floor rotated again just as the radioman pulled out a revolver and fired several shots.

The bullets pinged against the closing door.

Indy and Henry were out of the proverbial frying pan and into the fire. The carpet, drapes, and furniture were all ablaze. Greasy plumes of smoke burned their eyes; fire leapt for the ceiling. Indy coughed; he could hardly breathe.

"We were better off back there," Henry shouted above the roar of the blaze.

Indy didn't waste his breath answering him. He had been working at the burned rope around his wrists, and suddenly his bonds broke. He slid off the chair and quickly unraveled the ropes around his father's wrists.

He hurriedly looked around. He spotted a grating inside the chimney, and tested it with his hand. The fireplace started to rotate again. "Quick, up here." He stood on one of the chairs, and grabbed the grating and pulled himself up through the opening in the center. He wedged himself between the walls, reached down and grasped his father by the arm. He pulled him up through the grating just as the four radiomen revolved into the burning room.

Their pistols were drawn. They looked at the empty chairs, conferred a moment; then two of the men returned to the communications room. The other pair shielded their eyes and moved cautiously toward the flames.

Indy knew they weren't going to be able to remain much longer in the chimney. Besides the fact that their positions were awkward, the heat of the fire was funneling up the chimney. A minute passed, and the radiomen returned from the communications room. As soon as they ventured away from the fireplace, Indy, then Henry, dropped from the chimney.

Indy immediately pulled the lever to rotate the fireplace. As they started to revolve, he saw the door across the room open and momentarily glimpsed the startled face of Colonel Vogel. Flames swept toward the Nazi as air from the corridor was drawn into the room. The colonel leapt back, barely escaping the rush of fire and smoke.

"Halt!" one of the radiomen yelled as he spotted Indy and Henry disappearing behind the fireplace.

"They're going to be coming back again," Henry warned as soon as they were inside the communications room.

"I know. I know."

Indy smashed a wooden stool against the floor, breaking off a leg. The wall started opening just as he reached over his head and jammed it into the gears controlling the movement of the wall. The door stopped after only opening a few inches. The radiomen were sealed inside the burning room.

Henry stared at the door, listening to the men's screams. Indy knew his father was horrified at what he had just done. It was that or die. That was the reality. Kill or be killed.

He turned away and searched for a way out. There had to be another exit, another secret door, a window, something. He ran his hands over the walls, knocked his knuckles against them, listening for a hollowness.

"You won't find the way out *that* way," Henry told him. "Let's sit down and work this out."

"Sit *down*?" Indy's eyes widened. "Are you crazy?"

"Stop panicking. I often find if I sit down calmly, the solution soon presents itself."

Henry slumped down into an overstuffed sofa. As he did, it budged slightly, and started to tilt forward as a section of the floor opened.

Indy leaped onto the sofa, realizing that his father had found the exit. "I see what you mean," he yelled as they slid down a ramp for several hundred feet until they were deposited on a dock. They were inside an enormous cavern that covered an underground causeway. The cavern obviously had been transformed into a Nazi storage depot.

They hurried over to a stack of large shipping crates. "We must be inside the mountain, below the castle," Henry whispered.

Indy perused the array of gunboats, speedboats, and supply vessels. "Great. More boats."

They waited until a Nazi patrol had passed, then darted across the dock to one of the boats. Indy revved up the engine just as Vogel appeared on the dock.

The colonel stopped and glanced over the boats as the engine roared to life. He ran with several Nazis to the nearest speedboat and climbed aboard. A moment later Vogel's boat sped away from the dock in search of the two Dr. Joneses.

Indy and Henry had already abandoned the boat and appropriated a motorcycle and sidecar. Indy was at the bike's wheel, and his father squashed into the little connecting car.

"Would you say this has been just another typical day for you?" Henry shouted as they roared along the dock.

"Better than most," Indy yelled back, accelerating toward a circle of light he hoped was the way out of the mountain. If it wasn't an exit, he wasn't sure what the next move would be.

Maybe there wouldn't be any next move.

The road and waterway suddenly came together at the mouth of the cove. The rattle of machine-gun fire exploded from a boat. "Get down!" he shouted to his father, who complied without argument.

Indy ducked low on the motorcycle, and a moment later they burst into the bright morning sunlight. The road veered sharply away from the canal and away from the immediate threat.

Indy glanced down at Henry, who was peeking up over the side of the car now, checking to make sure the coast was clear. "And we're just starting a new day."

As the motorcycle raced toward a crossroad, the sign indicated Budapest to the right and Berlin to the left. Indy slowed at the intersection and turned right.

"Hold it!" Henry yelled. "Stop!"

"What's wrong?" Indy braked the motorcycle and glanced over at his father.

Henry just kept motioning him to stop so Indy pulled off the road and into the bushes, out of sight from any curious eyes.

He dismounted from the motorcycle and stretched as Henry climbed out of the sidecar. "So what are you waving your hands about?"

"Turn around. We've got to go to Berlin."

Indy pointed in the other direction. "But Brody is *that* way, Dad."

"My diary is *this* way," Henry answered, jerking his thumb in the other direction.

"We don't need your diary."

"Oh, yes we do. You didn't tear out enough pages, Junior." He glared defiantly at Indy.

"All right, tell me. What is it?"

"He who finds the Grail Cup must face the final challenge— devices of a lethal cunning."

"You mean it's booby-trapped?"

"Eight years ago I found the clues that would take us safely through the traps. They were in the *Chronicles of St. Anselm*."

"Well, can't you remember what they are?"

"I wrote it down in the diary so I wouldn't have to remember."

Indy heard a roar and glanced out to the road just in time to see two Nazi motorcycles racing by, headed in the direction of Budapest.

"The Gestapo and half of Hitler's Wehrmacht is after us now, and you want to turn around and head right into the lion's den."

"Yes. The only thing that matters to me is the Holy Grail."

"What about Marcus?"

"Marcus would agree with me. I'm sure of it."

Indy rolled his eyes. He'd heard *this* litany so many times, he could have recited it in his sleep. "You scholars. Pride and plunder. Jesus Christ."

Henry's hand stung Indy's cheek. The blow wasn't hard, but it surprised him. He had been joking, but his father had obviously taken offense. He touched his cheek and frowned at him.

"That's for your blasphemy," Henry snapped. "Don't you remember anything from reading *Parzival*? Didn't you learn anything from Richard Wagner or Wolfram von Eschenbach? In the hands of the knight, Sir Parzival, the Grail is a sacred talisman of healing. But under the control of the malefic Klingsor it is a tool for black magic."

He shook his head scornfully at Indy. "The quest for the cup is not archaeology. It's a race against evil. If the Grail is made captive to the cult of the Nazis, the armies of the darkness will march over the face of the earth." Henry glared at him. "Do you understand me?"

Myth and reality were intertwined in his father's world. They were virtually inseparable. He was living the myth. "I've never understood this obsession of yours, and Mother didn't, either."

He glared back at his father. The mention of his mother was a challenge. For the first time in more than thirty years, he heard his father talk about her.

"She did. Too well. Because of it, because she didn't want me worrying about her, she kept her illness from me until all I could do was mourn her."

Their eyes locked, and for those few moments Indy knew they were equals. At last his father had spoken to him of his mother's death and told him his feelings, even admitted fault. The very mention of her resolved an old wound between them.

He clasped a hand on his father's shoulder. "C'mon. Let's get on our way to Berlin, Pop."

FIFTEEN
Berlin Fireworks

FLAGS, BANNERS, AND STANDARDS displaying the swastika were waved frantically back and forth, over and over again, in a rhythmic motion that reflected the mounting frenzy of the massive crowd. At the center of the rally was a bonfire fueled by a ten-foot-high mound of books. At the periphery of the fire college students and Nazi Brownshirts fed the flames with more and more books. Many of them were classics that had been deemed blasphemous or unpatriotic by the Nazis and their sympathizers.

Indy walked toward the square, buttoning the tunic of a Nazi uniform that was several sizes too large for him. When they had arrived in Berlin, they had driven around on the motorcycle until they found a uniformed Nazi who was separated from his unit. Henry had acted as if he were ill and collapsed on the sidewalk a few feet away from the soldier. When the man had stopped to see what was wrong, Indy had rushed up and asked him to help carry his father to someplace quiet. When they reached the alcove of a building, Indy had knocked the Nazi cold and stripped off his uniform.

Henry, still dressed in street clothes, hurried along beside Indy, gawking at the chaos around them. "My boy, we are pilgrims in an unholy land."

"Yeah, too bad it's real life, not just the movies," Indy said, nodding toward a motion picture cameraman who was filming the scene.

Indy suddenly stopped dead and stared ahead at the platform.

"What is it?" Henry asked.

Indy nodded toward the raised dais. It was occupied by high-ranking officials of the Third Reich, who gazed out over the rally like royalty overseeing their subjects. Among them were two familiar faces: Adolf Hitler and Dr. Elsa Schneider.

"Oh, my God," Henry moaned, and shook his head. "On the right hand of the fiend himself. Do you believe she's a Nazi now?"

Indy said nothing. He threaded his way through the crowd, Henry right behind him like a shadow, and moved as close to the platform as he dared.

A woman stood next to a cameraman who was trying to get a shot of Hitler, Elsa, and others in the High Command. Indy pegged her as the director, because she kept shouting and waving her hands to attract the attention of those on the dais. There was so much noise and confusion, she was having a hard time of it.

"One step forward, please, Mein Führer," she called out in German.

Hitler took a step back.

"All right. That's fine. That's fine. Everybody else, one step back now."

Instead, everyone took a step forward, and Hitler was barely visible.

The director threw up her hands and shook her head. "Please, please. You are blocking the Führer."

Indy laughed to himself. "Looks like I understand German better than the High Command," he remarked to his father, who had forced him to learn several foreign languages before he was eighteen, something he resented at the time but appreciated now. "Thanks to you," he added, elbowing his father gently in the side.

Henry snorted. "*Now* he thanks me. *Now* he listens to me."

Indy laughed.

The rally was breaking up, and Indy pressed his way past a throng of torch-bearing Nazis. The zealots repelled him, but outwardly he maintained a placid look of indifference. He skirted the platform and snaked through Nazi officers and their staff cars. He perused the dispersing crowd and spotted Elsa walking alone, her hair thick and gold in the sunlight.

Henry trailed behind, keeping a discreet distance. He had agreed that Indy should be the one to approach Elsa, and they decided to meet in half an hour near one end of the platform.

Indy hurried after Elsa, approaching her from behind. He slowed as he neared her, waiting until she was well away from anyone who could overhear them.

"Fräulein Doctor."

"Indy," she gasped.

His voice was quiet and tough, his eyes hard and unforgiving. "Where is it?"

"You followed me."

She said it in a way that made him wonder if she was still attracted to him. It was as if her emotions pulled her one way, while her logic and her orders directed her on another course—a deadly one for Indy and his father.

Her hand touched his face, her mouth opened slightly, and her eyes shone with longing. "I missed you really bad, Indy."

He brushed her hand aside and slipped his hands over her body, searching her pockets for the Grail diary. "I want it. Where is it?"

His voice and the roughness of his search snapped her back to the reality of the situation. For a moment he thought she was going to beg him to forgive her. Her mouth quivered, her face seemed to come undone at the seams. But then something changed; he could see it happening, a pulling together somewhere deep inside her. Her reply was cool and crisp.

"Everything is right where it was the last time you looked."

Indy continued with his search, ignoring her. He slid his hand along her legs and stopped as he felt something. He glanced around, then quickly reached up her dress and pulled out the Grail diary, which she had strapped to her leg.

"Sorry about the inconvenience."

Elsa shook her head, confused by Indy's urgent search. "I don't understand, Indy. You came back for the book? Why?"

"My father doesn't want it incinerated in one of your parties here."

She glared back at him. "Is that how you think of me, like I'm one of these Brownshirts?"

"I don't know why I would think any other way," he answered coldly.

"I believe in the Grail, not the swastika."

"Yeah." He jerked his thumb over his shoulder toward the platform. "And you stood up to be counted with the enemy of everything the Grail stands for. Who cares what *you* believe?"

"You do," she snapped.

Indy's hand shot out and clutched her throat. "I only have to squeeze."

"I only have to scream."

It was a standoff, and he knew it. Love and hatred, back and forth, a tug-of-war. He wouldn't follow through on his threat, and she knew it, just as he knew she wouldn't scream. In spite of everything, the allure and fascination of her presence was as strong as ever.

Indy released her and backed away. They shared a look that said everything, that told of lovers whose lives met and diverged through matters that appeared beyond their control. But at the

INDIANA JONES AND THE LAST CRUSADE

same time some part of him knew it was their own choices that had brought them together and would separate them.

"Indy," she called out.

He took another step backward, then spun around and left. He found his father waiting near the platform. "Come on. Let's get out of here."

"Well, did you get it?" Henry asked as they walked away.

"Yeah. I got it."

"Wonderful. How did you get it away from that Nazi whore?"

The comment angered him. For some reason he felt compelled to defend her. He was about to lash out at his father for the crack when he realized that the crowd they were walking through consisted of Hitler and his entourage. About fifty kids surrounded the Führer, pushing autograph books at him for his signature.

Hitler paused to sign them, then looked at Indy, who towered well above the heads of the youngsters. Their eyes locked. The contact lasted only a moment, but Indy felt the pull of Hitler's charisma. For the first time, he understood the attraction and allegiance the man drew from his followers. But he also knew the horror of Hitler's regime, the devastation and suffering, and the horrible potential for worldwide chaos. And that made his appeal all the more frightening.

Hitler broke the spell when he took the Grail diary from Indy's hand to autograph it. He opened it before Indy could react, but his father's groan was clearly audible behind him. Then Hitler signed the diary and handed it back to him.

Indy quickly recovered his sense of place. He clicked his heels and delivered a straight arm salute. At the same time, he secretly countered his show of fealty. He held his other hand behind his back, and crossed his fingers.

A moment after Indy withdrew his salute and stepped back, Hitler was whisked away into the backseat of a waiting limousine and the crowd of students dispersed. But his direct encounter with

Hitler had created enmity from other Nazis who witnessed the incident. One of them, an S.S. officer whose obesity was wrapped in a long overcoat, lingered behind to castigate the low-ranking Nazi.

"What are you doing here?" the officer demanded in crisp German. "This is a restricted area. Get back to your post at once."

Indy stood bolt upright, raised his hand in another "Heil Hitler" salute. Realizing there was no one else around, he jerked back his arm, balled his fingers into a fist, and smashed the officer in the face.

Henry groaned again.

"Now we're going to do things my way," Indy announced to his father.

"Meaning what?"

"We're getting out of Germany."

Indy pulled up to the main terminal of the Berlin airport and parked the motorcycle. As he hopped off, he adjusted the overcoat he had taken from the overweight S.S. officer.

"If you're going to keep taking other people's clothes," Henry said, as they entered the terminal, "why don't you pick on somebody your own size?"

"I'll remember that next time."

They got in line at one of the boarding gates and waited to buy their tickets. "Any luck, we'll be out of this country in an hour, and we'll find Marcus tomorrow," Indy said confidently.

"Oh, oh." Henry nodded toward an area to the side of the ticket counter. Each passenger buying a ticket was being questioned by Gestapo agents.

"Yeah." Indy took Henry by the arm and turned away from the line. They had taken a half dozen steps when he spotted more trouble. Colonel Vogel was striding across the terminal. "Look who's here."

Both men quickly turned up their coat collars and lowered their hat brims, then briskly veered away from Vogel. Indy glanced back once and saw Vogel showing a couple of Gestapo agents a photograph.

"It's probably not a family portrait," he muttered to himself, and they left the terminal. The adjoining building was another terminal, but it was smaller, newer, and decorated in a florid art deco style.

They headed for the counter and stood in line behind several well-dressed men and women. Must be first class, Indy thought.

"Why this line?" Henry asked.

"Because, nobody's checking it."

The line inched forward. Minutes ticked by. Indy kept glancing around, anxiety churning across the floor of his gut. He hated this. He hated waiting around for something to happen. He would rather be confronting it—and getting it over with.

He started feeling conspicuous and forced himself to stare down at his shoes for a while. Then he raised his eyes and looked around again, but slowly, like a bored traveler who was wondering where he was going to sit once he was checked in for his flight. To keep from turning around, he read a plaque that was on a nearby pillar. It commemorated the zeppelin *Hindenburg*, which had flown from Lakehurst, New Jersey, to Friedrichshafen, Germany in forty-two hours and fifty-three minutes, August 9–11, 1936—a world record.

He looked back down at his shoes, tapping his foot impatiently. Then he couldn't stand it anymore, and his eyes roamed through the terminal again, hungry, curious. A burly woman, who was next in line, glared at him. He looked back at the plaque and read the last line: Certified by Federation Aeronautique Internationale.

"What are you doing?" Henry barked.

Indy jerked his head around and saw that the line had moved ahead, and his father was waiting at the window. They purchased their tickets, asking for the next flight. As they walked toward the door of the terminal, Indy asked his father if he knew where the flight was headed.

Henry rolled his eyes as if it was a foolish question, but to Indy's surprise said, "As a matter of fact, no. Do you?"

It didn't really matter where they were going at this point, as long as it was *out* of Germany. But he consulted his ticket. "Athens. Not exactly within walking distance of Iskenderun, but at least it's in the right direction."

"Athens, of course." Henry repeated, nodding his approval of their destination. "Things are starting to look up."

Indy stopped as he noticed the drawing on his ticket and realized they weren't taking an airplane to Athens. "Hey, Dad."

Henry kept walking and didn't hear him. Indy hurried after him. They stepped out onto the tarmac and saw their ride to Athens parked in front of them.

"Well, well," Henry said.

A zeppelin that was more than ten stories high and two football fields in length was moored on the tarmac. They not only hadn't bothered to find out where they were headed, but neither of them had realized they were taking a zeppelin. As they approached the boarding stairs, Indy and Henry exchanged glances. Both were excited and surprised by the turn of events.

"Hey, look at that," Indy said, pointing to a pair of biplanes suspended on large hooks below the zeppelin. "How'd you like to ride down there?"

Henry's answer was succinct. "No, thanks."

They found an empty compartment and made themselves comfortable as the zeppelin prepared to take off. Indy sank down in his seat, folded his arms across his chest, and exhaled.

"We made it, Dad."

Henry took out a handkerchief and wiped it across his forehead. "When we're airborne and Germany's behind us, I'll join you in that sentiment."

Indy gazed out the window. "Relax. In a few hours we'll be in

Athens and on our way to Iskenderun, and Marcus. Sit back and enjoy the scenery."

Just as he finished speaking, he saw a now too familiar figure rushing across the tarmac. It was Vogel, followed by one of the Gestapo agents Indy had seen in the airport. His body suddenly felt leaden as he watched the pair board the zeppelin.

He sensed it was going to be a rough flight.

SIXTEEN
Aerobatics

"S TAY HERE," Indy said to his father.

He flew out of the compartment before Henry could say anything, his mind racing, seeking a plan. His only advantage was that he knew Vogel was on board. He didn't know how he could use it for leverage but felt sure he'd come up with something before it was too late. He always had before, so why not now?

He felt like a cat with nine lives. Nine lives. Do I have any left?

He was barely out of the compartment when he spotted Vogel headed down the passageway in his direction. He ducked through a door marked Crew Only. As the Nazi colonel walked past the door, Indy heard a steward tell him that the zeppelin was about to take off and that he must find a seat. He opened the door a crack and saw Vogel following two other late-arriving passengers into a compartment, the same one he had just vacated.

"Oh, God," he whispered, wondering how his father would deal with Vogel.

Before he could do anything, the steward slid open the door and nearly ran into Indy. "What are you doing here?" the man asked loudly in German. "This is the crew room, can't you see? We're about to take off. Please . . ."

Indy pointed toward the ceiling, and the man glanced up. As he did, Indy connected with a short punch under the jaw. He disliked assaulting innocent bystanders, but with Vogel seated only a few feet away, he knew he had to deal quickly with the man.

Unlike the butler, the steward only stumbled back a step. In his concern about not hurting the man, he hadn't hit him hard enough. The steward gave Indy a startled look, then threw his own punch. Indy blocked it, and this time connected with a powerful blow to the man's cheek. He slumped to the floor, unconscious.

When the zeppelin rose from the tarmac a few minutes later, Indy returned to the compartment where his father was. But now he wore the hat and jacket of the steward. For a change, the borrowed apparel fit perfectly.

"Tickets please. May I have your tickets?" he said in German.

Henry peeked over the top of a magazine, and his eyes widened as he saw who was collecting tickets. Indy nodded as his father passed him his ticket.

"Your ticket, sir," he said to Vogel and held out his hand.

The colonel glanced up, recognized Indy, and reached for the gun inside his coat. But Indy grabbed his arm, collaring him, and jerked him out of his seat. He removed his Luger and, with a boost from his father, shoved Vogel out the window and onto the tarmac.

The other passengers in the compartment drew back, startled and frightened by the aggressive behavior of the steward with the foreign accent.

Indy smiled and shrugged. "No ticket."

Everyone in the compartment immediately produced his ticket and held it up in Indy's face.

As he collected them, Indy glanced out the window to see Vogel on his hands and knees, peering up as the zeppelin lifted off. "Next time, you get a ticket first," Indy yelled at him.

He moved out of the compartment and ducked back into the

crew quarters. He wondered what he'd do next. Vogel hadn't been alone.

A few minutes later the Gestapo agent hurried down the passageway. He stopped a few steps past the crew quarters. He looked worried and disgruntled, and it didn't take a genius to figure out why. After all, the poor sucker hadn't been able to find him or his father, and now he couldn't even find Vogel.

Indy stepped out of the crew quarters and tapped him on the shoulder. He was about to club him with the butt of the Luger when one of the passengers who had seen him toss Vogel out the window emerged from the nearby compartment. Indy asked the Gestapo agent for his ticket.

"I don't need one," the man snapped.

The passenger walked by, heading for the bathroom. "You'll be sorry," he mumbled to the agent.

"He's right," Indy said, and cracked him behind the ear with the Luger. The agent crumpled. Indy dragged him into the crew quarters, took his gun, and opened the storage closet. Inside, the steward was bound and gagged.

"Company." He lowered the agent into the corner.

The steward was wide awake and yelling into his gag. Indy brandished the gun over his head, and he immediately calmed down.

He noticed a cluster of wires running into a box marked Radio Transmitter and yanked them out. Then he saw a leather jacket hanging from a hook. It looked a lot like his own. He couldn't resist trying it on.

Another perfect fit.

At the bar in the zeppelin's lounge, Indy eavesdropped as a World War I German flying ace relived his daring exploits, using a pair of model airplanes as props. Several enthralled onlookers bought him one drink after another, and the stories grew more and more fantastic.

The steward arrived with drinks for Indy and his father, who were seated several tables away from the now drunken flying ace. Both men had settled for non-alcoholic beverages. Neither was now certain their ordeal with the Nazis was finally over. If it was, fine. But if more trouble was ahead, they wanted to remain as alert as possible.

Henry was so absorbed in the Grail diary, he didn't even know his drink had arrived. He was studying the pages that described the lethal devices defending the Grail. Now and then, he would mutter to himself, and all of it brought back old childhood memories for Indy, of his father in his study, lost in the ancient past. Some things, he thought, would never change.

Indy stared out the window, watching bright wisps of clouds sail past the zeppelin. He wondered what Elsa was doing and if she was thinking of him. Despite the fact that she had been standing up there with Hitler, he believed her primary interest was in the Grail, an obsession he could understand, since it was something she shared with his father. But he couldn't condone her association with the man who was quite possibly the most heinous human being to walk the face of the earth since Genghis Khan.

He turned away, shutting off his secret longings. He looked down at the Grail diary and focused on his father's tiny handwriting, which was inscribed in medieval Latin. There were three complex diagrams that made no sense to him. The only thing he understood was their labels. The first was called The Pendulum, the second, The Cobbles, and the third, The Invisible Bridge.

He was about to ask his father to explain the devices, when Henry looked up at him. "Sharing your adventures is an interesting experience."

"That's not all we shared," Indy said, thinking of Elsa again. "By the way, what *did* she say in her sleep?"

"Mein Führer."

"I guess that's pretty conclusive." He thought back to his last moments with Elsa in Berlin. He was sure that she had been sincere and yet . . .

"Disillusioned, are you? She was a beautiful woman, and I'm as human as the next man."

"Yeah. I was the next man."

Henry smiled as if he was thinking about his own experience with her. "Ships that pass in the night. Can we drink to that?"

He raised his glass, and Indy did the same. They clinked glasses. "Ships that pass in the night," Indy repeated. He thought a moment. "Also the afternoon."

Henry cleared his throat and straightened his shoulders. "Well, back to work."

He leaned over the diary and began reading. " 'The challenges will number three. First, the Breath of God; only the penitent man will pass. Second, the Word of God; only in the footsteps of God will he proceed. Third, the Path of God; only in the leap from the lion's head will he prove his worth.' "

"Meaning what?"

Henry tapped the page. "I think we'll find that out when we get there."

Sunlight broke through the clouds, casting a beam through their window and dividing the table into equal parts of light and shadow. As Indy reached for his drink, he noticed that the ray was moving across the table like the hand of a clock. He stared at it, puzzled by the phenomenon. Then suddenly he understood what it meant.

"Dad."

"What is it?"

"We're turning around. They're taking us back to Germany."

They quickly rose from the table and made their way to the crew quarters. The storage closet door was smashed open, and the Gestapo agent and steward were gone. Indy looked around and saw that the radio wires had been repaired with tape.

"Shit."

"Ah, Junior. I think we've got a problem here."

"I know. I know. You don't have to tell me," he said, as he tried to figure out what they should do.

"No, you don't understand. I forgot the diary in the lounge."

"You *what*?"

Henry smiled weakly at him and stammered: "Yeah, I'm afraid so."

Good going, Dad. "Okay, stay right here. I'll be right back." Indy hustled down the passageway, back toward the lounge. He started to push open the door but heard voices and stopped. He peeked inside and saw the agent and several crewmen standing in the center of the lounge near the table Indy and Henry had just abandoned. The diary was on it, but no one had noticed it.

The agent called for everyone's attention. "There are spies aboard the airship! Everyone loyal to the Führer, the Reich, and Deutschland come immediately with me."

Blasé passengers looked up, then returned to their conversations and cocktails, ignoring the agent's command. The only one who responded was the World War I ace, who struggled to his feet from his bar stool and wobbled forward.

Indy knew he had to act fast. He turned the collar up on the leather jacket and took out a handkerchief. He sneezed into it as he walked into the lounge, keeping his head down. He heard the agent giving orders.

"You," he pointed at Indy. "You come with us. We're looking for American spies."

Indy kept the handkerchief to his nose. "I've got a cold," he said in German. "Sorry." He reached around behind him and slipped the diary into his back pocket. He recognized the steward he had knocked out standing near the agent. He was wearing an undershirt, and his face was a question mark as he looked over Indy.

"I'll guard my compartment," Indy said, and hustled toward the door.

"That's him," the steward yelled. "Stop him." But Indy was already out the door and racing down the passageway.

He ducked back into the crew quarters and looked around for Henry. "Dad, where are you?"

Henry poked his head out of the storage closet. "Did you get it?"

"Yeah, but I think I got a lot more, too." Indy hurriedly prowled around the quarters, looking for a hiding place. He glanced up at the ceiling.

"Trouble, you mean?"

"No more than usual."

Quickly he pulled a chair across the floor, stepped on top of it, and hoisted himself up through a hatchway. He reached down to help his father.

"Not another chimney," Henry complained.

Indy lifted him through the opening, then climbed to the top of the hatchway. They crawled out the top of it and found themselves in the belly of the zeppelin. Its skin was attached to an elaborate metal framework, and narrow catwalks connected the huge helium gasbags that gave the airship its lift.

Henry paused in wonderment and awe. Indy glanced down the hatchway and saw the agent and steward peering up. He grabbed his father by the arm, and they rushed along one of the narrow catwalks.

But they weren't fast enough.

The agent pulled a small gun from an ankle holster and aimed it at Indy. He was about to fire when the steward knocked his arm aside.

"Nein! Nein!"

Indy looked over his shoulder and saw the steward point to the gasbag, then gesture with his arms. "Kaboom!"

The catwalk ended at a pair of doors framed on the outer skin of the zeppelin. Behind them Indy heard the pounding of feet along the catwalk. He opened one of the doors, and gripped the frame as the wind pounded him. He was staring into the blue sky and white clouds.

Several feet below, he saw the biplanes suspended on hooks that were attached to a steel framework. Indy pointed to the nearest one, which had an emblem on the fuselage of a pelican with its wings spread wide. "Climb down, Dad. We're going for a ride."

Henry looked terrified as he peered out the doorway. "I didn't know you could fly a plane."

Fly, yes. Land, no. "Let's go."

Henry ventured out of the zeppelin, climbing down a metal ladder to the biplane. Indy watched anxiously, then looked away. If his father fell now, he couldn't help and didn't want to see it.

He glanced back to Henry and saw he had made it safely to the biplane. He started to follow, when the Gestapo agent grabbed him by the arm and attempted to pull him back. He twisted free and pushed the man away. He was about to resume his descent when the steward scampered down the ladder and dropped on top of Indy, wrapping his arm around his neck.

Indy clung to the ladder and, to his surprise, saw his father climbing up toward him. Henry grabbed the man by the back of the collar and jerked him away. At the same moment Indy bucked as hard as he could.

The steward lost his grip and tumbled into space, arms pin-wheeling, grappling for anything to break his fall. He caught hold of one of the struts just above the hook that attached to the plane. His legs pumped in midair.

Indy stared at his father in amazement. "Look what you did!" he shouted.

Henry climbed down into the rear cockpit, and Indy leaped the last few feet, landing in the front one. He found the starter and switched it on. The propeller sputtered, coughed, then roared to life.

As Indy searched for the lever to release the hook, Henry shouted something. Indy's head snapped up, and he saw the agent standing in the doorway above him, aiming the gun at him, trying to hold it steady in the wind. He fired, but missed. Indy found the lever and pulled back on it, releasing the biplane.

Suddenly they soared away from the zeppelin, leaving the agent and dangling crewman behind.

Indy circled about and saw the World War I ace walk out onto a catwalk outside the zeppelin and climb down into the second plane. He signaled the Gestapo agent to join him.

The agent, mimicking Indy, walked out on the catwalk, and jumped into the rear cockpit. He struck hard, and his feet burst through the bottom of the fuselage, and the lower half of his body was suspended in midair below the plane.

The World War I ace didn't realize what had happened, and released the plane from its hooks. He was so drunk that he had forgotten to start the engine first. Instantly it spun straight for the ground. Indy knew there was no way the ace pilot, even with all of his experience, could start the engine and recover from the spin.

Less than a minute later the plane crashed into the side of a mountain, spewing flames and debris.

Indy's plan was to fly as far away from Germany as the biplane would take them, and as near as they could get to Iskenderun. He wasn't looking forward to landing. He decided he would take it down in a field rather than an airport, and that way they would avoid any questions. The last thing they wanted to do was attract attention and get the Nazis on their trail again.

He heard his father yell something to him. He turned back to him and saw Henry jerking his thumb up and down. Indy smiled and flashed the thumbs-up sign back to him, and beamed with confidence. But Henry shook his head.

Indy finally understood. His father was pointing up and yelling something he couldn't hear. What he did hear, though, was a sound that was both a roar and a wail. He couldn't see anything above them, but the sound was growing louder, eerier. He tilted his head back again.

Two Messerschmidt fighter bombers streaked out of the clouds and raced across the sky. Indy and Henry sank down in their seats as the fighters screamed toward them.

"Fire the machine gun," Indy yelled.

Henry puzzled over the gun, trying to figure out how it worked.

Indy turned in his seat and pointed at the gun. "Pull back on that lever, then jerk the trigger."

The plane's slow speed and small size worked to their advantage. The speeding Messerschmidts overshot them and whizzed by in a blur. Indy knew it would take the fighters miles to turn around. But he also knew the pilots would find them again.

On the second sweep Henry framed one of the fighters in his sight. He pulled back on the trigger and fired at the first one. The gun exploded with such force that he was nearly shaken out of his seat. The Messerschmidt banked to the left, and Henry swung the gun around. He kept firing, missed the fighter, and inadvertently cut his own rear stabilizer.

"Oops."

"Are we hit?" Indy bellowed.

"More or less," Henry yelled back.

Indy looked over his shoulder at the missing tail section, then at his father, and his heart plunged to his toes, then zipped up again. *Bad news, Pop. Real bad.*

"Son, I'm sorry. They got us."

Indy struggled to control the plane as it rapidly descended.

"Hold on. We're going in."

At five hundred feet Indy saw a paved road. It was their only hope, their only choice at all, in fact, because that was where the plane was headed. He did his best to stabilize the craft, and they belly-flopped onto the road. The plane skidded out of control and crashed into the parking lot of a roadside tavern.

Indy was shaken by the impact, but still managed to crawl out of the plane. He helped Henry out. "You all right, Dad?"

"I'm in one piece, I think," he said as they stumbled away from the plane.

Indy knew they had to get away as fast as possible. He spotted a customer who was about to drive off, and signaled him. As the man stepped out of his car, Indy leapt behind the wheel. He circled around the parking lot, picked up Henry, and shoved down hard on the gas pedal.

The man chased after them, shaking his fist and shouting. A moment later, the Messerschmidts screamed low, guns blazing. Through the rearview mirror, Indy saw the car owner dive head-first off the road and roll down a ditch as the fighters strafed the parking lot, ripping holes through the parked cars.

Indy shoved the throttle down and gripped the steering wheel tightly with both hands. He concentrated on the road as Henry twitched and turned and fretted.

"Are we out of the woods yet?"

"Hope so."

Indy heard the peculiar roar of a Messerschmidt again and glanced into the side mirror. One of the fighters was swooping toward them.

"Oh, shit."

"What is it?"

Gunfire ripped through the car, miraculously missing Indy and his father. As the Messerschmidt screeched away, beams of sun-light streamed into the car through the bullet-riddled roof.

"Good Lord," Henry moaned. "Take me back to Princeton. This is no way to live."

The whine of the second Messerschmidt raised the hair on the back of Indy's neck. "Here comes the other one."

Then he saw a tunnel cutting through the mountainside. He slammed his foot against the gas pedal and raced for it. But the fighter bore down on them, its machine guns chattering.

They sped into the tunnel, out of the range of the guns. "Let's stay in here," Henry said.

But even the tunnel wasn't safe. An instant later, they heard a resounding crash. The Messerschmidt couldn't pull up in time. It slammed into the mouth of the tunnel, the mountain shearing off its wings. The fuselage rocketed like a bullet down the muzzle of a gun. Sparks flew as it scraped the pavement and sides of the tunnel. Then the fuselage burst into flames.

A fireball grew in the rearview mirror, gaining on them. The accelerator was flat against the floor; the car was going as fast as it could. Indy leaned forward, as if the thrust of his body could somehow speed up the car. He gripped the steering wheel so tightly, his knuckles turned white.

Just as the fireball was about to slam into them, the car flew out of the tunnel. Indy swerved sharply to the shoulder of the road and struggled to maintain control of the car. The flaming fuselage shot past them, struck a tree, and exploded.

Indy swung back onto the road and raced into a wall of flames and greasy smoke. He shot out the other side, eyes wide, heart slamming against his chest.

Henry looked as if he was on the verge of a stroke. "They don't come any closer than that."

"Don't count on it," Indy said as he saw the other Messerschmidt screaming out of the sky toward them.

The fighter dropped a bomb; it exploded in the road directly ahead of the car, missing it by several feet. Indy turned the wheel hard to the right. The car smashed through a guardrail and bounced down an embankment. For several seconds they were airborne. It was all over, he thought, and squeezed his eyes shut.

As quickly as the car had pitched off the road, it landed with a thud, sinking into the soft sand of a deserted Mediterranean beach. The two men staggered out of the car. Indy held his head where he had cracked it against the steering wheel. There wasn't another person in sight for miles. The beach was populated by sea gulls, which had turned the sand into a virtual snowfield of white, feathered bodies.

Indy heard the deadly sound again and looked back, to see the Messerschmidt coming in for yet another pass. Father and son exchanged a wordless glance. They didn't even think about running. There was no place to hide.

Indy checked his gun. It was empty.

The fighter was coming in low, less than a hundred feet over the surf.

Suddenly Henry ran toward the sea gulls, waving his hands. He was a madman, screaming, shouting.

The gulls took to the air en masse, thousands of them rising in fright, wings beating the air just as the Messerschmidt howled overhead, its machine guns spitting, tearing into the beach, kicking up sand.

Then the fighter and the sea gulls met. It was a massacre. Hundreds of gulls were shredded apart by the whirling propeller blades. A feathery, white-and-red puree smeared the windshield and clogged the engine.

The Messerschmidt stopped firing just short of Indy and Henry. Its engines sputtered. The plane stalled and disappeared beyond an embankment.

A brief moment later an explosion shattered the silence. Smoke and flames rose in the distance.

Indy sank into the sand, completely drained.

Henry walked back to him and sat down next to him. "I remembered Charlemagne. 'Let my armies be the rocks and the trees and the birds in the sky.' "

Indy gazed off into the distance toward the burning fighter. "Good advice then; good advice now."

SEVENTEEN

Converging Forces

THE SAME DAY Indy and Henry were fleeing Germany, Marcus Brody arrived by train at Iskenderun. He was utterly exhausted and wished he was back home in New York in the safety of his museum. The problems he faced in his everyday life seemed minor to the frustrations he had already experienced on this trip. And who knew what was ahead for him and Sallah.

That is, if he even found Sallah.

He should have arrived at least a day earlier, but he had taken the wrong train out of Venice and found himself in Belgrade before he realized it. There, he wasted another day in confusion before finally boarding the right train. He had traveled nonstop through the day, the night, and half the following day. He was finally here, and as he disembarked from the train, he sensed that his bold proclamation that he would find the Grail Cup was brash and unrealistic.

His eyes burned as he moved along the railway station platform, through a crowd of Hatayans and Arabs. Bodies in flowing robes blurred into a collective mass. They seemed part of some mysterious coordinated activity, and only he, Marcus Brody, stood apart, confused and out of place. He rubbed his throbbing eyes. What he wanted most of all was a hot shower, a good meal, and about twenty hours of sleep.

He felt anxious and depressed because he had failed Indy and Henry. He should have found the Grail by now, or at least been close to it. Instead, he couldn't even find Sallah. But he was a scholar and a museum director, not a geographer . . . not an explorer. And certainly not an adventurer.

He needed a guide.

"Mr. Brody! Marcus Brody!"

He looked up, amazed to see Sallah making his way through the crowd toward him. He was so relieved by the familiar face, he almost threw his arms around Sallah. That was something he would never even consider doing in New York or in his native London.

"Old fellow, it's good to see you!" You have no idea how good, Sallah.

They shook hands; then Sallah embraced him. Brody patted his back, although his arms barely reached halfway around him. He blushed and grinned sheepishly, embarrassed by the public show of affection.

"Marcus, where have you been?" Sallah held Brody at arm's length and looked him over. "I've been waiting for you here. I've been worried."

Sallah was a bear of a man with black hair and eyes and distinctive Mediterranean features. His rich baritone voice and hearty laugh went a long way toward making Brody feel better, as did his reputation for loyalty. He was known for his fierce dedication to his friends and as a formidable enemy to anyone who opposed them.

"I was turned around for a while. Is Indy here?"

Sallah shook his head. "No, I thought he would be with you."

Now Brody didn't feel so bad. He had still managed to beat Indy here. "He's been delayed."

"Ah, yes. Delayed." Sallah laughed. He picked up Brody's luggage with such ease, the bags could have been empty. "Perfect British understatement, that," he added with a grin.

They left the station and emerged in an open-air market. Vendors' carts were everywhere, and people were shouting and waving their wares. The smell of ripe fruit and vegetables baking in the warm sun swirled around Brody, making him nauseous and dizzy. He felt as though he'd stepped off onto another planet and longed for the quiet solitude of the museum, for the cool silence of the artifacts that were entrusted to him. This, he thought, was not his world, not his way of life.

Sallah said everything they had discussed when Brody had called him in Cairo was ready, and he was anxious for the journey to begin. "As soon as we—" He stopped in midsentence. Two thugs in trench coats were blocking their path.

"Papers, please," one of them said in a foreboding tone, and held out his hand.

"Papers?" Sallah nodded. "Of course. Have one right here. Just finished reading it myself."

Sallah took out a newspaper from under his arm and shoved it in front of the agents' faces. "*Run!*" he hissed at Brody.

Turning to the men, he grinned and waved the newspaper. "The *Egyptian Mail*. Morning edition. Lots of good, timely news."

Brody frowned at Sallah. "Say again?"

"*Run!*" This time he yelled it.

Brody spun but didn't even move a step before one of the men grabbed him by the collar and pulled him back. Sallah bulldozed into both thugs with a flurry of punches. Bystanders scattered, and vendors' stands were overturned as the fight spilled into the open-air market. Fruits and vegetables fell to the ground and rolled away. Spools of costly silk and colorful cotton tumbled into the mud.

Brody pushed his way through the excited, chattering crowd. He tried to come up with a plan to help Sallah, but nothing came to mind. He didn't have the strength to overpower either man, and besides, Sallah *had* told him to run. He threaded his way through stalls, past vendors, and finally took refuge in a doorway.

He could still see the fighting and spotted Sallah just as he bumped into a camel. The impact stunned him long enough for the thugs to lunge at him. But Sallah quickly recovered and slapped the camel on the nose. The ornery beast jerked its head back and unleashed a huge gob of spit that splattered in one of the thug's faces. Sallah raced away, and Brody waved his arms, hoping to catch his eye.

Sallah raised a hand in recognition and cut toward him, jabbing a finger at a darkened doorway at the top of a ramp. A curtain hung over it. "Get away, fast! Go!"

Brody didn't feel particularly disposed toward hiding there, but Sallah kept shouting. So Brody stepped out of the doorway and ran up the ramp. He slipped behind the curtain and peeked out. In the moment Sallah had turned his attention from the thugs, they had caught up with him. They pounced on him like animals, pounding him with their fists and short, heavy clubs. But Sallah wasn't fighting back. He was still waving frantically at Brody and yelling something he couldn't understand.

Nearby, a couple of Nazi soldiers moved in to back up the thugs. Brody knew Sallah didn't have a chance. He hesitated, wishing he could do something for his friend, but knew it was useless. He didn't want to look any longer. He ducked behind the curtain and turned around. Before he realized where he was, he heard metal doors slamming shut behind him. He was inside a truck, and on the wall was a red-and-black Nazi banner.

Sallah lifted his head. He hurt all over, he was bleeding, dust filled his nostrils. The thugs were gone, but they had captured their target after all. Brody had misunderstood him and run right into the Nazis' grasp instead of away from it. Now the truck had disappeared—with Brody in it.

One day later, in a center of a courtyard in Iskenderun, the sultan of the region was seated on his royal chair. It was purple and high-backed and made the sultan appear larger than life. He was an aloof-looking man with eyes that somehow defined his royal bearing. His full beard was silky white and fell to his chest. He wore a deep-red coat embroidered with golden braids on the front and sleeves, and ornate epaulets on the shoulders. His midsection was wrapped in a wide, gold-and-red sash, and his hat was flat-topped and cylindrical and matched his coat.

He was surrounded by his minions, and standing before him was an American he had met more than once in his travels. "What can I do for you, Mr. Donovan? As I told you the last time we talked, I am not interested in selling any works of art."

Donovan nodded. "I understand that. Your Highness, I have something I'd like to show you."

He handed the sultan the missing pages of the Grail diary. "These pages are taken from the diary of Professor Henry Jones. They include a map that pinpoints the exact location of the Grail Cup."

The Sultan studied the map with superficial interest. The fact that the cup was in his territory didn't surprise him. Nothing really did, not since he had realized as a child that he had been born into a wealthy, powerful family in a land where most people were born into families with little or nothing. He was privileged. He accepted that as fact.

He folded the map and casually handed it back. "And where did you obtain this map?"

Donovan turned and nodded toward the group standing near the entrance of the courtyard. Among them were Elsa Schneider, several Nazi guards, and Marcus Brody. It was obvious that Brody was being guarded.

"The man in the center is an emissary to Dr. Jones. He was given the pages by Dr. Jones's son, Indiana Jones."

"And what was he doing with them?"

"We captured him in Iskenderun. He was on his way to steal the Grail Cup from your territory."

"I see."

The cup didn't mean much to him. He had heard of it, of course, and was aware there was an old story that it was supposed to possess great power. But he didn't believe in superstitions—as far as he was concerned, it was just another gold cup destined for a museum or a private collection. He was a modern man and much more interested in newer, up-to-date things, objects with real, believable power.

But he was also well aware of the law of supply and demand. It was obvious that Donovan was interested in the Grail Cup himself. With more than one party pursuing it, the cup's value was greater than if only one party was after it. He knew exactly where he stood in the matter—right in the middle—and if Walter Donovan wanted to go into the desert and find the old cup, it was going to cost him dearly. The sultan had no doubt about that.

"And what do you want to do?" he asked, as if he didn't already know.

Donovan cleared his throat. "As you can see, the Grail is all but in our hands. However, Your Highness, we would not think of crossing your soil without your permission, nor would we remove the Grail Cup from your borders without suitable compensation."

The sultan looked past Donovan. "What have you brought me?"

Donovan turned and signaled the Nazi soldiers. "The trunk, please."

Two of them lugged a huge steamer trunk to the feet of the sultan.

Donovan motioned them to open the lid.

They unlocked the trunk and lifted the top. When the sultan made no move to inspect its contents, Donovan told the soldiers to empty it. For the next several minutes, they removed a wide-ranging assortment of gold and silver objects. There were goblets and candle holders, bowls, plates, and cups, precious boxes of varying sizes, and swords and knives.

"These valuables, Your Highness, have been donated by some of the finest families in all of Germany."

The sultan rose from his chair and walked right past the trunk and the "donations." He headed directly to the Nazi staff car parked in the corner of the courtyard and began to inspect it.

"Daimler-Benz 320L." He lifted the hood and studied the engine. "Ah, 3.4 liter, 120 horsepower, six cylinders, single solex updraft carburetor. Zero to one hundred kilometers in fifteen seconds."

He turned to Donovan, who had trailed after him, and smiled. "I even like the color."

Donovan quickly sized up the situation. It was obvious the sultan wasn't going to settle for the gold and silver, and since they needed his help, there was really only one choice. However, he could still bargain. "The keys, Your Highness, are in the ignition and at your disposal. It is yours, along with the other treasures. I would only ask that you loan us some of your men and equipment."

The sultan smiled appreciatively. "You shall have camels, horses, an armed escort, provisions, desert vehicles. And a tank."

Donovan nodded, pleased with the agreement.

Elsa hurried across the courtyard toward Donovan. "We've got no time to lose. I'm sure Indiana Jones and his father are on their way."

The proceedings at the sultan's court had not been overlooked by another party interested in the Grail Cup. Standing off to one side under an arch was the man who nearly killed Elsa and Indy in Venice, the same man who told Indy where his father was being hidden.

Kazim slipped a hand inside his tunic and ran a finger over the outline of the cruciform sword tattooed on his chest. No one was going to take the Grail Cup from its hiding place as long as he was alive.

The train arrived in Iskenderun at dawn. Despite the early hour, the platform was crowded with arriving and departing passengers. Indy glanced around. He hoped to see Marcus waiting for them but knew that was unlikely. Even if he was in Iskenderun, he would have no idea they were arriving at this hour.

Henry apparently was thinking along the same lines. "I wonder where we'll find Marcus."

"No sign of—Look!"

Indy pointed at the heavyset bearded figure bounding through the crowd toward them.

"Indy," Sallah bellowed. "How I have missed you." He embraced him, lifting him off the ground.

He put Indy back on the ground and turned to Henry. "Father of Indy?"

"Why . . . er . . . yes."

"Well done, sir! Your boy has blessed my life. He is a wonderful man." He threw his arms around Henry, who looked as if he didn't quite know what to make of Sallah, or any of the rest of it. "I'm so glad I have met you."

Indy noticed the bruises and lumps on Sallah's face. "What the hell happened? It looks like a camel kicked your face."

"Something like that. I'll tell you all about it very soon."

Indy frowned, almost not wanting to ask. "Sallah, where is Marcus?"

"We can't talk here, Indy," he whispered, leaning closer. "Hurry. Into the car." Sallah pointed at a battered, dusty coupe parked at the edge of the market.

After they had all climbed into the car, Sallah gunned the engine, and the coupe shot forward. A moment later they were racing through the crowded, narrow streets, threading through animals and cars, bicycles and wagons, and throngs of pedestrians. He honked, accelerated, downshifted, and swerved.

Henry was speechless with terror; he gripped an armrest in the backseat, certain that at any second Sallah was going to smash into a cart or plow through a crowd, killing everyone.

He finally found his voice and sat forward. "Please," he gasped. "Please, slow down. I've had enough crazy driving for a lifetime on my way here."

"Sorry, father of Indy."

He motioned frantically with his hand and stuck his head out the window. "Move that goat!" he shouted at someone in the street.

The goat moved, they sped forward, and Sallah looked over at Indy. "About Marcus. There were too many for me to handle."

"Watch out!" Henry bellowed from the backseat.

Sallah slammed on the brakes and cursed as a man with a cart pulled into their path. "Get a camel!" he yelled, poking his head out the window.

The man ignored him, and Sallah veered around the cart and sped on again. He returned to the matter of Marcus. "My face will tell you I did what I could with what I had." He raised a bruised fist. "I am not the only one who is feeling sore."

"What about Brody?"

"They set out across the desert this afternoon after getting supplies and soldiers from a sultan. I fear they took Mr. Brody with them."

Henry jerked forward, leaning over the front seat. "That means they have the map and are on their way. They'll reach the Grail Cup before us."

"Calm down, Dad. We'll find them," Indy reassured him. At the same time he worried they were too late, for Marcus, and for the Grail.

"There's no silver medal for second place in this race, my boy." Henry had suddenly changed his mind about Sallah's driving and patted him on the shoulder. "Faster. Go faster, please."

Sallah grinned, pounded the horn, and stuck his head out of the window. "You blind Ottoman rug merchant. Out of my way."

Henry rolled down his window and joined in the haranguing. "Road hog! Move along now."

Indy was pensive. He knew that once Donovan and his gang of Nazis were certain they were on the right trail to the Grail Cup, Marcus's life would be worthless. "Can we catch them?"

Sallah gave Indy a knowing smile. "There are always short-cuts."

He leaned on the horn, shaking his head and cursing in three languages. He turned to Indy. "You'll see."

EIGHTEEN
Confrontations

MARCUS BRODY pushed his head up through the hatch of the World War I tank and peered into the blazing sun. He wiped his forehead with his handkerchief and muttered, "Nazi mad dogs."

They were moving through a desert canyon that looked just like the last one. To Brody, who thrived in urban environs, it was the end of the world—barren, harsh, ugly, and relentlessly hot. The irony didn't escape him: there was a good chance that this ghastly, forsaken land would be the end of *his* world.

"Care to wet your whistle, Marcus?"

Brody turned at the sound of Donovan's voice. An open-topped car trailed the tank. Seated with Donovan was Elsa Schneider, the betrayer, and a Nazi whom Elsa had called Colonel Vogel. Behind the car was the remainder of the caravan—camels bearing soldiers from the sultan's private army, each of whom was armed with a saber and carbine and garbed in billowy desert dress; spare horses; a supply truck, a German sedan, a jeep; and a couple of troop carrier trucks packed with Nazi soldiers.

Donovan thrust the canteen at him and grinned. Brody felt like spitting in his face rather than accepting his offer. But since he didn't have any spit, he caught the canteen when Donovan tossed it up to him, and took a swallow. They had stopped briefly at an oasis a couple of hours ago, but he was already parched. The sun had turned the inside of the tank into an oven, and up on top it was like a broiler.

The water ran down his throat, and he couldn't remember anything having tasted this good in a long time. He took a breath, turned the canteen to his lips again, and drank deeply.

Donovan held out his hand for the canteen, evidently worried that Brody was going to deplete it. "According to your map, Marcus, we are only three or four miles from the discovery of the greatest artifact in human history."

Brody wiped the back of his hand across his mouth and considered hurling the canteen into the bastard's face. But he knew that would only reduce his chances of surviving even further. Instead, he simply lobbed the canteen to him.

"You're meddling with powers you cannot possibly contemplate, Walter."

Donovan started to say something about power but stopped.

Brody followed his gaze. In the distance, somewhere in the hills, he glimpsed a reflection. He had a good idea what it was, and figured that Donovan did, too.

The sun glinted off the binoculars as Indy spied on the caravan moving across the canyon basin. Sallah and Henry were on either side of him, and the car containing their supplies was parked beside a rock outcropping thirty yards behind them.

"They've got a tank . . . six-pound gun. I see Brody. He looks okay."

Henry shaded his eyes and squinted. "Be careful they don't see you."

"We're well out of range."

At that moment they saw a flash as the tank fired a shell in their direction. Indy dove to the ground and covered his head. The others did the same. The shell whistled past and exploded less than a hundred feet away. Pieces of Sallah's car, destroyed by the direct hit, rained down on them.

Sallah groaned. "That car belonged to my brother-in-law."

"Bull's-eye," Colonel Vogel shouted. "Let's go claim the bodies."

Elsa took the binoculars and looked for herself. Part of her felt like weeping at the possibility that Indy might be dead. But another part felt immensely relieved: if he was dead, her own internal conflict would be over. She could get on with finding the Grail and wouldn't constantly be battling with herself. Ever since she met Indy, she had been on an emotional roller coaster. One moment she hated him, the next moment she didn't want to live without him. If he was dead, so be it.

The Grail, she reminded herself, was her true passion. Men and politics were simply means to another end. She would go along with Donovan, but only to a point. She needed Donovan to get her to the Grail, but somehow she had to get the cup away from him. The promises the cup held were too wondrous to pass up. It would be hers, or she would die trying to get it.

When they arrived at the spot where the car blew up, Elsa saw that there were no bodies. Oddly, she felt better. Indy was alive.

As Vogel hurriedly organized the soldiers to begin a search, Donovan walked over to her. "Well, maybe it wasn't even Jones."

"No. It's him, all right. He's here." She looked around, feeling that they were being watched. "Somewhere. I'm sure of it."

Donovan must have felt it, too. He looked around anxiously, then told one of the soldiers to put Brody in the tank. He turned back to Elsa. "In this heat, without transportation, they're as good as dead."

Suddenly, a bullet ricocheted off a nearby rock, and the crack of gunfire filled the air. Donovan ran for cover, forgetting about Elsa. She scrambled after him, angered more by the possibility that Indy might be firing at her than by the fact that Donovan had only been concerned about saving his own neck.

"It's Jones," Donovan yelled. "He's got guns."

Indy was hiding behind a massive rock when the gunfire began. He saw Elsa and Donovan rush to cover and the soldiers return the fire.

He exchanged puzzled looks with his father and Sallah. Who could be firing on them?

"C'mon. Let's take a look," Indy said.

They climbed down from their hiding place and, after a couple of minutes, reached a rock overlooking a chaotic scene, as Nazis and the sultan's soldiers exchanged gunfire with an unseen enemy positioned in caves on the canyon wall. Sallah gazed through a pair of binoculars, then passed them to Indy.

One of the figures emerged from the shadowy mouth of a cave, and Indy saw the man had a symbol on his shirt, a cross that tapered down like the blades of a broadsword. The man stepped boldly into the open, defying death. Indy focused on his face and recognized him. It was Kazim.

So the brotherhood of the Cruciform Sword was more than just one man's fanatic enterprise.

Indy handed the binoculars back to Sallah, then conferred with Henry. The three men agreed on a plan, and Henry moved off toward the tank where Brody was being held. Indy and Sallah, meanwhile, crawled down to the outskirts of Donovan's hastily made encampment.

From their position they could see the horses, and Indy picked out the one he wanted. They waited for the right moment to race across the open span.

"Look," Sallah said, pointing toward the canyon wall.

Kazim was climbing down the rocky face and firing as he ran from boulder to boulder.

"Now," Indy said, and signaled Sallah.

They were halfway between the rocks and the horses when one of the Nazi soldiers who had been firing at the caves turned away to reload his weapon. He spotted them and was about to alert the others when Kazim rushed forward and fired, killing the soldier. Kazim spun wildly around, firing like a madman until he was cut down at close range by a hail of bullets.

Indy and Sallah ducked down among the horses as Donovan rushed over to Kazim. He was standing just a dozen feet away from them.

"Who are you?" he demanded as Kazim lay bleeding.

"A messenger from God. For the unrighteous, the Cup of Life holds everlasting damnation."

Those were Kazim's last words.

Abruptly more shots rang out from the caves, and Donovan darted for cover as bullets kicked up dust within feet of him.

Indy and Sallah slipped onto the backs of two of the horses and rode off undetected amid the gunfire.

Brody was sweltering in the tank. He had been left alone and was searching for a spare key. He wasn't sure he would be able to figure out how to operate the tank, but he knew he needed the key before he was going to get anywhere. He heard the hatch open and quickly moved away from the front of the tank.

"Marcus."

The voice was familiar. He looked up at the hatch in surprise, and before he could respond, Henry dropped down feet-first next to him.

He grinned at Brody and recited an old University Club toast: "Genius of the Restoration . . ."

". . . aid our own resuscitation!" Brody finished.

They threw their arms around each other. "Hope you don't mind my dropping in this way, unexpected and all," Henry said, and laughed.

"Not at all. Glad to see you alive, old boy. What are you doing here?"

"It's a rescue mission, my good man. You thought I was coming for tea, or what?"

"You're a little late for that."

Suddenly a Nazi dropped through the hatch and aimed his Luger at the two men. Two more Nazis joined him, followed by Vogel.

"Search him," the colonel ordered.

One of the Nazis frisked Henry, but found neither weapons nor the Grail diary. Vogel was infuriated. He slapped Henry across the face.

"What is in the book? That miserable little book of yours."

When Henry didn't reply, Vogel's hand slammed across his face again. "We have the map. Your book is useless. And yet you went all the way back to Berlin to get it. Tell me why, Dr. Jones."

Henry remained mum, and Vogel smacked him across the face a third time. "What are you hiding? What does the diary tell *you* that it doesn't tell us?"

Henry's look burned with loathing. "It tells me that goose-stepping morons like yourself should try reading books instead of burning them."

Vogel slapped him again, much harder this time, and Henry staggered back under the impact.

"They've got your father in the tank," Sallah said, passing Indy the binoculars. "I saw the soldier go after him."

Indy cursed himself. He shouldn't have listened to his father. He should have gone after Brody himself and worried about the horses later. He gazed toward the tank, then turned in the direction of Donovan and the other soldiers. He saw they were still busy fighting the remaining members of Kazim's band.

"Let's get them before it's too late."

"Herr Colonel!"

One of the soldiers, who had moved to the driver's seat of the tank, motioned for Vogel to come to the viewing port.

Vogel looked out and saw Indy and Sallah charging toward the tank on horseback, through a cloud of dust. He turned back to the Nazi who guarded Henry and Brody. "If they move, shoot them both."

He took command of the tank's gun.

"Watch out, Indy. The guns!" Sallah bellowed.

Indy saw the six-pound cannon on the tank revolving and pointing in their direction. He suddenly realized that attacking the tank wasn't such a good idea. He pulled back hard on the reins and headed in a different direction—away from the tank.

Sallah was right behind him, yelling at the top of his lungs. "Smart move, Indy. Horses against a tank are no good. I totally agree."

They zigzagged across the desert as the tank gave chase, firing several rounds at them. Each time, Indy and Sallah emerged from a plume of dust as the rounds missed them.

Indy's head snapped around. The tank was gaining on them. Then he noticed they had company. A small German sedan with two soldiers was heading their way. It was going to take more than two of those guys to stop him. He knew that for a fact.

Just then another shell was fired, barely missing Indy this time. "Damn."

"That was close, Indy," Sallah yelled. "Ride for your life."

Sallah charged ahead, but Indy was starting to get angry. He scowled, glancing back, and this time realized that the gun that was firing on them could only pivot so far. It gave him an idea.

He jerked back on the reins and turned the horse. The tank turned and followed him, but now it was heading on a collision course with the small sedan carrying the two Nazi soldiers. The driver of the sedan tried to avoid the tank, but Vogel didn't see him; he was only concerned with keeping Indy in the sights of his gun.

With an earsplitting screech of metal, the sedan was struck from the side and lodged between the front treads of the tank. Not only was the tank stopped by the collision, but the sedan had blocked the front port and jammed the turret on the six-pound cannon.

Indy, meanwhile, reined in his horse. He leaned down and scooped up an armful of rocks from a wall along a culvert, then urged the horse on. He galloped up to the starboard cannon and jammed several of the rocks down the barrel. Then he steered the horse so that he was directly in front of the gun, close enough to be an easy target.

"I see him." Henry jerked his head up as he heard the side gunner's excited yell.

He knew the Nazi was talking about his son.

"Well, shoot him," Vogel ordered.

"No," Henry yelled, and lunged toward the gunner. But the guard blocked his way and shoved him against the bulkhead. He pointed his Luger between Henry's eyes just as the side gunner aimed the cannon at Indy and fired.

The gun backfired, blowing the breech into the face of the gunner. He stumbled backward, his face ripped apart by the blast. He was dead before he hit the floor.

Smoke poured into the tank. Henry and the others choked and

gasped for air. Vogel stepped over the dead gunner, reached up, and threw open the hatch to let out the smoke.

"Fire the turret gun," he yelled at the driver, taking no chance himself.

Henry grabbed Brody by the arm, and together they crawled on hands and knees until they were underneath the hatch. Henry was about to stand up and climb out when he bumped into the guard, who was also on the floor of the tank. The guard raised his Luger and pressed it against Henry's forehead.

The driver of the sedan was dead upon impact with the tank, but the passenger survived the crash and was attempting to cut his way out through the cloth top. He managed to cut away a flap, and pulled it down. He stuck his head through the hole and stared directly into the barrel of the six-pound cannon.

At that moment the cannon fired, emulsifying everything in its path and blowing bits of the sedan seventy-five yards through the air.

Indy was behind the tank. He had just spotted Sallah galloping toward him when the cannon blasted the sedan. Chunks of the car landed all around Sallah. His horse reared up, and Sallah tumbled off.

He quickly remounted, glanced once toward the tank, and charged off in the opposite direction.

Indy had the feeling he wasn't going to get much more help from Sallah.

Free of the car, the tank trundled ahead.

Vogel took over the turret gun and swiveled it around, looking for Indy. But now the turret would only move in a ninety-degree arc. He was sure Indy was behind the tank, and if the other horse-man joined him, they might try boarding.

If they did, he would shoot Jones's father, right in front of him.

But he needed reinforcements. He grabbed the microphone on the radio and called Donovan. "Forget about those crazies in the hills," he said tersely. "Bring the troops now."

There was a moment of silence, then Donovan barked, "Are you telling me you haven't taken care of Jones, even with that tank?"

Vogel fumed, and spoke between gritted teeth. "Not yet."

He stared out above the turret gun, looking again for Indy. He saw a narrow canyon opening on the port side, and an idea struck him. He smiled to himself and ordered the driver to turn into the canyon.

He clicked on the radio again. "By the time you get here, Jones will be taken care of, as you say."

He turned the turret gun as far as he could, as they entered the canyon. He aimed it at the canyon wall and waited for the right moment. He spotted a rock overhanging the wall and adjusted his aim. He fired a volley directly at it, and suddenly tons of rock tumbled down.

Vogel grinned. That should take care of Jones.

NINETEEN
One Against Many

MOMENTS BEFORE the landslide Indy lagged behind the tank, looking for loose rocks again. His plan was to jam the tank's port gun in the hope that it would backfire as the other had done. This time, when the hatch opened to clear away the smoke, he would overpower Vogel and commandeer the tank. A simple plan, if Vogel fell for it.

But the tank had maneuvered into a narrow canyon, and he couldn't find any sizeable rocks. There were pebbles and there were boulders, most of them half the size of the tank or larger. And that wasn't the only problem. The canyon had also cut him off from Sallah, who had galloped well out of the range of the tank's big gun. Now Sallah probably wouldn't know what had happened to him or the tank.

He concentrated on the ground. Rocks. I need rocks.

Just then, the cannon fired into the cliff, and suddenly more rocks than he cared to think about were careening toward him. He reined the horse sharply, turning, and galloped away from the landslide. Rocks bounded by on either side of him, barely missing him. But he escaped unharmed.

If he had been keeping pace with the tank, he wouldn't have been so lucky—he would be dead. No doubt about that.

But now he had another problem. The route through the narrow canyon was cut off. He would have to backtrack and go around the canyon to find the tank, and that would take precious time, maybe hours.

He didn't have hours.

Then he saw an alternative route. The landslide had worked to his advantage, creating a rugged trail along the side of the cliff. Time to take the high road.

He followed it as quickly as he could, maneuvering the horse around the rubble. He found that it not only allowed him to cross the canyon but it was also a shortcut. Before long he was nearing the tank, approaching it from above. He passed it and was wondering how he could work his way down to the canyon base when, unexpectedly, his luck ran out. The trail abruptly ended in a rock wall.

He glanced down as the tank motored along below him. He would have to turn around, or . . . He dropped from his saddle and, before he had time to change his mind, ran to the cliff's edge and leapt. He landed on his feet on top of the tank, and dropped to his hands and knees. He made it—but now what?

The tank cleared the canyon, and the desert opened again to the right. Indy glanced back and saw a cloud of dust on the desert floor. He squinted against the bright light. A jeep was rapidly approaching. Behind it, in the distance, were two carrier trucks filled with Nazi troops.

Company was arriving.

"Welcome aboard, Jones."

He turned and saw Vogel's face peering through the hatchway. His beady eyes speared Indy like darts. He stared back at him and held his gaze. He felt waves of hate from the man but refused to look away, to let him win the contest of wills.

Suddenly he felt a familiar prickling sensation on the back of his neck—a warning. He spun around and saw a soldier crawling behind him. He realized Vogel had been trying to distract him while the soldier boarded from the jeep. The man leapt like a spider and overpowered him, pinning him to the top of the tank.

He struggled to free himself, but his cheek was pressed against the hot metal. The position gave him a chance to see one of the troop carriers moving alongside the tank. A handful of soldiers vaulted aboard like pirates stealing their way onto a galleon. The odds were not looking good.

Indy shoved the soldier and grappled with him for his Luger. They rolled over, and Indy pinned him to the tank with the Luger wedged between them. He twisted the soldier's hand, trying to loosen his grip on the gun. They rolled over again, and the barrel of the gun neared Indy's head. He used the leverage of the tank and forced the gun away until it was turned toward the soldier.

He squeezed with all his strength, forcing the soldier to fire a round into himself. The bullet passed through the man's neck and continued through the stomach of another soldier and the groin of a third. The three bodies fell away, tumbling over the side of the crowded tank.

Three down, plenty more to go. He saw that Vogel had emerged from the hatch to join the huddle of Nazis surrounding him.

"That's my boy. Go get 'em, son."

Indy heard his father's voice, then spotted him looking up through the open hatch. He reached for the bullwhip on his hip, but realized it was too crowded to use it. The lack of space, however, was his one advantage. The soldiers came at him from all sides, wielding knives and guns, but he was an elusive target. He dodged the blade of a knife, which missed his side and slammed into the thigh of another Nazi. A blow struck him in the jaw, and he spun around and kicked a gun out of the hand of a second Nazi, who fell off the tank. A third soldier fired at him, missed, and hit one of his own men. A few more down.

"Go get 'em, Junior," Henry yelled.

Suddenly, Indy literally saw red. He seethed, his anger spurted through him like a shot of adrenaline, and he slammed his fist into the jaw of the nearest soldier. The man fell back into another soldier, and they both tumbled off the tank. Indy kicked at the next one, who fell onto the tank's tread and took one more with him. The two rolled forward, hit the ground, and were instantly crushed by the tread.

Indy, still infuriated, looked at the hatch. "Don't ever call me Junior again!"

No sooner had he spoken the words than Vogel swung a length of chain and snapped it twice around Indy's shoulders. A white hot pain burned through him; he crumpled to his knees, grimacing in agony. Still, he managed to keep his wits about him. He saw the Luger the first soldier left behind and kicked it toward the hatch. It was a shot that would have pleased a soccer champion. The gun skittered across the tank and fell right into Henry's lap.

Indy rose to his feet and faced Vogel and the one remaining soldier. The chain was still wrapped around his shoulders but he could move his arms, and neither of his opponents was armed. He smiled gamely at Vogel. After overcoming all the others, he was confident he could handle these two.

But Vogel smiled back, and then Indy saw the reason for his cockiness. A second troop carrier was about to pull alongside the tank with a host of reinforcements. More men than he could handle. Hell, more men than a half dozen of him could fight.

When the gun fell into his lap, Henry grabbed it by the barrel, just in time. Brody yelled for him to watch out. He heard a thud as his friend was knocked to the floor. The guard wrapped his arms around Henry's waist and pulled him down from the hatch.

"Let go of me," he yelled.

When he didn't, Henry acted decisively. "Fair warning, fellow."

He clubbed him over the head with the butt of the gun, and the guard dropped to the floor next to Brody. Henry climbed to the top of the hatch, and was about to join Indy when he saw the troop carrier. There was no way they could overcome that horde of Nazis. They needed help, and lots of it.

He ducked back inside and ran over to the port turret just as the guard stumbled to his feet. Henry aimed the cannon at the troop-laden truck and fumbled for the trigger. Just as he found it, the guard jerked his arm away and dragged him away from the turret.

Brody crawled over on his hands and knees, and the guard tripped over him. Henry slipped out of his grasp and lunged toward the turret. He quickly aimed at the troop carrier, and squeezed off a round.

Beginner's luck was with him: he scored a direct hit on the gas tank, and the carrier exploded, spewing soldiers and debris through the scorched air.

The blast blew Indy, Vogel, and the last soldier off the top of the tank. The soldier fell to the ground, but Indy and Vogel landed on the moving tread. Both were shuttled quickly forward and were inches from being crushed under the tank when they rolled onto the cannon mounting.

Vogel's feet slammed into Indy, forcing him off the narrow ledge of metal and back onto the tread. Indy latched a hand onto the cannon, then wrapped his other arm around it. His feet dangled over the edge of the tread as he fought to keep from falling.

Vogel, meanwhile, crawled forward, and kicked at Indy's hands.

Inside the tank the guard picked Brody up and hurled him viciously against the bulkhead, smashing his head into it. He slumped to the floor, lingering on the edge of consciousness, fighting the blackness that crept up on him like a nightmare. Vaguely he was aware that the guard was aiming his Luger at him. He closed his eyes, not wanting to see any more. He waited for the explosion, and death.

Henry jumped the guard, knocking his arm aside. The weapon fired, and the bullet ricocheted several times. Suddenly the tank veered out of control as the driver pitched forward into the gears, struck dead by the bullet.

Henry fought. He gasped for breath. The guard's powerful arm was wrapped around his neck, and he was squeezing. Both of Henry's hands gripped the guard's other arm, keeping the gun from turning toward him. Desperately he tried to stay conscious. If he passed out, he was dead.

Brody was jarred awake as the tank bounced over a large rock. He felt as if he had been raised from the dead. His body ached fiercely in a dozen places, and his head throbbed as though a spear were piercing it. But he pushed himself to his feet despite the pain and saw Henry struggling with the guard. Brody kicked the guard's hand, and the gun skidded across the floor.

The tank bounded over another rock, and Brody fell to the floor. "Who's driving this thing, anyhow?" he muttered.

Henry reached into his pocket the moment Brody kicked the gun away. His fingers were inside the pocket, moving, searching, groping for a fountain pen. His other arm clung to the guard, who was now trying to get away and retrieve the Luger. He pulled out the fountain pen and stabbed the guard again and again, but the man didn't seem to feel it. He finally managed to get the top off, raised his arm, and squeezed. A burst of ink shot into the guard's eyes.

The man bellowed, staggered back, clawing at his eyes. Henry gulped for air, filling his lungs, then smashed his fist into the stunned guard's face. The man's head jerked back and cracked against the bulkhead. He pitched forward and was out cold.

"The pen *is* mightier than the sword," Henry crowed, and helped Brody to his feet. This nonsense was a damn long way from the study of ancient languages and antiquities. But now the adrenaline was pumping through him.

They climbed through the hatch and onto the top of the tank. Neither Indy nor the soldiers were in sight. Then Henry peered over the side of the tank. Vogel and his son were locked in a deadly embrace on the cannon mount, and both were now fettered by Vogel's chain.

And Indy's head was only inches above the tread.

Henry carefully lowered himself over the side of the tank, determined to help his son in a way he had never dreamed possible. He would make up for his shortcomings as a father, all right. And when this was over, he would stand in front of Indy and spell out those shortcomings, just as he should have done years ago.

I'm a stiff ole coot whose stubborn ways never did him any good. That's what he'd tell him, he thought. It was time at long last to admit to it.

Sallah had galloped away from the tank after he had nearly been killed by the parts of the demolished car. A horse was no challenge to a tank, he had told himself over and over. But where was Indy? The tank and Indy had disappeared. Sallah backtracked and found the narrow canyon but was baffled when he came to the landslide. Fearing that Indy had been trapped in the rubble, he searched the rocks.

Finally, certain that Indy wasn't in the rubble, he had backtracked again and spotted the tank in the distance. As he neared it, he knew something was wrong. The tank was speeding directly for a gorge less than two hundred yards away, and he didn't see Indy. He spurred his horse and tore toward the tank. As he galloped alongside it, he spotted Brody clinging to the top. *"Jump!"* he shouted. *"Jump, man!"*

Brody heard Sallah yelling. He snapped his head around and saw the gorge for the first time. He slid down to the cannon mounting on the side where Sallah was galloping.

"Jump, I said!" Sallah roared.

He figured he was going to die, but leapt anyhow. He grabbed Sallah's neck as he landed half on the horse, half off. Sallah reached back, pulled his ankle over the horse.

"Hang on, Marcus."

"The other side," Brody yelled. "They're on the other side."

Indy and Vogel were still tangled in the chain, at an impasse. If one threw the other from the tank, they would both go over the side.

Then Indy saw the gorge barely a hundred yards away. *Who the hell is driving the tank?*

He fought to rip the chain from around his chest just as Vogel, who had also seen the cliff, tried to jump. But to Indy's surprise, his father appeared from nowhere and grabbed Vogel by the leg.

Vogel spun and jerked his leg away, then kicked Henry in the face, knocking him onto the tank's tread. Indy saw his father rolling toward the front of the tank and reacted instantly. He unhitched his whip and snapped it toward his father. The whip coiled neatly around Henry's ankle just as he was about to roll over the front of the tank.

Indy reeled in the whip with every bit of strength he had left, and Henry bounced back along the tread, a huge fish hooked on the end of a line.

Sallah drew his horse up next to the tread. "Indy, hurry. Get off the tank."

Indy glanced over at him. "Here. Give me a hand." He passed him the whip.

Sallah snatched it, reined back on the horse, leaned away from the tank.

Henry tumbled off the tread and rolled in the dirt. Sallah was about to dismount to help him, when he looked up to see Indy and Vogel racing to the rear of the tank. They were tangled in a chain, and both leapt at the same time. They would have made it, too. But one end of the chain hooked on the superstructure of the tank and both men were dragged toward the cliff.

"Oh, no. Indy," Sallah shouted.

In a final act of desperation, Indy struggled to slip out of the chain as he was dragged across the ground. But now the chain was caught on his leg. He ripped open his pants, and pushed them down over his hips and then his knees. He was like a stage magician performing a sensational death-defying escape trick. But it wasn't a trick, at least not one *he* had ever performed.

Next to him Vogel screamed in despair as he fought the chain.

Indy's pants were almost off when the tank hit the edge of the cliff and plummeted over the side, plunging toward the deep gorge.

In the distance Elsa saw a plume of black smoke rising from the gorge. She lowered the binoculars and ordered the driver to start the engine of her sedan.

"The tank is finished," she said to Donovan. "All of them are finished."

"What about Vogel?"

"What about him, Herr Donovan?" Her voice was terse and utterly cold. She had shed her emotional concerns, stripped herself of them. The point was the Grail. She couldn't expect Indy to be alive, and what if he was? What would it change?

Nothing.

Donovan nodded and joined Elsa in the car. "I guess it's destined that you and I would find the Grail Cup together."

Elsa remained silent, staring ahead, watching the heat ripple across the desert floor. *Dead. Indy's dead. Nothing matters but the Grail.*

"Make sure the supply truck and the others are ready," she said at last. "We've got work to do."

Henry stared down at the flaming wreckage of the tank, fighting a wave of emotion that threatened to drown him. He was cut, bruised, battered. But that didn't matter. He had lost his only son, lost him before he had ever had a chance to put things right, to make up for the years of misunderstandings.

"I have to go after him," Sallah said. "He's my friend." He started to charge toward the cliff, but Brody grabbed his arm, restraining him.

"It's no use, Sallah."

The big man pulled himself away from Brody, then sank to his knees and buried his face in his hands. Henry looked from Sallah to Brody, not knowing what to say, barely able to place his own grief in any sort of perspective, much less anyone else's.

Brody tried to comfort him. He slipped an arm around Henry's shoulder, offering his condolences. Henry's eyes burned with tears. Dust swelled around them. The hot sun beat down.

I never even hugged him, Henry thought miserably. *I never told him I loved him.*

Dazed and bewildered, Indy staggered from behind a cluster of rocks. He was carrying his pants, which had been slit from the waist to the ankles. Remnants of the pants were gathered around his boots.

He joined the others and gazed over the cliff at the wreckage. One by one they became aware of his presence. First Brody, then Sallah, then Henry.

Indy shook his head and whistled softly. "Now *that* was close."

"*Junior!*" Henry shouted, and threw his arms around Indy, hugging him hard. "I thought I'd lost you," he said over and over again and babbled on about love.

It took a moment for Indy's head to clear enough for him to realize his father was embracing him, telling him he loved him. It was something he hadn't heard in a long time. In fact, he couldn't recall ever hearing it, or his father ever embracing him.

He hugged him back, hugged fiercely, a young boy swept up in a blind love for his father. "I thought I'd lost you, too," he whispered.

Brody was moved by the sudden reconciliation, but Sallah was obviously confused.

"Junior? You are Junior?"

Indy made a face. He was in no mood to talk about *that* topic. He stepped back and did his best to improvise a way of putting on his pants.

Henry answered Sallah's question. "That's his name. Henry Jones, Jr."

"I like Indiana," Indy said resolutely.

"We named the *dog* Indiana!" Henry countered. "We named *you* Henry, Jr."

Brody smiled, and Sallah laughed.

"The dog?" Sallah exclaimed.

Even Indy couldn't resist a grin. "I got a lot of fond memories about that dog."

Sallah laughed even louder and slapped Indy on the back, causing his pants to drop around his ankles.

TWENTY

Grail Trail

THE MIDAFTERNOON sun was scorching the barren rocks around them. Elsa closed her eyes a moment, calming the anger she felt. She was doing her best to ignore the heat, but Donovan was another matter. She had dealt with her share of arrogant, overbearing men who preferred treating her like a piece of jewelry instead of a scientist, but Donovan was the worst. Even the Führer, for all his eccentricities, at least recognized her intellectual capabilities.

"It should be right here," Elsa said, pointing at the wall of rock in front of her.

"Nothing's there," Donovan replied in a flat, condescending tone.

"I've checked and rechecked the landmarks, Walter," she said evenly. "If the map is accurate, the hidden canyon is directly behind that wall. And that is where we'll find it."

Donovan shrugged. "We've already tried every possible route. There's no entrance. It's solid rock."

For someone who was as conniving as he was, Donovan wasn't

much help when it came to practical matters. He would be better off allowing someone else to find the Grail Cup, and then stealing it, she thought.

"Then, I suppose we make our own entrance."

"How do you propose to do that?"

"I guess you've never worked with explosives."

He regarded her a moment with an icy stare that even the desert heat couldn't counteract. "I don't suppose that I have."

Not surprising. She turned and walked back to the supply truck. She felt his eyes on the back of her head. Let him worry, she thought. She would lead him to the Grail, then she would watch, and at the right moment, she would act. The Grail would be hers, or she would die. Period.

Indy, like his three companions, was wearing a hat draped in white cloth and trying to get used to the way his camel moved. It was nothing like riding a horse or even an elephant. This was something completely unique—a steep dip, a rise, another dip, another rise, but the camel's lope never felt quite even. He couldn't grasp the rhythm and suspected you had to be born into a nomadic desert life to ever feel comfortable on one of these creatures.

The white cloth and his hat helped some against the relentless heat, but they didn't assuage his thirst. He thought of water, bottles of it, rivers of it, cool and endless. He thought of sliding into a pool, soaking his feet in cool, wet mud.

Sallah had recovered Indy's horse, and the four of them had backtracked—two to a horse—to where they had last seen Donovan's caravan. There had been no sign of either Donovan or Elsa. But they had found tire tracks, several abandoned camels, and even a couple of canteens of water.

Indy had urged his father and Brody to stay behind and wait while he and Sallah pursued Donovan on horseback. But neither would listen to him. Both insisted they were okay, and could continue on. They could all go on the camels, Henry had said.

They rested only a short time, attending to their cuts and bruises and discomforts. Indy had found a pair of pants among some of the supplies left behind, and they fashioned their headwear. Finally, they climbed onto the camels, and set off across the desert.

Without the map they would never be able to locate the place where the Grail Cup was hidden, Indy thought. But the route was clearly marked by the tracks left behind by the remaining vehicles of the caravan. Indy guessed that Donovan and Elsa believed he and his group were dead, because otherwise they wouldn't have been so careless about leaving a trail. So let them believe it. It might prove to be his group's only advantage.

A distant explosion resounded through the pass, snapping Indy to attention.

"What was that?" Brody asked.

"The secret canyon," Henry exclaimed. "They've found it."

Indy recalled the words from the Grail tablet. *Across the desert and through the mountain to the Canyon of the Crescent Moon, broad enough only for one man. To the Temple of the Sun, holy enough for all men.*

He urged his camel to pick up the pace. "Let's keep moving."

When they arrived at the site of the explosion, rocks were strewn about, and a gaping hole in the cliff led into a narrow canyon. Its walls were high and steep, the color of ocher.

Indy passed his canteen around. They were all weary, hot, and sore, but they knew they couldn't waste any time. Henry, who had taken off his jacket, led the way into the canyon. His shirt was open at the collar, and his hat was pulled low over his eyes. He didn't look like a medieval scholar now, Indy mused. If anything, his father looked like an aging adventurer who was secretly having the time of his life as he valiantly sought to fulfill his greatest desire.

As Henry entered the canyon, his camel stopped, snorted, and tried to back away. He cursed the beast, slapped it on the rear with his hand, and finally convinced it to move ahead.

They all experienced similar resistance from their camels as they followed single file behind Henry. Brody's animal was the most stubborn, and Indy finally was forced to dismount and pull it through. Once inside the canyon, the animals calmed down. It was the humans who felt wary, out of their element.

The farther they progressed, the narrower and steeper the walls became. The place was eerie, too still, too tight, too hot. The camels' hooves echoed, and the sound of them, Indy thought, had a strange quality, although he couldn't have said exactly what.

The air was more refined, as if they were at a higher elevation. Indy was light-headed and felt the dull throb of a headache. The light was different here, too, less harsh, gold against the stark canyon walls on either side of them.

He didn't like being here, he didn't like the feel of the place. None of them did—except for Henry. He was the optimist of the group, and why not: the project that had dominated his life was near fruition. The Grail wasn't in his hands yet, but it was close enough for him to imagine that it was. He actually seemed to be enjoying himself.

"Marcus," Henry said, "we're like the four heroes of the Grail legend. You're Percival, the holy innocent. Sallah is Bors, the ordinary man. My son is Galahad, the valiant knight. And his father . . . the old crusader, Lancelot, who was turned away because he was unworthy, as perhaps I am."

"I'm an old sot who'd rather be home safely with a nip of Scotch at hand," Brody replied. He was clinging to his saddle for support and glancing around, uncertainty etched in every line of his face. His fretting expression, Indy thought.

But Henry didn't seem to hear him. He nodded to himself,

musing over his comparisons. Then he turned to Indy. "But remember, it was Galahad who succeeded where his father failed."

Terrific, Indy thought. It was just the sort of responsibility he didn't want. "I don't even know what the Grail looks like, Dad."

"Nobody does," Henry replied. "The one who is worthy will know the Grail."

Like King Arthur and Excalibur. As if this was all some sort of glorious quest, not a dangerous predicament. It annoyed him. In his father's mind, they had been elevated to the ranks of crusaders.

While Henry gazed ahead expectantly, Indy looked down at the dirt. They no longer needed the tracks of the vehicles, but the fact that they were there, inches inside either wall, kept him cognizant of the fact that they weren't alone.

"Look!" Sallah burst out, and pointed.

They stopped and stared. The narrow canyon led into a broad, open area like an arena, and carved into one of the rocks on the far side was a spectacular Greco-Roman facade. Wide steps led up to a landing with massive columns, and beyond them was the entrance to a darkened chamber. The Temple of the Sun, Indy thought.

"Let's go," Henry said eagerly.

The camels complained again, but the men spurred them on, and they grudgingly trotted ahead, crossing the open area and stopping in front of the temple steps. Indy stole a glance at his father: his expression was rapturous, struck with a childlike wonder. Even Indy was awed by the sight, but not as his father was. Henry's elation swept out of him in waves, like an odor. It was infectious.

"Monumental," Brody uttered.

"Built by the gods," Sallah mumbled.

Indy understood. In the presence of a structure of such grand scale, it was easy to think that it had been built for immortals twice their human size and strength.

For a long time none of them moved from the bottom of the steps. The temple had *that* sort of magic about it. But Indy finally broke the spell. He looked down at the ground again and saw the tracks crisscrossing behind them. So what had happened to the vehicles?

He squinted to the west, where the sun hovered low over the wall of the arena. Among the shadows he made out the shape of a troop carrier, a supply truck, an auto, and several horses.

He motioned toward the temple. "Come on. Let's take a look. But keep quiet."

He led the way, followed by Henry, Sallah, and Brody. Slowly they ascended the steps toward the dark entrance. As they reached the top, Indy glanced back, making sure the others were still behind him. Then he pressed on into the temple.

It took his eyes a moment to adjust to the darkness. But then he saw someone standing directly in front of him—a knight dressed in armor, a magnificent Herculean figure that was two, no, three times, his size.

Indy stopped, stepped back, then smiled as he grasped the obvious. The knight was carved from an enormous block of stone.

The interior of the temple was ringed with exact copies of the stone sentinel, and beyond them was a ring of massive pillars. Indy relaxed and pointed at the knights. Then he heard something, a sound within the temple, and his senses instantly snapped to attention. His muscles tensed; he twitched nervously. In his fascination with the temple, he had momentarily forgotten that Donovan and Elsa were somewhere ahead of them.

He motioned for the others to follow and to remain as silent as possible. They slipped from one pillar to the next until they were close enough to see what was taking place in the center of the temple.

A soldier from the sultan's force, armed with a sword, cautiously climbed a set of stone stairs toward an arched opening in the back wall of the temple. Standing at the base of the steps, watching the soldier, were Donovan and Elsa. Behind them were several Nazis and more of the sultan's soldiers.

Elsa: Indy watched her. He noticed how she concentrated intensely on the soldier's progress.

She probably assumed Indy was dead. He was just another man from her past. Disposed of, forgotten. Despite everything she had said, it was obvious that her love affair was with the Grail, with its history and legends. Men were simply means of achieving her goal.

It didn't add up. There was something more, there had to be. It was something he wasn't seeing. Then he realized that perhaps it was simpler than it appeared. Maybe she believed the legends. Maybe she had convinced herself that the cup was actually a source of immortality.

And what about Donovan? He had discussed the myth with Indy. Did he actually believe it? He must. After all, he hardly needed to endanger his life to obtain another artifact. Sure, he was working with Elsa, but he wasn't about to let her claim the cup. Indy was sure of that.

He looked up at the soldier, who was nearing the top of the steps under the arch, and then saw something else. A body. A few steps away from the man was another of the sultan's soldiers, and near the sprawled corpse was something else. Indy leaned forward, trying to make it out.

Oh, God.

It was the soldier's head.

"Keep going," Donovan urged the soldier. "Keep going. You're almost there."

Elsa shook her head. "It's not possible."

The soldier stopped a step away from the body.

"Keep going," Donovan yelled.

The man took the next step under the arch, and it was his last. A loud whooshing sound like a sudden gust of wind swept through the temple, and suddenly the soldier's head was cleanly severed from his neck. It tumbled toward the steps, bounced down, and rolled toward Donovan and Elsa.

Donovan motioned to one of the other soldiers, who ran over

and picked up the head. He turned and tossed it in the direction where Indy and the others were hiding. The head rolled within several feet of them. The mouth gaped open; an expression of horror was frozen on its features.

Indy looked away.

"The Breath of God," Henry said softly.

At first Indy wasn't sure what he meant. Then he remembered the three challenges from his father's Grail diary. The Breath of God . . . What where the other two? He couldn't think clearly now. He touched his pocket, where he kept the diary. It was still there. He would need it to reach the Grail. But right now he needed to find a way to get past Donovan and his entourage.

Then he heard Donovan order one of his Nazi guards to get another of the sultan's soldiers.

"Helmut, another volunteer."

The Nazi pointed to one of the soldiers, but the man shook his head and backed away. Two of the Nazis grabbed the soldier and dragged him forward.

"No-no-no!" he shouted, struggling to free himself.

They shoved him, and he stumbled up the first couple of steps. He turned; his eyes were globes of terror. The Nazi guard named Helmut pulled out his Luger and aimed it at the soldier.

Reluctantly he turned and started the deadly climb to the top.

Out of the corner of his eye, Indy saw Brody look away in disgust, unwilling to watch another decapitation. He didn't care to see the slaughter any more than Brody did. He felt like a spectator in a Roman coliseum, but he didn't know what else they could do. They needed a plan of attack, but . . .

Brody tapped him on the shoulder. "Uh, Indy."

The lines on Brody's face were so deep, they looked like shadows. Indy touched a finger to his lip, but then he saw what Brody had seen. A few feet away a Nazi soldier held his revolver on them.

"*Raus! Raus!*" he yelled, gesturing frantically with his gun, indicating that they should move.

Just then three more Nazis surrounded them, each with a rifle. Indy realized they had probably been hiding near the entrance and had been watching them since they walked into the temple. The Nazi with the pistol searched them for weapons and confiscated the guns Indy and Sallah were carrying.

They were pushed forward into full view of the others, their hands raised above their heads. The sultan's soldiers swung around and fixed their rifles on them. Indy saw Elsa spin on her heels, gaping at him. Her mouth seemed to quiver slightly. Donovan walked toward them, hiding his surprise behind a broad smile. He made it appear as if old friends had just arrived in town, guests for dinner, and he was the host.

"Ah, the Jones boys . . . and not a moment too soon. Welcome, welcome. We can use your expertise. I'm so happy you're still alive."

"You'll never get the Grail," Henry exploded. "It's beyond your understanding and capabilities."

"Don't be so sure about that, Dr. Jones." Donovan spoke between gritted teeth. "You're not the only expert on the Grail in the world."

He motioned the Nazi guards to take them to the steps. They were shoved forward and lined up opposite the sultan's soldiers. Targets in a shooting gallery, Indy thought.

Elsa stepped out from behind the soldiers and walked over to Indy. "I never expected to see you again."

"I'm like a bad penny. I keep showing up."

Donovan laid a hand on Elsa's shoulder. "Step back now, Dr. Schneider." His tone was disdainful, as if he questioned her loyalty. "Give Indiana some room."

Elsa ignored him a moment, holding her ground. She stared at Indy as if she didn't really believe she was standing in front of him.

Indy looked away. It was no time to renew old acquaintances, especially with her.

"Dr. Jones is going to recover the Grail for us," Donovan said.

Indy glanced in the direction of the decapitated bodies and laughed. The third soldier had stopped halfway up the steps and was slowly working his way down, acting as if no one saw him.

"You think it's funny. Here's your chance to go down in history if you are successful. What do you say, Indiana Jones?"

"Go down in history as what, Donovan, a Nazi stooge like you?"

Donovan regarded him for a moment, and Indy couldn't tell if he was angry or amused. Then Donovan smiled and shook his head, as though Indy were a child who had said something stupid. "The Nazis," he spat. "That's the limit of your vision?"

Indy didn't bother to answer him.

"The Nazis want to write themselves into the Grail legend and take on the world," Donovan continued. "They're welcome. Dr. Schneider and I want the Grail itself, the cup that gives everlasting life. Hitler can have the world, but he can't take it with him."

He moved closer to Indy, jutting out his square jaw. "I'm going to be drinking to my own health when he's gone the way of the dodo."

He pulled a pistol from his pocket and aimed it between Indy's eyes. He took a step backward. "The Grail is mine, and you're going to get it for me."

Indy grinned, feigning indifference. "Aren't you forgetting about Dr. Schneider?"

Donovan smiled. "She comes with the Grail. Too bad for you."

Indy's eyes strayed to Elsa, who was standing a few steps behind Donovan. Her face was a mask—lovely, soft, a riddle.

Donovan cocked the pistol. "Move."

Indy pointed at the gun. "Shooting me won't get you anywhere."

Donovan knew he was right. For a moment he didn't answer. Then his eyes slid to Henry and back again to Indy, and a slow smile spread across his face. "You know something, Dr. Jones? I totally agree with you. You're absolutely right."

He turned to Henry, aimed the gun at him.

"No!" Elsa and Indy yelled simultaneously.

But Donovan fired, hitting him in the stomach at point-blank range.

Henry's hands covered his stomach. He stumbled, and turned toward Indy.

"Dad!"

Elsa ran forward. Donovan caught her and shoved her back. "Stay out of this."

Henry collapsed in his son's arms. Brody and Sallah rushed over as Indy gently lowered him to the ground. Sallah cradled Henry's head, and Brody knelt down next to him.

Indy ripped open his father's shirt; the gaping wound nearly made him gag. Brody pushed a handkerchief into Indy's hand, and he pressed it against his father's abdomen. He held it there to slow the bleeding. Then he noticed the bullet had exited through his father's side, where there was more blood. He spoke softly to him, telling him it was going to be all right, really it was, and hoped to God his voice was convincing.

"Get up, Jones," Donovan snapped.

Indy whipped his head around, hate filling his eyes, and leapt to his feet as Brody cradled Henry. He was about to go for Donovan's throat, then hesitated when Donovan cocked his weapon.

"You can't save him if you're dead," Donovan said, training the gun on Indy's heart. "The healing power of the Grail is the only thing that can save your father now." He paused a moment. "Do you doubt me? It's time to ask yourself what to believe."

Henry groaned and coughed.

"Indy," Sallah called out. "He's not good."

He turned and knelt next to his father again. Brody whispered that Henry was badly injured. Indy nodded. He knew, he knew, he had eyes.

"The Grail is the only chance he's got," Donovan said, smiling with certainty that Indy would accept the challenge, that Indy did not, in fact, even have a choice.

Indy looked up at Brody. "He's right. The Grail can save him, Indy. I believe it. You must, too."

Under other circumstances Indy might have laughed at the idea. But this was his father, and he was dying. He nodded to Brody, then reached in his pouch for the Grail diary. He was about to stand up, when Henry's hand fell on his wrist.

"Remember . . . the Breath of God."

"I will, Dad. And I'll get the Grail. For you."

TWENTY-ONE

The Three Challenges

INDY CLUTCHED THE GRAIL DIARY and peered warily up the flight of steps. He could see an archway at the top and a dark passage. He drew in a deep breath and slowly climbed toward the two headless bodies.

Halfway up he stopped.

The silence was broken by the sound of cartridges slamming into the chambers of the sultan's soldiers' guns. The sound echoed in the temple. Donovan had told the soldiers to shoot him if he attempted to flee. They were definitely following his orders.

Indy opened the Grail diary and looked down at it. The light was dim and the writing a blur. But he had to find a way past the arch—the Breath of God. His father was lying on the ground, bleeding to death; he had to help him. He had to get the Grail Cup and bring it back as fast as he could.

Rationally he knew no ancient cup could heal a bullet wound, but that didn't matter. He had had enough strange experiences in his life to know that things that weren't supposed to happen sometimes did. Maybe the healing capacity of the Grail Cup could never be proven, could never be repeated in a scientific setting, but he was willing to try. All it had to do was work once, that was all. Just once.

He took two more steps. He could hear his father calling out to him. Indy turned and saw Henry's glazed eyes looking up at him. He listened; his father was muttering the phrase over and over.

"Only the penitent man will pass.

"Only the penitent man will pass.

"Only the penitent man will pass."

Indy repeated it to himself and carefully climbed the remainder of the steps. The corpses were a few feet in front of him. The top steps were soaked with blood.

He took another step toward the arch and then one more. He could see down the passageway beyond the arch. He stopped, sensing that he was only a pace away from being beheaded.

"Penitent . . . Only the penitent man will pass," he whispered. "Only the penitent man will pass. Only the penitent man will pass."

He spoke it like a mantra, a prayer, and each time he said it, he felt himself becoming more and more aware of his surroundings, aware that what he was seeking was not an ordinary artifact, aware that his father's quest was now his quest. He remembered his father's words as they passed through the canyon. It was Galahad who succeeded where his father failed.

He noticed a huge cobweb across the archway just ahead of him. Why hadn't he seen it before? Neither of the men had reached the cobweb. He knew that whatever it was—*The Breath of God*—lay between him and the cobweb.

"Only the penitent man will pass. Penitent . . . penitent. A penitent man."

He started to take a step forward but held his foot in midair, like an oversized bird at rest. Penitent. The penitent man is humble before God. The penitent man kneels before God. Kneel.

He set his foot down and fell to his knees. As he did so, he heard a loud whooshing overhead, and he instinctively tumbled forward. He lay there on his stomach a moment, then slowly rolled over. He peered up, and now he could see it above him—a razor-sharp triple pendulum, and it was still whirring just inches over him. The pendulum was attached to a pair of wooden wheels connected to the inside of the stone arch. It was probably activated by the slightest breath of air created by a person's movement, and stopped after it struck its target.

The pendulum had been there for centuries and still operated perfectly, as if under a spell. This part, at least, he could understand. He knew it would take millennia before anything disintegrated in this desert. He had seen bodies thousands of years old that had been discovered under the desert sands. The skin was still on the bones and the clothing intact, with the threads appearing as if they had only recently been woven.

Indy saw a rope hanging from one of the wheels and worked his way over to the side of the arch. He grabbed the rope and hooked the looped end over one of the spokes in the nearest wheel. Instantly the mechanism ground to a halt, and the blades jammed.

He was through; he had made it. He stood in the archway, the cobweb tangling in his clothing. He signaled to Brody and Sallah that he was okay. He saw Elsa smiling at him. She looked pleased. The longer he survived, the closer she was to the Grail.

"True love," he said softly, his voice riddled with irony.

His eyes met Donovan's for an instant. He rubbed his neck, and turned away.

Brody gently patted Henry's shoulder. "He did it, old boy. Indy made it."

Henry nodded his head, indicating that he understood, but Brody could see the effort it cost him for just this small movement. Then he murmured something under his breath.

Brody looked at Sallah, who still cradled Henry's head. "What did he say?"

Sallah shook his head, worried. "He's out of his mind with the pain and loss of blood."

Henry muttered again, and this time Brody understood a few of the words. "In the Latin alphabet it starts . . ."

"What?" He leaned closer and listened.

". . . with an *I*."

"In the Latin alphabet it starts with an *I*," Brody repeated. "Okay. But what . . ." He shook his head, confused, and conceded that Sallah was right. Henry was delirious.

He looked up toward the passageway, wishing Indy luck. Then he noticed Donovan, followed by Elsa, climbing the steps. "Those wretched schemers. Perfectly abhorrent," he muttered.

Henry suddenly rose up slightly and spoke in a raspy voice. "The Word of God . . . The Word of God . . ."

"No, Henry. Try not to talk," Brody said.

A spasm of pain shot through Henry's body, and Brody feared they were going to lose him.

"The name of God," Henry croaked. He relaxed a bit as the pain eased. "Jehovah," he muttered. "But in the Latin alphabet, Jehovah begins with an *I*."

His body was wracked by another jolt of pain. "Oh, dear," he gasped, sucking in his breath.

Sallah placed a hand on his shoulder and glanced up at the passageway. "It's okay, Henry."

Indy lit a match, held it up to the Grail diary, and translated the phrases from Latin. "The second challenge. The Word of God. Only in the footsteps of God will he proceed."

The match winked out.

Indy stood in the darkness and gazed ahead, wondering what the words meant. When he reached the challenge, he hoped he would recognize it in time to save his life. At least with the first one, with the pendulum, he had had the advantage of two failed attempts ahead of him. With this one he was truly in the dark.

"Only in the footsteps of God will he proceed," he said, memorizing the words. "The Word of God—the Word of God." What could it mean?

He lit another match and read the rest of the section. "Proceed in the footsteps of the word. In the name of God. Jehovah."

He heard a noise and looked back to see Donovan and Elsa. They stood just beyond the entrance to the passageway waiting for him to make his next move.

Parasites, Indy thought.

"Don't stop now, Dr. Jones," Donovan said, derisively. "You've just begun your journey."

Indy reminded himself that the only reason he was here was for his father. It had nothing to do with Donovan. Or with Elsa.

He turned and continued along the passageway until he came to a checkerboard of cobblestones. "Cobbles." He remembered the word from the diary; it was on the page with the diagrams. Pendulum. Cobbles. And something about a bridge.

He lit another match and turned the page of the diary. Now he realized the checkerboard diagram was the cobblestone. He held the match up to get a better look at the pattern of stones. As in the diagram, each one was marked with a letter. "The Word of God. Proceed in the footsteps of the Word of God. Jehovah."

He stepped tentatively on the *J*. Suddenly his foot plunged through a hole, and he almost lost his balance. He steadied himself, pulled his leg out. As he did, he felt something crawling on his ankle. He quickly shook his foot back, then brushed away a fist-sized, hairy black spider. It scrambled down the passage, a plump, hideous thing, and a moment later, Elsa shrieked.

She did better with the rats under the library.

He looked back at the diagram and shook his head in disgust as he realized his mistake. Okay. Wake up. Pay attention. We're not dealing with English. The Latin Jehovah begins with an *I*.

He lit another match and made a quick search of the cobblestones. Then, saying the letters aloud, he jumped across them from stone to stone. As he landed on the *O*, his foot slipped partially onto the stone with the letter *P*. Instantly it dropped down. He wobbled, regained his balance, and stepped across the last two letters. He had made it.

He looked back and saw Elsa and Donovan approaching the cobblestones. He wasn't going to give them any hints, but Elsa had already figured it out from what she had overheard him repeat from the Grail entries, and what she had seen him do on the cobbles.

She smiled at him and stepped ahead as if she were playing hopscotch. "*I-E-H-O-V-A.* Jehovah."

Indy scraped cobwebs from his hat, turned, and walked on. Behind him he heard Donovan yelling for Elsa to go on, to keep Indy in sight, and that he was right behind her.

Sallah knew Henry was slipping fast. He was no longer talking to himself or moving. His breathing was so shallow, it was nearly inaudible.

He felt for a pulse at the side of Henry's neck, then glanced up at Brody and shook his head. "I'm afraid that he's . . ."

"No. He can't die," Brody said. He glanced toward the steps. "I'm going for Indy. He's got to hurry. There's no time to waste."

Sallah watched him run up the steps, thinking that Brody was acting as delirious as Henry. "Father of Indy. Stay with us a little longer. Your son will come soon. Your son will come."

He muttered a prayer to himself as his eyes turned upward to the heavens.

As he finished, he heard a voice. It was Henry. He leaned over, pleased that God had answered his prayer so fast. "Father of Indy. What are you saying?"

"You must believe, boy. . . . You must believe. You have to believe. . . . Believe . . . Have to believe."

Indy stood at the edge of an abyss, holding on to the rock wall for support. The passage had abruptly ended. Across the gulf was a triangular-shaped opening, and on the rock facing above it was a carved lion's head.

"The Path of God."

He glanced up, saw a matching lion's head above him, then looked back at the diary. "Only in the leap from the lion's head will he prove his worth."

He looked down into the abyss, then across to the rock face. No, it was too far to leap. Nobody could make that jump.

Then he remembered the page with the diagrams and found it in the diary. The pendulum. The cobbles. The invisible bridge.

The third diagram was wedge-shaped, with a series of dotted lines leading across the top of the wedge. He studied it a moment, then slapped the diary shut.

Useless. It didn't make sense. He didn't believe in invisible bridges.

"Indy!"

He turned at the sound of Brody's voice coming from inside the passageway. "Marcus?" he yelled back.

"Indy, you've got to hurry."

He leaned his head back against the rock wall and closed his eyes. He could turn around now and go back and watch his father die. Or he could jump, and hope . . . even though there was no hope. He suddenly remembered himself as a child of ten with his father and wondered how the hell his life could be flashing before his eyes when he hadn't even jumped yet.

His father had given him a bow and arrow set for his tenth birthday and had put up a target in the backyard. "You stand behind this line, Junior, and practice, and when you get a bull's-eye come and get me. But don't cheat. Stay behind the line."

"Yes, sir." He was happy and excited and more than anything

wanted to please his father. He practiced the rest of the afternoon, but didn't hit a single bull's-eye. Half of the time he missed the target completely and had to retrieve the arrows from the bushes at the far side of the yard.

The sun was low in the sky when his father came outside again. "Well, Junior?"

"I can't do it, Dad." His eyes were filled with tears. He was angry and frustrated. "I just can't hit the bull's-eye. I'm too far away."

"No, you're not, Junior. You're not too far away. Your problem is, you don't believe. When you believe you can do it, you will do it. *Believe, Junior. Believe.*"

He had scoffed that believing wasn't going to make him any better. His father had pointed at him. "Don't grow up to be cynical, Junior. The cynic is a fearful person who accomplishes nothing."

He had lowered his bow and stared at the bull's-eye, saying over and over that he believed he could hit it. He raised the bow, but he felt his doubts returning. He lowered it again.

I believe. I believe. I believe I can hit it. I'll do it. I can hit the bull's-eye. I believe. I'll do it.

And he did.

Indy opened his eyes. The memory had been as clear as if he were still ten. He stared across the abyss again. When he grew up, he had relegated the experience to a coincidence. But now there was no time to question the power of faith. I've got to believe. That's the only way. I can make it. I believe it.

He stuffed the diary in his pouch and focused on the rock wall on the far side, saying over and over again that he believed. If I don't believe, I won't jump. I'll jump when I believe.

He brushed aside his doubts, concentrating, and repeating his belief until he felt the grooves of that faith etched inside him. His breathing was deep. It came faster and faster. I can do it. Dad. I can do it. I'll make it.

He crouched down on the edge of the abyss. With every bit of his strength, he pushed off and sprang like a lion.

It was a strong leap, the best he could have done. But, of course, it was far too short. The gap was too wide.

He was going to die. Yet, he knew he wouldn't. At that moment he landed and fell forward on his hands and knees.

He looked down and saw he was on a rock ledge a few feet below the passageway. But why hadn't he seen it? It was obviously there all the time.

He leaned back slightly, trying to look at the ledge from the perspective of the opposite wall. Then he saw there was something unusual about the rocks. It was ingenious. The ledge was colored to blend exactly with the rocks one hundred feet below. From the sight line on the opposite wall, it appeared there was no ledge. It was a perfect camouflage until he leaped.

He laughed aloud. He had believed, and he had found the impossible. *The Invisible Bridge*. If he hadn't believed he could survive, he would have never leaped and never found the bridge.

He stood, wobbled a moment, and looked back across the abyss. He saw Elsa and Donovan staring at him in astonishment. He chuckled, knowing that from their perspective, he looked as if he was standing in midair.

Gingerly he followed the ledge as it gradually rose, a gentle slope that ended beneath the lion's head. He was now just below the lip of the aperture in the rock wall.

Then he remembered something else. The lion was one of the symbols in the search for the Grail—the fifth level of awareness. It stood for leadership, conquest, and the attainment of high goals.

He had overcome the three challenges; a high goal had been achieved. Now he was ready to move on and find the Grail Cup. He had the feeling, though, that the toughest challenge of them all was still ahead.

TWENTY-TWO

The Third Knight

INDY LOOKED BACK once before pressing on and saw Elsa throwing pebbles and dirt out over the abyss and onto the invisible bridge.

Bright woman. Bright and dangerous.

The passageway narrowed and the ceiling lowered as he continued forward. He banged his head on the ceiling and scraped his shoulders on the walls. He was forced to crawl, but it didn't do much good: he still banged his head.

If this gets any tighter, I'll have to start believing I'm a rabbit, for Christ's sake.

Darkness wrapped around him like a thick overcoat. His fingers led the way, penetrating the darkness ahead. He worried that when he reached the end, it would be a rock wall. Then what? He hadn't overcome the challenges just to find out there was no Grail, only a dead end. This was no time for cosmic jokes. His father was dying.

He banged his forehead and, fearing the worst, extended his arm and patted the wall with his hand, defining the contours of the tunnel. He realized it was curving, not ending. He moved slowly ahead and noticed the tunnel was now dimly lit.

He crawled another ten feet. He could see a light ahead and moved faster. The light grew stronger, brighter. He squinted as brilliant sunshine beamed into the tunnel. Then, forcing his way through a narrow opening, he tumbled out of the tunnel. Sweet, fragrant air swirled around him. His eyes quickly adjusted to the daylight.

He stood, brushed the dirt off his shoulders, and stretched his arms and legs. He was inside another temple, smaller than the other. His attention immediately focused on an altar in the center. It was draped in violet linen, and on it were dozens of chalices of various sizes. Some were gold, others were silver; some were festooned with precious jewels, others were less ornate. But all of them shone and glistened, and Indy was mesmerized by the spectacle.

He knew he had reached his destination.

He moved forward for a closer look, then saw another smaller altar off to one side—and something else. A figure in a tunic and a knit headdress knelt in front of the other altar with his back to him.

Indy walked closer. The man's thin, bony hands were folded, and his head bent in prayer. The skin on his fingers was paper-thin, translucent, and outlined the bones. He moved forward and saw a shaft of light striking the emblem of a cross that was stitched on the man's tunic.

Indy realized he was looking at the third Grail knight, the brother who had stayed behind to guard the cup.

He bent over and looked into the knight's face. His eyes were closed; his parched lips were slightly parted as if he were about to say something. The face had heavy, white eyebrows and a prominent nose. The body was dried and brittle by time and the desert, yet remarkably preserved, in far better condition than the gruesome remains of the knight's brother from the catacombs in Venice.

He leaned forward and frowned. For a moment, he thought he saw the knight blink. Then he smiled and shook his head. A candle was burning on the altar in front of the knight, and the flickering light was playing tricks with his eyes.

Indy raised his head. A candle. Who lit that?

He lifted his gaze and looked around the temple, wondering if he was being watched. "So who lit the candle, old fellow?"

The knight suddenly raised his head.

Indy drew back, astonished. "What the hell."

He watched in stunned disbelief as the knight rose slowly to his feet, then lifted an enormous sword with both hands. Before Indy even realized what had happened, the sword flashed in the air. The knight swung the weapon quickly, deftly, and the tip of it nicked the front of Indy's shirt and sliced the strap of his pouch, which slipped to the ground.

Indy leaped back as the knight hefted the sword again and took another swipe at him. This time the weight of the sword was too much, and the knight lost his balance. He stumbled back against the altar; the sword clattered as it struck the rock floor.

Indy moved over to him and helped him up. He was old but possessed an unmistakable vitality that made his eyes gleam. He opened his mouth, but no words came out. It was as if he were uncertain how to speak. Finally, he uttered a low groan.

"I knew ye would come," he said, looking Indy over, judging him against some image in his own mind. "But my strength has left me. I tire easily."

"Who are you?" Indy answered slowly.

"Ye know who I be. The last of three brothers who swore an oath to find and protect the Grail."

"That was more than eight hundred years ago."

"A long time to wait."

Indy smiled affably. The old guy was senile. "So when was the First Crusade?"

At first, Indy didn't think the old man heard him. Then he answered: "In the year of Our Lord 1095 at the Council of Clermont. Proclaimed by Pope Urban II."

"When did the Crusades end?"

The knight gave him a withering look that reminded Indy of his father. "They have not. The last crusader stands before ye eyes."

Indy nodded. He didn't have time to interrogate him, though. He needed to act. If this guy was the real thing, and still alive, then the Grail Cup could save his father.

He heard voices coming from the tunnel and started to turn, but the old knight tugged on the brim of his fedora. "Ye be strangely dressed . . . for a knight." He ran his fingers over Indy's bullwhip.

"Well, I'm not exactly . . . a knight."

"I think ye be one."

Indy shrugged.

"I was chosen as the bravest and the most worthy. The honor of guarding the Grail was made mine until another worthy knight arrived to challenge me in single combat." He lifted the hilt of his sword. "I pass it to ye who vanquished me."

"Look, let me explain. I need to borrow the Grail Cup from you. You see, my father . . ."

"Hold it, Jones."

Indy whipped around to see Donovan squeezing through the tunnel, aiming his pistol at him.

"Stay right there." Donovan glanced around, saw the altar of chalices, and moved over to it. Elsa emerged from the tunnel and quickly joined him.

Donovan glanced over at the knight, his gun still aimed at Indy. "Okay, which one is it?"

The knight took a step forward and rose to his full height as he stared at Donovan. "I no longer serve as guardian of the Grail." He nodded toward Indy. "It is he who must answer the challenge. I will neither help nor hinder."

Donovan grinned at Indy. "He's not stopping me."

"Then choose wisely," the knight advised. "For just as the true Grail will bring ye life, the false Grail will take it away."

Indy smiled wryly at Donovan. "Take your pick, Donovan. Good luck."

Elsa moved closer to the altar. "Do you see it?" Donovan asked under his breath.

"Yes."

"Which is it?"

Elsa removed her hat and carefully picked up a shiny cup encrusted with sparkling colored stones. Donovan instantly grabbed it from her and held it up to the light. "Oh, yes. It's more beautiful than I had ever imagined. And it's mine."

Indy expected Elsa to protest, but she remained silent. The knight's face was implacable, revealing nothing.

Donovan looked up toward a font and carried the cup over to it. Elsa followed him.

Indy knew that according to the legend, immortality was achieved by drinking water from the cup.

Donovan admired the cup again. "This certainly is the cup of a King of Kings. Now it's mine." He filled it with water and held it high in one hand. He gazed triumphantly at Indy and the knight. The gun was still in his other hand, but in his excitement, he no longer aimed it at Indy.

"Eternal life." He drank long and deeply. Donovan lowered the cup to his chest. His eyes were closed, and a beatific smile spread across his face.

Indy could have tackled him at that moment and wrestled the cup from him. But something inside him told him to wait and watch. He didn't have to wait long.

Suddenly Donovan's eyes opened wide. The hand that held the cup started to shake. He turned away and bent over the font. His face skewed in pain. His body shuddered. He dropped the gun.

With a great effort he pushed away from the font and stumbled toward the altar. He stopped several feet short of it, unable to take another step. "What . . . is . . . happening . . . to . . . me?" he gasped.

His features contorted into a grisly mask. His cheekbones projected. His skin shriveled and wrinkled. He looked frail and already ancient when he turned to Elsa, the cup still clutched in his hand. His eyes seemed to have sunk into his cheeks and lay there like old stones in dry sockets.

He then hurled himself toward her, hands digging into her shoulder. "What . . . is . . . happening?"

She screamed and tried to push him away from her as he kept repeating his question, his voice growing fainter by the second, his body aging rapidly now. His hair was growing long and gray and crisp. His face was sinking, his skin peeling away.

"No. No. No. No. No. No," he whispered. He shook his head and bits of skin flew away.

Elsa shrieked in terror.

Donovan's fingernails curled back on themselves. Milky cataracts coated his eyes. What remained of his skin turned brown and leathery and stretched across his face until it split and hung in flaps.

Then he crumpled to the ground, an ancient skeleton blackened with age.

Indy moved quickly to Elsa's side and pushed her away from the still-writhing remains. He kicked the pile of bones and cloth, and Donovan's skeletal arms fluttered, collapsed, and turned to dust.

Elsa clung to Indy, her face pressed against his shirt, sobbing as a cold wind swirled through the temple and gradually died away. Indy peered over Elsa's shoulder, looking at the pile of dust that had been Donovan. As she began to calm down, Indy let go of her and turned to the knight, an unspoken question on his face.

"He chose poorly," the old knight said, and shrugged as if Donovan's death was of no consequence to him. He had given him fair warning.

Indy glanced at Elsa and picked up the gun Donovan had

dropped and tucked it in his belt. Then he hurried over to the altar. He was thinking of his father, of his father dying back there, of his father bleeding and in pain.

He stood in front of the chalices, took several deep breaths and let his eyes unfocus. A feeling of acute awareness overtook him. He felt light-headed. He closed his eyes a moment, concentrating, telling himself that he could do it, he could select the correct Grail, the one that would save his father.

He opened his eyes and cast a quick glance over the rows of glittering, bejeweled chalices. Then his eyes came to rest on one that was different. It was a simple cup, dull compared to the others. He didn't know why, but it seemed right. He picked it up and looked it over carefully. He didn't know what he expected to find. He knew there wouldn't be any stamp of authenticity.

"Is that it?" Elsa asked.

"I guess there's only one way to find out."

Indy moved quickly to the font, scooped up some of the water. He breathed deeply, took a quick drink from the cup, and waited an instant, wondering if something was going to happen, if he was looking at the last few seconds of his own life. He didn't feel any different, for better or worse.

Then suddenly his vision blurred. He felt dizzy; he blinked and squeezed his eyes shut. God, had he chosen wrong?

Oddly, he realized he could still see. But it was a different way of seeing. The cup in his hands was growing and transforming. It grew wings, a head, a beak. It was an eagle, spreading its massive wings and taking flight. It was the eagle of his vision quest and the eagle that signaled the sixth and last level of awareness in the Grail search.

"Indy?"

At the sound of Elsa's voice he blinked and shook his head. The cup was still in his hands. He glanced over at Elsa. From the questioning look on her face, he knew that she hadn't shared his experience. He looked over at the knight, who smiled knowingly.

"You've chosen wisely."

That was all the verification Indy needed. He didn't wait a second longer. He headed directly for the tunnel and crawled through it. He moved as rapidly as he could, while still carefully balancing the water-filled Grail Cup. He worried about banging the cup into the ceiling or the walls, and he worried about going so slowly that his father might die before he reached him. But as the tunnel expanded in size, he stood up and ran, at first at a low crouch, gradually rising up to his full height.

He slowed as he came to the ledge above the abyss. It was now speckled with dirt and clearly visible. He realized that it wasn't merely a protrusion, but actually was a bridge spanning the chasm between the two lion heads. Now it was easy. He walked quickly out onto the bridge, holding the Grail Cup in front of him.

He was hurrying, thinking about his father, and not paying enough attention. He was halfway across when his right foot slipped on the pebbles and dirt. His leg swung out, and he tottered back and forth, the Grail Cup wavering precariously over the abyss. Just as he almost regained his balance, his other foot slipped, and he fell unceremoniously onto his butt. Miraculously only a few drops had wet the sides of the Grail Cup. He carefully stood up and cautiously walked to the other side.

Brody stood at the top of the steps looking anxiously at Sallah and Henry and the dark passageway. There was still no sign of Indy, and he knew Henry wouldn't last much longer.

"Marcus!"

He looked up, peered down the passageway, and saw Indy moving quickly toward him, clutching the Grail Cup in his hands. His eyes widened, and his face lit up. He stepped back as Indy rushed past him and down the steps.

He moved forward and was about to follow Indy when he

nearly collided with Elsa as she rushed out the passageway. By the time he reached the bottom of the steps, Indy was on his knees beside his father, and the sultan's soldiers had closed around him. Brody pushed his way through the soldiers as if they were of no consequence. They were without a leader now and simply watched out of curiosity.

Brody crouched down and helped Sallah lift Henry's head. Indy quickly put the cup to Henry's lips. Henry was too weak even to open his eyes. Indy poured, but the water just ran down the side of Henry's mouth.

"Come on, Dad. Drink. Please drink."

Brody looked anxiously at Indy and saw the worried look on his face. He had to do something. He leaned forward and helped him to open Henry's mouth. He felt Henry's throat move. He was drinking. He had swallowed some of the water. He was sure of it.

Indy then carefully removed the emergency dressing from Henry's wound and poured some of the water over it. Quickly he placed the cup to his father's lips again and poured more water down his throat.

They waited.

Indy was certain his father's breathing was growing stronger. He leaned over and listened to his heartbeat. It was steady and resolute. He could almost see and feel his father coming back to them.

Suddenly Henry's eyes fluttered open. They focused first on Sallah, then Brody, then his son. Finally, they settled on the Grail Cup.

Indy smiled, feeling a certainty in his heart that his father was out of danger. He probably would never be able to convince his skeptical colleagues that water from an ancient cup had healed his father, and there would be plenty of doubts and controversy about whether this was the real Grail Cup.

But so what? He knew. That's what mattered. He had seen and experienced the beauty and power of the Grail. In doing so, he had ascended in his own quest from cynicism to doubt to awakening. The quest was fulfilled, and with it the Last Crusade finally neared its end.

"Dad. You're going to be all right. I believe it. I know it."

TWENTY-THREE

End of the Quest

Henry's hands shook as he reached out for the Grail Cup, but now it was from excitement, not weakness. The color had returned to his face, and his eyes were wide open, clear, cognizant. His wound had been covered again, but it was no longer bleeding and didn't seem to be causing him any great discomfort. With Sallah's help, he had been able to rise up on his elbow.

As Indy proudly passed his father the Grail Cup, he heard a clatter behind him. He jerked his head around and saw the sultan's soldiers dropping their weapons and shrinking back. Their curiosity had turned to fear. They didn't want anything to do with guarding the wizards who had performed the miraculous healing, and suddenly all of them fled the temple.

All but a couple of the Nazi soldiers immediately gave chase, shouting and threatening to shoot the sultan's men. But they kept on running. Sallah swiftly made the most of it. As the two remaining Nazis called to their companions, he stealthily made his way toward the nearest rifle. He swept it up, spun around, and ordered the remaining Nazis to drop their weapons. *"Die Gewehr herunter,"* he repeated when they momentarily hesitated.

"Do as he says," Elsa snapped at them.

They hesitated but not for long. They set down their weapons and raised their hands.

Sallah, however, didn't realize that another Nazi had stayed behind and was standing a few feet behind Elsa. As the soldier reached for his pistol, Indy dove for his legs, tackling him. The Nazi twisted about and turned his gun on Indy. He was about to fire, when Elsa kicked the weapon from his hand.

Indy rose up on one knee, gazing at Elsa, amazed and baffled at what she had done. The Nazi took advantage of the moment and punched him. Indy grabbed his jaw, frowned, then collared the Nazi and landed a punch that was hard and direct. The soldier flopped to the ground and rolled over. Indy stood up and smiled at Elsa. He didn't know what to make of her. On one hand there was abundant evidence of her deceitfulness, yet she had just saved his life. Elsa's complacent look abruptly turned to horror. Her mouth dropped open, quivered a moment. "Watch out! Behind you!"

Indy turned just in time to block the arm of the same Nazi as he stabbed at him with a long, vicious-looking knife. Sallah ordered the soldier to drop it. The man looked up at the rifle barrel, his eyes flicked to Sallah's face, and he released the knife.

Indy grabbed it and spun the Nazi around. "Go join your buddies." He pushed him roughly toward the other two Nazis.

Indy looked over at his father and realized that when Sallah left him, he had remained sitting up, holding the Grail Cup to his stomach. Indy started to ask him how he felt, but Henry was gazing past him, eyes glazed, a rapturous expression on his face.

Now what?

Slowly Indy turned and saw the Grail knight standing on the steps.

"I know you," Henry called out to the knight. "Yes, I know you."

"Were we comrades in arms?"

"No, from the books. You're the third knight, the one who

stayed behind. But I don't understand. You had the Grail Cup. Why are you so old?"

The knight descended the rest of the stairs. "Many times my spirit faltered, and I could not bear to drink from the cup, so I aged, a year for every day I did not drink. But now at last, I am released to death with honor, for this brave knight-errant cometh to take my place."

Indy looked from the knight to his father, uneasiness churning a path through his gut. "Dad, there's a misunderstanding here. I didn't really . . ."

"He is not a knight-errant," Henry scoffed. "He's just my errant son who has led an impure life. Unworthy of the honor you bestow."

Indy nodded. "Yes, an impure life."

"Totally unworthy. Son, do something worthy, and help your father stand up."

Henry set the Grail Cup down and wrapped an arm over Indy's shoulder.

"You sure you want to try this, Dad?"

"Of course. I'm feeling better by the moment."

Brody took the other side, and they gently lifted Henry to his feet. Indy hoped his father's recovery was not just a temporary one brought on by the sight of the Grail Cup and the belief that it could cure him. He wanted the cure to be real.

"There, see?" Henry cringed a moment, then courageously straightened up. "That wasn't so bad."

"Are you really cured, Dad?"

Henry frowned at his son as if he were still a child asking silly questions. He took his arms away from Indy and Brody. "How many times have I told you, Junior, that belief creates reality. I believe—I *knew*—the cup could heal me, and it has. It has."

After everything that had happened to him today, Indy didn't see any reason to doubt him. He thought back to what the old Indian had said to him after he had climbed down from the mesa and told him about the eagle. *Now you know that you have the power within you to attain all that you seek, no matter how difficult the challenge.*

Eagles and the Grail Cup; the knight and the Indian. It was all a jumble. But his father was alive, and they knew each other now as never before. He watched as the knight stepped closer and peered into Henry's face.

"Is it you then, brother? Are ye the knight who will relieve me?"

"Alas, no. I am but a scholar."

The knight gestured toward Brody. "Is it you, brother?"

"Me? I'm English."

The knight looked baffled and walked over to Sallah, who had herded the Nazi guards away from the others and was still keeping an eye on them. He placed a hand on Sallah's shoulder, apparently confident that he'd found his replacement. "Ah, good Knight."

Sallah didn't understand. He looked at Indy.

"He said, 'Good knight.' "

Sallah nodded to the old man. "Yes. Good night. Sleep tight."

Indy bent down and picked up Henry's hat, tie, and watch. He froze as he saw Elsa out of the corner of his eye, inching closer to the Grail Cup. Suddenly she took two quick steps, grabbed the cup in both hands, and held it up. She gazed at it as if in a trance. Her eyes were fixed on it with such an intensity that Indy finally understood that nothing else truly mattered to her. Not him. Not the Führer. Not anyone. She was obsessed by the Grail.

Indy was distracted by the old knight, who stepped in front of him. "Why have these strange knights come," he muttered, "if not to challenge me?" He shook his head, bewildered, and walked away as Indy rose to his feet.

"For this, you fool," Elsa answered. She clutched the Grail Cup to her chest and bolted for the entrance of the temple.

Indy was about to give chase, when she stopped and turned. She was a few feet from the entrance of the temple, silhouetted in the late afternoon light. She must have realized, he thought, that she wouldn't go far in the desert on her own.

"We've got it. Come on. Let's go."

"No!" the knight yelled. "The Grail can never leave this place! Never!"

He looked over at Indy and Henry. "Remaining here is the price of immortality."

Henry glanced from the knight to Elsa. "Listen to him. He knows. The Grail will be nothing but an old cup if you take it from the temple."

"I don't believe him."

"You must not cross the seal," the knight warned, pointing past her.

Elsa turned and took several defiant steps toward the entrance.

"She will pay dearly," the knight said quietly.

"Wait," Indy shouted, running after her. The images of what happened to Donovan were still fresh in his mind. "Wait, Elsa. Don't move."

She neared a large metal seal on the floor but paid no attention to it. She was not only captivated but overwhelmed by the Grail Cup, and her eyes were glued to it.

"Elsa!" He reached her just in time and grabbed her arm.

She peered up at him with those incredibly blue eyes of hers, and he felt something shift and slide in his chest. "It's ours now, Indy," she said softly. "Ours. Don't you understand? Yours and mine. No one else matters. Donovan is dead; we'll keep it from the Führer."

He shook his head. "It's staying here."

With sudden and unexpected strength she pulled her arm free of his grasp. She cuddled the Grail, like a child with a stuffed animal, and stepped defiantly onto the seal. Then she backed across it out of the temple.

A moment or two passed, then a deep rumbling sound that was felt as much as heard erupted beneath the temple. The canyon walls started to shake. Dust flew as debris began to tumble from the shaking walls. Elsa spun around, terrified, and ran a few steps into the temple. Indy backed away from her as the floor shifted under his feet. He turned and saw one of the massive carved knights shuddering. The pillars rocked. He leapt aside as a stone cap shook loose and tumbled toward him, pulverizing at his feet.

Henry was holding his arms above his head, trying to protect himself from falling rocks. As the floor kept shaking, Brody lost his balance and fell to one knee. Sallah grabbed both men by the arms and jerked them away just as one of the pillars crashed where they had stood. The knight, meanwhile, fled up the steps toward the passageway and his inner sanctum.

Indy signaled the others to hurry toward the entrance. He turned and saw Elsa. She was looking up at one of the swaying columns of stone, her eyes wide with fear. The earth suddenly shifted again, and she lost her balance. She pitched forward, and the Grail Cup slipped from her hands.

As the cup rolled away from her, a jagged crack seared through the center of the seal and across the temple floor. Elsa struggled to her feet. Her legs straddled the gap, which was slowly widening.

The crack split apart the inner steps leading to the passageway and knocked the knight from his feet. He fell back, rolling down the steps. Another crack ruptured the floor of the temple, perpendicular to the first one. Henry toppled like one of the pillars, and Brody wobbled like a drunk next to him. Sallah and Indy both froze, uncertain which way to turn. Behind them the knight crawled laboriously up the steps.

The Nazis made a run for the entrance and leapt across the crack that Elsa straddled. At the same instant, she pushed off with one foot, but as she did, the ground bulged on the side she had chosen. She desperately clawed and scratched, searching for a handhold.

The Nazis were in the same predicament. They had almost reached the top of the incline when they slid back and fell into the abyss. Their screams echoed long after they were smashed to their deaths below.

Elsa clung to a boulder protruding from the side of the crevice. Below her she could see the Grail Cup lying on a rock jutting over the edge of the crack. Instead of climbing up and away from the abyss, she lowered herself on one side of it and reached for the cup.

Indy realized the danger she was in and dashed over to her. He stretched out on his stomach and extended his arms, shouting to her to grab his hands. Their fingers brushed; then he inched forward and clasped both of her gloved hands. He pulled with every bit of strength he had, but it wasn't enough; he started to slide forward.

"Junior, Junior," Henry shouted.

"Indy," Sallah bellowed.

As Indy pulled, Elsa wrenched one of her hands free. She reached down toward the Grail Cup, which rocked back and forth, inches from the chasm. Her fingertips grazed the edge of it, but she couldn't quite grasp it.

"Elsa!" Indy yelled. With his free hand, he grabbed hold of a rock.

"I can reach it," she gasped. "I can."

Indy's hold on her was slipping. She stretched toward the cup and was about to grasp it when her glove slipped off her fingers. They each clung to the glove, their hands no longer touching. The glove stretched. It started to rip.

"Indy!" Alarm riddled her voice. "Don't let go. Please."

The glove ripped more.

"Elsa!"

He let go of the rock and lunged for her wrist, but it was too late. Her fingers slipped, and she fell backward into the chasm, her screams ringing out in the temple.

Indy slid forward, plowing his hands into the earth in a desperate attempt to stop himself from hurtling after her. He was about to slide into the blackness when hands squeezed around his ankles like a vise.

"Indy!" Sallah yelled. "I've got you. I'm going to pull you out."

"Wait." He reached out for the Grail Cup, but his fingers fell several inches short of it. "Lower me a little more."

"Don't be crazy, Indy," Sallah grunted, struggling to hold on to his friend. His feet were inching forward, and it wasn't because he was trying to lower Indy toward the chalice.

"A little more," Indy gasped.

"No, Indy. Please."

"Junior, get back up here," Henry barked from behind Sallah.

"I can get it. I can reach it."

"Indiana."

"Dad?" It was the first time his father had ever called him by name.

"Let it go," Henry said calmly.

Indy abandoned the Grail and clawed his way backward as Sallah pulled at his ankles. The dirt he loosened tumbled down onto the Grail Cup. He looked up once just in time to see the cup slide off its perch and into the abyss with Elsa.

Sallah gave one final yank, grunting loudly as he pulled Indy over the lip of the crevice. Indy sprawled on his stomach, staring into the black chasm that had swallowed Elsa and the cup. The horrified expression on her face as she slipped away had burned a path through his brain. If he had done what his father had, if he had told her just to forget the cup, he could have saved her.

Henry's hand was tight on his shoulder. His voice was urgent. "Come. Now. We've got to get out."

Indy nodded, picked up his hat, took one more glance over the side, and stood up.

Sallah guided them forward. "Where's Marcus?" Henry called out in alarm.

"I'm here," he said from somewhere nearby.

More and more debris was falling around them. Indy tried to clear his mind of guilt, of the nagging certainty that he could have saved Elsa if he had tried a little harder, if he had acted differently. After all, he owed her. She had saved him. And he had failed her.

But he knew she was partly responsible for her own death. She wasn't leaving without the Grail. There was nothing more to do but let go of his guilt and save his own life. Somehow, he knew, she would want it that way.

He followed after the others, then noticed that his father had stopped and was staring toward the steps. Indy followed his gaze and saw the Grail knight standing impassively at the top of the steps a few feet from the jagged crack. Rocks and dust were tumbling around him, but he seemed completely oblivious.

The knight raised his right hand, a farewell. It was as if he were saying the Last Crusade was finally over, and the Grail was safe. To Indy it made sense. He now realized the Holy Grail was more than an ancient and sacred cup. It was more than a means of attaining immortality, more than a way of miraculously healing.

He had sipped the ambrosial waters from the cup, and had understood. It was the essence of a higher awareness that was in him and in everyone who bothered to look for it. Now, he vowed, he would do the best he could with the understanding and knowledge he had gained.

Henry smiled back at the knight and nodded.

"Dad."

Indy pulled on his father's arm and hurried him away as massive rocks thundered down around them and pillars collapsed. The walls were crumbling, and jets of steam hissed up through the crevices. But Indy knew they would survive. They had made it this far—they would make the final steps.

A moment later they reached the top of the outer stairs. Indy took one more look inside the temple and thought he saw the Grail knight still standing at the top of the steps.

"Henry, Indy. Come on," Brody yelled from the saddle of a horse outside the temple. "I know the way. Grab a horse and follow me."

Brody spurred the horse, which bolted ahead, then circled and careened around them, nearly running over Sallah. He floundered in the saddle, but finally took control and galloped into the narrow canyon.

Henry shook his head and swung his leg over the back of a horse. "We better catch up with him. He got lost in his own museum."

"I know."

Henry gestured to Indy. "After you, Junior."

"Yes, sir," Indy said with a smile. It didn't matter any more what his father called him. The quest had been fulfilled.

For Henry, and especially for Indy.

He slapped his horse with the reins and galloped after Brody.

CAMPBELL BLACK was born in Glasgow in 1944 and educated at Sussex University. His first novel was published in 1968, and three years later he moved to the United States, where he taught creative writing. He lived there for twenty years with his wife and children and produced twenty novels before moving to Ireland in 1991. Following the international success of *Jig* (1987), many of his books, including *Brainfire*, *Asterisk*, and *The Bad Fire* are once again available in the United Kingdom.

JAMES KAHN is a recovering emergency-room doctor who has published a science fiction trilogy, as well as a couple of murder mysteries and a handful of novelizations, including the novelization of *Return of the Jedi*.

ROB MACGREGOR enrolled at the University of Minnesota in the late 1960s, planning to study archaeology. He never gave up his interest in ancient civilizations, and between jobs and on vacations he explored archaeological sites in Mexico, Central and South America, Europe, and North Africa. Those experiences would later come in handy when he wrote the novelization of the blockbuster movie *Indiana Jones and the Last Crusade*, and then went on to write six original Indiana Jones novels for Lucasfilm Ltd. and Bantam Books. In addition to writing, Rob teaches yoga, based on his own system called Astro-Yoga.